*Seven are they! Seven Are They!*
*In the Ocean Deep seven are they!*
*Battling in Heaven seven are they,*
*Workers of evil are they,*
*They lift up the head to evil, every day to evil*
*Destruction their work.*
*Of these seven the first is the South Wind*
*The second is a dragon with mouth agape*
*From which flames leap*
*The third is a grim leopard*
*That carrieth off children*
*The fourth is a terrible serpent*
*With many heads*
*The fifth is a furious beast*
*That none can restrain*
*The sixth is a rampant*
*against god and king*
*The seventh is an evil windstorm*
*That none can with stand*
*Baleful are they, baleful are they.*
*Seven are they, seven are they, seven twice again are they.*
*May the spirits of heaven remember, may the spirits of earth remember.*

- The sixteenth tablet of the "Demon Series," translated from Sumerian, dated 3100 BC

# The Ancient

**By Matthew Bryan Laube**

Cover art by Mauro Balcazar

"Seven are they" based on translations by R.C. Thompson, published in The Devils and Evil Spirits of Babylonia, London, 1903.

Book 1

# Awakening

# 1- Miller

Outside of Vannes, France - 1908

The monsters were out there, just beyond the bonfire's light. Dallas strained his eyes to make them out at the top of the hill in front of him. He counted six werewolves at least, prowling just out of view. For any other group of men this would be something truly terrifying; for Dallas' group of soldiers, it was Wednesday. They were "The Terrible 13th," a unit that didn't strictly exist in any army. Instead, the unit was made up of various volunteers from around the world. Most of the men were English, a few were French, and two were Russian. For the first time last year, an American had joined the group. They had the dangerous and highly classified job of dealing with those things that were not supposed to exist-werewolves, vampires, demons. The list was long and not particularly pleasant.

"At least six of the wolves," Dallas said to the old man.

The old man was staring up at the night sky. That mad grin he always wore was plastered to his face. "Seven," he said, "but those are not the ones we need to worry about."

That bothered Dallas. When the old man was nervous, it meant something. Dallas had been working under Joseph Miller for about a year now. Because of him, Dallas had seen some terrible and wonderful things, none of which he had believed possible just a short twelve months ago. Dallas had been recruited as an explosives expert. Miller and Dallas had hit it off. Something about the Texan's hard-living manner seemed to mesh well with the old man's point of view on life. Although he kept no second in command, Dallas had quickly become Miller's go-to man.

"Dallas, there is a demon out there, one of the Fallen. You might say the king of them all." Miller looked directly at Dallas, his face suddenly becoming grim. "When you see him, you pull these men back. This is not something that you can help me with."

"Yes sir," Dallas responded, glancing back up the hill. "Well, do you think we look enough like a tasty doggy treat?"

"Oh I think we will do." Miller's eyes lit up at Dallas' attempt at humor. He was a big man with long white hair, wrapped into a ridiculous looking ponytail, and a white beard. He looked maybe 60 years old to Dallas, but moved like a man in his 20s.

The Thirteenth had made camp directly at the base of a hill. This was, tactically, an unwise move, but then they were not fighting a traditional war. Behind them, they had built a huge bonfire that lit up the night. In front of them, they had hidden an extra surprise under a tarp. Dallas was never sure how the old man knew where to set up, but he was never wrong. Sure enough, a few short hours after making camp, he began to notice the hulking shapes of wolves shifting in the dark.

"All right lads, listen up," Miller shouted. His accent was almost Scottish but not quite, like he was pretending. "There are some big bad beasties out there tonight. They will be down here shortly for dinner. You know the drill at this point. Stay sharp. The big one, leave to me. You will know him when you see him." The twelve nodded in agreement and readied their rifles. They had done this before.

As if the monsters knew they were ready, they suddenly attacked, seven wolves running down the hill, side by side. Dallas could see them clearly now under the moonlight, six males and one female. Looking at the figures running at him, he couldn't help but struggle again with the question. Why did they call them werewolves? The huge figures, while covered with thick black hair, looked nothing like wolves. Rather, they reminded Dallas of the apes he had seen in a book he had once read about Africa. They looked like immense men with huge claws like five large knives sticking out of each hand. Even the one that had been a woman was at least twice the size of Dallas. She still wore the remains of what appeared to be a pink dress. Most disturbing, though, were their eyes, black and empty things, reflecting the light from the bonfire.

As the werewolves bore down on them, Miller shouted, "Now!"

Dallas brought the plunger down, igniting the explosives he had set into the hillside just hours before. The hilltop seemed to jump under the wolves, tossing them into the night sky. Three of them appeared to come apart in the air. A fourth crumpled into a ball and skidded to a stop. The remaining three carried on down the hill, undisturbed by the deaths of their comrades. Dallas could clearly see the white foam streaming out of their mouths.

"Shields!" Miller shouted. The men grabbed their huge metal shields, the likes of which Dallas was sure had not been used since medieval times. They drove them into the ground just as the wolves reached the first row of men. Not even this form of protection could slow the wolves down, however. The lead wolf's claws knocked three men aside with a single swipe. The female pounced on one of the fallen men, tearing at his shield.

"Down!" Miller yelled. The rest of the men dropped, covering their bodies with their shields. With one smooth motion, Miller removed the tarp in front of him like a magician revealing his next big trick, and lit the fuse to the short-barreled cannon. Dallas covered his ears and opened his mouth to better handle the shock of the blast. The wolf-man in front of the cannon seemed to pause for a second, as whatever remained of its human mind recognized the device. Then it vanished in a red mist as, with a huge boom, the pellet-shot fired on it almost point blank. The force of the cannon made Dallas' teeth ache. The she-wolf was caught by the edge of the blast. She spun around, her arm a mangled mess, and fell to the ground. Several pellets bounced off the men's shields, which were now covering their bodies as they lay flat on the ground.

The remaining wolf seemed to pause for a second to note his missing siblings. Seeing Miller, the only man standing, he dove at him with a howl. The old man was ready though, and simply side-stepped the beast, drawing a large and ancient looking broadsword from a sheath on his back. Using the momentum of his step, Miller spun around and brought the sword through the wolf-man's neck, slicing his head clear off his shoulders. Black blood spurted from the wound as the head hit the ground and the wolf's huge body toppled over. Then the she-wolf was on her feet again, managing to tag Miller in the back with three of her claws. Miller stepped forward, away from his attacker, but tripped over the newly-dead wolf's head on the ground. Recovering in mid-fall, he spun to face his new opponent, drew a pistol from his belt, and fired one clean shot before landing on his back. Dallas heard the old man grunt with the pain as he landed on his shredded back. The she-wolf stepped back. The bullet had passed straight though her eye, leaving a gaping black hole. For a second, the wolf rocked back and forth on her heels, stunned. Then, with a sickening "pop", black fluid seemed to leap out of the wound, reforming the missing eye.

Dallas was back on his feet. Tossing his metal shield to the side, he drew a saber from his hip and slashed at the she–wolf's back with all the might he could muster. The blade struck the creature's shoulder and stuck. Freddie, an Englishman from London, was in front of the wolf. He drew an axe and drove it deep into her chest. She screamed with rage and gored Freddie with one huge claw. The man fell back, a large chunk of his face torn open. The she-wolf then turned to face Dallas, moving fast enough to rip his saber from his hands. He cringed and backed away. She was a truly terrible creature. The fact that she had at one point been a woman, maybe even an attractive one, made it somehow worse. Here was a creature of beauty, twisted and misshapen into the stuff of nightmares, and she was hungry. It took all his strength of will not to turn and run, which he knew would mean certain death. Instead, he continued to step back as the wolf advanced, arms in front of him as if trying to calm the creature. "Um, sorry about this miss. I'll just be going," he joked. She wasn't listening.

"The head, man, go for the head!" Miller's voice came from behind the creature. A second later, the edge of Miller's broadsword flashed though the wolf's neck. The wolf seemed to freeze for a moment and then her head simply rolled off her shoulders, dropping at Dallas' feet. "It is the only way to kill them. How many times do I have to repeat myself?" Miller seemed to stumble a bit, as if the sword he always carried was suddenly too heavy. Turning away from Dallas, he shouted to the men, "It is a fine start, people, but our work is not done. Time for clean-up. Make sure that they stay down. Medic, take a look at Freddie." Responding to his words, several men pulled axes from their packs and went at the messy work of dismembering any werewolf that looked like it might still get up. Staring at Miller's back, Dallas noted the blood flowing freely from the new scratches.

"James can look at that for you, sir," he said, referring to their medic. "It'll be fine. The big one is still out there."

Miller grinned at him. "Trust me, it takes a lot more than such scratches to slow me down."

At the sound of a woman's voice, Dallas' attention snapped back to the hill.

"Oh thank God, those beasts were about to kill us." The woman was speaking in French, walking briskly down the hill towards their group. She had an almost eerie sense of calm about her. Even in the dim moonlight she was striking. Dressed in fine silks, she appeared to be a noblewoman or at least a rich man's wife. The men all stopped, distracted by her beauty. Everyone, that is, but Miller, who raised his pistol and shot her.

Dallas was stunned for a moment. The woman, however, did not crumble as the bullet struck, only missing a step before quickening her forward pace. Miller fired three more shots and broke into a jog. "Get away from it!"

The men were sluggish, as if coming awake from a dream. At last becoming aware that something wasn't right about this woman, they began to raise their axes. Closing in, the woman shrugged off Miller's bullets and opened her mouth wide as if to scream. Instead, a huge black tongue snapped out of her mouth like a lizard's. It wrapped itself around one man's throat. Instantly, the man stiffened and then appeared to shrink as the woman sucked the life from him.

"Vampire!" Miller shouted, "Vampire!" The woman's arm seemed to double in size. She used this club to swat aside a man who was trying to save his friend. More bullets struck her, and then an axe, but she simply grinned an unearthly smile as she finished her meal. Then Miller was there at her victim's side. With one smooth motion of his sword, he sliced the tongue in two with his sword. The man dropped to the ground as the vampire screamed, black blood gushing from her mouth. In an instant, several men were upon her, chopping away with their axes. Her shrieking ended with a gurgle.

Miller strode past the men exacting their vengeance and up the hill into the darkness. Dallas did his best to follow. Several feet beyond them, a man was waiting in the dark. In the moonlight, Dallas could not make out his features. Keeping in mind what had happened with the woman just moments before, he unsheathed a long dagger with his left hand from his belt.

"So you are the Ancient One," the man said. His voice seemed to shake in fear. Dallas raised his pistol. He knew it would do little good, but it made him feel better. His other hand still held the dagger.

"I am," Miller said, stopping before him. "And you are the demon Asmodai, the last of your kind. I have searched for you for many long years. Tonight, I end this." Miller towered over the strange man in the darkness.

"You may be right, old one, but know this: I can never truly die. Even if you win this battle tonight, in time I will rise up again..."

"Yes, yes I know!" Miller cut him off. "A great evil that will retake the earth from the filth that is humanity, and not even I can stop you. Do you have any idea how many times I've heard this speech? Demon, you need a new line!" Miller raised his broadsword and lunged at the smaller man, who sprung backward and out of reach with an incredible leap. The man seemed to smile, although Dallas could not be sure in the darkness.

"It is not that easy, old one." With that, the man seemed to explode. He tore at his chest, ripping through both cloth and his flesh, revealing dark black scales. His mouth opened impossibly wide, his jaw seeming to melt, and a huge black head rose out of his throat, snout first, followed by a long neck. It tore the remaining flesh of his face to shreds. Huge black wings emerged on his back and his hands exploded into massive talons. The monster seemed to stretch and stretch, tripling its size in seconds.

Dallas pulled the pistol's trigger, backing away from the still-growing beast. Although Miller had called it a demon, it looked more like a dragon from an old storybook, complete with wings and snout but oddly missing a tail. It stood like a man on its massive legs and must have been 10 feet tall! Miller seemed unimpressed.

"Aye, you are a big one. Good, I like a fair fight."

Miller charged the beast, not flinching for a second. He dodged the first swipe of its massive talon, rolled between its legs, and slammed his sword into its back. The dragon roared in pain and leapt into the air, with Miller still clinging to the embedded sword. The two figures rose high into the air over the hill.

Dallas stood below, watching in terror. He did not notice that he was still pulling the trigger on the pistol, although he had long ago run out of bullets. Several men raced to his side, raising rifles at the sky, trying to track the monster.

"My God, was that really a dragon?" he asked no one in particular.

The demon reappeared, swooping low over the camp. Miller was still hanging on. In fact, he had somehow managed to move up its back toward its head. The monster was spinning madly, trying to shake him off. Then they were gone again, disappearing into the darkness. Belatedly, several of the men fired their rifles.

“No! You’ll hit Miller!” Dallas shouted, becoming aware of his surroundings once more. The men lowered their guns.

“Follow me, back to the cannon. Once Miller gets clear, we're going to need to hit that thing with something big!” Dallas ordered. The chain of command after Miller was a bit unclear, but no man argued with Dallas and they all took off, heading back to the base camp at a run.

Somewhere in the darkness above them, the beast screamed. The sound of it made Dallas's head ache. Everyone froze, looking up at the night sky, trying to find the source. Then, the monster dropped out of the sky, smashing into the ground like a cannonball. The troop of men again reversed course, racing back up the hill to the crash site.

Something grabbed Dallas's leg as he ran by. A werewolf, blown farther away than the rest of his pack by the initial explosion, was still very much alive.

“Help me. Please help me,” it begged in French. Dallas reached for the now-empty pistol and paused. The werewolf's eyes were a bright and very human-looking grey, instead of the pitch black that they normally were. Dallas pulled his leg free but did not strike the wolf, suddenly unsure of what to do. Instead, he ran on up the hill to check on Miller.

Arriving at the crash site, he pushed his way to the front. The monster was most certainly dead, its head attached to its neck by only a few strings of flesh. Black blood still pulsed from its trunk. Miller must have somehow managed to cleave its head off in mid-flight. But where was he?

“He’s here!” someone shouted. The men turned toward the voice. Miller had been crushed underneath the demon’s massive bulk. Blood ran freely from his mouth. He laid still, eyes staring blankly at the stars above in the night sky.

# 2 - Arrival

Someplace in New Jersey - Today

He was staring up at the stars as if waking from a dream. He had been dead, he was sure of that. For him, being dead was no new experience, but the act of dying was not what he considered a good time. Being dead was not awful. It was not cold, it was not dark. There was no bright light, at least not for him. There was simply nothing, and nothing was not so bad.

Then just like that, with a blink, he was back. He never understood why or how, but there was no arguing against it. For thousands of years, he had been mankind's protector. He had had many names throughout time. He had been Gilgamesh, Orion, Beowulf, and Theseus. In China he had been called Lu Tung-Pin, the great slayer of dragons. The demons called him "The Great Hunter" and "Ancient One." In recent times, he had taken the name Joseph Miller. The demons would appear and he would be reborn and hunt them down. It was the natural order of things. Perhaps it was done to strike some kind of balance between good and evil, or maybe some god just found it amusing to toss him at the monsters of the world again and again. He supposed it was a curse of sorts to never truly rest, but it rarely bothered him. After all this time, it was just what he did, what he was, as natural as breathing. Maybe it had driven him mad long ago and he no longer noticed. One of the two.

He took a long, deep breath and his face twisted in disgust. The air tasted terrible here, like his time in London, and the smells were all new, and not exactly pleasant. Looking around, nothing resembled the things he had seen in all of his many years. Huge buildings of glass, like giant trees, sprung up in every direction. "Well, well, this should be interesting," he thought, and took his first step forward.

A loud screeching noise filled his ears as a huge metal beast sprang at him, striking him full on. As he felt the darkness retake him, he thought, "This is not starting well."

*****

The truck driver didn't see the small Hispanic man until it was far too late. "Why was the idiot standing in the middle of the road past midnight? Fool deserved to be hit by a truck," he told himself as he dialed 911.

# 3 - Ann

In her dreams, all she could hear were the drums.

All she could see was darkness.

All she could feel were the snake's dry scales against her flesh.

Ann woke with a start and thrashed wildly about the bed, trying to break free before realizing she was alone on her couch in her living room. Safe. The dream faded quickly. Her head pounded and her stomach again had that tightness that had been so common of late, the feeling that her muscles were twisted in knots. Enough with the nightmares!

"Ugh," she said to herself, "No more all-night movie marathons for me." She had inflicted herself with some modern Sci-Fi channel "classics," including "Girlsquito" and "Raptor vs. Rattlesnake," in an all-night girl geek-out with her friend Lizzie. It was not a typical girly thing to do, but Lizzie was hardly typical, and of late Ann couldn't handle sappy dramas. So, bad sci-fi it was. Ann was not supposed to drink, as she was taking large dosages of antibiotics to help fight off Lyme disease, but Kahlua mudslides were required to deal with such terrible movies. Her head spun and her stomach churned, reminding her far too late just how bad of an idea it had all been. It had been fun while it lasted, but she was going to pay for it today. She struggled off the couch and headed to the shower.

Lizzie was apparently long gone, off to do God knew what. Lizzie was a computer programmer who had struck it rich years ago with some minor but useful piece of software and now drifted through life doing whatever she pleased. She liked to slum with her poor student friends from time to time, and as long as Lizzie was buying the drinks...

Ann quickly showered and dressed. After a quick glance, she studied herself more carefully in the mirror. She was a short girl with long blond hair, and was far, far too skinny, according to her friends and family. Now though, looking in the mirror, she looked old, her face swollen and puffy. Her hair just did not want to lie correctly. It shot off in random directions, giving her the "stuck a fork in an electrical outlet" look. She fiddled with it for a long time before giving up and just forcing it into a long ponytail.

She managed to down some toast without vomiting up a lung and used some day-old coffee to knock down yet another horse-sized dose of her meds, plus a handful of Motrin. She spent a minute just staring out of the one nice part of her tiny seventh-floor apartment - a large window through which she could make out most of the New York City skyline. Then, grabbing her coat and her phone, she was off to another fun-filled day at the lab.

Outside it was a clear, cool spring day in Newark. The sun did little to lift Ann's spirits and she dug in the pockets of her oversized coat for her emergency hangover sunglasses. For two years now, Ann had been a full time PhD student at the College of Medicine and Dentistry of New Jersey (CMDNJ), studying biology. It saddened her to think that her whole academic career had been built around her high-school boyfriend, Keith, who was a doctor. He had dumped her just six months ago, leaving her somewhat adrift in life. That was, of course, until last week, when sparks flew between them again, leading to what she hoped wasn't just a one-night stand.

She checked her phone. Keith had not returned her calls, or her emails, or her text messages. It had been a full week! The jerk could at least let her know he had made it home okay. Was Keith really so cruel that he would do this to her again? Their first breakup had been devastating, tearing her whole life into tatters. Well, that wasn't going to do. If she was going to be miserable, so was he. He worked just across the street in the College Hospital emergency room. There was no hiding from her. During her lunch she could just drop by and have a word. "Yes," she said aloud, a grin covering her face for the first time this morning. "That would be just fine." The decision made Ann begin to feel a little bit better.

Newark was not normally the prettiest of cities. In April however, flowering trees on almost every street would come into bloom. The city itself was going through a rebirth. In recent years, a new mayor had begun turning the city around. The crime rate was down, several large office buildings were being built, and many of the older, ruined buildings were demolished. The city's skyline seemed to change almost daily.

Something that had not changed in the city was the homeless. One particular old, blind, and homeless black man had recently taken up residence in front of a closed-down movie theatre on Ann's way to work. He was the strangest man Ann had ever seen. He wore a suit that was extremely old-fashioned and incredibly dirty, complete with a bow tie that at one point, many centuries ago, may have been red. On his face were dark sunglasses, hiding ruined eyes that Ann would sometimes get a glimpse of as she passed. He had a thick wooden cane always by his side as he lay sprawled out in front of the old ticket box. He must have been quite tall, as his legs seemed to go on forever, but Ann had never seen him standing. In front of his usual resting place, he had placed a ruined top hat, which held a few pieces of loose change. Next to the hat was a cardboard sign. This sign changed every day. Today, it said in shaky black ink, "I believe in angels" with a little winged stick figure. Every day he sang the same song. When Ann got close enough she dropped a dollar into the hat.

"Good morning little sister!" he said in a low, scratchy voice.

"Good morning," Ann said as she passed, quickening her step a bit.

"May I just say," the homeless man continued, staring at nothing in particular, "you look positively radiant today." He then laughed a low, sickly laugh. He had never said anything to her before and Ann found the whole experience creepy. She would have to find a new way to work.

Ann arrived at the lab of Dr. Larry Conners. He was Ann's advisor and a nice guy, but a bit of a has-been. He was older, maybe in his early 50s, with just a few strands of white hair combed over in a feeble attempt to imitate a head full of hair. He was missing a large chunk of his left arm, due to an alligator incident years ago. Still, at one point he must have been someone important, because he still had funding for real cancer research.

Entering the lab, Ann saw Wen Li, Dr. Conners' other PhD student, talking to someone Ann didn't know. Wen was a Chinese man of about thirty who was frustratingly intelligent. He was also always extremely happy, which made it hard not to like him. They were conversing in Spanish. Ann wondered to herself how many languages this man knew. She knew that he spoke several dialects of Chinese, perfect English, and now Spanish. She was jealous.

Seeing her enter the room, Wen gave her a friendly wink. Attempting not to disturb the discussion, Ann went directly to her bench and began to prepare for the day's work. She opened her lab journal and scrawled the date on a blank page. She noted that she had not actually written anything inside in several days. She promised herself she wouldn't let Conners sere her slipping like this.

In time, Wen and the stranger's discussion came to a close and the slim, energetic man bounced across the floor to say hello.

"Ann Melakh, you have killed my father, now prepare to die!" He took on a fencing stance and mimed running Ann through with a sword. Despite herself, she grinned.

"So you liked it then?"

"The Princess Bride? How could I not? And my daughter loved it!" Wen's face nearly split in half with his huge smile.

"I'm still kinda surprised that you'd never seen it," Ann shot back.

"Believe it or not, I have not seen every American movie ever made. Now it's my turn to pick the movie. Have you ever heard of 'Drunken Master?'"

"Umm, a kung fu flick? You know I'm a girl, right?"

Wen pulled a DVD out of his lab coat. "Try it. It's a very young Jackie Chan. My wife says he was very hot."

Ann took the offered DVD between thumb and index finger, keeping it as far away from her person as possible, as if it smelled bad.

"If you say so. Hey - what was that all about?" Ann gestured towards the place where the stranger had been. "You know Spanish?"

"Of course I speak Spanish. I don't know how you function only knowing one language. And that was housekeeping."

"Housekeeping?"

"Yes. It appears our employer recently fired our regular janitor. He stopped showing up to work a few days ago and the good Dr. Conners took offense."

"Hmmm, I had noticed it was a bit messy in here." Ann eyed her overflowing garbage can.

"So that was our new janitor and I was just introducing myself."

"In Spanish? You suck-up."

Wen looked a bit sheepish. "By the way, Conners was looking for you before."

"Really? Thanks, I'll check in with him in a few."

A few minutes later, Ann slipped into Dr. Conners' small office.

"What can I do for you?"

The older man looked up from his work, giving her a dry smile. "Ann, ah good. I wanted to ask how you were coming along with Dr. Dupré's sample."

"The lily? I'm pretty much nowhere. It seems to be just a regular old lily. Are you sure this Dupré lady isn't just messing with us?"

"Oh, quite sure. Dr. Dupré was my mentor many, many years ago. She's done some pretty amazing research. If she says that sample is something useful, then we need to take a look."

"She was your mentor? That must make her, like, ancient…" Ann trailed off, suddenly realizing how rude she was being. "I mean, not that you're old. I'm just saying…"

Conner waved a dismissive hand at her. "Don't worry about it Ann. In truth, she does have to be getting up there. She wasn't exactly young when she was teaching. I had expected her to retire a long time ago. Still, the research could mean some new funding for us, which is always a good thing."

"And she knows we don't usually work with flowers?"

"Ann, this is a special one-time deal, and I'm letting you take care of it for me. She's actually coming here in person to talk about your research, so do your best with it, okay? If you get stuck, maybe ask Wen to help."

Ann sighed. "Of course. I'll do my best." She left the office.

Back at her bench, she took out the sample and looked it over again. It appeared to be a normal lily, its petals already turning black and wrinkled. Somewhere in the back of her mind, she half remembered a nightmare about the flower. There had been something dark and sinister about it.

She really had to lay off the late-night horror films. She placed the sample to the side. Like all great procrastinators, she planned on doing something about it later and never did.

When noon came at last, she headed across the street to the hospital. College Hospital was a bland concrete structure with dark blue tinted windows. Ann had always wondered why people didn't make hospitals look more inviting. At least for her, they always seemed to hold a sense of dread. It probably had to do with all the dying people.

She snuck in the ambulance entrance, something she wasn't really supposed to do, but then again, rules were for those who got caught. She had been here many times and several people knew who she was. She waved to a few EMTs on the way in and headed to the emergency room reception area. Stacy Kline was working at the front desk. A nurse in her early 40s, she had always been friendly enough.

"Hi Stacy, is Keith around?"

Stacy looked up from some papers she was sorting.

"Little Ann! Long time no see. You and Keith dating again?"

Ann blushed a bit. "Well actually sorta. At least, I thought so." She paused, feeling a bit sheepish talking about this with someone else. "I'm actually going to try and find that out today. Is that too much information?"

"Ah," Stacy said with a grin, "I'm not getting involved. Just try and keep the drama off hospital grounds."

"Yeah, like that's possible with the hours you people work," Ann grinned back. "So, have you noticed him sulking about?"

"Dr. Malone was here earlier. However," Stacy leaned forward and lowered her voice, "don't let him know I said that." They shared a conspiratorial grin.

"Lab rat's honor." Ann waved as she took off down the hall.

It seemed to be a really slow day, and Ann passed very few patients as she made her way through the long tangle of corridors. She glanced in each room that she passed for signs of Keith. Not seeing Keith on the first floor, she went up one flight of stairs. In one of the rooms, she noticed a friendly face.

"Cynthia!" The plump older woman looked up from a patient's chart.

"Little Ann! How are you?"

She raised her arms in the universal sign, showing that she wanted a hug from the older woman. They shared a quick embrace. Cynthia was a tech and a near-stereotypical older Irish woman. Her hair was curly red with just a bit of white mixed in, and her face was covered in freckles. She was on the plump side, free-spirited, and loved to hit the bars with her husband, Scott. Ann and Keith had gone on quite a few pub crawls with the couple but could never keep up.

"Oh, sorry," Ann said, noting the unconscious man on the bed.

"Oh no worries, he's out cold. He was admitted a few days ago. Hit by a truck and on enough drugs that he won't be waking up for a long time.

A good thing too."

Ann inspected the short Hispanic man. His left arm and leg were immobilized in casts that were wired in place. One of his eyes was covered and enough bandages were wrapped around his chest to give the impression of a mummy.

"Ouch," Ann said, "That had to hurt." Looking at the man, she thought he looked very familiar, although she couldn't quite place him.

"I almost socked Dr. Malone when I heard what he did to you." Cynthia threw a punch out in the air, somewhere above Ann's head. "Men are beasts. Monsters, I tell you! But why are you here? Did he come to his senses?"

"Well," Ann began, "I thought so. We kinda had a thing last week…"

"A thing, eh?" She nudged Ann in the ribs a bit and then sighed. "Ahh, to be young again."

"... but then nothing all week."

"That dog. That low dog." Cynthia shook her head.

"Hello ladies," said a voice from behind. Both women jumped and turned toward the patient, who was very much awake. They stared open-mouthed at him.

"I am sorry. Where are my manners? Was I interrupting?" he continued. His accent was strange, almost Scottish but then something else. Ann struggled to place it. It was like one of the characters from the Lord of the Rings doing a bad Sean Connery impression.

Cynthia recovered. "Oh no sir, we were just chatting a bit. We didn't wake you, did we?"

"Oh yes, but that is fine. I think I have been sleeping enough of late," the man answered back. He seemed to notice his surroundings for the first time. "Would you mind telling me where I am?"

"Of course, you're at College Hospital in Newark."

"Newark?" he asked. Ann and Cynthia exchanged glances.

"In New Jersey," Ann offered.

"Jersey?" The man seemed to chew the word in his mouth for a long moment. "Oh, New Jersey. In the Americas." He put on a broad smile and grinned at the girls. "That is fine. I have not been here in, oh," he paused, "you cannot imagine how long."

The Americas? Ann thought that bump on the head must have done some real damage.

"Are you from Scotland?" Ann asked.

"Oh no," replied the man, "Africa originally, but I spent a lot of time in Scotland over the last, err, several years. Lovely place!"

Cynthia cut in, trying to get to her job. "I should get you a doctor in here." She keyed the intercom. "This is room 269. Can you page Dr. Black? Her patient is awake." She looked back down at the strange man. "Sir, what's your name, and do you have any folks that I should have a nurse contact?"

"Oh, how rude of me. Joseph Miller, at your service, ladies."

Ann giggled a bit at that. There was something truly goofy about this man. Her giggle only made the man's smile broaden. "Is my name amusing to you, lass?"

"Oh no. Sorry." Ann looked down at the floor.

"Mr. Miller, do you have any health insurance?" Cynthia asked.

Miller seemed to consider this for awhile. "I don't think so. Should I?"

"Ann, you stay here, I'm going to see if I can find Dr. Black," Cynthia said, heading out the door. As she passed Ann she added under her breath, "and maybe get someone from the psych ward up here for this one."

"Umm, sure." Ann grinned and shrugged. It wasn't like she worked here, but then this guy wasn't in any shape to hurt her or anything. "Let me know if you see Keith though!"

With Cynthia gone, there was an awkward silence as Miller grinned at Ann.

"Husband?" Miller offered.

"What?"

"This Keith fellow..."

"Oh no, he isn't even much of a boyfriend anymore," Ann said bitterly.

"Fantastic," Miller said. The grin did not move from his face. It made Ann very uncomfortable. Was he hitting on her?

Dr. Vanessa Black entered the room, nodding a curt hello to Ann. She was a tall, dark-haired woman who was smart, sexy, witty…and a complete bitch. Ann couldn't stand her. She was very happy to make room for her now though. It was good to put some distance between her and the strange, broken man. Doctor Black went through a series of tests, asking Miller various questions. Miller answered them all in his own vague way, suddenly seeming less playful. He stared at his doctor like a hungry wolf. Ann waited until the doctor left and then, letting some disgust creep into her voice, she said to Miller, "You really shouldn't stare at women like that."

Miller seemed to jump a bit, as if switching gears in his mind. The grin reappeared on his face. "I am sorry lass, you speak true, but although it's been a long time since I have been with a lady, you misunderstand me."

"Oh really?" Ann crossed her arms on her chest, trying her best to look stern.

"Oh yes. You see, lass, that's no woman."

Ann gave him a sarcastic smile. "Right…"

Miller looked defensive.

“She is one of the ‘Fallen.’”

“The what?” Ann asked.

“A demon.”

# 4 - Samson and the Wolf

He was awake. He wasn't sure why yet, but he was. It wasn't the usual nightmare. He was sure of that. Mike glanced at his wife's spot on the other side of the bed. It was still a bit of a shock seeing it empty, even after six months.

Then, the baby monitor on the nightstand grabbed his attention. From it, Mike could make out a faint scratching noise. Odd. What would make that noise? He struggled over to the nightstand and slowly cranked up the volume on the monitor.

A woman's voice drifted through, at last loud enough to make out.

"Help me. Please help my baby!"

Electricity seemed to snap down his spine. Someone was in Sam's room. "Oh God," he whispered. He threw himself out the door of his bedroom and down the short, narrow flight of stairs to the first floor. "Oh God, oh God, oh God…"

His body was moving much faster than his mind, the fog of sleep slowing his wits. Someone had gotten into the house and was now doing God-knows-what to little Sam.

He rounded the corner to Sam's room and threw the door open to see...nothing. The boy was sleeping peacefully in bed. Mike stared for several minutes, watching his young son breathe. He glanced at the matching baby monitor that sat on his son's nightstand. It wasn't on.

"Damn, I forgot to turn the damn thing on. Hell of a father I am," he said to himself. But where had the woman's voice come from? He knew he hadn't dreamt it. Racing back up the stairs, he confirmed that the monitor was still getting a signal from somewhere.

"Please…" the woman's voice was back, seeming to trail off. Turning up the volume, he could hear a terrible gurgling noise.

It must be another baby monitor running on the same frequency nearby. It had happened before. Here in the suburbs of New Jersey, the houses were more than close enough for that. The house that made the most sense was Ted and Susan Zhang's, a Chinese-American couple who had a girl just a little younger than Sam and lived directly across the street. The couples were close friends and when the Zhangs found themselves pregnant, Mike and his wife Melissa had recommended several items, including the baby monitor.

Was it any of his business? The woman, who had to be Susan Zhang, sounded hurt. Well, he was a police officer, even though he had not done much more in his short career than traffic duty. "To protect and serve" still counted, though, even in your pajamas in the middle of night. And if his neighbor was hurt and he did nothing, he would never forgive himself.

He picked up the phone on his stand and quickly dialed his neighbors' number. Four rings, then the click of the answering machine. Okay, so much for the easy way. He grabbed his coat and then, on a hunch, took the hand gun from his room and pushed himself out into the cool spring night air. Outside, the moon was as visible as a fingernail, failing to do anything useful even though the sky was clear. In the electric light of the street lamps, all of the houses looked the same, like in that old episode of The Twilight Zone. Mike took a moment to organize his thoughts. Would he just knock on the door and explain that he had heard someone asking for help on his baby monitor? Yeah, like that would fly well.

As he crossed the street, Mike thought back to a few days ago, when he had last seen the Zhang family. It had been a bright spring afternoon. He had just pulled up to the house after picking Sam up at his in-laws and was helping him out of his booster seat in the car. Sam noticed the Zhangs across the street.

"Sally!" he shouted and waved. The girl was out with her father taking a walk. She giggled in the way that toddlers do and waved back at Sam. Sam made a dash to cross the street, but Mike snatched his hand.

"No crossing a street without an adult," he said and together they walked over to their neighbors. Once they had reached the other side, a game of tag started, with Sam as "it." The kids ducked in and out of their parents' legs, screaming and laughing. "The toddler screech," Melissa had called it.

Ted had a cast around his hand. Mike pointed it out. "Everything alright?"

Looking down at it Ted said, "Oh it's nothing big. Fell down the stairs and busted my hand. Ended up in the emergency room this morning. Hurt like hell."

After more small talk, Mike picked up Sam to bring him home and inflict more of his terrible cooking on him. The Zhangs had seemed fine at the time. Now, in the chill of the night, Mike's concern grew for his neighbors.

Mike bounded up the short flight of stairs that led to the front door of the Zhangs' small two-story home. As he reached the top step, his shoes crunched on glass. The house had two doors - a screen door that was half glass and half metal screen, and a sturdy metal door behind. The glass of the first door was shattered, with pieces lying as far as several feet away. He made to reach for the doorbell but then noticed that the metal door was open as well, just a crack. Something was definitely wrong here. Mike pulled his revolver, a strong sense of dread forming in the pit of his stomach. After several deep, calming breaths, he carefully pushed the metal door open and slipped inside.

Mike thought back to his detective studies. He had tried to take the detective test several times, but had yet to pass. Still, some of what he had learned came back to mind. This had to be a break-in, but the glass on the front step would imply a "break out." Someone had broken the glass on their way out, which didn't make much sense. Maybe they were leaving in a hurry and had come in through another point of entry, perhaps a window that had been forced open somewhere in the house. If so, the chances were good that the perp was long gone. He kept the gun out, just in case.

"Ted? Susan? It's Mike," he called out into the darkness of the house. Then, thinking better of it, he followed up with, "This is Officer Samson." There was no answer. He had been in the house several times and knew the little girl's room was upstairs, so made that his first destination. Moving slowly in the dark, he found the light switch and flicked it quickly to the "on" position. The sudden light was blinding and it took a few painfully-long seconds for his eyes to adjust. A look around revealed no armed criminal in waiting. The house was generally quite neat. Mike noticed that the front door had been knocked out of its frame a bit. The plaster around the door was destroyed and the frame could plainly be seen under the wood trim. That was really odd. Very sloppy yet extremely strong thieves.

Mike made his way upstairs, which was a mess. Something had definitely gone down here. The light from the street poured in through a broken window at the end of the hall. Clothes and furniture were tossed about and there were dark stains on the floor which Mike was pretty sure were blood.

Mike could sense that something terrible had happened here. He poked his head into the first room, a bathroom. It looked generally normal, apart from the hideous pink and black floor tile. The next was a bedroom. It was a bit disheveled but much better than his room at the moment.

The last room in the hallway was the kid's room, made obvious by the various toys that were scattered in the doorway. The sense of dread that had been slowly building in him reached a screaming pitch.

The room was dark as Mike entered. Feeling along the wall, he found the switch he was looking for. The light snapped on, and Mike almost vomited. He had witnessed some terrible car accidents in his time, seen his fair share of mangled, mutilated bodies, but this was so much worse. Susan lay sprawled on the floor, covered with blood. Her torso had been torn open and, judging by the amount of blood around the room, she had taken a long time to die, crawling towards her child. Worse still was the tiny body that lay sprawled on the child's bed. Most of the flesh was gone, revealing a tiny white skull. Only the right hand of the little girl remained unmolested, standing out as proof that this pile of flesh and bone had once been the little girl he had seen in the sandbox, laughing with his son.

“Oh God.” Mike's courage broke and panic took him as he dashed down the stairs, away from the nightmare. He would have kept running, but once outside he spotted someone standing in the middle of the street. Mike skidded to a halt and drew his gun, his heart hammering in his chest.

“Freeze! Police!” For a second Mike and the man stared at each other. The man was not much taller than Mike, but was built like a bodybuilder. His hair stuck out at all sorts of odd angles and he seemed to have long knives attached to his fingers, which looked like inch-long claws. Terror ran up and down Mike's spine again as the man charged at him like some kind of crazed animal. A strange howl erupted from the charging beast-man. This had to be the thing that had so brutally murdered his neighbors. That thought, and the fear that followed, made Mike pull the trigger of his gun, not once but three times. The bullets all found their marks. Mike was a decent shot and the range was short, but the man didn’t slow. He collided into Mike, knives biting into flesh, pinning Mike’s arms against his chest and driving both men to the ground.

For a second, the attacker paused and Mike could see his face clearly. It was covered with wiry hair and the teeth were all wrong, but he could see that it was Ted. The most disturbing thing was his eyes, which were a solid black. Like pitch. Ted growled and brought a hand up to strike. It was covered with the remains of his cast. Mike screamed as he realized that the blades he had seen were not knives, but claws that were digging into him. The fear gave him strength, and he bucked and kicked. Mike managed to bring his hand, still carrying the gun, straight up to his chest. As Ted’s claws came down, he pointed the barrel of the gun at his attacker’s chin, firing it just as the claws dug deep into his chest. The bullet tore though Ted’s chin, through the entire length of his head, and blasted out of the top of his skull in a spray of brains. Ted made a choking noise and rolled off of Mike.

Pain radiated all over Mike’s body and blood gushed from his chest. It took him a few moments to notice that he was screaming and few more moments to make himself stop. He glanced to where Ted had landed, but he was gone.

“What the hell?!” he shouted, once again raising his pistol. There was nothing there but a trail of what Mike assumed to be blood. A million questions ran through Mike’s fear-ridden brain. Had that really been Ted? If so, what the hell had happened to him? How the hell did he get back up after having his brains blown out of the back of his head?

Mike struggled to his feet, one hand still pointing the gun out at the darkness, the other pressed against the cut on his chest, trying to keep pressure on the wound. He limped toward his house. He had to get back to his son. With several painful steps, he managed to cross the street. He fought with the lock for a bit before managing to throw the door open and push through. Spinning around, he slammed the door and locked it again, and then dashed back to Sam's room. The sight of his sleeping son, breathing quietly, calmed his mind a bit. He slid down onto the floor, suddenly remembering his wounds. They throbbed. He needed to call this in and then he needed to see a doctor. Then maybe he would have a nice mental breakdown. He got up and made the call.

"This is Officer Mike Samson." He gave the woman on the other end of the phone his badge number. "I need to report a double homicide." He gave the address.

"Officer Samson, we have a car heading there now," the woman's voice on the other side stated. Hanging up, he headed to the bathroom, stripped off his shirt, and quickly bandaged his cuts. He could see the lights from the arriving squad car outside. He would deal with them in a moment. First, though, he crawled into his son's bed and held him, tears rolling down his cheeks.

# 5 - Monsters

Catharine's first two days on the job for FedEx had been pretty rocky. She had dropped packages, gotten lost twice, and fallen down a flight of stairs. Still, the job had been a stroke of good luck after a string of terrible disasters. No one wanted to hire a junkie, even an ex-junkie. An old high-school friend she had bumped into at church had pulled some major strings for her. Yes, she had been to church, and how funny was that? But she had a lot to repent for and if she was going to turn this worthless life around, it seemed like a good place to start. Her manager had been the one that had interviewed her, and he had somehow managed to see past her messy dreads and nervous stutter to find someone worth hiring. She was determined to prove him right.

On the third day, when she arrived at College Hospital, she was having a better time with things. The box for the delivery at this address was quite heavy and she made sure to strap it to her little cart correctly. There would be no dropping this one. With her luck, it was probably some cure for an incredibly rare disease and dropping the box would mean a roomful of kids would die. As she weaved her cart through the hospital entrance, her mind came up with more and more incredible items that could be in the box. The last of these was a new liver for the President of the United States, with her screw-up would mean the downfall of modern western civilization.

As she approached the front desk, a nurse noticed her.

"Package delivery," Catharine said in her most professional voice.

"Oh, I bet that's our new coffee machine. Hey Mary, can you show her where to store this?"

"Sure thing." Mary was a tall, good-looking white nurse who had been busy chatting with a handsome doctor. Heck, the pair looked to be right out of some soap opera. Mary waved her over to a nearby elevator and Catharine followed. She struggled to get the box through the door before the elevator doors clamped shut. Can't ruin the coffee maker, doctors need their caffeine. She still had the lives of hundreds of people in her hands. She smiled at the thought.

Mary made no attempt at small talk as the elevator descended one floor, so Catharine kept her mouth shut as well. She figured that was the professional way to go. When the elevator doors opened, Mary stepped out and waved her on.

"This way."

Catharine again struggled with the cart and then followed the nurse down the hall and into a sort of break room. "It'll be fine in here," Mary told her.

Catharine began unstrapping the box from the cart, and as she did, she noticed that the nurse was standing far too close to her. It made her uncomfortable but she tried to ignore it.

"Umm, sign here."

"Of course," Mary replied, scrawling something on Catharine's data pad. Handing it back, she said, "Now let's see what we can do with you." She stepped in closer, lightly brushing Catharine's cheek with a perfect hand. Her eyes locked with Catharine, looking somehow hungry.

"Look, I don't…" Catharine began to argue.

"Ssssh," Mary stopped her. Catharine knew she should step back, get away, and yet she couldn't. There was something odd about this woman, something horrible in that perfect face.

She felt a strange panic rising up in her stomach. Some small voice was telling her to flee, but she could not seem to bring herself to run. Suddenly and violently, the nurse grabbed the back of her hair and pushed their mouths together in an awkward kiss. The nurse pushed Catharine's mouth open with her tongue. At last coming awake, Catharine tried to break free, but the nurse's grip was too strong. There was a sound like a wet cough and something slimy filled her mouth! Catharine at last pulled away and started to gag as whatever it was slid down her throat. She fell to the floor, trying to scream as she stared up at the nurse, but couldn't get any air into her lungs. The nurse stared back, stroking Catharine's hair. Her eyes were perfectly black, as if filled with ink.

"There, there, it will be alright in a minute. Welcome to the family."

And then she could breathe again, as whatever it was traveled back up past her throat. She did not waste time on screaming and instead struggled to her feet and ran. She moved faster than she ever had in her life, out of the door and down the hall. She collided with a woman on the way, but picked herself up and kept running.

She ran and ran, bursting out of the front doors of the hospital. She charged toward her truck, tearing the key out of her pocket. She slammed the key into place and gunned the engine...and then stopped. What was she doing? She couldn't remember. She shook her head. She must have nodded off for a second. She couldn't be doing that. She had more work to do. She did feel good though. In fact, she felt better than she had in a long time.

*****

Ann did not find Keith that first day, nor did she find him the next. The people at the hospital all said that they had seen him around recently, but none could say exactly when. It was driving her crazy. Near the end of her second tour of the hospital, she once again passed Mr. Miller's room and was drawn inside.

"Miss Ann." The sound of his voice made her wince a bit. She was unsure what to make of him. Somehow he managed to creep her out and make her laugh at the same time. And then there was the whole demon speech from yesterday. She also couldn't shake the feeling that they had met before

"Hiya," Ann said, and gave him a halfhearted wave.

"Come over here. I have something amazing here," he said, quickly waving his one good arm, beckoning her. He reminded Ann of a four-year-old who wanted to show off his latest toy. "Look. Look. Look." He pointed to a television screen showing the hospital welcome screen. Relaxing photos of happy doctors and patients moved across it.

"Um, so?" Ann asked, a bit baffled.

"The pictures. They move by themselves! No moving parts whatsoever. It's brilliant!"

"You mean the TV? You've never seen a TV before?"

"No, never. Are they common? What fantastic things! I was impressed with the electronic candles but when the nurse turned on this box..."

"You really don't get out much do you? Look, here, let me show you." She snagged the remote from the bed-stand and changed the channel. A talk show was on.

"Ah. It has more than one picture? Wait, are they actually inside there?"

Ann shook her head. How could someone not know what a TV was? "No, it's television. It's a show recorded someplace else and then played back here."

"Like a camera with moving pictures." Miller was breathless. "How many *shows* can it do?" He said the word "shows" slowly. It must have been his new word of the day.

"Oh, sometimes hundreds at once."

Miller's jaw dropped. "That is truly amazing! Now if it could only make sound. Music maybe."

Ann rolled her eyes, smiled, and pushed up the volume.

Miller gasped.

Ann sat down in the empty chair by the bed and for a moment they sat in silence, absorbed by the TV.

"Thank you for showing me this," Miller said.

"Oh it's no trouble. I figure one of the nurses or techs would have shown you. No kidding, you've never seen a TV before?"

"I do not 'kid' you. This is a first for me." He paused, glancing back at the screen. "People must never leave their houses!"

Ann shrugged. "Actually, that is kind of an issue."

"I guess that I missed it. I have been away for a bit."

"Really? How long?"

"Let us just say a long time and leave it at that." Miller's grin was back on his face.

"Right," Ann said, "Whatever. Look, I have to go. Apparently, I've become my ex-boyfriend's stalker and I need to finish up my rounds."

Miller's face was suddenly serious. "Ann, you will think I am mad for this, but please do something for me."

"I make no promises, crazy man."

"Just stay away from Dr. Black. She is very dangerous and it would be a shame for a nice young lass like you to be injured." There was genuine concern in his eyes. "Perhaps stay away from this whole area for a few days."

"Look, I've known Vanessa Black for a few years now. She's a bitch, but she's harmless."

"Take my word, Ann. That person you knew is no longer with us. Just give her some space." He tapped the cast on his right arm. "I'll handle her in a few days, once I get this off."

Handle her? Good lord, this guy should be in the psych ward. She stepped away, wondering for a moment if you could catch crazy.

"And on that bizarre note, I'm out!"

She gave Miller a quick wave and dashed out of the room. She wondered why she had stopped there in the first place.

Moving on down the hall, she poked her head into the last few rooms with open doors. This was getting crazy. She *was* becoming a stalker. Obviously Keith was hiding from her, and if he was too much of a coward to face her, what could she do?

"Okay then, one more floor and then back to work, and Keith Malone? You're dead to me."

It wasn't the "great telling off" that she had planned in her head, but it would have to do.

She headed past a nurses' station where Vanessa Black was talking to a nurse. She paused, wondering if she should warn her. Just because she really didn't like Vanessa didn't mean she wouldn't feel horrible if, a few weeks from now, crazy man managed to get out of traction and attacked her, thinking she was some kind of monster.

"Umm, excuse me Dr. Black. I think you should know something."

Vanessa silenced her with an open hand and finished talking to the nurse. They were chatting about American Idol. For a second Ann considered storming off but then held her peace. Finally turning to Ann,

Vanessa said, “Now Miss Melakh, what can I do for you?”

“Look, I just wanted to warn you, the patient in room 269…”

“Let me stop you right there.” Again Vanessa put her hand in front of Ann's face. “I've heard you’re looking for Dr. Malone. I know you and he had a relationship in the past. However, this does not give you the right to run around my hospital bothering my staff and my patients.”

“Hey, listen, you...”

“No. You listen,” Vanessa shouted, the anger slipping into her voice. “If I see you in here one more time, I will call security and have you dragged out of here.” The sentence seemed to end in a snarl. The two women stared at each other..

“Fine,” Ann turned to leave, “Bitch.” She stormed to the nearest elevator, pushing past the two nurses getting out. As the doors closed, Ann gave Vanessa the middle finger and slammed the button, not for the ground floor, but for the basement.

“You won't be rid of me that easy.”

She had actually never been in the basement. She had first imagined that Keith was just working, not avoiding her, but now she was going to widen the search a bit. The elevator stopped and as she stepped out, another woman plowed into her. They tumbled, forming a mass of arms and legs on the floor.

She was young, dark-skinned, and a bit overweight. Her hair was done up in dreads and she wore a FedEx uniform.

“Are you okay? I can...” Ann asked, pushing herself up and offering the woman a free hand.

The woman ignored Ann and dashed down the hall. Ann watched her run, heading for the stairway. Turning around, she caught sight of a familiar-looking nurse who winked at her, waved, and entered a room on the right. Glancing back and forth between the fleeing figure and the nurse, Ann shook her head.

“Okay, that was odd,” she said aloud.

Heading down the hall, a bit shaken, she noticed two orderlies farther down the hall. The two massive, hairy men nodded at her as she passed. Their huge uniforms could barely contain them, as if they had shrunk in the wash.

“You new here, fellas?” she asked in passing. The man on the right, who looked vaguely Asian, simply grunted. “Not much for talking then. I'll just move along.”

This looked like a psych ward. At least that’s what her extensive movie-watching experience told her. Mean-looking orderlies? Check. Lots of rooms with locks on the outsides and windows to peek in through? Check. Crazy people, like the woman by the elevator? Check.

She glanced into a room at random. Through the window she could see a man in a *straight jacket,* drooling. Double-check. There was no way Keith was hiding here. It was way too creepy for that big chicken. Ann decided to turn back.

Just as she was about to head back to the elevator, something slammed hard against the door of one of the rooms, making the door vibrate in its frame. Curiosity got the better of her and she walked down the hall and put her head to the glass.

"Oh my God."

Inside was a man, or at least something like a man, completely naked. Black scales like a snake's covered most of his chest and shoulders. One arm was massive, its knuckles dragging on the ground. Foam sprayed from his mouth and his eyes were jet-black. From his back jutted one massive bat-like wing, which flapped aimlessly. The man-creature, whatever he was, was in a rage. He smashed the door with his oversized fist, tossed himself to the ground, and then flung himself against the door again. He seemed to be screaming, though the room was apparently soundproof, as no noise reached Ann's ears.

She stared, wide-eyed, at the thing. Was it a man with some kind of new disease? Was this even possible? A wing?

Suddenly, someone grabbed her shoulder and flung her back, slamming her into the wall across the hall. Black spots briefly blurred her vision. When they cleared, Vanessa Black was over her, her face misshapen with rage.

"Vanessa, what the hell...urk," Vanessa's right hand latched on to Ann's neck and lifted her off the ground. The wind had been knocked out of her and her lungs instantly started to burn. Her feet dangling, she grabbed Vanessa's arm, desperately trying to get free and breathe.

"I know what you're doing," Vanessa said, "and he is mine. Mine!" The "mine" was more scream than speech. Vanessa's hand suddenly seemed to bulge and the skin split. Underneath, Ann could see the same black scales that the man in the cell in front of them had. Vanessa growled and tossed Ann down the hall. She flew a good fifteen feet before hitting the ground and skidding to a stop.

Ann lay on the cold floor for a second, panting. Vanessa was standing over her, her hand now a huge black talon. She rubbed her claws together, creating a sound disturbingly like nails on a chalkboard.

"Be happy the law keeps me from killing you."

Vanessa's words seemed to knock Ann out of her shock. To put it plain and simple, she lost it. Picking herself up, she took off at a mad sprint down the hall. There was no screaming. She didn't have air in her lungs for more than running. She ran past the two orderlies, who had watched the exchange, unimpressed. She ran past the elevator and made a sharp turn at the stairway, flying up the stairs two at a time, following a similar path to the woman before her. She didn't stop running for a very long time.

In Ann's panic to escape, she did not notice the extremely tall blind man in the old suit and ruined old top hat leaning against the building. As she ran by, a large, toothy grin appeared on his face.

# 6 - The Morning After

Mike hadn't slept that night. The first officers on the scene were a man and a woman. He didn't know the man but had met the woman, Jones, before. He did his best to explain what he had seen and done. His story sounded crazy even to himself, so he could imagine how bad it sounded to them.

"So you heard one of the victims on your baby monitor. Does this happen often?"

"We had recommended the same monitor to them, so it makes sense. It's what happened tonight."

"And you think the man who attacked you was the husband, Ted Zhang?"

"Honestly, I don't know. His face looked like him, yes, but the build was all wrong. Maybe..." he paused, trying to make some sort of sense of the memory, which was more like a nightmare. "Maybe it was his brother, although I didn't see Ted's body in there." At the time, he had been so sure that it was Ted.

Little Sam stood next to his father, his "Toy Story" pajamas covered with a blanket. There was no way the kid could walk without tripping, but then Sam was so out of it from being woken up in the middle of night that he hardly moved. Mike wasn't letting him out of his sight now. Not with whatever, or whoever, it was still out there.

"And you shot him?"

"Oh yeah, four times. The last hit him in the head."

The male officer shook his head. "Right." The word had a mocking tone to it. "I don't think you walk away from that one. I think you missed and scared him off."

Mike tried to make what happed seem rational, at least in his own head. "I think the guy was high on something, some messed-up sh…" He glanced down at Sam. "Stuff."

"Well, judging by that little horror movie across the street, there was something obviously wrong with the guy." All three officers were silent, replaying the scene upstairs in their heads. Mike felt a bit nauseous.

More officers arrived, along with an ambulance, although it didn't do any good for the Zhangs. They asked more questions, which Mike tried to answer. He was coming down from his adrenaline rush and it was making him feel sick and sleepy. The cuts on his chest throbbed and he could feel blood seeping through the bandages. Eventually he gave up and asked if he might get some medical attention himself. One of the EMTs looked his chest over.

"Looks pretty deep, I think you're going to need stitches at least. Why don't you take a ride with us? We'll patch you up good."

Jones, who had been following him and Sam around and generally being as helpful as she could, spoke up. "Why don't you and Sam go? I can handle this here. You just meet up with us at the station in the morning. I'm pretty sure you know where it is and I'll still be on shift." She smiled at Mike. It was a friendly smile but there was a bit too much pity in it.

"Sure, thanks. I need to call my in-laws to pick up Sam, but they can meet us at the hospital. Which one are you taking me to?" he asked the EMT.

"College."

# 7 - Lizzie

Lizzie was sitting in front of the computer when the phone rang.

"Lizzie! Lizzie!" It was Ann, and something seemed to be bothering her.

"Hey, girl."

"I need help. I think something ate Keith."

"What? You're not back together with that spineless dweeb are you?"

"No. Well…yes. Well, we had a thing. But look, that's not important..."

"A thing? Don't tell me you got laid and didn't tell me."

"No. Well, yes, but just listen…"

"We've been through this Ann. The guy is no good. He's going to keep stringing you along. Now if you want to use him for a little action on the side, I can understand that..."

"Will you please stop being Oprah?" Ann raised her voice, cutting Lizzie off. "Look, something happened. It's really freaking me out, and I need someone to tell me I'm not crazy."

"Oh, you're not preggers are you? It takes more than a week for those tests to tell you anything, you know."

"No. Just shut up and come get me. I need a ride. I don't have taxi fare, I'm in downtown Newark, and it's getting late. Pick me up off Broad Street by that Army surplus you got those fancy boots from."

"Ann, I'm kinda in the middle of something here."

"This is way more important than any stupid World of Warcraft raid." Ann hung up.

Lizzie swore to herself. Putting down the phone and picking up her headset, Lizzie said, "Sorry guys, family aggro. I gotta bail tonight." Her announcement produced a chorus of male voices, their disappointment ringing clear as a bell in Lizzie's ear.

Had it been anyone but Ann, she would have told them to go screw themselves. But poor, sweet, naive Ann was her oldest, closest friend. She had been her only friend in high school, before the money, before the surgery, before the expensive personal fitness trainers, before she had become the successful chic-geek she was today. Back when Lizzie had been the fat, shy Asian kid, Ann had been there, solid as a rock through many of Lizzie's bad times. Now after all these years, it was Ann who needed the support.

Of late, Lizzie had spent a lot of time worrying about her friend. The break-up with that deadbeat Keith had crushed her. Lizzie had thought that

Ann was finally starting to recover but this last week she had been so distant. It explained a lot that Keith was back in her life. On the phone now, there had been real fear in Ann's voice. That was unusual.

She tossed a beaten leather coat over her “Rogues do it from behind” t-shirt and strapped on her Army boots. Grabbing the keys to her Honda she headed out.

Lizzie lived in Springfield, New Jersey, which was far enough away from NYC for her. She had her space in one of the better neighborhoods, but close enough that she could be in Manhattan for business reasons in under an hour. It took her about 20 minutes to get to Ann, who was right where she said she would be. She was pacing back and forth and looking an awful fright. Lizzie pulled to the curb and popped the locks on the car.

“Oh thank God,” Ann said, getting into the car. She reached over and hugged Lizzie.

“Ugh! You smell like shit, girl. What have you been doing?”

“A lot of running, actually,” Ann answered, letting her friend go. “I owe you huge for this. Something amazingly messed up happened.”

“Look, just calm down. You need a drink or something?”

“God yes, strongest thing you can find,” Ann paused and grinned. “You’re buying, right?”

“Ugh. I'll put it on your tab.”

“Good, then let’s go. The farther from this place the better.”

The name of the restaurant they ended up at was “The Office.” Lizzie knew the bartender there well, Ann did too, and they had great burgers. Lizzie generally hated public places, but this one was okay, as long as she didn’t have to talk to anyone.

Ann hadn't said much on the way there. She claimed she needed a stiff drink before she could even think about it. They ordered dinner, Lizzie ordered her usual Grey Goose martini, shaken not stirred, and Ann got a whiskey, neat.

“Whiskey? Really?”

“God yes, can't stand the stuff.” Ann pounded it down the instant the waiter brought it and after gagging for a moment ordered a second. Lizzie stared at her friend.

“Aren’t you supposed to avoid drinking on your meds?”

“After this afternoon, I'm drinking every day for the rest of my life.”

“You aren’t going to try to kiss me again, are you?”

“What?”

“The other night, when you were wasted on mudslides, you tried to lock lips with me.”

Ann was horrified.

“I’m so sorry. I don’t remember that at all.”

"It's okay. I am pretty stunning." Lizzie gave her a wink and then turned serious. "This drinking is a new side of you. What's going on?"

"I..." Ann started to explain, and then stopped. "I don't know where to start. Look, this is going to sound nuts."

"Try me."

Ann rubbed her face for a minute. When the waiter came back with her next drink, she threw the whole thing back again. "Look, can I just get two more of these? Save you a trip." She held up the glass to the waiter, who scurried off to fetch more booze. Again turning her gaze to Lizzie she asked, "What do you know about demons?"

"Domains? Oh a shitload, you know me. Ultra geek girl to the rescue."

"No, *demons*. Like fallen angels out to capture men's souls and such?"

"Oh." Lizzie took a sip of her drink. "Nothing much, really. I mean, nothing much outside video games and movies. Why in God's name would that matter?" The waiter appeared, this time with double the whiskey.

"Ha! Good choice of words there, but I'm pretty sure God has nothing to do with this." Ann began to sip her third whiskey, cringing at the taste and no longer drinking like she was pledging to a frat. "This is going to sound nuts, I mean downright bat-shit insane."

"Just spit it out!" Lizzie let her frustration edge into her voice.

"Okay. Well, you know about my, err, event with Keith about a week ago, right?"

"I do now. I knew you were down about something the other night. I guess you're not back together then?"

"I'm not sure. We had a great time that night, slept together, you know, the works, but in the morning he was long gone. No note, no phone call, nothing. So I gave him a few days. I thought maybe something came up at the hospital. Whatever. Anyway, a few more days and still no call. I left him messages on his phone, wrote him emails, even stopped by his place once. Nothing. So yesterday, I get the big idea of going to the hospital and confronting him, really giving him a piece of my mind."

"Everyone thinks they've seen him recently, but no one knows where he is now. So, I kick around the place, run into our old buddy Cynthia, you remember her."

"Older Irish chick, can drink any man under the table."

"Yeah, that's her. Anyway, she's working on this patient there. Guess a truck put him into traction or some such thing."

"Ouch!"

"Again, anyway, the guy wakes up and he is fricking crazy. He talks like Sean Connery, or maybe Patrick Stewart, but he's this little Mexican guy. He takes one look at his doctor and says she's a demon. So I'm like, whatever, crazy guy."

"Which doctor?"

"Vanessa Black." Ann paused a bit after saying the name and shivered.

"Oh yeah, I met her once. Hot," Lizzie said. She did not know for sure, but suspected Vanessa and Keith were friends with really good benefits. Ann still seemed oblivious to this fact and Lizzie was not about to break the news.

"I...well I guess. Anyway, she's a complete bitch and apparently the crazy guy has her dead to rights, 'cause she either is a demon or has the world's must frakked up rash ever. Speaking of rashes, does my neck look okay?"

"It does look a little red, now that you mention it."

"The demon lady tried to choke me out."

"What?" Lizzie almost stood up.

"Yeah, then tossed me a good 15 feet. I'm going to be bruised."

"Wow, what? Slow down, this conversation just took a left turn. I'm not following you."

Ann explained the whole confrontation with Vanessa Black, the threats to have Ann removed from the building, and her trip to the basement of the hospital. She told Lizzie about Vanessa's remarks about Keith and her mad run out of the building. Lizzie fidgeted a bit in her seat.

"Look, I don't think Keith did leave me, well, not for the second time. I think Vanessa ate him or has him under a spell or something. Well, I don't know what happened, but I know I'm worried about him."

There was a long pause as Lizzie stared at her friend. Was this what a nervous breakdown looked like? At last she said, "Um, honey, I don't know how to say this, but half that shit you just said is impossible. Also, the whole stalking thing? Sad."

"I know, I know, and if I hadn't seen that talon thing grow out of her arm, I wouldn't believe it either. I mean, it was bigger than my head." Ann spread her hands to show just how big. She was beginning to rock a bit in her chair, her words slurring together. "Have I gone crazy?"

Lizzie stopped for a minute, and rubbed her chin. The answer that immediately jumped to mind was yes. She took a deep breath. "Did I ever tell you the story of how I got the name Lizzie?"

"Umm no, I don't think so."

Their food arrived, and Lizzie paused to grab a bite. Ann attacked a salad as if she hadn't eaten in a week.

"Well, when my parents left Korea when I was ten to come to your messed up country, of course no one could say my name. Goddamn Americans. Anyway, I decided I needed a name you people could pronounce. Back in those days, I never left the arcades and I was the only girl there. There was this game called “Rampage.” It had the only female character I had ever seen in a video game and she turned into a giant lizard and trashed cities. Well, besides Miss Pac-Man, but she was a bitch and the yellow thing seemed like a terrible stereotype. Anyway, her name was Lizzie and I wanted to be just like her. So during class, I used to imagine I changed into a giant lizard and ate all the rest of the kids in the class.”

Ann giggled a bit. “You know, when you told that story, you got a bit of your old accent back. You sound like that character from Mad TV, Ms. something? Swan? Also, you may have some aggression issues.”

“Oh, screw you.” They laughed together for a minute.

“So, what does this have to do with my adventure into the Twilight Zone?” Ann asked.

Lizzie squirmed in her seat a bit. “Well, you know, when I was going through that rough spot after my parents...passed, there was a time,” she paused again and blew out a long breath, “There was a time when I thought I could really turn into a lizard and...”

“Is this your bad acid trip story again?”

“No, well yes, but I know sometimes you can get carried away with...”

Ann interrupted. “See? Now, I knew you wouldn't believe me. I mean, I can't blame you, I don't believe me either. You going to finish that burger?”

“Um, no. Go ahead. Well look, you are on these new meds.”

“They’re antibiotics! Not LSD.”

Lizzie sighed. Oh Ann, she thought to herself, how can I fix you?

“Look, I'll tell you what,” Lizzie said, “We'll go back to my place, I'll put on my hacker cap and see what I can find out about your missing man and maybe your demon doctor chick.”

Ann slammed down her drink and gave Lizzie a huge smile. “You know, for an anti-American computer geek, you’re not a bad person at all.”

“Just don't tell anyone, ok?”

# 8 - Malpractice

Mike and Sam rode in the ambulance, Mike in the back and Sam up front with the driver. The driver must have done this type of thing in the past, as he had a whole speech pointing out all the various switches and dials for the boy. Mike didn't pay much attention. His mind just kept repeating the night's events. The first rays of sun could be seen through the rear window of the ambulance. He tried to block the scene from the bedroom out of his mind. Going over things wasn't helping. He had to think. He needed to figure this out.

The man-beast had to be Ted. Otherwise, where was he? The thing had been in the house, obviously. There were no signs of forced entry, besides the front door, which appeared to be more of a break-out, so the murderer had to be in the house. It was a like a bad movie with the wolf-man or some nonsense, but...no, that was impossible. There was no such thing as a werewolf. The moon wasn't even full. He smiled at that thought. It was insane. He was no detective, he just did speeding tickets, but this was something that he needed to figure out. Otherwise, he would go mad. One thing was for sure: he would take a few days to heal and then look into things himself.

If it had not been a monster, because there was no such thing, it had to be something else. Where did these legends come from anyway? He would have to check it out later. Maybe it had been some drug reaction. That seemed much more likely, but Ted had never struck him as a user. What about the last time he saw him? Mike thought back to the day in front of his house. Ted had been at a hospital. Maybe he'd had a reaction to a medication or something. It seemed far-fetched, but it was a lead. And as fate would have it, he was heading to the hospital right now. Maybe he could follow it up.

Arriving at the hospital, he met Melissa's parents in the emergency room. They were good people and he had become even closer to them now that Melissa was gone. He reassured them everything was fine and that he just needed some stitches, and told them that if they could bring Sam to daycare, it would help a lot.

He said his goodbyes to his son and checked in with the nurse at the triage desk. He briefly showed her his chest when she asked what was wrong. The blood was again flowing from under the bandages, making them a sticky mess.

"Ouch. What did that? A bear?"

"Um, no it was, ah, a very large dog." Mike figured that the lie was easier than the truth.

The emergency room was empty and, after taking a seat, he began to doze a bit. Even with the horrific images in his mind, the fatigue and blood loss were too much, and sleep slowly took him.

*****

Mike was in the patrol car when his cell phone rang.

"Hey!" It was Melissa. He was so relieved to hear her voice, although he couldn't quite figure out why.

"Hey baby, how's it going?"

"Just out in the front yard, playing catch with the boy." The image of Melissa and Sam playing together lifted his heart. "What are you up to?" Mike glanced around the car, looking over a report of a speeding ticket.

"Oh you know, fighting the *criminal* masterminds of New Jersey," he quipped. "Sounds like you guys are having more fun though."

"You know it! Say hi to your Dad..."

Sam's voice popped into the cell phone, "Hi Dad!" and then was gone.

"Hey kid," he responded, but knew he was already too late. "Man, in a hurry as always."

Melissa's voice came back on the line.

"That's our little man, always on the move. Good catch Sam!" He could hear the game continuing as she spoke. "So, tonight for dinner, I'm planning..." She paused. "Hold on a second baby, we have a runaway ball."

"Sure, no problem." Mike busied himself with some buttons on his computer.

"Sam, stay out of the road. I'll get it." Melissa's voice was distant now, the phone away from her mouth. Another pause, then, "Geez, what is that guy doing?" Suddenly, there was the sound of screeching brakes and Melissa screaming. With a loud crunch, the phone went dead.

*****

"Melissa!" Mike screamed as he snapped back awake. That's not how it had happened!

He was still in the waiting room, still alone. Melissa was still dead. The dream, the daily nightmare, left him with an ache in his heart so deep a small sob escaped his lips. For awhile he did nothing but resist the urge to tear up. This wasn't the time or the place.

"You okay?" asked a sweet voice. Mike looked up to see a stunning nurse looking down at him.

"Yeah," his voice was choked. Then he added, "I'm good." He

sounded much more like himself.

He tried not to stare at the woman. She was amazing. Tall, strongly built, full-figured, with long, dark hair. Everything combined to form a picture so attractive, even the scrubs she was wearing couldn't distract from it. It was like waking up from a nightmare to find an angel!

"Mr. Samson?" she asked politely.

"Yes that's me." He glanced to his left and his right. He was alone in the waiting room. Who else would he be?

"Follow me, please."

"No problem." He tried not to sound too eager. "Is this place usually so empty?"

"Oh, we've been pretty busy," she looked back and shot him an odd grin. It was a creepy expression, and suddenly Mike felt a bit uneasy. She led him to a room with several beds broken up by curtains.

"Let's get that shirt off and take a look." Mike obeyed, noting the pain in his shoulder as he removed the blood-soaked t-shirt.

The nurse began to clean the wounds. She didn't ask how he got the cuts, but just went about her business. Mike couldn't help but continue to notice how attractive she was.

"So, you're a police officer?" She started to glue the two deeper cuts, her touch oddly hot. He couldn't help but fidget.

"Yeah, just a traffic cop. A run-of-the-mill police officer. I might try for detective in…OW!" The nurse had actually pushed hard against one of the cuts. "In another year or so."

"I'm so sorry." Then, her eyes locked with his and sparks flew. "You might be very useful..." She ran her fingers slowly up his chest, sending little shocks of pleasure through his skin. This was suddenly going very differently than he had expected. He wanted this woman. He needed her. She grabbed the back of his head and slowly moved his lips towards hers. It seemed wrong somehow, but he was so light-headed, he couldn't think.

"I…I can't," he stammered. But it was a lie, he could. He had been so lonely without Melissa.

"Shhh," was her only response. Their lips just brushed and then…

"Let's see what we have here," said another voice. The nurse pulled back and snapped her head around, looking for its source. Mike stiffened, the spell broke, and suddenly, he felt confused. A female doctor, dark-skinned and pretty in a normal sort of way, pulled the curtain aside and stared at them both.

"Everything alright, Mary?" She gave the nurse a searching look.

"Of course, Doctor," Mary smiled back.

The nurse patted Mike on the cheek, and whispered, "I'll be right back, don't go anywhere." She opened the curtain and stepped out. Mike caught sight of a handsome man, right outside.

What the hell was that about? Mike watched her leave. Had she really just come on to him like that? That didn't really happen, did it? He could see the letter to Penthouse in his head.

*Dear Penthouse, I never thought this sort of thing could happen to me, but there was this really hot nurse and...*

No, there had been something very wrong about the situation. Something was odd about the woman. She had been so attractive, so amazing, yet Mike sensed that something was off.

"Hi, I'm Dr. Tyler. Sorry I took so long. Sometimes it seems like I'm the only one here seeing patients." She gave Mike a quick smile. "Let's see those cuts, Mr. Samson."

For a moment, the doctor inspected his wounds, and then started stitching them closed. After several minutes of poking him with the needle, the doctor applied new bandages.

"Do you mind if I ask where you got these? They look like a bear or something."

"Police business. I can't really talk about it."

"So you're an officer then." It wasn't really a question.

"Yeah. Look, I was wondering, is it possible to check if you had a patient in here a few days ago?"

"Well I'm sure I can't help. I've been away for a few weeks. First day back. I'm pretty sure you would need a court order to get any details, but they might be able to help you at the front desk." She quickly gave him directions and hurried on to her next patient.

Mike replaced his shirt, regretting that he hadn't brought a clean one. Heading back into the hallway, he made his way to where he thought the front desk should be. The halls were quite empty. Maybe it was just that time of morning. *A* movement caught his eye as he passed a room, and glancing inside, he saw two figures locked in a passionate embrace. He recognized the nurse named Mary and the tall male doctor. In the dim light, Mike could just make out the doctor's name tag.

K. Malone, MD

# 9 - Bad Dreams

Ann could hear the drums pounding, so loudly that they seemed to rattle her brain. No matter how she covered her ears, the sound still made its way through. She stumbled through the darkness, struggling to cover her ears against the noise while keeping a hand out in front of her.

"Help me!" Keith's voice called out, sounding surprisingly clear despite the drums. "Help me."

"I'm coming!" Ann was yelling but couldn't make out her own voice. Suddenly, she tripped over something and landed flat on her face. Looking up from the floor, she found herself staring into the eyes of a giant black lizard. Ann screamed and pushed herself away, but it simply hissed at her and then made its way farther into the darkness. On her hands and knees she pushed forward, eyes darting back and forth for more lizards.

"Keith!" she shouted again, still not hearing her own voice.

"Here, Ann, I'm here. Save me please," Keith pleaded.

Abruptly, the ground underneath Ann seemed to tilt forward and she slid face-first down a hill. She tried to dig her hands in to gain purchase but fell faster and faster into darkness. Then, just as quickly, she was underwater. No, this wasn't water, but something thicker, like oil. Ann struggled to right herself and get her head out of the liquid, which turned out to be shallow. She found the ground with her hands and pushed herself up. Bursting out of the goo, she gasped, trying to recover lost air. She clawed at the gunk, trying to clear her face and eyes, panic rising. She found that she could stand, the stuff just reaching her waist.

"Well, if it isn't little Ann!" The voice was almost Vanessa's, although somehow deeper and more terrible. "You aren't looking for this, are you?" It was Vanessa, a monster version of her. Her head was human but her body was that of a black-scaled demon. Giant bat-like wings protruded from her back, and in one giant talon she held Keith by the neck. "Give us a kiss, lover," Vanessa said and raised Keith's head to hers. He did not resist, and just lay where he was. They kissed. "I told you before, Ann. He's mine. However, because I'm a nice person, I did bring some friends for you to play with." At her words, huge black snakes leapt up out of the black goo, coiling themselves around Ann. She screamed and tried to pull them away. She tried to wade forward but a snake had wrapped itself around her legs. Ann bucked forward and then managed to right herself, regaining her balance. She ripped off snake after snake, until one finally pinned her arms to her sides. Ann kept screaming, trying to break free, but its grip was like iron. Another snake had gotten around her neck and for a moment, locked eyes with Ann. Then it dove into her mouth, sliding its way down her throat.

Ann woke with a start, sitting up in bed. Sunlight filled the sparsely decorated apartment, giving everything a clean, pure look. Glancing around, she was stunned to find that she was in Keith's apartment, totally nude. Keith's sleeping body was next to her, his naked back showing clearly in the tangled sheets. A feeling of pure joy filled her heart. Everything was alright now. It had all been a strange dream.

"Oh Keith, honey," she said, tugging at his arm. "You would not believe the dream I just had."

He didn't respond. With some effort, she rolled him over to face her. His eyes were open and completely black and there was something dark and sticky oozing out of the corner of his mouth.

For the second time, Ann awoke with a scream, falling off the couch. On the floor, her body spasmed as her mind again tried to take in her new s*urroundings*. Her eyes darted around the room. She was at Lizzie's place. Safe at Lizzie's place. She heaved a huge sigh of relief and tried to stop *trembling. A nightmare double feature.*

It was still dark out and the clock showed 5:00 am. Ann was covered in sticky sweat and found 2 large clumps of her own blond hair in her hands. Ouch. She spent a few moments on the ground, trying to control her breathing. The nightmares of the past few weeks were getting worse. Always in the dark, with the drums, and always with those black snakes. What had that last part been about, in Keith's apartment? That had seemed so real. Which was worse, the nightmare or what had gone down at the hospital? Did that even really happen? Now she seemed unsure. Had Vanessa really started to turn into something else? Had there really been some kind of monster in that locked room? Looking back now, it was hard for her to believe. Something had happened though. She was convinced that whatever horror was at the hospital, Keith was involved. She needed to rescue him. Of that at least, she was sure.

Finally she stood, her mind made up. Her head hurt from the drinking the previous night, but not as badly as she had thought it might. Her stomach hurt too, but felt less like she was going to be sick and more like some muscle had tied itself up in a knot. She would find Keith and get to the bottom of this, even though it meant going back to that hospital. She shuddered at the thought but did not change her mind.

She found that she had no pants on and was wearing one of Lizzie's shirts. Lizzie was taller and broader than she was, so the shirt made for decent pajamas. She did not remember getting undressed, or much after the restaurant.

"Step one: find pants," she said to herself, "Can't save ex-boyfriend with no pants."

After gathering her clothes and spending some time in the bathroom cleaning up, she found Lizzie in her computer room. Lizzie's ears were covered by large headphones. She jumped when Ann tapped her on the shoulder.

"AHHHH!"

"Sorry. It's just me," Ann raised her hands in front of her, fending off Lizzie's defensive slaps.

"You scared the shit out of me!" she said, tearing off the headphones and sending a few more slaps her way. "How are you awake? You had enough booze last night to kill an elephant."

"Ah, come on. I wasn't that bad." Ann shrugged.

"You were. I thought I was going to have to hold your head over the toilet all night. You really aren't known for holding your liquor, you know."

"Well, I'm fine. Hungry, actually." Then, in a softer voice, Ann said, "Thanks for listening last night. I must have sounded like a crazy. I owe you huge."

Lizzie smiled. "Yes, yes you did. And I charge extra for getting drunk bitches undressed and ready for bed on my couch."

"You charge? I thought you paid extra for that."

"Bitch. See if I tell you what I learned about your monster doctor."

"OK, ok, I'm sorry. Thanks for that too." She gave Lizzie a little hug. "Did you find anything?"

"You're lucky you're cute," Lizzie grunted. "So first, this deadbeat of an ex-boyfriend of yours. I checked in on all his credit cards, no activity this week. Though for him, that's not all that strange. He must live in that hospital. Also, no bank activity and he's only been back to his house once."

"How do you know that?" Ann broke in.

"I hacked the security cameras outside his apartment like 3 months ago. You know, just for fun. Thought I might get some embarrassing shots of you begging him to come back. "

"Ouch. Now that was uncalled for," Ann shook her head.

"However, this one night, you should probably see." Lizzie brought up a screen, showing the parking lot outside Keith's place. A black Nissan pulled up and Vanessa Black stepped out of the car. She was dressed in an evening gown, dolled up like she was going on a date.

"What day was that?" Ann snarled.

"That was Saturday night. She looks pretty human to me. I mean if you were a demon, wouldn't you fly or teleport or something?" There was a mocking tone to Lizzie's voice.

"Um, yeah right. Maybe she's trying to stay undercover or something."

Lizzie gave her a long hard look. After a moment she turned back to her screen. “On to demon woman.” She started again. “Let’s see, 5'10”, 36 years old, divorced, no kids. I have less info on her recent life. I know she's been at the hospital all week, except the one evening I have her on film.” Lizzie sighed. “It’s pretty obvious to me that she and Keith have a thing going on. Other than that, I can't really say. Look, Ann, there’s nothing odd here.” Lizzie's voice became soft, gentle. “Maybe the other night between you and Keith was a goodbye and now he’s moved on. It’s a really shitty way to go about it, but the guy was never the most…” she paused, searching for the word, “tactful.”

“And so the whole monster in the hospital thing was?” Ann asked dryly.

“Well, maybe the patient you talked to got the idea of demons into your head, like a suggestion of sorts, and later on, when you had your little break...”

“Break? Like a breakdown? So now I'm crazy?” Anger began to boil up and out of Ann. Some of it was directed at Lizzie but she knew a lot of it was focused on Keith and herself. She glared at Lizzie, who put her head down, and let out a long sigh.

“Yes, well, just a little.”

“What?” Ann shouted.

Lizzie put a calming hand on her arm. “Look, you took this whole break-up thing really, really badly six months ago. You've been depressed ever since. I think…” Lizzie paused. “I think you need help.”

The rage came to a boil inside Ann. “Fine,” she stammered, “I've lost it. Poor crazy little Annie’s gone and lost her boyfriend and now she’s seeing monsters. No, okay? Just no! I saw something, I’m not nuts, I didn’t have any sort of a breakdown, and I was *so* over Keith!” She was shouting now. “There’s something going on and I'm going to get to the bottom of it, without your help.” She turned and stormed out of the room.

“Ann, wait...” Lizzie called, but Ann was done waiting. She ran out of the house, not turning back. She was doing a lot of running out of places lately. She might have to look into that.

*****

It had been an angry bus ride home. Ann had had to walk to the bus station, which was not far, but the buses just seemed to take forever. She hated buses and wished she could afford a car. They were slow, dirty, and filled with big fat hairy men who liked to hit on her or chat about the weather. People just wouldn’t shut up and let her be. Today though, no one talked to her. Her black mood must have kept them away. She sat in her dirty seat and stared forward, giving the world her best “I will tear your head off if you come near me” look.

It was still morning when she arrived at her place. She quickly showered, dressed, and ate an apple. The food helped but the big knot in her stomach didn't go away. She had been trying to work out a rescue plan in her head but hadn't really come up with much. She decided that first she would visit Miller, the strange man at the hospital. He had said that Vanessa was a demon and might know more. After that, she planned on storming the place. Sadly, Ann didn't have much in the way of weapons. She felt like she should have some protection if it did turn out there were horrible monsters and demons running around the place. Maybe some holy water or garlic? No, that was stupid. These were demons, not vampires. What she really wanted was a big-ass gun. She had never had even the faintest desire for a firearm, but at the moment, carrying one seemed wise. The best she could do on short notice was a bottle of pepper spray. Maybe demons had very sensitive eyes? Ugh. This wasn't going to end well.

Horribly under-equipped, Ann grabbed her coat and headed out. It was turning out to be a sunny day, and she had the short walk there to try and psych herself up.

"You can do this, Keith needs you," she chanted to herself. Exactly how she was going to rescue him was still a mystery to her, even after she had opened the door to the hospital. She decided to keep her head down, walk straight to Miller's room, and make the next move from there.

Ann dashed past the front desk, though they took little notice of her. She quickly grabbed an elevator to the second floor and found Miller's room.

"So far, so good. No sign of ol' black scales," she whispered. Poking her head into Miller's room, she noted that it was empty. A quick blast of panic ran up her spine. She snagged a passing tech, a big man that she hadn't met before.

"The man in this room. Was he moved?" she asked.

"Miller? The one that was hit by a truck?" Ann nodded and he continued. "I'm sorry, but he passed away last night."

# 10 - Miller Time

Joseph Miller had been in the hospital for several days. He was quite impressed with it. Apparently, man had gotten by just fine without him. Had it really been over a hundred years? There had always been gaps, but none this large. They had made such progress. This "TV" was truly amazing, although he could follow very little of what it showed him. It was like a magic mirror into a world he no longer understood. But then, figuring it out was the best part, and he was dying to try everything. Perhaps "dying" was a bit too appropriate in his case. Unfortunately, the wounds he had received on his first night back in the land of the living were serious. The bones in his right arm and leg had shattered, as well as several of his ribs. At least, that's what the nurse had told him. Wounds like this took time for even him to recover from, although he healed much faster than normal men if he survived the initial violence.

There were demons here, and of course their offspring, the Cursed. He could see the dark mist that clung to them. He was so close, and yet could not make a move against them, or at least not yet. And so he waited and enjoyed the magic of the TV and healed. Nurses and doctors would come and check in on him from time to time. Some were human, most were not. After the first day, he paid them very little attention, transfixed by the television. This turned out to be a small tactical error on his part.

He registered the nurse that had entered almost unconsciously. His attention was wrapped up in "The Price is Right." He shouted out random numbers, trying to imitate the people on the show. He had no idea what it was about, but they all looked so happy to be there. He didn't acknowledge the nurse for a whole minute and then, at last, and far too late, he turned to face her.

She was a demon and a young one too, by the looks of it. No more than a few days old. Like all demons, who were vain and could shift shape, she had made herself quite beautiful. Judging by the look of her uniform, she had been a nurse until recently. She stood preparing some sort of device. There were so many in the room and Miller didn't understand any of them. The nurse was possessed by an ancient and terrible evil, which fed on man, woman, and child alike, and in a few days he would most likely have to cut her head off, but for now, he saw no reason to be rude.

"Well, hello there Miss. Care to watch this wonderful TV with me?"

She responded by jabbing something small and sharp into his arm. The world darkened around him.

"Actually, we're off to get a bite to eat." She grinned.

"So, no then?" he asked weakly, before falling silent.

*****

Time moved forward without him. It hadn't been long, not more than a few minutes. He was still on the bed, being rolled down a hall. It was not hard for him to feign unconsciousness, as half of his body still was bound by the thick casts and braces that had been used to reset his bones. A normal man would still be unconscious, and he had no intention of letting it be known he was anything but normal.

As he rolled down the hall, he considered his options. He was quite sure that his arm and ribs had mostly healed by this point, but was equally sure that his leg had not. Without a weapon and with one damaged leg it would be nearly impossible take a demon head-on, even a young one such as this. He would have to wait for his moment and hope that his luck would change. Otherwise, it might be another hundred years before he had another chance. God only knew what the state of things would be by then.

Suddenly the bed stopped.

"I have a meal for my brother," the demon-nurse said to someone. "Is he calm?"

Miller risked a quick glance. Two huge men were standing next to his bed. Wolves, and just like the demon, very young. This kept getting better. Things were further along than he had thought. He guessed that his holiday was over.

"For the moment," was the husky reply of one of the men. Miller tensed his stiff muscles, trying to ready himself for whatever came next.

"Perhaps cracking this one open will be good for him." He heard a door open and was wheeled into a new room. The smell hit him like a wave. The stench of death and decay assaulted his senses. The door was quickly shut and locked behind him.

Miller took a chance and opened his eyes wide. He was alone in a large white padded room. No, not alone. Someone or some*thing* was in the room with him. He sensed it but couldn't manage to see past his right arm, which was still locked into position on his bed. The first thing to do would be to stand up and see what was going on. He rocked back and forth, trying to tip the bed over. A loud slurping noise stopped him for a moment. "Well that's a new sound." He thought.

He began the rocking motion again. Whatever it was, it was coming closer. He heard the padding of feet and something heavy dragging along the ground. The creature was panting and something was dripping. Drool, perhaps? Fantastic!

At last, the bed rocked far enough to tip over and crash to the floor. Pain flooded his right leg. That one definitely needed a bit more time. The fall had freed his good arm and loosened up his right. He began fighting with the straps, keeping his legs in place while stretching his neck to try to see his playmate over the side of the bed. He could not see anything yet but managed to undo the belt at his waist. He then went back to freeing his right arm from the various bits and pieces that kept it locked into position.

Suddenly, a large black claw latched onto the side of the bed and lifted it straight up. Miller's arm came free with a snap but there was still a strap on his right leg that managed to hold it in place. His head hit the floor, while most of the rest of his body dangled in the air. He twisted again to try to see, helpless at the moment to do much else.

It was a horror that he had not had the pleasure of experiencing before. The one arm was a massive claw, as if borrowed from a larger demon, much older than this creature could possibly be. Most of the rest of it was young, and clearly male. The black scales on his arm stretched up to his shoulder, across his chest, and down his belly. His eyes were the black of those touched by the Fallen, but empty of intelligence. A long, black, barbed tongue hung out of his fanged mouth and drool ran down his cheek. Miller could see the very faint tracks of tears on the creature's face. Most of his hair had fallen out or been torn out, but some bits remained, sticking out in odd directions. One large wing twitched on his back, like something from a huge insect. He wore no clothes, and the spots where his remaining skin met the dark scales looked red and blotchy.

"Hello. Joseph Miller. A pleasure to meet you."

He started again, not feeling that he should be rude to this creature. He meant to keep this civil, at least until they started trying to kill each other. Perhaps someday he would find a monster who, instead of feeding on the flesh of mankind, enjoyed knitting.. This beast's only response was to lick the back of the bed. It made a slurping, scratching noise.

"Hmm. You seem to have me at a bit of a disadvantage."

Apparently not liking the taste of "ye olde hospital bed," the monster chucked it aside with inhuman strength. Miller, unfortunately still attached, was tossed along with it. He landed in a heap but managed to keep the bed between him and the monster. Pain exploded all over his body, but at least now he could finally reach the belt that stubbornly held him in harm's way. In a moment, he was free and pushing the bed away. Leaning against the wall, he managed to pull himself up to a standing position. His left leg was stiff but workable. He was surprised to find that he could put some weight on the right with only minor pain. Much better.

The demon-man was facing away from him now, seeming not to notice him. It howled and smashed its giant claw into the wall, tearing into the padding that covered the room. The black scales ran down most of its back, and several spikes poked out from its spine. In one corner of the room he noticed a pile of bones, which had been sucked clean. In some way, this comforted him. So many things had changed, but monsters' habit of piling up bones in their lairs had remained constant. Just like the good old days.

Miller focused on the new creature. It was as if a demon had miscarried as it possessed the man, creating some sort of mindless creature. This was something that, in all of his thousands of years, he had never seen. But then, he had been seeing a lot of new things of late. Why not new monsters as well? It seemed only fair. Apparently, in an effort to prove they could be a decent folk, the other demons were caring for this one like a sick sibling and he was meant to be lunch. He almost felt bad that he had to kill it, seeing as nothing similar had ever existed before. He did have a job to do, though. Thinking better of it, he hit on an idea.

"Lad, I think you and I can help each other out." The beast did not respond. Perhaps it could not hear? Finding an old bone on the floor, he picked it up and tossed it at the creature's back. It bounced right off. The beast spun around with a growl, at last taking notice of him. It howled and charged, its lopsided body lurching forward with impressive speed. Miller just barely managed to hop to the left as its huge black claw smashed into the wall. Leaning back, he drove an elbow hard against the side of its head with a loud crack. It staggered, but the claw embedded itself into the wall, and the beast could not move far. Its head seemed to flop to the side for a second, before snapping back up and locking eyes with him. To Miller's surprise, the eyes were now human!

"Please," it pleaded, the word slow, drawn out, and slurred as it came from its mouth, the long tongue making speech difficult. "Please kill me."

Miller was struck mute, a rare thing for a chatty man like him, and stumbled backward, falling over. There was still something human in there. This was impossible. Once cursed by a demon, there was no coming back. Or was there? Impossible! He thought about the trails of tears that clung to its cheeks. After all these years, had the rules changed?

"Good Lord," he stammered. The creature stepped forward and screamed. The noise started off almost human but then become an angry howl as the demon's eyes filled with inky blackness. Whatever part of the creature that was still human had left again. The beast started for him, lifting its giant arm as if to crush him into the ground. Recovering from his shock, Miller rolled across the room, briefly held up by the arm in the cast. This time the beast's claw missed him by some distance. Stopping at the wall on the other side of the room, he once again propped himself up and faced the half-breed demon. They stared at each other as Miller shifted toward the front door. Using the wall to help keep the weight off his injured leg, he moved very slowly, waiting for the beast's next move. He knew that if the black claw reached him, he would go back to nothingness, and then how could he watch more TV?

No move came from the beast. It stepped forward and then stopped, as if unsure. It seemed to be quite literally of two minds as to what to do next. At last reaching the front door, and not taking his eyes off the beast, Miller gave a quick polite knock to the small window and waved at the man outside the door.

"Hullo. Joseph Miller, nice to meet you." Miller grinned at the now panicked man. Turning to face the beast he said, "What's the matter, don't want your dinner? You're going to have to do a lot better than that!"

In response, it shuffled forward, dragging its oversized arm behind it. He hoped whatever was human in the creature wouldn't feel what was coming next. Miller didn't wait this time. At last putting weight on the bad leg, he went into a fighting stance, and drove the palm of his good hand forward, catching the beast full in the face. Black blood exploded from its nose and its head snapped back. Keeping the momentum going, he shifted his weight back to the good foot, dropped his weight and spun, sweeping out with the leg in the cast. He let out a loud yelp of pain as he made contact with the beast's legs. It collapsed to the ground.

Hearing the door click open, he kept the spin going, turning to face the door and hopping on one foot. One of the cursed men leapt through the door at him, trying to protect his charge. Moving with the new man's force, Miller placed his good foot on the cursed man's chest and dropped back to the floor, tossing the man over Miller's shoulders and right on top of the demon. The two collided, falling to the ground. Rolling to the right, Miller again used the wall to pick himself up and then hopped on his good foot.

The cursed man and the half-demon struggled for a moment, until the demon managed to snatch up the man in his giant claw, immediately starting to crush him. The man, who howled as he struggled to escape, began to grow, trying to change into his stronger, hairier, less-fun-at-parties form. The demon would have none of that. Its tongue snaked around the wolf's throat, tearing it open and beginning to feed off its blood.

"Ahh, that's a good lad." As Miller had hoped, the beast had no concept of friend or foe. Whatever was left of the human in him could enjoy the meal. "That worked well."

Then, a thought occurred to Miller. Hadn't there been two men at the door?

He turned to face the door just as the second cursed man charged in. Miller didn't have time to dodge the fist that swung at him, knocking him back. It was a good solid hit to his face. Reeling, Miller tucked in his chin and covered his face with his elbow as a second fist followed. He managed to partially block this one, but its force was still enough to drive him off his unsteady feet to the ground. He didn't fight the motion, and dropped straight down onto his back. The wolf-man stood above him, massive and powerful even in his human form. Once they transformed to beasts for the first time, werewolves never completely changed back. Most of them kept their huge muscles and height, making them formidable fighters in any condition. That is, of course, if one fought fairly. Miller drove his good leg up between the wolf-man's legs with all his might. The man seemed to buckle with the blow, releasing a soft grunt and falling over to his side before rolling into a ball and rocking back and forth. Miller slowly stood up and limped to the door. "Well, lad, this one here should make a fine dessert. I'll be back later for you. I promise."

The beast was busy tearing the first wolf-man apart, piece by piece. He no longer struggled, and was already quite dead. Miller closed the door behind him and, after a moment, managed to work the lock into place. He took a last glance through the door's window. The remaining wolf-man was getting back to his shaky feet and was staring at Miller. Miller gave him a friendly wave and walked away just as the huge black claw appeared above the wolf-man. From outside the padded room, Miller could just make out the soft crunch.

# 11 - Allies and Enemies

Mike had gotten himself lost. He had taken a wrong turn someplace and was now wandering aimlessly. It wasn't completely his fault. His mind was still on that nurse, Mary, not to mention the shock of last night. He was also very tired.

Passing a nursery, Mike stopped and leaned on the glass. Inside, he saw several rows of newborn babies, each in their own little cart. On the front of each cart was a piece of blue or pink paper. The babies themselves looked tiny to Mike, and very angry. Not one was sleeping. Being a father, he knew that sometimes this was the case, but he thought it was odd that all of them should be awake.

"They're crack babies," a woman's voice said. Mike spun to find the source. It was a short blond woman. It looked like she was having a pretty poor morning as well. Her hair was a mess and there were bags under her eyes.

"I'm sorry...what?" Mike asked.

"Crack babies. They're all kids whose mothers are addicts. There's a program here for them. Junkies just drop off their kids, or even worse, have them here and then just leave without them. They don't have a real maternity wing here."

"Oh," was Mike's only response. The woman walked up to the glass and put her head against it, looking miserable.

"It's pretty terrible. The mothers are using while pregnant and it really screws up the kids. Some of them die, and none really ever recover," she continued. Mike didn't know what to say to that. It was horrible. There was a moment of silence while both of them looked at the struggling children. A great sadness hung over them.

"Um, are you ok?" Mike asked. The woman didn't lift her forehead off the glass, but moved her eyes to look at him. The position looked pretty silly.

"No, I don't think so. It's kind of a long story, and I don't think you would believe me."

"Oh, one of those," Mike responded. "I have one of those as well."

The woman straightened and gave him a stern look.

"I didn't mean it as a challenge, you know." There was another stretch of silence.

"Look maybe if you help me, I can help you," Mike started. "You see, I'm a bit lost and

you seem to know your way around."

“I don't think you could help me and, strictly speaking, I'm not even supposed to be wandering around here.”

Mike raised an eyebrow. “Why is that?”

“Oh, that’s that long story again.” She paused and stared him up and down. “I'm Ann, by the way.”

“Mike Samson,” Mike said and shook her hand. “I'm just trying to get to the front desk. You see, I'm a police officer and I'm trying to...”

“Wait, you’re a cop?” Ann interrupted.

“Well, technically off-duty at the moment, but yes.”

“Maybe you *can* help me then.” Her spirits seemed to rise. “I think something is going on here, in this hospital. My boyfriend, well technically ex-boyfriend, Keith, is a doctor here, and he’s gone missing.”

“Missing? Have you put in a missing persons report?”

“No. Until yesterday I thought he was just avoiding me. But then I saw something.” She stopped and rubbed her hands together. “Look, you’re not going to believe this part, but I swear it’s true.”

Thinking back to last night’s little nightmare, Mike said, “Try me.”

“Down in the basement, there’s this, like, psych ward or something. And there’s a monster in there.” The hair stood up on the back of Mike's neck. He couldn't call her a lunatic. Last night he had seen a monster as well. Maybe it had been Ted, doped out on something, but then again...

“A monster? What kind of monster? It didn't happen to be really hairy with big claws like knives sticking out of its fingers, built like an ape?”

“Umm, no.” She scrunched up her face at him. “And that’s stupid. No, it was this demon-guy thing, all black and scaly with this one huge arm and a bat wing sticking out of its back.”

Never mind. She was a lunatic.

“So wait, my monster is stupid and yours isn’t?” he asked.

“Well, no, I mean, wait...you didn’t actually see something like that did you? I thought you were just making fun of me.”

Mike came clean. Maybe he had gone crazy too. “Oh yes, I did.” He lifted his shirt to show the bandages across his chest. “Sucker ripped me up pretty good too. I shot him in the head. It didn’t even slow him down.” Ann's eyes widened. “Worse yet, he ate two of my neighbors. One was this sweet little girl that used to play with my son.”

“Are you serious? You’re not shitting me ‘cause I started talking about monsters, are you?”

“No, I'm dead serious. I don't think I would have ever even considered telling you if you hadn’t started to talk about monsters. Maybe it was a werewolf.”

“Except,” Ann added slowly, “there’s no such thing.”

"And there's no such thing as a demon-guy thing either, although I give you points for being more original with your monster."

Ann gave him a sour look. "Yeah, sorry. Look, there's more. One of the doctors here, she threatened me and smacked me around a bit. Her hand went all black and scaly and grew huge. It just, like, burst out of her skin. I think she has my boyfriend, Keith, captive someplace."

"Wow," Mike said, "that does sound a little crazy."

"Says you, werewolf boy." Ann balled her hands into fists and punched the wall. "To top it off, I think patients are disappearing. There was this one guy, named Miller. He took one look at the doctor and knew she was a demon. I think they killed him off to hush things up."

Something clicked in Mike's mind. "Wait, your ex, he's a doctor here named Keith. He's not Dr. Malone is he?"

"Yes, yes that's him. Did you see him?"

"Yeah just like 30 minutes ago, he was..." He trailed off, not wanting to add "making out with an incredibly hot nurse." He couldn't tell her that. Instead, he finished with, "downstairs in the emergency room."

"I have to find him." Ann turned and headed down the hall.

Thinking for a moment, Mike yelled, "Ann, wait!" She turned back to face him, looking like she was about to cry.

"I know it sounds nutty to you, but I need to work this out too. Something is happening here!" Ann said, her voice shaky.

Mike jogged a few steps to her side. "I think you're right." He still thought she might be crazy. "Let me help."

Ann gave him a warm smile and, with a nod of her head, said, "Thank you."

*****

Joseph Miller knew what a lift was. He had seen one in Saint Petersburg many years ago. He even understood the general concept of how it worked. This did not mean that he had any idea of how to operate one. After leaving the two wolves alone with their dinner date, he had limped off in the direction he was pretty sure that he had come in, only to be stopped in his tracks by the stairs. In his current rather itchy state he could not even manage to take the first step up. His injured leg could not support enough weight to move up to the next step. The hero of ages had been stopped in his tracks by stairs. Miller got a good chuckle out of this.

So here he was at the lift. He stared at the door for some time. There appeared to be no handles, just a small arrow to the right of the door that pointed up. He understood that it went up, but how should he open it? Perhaps if he just asked?

"Excuse me, fine, uh," he lacked the words, "contraption. Would you mind taking me to the next floor?"

The door did not respond. He knocked politely. Still the lift stayed shut. He tried to pry the door open with his free hand. It did not move an inch. He shouted. The lift ignored him. Frustrated, Miller leaned on the wall to the side of the elevator and let out a long sigh. The TV had been so much easier.

Suddenly a bell dinged and the doors to the lift slid open. "Aha!" Miller cried, limping his way inside. Perhaps the door had finally found him worthy. He was not was about to question his change of luck. He leaned hard against the wall of the lift, taking the weight off the bad leg. It still hurt to walk but he had dealt with worse in the past. Glancing around the inside of the lift, he found it to be empty except for a panel of numbers on the wall. Was it as simple as pressing a number? The doors closed again as he pressed a number at random. The number lit up at his touch, and he felt the lift move up.

"Fantastic!" Miller grinned to himself, once again taking his place against the wall at the back of the lift. Now he needed a plan and weapons. Also, a few more working limbs would be helpful. If he could find a way to free his arm, it would be a great help. But where to start? He knew nothing of this place or time. He needed help.

As if heeding his call, the elevator stopped. Before Miller could begin to move out, two figures entered the lift. One was an attractive, dark-skinned woman. The other was the demon that had tried to feed him to the beast downstairs.

This was awkward. He tensed, ready for battle, but the two were in the midst of a conversation and did not seem to notice his presence.

"Mary, I have to say, you look amazing!" the dark-skinned woman said.

The demon smiled almost shyly at her in response. "Thank you, Martha."

"I didn't even recognize you. I was only in Cardiff for two weeks. It's like you're a whole new person. Where did you get your work done?"

"My work? Oh yes, here actually. If you like I can introduce you to the doctor who did it." The demon grinned at its little joke. There could be no mistaking its intention. It planned on eating this woman or adding her to the brood. Miller would have to stop the demon here and now, but how? He had only just managed to avoid the crippled one. What could he do in such a tight area? At last the dark-skinned woman called Martha seemed to notice him.

"Sir, are you supposed to be out of bed?" There was a look of concern on her face.

"Of course, lass. I'm just out for a bit of exercise. Good for the blood." He smiled at her, but couldn't hold onto it as the demon's eyes focused on him. Uh-oh.

"You? But how?" it stammered. Miller braced himself. Maybe if he moved fast enough he would have a chance. The demon suddenly lurched forward, so violently that Miller paused in his offensive. It seemed to be hearing something Miller could not make out.

"Arrrgh! Not now!" It held its head in its hands. "It is too early. That idiot!" The lift dinged again and the doors slid open. The demon stepped into the hallway. "No matter, I'll still have you two." It reached for Martha and Miller. He sidestepped the grab and tried to get a grip on Martha, but he was too slow and before he could get to her, the demon had her by the throat and was out in the hallway. He followed, intent on rescuing the woman, but as he made it out of the lift they were already far down the hall. In the time it took for another few of his limping steps, the demon and the woman had vanished.

*****

"Is it just me or is this place, like, empty today?" Ann asked Mike as they reached the first floor.

"It does seem kind of quiet for a hospital," Mike agreed, "but it's early in the day. I would imagine it gets busier in the evening."

"I'm not so sure about that. I've been here plenty of times."

Mike had a loose idea of how this was going to go. They would find the boyfriend hanging out, there would probably be some harsh words, maybe some slapping, and then he would try to take Ann to her home. Maybe have her see a doctor. But what if there really were demons running around the place, or werewolves for that matter? No, such things were impossible. There had to be another answer. Ann seemed nice enough, but troubled. She looked a bit ill and her hair was a mess. She wore an oversized coat that hid her frame and she constantly had her hands in her pockets, fiddling with something. She didn't paint a portrait of sanity. But then he must look like hell too. He still had blood all over his T-shirt.

They entered a long room filled with beds and curtains on the walls that could be drawn around them to give each patient some privacy. It was very similar to the room he had been stitched up in. A part of him really didn't want to meet Mary the nurse again. He was almost ashamed to admit it, but there was something about her that scared him a little.

Ann peeked her head through the first curtain. "Nope." Mike looked in after her, to find an older woman asleep. He quickly closed up the curtain.

"Ann, we can't just disturb these patients until we find your doctor. Don't you think it's a little rude?"

Ann stopped in front of the next curtain and gave him a hard look. "Mike, this is a life-or-death situation. At least," she fidgeted a bit more with her hand in the pocket, "I think it is." She looked down at the ground, then gathered herself up and threw open the next curtain. Not seeing what she wanted, she moved on.

Mike followed her and closed the curtain, but when what was behind the curtain registered in his mind, he opened it again.

"Ted?" he asked the man on the bed. The figure shuddered briefly and turned towards him. It looked so much like Ted, but this man was taller and had a bigger build. Not quite the hulking mass that his "werewolf" had been last night, but still impressive.

"Mike? Mike Samson?" the man asked weakly. His voice was very quiet. It was Ted! Mike stood dumbly in front of the curtain. Ann pushed in behind him, suddenly interested.

"You know this guy, Mike?" she asked. The question was enough to knock Mike out of his stupor.

"Yeah...at least I think so."

"Mike, have you seen my girls?" the man who might be Ted continued. Ted always referred to his wife and daughter as "his girls."

"I..." was as far as Mike got. How could he explain to his neighbor and friend what had happened? The man's loss made him want to cry right there. Worst yet, it echoed with his recent grief. He knew about death and broken families all too well.

"Hi Ted." Ann stepped in. "I'm Ann, a friend of Mike's. We just met actually, but I'm terribly interesting, so I'm sure we'll be good buddies." Ted cradled his head and winced. Ann continued, seeming not to notice. "Can you help us? We're looking for a doctor. Tall handsome white guy, name of Malone?"

Ted moaned and held his head in his hands, rocking. "I'm sorry, I…" His words were slow and he stuttered. "I haven't seen him. Mike, have you seen the girls? Did you bring them here? I have this terrible..." he moaned again, "headache. Ugh, like you wouldn't believe." He lay back down on the bed. As he did, Mike noticed a large, fresh-looking scar right below his chin. It was in the exact spot that Mike had placed his gun and pulled the trigger, just this morning.

"Oh my God..."

It had been Ted. And Ted was a werewolf. How else could he survive that shot? He had killed his wife and daughter and had no memory of the event. The horror of the situation stung Mike down to the very root of his being. To find your family violently murdered was a nightmare above all others. To find that you were the murderer was something beyond any bad dream he had ever imagined.

Suddenly, the curtain behind them was flung open.

"Miss Melakh! What did I say I would do the next time I found you in my hospital?" It was a doctor. She was tall and beautiful like the nurse, but somehow much more frightening. Her voice was stern, like she was lecturing a toddler. Ann jumped at the sound of the woman's voice and turned to face her. For a moment there was a stunned silence, as the doctor glared at Ann with a look that Mike was sure could kill small animals. Ann was shaking like a leaf.

"Excuse me doctor." Mike started with his cop routine, but had trouble finding his usual authoritative tone of voice. "Miss Melakh was just helping me find a patient."

"And you are?" Her words were icy.

"Officer Mike Samson." He flashed his badge quickly, just as he had seen cops do hundreds of times on TV. It was actually kind of fun. This seemed to take her down a notch.

"Oh, well Officer..." Just then, Ann came back to life again, tearing some sort of spray can out of her pocket and sticking it in the doctor's face.

"You can't have him, you demon bitch, but you can have this!" Ann pushed the spray can's release, puffing a fine mist directly into the doctor's eyes.

"Ann, no!" Mike called, pulling her away far too late. The doctor screamed and clawed at her own eyes. The scream turned to a shriek, as if Ann had lit the doctor on fire. Black ooze ran out from underneath her hands.

"God, Ann, what the hell did you do that for?"

"Mike, just look at her," Ann stammered, staring at her victim. Large chunks of the doctor's flesh were dropping to the floor. Her screaming was becoming something far less than human. The doctor seemed to expand then, like a strange balloon. The lights flickered, on and off, and then on again.

"Ann, what the hell was…?" Mike's question died on his lips. The doctor looked up at them, her formerly pretty face unrecognizable, replaced by something only vaguely human in shape. It had a flat nose and pointed ears and was covered in black scales. The eyes were as black as Ted's had been. They did not look at Mike and Ann directly. In fact, they stared blindly at a corner of the room.

"Kill them!" the thing growled. Mike glanced back at the bed as Ted began to convulse, foaming at the mouth. The muscles in his arms and chest expanded rapidly. Mike pulled Ann away as he stepped back, unable to take his eyes off of the transformations that were taking place.

"Oh hell," he said.

"I second that," Ann muttered in a low shocked voice, "Time to go." She turned and ran. Seeing the wisdom in this, Mike followed her example.

They took off at a sprint, away from the demon woman and wolf-man.

"Oh my God. Oh my God. Oh my God," Ann chanted.

Suddenly, another curtain was torn open in front of them, and a huge black man stepped out. Just like Ted, he was growing in size. Dark black hair was sprouting up along his arms. He staggered toward them slowly, like something out of a terrible zombie movie. Ann screamed and lost her footing, but Mike scooped her up with one arm and kept running to the hallway beyond. They could hear the demon woman screaming behind them.

"Kill them!"

Mike did not turn back. He took the first turn that they came to found, and then took another. He needed a gun. A big gun, and a SWAT team, and an army, and maybe Chuck Norris.

He skidded to a stop, narrowly escaping a collision with a woman running in the other direction. Though she said nothing, her face was a mask of terror as she fled past them down a third hallway. Seconds later, another werewolf leapt from a doorway. Mike jumped at the sight of the new monster, quickly turning to follow the fleeing woman.

The little threesome fled down two more hallways. The monsters were behind them but seemed to be losing ground. Mike slowed for a second and put Ann back onto her feet.

"Thanks," she said, before they both took off running again. Then, the sight ahead of them slowly pierced his panic-stricken brain. It was the front desk. A nurse stood at the desk, staring down at something on her desk. They were so close to the exit, just a few feet away.

"Lady, run! Something…" Mike didn't bother finishing the sentence though, noticing that the nurse's eyes were a familiar black color. A low growl was coming from her throat. She suddenly spat something out, her body beginning to spasm. It took several moments for Mike to work out what had come out of her mouth. It was the woman's teeth, all of them, sitting in a pool of blood on the desk. The sight stopped him in his tracks for a moment, before Ann's voice snapped his attention forward again.

"Mike, help!"

Two more werewolves had appeared out of nowhere and grabbed the woman who had run with them. Ann, in what Mike could only imagine was a fit of madness, charged one of the beasts, slamming her fist hard into its face. To her credit, the monster stopped in its tracks, a dumbstruck look plainly visible through the extra hair and fangs. "Well, if she can do it... " Mike thought, following her lead and slugging the nearest wolf-man as hard as he could. He was a little surprised when the beast staggered and released its victim. The woman was free for a second and Ann reached over to help her up.

"Come on!"

The ex-nurse from the front desk was upon them now, her mouth full of long, sharp fangs. She smacked Mike aside with one glancing blow and went right for the woman, who was still struggling to get up.

Reeling from the blow, Mike could do nothing to stop the nurse from picking the woman up and running with her. The woman at last made a sound, a cry for help, as the wolf-nurse tossed her over her shoulder like a bulky gym bag. In the meantime, Mike's boxing partner had recovered and was going for a little payback for the punch to the face. It dove at Mike but, by luck, missed when Mike ducked.

"Mike, this way!" Ann was reaching for him. He grabbed the hand she offered and together they were on the run again. A few steps In front of them was a door marked "Stairs."

"No Ann, we have to save her before we get out!" Mike yelled in frustration, noticing the increasing distance between him and the escaping ex-nurse. His noble intentions were quickly abandoned, however, when he noticed yet another werewolf bearing down on him. He quickly followed Ann through the door to the stairwell and swung it closed behind him, hard. It connected with their closest pursuer, giving off a satisfying crunch.

Ann was ahead of him, heading up the stairs. "This way. Move!" she shouted, like he needed to be told that it was a good idea. He bounded up the stairs two at a time, fear erasing any memory of his injuries.

On the next floor they burst through a door and ran down a new hallway. After a moment, noticing no pursuit, they slowed.

"Ann," Mike panted, "can you find us another way out of here?"

"Not without Keith!"

"What? Are you insane?" Mike shouted. He grabbed her arm, wanting to shake some sense into her.

"No, look! Now I have proof that something horrible is going on and I'm not a loon. I have to find him!" There were tears in her eyes. "Please, Mike. Please. You and I are his only chance. And I love him," she pleaded.

Mike frowned and shook his head. "But what can you and I do against those...things, whatever they are?"

A growl from down the hall ended the conversation. At its end, a werewolf was sprinting towards them. It was huge, far larger than Ted had been. Foam streamed out of its fanged mouth and huge claws jutted from its fingertips. It still wore pants but its shirt had been torn apart by its massive chest muscles. Once again, they broke into a run.

As they sprinted past an intersection, Mike caught an odd sight. While perhaps not as odd as the man-beast that was chasing them, it was enough to catch his attention. It was a small Hispanic man, in a hospital gown, leaning against the wall. Both his right arm and right leg were bound up in large casts and he looked ready to pounce on something. He winked at Mike as they ran past.

"Look out!" Mike shouted, but the man ignored him. As the wolf-man passed the man, he spun out from his hiding place and smashed the arm with the cast into the creature's face. There was a loud crack as the wolf-man was knocked to the floor. The man quickly followed through, bringing the cast down on its head two more times. The first time there was another thunderous crack, and the second, a wet crunch.

Mike grabbed Ann by the arm and they came to a stop, turning to look at their savior. As they walked toward him, the man worked on pulling apart the remains of his cast..

"Ah, thank you sir," the strange newcomer said to the downed monster. "I've been trying to get that off for quite some time. Amazingly itchy."

"Mr. Miller, is that you?" Ann asked as the pieces of the cast fell to the ground. Miller rubbed his arm. The skin there was a bright pink. He turned toward her and gave her a friendly wave.

"Miss Ann!" He had an odd, almost Scottish, accent.

"I thought they got to you," Ann replied. "I thought you were demon food or something."

"Oh they tried. As it turns out, Scottish food is terrible." He grinned. There was a long pause as both Mike and Ann tried to figure out what he meant.

Miller ignored their confusion and gave Mike a once-over. "Joseph Miller, a pleasure to meet you." He put the hand of his recently-freed arm out to shake. Mike slowly took it, confused by the odd man but happy to have the help.

"Mike Samson."

"Samson? Fantastic name!" Miller smiled and slapped Mike on the back.

"Is that thing dead?" Ann asked, kicking the wolf-man a few times.

"Oh, most likely," Miller said. "Generally, crushing their skulls works fairly well. It's a bit less effective than chopping off their heads, but I really don't have any better tools at my disposal at the moment."

"What exactly was it?" Mike asked.

"Oh, that's a lesser demon spawn, commonly referred to as a werewolf. Although where the actual wolf reference comes from, I have no idea," Miller continued, as if describing a type of mold, or a model of vacuum cleaner. "Generally quite vicious but not really dangerous unless in packs."

"Miller," Ann asked, staring at his arm, "how did you do that with your arm? Cynthia said it was shattered."

“Oh, that.” Miller looked a bit embarrassed. “I heal much faster than you regular folk.”

“You’re not one of them, are you?” Ann asked. Mike wasn't sure if the “them” she was referring to meant demons or werewolves.

Miller laughed and then, with a grin, answered, “Lass, I'm not one of them. I’m the one that hunts them.”

# 12 - Lawyers, Guns, and Money. Well, Guns Anyway.

Quite some time ago, Ann's mind had reached its maximum level of tolerance for freaky shit. The fact that she had not simply rolled up into the fetal position at the sight of Vanessa's true face was nothing short of a miracle. She was so far past losing it, she was almost giddy. When the little Hispanic guy who had been hit by a truck just days before (and was probably loaded with pain killers) was up out of bed, walking around and beating a mythical beast to death with a cast he apparently no longer needed, Ann almost giggled. She knew this was not the right reaction, but what could she do?

Ann was relieved to see Miller alive, until she was reminded just how nuts he was. Then again, the world seemed to have recently gone mad, so maybe that worked. Lyrics from an old song popped into her head. You may be right, I may be crazy, but it just may be a lunatic you're looking for.

"So you're some kind of demon hunter?" Mike asked. The big guy seemed pale. He had wanted nothing more than to run the hell out of this place and maybe that was the smartest thing to do.

"Aye, something like that. But I've been out of the game for some time, and things may have changed. Now, while I do love to chat about myself, I think it's wise for us to retreat and find some supplies." He looked himself up and down. "And maybe some pants."

"Supplies? Like what? An army?" Mike raised his voice. "I say we get our asses out of here while they're still in one piece."

"Not without Keith," Ann said firmly. She had come this far, and heck, now she had a professional demon hunter on her side. She briefly wondered where you went to school for that? Transylvania?

Miller rubbed his chin. "Yes, I'll do what I can to help you, lass, but what we find may not be pleasant."

"Are you crazy? Did you guys see that thing? And that other...thing?" Mike asked. The lights in the hallway flashed off again and then came back on.

"Look Mike, thanks for trying to help me, and you don't have to stay, but I need to find Keith. I'm not leaving until I do. It seems Mr. Miller here is going to help me out."

For a second Mike just stood there and fumed. Then he kicked the wall and shouted, "Fine! If you idiots want to die, I can't stop you." He made no move to leave.

Miller turned to Ann and said, "Ann, I am going to need some weapons if we are to survive this."

She thought hard. "Well, there's a security station down the hall. We might be able to find something there."

"Good," Miller said. "Lead the way." They were off down the hall.

Mike glared at them. "Damn it, I can't just leave you two here."

Suddenly, they heard a crashing sound from the direction that the wolf-man had come, as if the ceiling was collapsing. They turned to see what Ann assumed was a giant black demon making its way around the corner. It moved slowly, as it was far too big to fit into the hall. Its pointed horns dragged against the ceiling, smashing lights and knocking down tiles. It had the head of a bull and giant hooves for feet. Its body was a huge mass of muscle and black scales. The creature seemed to be blind and was smashing into everything in its path.

"Melakh! I'm going to rip you into little shreds!"

"Good Lord, it's Vanessa!" Ann was stunned for a moment.

"*Was* Vanessa. How odd. It seems to be blind." For a moment, Miller's voice sounded solemn, as he inspected the creature. Then, far too cheerfully, he yelled, "Run for your lives!" and broke into a run. Mike quickly passed the limping Miller, who was following Ann down the hall. She led them through two more rights and a quick left, arriving at the security station.

It was a tiny room, just a bit bigger than a walk-in closet. There was a desk covered with monitors on one side, while the other side held a simple coat rack. On a third wall stood several lockers. A security guard was pulling off his coat. He looked up at them as they entered.

"Can I help you?" he asked.

"Yes," Miller said, picking up the man by his shoulders and shoving him into the hallway just as the massive demon turned the corner.

"Mother of God!" the man screamed, as Miller pulled him back inside and slammed the metal door shut. Mike grunted as he shoved a metal cabinet in front of it. The extra precaution made sense, but was the door demon-proof?

"Now that you've seen our problem, can you spare any weapons?" Miler asked.

"My God, what the hell was that?" asked the security guard.

Ann put her hands on his shoulders and shook him. "Focus, buddy. That thing is going to be at our door very shortly. We need something to stop it from eating us."

The man's obvious fear made her feel a bit better. It was not unreasonable to simply want to run away screaming.

"Uh…" his eyes darted wildly around the room, at last stopping on a cabinet.

"Here?" Miller asked, beginning to shake the cabinet. Suddenly, there was a bang at the door. Mike braced the cabinet blocking it with his body.

"Melakh, I can smell the cop's blood in there. This door won't stop me!"

"Be right with you!" Miller responded, sounding calm and polite. Returning his attention to the guard, he said, "I don't suppose that you have the key for this?" Just then, the door seemed to hop out of its frame, briefly knocking Mike back.

"Anytime now!" Mike shouted at the security guard. He was fiddling with his keys, but dropped them as something huge hit the door, bending it slightly. Ann snatched the keys from the floor and quickly worked out which one she needed. She flung the cabinet doors open to reveal two shotguns and several boxes of ammunition.

"Shotguns?" Mike asked, still leaning his weight against the door. "And combat ones at that. Isn't that a Mossberg? A bit much for a security job."

The security guard only shrugged. "It *is* Newark."

Leaving his spot at the door, Mike snatched a shotgun out of the cabinet and did a quick ammo check before giving it a pump.

"Those won't help much. You need a sword or an axe," Miller pointed out.

"They make me feel a lot better. You know how to use one of these?" he asked Miller.

"Not exactly the shotguns of my time, but I am a fast study."

Once again the lights flickered, the computer screens in the room dimming with the power loss. Then, just like the last two times, the power came back on.

There was another loud bang, this time at the wall next to the door, which suddenly splintered, long cracks running from the corner of the room to the edge of the doorframe. This was instantly followed by another blow. Brick and plaster exploded, showering Ann in dust and pebbles. She couldn't help but let out a little scream as a huge talon pushed its way through the new hole in the wall. Mike shoved the shotgun point blank at the talon and pulled the trigger. The demon's hand exploded into black chunks. In the closed room, the sound of the gun was even louder than the beating on the door, and Ann slapped her hands over her ears. Black blood from the demon splashed over the front of her coat.

From outside came a loud howl and the bloody talon was quickly pulled back out of the room. Loud crashing noises accompanied the beast's retreat down the hall.

Miller whistled, clearly impressed by the shotgun's effect. "I stand corrected." He picked up the other shotgun. "Show me how it works."

Ann turned back to the security guard. "Can you call for help?"

"I...I…yes." He started pressing buttons on a phone on the wall, and then paused to look back up at Ann. "But what the hell do I tell them?"

Ann shrugged. Massive bear attack probably won't cut it.

"Tell them there's a group of armed gang members shooting up the place. They'll believe that and come with the heavy equipment," Mike broke in, before continuing to show Miller how the shotgun worked. It was handy having a cop on your side, even if he had wanted to run away. To be fair to Mike, he was handling himself pretty well.

Ann looked down at a row of security screens. Those that had not been destroyed by flying debris were flipping through camera views from around the hospital. Several showed werewolves roaming the halls. One was dragging an unconscious man across the floor. "This place has gone to the dogs," she joked, trying hard not to break into a panic.

"You have a very odd sense of humor, lady," Mike noted while stuffing ammo into the pockets of his jeans.

"It's either that or the fetal position."

Mike nodded. "Yeah, I know that feeling."

The security guard jerked the phone away from his head. "It just went dead!"

Of course it would just go dead. Ann had seen this movie before.

"Did you get through?" Mike asked.

"Well, I started to, so they do know something's wrong."

Miller pushed his way between them. "What's your name, son?" he asked the security guard, who gave the seemingly much younger man a hard look that lasted a moment.

"Bill Tirhsred," he responded.

"Joseph Miller. Welcome to the good fight." They shook hands.

"I just got here for my shift, thought it was odd no one was around," Bill said. He was a slightly bald, middle-aged man. "What the hell was that thing?"

"A demon, apparently," Mike responded.

"That's Vanessa Black, one of the doctors here. Apparently she's been infected or cursed with something."

"Dr. Black? Tall woman with really nice..." he looked over at Ann, "...hair?" he finished lamely.

"Yeah, that's her. And she's not alone. A bunch of patients seem to have the same problem, except it's making them big and furry with claws," Ann explained.

"Wait," Mike put up a hand in warning. "How do we know this guy is human?"

Ann nodded. It was a fair question.

"He is as human as you are, Mr. Samson," answered Miller.

"How do you know?" Ann asked.

"Trust me, I've done this before." Miller grinned.

"So you've been trapped in a hospital with a gaggle of werewolves and a demon?" Ann raised an eyebrow.

"Well not this exact situation," Miller waved his hand around the room, "but similar ones."

"Does anyone have a cell phone?" Mike asked.

"Here." Ann tossed her phone over to Mike. Snatching it out of the air, he quickly dialed and put the phone to his ear.

"This is Officer Mike Samson. I need to report an emergency, my badge number is..."

Miller tugged on Ann's arm, stealing her attention away from the phone call. He whispered in her ear. "What did you see before we crossed paths?"

Ann shrugged his hand off of her arm. "I gave that bitch, Vanessa Black, a taste of this pepper spray and she went all…demony? Demonie? Demonic, that's the word."

"Pepper spray? A weapon of some kind?"

"Umm, yeah, it's like an anti-rape thing, you spray it in their eyes and it burns them."

"Hmmm." Miller rubbed his chin again.

"Why? Is that important?"

"Have you ever hit a bee hive with a rock, Miss Ann?"

"No, what kind of a stupid question is that?"

"Well you just did. This hospital is the hive and that doctor is the queen. When you hurt her, you woke up every cursed creature nearby."

Ann went a bit paler. "So all this chaos was my fault?"

"Well, yes and no. Chances are, this was going to happen soon enough, and you just moved things forward a bit. Don't worry about it." He shrugged. "These things happen to me all the time."

Mike snapped the phone closed. "I got through. Help is on the way, but there was some kind of odd static."

There was another thump at the door. This one was not nearly as loud, but a little scream of surprise popped out of Ann's mouth.

"What now?" Bill looked toward Miller.

"Wolves this time, I think. I believe Mr. Samson did enough damage with his wonderful new toy that our demon friend has sent in the reserves."

A furry and clawed hand reached through hole in the wall. The four of them stood against the wall to get as far away as possible from the new invader. Mike breathed out hard. "Not again."

The pounding on the door continued. It sounded as if many fists were knocking at once.

"Everyone, this is how it is going to work." Miller pumped his shotgun for dramatic effect. "Our mission here is a rescue one. We are to find as many people as possible and get them out. We also aim to keep you three alive."

"Just the three of us? Not you?" Ann asked. Miller grinned that stupid, crazy grin.

"I always make it out alive." He paused for a moment, as if mulling something over. "Well, almost always," he corrected. "Your job is to help any curse-free humans you find, and maybe..." Miller paused to look down at the hospital gown, "to find me some pants. Leave the monster killing to me. That includes you, Mr. Samson." Mike nodded at that. "Try to avoid the wolves as much as possible. The demons are the real threat. If you do need to take down a wolf, aim for its head. I am not sure how well these shotguns will work against them, but I have high hopes." There was another louder bang on the door as several bodies hit it at once. "Everyone against this wall here. Let them open the door. I'll make a path out for us once they enter. I expect it to get very messy, so Miss Ann, you may want to cover your eyes."

"Bite me, Miller. Give me something to hit 'em with and I'll be right there with you." Ann's tough talk sounded a bit weak, even to her own ears.

Miller gave her a smile. "Good lass. Well put."

Mike spoke up. "Is there any way to turn these people back?" There was a bit of pleading in his voice. "I mean, these are innocent people, infected with some sort of disease. Maybe there's a cure."

"Mr. Samson, while I have no idea what the word 'infected' means, I assure you that we will do what we can for these people. Our first task, however, must be for you to survive." Miller paused. "Now, any other questions?"

There was another slam at the door. It was beginning to buckle. Bill meekly raised his hand. "Can I have a shotgun?"

"No!" Miller and Mike said at the same time. There was a moment of silence between them as they all looked at the door. Another crash and the frame was pushed further out. A clawed hand appeared at the top of the door. Another bang, and another. Bill let out a small whimper and Ann's already-cramped stomach spun.

Suddenly, the door fell into the room, taking a chunk of the wall with it. Three werewolves spilled into the room, hopping over the cabinet, clawing and howling their way into the room. Ann noticed with a shock that the lead wolf was the little old lady they had found asleep in one of the emergency rooms. Her green hospital gown still clung to her, though the sleeves had been shredded. Her gray hair shot out in wild directions. Miller stepped forward and fired his shotgun directly into her face. Her head exploded in a horrible red mist, like a rotten pumpkin.

Ann screamed. She couldn't help it, but didn't look away. Mike stepped forward and shot the second wolf, but missed the head, instead catching it in the chest and knocking it straight back into the hall, taking down a third wolf on the way.

"Move!" Miller commanded. It became obvious Miller had spent a lot of time in charge. He barked the order with such authority in his voice that there was nothing else to do but follow. Mike took the lead, with Ann and Bill following and Miller watching the rear. The wolf at the bottom of the pile was struggling to get free but Miller quickly stopped him with another blast of his shotgun.

"Fantastic weapon!" he beamed, his grin growing wider.

"Where to, Miller?" Mike shouted back. Apparently his desire to run like hell had left him. Ann was glad for it. He seemed more competent than Bill, who was quaking like a leaf and waving his little handgun around in front of him, but far less insane than Miller.

Miller pumped the shotgun and hobbled forward. "Room-to-room search. Might as well start with this one on your left."

Mike obeyed, and took cover next to the doorway. He nodded at Miller. "Monster hunters first."

"Aye, that's a bright lad." Miller limped past him and moved to give the door a kick, but then thought better of it and slammed it open with his left hand. Ann held her breath as he walked in, but there were no gunshots. His voice came out shortly after. "Empty."

The next four rooms were empty as well. Each time Miller went through a door, Ann cringed and the twist in her stomach worsened.

"Where is everyone?" Ann asked.

"No place good," Mike grunted.

"Aye," Miller put in, "Something very odd is afoot here. I couldn't be this late."

Ann wasn't sure what to make of that, but so far only about half of what Miller said made sense, even on a good day.

"I only passed one person on my way in. I thought that was strange," Bill added in a shaky voice.

Miller stopped abruptly. "Well hello, beautiful!" He whistled. On the wall, behind glass, hung a red fireman's axe. Miller smashed the glass with the back of the shotgun and pulled it out. Moving the gun to his left hand, he hefted the axe with his right, trying to get a feel for the weight.

"What are you going to do with that?" Mike asked.

The old grin crawled back over Miller's face. "Oh, I think it will come in handy."

They repeated the same exercise in every room. Miller entered first, with Bill behind him and Mike and Ann watching the door. Ann had her pepper spray ready. It was no gun but had worked so well on Vanessa that it had to be better than nothing.

A few seconds after entering the fifth room, Miller let out a loud "Ah ha!"

"What is it?" Mike shouted as he spun around the corner, Ann close behind.

"Trousers!" Miller was ecstatic. They had entered a locker room of sorts. Clothes lay tossed about the place. Miller was holding up a pair of green scrub pants. Ann quickly averted her eyes as, with one smooth motion, Miller ripped the hospital gown off.

"To finally get out of that dress!" There was a bit of banging around as Miller struggled with the scrubs. Ann turned around again after hearing a loud rip. Miller had torn off the one leg to make room for his cast, but otherwise he was decent. He shuffled through the room looking for something else to put on.

Ann marveled at the fresh scars on the man's chest and arm where he had been hit by a truck just a few short days ago. Although the flesh was still the bright pink of the newly healed, there was no swelling at all. It seemed impossible, but following the laws of reality didn't seem to be all that popular today. Miller noticed her stare and stopped.

"Try this," Bill said, tossing him a shirt. It was a white t-shirt with the words "New Jersey Devils" on the front.

Miller shrugged it on. "It will do. Many thanks." He evaluated his new outfit. "I look much improved. Wait…" He dug into the pockets of his new pants. "What is this?" He pulled a blue pen out of his pocket and held it up for the others to see. "A medical tool of some kind?"

"That's a pen," Ann said, barely managing not to add "idiot."

Miller's face fell. "Oh, that is far less useful. Still, it is a rather nice pen." He shoved it back into his pocket.

"Someone was certainly looking for something here," Mike said after a few minutes of rooting through the open lockers. Each door had been torn clean off the hinges.

"Someone not human, by the look of the lockers," Ann noted. "How many of these demon-things are there?"

"They call themselves the 'Fallen.' There are always seven," Miller said, retrieving his gun.

Mike picked up the thread. "So we know that Dr. Black is one."

"And a nurse named Mary as well," Miller continued.

Mike gulped. "Mary? Damn I knew there was something off about her."

"You know her?" Miller asked.

"Yeah, let's just say she tried to get, err, personal with me earlier. I guess I'm glad we were interrupted."

"Aye, so am I. Otherwise we wouldn't be having this lovely conversation. You would be one of them." Miller jabbed a finger out toward the hallway.

"Well, great," Bill put in, a sarcastic edge creeping into his voice. "Now we just have to work out the final five."

"Four," Miller announced. "I know of one more."

Mike somehow found a way to turn even paler as he digested what Miller had told him. Then something seemed to dawn on him. "Wait, I was attacked by a werewolf earlier." He lifted his shirt up to show the fresh cuts. "Does this mean," he stuttered, "does this mean I'm going to become one of them?"

Miller laughed. "Hah! Lad, that is the most ridiculous thing that I have heard in some time. If it was that easy, everyone would be cursed. Where on earth did you get such a ridiculous notion?"

Mike pulled down his shirt, looking rather stung but relieved. "I just…well you know…the movies and such."

Ann backed him up. "It's like a classic werewolf movie. A guy goes out for a hike in the woods, gets bitten, eats all his friends. You know. It's how the legend goes."

Miller laughed. "These movies are like the shows on the TV? I have to see one! They must be fantastic!" Miller seemed to notice the stunned looks on the faces of the others, and dropped the subject abruptly.

"What's with those eyes anyway?" Ann asked. She shivered.

"The mark of the Cursed. Well, one of them, anyway. All those touched by the Fallen have it, though wolves and vampires can hide it for short periods in their human forms." Ann saw Bill jump a bit at that.

"Wait! Vampires? Those are real too?"

Miller laughed again. "Sadly yes, but again, the stories about them are completely incorrect. Some poor sod wrote a book about them where they had pointy fangs and could turn into bats or some such nonsense."

"Wait. Vampires don't have fangs? Then how do they suck?" Ann asked.

"I hope for your sake you never have to find out. Filthy creatures. They should never be trusted."

"So if there are seven 'Fallen'," Mike said the last word slowly, trying to get a feel for it, "How can the four of us possibly do anything against all of them?"

"It is no small task, Mr. Samson. We do have a chance, however. The demons here are young and not yet completely themselves. Once they have had enough time to feed and grow, they will become even more unstoppable."

"That was pretty much the opposite of reassuring. Thanks, Miller," complained Ann.

A brief silence fell on the room until Mike broke it with a question. "I wonder if the Newark PD is here yet?"

"I don't know. Everything seems so quiet. Let's see if we can find a room with windows and take a look around," Ann suggested.

"Aye. Let's head out to the next room. Keep your eyes open." As if hearing him, the lights went out. This time, they stayed out.

*****

It had been a particularly rough shift. Officer Jessica Jones was trying to keep herself going for as long as possible. She knew that once she stopped and curled up in bed, the image of the mutilated girl would come back to haunt her. She had never seen anything like it and hoped she never would again. Poor Mike Samson had known the people, discovered the body, and even seen the perp.

She was in her patrol car, filling out more paperwork when the call came in. "Gang shooting at College Hospital."

"College? Isn't that where we sent your buddy Samson this morning?" Andrew Fox, Jessica's partner, asked. Andrew had been busy snacking on a doughnut. This habit of his made Jessica's eyes roll. She only ate fruit on the job, just to break with silly stereotypes.

"Buddy? I know the guy, ok? He's a fellow officer, and I heard he lost his wife in some sort of accident a few months back. I just feel for the guy, you know?" She had truthfully only met Samson a few times and had really only spoken to him at length once at a Christmas party. His son, Sam, had been there, and had been the one to make the lasting impression on her. "We should check this out. It's not far from here."

"Jessie, our shift ended an hour ago. We need to go home. My wife is going to kill me as it is."

"You know you don't want to go to bed anymore than I do."

Andrew sighed at that. He had three little girls at home, all at school by now. "No, not really. Okay, let's go."

The hospital was only five minutes away and when they arrived, four other squad cars were already there. The other officers were getting out of their cars. Jessica and Andrew quickly hopped out to join them.

"You guys still on shift?" someone asked Jessica.

"Yeah, a bit of overtime. What's the situation here?"

"We're still working that out. There's no response from the hospital front desk at all."

"Not good," Andrew grunted.

"We received a call from a security guard and from one of our own, Samson." Jessica started at the name. Damn, she had hoped he would be home by now.

"But no gun shots, no hostages, nothing?" Andrew asked.

"Not yet. I'm guessing we're going to have to take a look," the officer said. Several more officers had drawn guns and were approaching the front door. Jessica made to follow them.

The inside of the hospital was dim. All of the lights were out, except for one that was hanging from the ceiling by a cord, flickering on and off. As the officers moved through the front doors they saw no one. The place was a mess of papers, overturned chairs, and garbage tossed around the floor. The sunlight of the front windows only just penetrated the darkness of the waiting room. Beyond a certain distance, darkness filled the area like a pool.

"No one home," Andrew whispered, his gun out and pointed forward into the darkness.

Another officer raised his voice. "This is the police! Is anyone here?"

Jessica flinched at the sudden noise. "Great. Just let the bad guys know what to shoot at," she muttered under her breath.

No shots came. There was nothing but terrible silence.

"Looks like we're going to need to go further in. Someone see if they can fix the lights." The man who spoke appeared to be the officer in charge.

Jessica pulled out her flashlight and followed the others deeper into the building. She kicked at the random papers and hospital equipment that was scattered across the floor. She found a rag which, on closer inspection, turned out to be the top of a nurse's uniform. It was so badly shredded that it took her some time to recognize.

"What the hell?"

Somewhere in front of her and to the right, a man screamed. The sound cut through the silence like a knife. Andrew yelped and everyone pointed their guns in the direction of the noise.

"I think it was over here," she waved the flashlight to her right. Several officers rushed to her side. Taking the lead with her gun in one hand and her flashlight in the other, she moved quickly. She could not understand how it was so damned dark in here in the middle of the day.

She entered the room that she believed the sound had come from and started to cover as much area with the small beam of her flashlight as possible. Something wet caught her eye and she flipped back to double-check. It was blood all right, and it looked like it was coming from…she panned the light over to the right. It was one of the officers that had walked into the building just a few moments before her. Or, to be more precise, it was his body. His empty eyes stared blankly at her from across the room. She moved the light just a little to the right, and revealed someone chewing on the body.

“There!” she shouted. Several of the other officers pointed their lights at the same spot. It looked like a young boy, but he was horribly misshapen. He was very broad across the chest and his arms were large and covered in hair.

“Freeze!” someone shouted. The boy’s eyes snapped up at the sound of the voice and looked in the general direction of the officers. His eyes were empty, black pools. He hissed at them like a big angry cat and jumped to the right.

“Good God, what’s wrong with him?” someone shouted, as Jessica desperately tried to follow the boy with her light. He moved incredibly fast. Her light exposed two more creatures like the boy. These were bigger, obviously adults, with the same black eyes glinting in the dark. Another officer to Jessica's right yelled and fell over. Guns fired into the darkness as more screams rang out. With her flashlight, Jessica tried to find a safe target. An officer was being dragged away by one of those things. She squeezed off four shots, three of which hit the creature. It jerked with each hit but did not stop dragging the officer away. At that moment she felt a hand grab her ankle. Jessica dropped the beam of light to see what had gotten hold of her. It was Andrew.

“Jessie, help,” Andrew pleaded, “One of them has my leg.”

“I got ya, buddy.” Biting the flashlight in her mouth to free up a hand, she reached down and tried to pull him up. The creature was too strong.

“Aggh! It’s ripping my goddamn leg apart!”

Jessica fired a random shot into the dark where she thought the creature was. It had no effect. Moving the flashlight with her teeth, she found the beast’s head. It looked like a cavewoman. Jessica lined up her shot, fired, and hit the creature in the bridge of the nose. Its head snapped up and it howled in pain. Andrew came free and tumbled back through the door with Jessica. The force of the fall was enough to knock her flashlight free of her teeth and it dropped, rolling across the floor.

She picked herself up and grabbed at Andrew's shoulder to drag him away, but something else got to him first, yanking him hard into the darkness. He was gone instantly.

“Jessie, help...” the sentence ended in a horrible gurgle. Jessica turned to run back into the light. As she did, she snatched out her radio and began shouting into it.

“Officers down! I have several officers down. There are some kind of creatures here, maybe, I don't know...”

Something knocked her down, ending her sentence. Her radio flew one way and she flew another, spilling onto the floor. She rolled over quickly and tried to stand back up. Now, back near the main entrance of the hospital, she could see her attackers. They were flowing out of the darkness like water. There were too many of them, furry beasts with black eyes. Some had clothes on and were dressed as doctors, nurses, EMTs, and regular street folk. They surged forward like a terrible tidal wave.

Jessica managed to scream just once before they reached her.

# 13 - Darkness

"Great," Mike said. "This just keeps getting better and better."

He still wanted to run, to just get out. He was all Sam had now and he was sure as hell not going to let some insane people drag him away from his real responsibilities. On the other hand, innocent people here needed his help. It was, in a way, his job. And, like it or not, he had formed a bond with these people. Their best chance of living through this was to stick together. At least now he had a gun that seemed to do something against the wolf beasts.

"Give it a sec. The emergency lights should kick on automatically," Ann said. Her hands were still deep inside her huge coat. The crazy girl look had gotten worse over the last hour or so. She looked like she was ill, but then, that's pretty much how Mike felt as well.

"Any second now," Ann continued. Several moments passed. "Well then, maybe not."

Bill snapped on a flashlight. His hand shook terribly. Of all of them, he seemed to be the most terrified, and he hadn't even witnessed the doctor's transformation. That in itself was a nightmare that Mike was pretty sure was going to replay in his mind many, many times.

Bill gave the impression that he was going to bolt off screaming in at any minute. But, so far, to his credit, he had kept it together.

"An electric torch! Brilliant! I don't suppose that you have any more of those?" Miller asked.

Bill shrugged. "Nope. Sorry."

Mike couldn't make sense of Joseph Miller. He looked like a guy in his early 20s. Hispanic, maybe Mexican? But he spoke and acted with the confidence of a much older man. He also seemed to be unaware of pretty basic things, like flashlights and how pants worked. He handled himself well in a fight, and for that Mike was grateful. He seemed to know a lot more of what was going on around here than anyone else. Mike was planning on having a long talk with Miller if they got out of this, preferably at the police station.

"Okay then, let's start moving. Mr. Tirhsred, I am afraid you're going to have to take the lead this time. I'll be right behind you." Bill gulped hard at Miller's words, but led the way out of the room.

The sudden darkness of the hospital unnerved Mike. There were not many windows and the ones there were didn't seem to let enough light in. In the hallways, the dark pools between doors held a deep sense of dread.

Mike needed a distraction from his fear.

"Miller, what else can you tell me about these werewolves?" he asked. They had formed a line, with Bill and Miller at the front, followed by Ann. Mike was at the back, attempting to stare into the darkness behind him and the faint light ahead.

"Well, as I mentioned, I am not sure where the wolf part comes from, although I believe they are the root of much of the werewolf lore. I can assure you that they do not become wolves."

"They look like cave people, well a bit, anyway. Like people that have devolved or something," Ann chipped in.

"Cave people?" Miller asked.

"Yeah, like Neanderthals, ancient men. Although the bone structure isn't right exactly, they seem to have increased body hair and muscle mass, but fewer cerebral capabilities. Not sure about the claws though, that's certainly not from anything I've seen in the history books."

"Miss Ann…"

"Just Ann please, Miller," Ann cut in.

"Ann, then. I had heard some talk back in the 1880s that there was a race of men before our current one. I had thought it nonsense at the time."

Had he said1880s*?*

"The thing that really gets me is how quickly they…" Ann hunted for the right word, "transform, I guess the term is. That amount of cell growth, it's just not possible."

"I think someone missed the 'super' part in 'supernatural'," Mike jumped back in.

"No, really, it would take a massive amount of energy."

"Energy?" Bill asked.

Ann continued. "Well, food. Ok, let's say that this is some kind of virus. Maybe it's possible that this virus is rearranging people's DNA. But even with that, to completely transform a person's body in a matter of seconds…" She trailed off, lost in thought.

"You a doctor or something?" Bill asked, not looking back.

"Scientist, actually. Well, PhD biology student," Ann answered.

"Come on. There's another room up here." Miller again took the lead, pushing the door open. This time Bill was right behind him with the flashlight. It turned out that it wasn't needed, as the room had a row of windows. Mike rushed into the room and stood in the weak sunlight. His sense of panic died back down. Then he thought of his neighbor.

"Is there any way to help them? Like, cure them, I guess?"

Miller let out a long sigh and then started to explain slowly.

"It is possible to free the Cursed from their demon masters, but they do not become human again. They remain forever cursed. They live out their remaining years misshapen. Worse yet, they recall everything they have done while under the Fallen's control. It is not a fate that I would wish on my worst enemy."

"But how would we free them?" Ann asked.

"Ah, that's no easy task either. You need to kill the demon that cursed them."

"So if we could find the demon that infected…err, cursed these people, they would at least stop trying to kill us," Ann said.

Mike swallowed hard. Could he free his neighbor Ted, and condemn him to hell on Earth, with the knowledge of what he had done to his own family? No. He decided he couldn't do that to anyone. Better to be dead than live through that torment.

"So if there are these demons, vampires, and werewolves out there, why don't we hear about them all the time?" Bill asked.

"A fair question. What do you know about locusts, Mr. Tirhsred?"

"Um, the car?" Bill responded.

"I think he means the insects, not Lotus," Ann said. "Don't they only show up every few years or something?"

"Exactly, Ann. Demons are like locusts, with a slightly longer cycle. This room is clear. Let's keep moving." Mike was sad to leave the light behind.

"How long is a cycle, Miller?" Mike asked, once again stepping into the darkness. Bill turned back on the flashlight.

"Well, there seems to be a range. The last one started in 1793, I believe."

Ann whistled. "That kinda makes sense. Every few hundred years they show up, do some damage, make some famous fairy tales, and then die off somehow."

"Aye, you have it right, lass. Usually I'm the one that kills 'em. Generally with help."

Now it was Bill's turn to laugh. "You? That would mean you're like, 300 years old or something."

"Oh, much, much older than that," Miller responded.

"How old *are* you?" Ann asked, apparently ready to believe the delusional man.

"Let us just say I could almost give your ancient race of man a bit of competition."

"Are you even human then?" Bill asked.

Miller stopped and turned to face them. For once his grin was replaced with a hurt look. "Of course I'm human! Just not…" he waved his hand around at the three of them as if he was having problems remembering the word. "Mortal."

"Hey! Over there!" Bill cut in, his voice shrill with panic.

"Something moved!" He started to wave his flashlight around the room, trying to catch whatever it was with the beam. Suddenly, something collided with him. The flashlight in his hands spiraled down the hallway. "Help!" he screamed, as the thing lifted him into the air. Mike dove for the flashlight, but in the few seconds it took him to pick it up, Bill had already been carried halfway down the hall.

"Damn!" Miller shouted, "I can't get a good shot." Mike trained the light down the hall, and was just able to make out the fleeing werewolf's back. Miller squeezed off a shot and the werewolf stumbled but did not stop. Miller took a few limping steps forward, giving chase. "Samson! Go slow him down! I cannot move that quickly!"

Not thinking, Mike did exactly what he was told. He sped after the werewolf, trying to keep the fleeing creature in the flashlight's beam. The beast was made easier to track by Bill, who was screaming his lungs out, sounding more like a teenage girl than a grown man, not that Mike blamed him.

The werewolf cut left through a doorway. Mike followed it, entering a stairwell. It was pitch-black. Using the flashlight, he quickly found the beast just 10 stairs below. Apparently Miller's shot had done some damage, as it seemed to be slowing down. Mike considered how to take the werewolf down while it still carried Bill. A shotgun was hardly a precise weapon. Mike could only think of one tactic that might work without killing Bill, and 'might' was the key word. He dove down the stairs three at a time. Then, closing the distance, Mike tucked his weapon and flashlight to against his chest and jumped. He connected with the wolf's back in a flying tackle. Bill, Mike, and the beast tumbled down the rest of the stairs in a confusion of arms and legs. At the bottom of the stairs, next to the doorway to the hall, Mike freed himself from the tangle and grabbed Bill with one hand while attempting to aim his gun at the wolf with the other. Bill came partly free and Mike shifted his weight to get a better grip. Suddenly, a large furry hand wrapped around Mike's chest and pulled him into the hall. The shotgun was knocked aside and Mike was slammed hard against a wall. Here, some sunlight snuck in from beneath one of the doors, and Mike could see without the aid of a flashlight. He stared directly into the black eyes of his neighbor, Ted.

*****

Miller did his best to follow the wolf, Bill, and Mike. He cursed his shattered leg once more as he limped along, moving as quickly as he could. Ann stayed behind him. Reaching the door that his companions had recently passed through, he paused.

“Ah stairs, my old nemesis,” Miller said.

“What? What are you waiting for?” Ann yelled. Miller looked at the shotgun in one hand and the axe in the other. He passed the gun to Ann.

“Lass, would you be so kind as to hold this for me?”

“What am I supposed to do with it?” Ann demanded.

“Just hold it. It looks lovely with your,” he paused, looking Ann over, “trousers.” Miller then hopped down the first stair, holding onto the railing and using the axe, blade down, as a sort of crutch. Seeing that this seemed to be a manageable mode of transportation, he repeated the maneuver as rapidly as he could down the rest of the stairs. The vibration was not kind to his wounded leg, but speed was of the essence.

At the bottom of the stairs, he found the wolf that he had wounded, still trying to drag Mr. Tirhsred away to whatever den these creatures were using. The man was still screaming like a wee girl, which Miller found shameful, but his task was not to judge. He was here to rescue. Miller swung the weapon up by its handle, catching the wounded wolf under the chin. Its face split, a fountain of black blood spraying Mr. Tirhsred. Ann let out a short scream and turned her head away.

“I do apologize for the delay. I got here as quickly as possible.” Miller lowered a hand to Mr. Tirhsred, who was still in too much of a panic to take it.

“Mike? Where’s Mike?” Ann shouted, coming to her senses.

Where was Mike? That was certainly a good question. Miller limped into the hallway to see him pinned against a wall, locked in a contest of strength with a werewolf. His arms were at the wolf’s throat, trying to keep its deadly fangs away from his face. This was not a contest that Mike could win and Miller knew he had precious little time to act. He threw the axe overhand and prayed that his aim was still true after all these years.

It struck the wolf in the center of the back. The thing let out a howl and released Mike, who dropped to the floor.

“Ann! Gun!” Miller commanded. Ann, who was still in the hallway seeing to Mr. Tirhsred, stumbled a bit at this request. She tossed the gun in the air but it did not quite reach Miller. He flinched slightly, but the gun did not fire when it hit the ground. She would need to work on her throw. Miller snatched the weapon off the ground and raised it in the direction of the beast. The wolf, bested, was long gone, leaving behind a bloody axe and a winded Mike.

*****

Ted was long gone, wounded by the look of it. Mike considered following his neighbor but he was unsure of whether he could be trusted to put him out of his misery. Besides, to separate from the group at this point would be suicide. He had learned something from years of watching horror movies as a kid. He glanced up at Miller as the wounded man approached. "Thanks. It almost had me there,"

Miller waved a dismissive hand at him. "Think nothing of it, lad."

Mike picked up his gun and quickly walked over to Bill. "Bill, you ok?" Bill had not stopped screaming. "Bill, it's ok. It's dead now."

"Is Mr. Tirhsred hurt?" Miller asked.

"Aaagh!" was Bill's response.

Ann was beside Bill, trying to calm him down. "Sshh, it's ok Bill, you're going to be ok." She squeezed his hand to reassure him.

"I think he's just in shock." Mike gave him a gentle slap. "Pull it together."

After a few moments, Bill managed to move from screaming to manic panting. Mike got up and started looking around for the dropped light. He found it just as it made a loud crunch under his foot.

"Shit!"

"What?" It was Ann's voice.

"Flashlight's broken." He picked up the crushed flashlight and tried to switch it on and off for a few seconds.

"Help me get Bill into the light," Ann said.

"Yeah, okay." Miller took the lead while Ann and Mike dragged the still-panting Bill behind them. The next door was close by and easy to make out by the weak sunlight that peeked out from under it. Sliding Bill near to the wall, Mike took position next to Miller, ready to back him up. As before, Miller slammed the door open and charged in. A new voice screamed from inside.

"Please don't hurt me!" It was a woman's voice. Mike charged into the room to see Miller covering a middle-aged, red-haired woman with his shotgun.

"It's okay, we're the good guys," Mike said. He walked out of the room and helped Ann drag in Bill.

"Cynthia?" Ann asked.

"Little Ann?" the woman responded. The two women hugged, tears visible on both of their faces.

"I was so worried that you didn't make it," Ann said, still hugging the older woman.

"Ann." It was Miller, his voice low and menacing. "Please step away from her!"

"Miller? What's wrong?" Ann said, not letting her friend go.

"She's cursed."

"What?" Cynthia asked. "Wait, aren't you the guy from 269? Didn't you die?"

"Aye, technically. Many, many times over, but I always get better," Miller said, and pulled at Ann's arm, still training the shotgun on Cynthia.

"No, no, no, she's fine. Look at her, she's right here, no crazy black eyes, no claws!" Ann was sobbing.

"Miller, are you sure? How can you tell?" Mike cut in. Was Miller insane? She looked fine to him.

"Why isn't she all furry like the rest of 'em?"

"Ann, think about it. The one person we find happens to be a friend of yours? She is a trap."

"Listen boy, I think you're still confused from that truck hitting you," Cynthia said. "Let's talk about this."

"No, I don't think so." Miller pumped the shotgun and drove it into Cynthia's face. He pulled hard on Ann, finally tearing them apart.

"NO!" Ann shouted. Cynthia fell back with a whimper. She brought her hands up to protect her face.

"Miller, stop!" Mike raised his shotgun.

"Stay calm!" Miller raised his voice. It held that tone of command again. "I'm not going to shoot her. Not yet anyway." Mike relaxed a bit, but still kept his gun trained on Miller.

"Miller, please. If it was a trap, why isn't she changing now?"

"I am not sure, but I can see the curse on her as plain as day."

Ann looked hard at her friend, tears streaming down her face. "No, it's just Cynthia. I'm telling you, she's human."

"And I say she is not."

"Ann, don't listen to him. You know he's crazy, we joked about that," Cynthia pleaded.

Bill moaned from the ground in the corner. Mike lowered his gun, and approached Miller's side. "Miller, I know you think you can tell, but she looks perfectly normal to us."

"Trust me, Mr. Samson, something is very wrong here." To reinforce his intentions he poked Cynthia with the barrel of the shotgun, producing another whimper.

"Miller, stand down, man! I can't let you go threatening innocent people," Mike shouted, stepping closer to Miller.

"Listen to Mike. She's my friend!" Ann pleaded.

"You do not understand," Miller shouted. "Just because she looks human now does not mean that she is." He lowered the gun and gave Mike a shove. "Stay back!"

Mike was knocked a few steps back. Miller had lost it and was going to shoot the woman. He needed to stop him.

"That's it, you lunatic!" Mike rushed forward and slapped the shotgun up out of Miller's hand, then drove his shoe into the man's cast. Miller howled out in pain and stumbled back. The shotgun rattled to the floor. Mike threw his arms around Miller, attempting to pin him down.

"You idiot!" Miller yelled, "You have no idea what you are doing." They rolled on the floor for a moment, both struggling to gain the advantage. Mike was surprised by how hard it was to pin the wounded man. Every grip he tried, Miller countered instantly.

"Samson! Do not make me hurt you!"

Somewhere in the back of Mike's mind, he registered an odd slurping noise. Ann was screaming. Instantly, both men stopped their fighting and looked up.

"Cynthia, NO!" Ann cried.

Cynthia stood over Bill with her mouth open unnaturally wide. A long, black tentacle-like tongue hung out of it. It had wrapped itself around Bill's neck and appeared to be sucking. For a moment everyone stared. Noticing the attention, Cynthia looked back up at them, seemingly ashamed. The tongue-like thing disappeared back into her mouth.

"I'm sorry, were you going to eat that?" she said.

Mike and Miller exchanged a brief glance. Mike rolled one way, Miller rolled the other, both reaching for their guns. They brought them up almost simultaneously and fired. The distance was not quite as close as Mike would have liked with a shotgun, but both shots hit Cynthia, sending her sprawling. Her chest exploded in a black mist. She let out a scream, rolled on the floor, and then was back on her feet, taking off in a run down the hallway.

"No, not Cynthia, please..." Ann choked as she wept. She slid down to her knees, and laid her head against the wall, tears rolling down her cheeks.

Mike bent over Bill. The security guard was definitely dead, his flesh a dull white. His face looked sunken and his neck was crushed and covered with small cuts. Mike cursed and turned to Miller.

"I take it that's what a real vampire looks like," he said. Miller nodded. "Did you know?"

Miller looked grim. "Not exactly, no. I could see the curse but couldn't tell the kind. She might have been a wolf that just had not changed. Or she could have been something new. Demons can be pretty creative."

"And it's still out there..."

"Aye. Vampires are much harder to kill and far more intelligent than any wolf."

Mike looked back down at Bill's body. "I'm so sorry, man. This was my fault." He looked back up at Miller. "I should have trusted you. It's just so..."

"Say no more." Miller gave him a hand, helping him to his feet. "You thought you were doing the right thing. I know this is hard to accept.

To your credit, it was a brave thing you did." Miller winced a bit. "Just please don't kick me like that again."

Mike couldn't help but thinking that maybe Miller actually was what he said he was. "What should we do with him?" Mike asked, pointing back down at Bill.

"We cannot do anything for him, although I am a bit worried about her." He pointed to Ann, who was still leaning against the wall, crying.

Mike walked over to her. "Ann?" He almost asked if she was okay. She obviously wasn't. "Is there anything I can do?" Ann just shook her head.

"How are you for ammunition?" Miller asked. Mike rooted through his pockets, finding four more shells. He tossed two to Miller and loaded the others into his own gun. Only four more shots. Things were looking grim.

"Miss Ann, we have to go." Miller's voice was low and respectful. He put a hand on Ann's shoulder. She shrugged it off and wouldn't look at him. "I am sorry about your friend. I know how terrible it is to lose someone you care about like that."

"Really?" Mike asked.

"Oh yes, I've lost a wife and two sons to the Cursed. Well, more in the past thousand years, if I think about it."

Mike shook his head. Just when he started to think the guy was sane, he went and said something like that. "Ann, he's right, we need to get out of here." She ignored him. "We need to find Keith."

She snapped her head up at that and looked at him hard. "I don't know..." she sniffed. "I don't know if I want to find him. He could be…could be," she pointed down the hall, "one of those!"

"I know, but we need to try, don't we?" Mike followed his instinct and put his arms around her in a hug. She didn't resist, and instead dug her face into his shoulder and wept. Mike scooped her up with one arm.

"I'll carry her for now."

"Aye," Miller nodded. "I think it best if we keep moving."

They headed back out into the dark hallway. Without Bill's flashlight, it was slow going. Dim light came in through the doors on the right, but at times the hall was close to pitch-black.

After walking for a few minutes, Ann began to struggle in his arms. "It's okay Mike, I can walk now. Thanks." She gave him a light kiss on the cheek as he put her down. She swayed a bit at first, but gradually became steady. "You're right. I still need to find Keith, one way or the other."

"Here," Miller said, "Take this." He gave Ann the small pistol that Bill had been carrying. "If you have to use it, aim for the head. It won't do more than slow them down, but maybe it will buy you some time."

"Thank you," Ann said, stuffing the gun into one of her front pockets.

Together, the three of them made their way through the darkened halls. They checked two more rooms. Both were empty. Mike enjoyed the brief sunlight both times. In the hallways the darkness was suffocating, as if the air was too thick. The rooms were better, although still a bit dim. He could see the sun clearly through a window in a cafeteria. It was fairly low in the sky, meaning that it was still before noon. So much had happened in such a short period of time. It took his breath away.

In the empty cafeteria, while he was briefly enjoying the sunlight, he heard the first gunshots.

"What's that?" Ann asked.

"Small arms fire," Mike responded, trying to sound professional. "Maybe it's the police, finally."

"Aye, I bet they are going to need help as well. Let's see if we can find them," Miller put in.

They all headed back into the dark, Miller in his normal spot in the lead. This time, they did not stop to check the doors they passed. Instead, they rushed toward the sounds of fighting, almost at a run.

"I think we're getting closer to the main entrance," breathed Ann, "although it's hard to tell in this light."

Miller slid to a stop and put up a hand. "Hold!" Mike and Ann obeyed, nearly tripping over each other.

"What's wrong?" Ann asked. Miller stared ahead into the darkness. Mike followed his look.

"It's darker here," Miller observed. "Something feels off."

"It looks about the same to me," Mike offered.

"No," Miller spoke slowly. "Definitely..." He trailed off, raising the axe in one hand like a shield in front of them. Mike focused hard on the area in front of them.

"I don't see..." No, he could see. Little black pools reflecting the faint light from behind them. There were too many to count. They were eyes!

"Mike, Ann, run!" Miller shouted.

They were wolves, so many wolves. They seemed to pack the hallway, waiting in the dark, not making a sound.

"Oh my God," he mouthed.

"Go!" Miller yelled, "Now!"

Mike grabbed Ann's hand and they turned and ran. He made sure to keep his body between her and the pack. Ann, for her part, was zigzagging, taking a right, then a left, with only the pale light from underneath the doors showing her the way. Mike split his focus between her feet and their pursuers. After a few moments, he shouted, "Wait!" and they skidded to a halt.

"Where the hell is Miller?" Mike looked around.

"Maybe he couldn't keep up, with his leg?"

"No, I don't think he was planning on coming."

Suddenly, something smashed into Mike, knocking him to the floor. The shotgun dropped out of his hand with the force of the blow. A large gray wolf had him pinned, its claws digging into his sides.

"Mike!" Ann screamed.

Mike managed to get his elbow under the beast's chin, keeping the sharp fangs away from this throat, but he had no defense against the claws. He felt blades dig into his flesh for the second time that day. Then Ann was there, gun in hand.

"I can't get a clear shot!"

"Just shoot!" he shouted back, "Shoot!"

"Oh, the hell with this!" Ann took a running step forward and kicked the wolf in the head, as if punting a football. Its head jerked hard with the blow, stunning it. One second was all Mike needed to kick the beast off of him. With a neat roll, he snagged the shotgun from the floor and aimed it. The wolf was already pouncing again, but too slowly. Mike pulled the trigger just as the wolf was at the height of its jump, hitting it dead in the face. Its head reversed direction, spinning its body around, but its momentum was too great, and its legs still caught Mike in the chest. They fell in a heap.

"Mike! Are you okay?" Ann was there, trying to move the wolf's body off of him.

"Ugh...yeah, I think so, just a few more cuts. God, those things hurt." With her help he slid free from under the body. His shirt was torn to pieces, but then it hadn't been in great shape to begin with. His new cuts were not as bad as he had first thought. They stung but certainly didn't look fatal. He noticed that the wolf's body was still wearing most of a uniform. Apparently it had been another security guard.

"Help me check this one out. He may have more ammo on him." Ann helped search the body while Mike tore off a large swath of its shirt, which he tied around his chest as a makeshift bandage. Ann grinned at him.

"That's a nice look for you. It's almost a toga."

"Yeah, well, if this keeps up much longer I'm going to be running around here in my birthday suit."

"Hah, I bet it's not a bad view."

Mike flushed at that.

"Ah, there you are!" It was Cynthia. The woman was covered in dark blood, her clothes torn to ribbons.

"Ann, get behind me!" Mike pushed Ann behind him, and raised his gun. Cynthia stepped forward and in one fluid motion, struck Mike in the temple with her right hand. It was the hardest Mike had ever been hit in his life. Black spots blossomed in his vision as he was lifted off his feet and tossed into the air. He hit a wall hard and crumpled into a ball.

"Mike, no!" Ann screamed.

"Come on Little Ann, there's someone who really wants to see you." Mike heard Ann's gun go off as he struggled to fight the blackness. "Enough!" There was a sound like a slap, and then the gun hit the floor. The last thing Mike could make out as he fell unconscious was Cynthia dragging Ann away by her hair.

# 14 - Extreme Violence

Miller stood alone against the darkness. It was better this way. Maybe Ann and Mike would escape, but he knew he had no chance if he tried to run. His damn crippled leg was just too much. If only he had had only a few more days to heal. Well, nothing to be done about it now.

It had been a long time since he had seen a pack this big. There had been a bad night in London, about 200 years ago, and he could never forget his short stay in India, but this was impressive. He counted at least 20, which was already without the several he had dealt with earlier in the day, but between the darkness and the relatively tight quarters it was hard to get an accurate count.

"Good afternoon gentlefolk," he said, "Joseph Miller, at your service." He heard a growl from somewhere in the crowd as they began to approach. It was as if his manners, always perfect, had awoken them from their slumber. It had been odd that they did not attack before. Why had they waited? There was something more to this and he strongly hoped that he would have the chance to figure it out.

"I think you have had quite enough to eat this morning," Miller quipped, as he surrendered a few more steps to their slow advance. He supposed that Ann and Mike had had enough time to get clear. There was no more reason to wait.

An ancient battle cry forced its way out of his mouth as he jumped forward. He was no longer sure what language it was in, but it was loud.

The pack surged forward like a furry tidal wave. For Miller, who had been in millions of battles in the past, time seemed to slow. Now, at last, he faced a real challenge. He fired his shotgun at the wolf in the lead, knocking several wolves back in the process. As he hobbled forward, he tossed the shotgun up, caught it with the same hand at the pump, pumped in the next round, tossed it forward, and caught it by the handle, firing again. Several more wolves were launched back. He knew he had one more shot. With the other arm, he swung the axe wide, not yet trying to hit anything, just making space. Wolves ducked and jumped, dodging the axe, but they did not close in.

Miller repeated his one-handed pumping trick, this time firing directly in front of him, blowing another three wolves back. He dropped the spent shotgun and gripped the axe with two hands. It was time for the messy part. Stepping forward, he again swung the axe, this time for the nearest wolf. Its head came off cleanly and was launched though the air. Miller ducked into a roll as several wolves dove for him. The now-dead wolf's body landed on top of him. He braced it for a moment, holding it like a shield. The wolves pounced on the body, thinking it was Miller, and he let them carry it away. Another roll brought him clear of the wolves and, using the axe as a lever, he sprung back to a standing position. He then plowed the weapon into the head of a wolf in front of him. It slashed through the monster's face and got stuck in the base of its spine. Moving forward, he pushed the axe down, bringing the dead body down flat with the ground. Then, he vaulted forward, freeing the axe from its victim and sending himself into another forward roll. He was clear of the pack and spun to meet them for another pass.

In trying to reach him, the wolves had collapsed into a confused, howling mass.

"Come on people, I'm over here!" After this he would have to come up with a name for his fine new axe. Wolfsbane? Perhaps that was a bit too much.

He took one step backward and lobbed another head off with a single swing. A wolf leapt at him, foaming at the mouth. Miller did not have time to pull back the blade of the axe, but still managed to deflect the attack with the blunt side of the weapon. Two more launched themselves at him. He hopped to the right and swung the axe again in a wide arc. It caught one of his attackers in the side of the face, splitting it open. Miller stepped back, his axe spinning again. He caught another wolf in the leg, and it fell, stumbling into another two. Miller quickly finished off another and kicked its body into the remaining wolves in front of him.

He continued his bloody work as more wolves freed themselves, attempting to charge at him by leaping over the bodies of their fallen pack-mates. Miller was faster than them all, killing at least one and dodging the rest. Black blood pooled across the width of the floor. It was quickly becoming so thick that Miller's bare feet were sticking to the floor. What he wouldn't do for a good pair of boots!

In that instant, the lights came back on. Both Miller and the wolves froze for a long moment. It was an odd red light, but it was welcome. At least he could see his handiwork. The wolves were in a tangled mass, some dead, some alive. Several pulled themselves free, but by now it seemed that some semblance of fear was beginning to dawn on them. Their numbers had been too great for the narrow hallway and they simply could not get around their own dead quickly enough to reach him without feeling the touch of his axe. After a few thousand years, Miller had gotten pretty quick with an axe.

Behind him, he could hear the sounds of fighting and men screaming. He was getting close to their original goal, which meant that very shortly he would either be surrounded or have new allies.

The pack was thinning at this point. He had lost count of the dead. The row of bodies marked his path backwards. Suddenly, his cast hit something heavy and he fell, dropping the axe. Instantly, there was a wolf on him. Claws penetrated his chest and fangs dug deep into his shoulder as the wolf took vengeance for its pack-mates.

"None of that!" Miller shouted. The palms of both of his hands shot forward and clapped over the wolf's ears. It howled and rolled off. He caught another wolf by the throat in midair as it tried to attack and snapped its neck with a quick jerk. He let it continue its trajectory, hitting a third wolf. Then, he snatched the axe off the ground and brought it down on the head of the wolf that was still cupping its ringing ears.

He quickly glanced at what he had tripped over. A man in blue lay sprawled out in front of him. Miller did not have time to check if the man was still alive. He was too busy trying to work the axe loose of the wolf's head. His chest was a bloody mess, the bite mark on his shoulder being particularly deep. Looking behind him, he could see four more wolves approaching him tentatively. He chuckled. They could be taught, and he had taught them fear!

The axe was stuck. A trickle of panic crawled up from some dark hidden part of his mind. He grunted with his growing effort but the axe would not budge! He forced down the rising panic. There were only four left. No need for an axe.

The wolves smelled the hint of fear and approached more confidently, foam dripping from their fanged mouths.

"Come on then." Miller abandoned the axe and waved his opponents forward. The first raised a clawed hand, preparing to slash. It had been a tall red haired woman, and was now covered in red fur. None of her clothes had survived the transformation, so Miller had no clue as to who she may have been. He focused only on her advance, readying himself for her blow.

All at once there was a sound like rapid thunder and the wolf's chest exploded. Miller tossed himself flat on the floor as the other three wolves were cut down by what might have been gunfire. Two men dressed in blue appeared from behind him, firing the meanest looking guns he had ever seen. He stared in amazement. What awesome weapons. Of course, man had always been good at finding new ways to kill.

"A survivor!" One of the men shouted. "Sir, are you alright?"

"Aye!" Miller said, grinning at them. "You have fantastic timing!" Without further ado, the axe fell free of the wolf's head with a clunk.

"Wait, did you do all this?" one of them asked. He was a huge man who whistled while surveying Miller's handiwork. Suddenly, the red-haired female leapt up, charging the man, the wounds on its chest already closing. Miller snatched his trusty axe and tossed it from a sitting position. It hit the wolf, splitting its head open. The big man shuddered, staring as the wolf crashed to the ground.

"I suppose that it was my handiwork, yes." Miller grinned.

# 15 - Lovers

Mike was sure that he hadn't been out for more than a few minutes, although in the dark of the hallway, it was impossible to tell. He struggled to his feet, every inch of his body aching with cuts and bruises. It had not been his best day. That was for sure, although, thinking back, it had not been his worst either. Just very close to it.

"It's all right Ann, I'm coming for you," he said aloud, more to convince himself than anything else. He broke into a shambling run, head throbbing with each step. Where to find them?

Passing a stairwell, he paused, hearing voices.

"He asked me to bring her to him." It was Cynthia. Mike stepped into the stairwell as quietly as he could manage. Sticking his head over the railing, he could barely make out the exchange.

"I don't care what he said. This is the one that hurt me!" another voice hissed. Mike couldn't be sure but he thought it might be the demon doctor that had started this whole mess. Unexpectedly, the hospital's emergency lighting snapped on, filling the stairs with red light. Mike quickly ducked his head back. It took him a few moments' concentration to make out their speech again. He caught the demon's voice first.

"The police must have repaired the emergency generator. We'll have to go shortly."

"Mary's pack will keep them at bay for a long time. I must deliver this one."

Mike chanced another look. He could make out Ann's unconscious form at the bottom of the stairs. Cynthia was just barely in view through the doorway, and she had a hand full of Ann's long hair still clutched in her hand. Ann was not moving.

"No, give her to me," the demon hissed. Mike could not see her from his vantage point.

"I cannot disobey..." Cynthia's voice was cut off as a huge black talon snapped around her head and pulled her out of view. Mike took off down the stairs but could not reach Ann before they disappeared. He ran down the stairs to a door and peeked around its frame.

The demon was there, holding Ann upside down by one leg and shaking her.

"Ahhh!" Ann woke up. "What the hell?"

"Wakey, wakey little one," the demon said.

"Vanessa?"

"Oh yes. We finally meet again."

“God, Vanessa, you've really let yourself go. You've gained a ton of weight and your skin is terrible.” Ann sounded oddly calm. He was sure that it was a bad idea to make the demon-woman angrier.

“Hah! Witty little thing. Let’s see how funny it is when I pop your scrawny head off.” Mike stiffened. It was now or never. He hoped a few point blank range hits with the shotgun would scare off the demon, but had no way of knowing for sure. Then, just as he was about to jump out and start blasting, he heard something else.

“Vanessa! You will not touch her.” It was a man's voice. Mike stole another quick look and saw the male doctor from earlier that day striding towards the demon.

Keith Malone was a tall, handsome man. He seemed an odd pairing for Ann, who was small and not particularly good-looking. He fearlessly strode up to Vanessa.

“What do you think you’re doing? You will not break our laws.” With that, he backhanded the demon. Vanessa was thrown up into the air by the force of the blow, dropping Ann. She smashed through ceiling tiles and left a huge gash in one wall as she toppled over. Keith was not done. He walked over to the fallen Vanessa and grabbed her by the throat.

“You will do as you are told, little sister.” At his touch, the demon seemed to shrink and fold in on itself. Human flesh appeared around its chest and crawled out over its body. The horns shrunk and vanished, replaced by brown hair. In mere seconds, the demon had fully returned to the very naked form of Dr. Vanessa Black, and was struggling to escape Keith's iron grip.

“Brother, she blinded me. She hurt me,” Vanessa hissed.

“Bah! You have already healed.” He tossed her aside. He approached Ann, who was struggling to sit up.

“Keith?” she asked meekly.

“It's me Ann, it’s really me.” He bent over to help her stand. “It’s so good to see you again.”

“Keith, what’s going on here?” Mike was wondering this too. “You look different.”

“Oh Ann, I have so much to show you. We've worked so hard to make this surprise for you today. Although,” he gave Vanessa another dirty look, “it would have been a much simpler matter had our sister not thrown her little temper tantrum.”

Keith walked over to the crumpled form of Cynthia, who had been thrown to the ground. She lay on the floor with her neck broken, eyes staring at her shoulder blades. Keith picked her up and, placing his hands on either side of her head, gave her a tug. Her head snapped back into place with a loud pop. She smiled at him. “Thank you, father,” she said.

"Look Ann, it's your friend Cynthia! She was hesitant to join our family at first but now I think she's quite happy here." Cynthia bobbed her head up and down in response, like an overexcited puppy.

"Oh yes, father, very happy."

Mike was pretty sure that this ruled the possibility of any of them being human. He could read the deep sadness in Ann's eyes. Her shoulders drooped and her arms hung limp by her sides. Had she given up? He had to get her out of there.

"Oh Keith, what have they done to you?" Her voice came out as a croak.

"Done to me?" Keith asked. "Done to me? Oh no Ann, it's what *I* did to *them*." He threw an arm around Cynthia's shoulder and motioned Vanessa to him, putting his other arm around her. Vanessa gave him a sisterly peck on the cheek. "It's our family, Ann. I made this family for us. It's like we always wanted."

Ann's mouth hung open, stunned.

"What are you talking about?" There was anger in Ann's voice. "I wanted babies with you, the key word being 'wanted,' as in past tense, as in before you dumped me six months ago!"

What was Ann doing?

Keith paused for moment and then smiled. "Of course you're upset. But I have so much more to show you. Come see! You're going to love this!" He shrugged off his posse, waved Ann forward, and marched off down the hall. Both Cynthia and Vanessa stared at her.

"Ok, ok, I'm going." Ann shrugged and followed Keith.

Mike waited until they were out of sight and followed from a safe distance. He watched the four of them walk down the hall, stopping into what Mike could only guess was a large storeroom. He counted to five and then raced to the door and poked his head in. He stifled a gasp as he realized that there were at least thirty people huddled together inside. He recognized Dr. Tyler, who had treated his cuts just a few hours ago. She was bound and gagged, and appeared unconscious. He also recognized the nurse, Mary, who stood guard over some people that Mike guessed were hostages. She looked particularly unhappy with her task.

"See?" Keith began. He pointed to the gathering of people. "All for you. You will be my queen..." He spun back to face Ann.

"Err, what am I supposed to do with them? Start a football team?"

Keith's face fell. "No, silly, they're here for you to eat."

"Eat?"

"Of course," Vanessa put in. "Unless you think one is worthy of joining the family."

Keith put his hand out to Ann. "Join us. Be with me…" he paused dramatically, "forever, my love."

Ann froze, staring at the offered hand. She had no sarcastic remarks left. Mike could see that she was actually considering the offer. Was she really that lonely, that desperate to be with him again? Mike thought back to his wife. Wouldn't he be tempted if he could somehow undo that one terrible night six months ago and be with her again? Tempted? Hell, he would sell his soul. Perhaps that was a poor choice of words.

Ann reached out slowly, and then her eyes fell back to the people restrained in the corner of the room.

"I…I can't," she said. "I loved Keith with all my heart, but you're not him." There was a moment of awkward silence as the three monsters stared at Ann, stunned by her rejection.

"Ahhhhh!" Mary shouted, breaking the silence. She collapsed to her knees. "He is killing them. Killing them! My children!"

Vanessa rushed to her side. "Sister, what is it?"

"That man. That man that came with her!" Mary pointed at Ann. "He's killing my pack. My whole pack! By himself!" Mary sobbed. "My children!"

"Umm," Ann spoke up, her voice regaining its mocking tone. "That would probably have to be Joseph Miller. Apparently he does this for a living."

Mike smiled to himself. He was relieved to hear that Miller was alive and kicking a fair amount of ass. Now, if only he could get Ann out of this, alive and still human.

"What? Who is this Joseph Miller?" Vanessa cried, with such fury that Ann took a step back.

"OK, ok, no need to shout. He says he's a professional monster hunter. Been doing this for long time." Ann shrugged. "He seemed to know his stuff. He managed to take out several of your furry people even with his leg in traction."

"I sent those children to bring you to me! They wouldn't have hurt you!" Keith seemed angry now. "You even shot your good friend Cynthia when I sent her. What's wrong with you?"

There was a sob from Mary's corner. "Gone! He has killed them! So many dead."

"Do you think this Miller is..." Vanessa began. Mike could see the fear creeping into her eyes. "Do you think he might be the Great Hunter?"

"No! Impossible!" Keith said, "There is no way he could find us so quickly." He paused, thinking. "But the name, the name sounds familiar…"

"The great what?" Ann asked. The demons ignored her.

"I say we find this Miller and avenge the pack's death!" Vanessa snarled, "He cannot possibly stand against the three of us."

"Oh, he can and he will," Ann put in. She was trying to sound tough, but failing. Mike thought she should just stick to sarcasm.

"Ann's right," Keith said.

"I am?"

"The ancient one has plagued our race since the dawn of the humans. If we strike him down, he will just come back the next day with a new face. No. It's better to retreat for now and build our strength."

"You coward!" Vanessa yelled, "I say we fight!"

"My sister is right for once," Mary said from her spot on the ground, tears streaming down her cheeks. "He needs to pay for what he did to my children!" she howled. Black scales appeared as her skin stretched tight in demonic growth. Mike turned his eyes away. He had no desire watch yet another gruesome transformation. This was the one that had tried to kiss him earlier. He shivered at the memory. He heard the Mary-demon howl, and had to look.

Mary was a very different looking monster from Vanessa. For one, he could tell that she was female. Although she was at least a foot taller, she kept all the curves that made her so stunning as a human. Now, though, they were just creepy. She still had hair, but it was thick and strangely corded. Her eyes were the black pools. On her back were bat-like wings, ridiculously small in proportion to her demon size.

"I will rip his heart out and feast upon it!"

Mike wondered why they needed to talk like that.

Mary stormed out of the room, heading directly toward him. Mike sprinted down the hall and slid around the next corner like he was stealing first base. He didn't pick himself up off the floor but lay still, trying to control his breathing. After a moment, he crawled over and glanced around the corner, just in time to see both Mary and Vanessa heading into the stairwell and up the stairs. It looked like Miller was about to have his hands full.

He waited until the count of five and dashed back up to the storeroom where he had last seen Ann, only to run headfirst into Keith. Smacking into the man was like hitting a brick wall. Mike bounced back and landed on his ass, once again dropping his shotgun. He was going need to tie that thing on.

He looked up to see both Keith and Ann staring down at him.

"Who is this one?" Keith asked. His voice was low and dangerous. "Is he one of yours?" He had a tight grip on Ann's arm. It looked uncomfortable.

"Mike! What are you doing? Run, you idiot!" Ann shouted at him. Mike pushed himself back with his hands, sliding across the floor. One hand reached the gun, which he snatched and raised to fire. Keith was too fast for him. He smacked the weapon out of Mike's hand and sent it clattering down the hall, out of reach.

"Well now, maybe this is why you are so hesitant to join me. This…human." Keith bent over him and seemed to be sniffing him, as if he was a flower or something.

"Him? It's not because you're a crazy demon feeding off innocent people? It's because of this guy? Keith, I met him like three hours ago. He's just overly heroic. He's a cop. It's his job." Ann tried to break his grip but Keith held her still. "Keith, you're hurting me."

"I'm hurting you? Hurting you? I have done so much for you! I built a family for you. I was creating an empire for you. But you reject me for this, this human!" Ann stared back at him. Mike started crawling very slowly down the hall toward his gun.

"No really, I just met the guy. Honestly, he's not even my type. And how can you be jealous after you dumped me? After I spent all week looking for you? Why didn't you come to me? Hell, you could have just emailed me that you were busy and we could do lunch in a week or so, once you were done enslaving mankind."

"Shut up!" Keith snapped. "I was busy making this," Keith motioned to the hall around him, "something worthy of my queen!"

Mike was nearly at the gun. Ann just had to keep him talking a little longer.

"Next time, maybe just send some flowers!"

"You mock me!"

"Yes! Absolutely I mock you!" Ann was crying again, but her eyes were filled with determination. "I've seen so many horrible things today, so many people dead. Cynthia a monster, that bitch Vanessa, who I always knew you had the hots for, some kind of demon. And sweet little Mary, transformed into some kind of demonic playboy bunny." She sucked in a breath and readied another barrage. "I came here looking for you. At first it was because I thought you had ditched me *again*, but then because I thought you were in danger. And," she sobbed, "I loved you. The old you. Not this *thing* you've become. What happened to you, Keith? Is there any small part of the human you were still in there?" There was a long silence as Keith and Ann stared at each other.

Mike dove for the shotgun.

"I am only what you made me to be, Ann," Keith said finally.

Mike was up and charging back at them. Go, go, go!

"What?" Ann said, her voice small. They both turned to face Mike at the same time.

Mike fired his first shot, catching Keith in the belly. Black blood gushed out and he was knocked backward, releasing Ann. Two shots left. Mike pumped the gun and fired a second shot, advancing at a run. This time he hit Keith in the face, throwing him to the floor. One more shot. Keith's body slid to a stop and Mike followed it. Standing above Keith, he put the gun into the remains of his face and pulled the trigger. It made a loud click. He had miscounted!

"Stop!" Cynthia was coming around the corner. He tossed the gun to the side, turned, and ran. Behind him, Keith let out a low gurgle, which was followed by some popping noises. Mike didn't have to look back to know Keith was still alive. Ann stood there, stunned, looking at him. Mike grabbed her by the arm.

"Run!" he shouted. It seemed to bring her to her senses. She sprinted with him.

"Mike, we have to rescue those people!"

"First we have to get away from your ex and the lady who eats people with her tongue!" There was a deafening roar from behind them. Keith was really pissed now.

"Shit, is he still alive?" There was a loud crash and the sound of glass breaking.

"I'm going to say yes. And we've made him very, very angry," Mike yelled back. He threw himself up the stairs two at a time, promising himself that he wouldn't look back.

# 16 - Mad Scientist, Anyone?

Dr. Larry Conners was mad. As he stood at the side of the road, waiting for what was probably one of the most important meetings of his scientific career, he wrestled with his anger. More accurately it was what *should* have been one of the most important meetings of his career. Now it was going to be a disaster. To be fair, he was mostly mad at himself for putting his faith in Ann. She had been such a promising young scientist, bordering on brilliant even a year ago. But then her personal life had fallen apart and, with it, her work.

Dr. Renée Dupré had been Larry's mentor many years ago and had helped him a great deal with his funding issues. She had been old then, and must be ancient by now, but was still a leader in her field. When she had sent her sample to Larry for his opinion, he'd seen the opportunity to impress his old teacher. Ann had been given the package and begun the basic work, just as she had been doing for the past two years. She had seemed to be almost finished, just in time for the meeting with Dr. Dupré, when she vanished. She had gone out for lunch the day before and simply not returned. Worse yet, this morning when Larry had gone to check on the sample, which was some type of rare lily, it was gone. All that remained where it had been stored in the refrigerator was some dark black sludge. Now he and Wen Li had to meet Dr. Dupré without Ann there to present her research, and without the original sample. He hoped that she had been meticulous in recording her results in her lab notebook. When Ann did show up, there was going to be quite the reckoning.

Larry glanced up at the blue sky and then down at his watch. The day was cold for spring, but the sun was out in full force, so that if you stood in its light it was almost comfortable. He and Wen had been waiting out in front of the building containing their lab for about ten minutes. Something was going on at the hospital on the other side of the block. A few police cars were parked out front, their lights flashing. Larry's mind registered this, but his attention was focused on the direction from which his guest would soon be appearing.

A white van turned the corner, slowed, and then stopped in front of Larry. Out came the tallest Asian man he had ever seen. The man seemed to unfold himself as he exited the van. He wore a neat black suit and dark glasses that screamed "federal agent." His look was solemn as he shut the door behind him. That changed in an instant, when the man snapped off his glasses and gave both men a warm smile. It instantly made him seem friendly, despite his huge height.

"Hello there. You must be Dr. Larry Conners. I'll have Dr. Dupré out in a second," he said, and began to slide open the large van door.

"I am. And you are?"

"Agent Takahashi is my caregiver these days," said the old woman, as the door slid open. Inside, the considerable frame of Renée Dupré, almost completely unchanged with time, could be seen. She was sitting in a large, complicated-looking wheelchair. The woman was oddly broad, with outsized hands and a wide face. Her eyes were brown, almost to the point of blackness. Most of her figure was hidden by the many, many blankets heaped on top of her. "It seems that your federal government likes to make sure I'm quite well taken care of."

A ramp extended automatically from the van and down the wheelchair came, giving the old woman a bump as the wheels hit the sidewalk.

"Conners, time has not been kind to you." She looked Larry up and down, her eyes landing almost with an audible thump on his cane. Larry tried to smile.

"No, I guess that it hasn't. It apparently hasn't affected you at all though. You look exactly the same as you did twenty years ago."

"And I see that you are still a suck-up." The words were cruel but there was a lightening to her features which led Larry to believe that she was trying to be funny.

"Now, I believe we have business to attend to inside," she continued. She gave Agent Takahashi a hard look. "John, I'm with an old friend. Why don't you stay with the van?" She did not wait for his response. "Conners, let's see this lab."

Larry looked from the agent to the old woman. There was an odd tension between the two.

"Of course. This way." Larry waved her to the front door.

Out of the corner of his eye, Larry saw Wen step up to the tall Japanese man and ask the agent, in a quiet undertone, "Why is she under federal protection?" John Takahashi looked him in the face, and then flashed that easy grin.

"Well, I'll tell you this much. It's not because of her sparkling personality."

*****

In the elevator, Larry introduced Wen to Dr. Dupré.

"This is your only lab assistant at the moment?" she asked. She gave Wen the same long, cold stare that she had given Larry only moments before.

"Yes, at the moment. Wen is a PhD student here at CMDNJ, quite bright." Larry nodded with the compliment and Wen responded with a thankful smile.

"At the moment?"

"Well, I did have another young woman working for me but I recently had to let her go." By "recently," Larry meant the next time he saw her. Dr. Dupré grunted something under her breath that Larry didn't make out.

"Excuse me?"

"Nothing, nothing at all. Just clearing my throat."

The elevator doors opened and Larry stepped out.

"Just over this way," he said, leading the wheelchair and Wen out into the hallway. He took the next right and stepped through the door of the lab. "And this is home." He smiled at Dr. Dupré as she entered the room. She ignored the smile, craning her neck around to Wen as he entered.

"Would you mind closing that door behind you, dear? There is a bit of a draft."

"Of course, doctor," Wen responded, shutting the heavy door behind him and making his way past the wheelchair to join Larry.

"Now, if you don't mind if we cut to the chase, I would like to see the lily."

Larry and Wen exchanged worried glances. Larry gave a nod, and Wen went to retrieve the empty container.

"Well, you see, there seems to be some..." As Larry turned to face the old woman, he noticed her pulling a large gun out from under one of her blankets. The sight was so out of place that he simply stopped talking, staring as the woman aimed and fired at Wen. The gun made almost no noise but the bullet must have been huge. Wen's head exploded like a water balloon, splattering his brains in every direction. His body remained standing for a second in mid-step, blood pumping out of the stump of his neck. Then it collapsed to the floor. Larry screamed.

"Hmm…human," said Dr. Dupré, "That's very disappointing. I was sure that he was the one." Then, the gun was pointing at Larry.

"My God," Larry stammered at her, "Why…" He couldn't finish the question, and trailed off, staring dumbly at the woman.

"Oh, it was nothing personal," she said. Then, pulling off the rest of the blankets, she stood and stretched. "Well, I guess it is rather personal, in a way. Nothing against your student. You see, I didn't think he was human. Good God, how I hate that chair. I can't wait until I can ditch this old lady routine."

Larry caught his breath back again for a second. "But how…why?" His brain was working its way out of shock and into pure panic.

"I'll let you in on a little secret, Larry, since I know you won't be telling anyone." She walked over to him and gave him a hard shove, knocking him to the floor.

"How old do I look to you? Go ahead. Guess."

"What? Why should I care how old you are?"

She poked him with the gun, the tip of its long silencer still hot. "Just guess," she said, her voice low and menacing.

"75?"

"Not even close." Dr. Dupré seemed to be working herself up for a show. "I'm 138 years old. Not so bad-looking for the world's oldest living woman, right?" Larry did not respond. It was, of course, impossible. She was surely insane.

"Does it sound crazy? No, it's true. And oh, it gets better." She grinned, and then seemed to reconsider. "I'll spare you the details. Let us just say I've been working on my current project for a very, very long time and now it seems to have gone slightly askew. A shame really, but it turns out that even we of the Cursed still can get a bit senile with age."

The Cursed?

"What would you say, my dear student, if I told you all the stories of monsters were true? What if I told you that werewolves existed, and vampires, and demons? Why, pretty much every story ever told about things that go bump in the night has been based on some truth." She stared hard at Larry, waiting for an answer.

At last he picked up his cue. "I would say you're pretty crazy." His response was weak but it was hard to talk at all with that big gun pointing at him.

Dr. Dupré coughed out a laugh. "Ha! Of course you say that. It's been a hundred years since they walked this earth. Much longer than that since they did so in any large number. Too long for anyone to remember."

"So they went extinct?" Larry asked. He had to keep her talking, there had to be a way out of this.

"You might say that. But you're missing the best part. What if I told you that I had found a way to bring them back?" She seemed to bounce with excitement.

"Why…why would you want to do such a thing?"

"Oh, that's a long story. Let's just say I did it for love. Anyway, amazing creatures really. If my theory is right, they can rebuild themselves completely from just one single cell, much like a starfish. Of course, it's less of a cell and more like a virus."

"You mean werewolves?"

"No, silly boy, we're talking about demons."

Oh, of course, how silly that was.

"Still, the plan wasn't to have them just run around New Jersey unchecked. They tend to, well, eat people, and that's never really a good thing. Now, since my 'help' seems to have wandered off, I'm here cleaning up my own mess."

Larry shook his head. "I'm not following you. Why come here? Why kill Wen? What did he have to do with your monsters?"

Dr. Dupré let out a long sigh. "I don't remember you being this slow when you were my student. The sample, Conners, the white lily. It's actually a very clever delivery system."

"For what?"

"For the demon seed!" She said it as if talking to a child about the number ten coming after nine.

"The what?"

"The demon seed. You see, demons require a host. Preferably a human one."

"So the plan was to infect me and my lab assistants with some sort of disease?"

"Not a disease, a life form. One that hasn't walked the planet in a hundred years. One that will change science as we know it."

"A life form that eats humans?"

"Well, among other things, yes. I didn't say it was the perfect plan. You have to believe it was nothing personal. You *are* going to die, but it's for a very good cause. Sadly though, before you go, I am going to need the name of that other lab assistant. She has to be the one."

It was Ann she was after, but Larry couldn't begin to imagine why. Dr. Dupré moved closer still until something caught her eye. Guessing at what she saw, Larry tried once more to distract her.

"So you kill us all in the name of science?"

She ignored him. "Ah ha!" The old woman picked up a notebook from the counter. "The lab journal of one Ann Melakh." She held it triumphantly up to Larry, and then turned solemn. "No, this isn't about science. It's about my husband."

The cough of the silencer was the last sound Larry heard.

# 17 - Out About

Miller leaned hard against the wall. Most of his minor scratches had already stopped bleeding, but his leg ached, and the bite on his shoulder was going to take a while to heal. One of the two soldiers was talking into a little black box. Something about finding a survivor, which meant him, he guessed. It was something he was good at, surviving. What he wanted was to rest and let his body finish healing. Another two days maybe, that's all it would take. But there were more people in here, alive. There were still Mike and Ann to find. He hoped that they had run away and were safe somewhere, but he knew that Ann would be stubborn about finding Keith. Miller was sure that that would not end well. Perhaps Samson could talk some sense into her.

He had taken the time to finish off the last of the wolves. His axe, now stained completely black with blood, had quickly made sure that they would not be attacking anyone else. The soldiers did not seem willing to listen to him, although they did not stop him from finishing his gruesome task.

Just then, he heard a noise from down the hall, something like scratching, a steady rhythm. Like claws on stone. Miller knew the sound well. The parents have come out to join them.

"Sirs, if I could have your attention for just a moment. We are about to have guests. I suggest you ready those fine weapons."

"What?" the black soldier asked. "More of these furry things?"

"Oh I don't think so. Those don't tend to make any noise. No, these are much bigger and meaner."

The man gulped and checked his gun. His companion looked a little less impressed but stared down the hallway nevertheless. A moment passed, then another. The sound was slowly becoming louder.

"I do hear something," the second soldier said. Then, from around a corner stepped a female demon. It was certainly not the biggest he had seen. Oddly enough, she still had a mostly human shape.

"What the hell is that?"

"I think it's a woman with...wings?"

"Lads, you are going to want to shoot that. I suggest aiming for her head. They do not die easily unless you can get that head all the way off." Both men glared back at Miller.

"Just a suggestion. I do this often, you see."

"Listen freak, you and I are going to have a long talk once we get you out of here."

"Less talk, more bang bang." Miller gestured to the demon. He readied his axe but eyed the guns with envy.

"Freeze!" said a soldier.

"I highly doubt that that is going to work," Miller sighed. The demon stopped advancing. "Oh, well, would you look at that." Its chest seemed to grow as it sucked in air, and then it opened its mouth and screamed. All three men dropped their weapons and clamped their hands over their ears.

A Banshee! Oh, how he hated these creatures. They made his ears ring for weeks. Still, he had an easy solution that he was dying to try out. He just needed to get to one of those fancy quick-fire guns. Of course, this was easier said than done. He walked forward slowly, approaching the first man. He knew his inner ear was not to be trusted and it took all of his focus to continue moving in a straight line and not stumble. With each step, the noise grew louder. His teeth rattled. His ears bled. Two more steps. His vision began to blur and grow red. Were his eyes bleeding? One more step. He lowered his hands from his ears and reached for the gun, noting how slick they were from his blood. He fumbled briefly but managed to get a good grip on it. The gun fired silently as he pulled the trigger. The kick was amazing, making it impossible to aim. Miller tried again, bracing the gun on his shoulder and firing. Again, the kickback was too much for him to control, but this time at least one round hit the demon in the chest.

Air hissed out of it, and the scream stopped.

"Thank the Lord." Miller stood up and took a proper second to compose himself. The last shot had bruised his shoulder, so this time he placed the gun against his right breast, and got a good strong grip. He held the trigger down. The demon was readying for another yell when the first bullet hit it in its right leg. Miller moved the stream of bullets up, hitting the creature's belly, chest, and, at last, head.

Black blood exploded out of the demon as each bullet hit, making the creature appear to dance a jig. Finally, the gun clicked empty and both the demon and Miller collapsed to the ground.

Miller's world was pain. His ears rang out with a single note that droned on and on. His jaw hurt and his vision was blurry. He took a few seconds to wipe the blood from his face and then inspected a nearby soldier. Amazingly, he was still alive and breathing steadily, but blood was streaking out of every opening on his face. He would live but probably never hear again.

Miller crawled to his axe. He wanted to finish the demon here and now, and then rest for a few moments before trying to find Ann and Mike. Using the axe to steady himself, he again got to his feet, cursing the crippled leg that made him so slow.

His hearing had not recovered, so he could not possibly have heard the approach of the huge demon that had once been Dr. Vanessa Black. He heard only ringing as she wrapped a giant talon around him, but he sure as hell felt it. The demon hit like a tidal wave, sweeping him away.

He still had the axe, but it was pinned to his side and he was far too weak to break free. The demon brought him up, inches away from her face. She was shouting something, and in fact seemed rather distressed. He shrugged.

"I'm sorry, but I cannot understand a word you say. Your sister there has broken me." He nodded to the still form of the banshee. The response was full of rage but still completely unheard. The demon lifted Miller over her head and prepared to smash him against the floor. Instead, something struck the demon in the chest, forcing her to step back. He could not hear the gunfire, but felt the force of it. More of those rifles. Brilliant things.

Miller was dropped like a child's broken plaything. Pain lanced through him as he landed face-first on the floor. He felt his collarbone crack and his vision flashed with blue spots. For a brief second, darkness took him.

Then he was back, watching the boots of several soldiers stream past him. He wanted to thank every one of them for saving him a trip back into the darkness. Perhaps he could buy them all a drink at the local tavern when this was done. Did they still make mead? At the moment, he would settle for ale. Even water would do.

He lay still for a long time, trying to gather the strength to get back to work. It did not come. Pain rolled though him in waves, each one just a mite weaker than the one before it. He needed time to heal. Just a few minutes.

The building shook him back to wakefulness. He could hear something. The single note humming in his ears was already beginning to fade. He heard more gunfire. Men screaming. Debris was everywhere. He looked up to find the soldiers and demons both gone. In the distance, however, he could see Mike and Ann running in his direction. Thank the Lord, they had made it. Ann ran past him but Mike stopped and waved her back. He was saying something but Miller could not make it out. He shook his head no. Samson glanced back down the hall, then back at Miller. Ann was suddenly above him looking concerned. She was a good lass. Dirty mouth, but brave. He liked that. Far too skinny though.

Mike and Ann each grabbed one of Miller's arms and began to drag him forward as his world faded away.

*****

Ann and Mike had seen the men battling the demon. It appeared to be an entire SWAT team. Vanessa had been about to toss something at them but had been struck by machine gun fire. The guns did not seem terribly effective against the giant demon woman but she did drop whatever she had been carrying and step back.

Ann had told Mike that the main exit of the hospital was straight ahead, right beyond the huge angry demon lady, who had demonstrated a strong dislike for Mike's traveling companion. They had been about to turn and try another exit when the gunfire caught their attention.

"Sounds like back-up has finally arrived," Mike muttered from his hiding place around the corner.

"About time," Ann agreed.

The bodies of the wolves were everywhere. Most were missing their heads, while some were still attached, but split like ripe pumpkins.

"Damn, Miller did all this with an axe?" Mike whispered, clearly impressed.

"The man loves his work," Ann whispered back.

Some distance in front of them, Vanessa backed away from the machine gun fire, covering her face. She picked up something and began to drag it behind her. It was the demon Mary, looking quite the worse for wear. Her face and chest had been torn apart by gunfire. Miller's work? Maybe the SWAT team's? Impossible to tell. Vanessa squatted down and then jumped straight up, smashing through the ceiling and disappearing onto the floor above. The police officers were driven back as the ceiling caved in.

"Now!" They ran forward, before the dust had even begun to settle. In front of him, Mike could see the afternoon sunlight streaming in through what was left of the front lobby.

As he ran to the exit, one of the bodies on the ground moved. It was Miller! Mike skidded to a halt next to him. "Ann! Wait!" Miller looked terrible. His face was covered in blood, and his neck seemed to be at an odd angle. He was alive though, his strong blue eyes focusing on Mike as he moved closer.

Miller tried to raise an arm, as if saying hello, but it flopped limply back to his side.

"Miller, are you alright?" Stupid question. Mike noticed the blood coming from his ears. "Can you hear me?" Miller shook his head slowly. "Ann, help me drag him out of here."

The ground shook again. Mike had a feeling their time was running short. He wasn't sure why, but it was clear in his mind that he had to get Ann away from here.

"God, is he still alive?" Ann asked.

"Yep. He's supposed to heal fast right? Isn't that what he was bragging about when I first met him?"

"Maybe." Ann glanced back nervously the way they had come. She grabbed an arm and began to pull Miller's body towards the exit. Mike followed suit, stopping for a second to recover Miller's bloody axe from the floor in front of them.

They dragged Miller forward as fast as they could manage. Wreckage and bodies were everywhere. There had been a hell of a fight. After the carnage, the sunlight might have been the most beautiful thing Mike had ever seen. They approached the front doors.

At the doors were several members of the SWAT team, who raised their weapons the moment they saw them.

"Freeze!" one man shouted, the edge of panic in his voice clear to Mike's ears.

"Do as they say, Ann," Mike whispered, "I imagine these guys are a bit jumpy."

"And we aren't?" Ann shot back, raising her hands. Mike laid Miller down on the floor and followed. Two men approached, assault rifles raised.

"Officer Mike Samson," Mike said, "If you let me reach into my pocket I can show you my badge." At the sound of Mike's voice, the men seemed to relax a bit.

"You look human."

"Thanks," Ann quipped, "we try."

"We are not…" How should he put it? "Infected," Mike tried. "We're survivors. There may be a few more back there. We could only carry our friend here." Mike pointed to Miller's still body. One of the men, a tag on his chest reading "Johnson," gave Miller a quick once-over.

"This man needs a hospital…" he said, catching himself and then lamely adding, "Another hospital…medical attention."

"Yes, but I believe this man and this young lady may have information as to what's going on in this building," Mike responded. He glanced back at Ann, trying to look reassuring. "Of course, I don't think the lady is at any fault. We just need to get them someplace safe away from here, where maybe we can work out some answers."

Johnson looked at Mike and the other two in his party. "Ok, we can bring them over to the precinct. Do you think this is a containment issue? Biohazard, I mean?" Johnson asked.

"I don't think so." If he was wrong he would be really screwed by now. "I'm not sure…There's another group of survivors downstairs. If you can get a team of men together, well-armed, I can lead you to them."

"Mike, no!" Ann cried. "You can't go back there. Come with us. You can't go back down there with those…things."

Mike again turned to face her. He could tell she was breaking. Whatever last bit of strength had been holding her together was dwindling.

"I can't, Ann. You were right earlier. I can't just leave. It's my duty to help those people down there, to work out the truth, to see what's going on here. I might be the only one that can now." Mike glanced over at Miller. His eyes were still open but the sharp focus from before was gone.

"No, I was wrong," Ann sobbed, "Sometimes," she fell to her knees, "Sometimes the truth is so much worse. Come with us. You've done enough. Please," she pleaded. It was tempting.

Mike bent down to look at her eye-to-eye. It was funny, he had only known Ann for a few hours but they already had a tight bond. They had been through hell together.

"I can't do that Ann. Look," Mike reached into his back pocket and dug a business card out of his wallet. "This is my contact info. When we get through this, I'm going to come looking for you. We'll work out what's really going on. Me and you. I promise, OK?" Ann sniffled and tried to put on the sarcastic smile she used when she wanted to sound tough. She couldn't quite pull it off, but managed a weak "OK" and took the card. She looked paler and was shaking quite a bit.

They were separated then. Mike and the man named Johnson went to find his superior. Ann, with the help of two other SWAT members, brought Miller out to a squad car. Mike didn't pay attention to the car or where it went. He was focused on getting up the nerve to go back into the hospital and rescue those people. It was no small task.

Captain Habermathy was the man in charge. Mike knew the face, but had never spoken to him. The Captain nodded to him as Mike approached.

"You Samson?" he asked.

"Yes sir."

"You called this in?"

"I did, although I'm still not sure what to call it."

"Any idea what the hell is going on here?"

Mike ran it over possible answers in his mind. You see, sir, there are these demons that are reborn every couple hundred years that take over people's bodies, and, oh yeah, eat people. Mike didn't think it was the way to go.

"Not sure sir. People inside seem to be infected with some sort of disease. Makes them extremely violent." That was a start. Was it lying if the truth was this crazy? "There are people down in the basement that are not infected, but guarded by," Mike paused, "some extremely dangerous people."

Habermathy gave Mike a strong look. It was clear the Captain wasn't completely sure what to make of Mike's story.

"I can believe the dangerous part. I've lost contact with almost every officer that's stepped through the front door. What can you tell me about the inside?"

"It's a madhouse sir. Bodies everywhere. We searched the first and second floors ourselves and didn't find any other survivors, but the group in the basement is large and some may be hiding higher up."

"Are these other survivors hostages? What do these 'extremely dangerous people' want with them?"

Mike didn't hesitate. "Food, sir. They plan to eat them."

The captain just stopped, stunned. Mike didn't blame him. But while he had the guy on the ropes, he might as well finish him off.

"Captain, there is one other thing. There are things inside that I can only describe as monsters. I don't know if that's how this infection works or what. I know they used to be people, doctors and nurses, but they aren't anymore. I know it's hard to believe…"

The captain seemed to recover. "Less hard to believe than you might think. You're not the first person to talk to me about monsters today."

Mike let out a little sigh of relief. He had expected to be called crazy. Johnson reappeared by Mike's side, passing him a bulletproof vest.

"Here, this might help," he said.

"Thanks."

"OK, you and Johnson here will push a second wave into the building. Get to those survivors and then get out. I've already called the National Guard in on this and the FBI. At some point very soon, things are going to get out of our control. Until then we need to save as…"

He was cut off by sudden screams from the front door. Three officers dashed out in a full run. The last one out the door only made it a few feet before bursting into white flames. The noise that came from the burning man was drained of humanity. It only lasted seconds before the man stopped running, crumbling into a pile of charred bone.

Everyone seemed to freeze in place, horrified.

"Good God!" someone said. It may even have been Mike. He wasn't sure. Then, the front doors to the hospital exploded, sending glass and metal flying in all directions. Something large, black, and snake-like was suddenly in front of them. It had a huge head like that of an alligator and the body of a snake. Two thick arms jutted out at its sides. It coiled and leapt into the air, unfolding massive red wings. Mike was sure that it was another of the Fallen, and based on the two large bleeding gaps in its trunk, it was Keith. Mike's shotgun had left its mark after all.

For a moment, it hovered above them all like a dragonfly on steroids, and then spit a trail of clear fluid from its mouth, which splashed out in an arc through the officers.

Mike was one of the first to recover. "Don't let it touch you!" He grabbed Johnson's arm as the spray covered a car in front of them. Several drops hit the captain's back as he jumped aside. There was a long pause as nothing happened.

"What just happened?" Johnson asked.

Suddenly, flames burst from everything that the fluid had touched. A car, less than ten feet away from Mike, exploded into a ball of fire, tossing the three men into the air.

For several moments there was mass confusion. People were screaming and running. Some were on fire and others had been thrown to the ground by the explosion. Someone had the good sense to shoot at the demon. Mike, for his part, was winded. His ears rang from the explosion and he could feel new burns on his arms. Johnson was trying to help him up. The nearby screams made any sort of communication between the two men impossible. Johnson had him and was pulling him away from something. Getting to his feet, Mike managed to glance over and see the captain, completely engulfed in flames. Thrashing about blindly, his flesh was dissolving.

"Jesus," Mike stammered. He had thought Vanessa's transformation was the most terrifying sight a man could see! Turned out there was always room for improvement.

Above, the demon darted forward with impressive speed, ignoring the chaos below. Apparently, it had someplace to be. Mike had one good guess where that was. It still wanted Ann. But why?

Pandemonium swarmed as Mike watched the form of the monster disappear from sight. Someone was attempting to extinguish the flaming car behind him. Several officers were firing guns at where the demon had been. Johnson was trying to say something.

"What?" Mike asked.

"That thing will light up the city. We have to stop it."

Mike didn't answer for a long moment. The truth of what he was going to have to do dawned on him slowly.

"No. You need to go rescue the hostages. They're down in the basement. First stairwell, make a right, big storage area. You can't miss it." Mike began to walk forward. He stopped at a nearby police car that was still in one piece. Someone had left a shotgun on the hood.

"What are you going to do?" Johnson asked.

"I know where that thing is going and I think I know the one man who might be able to stop it. Besides, there are more of those things in the hospital." Mike eyed a motorcycle a few yards away. It was far enough from the fray that he could get it out of here quickly. He dashed over to it and found the key still in the ignition. The bike came alive with a growl. He gave Johnson one last look over his shoulder. "Good luck, Johnson."

"You too," Johnson said. "You're going to need it."

*****

Ann wept. Here, in the relative safety of the squad car, the events of the last twenty-four hours finally caught up with her. She grieved for all the good people who had died in the hospital, and for Keith and Cynthia. Even if they still were alive as the empty puppets of some ancient evil, it was a far worse fate than death.

She had insisted on sitting in the passenger seat, putting on a strong act for the officer driving her to the station. He seemed relieved to get away from the action. Miller was sprawled across the back seat, muttering to himself. The "immortal" was in bad shape, but the constant jumble of words pouring out of his mouth told Ann he was still breathing. Once Mike was away and the car safely on the road, she had collapsed into a whimpering puddle. She had earned it.

Ann thought the name of the police officer driving the car was Carl. He was just a kid, younger than herself. He tried to put a comforting hand on her shoulder, which she did not reject or acknowledge. Then, his sudden swearing brought her out of her trance.

"What the hell is that?"

Ann's head snapped up. Through the back window, she could make out a demon winging its way toward them. She hadn't thought it possible but this one was even uglier than the last. It had the body of a snake, and looked almost like the dragons in Chinese parades. It slithered as it flew on crimson wings. It was catching up with them fast.

"Lizzie always told me he was a snake."

"What?" Officer Carl stammered, panic making his voice squeak.

"I think it's my ex. You'd better floor it." Carl was already on it, the squad car leaping forward, sirens coming to life to warn the traffic ahead of them.

"Oh my God!" the policeman shouted, but continued to stay focused on getting them out of there as quickly as possible.

"Miller!" Ann pounded on the wall of Plexiglas that separated the front and back of the car. "We need you!" Miller seemed to look at her then, the blue eyes focusing for a second.

"Who is Andres Soliz?" Miller stammered, a look of confusion on his face.

Desperation boiled up in Ann. "Focus, you jackass." She pounded on the glass. The force of her blow caused a small crack to appear. "What?" she asked, eyeing her handiwork. How had she done that? The car jerked hard to the right, snapping her attention back to the situation, and tossing her into the door. It jumped down a side street, tires screeching.

The demon took the corner as well but misjudged the space a bit, smashing its wings into a hot dog cart on the side of the road. The beast spun up into the air, then arced back down, bouncing on the ground, until it skidded to a stop.

“Yes!” Ann shouted, “Apparently he can’t corner to save his life! Nice driving!”

“Thanks.” Carl did not look at her, but continued to put as much distance between him and the demon as possible. “How did it find us so fast?”

Ann shrugged. “No idea.” She continued scanning the sky. Then she noticed Miller staring at her. His voice was weak when it came.

“Ann? Where are we?”

“You finally back with us Miller?”

“Aye. I woke up bouncing off this clear wall between us. What is this?” He tapped on the wall.

“We’re in a police car, heading to safety.” She hoped that was true. “Someone was following us.” Her eyes lifted to the sky to give Miller the clue as to ‘who’ she meant.

“They could be after me,” Miller said. “Are we inside some sort of carriage?”

“It’s back!” Carl yelled.

Sure enough, the flying snake-demon was diving out of the clouds again. Ann noticed that it had two spindly arms. Its speed was incredible. “Turn!” she shouted.

Carl weaved the car back and forth instead, which didn’t help. The demon smashed into the roof of the car.

*****

Mike had no problem following the beast. He weaved through traffic quickly. This was his city and he knew every last street.

The demon suddenly dove down to street level. Mike could guess why. It must have spotted the police car carrying Ann. Cutting hard, he took a right turn the wrong way down a one-way street. He nearly ran head first into a minivan, just barely missing it. He ended up on the sidewalk, forcing an old man to dive out of his way.

At the next corner he cut left, just in time to see the demon take a right. Mike gunned the throttle and charged after it. He heard a loud crash and a howl as the monster hit something big. As he rounded the next corner, leaning the bike far too low in order to make the turn at speed, he saw the beast shoot back up into the air, vanishing. Ahead, he made out the flashing lights of the police car.

He noticed a hot dog cart that had been launched into the storefront behind it. People were rushing out, pointing to the sky and helping others up. It must have been what the demon had hit. *Demon Stopped by Hot-Dog Vendor*. Now that was a headline.

Maintaining his breakneck pace, he reached the end of the street, taking yet another right. The police car was moving fast, but he had it in sight now. If he could catch up, he would…well, he would do something.

He followed the car through more turns, attempting to make up the distance. The demon seemed to fall out of the sky in front of him, throwing its wings out for a moment before hitting the ground and leaping forward at an awesome speed. The car weaved left and right but the demon sprang onto the roof, smashing the siren and rear window in the process. The suspension of the car bottomed out for a moment, throwing sparks and slowing the car down.

Mike had the bike going full out and finally started to catch up. He slid the shotgun out from the saddle bag. He would need to get very close and be particularly lucky for this to do any good. Luck wasn't really his strong point.

Mike inched closer to the car, trying to avoid both the swinging tail of the demon and the weaving police car itself. The demon had smashed through the driver's side window and was reaching inside. By some miracle, Mike managed to pull to its side. He raised the gun up to the demon's head and said "Hey ugly, remember me?" He pulled the trigger. The left side of the demon's face exploded into black pulp, taking the left eye and a good part of the jaw with it.

Of course, this was not a wise move. Unfortunately, unlike what the action movies Mike had always loved suggested, firing a shotgun one-handed while driving a motorcycle at high speed was not a safe or practical maneuver. The recoil from the gun was enough to jerk him hard to the left, which cut the wheel right, directing the motorcycle into the side of the police car.

This sent Mike forward over the handlebars, over the hood of the police car, and onto the very hard concrete. In the flash of time that the fall took, Mike only had time for one thought. A helmet!

Then, it was over.

*****

A black clawed hand burst through the driver's-side window, showering Carl and Ann with glass. It went right for Carl's chest, cutting huge gashes in his flesh. The young officer screamed but held on to the wheel. He was weaving madly, trying to shake the monster off the car. Ann dove for the demon's arm, trying to pull it off Carl. She noticed that they were slowing down but couldn't worry about that. The demon had too good of a grip on Carl's chest. To his credit, he kept on driving, screaming wildly in pain and fear.

Suddenly, Ann noticed a motorcycle pulling alongside of them, the rider wearing torn jeans and a black vest. Mike?

It was Mike Samson, playing hero. He had a shotgun and was pointing it toward where the demon's head should have been. The gun went off and two things happened. Mike's motorcycle hit the side of the car, launching him forward, and the demon was blown off the top of the car. Ann grabbed the wheel to stop the car from hitting Mike. Carl slammed on the brakes and Ann was thrown forward against the dashboard. The car slid to a stop, maybe fifty yards beyond the still body of Mike Samson and the twitching, screaming demon.

It took a few seconds for the earth to stop spinning. Then she heard a familiar voice.

"Ann!" It was Miller. "Ann, you have to get away. Let me out, I can slow it down." Ann sat up, now in Carl's lap.

"You ok?" she asked the officer. But he was about as far from "okay" as he could be. Empty eyes stared back. Carl was dead. His chest was crushed and blood poured out of his mouth. For a moment, she stared at the latest innocent person who had died helping her.

"Ann. Please, for God's sake, woman. Help me out."

Her response started low but rose as rage overtook her. "No. No one else dies today. Except for that thing!" She pointed at the demon, still howling in pain and holding its face with its two clawed hands. It was a very human-looking pose. "I'm sorry about this, officer." Ann unsnapped Carl's seat belt, popped the door open and pushed the lifeless body out. "Miller, hold on to something!" She snapped the seat belt back on herself and gave the car some gas. She drove about 100 yards forward, braked hard, and made a quick three-point turn. She was now facing the demon again, who seemed to be coming to its senses. It noticed Mike's body on the ground in front of it and slithered over, lifting him up into the air. Ann wasn't sure if Mike was alive or dead, but there was no way that thing was getting him.

"Hands off!" She slammed the gas pedal down and the car was off.

"Ann, don't!" Miller made one last protest.

The demon didn't seem to notice as Ann approached. A large tentacle-like tongue slowly emerged from its jaw, wrapping itself around Mike's neck. Ann alternated between watching the speedometer and lining up her weapon. Ann, Demon Slayer. It had a nice ring to it. The car hit forty-five miles per hour before the demon noticed it. Its tongue went slack and its remaining eye turned on Ann. Its jaw loosened a little in surprise, and then the car hit it dead on.

The demon's snake body collapsed around the car's mass of metal. The head of the beast slammed down on the hood of the car, and a second later seemed to be sucked under it. The back end of the car launched into the air and it flipped over, landing on its roof and skidding forward several feet. Ann braced her hands on the ceiling.

In a moment, all was silent. Hanging upside down in the car, Ann slowly looked around.

"Ouch," Miller's voice came from the back seat, "This has not been an enjoyable day."

Ann laughed. "I hope that hurt, you son of a bitch!" She howled a victory cry.

"Yes," a new voice said, "Yes, quite a bit, actually." It was low and hard to make out but Ann knew it was Keith's. The demon ripped the door off the hinges and grabbed her with both hands.

Ann managed to scream just once before she was pulled out of the car.

# 18 - Fallen Down

Panic, anger, and fear no longer filled Ann's heart. She was way past that. Now she felt an odd acceptance. She was not going to make it through this day alive.

She felt terrible. She was too weak to struggle in Keith's grip, not that it would have been wise to do so. His touch was hot, like he was feverish. Or maybe that was just how demons felt. They flew far above the streets of Newark, the sun high in the early afternoon sky. The view was quite nice, even if the circumstances of the little trip were not. She hoped Mike was okay. And Miller, although, from the sound of it, he was always okay.

Keith released her and for a moment, she again knew fear as she fell several feet to the roof of a building. She struck the surface hard and for a second, the world dimmed. Recovering, she tried to sit up, but her head was pounding too much. She had to lie down to keep from vomiting.

She thought she was hearing drums but realized it was her blood pounding through her ears, so loudly that it hurt. There was a bubbling noise from her right but she could not turn her head to see what it was. After a moment, Keith asked, “Why do you torture me like this?"

"Me, torture you?" Ann said weakly. It hurt to talk. Actually, it just hurt in general.

"Yes! I have done everything to please you. Everything to make my sire proud, to make her join me as my queen."

"I don't know what you’re talking about,” Ann said. She was distracted by a tightness in her belly. It seemed about to explode.

"You! You created me! You brought me into this world and then you rejected me!"

"What? I did no such thing," she groaned. Suddenly, the tightness seemed to be relaxing, her muscles uncoiling.

"You lie!" Keith yelled. The pain was fading, but it felt like she was stretching. She moaned, again trying to sit up. She had more success this time and managed to pull herself up to face Keith. He was human-shaped again but still had the blast marks from Mike's shotgun. His face was a twisted black mess and a good section of his chest had been torn open. One good eye stared back at her.

"Keith. You’re confused. That woman, Vanessa, she did something to you. Made you into this."

"Hah, my little sister did no such thing. Although she has been jealous of you since I sired her." A wet choking sound came out of his ruined face, which Ann assumed was a chuckle. "You honestly don't know, do you? You don't know what you are," he continued, becoming serious. "You are sick, just like little Jamie was."

“Jamie?" Ann thought back, she remembered a young intern by that name. He had started working at the hospital at about the time that Ann and Keith had broken up. Ann hadn’t seen him in a long while, but that was not unexpected. Interns rotated in and out of the hospital. "What about him?"

"He’s ill. Sometimes he still thinks he's human. Other times he’s a mindless beast." Keith sounded downright grave at this point, concern for the young man in his voice. "I think the humans have done something to us or themselves, to help resist our seed." The pieces suddenly fell into place in Ann’s head. The thing in the basement. That was Jamie.

"Your seed?" It felt like Ann's skin was getting too tight. She slid out of her coat, which was drenched with her sweat, and tried to stand.

"Our seed, Ann. You are one of us. The oldest of us."

"What? You’re crazy..." She was on her feet now, her body shaking from the effort. She took a step away, but her mind was spinning. She remembered what Vanessa had first said to her, "The law doesn't allow me to kill you.”

"Join our family," Keith had said. She had been compelled to take his offer. What was going through her mind? There had been all the dreams, the black scales and drums. She could hear the drums now, the blood thrumming though her ears. Good God, it wasn’t possible, was it? Miller had said Bill was as human as Mike was. He had made no mention of her. Did he know?

Ann felt something rip on her arm, and her flesh tore away, revealing white scales. "No, it can't be," Ann muttered under her breath. How was this possible?

"See?" Keith's ruined faced turned up with a smile. "You begin to see the truth."

"No!" Ann stumbled back to the ground as her spine stretched forward. She felt the flesh around her stomach give way. "God no, this can’t be real." Her shoulders spread apart, tearing both flesh and the cloth of her shirt. One hand suddenly doubled in size, the skin snapping away.

"No, I won’t let this be true." Ann struggled to crawl forward.

"You cannot deny what you are," Keith said. "Join your family. Come to where you belong."

Ann was silent for moment as she dragged her shifting body forward. One of her sneakers popped open to free a clawed foot. She saw only one way to end this nightmare. "I will not become a monster,” she said as she pulled herself up to the edge of the roof.

She had been right. She was not going to live through this day. With one long final stare at Keith, she pushed herself over the edge of the building.

Keith screamed and leapt forward, but was far too late. She closed her eyes as she dropped toward the ground, seventeen stories below, the air ripping through her few remaining strands of hair.

*****

Miller finally came to his senses and freed himself from the wreck of twisted metal. It took him several moments to gain the strength to get to his feet, the still-broken leg sending up shocks of pain in protest. He had to move faster. He had to get to Ann, to save her from whatever that demon had planned. Not far ahead, he noticed the still body of Samson on the ground. He quickly hobbled to his side, looking him over. He was still alive. Now for Ann. Where had the demon taken her?

As if on cue, a sudden movement caught Miller's eye. It took several minutes to work out that it was Ann, falling from the top of the building.

"No. No. No." He breathed and turned away, not wanting to see his new friend's end. He had seen so much death, but watching it happen to the people that you liked never got easier. He heard the body hit the ground with a strange metallic clank. Anger boiled up inside of him, anger at the demon, at this modern world, at himself for not doing more. He resolved to make the demon pay. He swept up a large shard of glass with one free hand and headed to the building that Ann had fallen from.

As if answering Miller's call for revenge, the demon dropped from the roof. It was now almost human, except for the massive wings jutting out of its back. Perhaps it planned to make some use of Ann's corpse. "We'll put a stop to that." He swore under his breath. Glass raised, Miller attempted to charge, limping as fast as he could. The demon did not turn to face him, instead standing motionless, black blood dripping onto the ground from its various wounds.

As he at last came into range, a battle cry escaped Miller's lips, and he brought his makeshift weapon to bear. He put all of his remaining strength into a blow aimed at the back of the demon's neck. The attack might have worked, had he been in better shape. The demon suddenly came to life, catching the "blade" with one hand and grabbing Miller's throat with the other. The move was either impossibly fast or Miller was moving much slower than he had thought.

"Gah!" was all that he could get out before his throat was forced shut. The demon screamed and tossed Miller into the air. He hit the concrete hard, falling again into darkness.

*****

The sudden pain of regaining consciousness was a welcome one. Miller was still among the living. All was not yet lost. He hung in the air, carried by the demon. It had him at arm's length and was inspecting him closely.

"Mr. Miller, I presume." Miller tried to respond but could only choke. For a moment, he coughed up blood. Then, recovering, he whispered an "Aye" through his blood-stained teeth. He looked the demon-man over. It had apparently not been a good day for it either. Several large chunks were missing from its chest and the left side of its face was a black, mangled mess. Black blood still oozed out of several wounds. Miller pondered why it wasn't healing.

It was then that Miller noticed how high up they were. Below him lay the city in all its modern glory. He had never seen such an alien landscape. Massive buildings of glass shot up everywhere, vehicles clogged the streets and the sky. He could see giant metal birds drifting in the distance, which he assumed were man-made. Directly below them was an enormous cathedral, all grey stone with green highlights. It stood out as something familiar in all this madness, reminding him of earlier centuries in England and France that had seemed only short weeks earlier. He turned his focus to the demon.

"Aye, I am Joseph Miller. You have heard of me?" He grinned. The demon man did not return the smile. Perhaps it was hard to smile with only half of its face left.

"Oh yes. We last met in France." It had started to remember then. How soon before it would remember its real name? For a moment, it said nothing, seeming to consider. Finally, it said, "I find it amusing that humans see hell as a place where the evil are punished by demons for their sins. It is ironic I think." He paused for a second, as if expecting a question. Miller just blinked back at him and said nothing. "You might ask why I find this ironic?"

"Oh, I see," Miller picked up his cue, baffled by the exchange. "Why do you find it ironic?" This was bizarre. Shouldn't the creature just kill him and get it over with? Miller was sure this was somehow television's fault.

"You see, my version of hell would be a kind of immortality, a cycle of constant rebirth, where I was born again and created a family, only to have them brutally murdered by the same man, who would, again and again, come for me and kill me. In time, I would be reborn again and the cycle would repeat itself."

Miller shrugged. "That does seem to fit the description, yes. Although is that what ironic means? I have always had some trouble with that word."

"It is ironic, because you are that man. You are my 'demon,' my tormentor, and this planet, this is my hell." He growled the last part.

Miller let out a weak laugh, which hurt horribly. "That is a pretty speech. How long did it take you to come up with that?" The demon man just stared at him. Miller could almost see the anger steaming off of it.

"I suppose this is where you tell me I've lost and send me screaming to my death?"

The demon smiled. Apparently he *could* do so. "Oh no, that's too easy. You see, I know your face now. Killing you won't stop you. At least now I know what you look like. Why should I lose that advantage? I will hurt you, but you'll live."

Miller was shocked. It was the most intelligent thing that a demon had ever suggested.

"But your friend," the demon continued, "What was it…Samson? I'm going to suck every last bit of marrow from his bones. You can count on that."

Miller stiffened. So it was to be his life for Mike's. That was not acceptable. He had failed too many people already. There had to be something he could do. He looked into the demon man's ruined face, staring at the one good eye. Why was it taking so long to heal? With his right hand he dug deep into his pocket.

"Lad, that is the single most intelligent plan your kind has come up with in at least a thousand years. I have only one question."

The demon seemed taken aback by this compliment. "Ask."

"How good is your sense of smell?" With that Miller ripped the pen from his pocket and jammed it into the demon's remaining eye, pushing it into the socket so hard that it completely disappeared into the skull. The eye burst and the now blind demon screamed, tossing Miller away into the open sky.

Miller had hoped to say something wittier. Like maybe "The pen is mightier than the sword." At least he had hoped for a "See you later." Instead, he just screamed as he fell, the moment of his previous death replaying clearly in his mind.

Death did not come. Instead, he smashed into the angled roof of the large cathedral he had seen just moments before. He bounced once and started to slide down the slope, throwing his hands out, trying to grab onto anything that might slow his fall. He failed, but as he slid past the edge of the roof, his right hand managed to find purchase on a loose tile. His broken collarbone screamed at the impact as his body came to a stop. For a moment, he hung in space, looking at the ground below, still a good fifty feet away. To his terror, the tile was slowly coming loose under his weight.

"Wonderful!" Miller went about shouting as many curses in as many languages as he could recall. Some of them had not been spoken in thousands of years. He was rather proud of his ability to swear, but that did not keep the tile from coming free. Once again he was falling. He hit a windowsill, then crashed through a paned glass window into the church below, hitting the ground with a solid thud. He thought of Samson and hoped he had done enough.

# 19 - The End and the Beginning

The world slowly came back to Mike. He awoke to find it was dark, which instantly terrified him. Realizing he was in a hospital bed made it much worse. He panicked and tried to get out of bed, but his head spun too much. Panting, he lay back down and waited for the spinning to stop. On his bed was a sleeping shape that he recognized as his son.

"Sam!" He gave a shout of joy. The boy snapped awake and glanced around the room in surprise.

"Dad?" Then, after a second of focus, "Dad!" Father and son embraced for a long time.

"I thought you went away too, Dad."

"Never," Mike swore.

In time, a doctor came to check in on him, and Sam fell back to sleep in his bed. Mike stayed awake, too busy processing the events of the past day to find rest. He had learned and seen so much. He knew now that there were monsters out there, and not the human kind. He had seen the basis of the vampire and werewolf legends. It was all a bit much to take in. It had to have been an insane dream.

In time, he realized that he was at St. Michael's Hospital. They had found him in the street, unconscious. Besides several deep cuts, heavy blood loss, and a concussion, he was actually in fairly good shape. Obviously, with the situation at College Hospital, they were not taking patients there, much to Mike's relief. It would be a long time before he could set foot in that building again, if ever.

According to the news, a gas leak at the hospital had killed close to 70 people. Twenty-seven people were apparently rescued from the basement and had managed to escape unaffected. No mention was made of the demon flying through downtown Newark. It sounded like the weakest cover story Mike had ever heard. But then, the truth sounded even worse.

Mike had been in the hospital for a good twenty-four hours before they came to visit. Mike was watching "Power Rangers" with Sam when two tall men in dark suits and dark shades entered the room. Seeing them, Mike couldn't help but whistle the theme music from "Men in Black." One was quite large. The other was a much smaller man with a cruel scar on his cheek that started at his chin and made a line directly to his ear. The ear was missing its lobe.

"Mr. Samson," the scarred man said, "I'm Agent Smith from the FBI."

"Smith? Like in the Matrix?" Sam asked. The man stiffened for a moment. He responded in a voice so dry with sarcasm, Mike thought it might snap.

"Yes, just like the guy in the movie. We were wondering if we might have a word with you, alone, for a few minutes," Smith said, glancing at Sam and his grandmother, who were both sitting in the room.

"Of course. Sarah, can you take Sam to the cafeteria and get him something to drink?" She nodded, taking Sam by the hand and leading him out the door. As it closed behind them, Sam said, "But I want to see the secret agents!" And then they were gone. That put a smile on Smith's face, and he took a seat next to Mike's bed. Smith's backup remained standing..

"So, what can I do for you? I'm guessing this has something to do with a gas leak."

Another smile from Smith. "Yeah, you might say that. We understand that you may have seen some pretty strange things."

"Pretty strange doesn't even begin to cover it. The stuff of nightmares is more like it," Mike responded.

"Can you tell us what you saw?"

Mike licked his lips. Could he? Would it even make sense? He had to. The world should know, even if no one would believe him.

So he told them the truth, or most of the truth. He left Miller completely out of the picture, but told them all about troubled Ann, who was looking for her missing ex-boyfriend, and the things they witnessed together. He told them about the monsters' plan in the basement. He told them about their escape from the hospital. Finally, he told them about Ann's abduction.

"Did she make it?" Mike asked.

"Who?"

"Ann…Melakh, I think her last name was."

Smith flipped through a pad before answering. "Looks like we aren't sure. She's on the missing persons list."

There was a long pause, and then Smith spoke again. "I think you'll understand when we ask that you tell this to no one."

"Who would believe me? But I need to know that you guys are doing something. That you understand that I'm not just some crazy guy seeing monsters in the shadows."

"Well, I can't really release any details at this time, but we are investigating the matter. I've had a talk with your chief and arranged two weeks of paid leave for you." Smith stood up to leave. "Spend some time with your son and try to forget all this." With that, he and his silent partner left.

The next day, Mike went home and tried to get on with his life. Several of his fellow officers and friends had been killed by the "gas leak," and so he found himself in his dress uniform three days later for a large funeral. Jessica Jones was one of them, as was her partner. While he had not known her well, her death saddened him. He brought her a single white rose. While there, Sam and Mike also visited Sam's mother. As Mike did every time he visited his dead wife, he made the sign of the cross and asked for her forgiveness. Not that it ever helped.

And so, Mike Samson tried to move on. His nightmares were still the same nightmares, except that sometimes Ann would appear, or Miller, crazy grin and all. He didn't dream of demons or werewolves or vampires. His own monsters remained center-stage in his dreams. Maybe he felt that the things he had seen were too terrible to possibly be true, or maybe his mind just wanted to pretend the whole thing had never happened. For nine days, he managed to pull it off, even with the Zhangs' empty house across the street.

On the tenth day, there was a knock at the door.

"I think it is one of the joyless witnesses," Sam said, peeking from behind a curtain.

"It's Jehovah's witness, Sam." But it wasn't a Jehovah 's Witness. It was Joseph Miller.

He stood at the door of the house, dressed in beat-up old jeans, ruined sneakers, and a black t-shirt. He no longer had a cast on his foot, and in fact, looked as good as new.

Mike hesitated before opening the door. Having Miller outside his house was like having a visitor from another world, a flashback from the day things went mad. What would happen if he let this man back into his life?

Miller had saved his life; he could at least see him. Mike opened the door.

"Mr. Samson!" Miller's face split with that God-awful grin of his.

"Miller?" was all Mike said before the strange Hispanic man had him wrapped up in a hug, pushing himself inside.

"Oh, this is a lovely place you have here. And look! You have your own TV." Sam looked sheepishly at this new stranger in his house. They certainly didn't get much stranger than Miller. "And a boy! What a fine looking lad you are." Miller rustled Sam's hair playfully.

"Err, Sam, this is a friend of Daddy's. His name is Mr. Miller. Miller, this is my son, Sam."

Sam looked Miller up and down. "Are you a bum?" Sam asked. There was such an honest tone to Sam's voice that Mike had to laugh a bit.

"A bum? Is that good?" Miller asked, looking confused.

"It's your clothes, they just look a bit, err, dirty."

"Aye, well I obtained them from a kindly priest. Many things have changed but the good folks of the cloth are always there to lend a hand when in need. Too bad they are such prudes about the ladies. Otherwise I could quite see myself as a holy man. ”

“Right. Look, I’m happy to see that you’re alive, but what are you doing here? How did you find me?”

“Ah. It was easy! As I think you may have guessed, after our little run-in with,” he looked down at Sam, “that rather rude fellow, I found myself a bit under the weather. Luckily, I managed to drop in at a nearby church, where some very nice folks took care of me. Once I had had a few days to pull myself back together, I expressed my need to find my long lost cousin, one Mike Samson. After a bit of doing, they kindly gave me a ride in one of those fine horseless carriages...”

“Cars, Miller, we call them cars.”

“Cars. Right. I will remember that. In any case, they brought me here. As I said, good people. Do you have anything to drink? Preferably ale?”

“Umm, yeah, in the fridge, hold on. You’ll have to deal with root beer. I don’t keep alcohol in the house anymore.” Mike motioned to the couch and moved to the kitchen. Miller took a seat and Sam followed his father into the next room.

“Mr. Miller seems kinda funny. And he smells bad.”

“Yes, yes he does,” Mike agreed. Of course, bathing habits had changed in the last hundred years. “Listen, why don't you play in your room? I think I need to talk adult stuff with Mr. Miller.”

“It’s not about sex, is it?” Sam asked.

“No, and what did I tell you about sneaking out and watching HBO after bedtime?”

After sending his son off, Mike returned to the living room. He tossed Miller a can of root beer. Miller caught it and stared at it.

“Err, need help?” Mike walked over to him and popped the can open.

“Ah, thank you.” Miller took a quick slug, made a surprised face, shrugged, and drained the can.

“Before we start…Ann?” There was no need for a clearer question. The smile drained from Miller’s face and he shook his head slightly. “No.”

There was a long pause as both men stared at the floor. At last, Mike let out a shaky sigh.

“So what can I do for you, Miller?”

“Straight to business. I like that in a man.” Miller grinned. “Well, to just come out with it, I am here to offer you a job.”

“A job?”

“Aye. You have shown me that you can handle yourself,” he paused, looking for the words, “under less than normal circumstances. I have need of a man of your caliber.”

"I'm sorry Miller. I don't see myself doing the professional monster hunter gig. It's just not me. I'm a single dad now. To be honest, I've been thinking about retiring from the force, finding something safe. For Sam's sake."

"You have a fine boy there, Samson. I can see why you would say that. But men like you and me cannot give up the good fight. It is in our blood."

"Maybe in your immortal blood, but I have a child to look after."

"That is fine. I am not looking for another monster hunter."

"You're not?"

"No, I am looking for a guide. This world is a strange place to me. I need a local guide. Someone to show me how things work. Being in my line of business, it is handy to have a guide who is also a fair shot with a rifle."

"Look, I'm sorry. I still can't." Mike paused a second, and for once Miller did not break in. "I've tried to help with things before. Many times. And, well, I don't have the best track record. Look at poor Ann."

There was another moment of silence between the men. For some reason, Mike's eyes drifted across the street at the now-empty house of his neighbor. The massacre that had happened across the street would happen again. Shouldn't he try and stop it if he could?

"Aye, we did lose that one, did we not?" Miller said. Then he slapped his hands to his knees and got up. "But that does not mean that we get to stop trying. Those beasties are still out there, and they like to stay busy and do exactly what you saw the other day. Many more folk like Ann will come to the same end. That is, unless you help me stop them." Mike looked down at his drink. Miller tried again.

"We failed Ann and many other people in that hospital, Samson, you and I both. We must redeem our honor. Otherwise, those people died in vain." That struck a deep chord for Mike. Redemption? Was that even possible for him?

Mike could not believe it, but he found himself seriously considering Miller's request. He had to be crazy. After a bit more thought, he said, "Ok, Miller. You've got yourself a guide, but under two conditions."

"Name them."

"One. Sam always comes first. Always."

"I have been a father many, many times and would expect no less."

"Two. We find a way to help these people whenever possible. Most of the people who died in that hospital, at least the ones we killed, were just innocent people infected with some sort of..."

"Curse?" Miller offered.

"Disease or something. A lot has changed in the last hundred years, buddy, and we don't just go chopping people's heads off. We try to help them. There must be a way."

Miller rubbed his chin. "That is no easy task." He stopped and considered. "But I accept. If we can find a way to help the Cursed, then of course we will. The world has changed so much. Perhaps I should as well. Although I'll warn you, like the events of last week, sometimes it's us or them. And, in my mind, it's always them."

"Fine. Deal."

They shook hands. Miller grinned his mad grin and slapped Mike on the back.

"So it begins!" He laughed.

# 20 - Next Time

Catherine stared at herself in the mirror. She was going out dancing tonight. Dancing. Her. It just seemed so unbelievable, but it was happening. She had felt so good lately, like she was a whole new person. Except the hunger. She had been so hungry lately. Well, it was really nothing to be concerned about.

She had been slightly freaked out when she heard what had gone down at the hospital. So many people dead and she had only missed it by only twenty-four hours. For once, she had been the lucky one.

A little girl's squeal distracted her. Missy, her sister's six-year-old was chasing the poor dog again. "What a cute little girl she is." She thought to herself. "Why I could just eat her all up."

# Epilogue

It was warm in the sun. Well, warmer. The morning light crept into Ann's hiding place every day around eight o'clock. By then, she had already long ago returned from her nightly errands and was ready to pass the daylight hours sleeping as best she could. Since her transformation into, well, whatever she was, she never really felt warm. The sun helped a bit, though. She curled up in a sunbeam like a large white-winged cat and attempted to rest. Her dreams were filled with images of her pink flesh, her blond hair, and her friends, and of regular food. Her waking hours were the time of terror. In the darkness of night, however, the bright white scales were easier to pass off as skin.

Ann had done a piss-poor job of offing herself. While many people dream of sprouting wings and flying away, in her case it had happened. When she had fallen almost ten stories, her wings had emerged, catching the wind and slowing her descent. In the end, she landed in a dumpster. Of course. A fitting end to a depressing life. In reality, Ann Melakh had died that day. She could not stand to look at what she had become. She was covered in white shiny scales. Her fingers were long and narrow and ended in large claws. She had no hair anywhere on her body and was taller now, by more than a foot, with ears that came to a sharp point. She had not brought herself to look at her face in a mirror, but could feel the sharp, pin-like teeth that now lined her jaws. And her eyes! She could not bear to see empty black eyes on her own face. Her tongue, at least, seemed normal. She had not grown the large tentacle-like thing that the demons seemed to use to feed. In fact, one thing she had been surprised and pleased to learn was that she still craved normal food. She would have thought that she would develop a taste for human blood, or babies or puppies or something. Perhaps that came later? Or perhaps she sucked at being a demon as much as she had at being a human. Then there were the wings. Giant bat-like things that jutted out of her shoulder blades. Made of a fleshly membrane, they were incredibly flexible. She found she could wrap them around herself like a cloak or fold them flat against her back.

Her first few days had been a haze of pain as she adapted to the new body. She remembered very little of that time. In her first real recent memory she had already found this place, an abandoned factory off Broad Street. The other homeless folk that lived there gave her plenty of space, which suited her just fine. She had found an old coat which covered her wings, and an old scarf to wrap around as much of her face as possible. At night she almost passed for human.

The night before, she had walked into a 7-11 and stolen some generic brand of canned pork and beans. When the shopkeeper tried to stop her, she simply pulled the scarf down and smiled at him. He gave her no more trouble, and later she had feasted. Now, in the morning sun, she was as content as a snake on a stone. She had wrapped her wings around her and used the coat as a makeshift blanket.

Comfy.

Then something poked her.

"Rise and shine, little sister," said a deep, dry, cracking voice. It sounded familiar. Ann jumped from her resting place and spun to meet the intruder. Her wings spread wide and she bared her teeth.

It was the tall blind homeless man from the street. Now though, the man seemed blurry, as if surrounded by a fine black mist.

"Whoa! Peace little sister. I'm not here for a fight." This did not make Ann relax one bit. She sensed something about the man.

"Who…what are you?" she stammered.

The man smiled. "Funny, I was going to ask you the very same thing. You can call me Abraham, and I think you know what I am." A long black tongue slithered out of his mouth to push up his top hat, and then slipped back.

"Demon," Ann hissed.

"Of a sort, yes, but I am not one of the seven. Oh no, not me, Madam. I am just one of their long forgotten children. Cursed by them, if you will, but no longer bound by them. I am a free agent."

"A free agent? You mean they don't control you anymore?"

"No more voices in this head. Well," the old man shrugged, "fewer." He leaned on his cane and laughed hard at that. "I bet you see their mark on me now though, don't you?" He raised his glasses, revealing empty sockets. Ann was repulsed. "I took out this mark but you can't hide from those with the sight."

"The mist that's all around you, that's what you're talking about?"

"Yes, the sight." Ann looked down at her own hands. She didn't see anything odd. Well, besides the white scales and claws.

"You see, I hunt the seven. It's a little side job I do, you know, till my singing career takes off. It's payback for what they did to me all those years ago."

"Wait, you hunt demons? Like Miller?"

"Miller? Oh, you mean the Ancient One. He still using that name? He isn't here, is he?" Abraham glanced around. How could he see?

"No, I don't think so. I haven't been in much of a hurry to find him either. I don't think we'll get along as well as we have in the past."

"That's wise. The Ancient One has no love for us Cursed. I try and stay out of his way.

But you, I think he is going to want to meet you. I think everyone is going to want to meet you."

"What do you want?" Ann asked.

"Want? Me? Just want to welcome you into the family. You see, I've been watching you for a while now. Truth be told, I was asked to kill you."

"What?" Ann backed away.

"Well, not you exactly, any of the seven that came out of that school. You were the only one I ever found there."

"Me? I'm not one of the seven. My boyfriend, my ex, he did something to me. Infected me with this…" Ann motioned at the wings on her back.

"Oh no, little sister," Abraham cut back in. "You were the one. Lilith, the queen of them all. The mother of them all too, if you like."

"No..." Ann started. "That's crazy."

"Oh it's crazy. I'll give you that. But it's also true. I saw her light flickering inside of you as you walked to and fro. Flickering and dying. The most amazing thing." The old man stepped closer and spread out his arms to the sky above.

"Somehow, you killed it. Somehow you stayed you. And that, little sister, is a first. No one has ever come back from being taken by a demon. A miracle! God be praised!"

Ann didn't know what to say to that at first. "So I'm not a demon?"

"I don't know. That's the fun part." Abraham smiled and tipped his hat to her. "You are something new. There isn't any demon mark on you anymore. You are clean. Pure. Which is why it's taken me so long to find you. To show you…"

Out of the hat Abraham pulled a small, dirty mirror and raised it to Ann's face. Her own blue eyes stared back at her.

"To welcome you to the family, little sister, and to welcome you to the war."

# End of Book 1

# Intermission 1

July 16, 1099

Behind him, the city of God burned. The Ancient One did not look back. The seven Fallen were dead. The last, Lilith, had met her end in the great city of Jerusalem as it fell to the Crusaders, who had slaughtered all in their path. The Ancient One had won and escaped, but he took no joy in it. In time, the Fallen would return, and again he would be compelled to hunt them.

He rode a white stallion and was wrapped in a worn cloak to conceal his dark skin, with a hood covering his bald head. He was a tall man, a massive sword strapped to his horse within easy reach. He wanted nothing more than to be left alone. Although he had been known by many names, Maliik Tahri was the most common at the moment. He had not yet taken the name Joseph Miller, though that time was coming, and very soon.

His melancholy was so great that he was slow to notice the first crusader with the crossbow. The man stepped out of a ruined building, moving to block his path. Dressed in armor from head to toe, with the crest of a Turkish king on his chest, he should have been hard for Maliik to miss. The man pointed his weapon at the Ancient One but said nothing. A second man stepped out from the other side of the path, armed in a similar fashion. Maliik slowed his steed, lifting a hand in a gesture of peace.

"Friends, there is no need for violence. I have no quarrel with you." He spoke in French, his best guess at a language they would understand. The men did not respond. Instead, they were joined by another three of their fellows, whose weapons were soon all leveled at Maliik. The silence continued for a moment. Maliik considered simply bolting - he was in no mood for another fight - but at this range it would be impossible for the men to miss his horse. He had grown rather fond of the stallion.

"So, you are the Ancient One?" asked a voice from behind him. He turned to face the newcomer and let out a small sigh of fatigue. The speaker was a short man, dressed in the clothes of a lord. The mark of the Cursed clung to him like a black mist. Maliik could guess what he really was from the age of the curse and the small size of the man.

"Your masters are dead, vampire. At the moment I have no need to kill you. Have your men allow me to pass and we will keep it that way. Unless of course, you would like me to end your cursed existence." Maliik was surprised by the note of weariness in his own voice.

"Well, well, well. You are confident. I have you outnumbered six to one, but I suppose those numbers do not frighten you much." The vampire laughed.

"Very little does. What do you want?" Maliik replied. Very slowly, he unclasped his cloak, revealing three throwing knives strapped across his chest. They would not cause the vampire much pause, but he hoped to inspire some dread in the men. He weighed his options, measuring angles, trying to get a feel for his opponents.

"Oh," the vampire smiled a wicked smile. "I just want to talk to you. In private."

"This is private enough, I believe. No one is here but us, and whatever dead bodies remain from your Christian friends' pyres. I imagine they have no idea what kind of creature you really are, do they?" For the first time today, Maliik felt his old grin spread across his face. He patted the horse's neck and bid him a quiet goodbye. There was no question where this was going.

"Oh, they know enough." With that, the vampire raised a hand. "Fetch him for me, will you fellows?"

The world seemed to suddenly slow as Maliik heard the crossbows release their bolts. He dove to the right, reaching for the blades at his chest. A bolt dug deep into Maliik's shoulder. Another scraped the horse's neck. Two more passed harmlessly overhead. The first throwing knife left his hand a moment before his back slammed into the ground. The second and third blades had been thrown a moment later. He did not have to look to know his blades had found their mark. The first of the men gasped as a knife entered his eye. Another let out a gurgle as a blade opened his throat. The vampire was faster, managing to move *almost* quick enough to escape.

The third knife carved a deep gouge along the length of his face and lopped off the bottom of his ear. The cursed man let out a howl of pain.

Maliik rolled back to his feet, tearing off his cloak and throwing it toward a man who had not yet fired his crossbow. It was nothing more than a distraction, but every second he could gain was a major advantage. As he tore the broadsword and sheath free of its housing on his horse, he heard the last crossbow release. The bolt just barely skinned his back, but the impact caused him to stagger for a moment. He regained his footing quickly, but not before the three remaining men had dropped their crossbows and drawn their swords. Maliik dove at the closest man, thrusting his sword forward, only noticing then that the blade was still sheathed. The man doubled over with the force of the blow but was merely stunned. The next man was too already too close. Maliik had no time to free the blade. He swung the huge weapon like a staff, clipping the man on the side of the head. It made contact with a loud crack, and the man collapsed. At last having gained some breathing room, Maliik unsheathed the sword and turned to face the last man standing.

For a moment, the two simply stared at one other. Maliik was almost unaware of the bolt embedded into his shoulder, noticing only a growing warmth running down his arm.

The crusader stepped forward, slashing high. Maliik saw it coming and returned the attack with a parry. The crusader stumbled, surprised by the strength of the parry, and Maliik followed through with a slice to his target's midsection. The broadsword cut almost halfway through the man's body before lodging firmly in his spine. Maliik struggled for a moment freeing his weapon, and then let the man drop to the ground and die. The Ancient One walked past the first man that his broadsword had felled, now struggling to stand, and simply kicked him in the head as he passed. Now it was time to deal with their master.

The vampire was just a few feet away, his hand covering the new wound on the side of his face. Inky blood poured out between his fingers.

Maliik gave his horse a glance. Amazingly, its cut looked minor. The creature, accustomed to war, had not run, merely taking a few steps forward. Maliik gave it an affectionate pat as he passed and returned his attention to the cursed man.

"Now then, what were we talking about?" Maliik asked.

The vampire looked up at him. "That was impressive," he said. He was trying to smile, but even vampires didn't enjoying having their faces carved open. "I was told that my approach would not work, but please understand that I had to try."

"Oh, that is perfectly alright. Please also understand, though, that I now have to try to hack you to pieces with this sword. It is only fair." Maliik raised the weapon above his head. The vampire did not move.

Suddenly from behind him, the horse let out a terrible shriek, of a pitch that he had not been aware that horses could make. He spun around to see the animal's eyes rolling up in their sockets. Maliik watched, stunned, as the animal collapsed into the dirt. He looked back at the vampire, who was now smiling with his success. Very slowly, a burning sensation crawled through Maliik's chest.

"Poison on the bolts?" he asked, matter–of-factly. The vampire nodded. As the world darkened around him, he managed to mutter, "You cheat!" before blacking out.

*****

The strong smell of earth was the first thing that came back. Maliik tasted it in his mouth and spat mud. His face was covered in something. He tried to brush it free but could not move his arms, his legs, or anything below his neck.

"Ah, there you are. You had me worried. I thought for a moment that I had overestimated your legendary vitality." It was the vampire's voice, high and mocking. "Help him see."

Rough hands grabbed his face and scrubbed his eyes clean of mud. Maliik blinked several times, realizing with a start that he was buried up to his neck in dirt. Before him was the one attacker that he had not killed. His nose was bandaged and still coated with dried blood. Behind the man was the vampire, sitting on a stool, his face roughly stitched back in place. They appeared to be in a cave lit by torches. The entrance was not far, and he could see the light from the sun just meters away. Was it the light of the same day?

"What is this?" Maliik demanded.

"Oh yes. I must apologize for the poor arrangements. You see, I am far from home and had to make sure you stayed put for our little chat without my usual tools. However, I think this will do nicely." The vampire stood and came closer. "But how rude! I have yet to even introduce myself. I am Louis Fevre. I work for certain…" He paused for a moment, trying to find the right words. "Let's call them 'interested parties.' These parties have hired me to obtain information. Information known by only one man."

"You would have been better off offering me ale. If you know me as well as you claim, you should know that this will not hold me," Maliik dropped his voice to a low growl, "And I am very good at finding people."

"Well, your feelings for people with my particular…lifestyle, are well known to my employers. This way, you will tell me what I want to know. You will tell me all you know about The Fallen."

Maliik spat again, this time hitting Fevre's boot.

"We'll see about that," he grinned.

"Oh, there is one more thing. I must thank an old friend of yours for helping us find you. I believe he goes by the name of Abraham now."

Maliik's smile faded, replaced by a look of shock.

The vampire continued. "Oh, I see you do remember him. Yes, he was quite helpful."

Rage made Maliik's body shake, but he could not move. "You will pay for this," he stammered.

"Maybe, but not today. You look tired." Fevre gestured to the man with the broken nose. "Help him rest." The wounded man's eyes lit up. He took one step forward and kicked Maliik hard in the nose. Blood streamed down his lips, running into his mouth. Pain flared, feeding his anger. A second kick came, this time to the temple. Red and black darted across Maliik's eyes and then he saw only darkness.

Book 2

# Enemies

"Fairy tales since the beginning of recorded time, and perhaps earlier, have been "a means to conquer the terrors of mankind through metaphor."

— Jack Zipes

# 1 - Flashback for Foreshadowing

New Jersey, a little over 6 months ago

Lizzie smashed her fist down on the dashboard of her car. The little silver hybrid was parked on a suburban street in New Jersey.

"I can't believe you're making me do this!" she yelled.

Ann rolled her eyes at her friend. "Overdramatic much? It's just a party."

"I have a medical condition," Lizzie yelled. Her plea sounded weak even to her own ears.

"Oh stop. You took your meds, right? You're fine!"

Ann sounded too much like Lizzie's mother.

"Besides, the doctor recommends you get out more. It's called 'socialization.' You can't always be home in front of that computer. It's not healthy. Besides, maybe you'll meet someone!"

"I have a boyfriend!" Lizzie shouted.

Ann raised an eyebrow at that claim.

"Have you ever actually seen him in person?"

"Well no, but that's beside the point." Lizzie lowered her head in shame. "There are only going to be doctors at this thing. I know the crowd you run with."

"What's wrong with a doctor?" Ann asked as the two women stepped out of the car. She was dressed in a tight-fitting dress, covered by her usual oversized coat. Lizzie had on her traditional leather coat, jeans, and army boots combo.

"When was the last time you saw Keith?" Lizzie countered.

"Well, two weeks ago…but things have been crazy at the hospital. "

"See! Even I get laid more than you!"

Ann made a disgusted face. "Really?"

"Well no, that would involve leaving the house," Lizzie lowered her voice. "But still, you hardly get to see each other."

"He *is* busy saving lives, you know." Ann smiled. "But I'm seeing him tonight and we're going to par-tay!" She did a short, embarrassing dance that made Lizzie grin in spite of herself.

"Fine. You and your boy-toy par-tay the night away and I'll sit alone in the corner until I have a nervous breakdown!" she said.

"Ah come on, we'll have fun. I won't ditch you. Scout's honor. I know this isn't your thing."

"I happen to know you were never a scout," Lizzie answered, and then let out a long sigh. She continued in a much more serious tone. "I don't know if I can do this."

Ann walked around the car to her friend and put an arm around her. "Honey, you'll do fine. If you start twitching, we'll leave. No worries, okay?"

Lizzie shrugged. "Okay, but if I flip out and tear some poor fool's head off with my bare hands, their death is on your conscience."

Ann laughed at that. "Hah! Whatever."

"No really, Korean girls all know taekwondo. It's genetic." Lizzie took on a fighting stance.

"Come on, Ninja Girl," Ann said, starting to walk down the sidewalk.

"Hey, ninjas are Japanese! I'm Korean, you racist!"

"Oh, just move it!" Ann yelled in mock anger.

The house, "party ground zero," as Ann referred to it, was packed with people. Stepping inside, Lizzie felt a little light-headed but otherwise okay. She made a conscious effort to keep the front door in sight at all times. For a while, the two friends just milled around, trying to look like they belonged. Finally, Ann spotted the tall, lanky figure of Keith Malone.

"Ahh, there's my man." Ann moved toward him, dragging Lizzie with her. Keith was talking to a smaller white guy with messy brown hair. They were obviously deep in discussion about something, and Keith was waving around the beer he held like a wand. As the ladies approached, Keith spotted them, freezing in place.

"Ann, you made it!" He seemed surprised.

"Lizzie gave me a ride."

"Of course, that's me. Whitey's taxi service," Lizzie said, doing her best disgruntled minority impression. No one looked at her. There was suddenly an odd tension in the room. Ann didn't seem to notice, but Lizzie sure as hell did.

"Well…good," Keith continued. "There's a few things I," he took a quick swig of the beer, "things I've been meaning to talk to you about. Maybe we could talk in private for a minute."

"Ah well, I mean sure, but I promised Lizzie I would stay with her," Ann stammered, suddenly confused.

"It'll just take a minute. That would be okay, right Lizzie?" Keith eyed her.

"Sure," Lizzie lied. "I'm fine. Just don't be too long, okay?"

"No problem." Keith took Ann by the arm and dragged her away. Ann managed to mouth the word "sorry" before being swallowed by the crowd.

Lizzie knew, right then and there, that Keith planned on dumping Ann. She stood stunned, unsure what to do to help her friend.

"Who's the blonde?" Keith's chatting partner suddenly asked, breaking the silence.

"That's Ann, his girlfriend." She emphasized the word 'girlfriend,' as if everyone in the world should know.

"Really? I thought he was dating that Vanessa chick. That sly dog!"

"What? That little snake, well, big snake. I'll…" Lizzie was suddenly dizzy, her hands shaking. The new guy looked concerned.

"Hey, are you okay?"

"I'm, I'm…no." Lizzie steadied herself against the wall, feeling a panic attack coming on. There were just so many people. So many! "I have this thing with crowded places. They bring on attacks."

"Agoraphobia?"

"Well, yes, how did you know that?" Lizzie asked breathlessly. "Oh, it's a doctor thing, right?" She wiped her sweaty palms on her jeans.

"Hah. Well, I'm just an intern, but yeah, that has come up. Why the hell are you here then?"

"Usually if I'm calm it's okay. It's just… Look, I need to get out of here." Lizzie pushed off the wall.

"Okay. Hey, here's an idea. Let's just find someplace with less people. Maybe get you a drink. There are a few rooms upstairs. That way you don't have to run out on your friend." The new guy offered Lizzie a hand, then froze. "Okay, that so sounded like a pickup, but honestly it wasn't."

"Yeah okay, just anywhere but here."

New guy helped Lizzie up a flight of stairs, snagging some water on the way. The house was large and they found an empty bedroom upstairs with a TV. Lizzie quickly dashed to a window and opened it.

"I'm Jamie, by the way. Jamie Ortez," New Guy said. Lizzie breathed in the cold air, feeling herself calming down. She could always jump out the window. Yeah that made sense. God, she was crazy.

"Lizzie," she said, finally. Feeling a bit more like herself, she flopped on the bed, grabbing the TV remote. She never gave out her last name. You never knew who was a data thief.

Jamie moved to close the door, but Lizzie shot him a look that made him freeze.

"Feeling a bit better, I take it?" he asked, sitting down on the other side of the bed.

"Actually, yes," she said. She gave him her best smile. "Thanks." There was a brief and awkward silence.

"So…agoraphobia? Brian Wilson had that. It's treatable."

"Who?" Lizzie didn't look at him again, focusing on flipping channels.

"From the Beach Boys."

"Who?" Lizzie repeated. Jamie let it drop. Lizzie got that he was trying to start a conversation. She just wanted no part in it. For a moment, the awkward silence returned. She was going to have to say something.

"God, would you look at this crap? I hate these stupid vampire movies. I mean the whole blood-sucking, turning into a bat thing, it's just idiotic."

Jamie picked up the thread. "Ha. Not a fan?" he laughed, "I always thought the undead chicks were kinda cute. I mean, besides the whole wanting-to-suck-the-life-outta-you thing."

"Ah. Actually, all of us women are like that." Lizzie gave him a grin. This was going okay, she could do this. "But come on, do you really enjoy this stuff?" She pointed at the TV, where a cloaked figure with plastic fangs stood over a sleeping woman.

"Well, I never much cared for vampires. Besides the hot ones, that is. Or werewolves." A big smile suddenly lit up his face. "But I have to admit, I have always, always loved…" He put his arms out in front of him and laid his head down on his shoulder.

"Zombies!"

# 2 - Boys Night Out

New York City, New York, now

It was Friday night in the city. The Ancient One kept stopping to look at some new wonder and it was driving Mike Samson crazy. Mike had come to accept that his new "boss," the Ancient One also known as Joseph Miller, had, in fact, come from 1908, which was pretty easy after coming to terms with the existence of werewolves, vampires, and demons. At this point, he was thinking he may have been off about the whole Santa Claus thing as well.

Their third night of "hunting" had brought them to New York City. By "hunting," Miller seemed to mean wandering the streets, visiting bars, and hitting on women. He was now pondering a large neon sign that showed a martini being poured. Moving to his side, Mike asked, "Miller, what are we doing out here again?"

"My dear Mr. Samson, as I have stated the last three times that you posed this exact same question, we are looking for the Cursed," Miller answered. He did not look away from the sign. "Truly amazing."

"Wait 'til you see Times Square," Mike said. "Ok, yeah, I get it, but you really think 'the Cursed' are just wandering around the streets with nothing to do? I thought you said the demons were most likely long gone."

"Oh, I'm sure the demons are long gone, as you put it. They know I am here now, but their children are not quite as intelligent. If we can find one, perhaps one that hasn't been turned yet, we can use it to track its parents."

"Turned yet?" Mike asked.

"Turned."

"Please stop talking in bad horror movie clichés," Mike pleaded.

Miller ignored him. "Ah. That establishment looks promising." Miller pointed to a rundown-looking bar, stuck between a nightclub and an all-night grocery store.

"Here? Miller, if you want a bar, we can at least find a decent place."

"No, lad, this should do nicely."

Mike shrugged and followed Miller in. The bar was quite full. There were a few young kids, probably with fake IDs, Mike thought. Vacation or not, he still thought like a cop. Some blue-collar folks were enjoying their Friday night. In the back, there was a jukebox, near which several people were dancing. The entire side of the building was set up with a long bar, most of it packed with thirsty patrons. On the other side of the space, near the door, there were several booths occupied by couples and larger parties.

"Samson, procure some drinks. Ask if they have mead," Miller said, finding a spot near the front of the bar that gave him a fairly clear view of the back.

"Miller, no one has mead anymore. I'm pretty sure bars stopped having mead somewhere before the last crusades ended."

"Bah, fine. Just none of that Budweiser. I've had better ale than that brewed in old boots."

Mike shrugged and made his way through the crowd. He preferred to be the one interacting with regular human beings. Miller, with his whole "man out of time" theme, managed to confuse and often offend pretty much everyone. Women were by far the worst, as times had changed quite a bit. After Miller had patted a woman's rear for helping him in Walmart, Mike had to beg and plead with the woman not to press charges, explaining that his "cousin" was mentally ill. That whole trip had been a complete disaster anyway, but they had needed something for Miller to wear, other than the outfit that he had been given when he had dropped in at a local church. After being nearly arrested twice, and banned from one store, they had managed to get Miller some standard jean/t-shirt combos. They had also found him some work boots, which he seemed to like, as well as a long, dark coat, which Mike thought worked with the whole monster-hunter theme. Now, Miller looked like nothing special on the street. A Hispanic man in his early 20s, not terribly tall or broadly built. Only the wild eyes, wicked smile, and almost Scottish accent told you there was something off about the man.

After a short talk with the bartender, Mike returned to Miller with the drinks. Miller gladly accepted his beverage and took a long pull on the mug.

"Ahh, much better," he said.

"Good. Now as much as I like hanging out and drinking on a Friday night, why this bar?"

Miller looked at him thoughtfully. "Mike, you must learn to celebrate your life. There are two things that make this all worth it. Drink!" he raised his glass and his voice, "and women!" This little speech produced some giggles and hearty laughs from nearby patrons.

"Miller, please don't get us kicked out of another bar for harassing women," Mike pleaded.

"Bah, your women are far too sensitive. I only wish to show them my gratitude for sharing their beauty with the world."

"I don't thinking groping is the way to go for that," Mike broke in.

"Fine, fine," Miller said dismissively. "Actually, this time I was referring to a woman for you. Good God, do you need it."

"Hey!" Mike protested. Technically he was still mourning his wife. It would be inappropriate to go chasing every girl he saw. Besides, he knew he wasn't ready.

"Yes, you need to meet a fine lass who can teach you how to freeze."

"Chill," Mike corrected after a moment, translating from clueless, "And stop trying to sound hip. It never works."

"I think you should go dance with her." Miller pointed to a woman who was dancing alone by a jukebox. She was brown-skinned, a little pudgy, and on the shorter side. Her hair was done in long dreads and she was dancing far too fast for the rhythm of the music.

"Yuck. Why her? Why not the cute blonde over there?" Mike subtly indicated a striking blond woman who was quite a bit younger than him. Miller drew Mike's attention back to the original woman. He leaned in close to Mike's ear and whispered.

"Because in about five minutes, that lass is going to become a wolf!"

"What?" Mike almost jumped out of his skin.

"Aye. She is the one I've been tracking for days. Do you think I just like hanging out in strange bars?"

Mike stared at Miller for a second. "Actually, I did. Miller, I'm not going to go over there if she's suddenly going to sprout claws and fur," Mike protested. He flashed back to an image of his neighbor, transformed into a raging monster, pinning him to the ground, shuddering at the memory. "Aren't you supposed to be the monster hunter? I'm just supposed to play sidekick."

"But lad, it was part of our 'deal.' You wanted to be kinder and gentler to the Cursed. Go find out something about her. Keep her talking and away from anyone else. And do not let her leave the dance floor."

"Why? You think it'll stop her from changing if she stays in public?"

"Not at all. Mike, she's looking for someone to eat. That is why she is here. Well, not her, but that thing inside her." Mike gulped. "She's going to try to get someone to go someplace private with her so she can have a nice easy snack once she's..." he paused.

"Playing for the other team?" Mike offered.

"Ha! Yes that works." Miller gave Mike a little shove. "Go have a word with her. I'll be right here. Wait. First, finish your drink. I think you will find that it helps."

"Miller, I'm going to get you for this," Mike hissed. He slugged down his beer in one long shot. How did he let himself get talked into this? He put down his mug and began his approach. He wanted to help these people. Well, at least he wanted to avoid having to kill them. Still, he wished there was another way.

The woman was still dancing to her own rhythm. Looking at her closely, Mike noticed that she did have a pretty face, even if she was a bit overweight. It was mainly the spastic dancing and the sweat pouring off of her that was repelling the rest of the men. They just weren't drunk enough yet, he figured. Letting out a long sigh, he moved up next to her.

"Hi," he said. He had no opening line and had not hit on a woman in 10 years. He'd forgotten how. He tried to break into a bit of a dance but all he could manage was a weak shuffle. The white boy shuffle.

"Well, hellooo," the woman said, sliding closer to Mike. Much too close for his liking. "Aren't you a cute thing?" Mike smiled but then remembered her goal and immediately felt a bit ill. "What's your name?"

"I'm Mike." He almost stuck out his hand to shake, but resisted the urge.

"I'm Catharine, but my friends call me Kate. Will you be my friend?"

Mike was working hard to stay cool. His mind kept flashing back to the scene outside his home when he had met his first wolf. "Sure," he answered, giving her a weak smile. She moved even closer in reaction, almost rubbing her hips against him.

"Oh, I love the drums in this song."

Mike looked at the jukebox. The song was "Tiny Dancer" by Elton John. He couldn't hear any drums. "Umm, yeah. Me too." He gave Miller a nervous glance. Miller grinned back and gave him a thumbs-up. He hated that guy so much. "Can I get you a drink?" He'd do anything he could to get off the horrible dance-floor. He was pretty sure no one was pointing and laughing at his lame dance moves yet, but it was just a matter of time.

"Oh no, I'm just loving dancing right now. Although I am feeling a bit hungry." She smiled at him, and again his stomach did a little flip-flop. They danced for a few minutes in silence.

"So, what do you do?" Mike asked, trying to take his mind off his terrible dancing skills and the looming near-death situation.

"Oh, I work for FedEx delivering packages. But I don't really want to talk about work." She grabbed his butt and pulled him towards her. She gave him a nervous laugh. "Look. This is going to sound really forward, but um, do you wanna go someplace a bit more private and, ah, you know…" she dragged a fingernail from his chest down to his belt buckle, "mess around a bit?"

"Hah, ah well…" He returned the nervous laugh. "That is pretty forward. Uh, well, my friend and I only got here a few minutes ago, and um, I really don't want to ditch him. He's new in town." He pointed at Miller, who waved at them both.

"Ooh, he's cute." She put her arms around Mike and said, in a deep, sultry voice, "He can come too." Mike could feel the heat coming off of her in waves. She leaned forward as if to kiss him, but instead licked his chin. "Mmmm, you're a tasty one." Rubbing against him, she let out a little moan. "What do you say?" For a moment, Mike was too horrified to answer. Then Miller was beside him.

"Well, hello lass! Aren't you a pretty little thing?" he said. She giggled at his accent and seemed to stumble a bit. She pulled hard on Mike to keep her balance.

"Sorry, a little dizzy. Must be all the heat in here." The look she gave Mike was so full of lust that he somehow managed to blush a deeper shade of pink. "I think I might need to lay down a bit," Catharine said, sliding down to the floor. Her entire body began to quake and her eyes rolled up toward the top of her head. People turned to see what was going on.

"Is she okay?" someone asked.

"Just give her some space," Miller said. He put up his arms to push a few curious people back.

"I think she's having a *seizure*. Make sure she doesn't swallow her tongue," a man said. Mike grabbed him by the shoulders and pulled him back.

"Trust me; you really don't want to put your hand near that mouth." Turning to Miller he said, "Don't we need to get these people out of here?"

"Worry not, Samson, I will make sure your new friend does not hurt anyone." Mike looked down at Catharine's body. Her eyes had filled with an inky blankness and foam was streaming from her mouth and down her cheeks.

"Give her some space!" Mike yelled, pushing people away.

"Oh my God, what's wrong with her eyes?" someone else screamed. The sound of tearing cloth brought Mike's attention back to Catharine. Her pant legs had ripped open to make room for the huge masses of muscle forming down her legs.

"I hate this part," Mike said. Someone screamed. Catharine rolled over and spit out a mouthful of teeth and blood. Her spine stretched and the muscles in her arms expanded like balloons. The crowd backed further away, but did not run, caught up in the horrible spectacle. Mike kept his distance. He had seen this before, and didn't want to watch it again.

After a terrifying moment, the beast that had been Catharine rose from the ground. Its hands were dripping blood from the huge claws that had just burst through its fingertips. New, sharp fangs stuck out of its jaw. It was taller than Catharine had been by only a few inches but it was no longer fat. Muscle rippled through its arms and across its stomach. Its clothes had, for the most part, stayed together, giving the beast an almost comical "werewolf on the town" look. Its face was still mostly Catharine's, besides the black, empty eyes and the short fur covering its entire body. It howled at the crowd that encircled it, prompting a gasp. For a moment, no one moved. Then, the beast charged towards Mike and the crowd exploded in a panic. Miller was thankfully fast enough to stomp down on one of the beast's legs with a steel-toed boot just as it leapt, and the beast howled as its bones crunched, falling face–first, only inches away from Mike.

"Do *not* let it feed!" Miller yelled.

"Oh really? I was going to just let her nibble on my arm," Mike said. He moved farther away from the creature. People were running in all directions, screaming and trampling each other. Next time Mike would make the game plan. There had to be a better way.

The wolf limped toward the door, dragging its busted leg behind it. Miller let it pass, helping an Asian woman back to her feet.

Mike followed at a distance. The beast took a swipe at a passing patron, but was too slow to connect. It leapt at another man, managing to pin him down. Mike ran up and gave it a quick kick to the ribs, knocking the man free. The beast howled in frustration.

"Sorry, lady. None of that." Mike and the wolf locked eyes for a moment before it fled through the door. "Miller! What now?"

"I follow it and make sure that it does not hurt anyone. You track us."

"Got it."

"Make sure you find us by daybreak!" Miller shouted.

Mike took off in the other direction, toward where the van was parked. "Okay, no problem."

"Daybreak, Samson!" Miller repeated once more, and was gone.

# 3 - For Whom the Doorbell Tolls

Springfield, New Jersey, now

When Lizzie finally found the official list of missing people related to the 'incident' at College Hospital, she was shocked by the length of it. A total of 54 people were still missing, although the list grew shorter each day as officials managed to piece together the bodies and identify them.

Every morning, Lizzie rechecked the list. If Ann's body was found, well, that would be it, but as long as her name remained, there was hope. This morning, she again performed her daily vigil, skimming down the familiar list of names. A few stood out.

Vanessa Black. Lizzie had only met her once. She had come off as stuck-up, but that didn't warrant her getting killed. Keith Malone. Ann's ex, who Lizzie hoped had been chopped to small pieces. Then there was Jamie Ortez, who she had missed on her first few read-throughs. She remembered meeting him once at a party and he had seemed nice. Well, nice enough that she had let him get to second base. Maybe 'nice' wasn't the right word. She looked at his name with some regret and moved on.

Short of her daily check of the list, Lizzie had exhausted her ideas on how to find Ann. She had checked Ann's credit cards and bank account. She had not made any purchases. Lizzie had even spent a day soon after the incident tracking down Ann's cell phone. She found it at the top of a seventeen-storey building near Broad Street, along with one torn shoe. God knew how it had gotten there.

That had been almost two weeks ago, and since then, there had been no leads. She had called the police and then, far worse, Ann's mother. No one knew anything. It was horrible the way she had last seen Ann, storming out of her house so angrily. The image of her exit replayed in Lizzie's head. That couldn't be the way she said goodbye. It just couldn't.

It was during this morning ritual that the doorbell rang. Lizzie wasn't expecting any visitors. Though it was late in the day, she was still in her pajamas, which in this case meant undies and an oversized Pink Floyd shirt. She had no idea who "Pink Floyd" was, probably some American rocker chick, but she liked the floating pig on the front.

She was slow to respond to the door, figuring it for some salesperson. She glanced around her office, considering the few pairs of pants tossed around the place. She grabbed one at random, giving them a sniff to make sure they weren't too dirty. She'd let the place get a little run down in the last few weeks.

The doorbell rang again. She tried stepping into the jeans while heading towards the front door, tripped, and landed face-first on the carpet.

The doorbell rang again.

"Jesus! I'm coming! Give me a second here!" she shouted. She managed to get one leg in as she stood up, hopping her way to the front door. On the way, she stumbled again, taking out a perfectly good flower vase.

The doorbell kept chiming.

"Damn it!" She was going to have to clean that up. Well, she was never really a flowers kind of girl anyway.

She approached the door, at last decent, and put her eye to the peephole. There was an old woman at the door. Not a regular little old woman. This was an extra-large version, not fat but built like a retired tank. She was dressed professionally and was leaning heavily on a large metal cane.

"Do I know you?" Lizzie called loudly enough to be heard through the door.

"I'm looking for Bong Cha Namgung," the woman replied. Lizzie was stunned to hear her full name. No one called her that. It wasn't even on her license. More surprisingly, this woman pronounced it correctly.

"Yeah, that's me." Sort of. "Who the hell are you?"

"Dr. Renee Dupré. I want to talk to you about a friend of yours, Ann Melakh." She even said Ann's name correctly.

"What about Ann? Do you know where she is?" Lizzie asked.

"Perhaps we could talk about this inside? At my age, I'm not much for shouting through doors." Lizzie hesitated. She hated having people she didn't know in her house. It drove her nuts, which, she often admitted to herself, was not far to go some days. On the other hand, this woman might have information about Ann. There was really no choice. Lizzie quickly slid back the dead bolt and unhooked the several chains on her door, swinging it open. She eyed the strange woman for a long moment.

"Can I come in or would you like to gawk at me for a few more minutes?"

The comment shook Lizzie out of her stupor. "Yeah, come on in. Of course." Lizzie waved Dr. Dupré inside. Dupré followed her into the living room, which was far less messy, since Lizzie was rarely in there. The old woman didn't seem to need the cane at all.

"I must say you are looking quite fit. Much more so than the pictures I've seen of you," she said.

That made Lizzie's hair stand up on the back of her neck. "What? You have pictures of me?"

"Oh just some old school shots I dug up, nothing so recent or private. You were a rather rotund creature in high school." Lizzie was stunned by this comment and did not respond, so Dupré continued. "But now, look at you. Perhaps still a touch on the plump side, but rather pretty. That's beside the point. I understand you are a successful engineer of some sort. Invented something useful, I take it?" She waited for Lizzie to respond. When she did, her voice was low and careful.

"Yes, I wrote some very popular imaging software. It, well, have you seen those diet ads, with the pretty people? 'I lost 200 pounds in 3 weeks?' That sorta shit? Well it makes the pretty people look like they actually did weigh 300 pounds."

There was a delay as Dupré processed this information. "Ah, I see."

"How do you know me and what do you want?" Lizzie asked.

"I got your name from a Janet Melakh, your friend's mother. She said you might know something about Ann's whereabouts before she disappeared."

"How do you know Ann?"

"I think she may have been involved in the murder of a very old student of mine. I want to ask her some questions," Dupré said.

"Ann would never kill anyone."

"Of course not," Dupré said, soothingly. "But she may have some information that could help. Have you seen her since the 14th of April?"

"Oh sure, several times. We hung out all the time. She's my best friend. But she went missing two weeks ago. I picked her up in Newark the night before..." She wasn't sure why she was planning to tell this woman what she knew, this rude ugly old woman. Maybe she had to tell someone. "She was going on about demons running off with her ex-boyfriend. She was really worked up. She drank enough to kill a man, and then passed out on my couch. We spoke the next day. I tried to talk her down, explain the 'no such thing as a demon' thing," Lizzie flashed Dupré a nervous smile, knowing how nuts the whole thing sounded. "But it didn't take. She got pissed and left in a huff. I figured she was blowing off some steam, but then I heard about what went down at College hospital. The police said she had been seen there." At last Lizzie stopped. Telling her story had actually made her feel a bit better. "I don't know what happened there, not really. I don't believe what the feds are saying."

"You're a smart girl, aren't you? Even with all your little mental issues. It's a shame," Dupré said, shaking her head and fiddling with something in her pocket.

"Well I haven't given up hope on her yet..."

"Oh not Ann, you! You see, I'm afraid..." The doorbell rang again, freezing Dupré in her tracks. She released whatever was in her pocket. Lizzie stared at her, confused. The doorbell rang again. At last Dupré said, "You should probably get that."

"Umm, right," Lizzie agreed and stepped back towards her front door. She didn't want to take her eyes off the strange woman. She was up to something. Her raging paranoia might actually be coming in handy for once. Then another thought struck. Lizzie had been so thrown off by Dupré's entrance that she had completely forgotten about relocking the door! Any crazy from the street could be inside. She raced back to the door, which swung open just as she was reaching for the doorknob. She was tossed back by the sudden force of the entry and, for the second time that day, landed on the floor. In front of her loomed a giant of a man. He wore a very plain suit, dark shades, and was the tallest Japanese man she had ever seen. The feds! How had they known? How did they catch her? Lizzie was on the verge of a full-out panic attack. It was lucky that she had taken her meds that morning, otherwise she would have collapsed into a crying mess on the floor.

"I, uh, it wasn't me, I mean, I'm sure someone spoofed my IP and…" Lizzie started.

The big man smiled. It was such a warm smile that Lizzie stopped talking.

"Miss, is it really that obvious that I work for the government?" he asked, in a calm voice.

"No?" she responded, more question than answer.

"Here, let me help you up." He offered her his hand. She took it. "First off, I'm not that kind of agent. Second, I'm looking for someone. Maybe you can help. She is an older woman, very large. Kind of mean. Looks like she ate just one too many babies?" Lizzie laughed out loud. She liked this man. Well at least for a Fed he was okay. Her feeling of panic was subsiding. She was no longer feeling compelled to flee to her computer room, tear out her hard drives, and light them on fire.

"Dr. Dupré is in my living room."

"Good!" He smiled again and walked further into the house. "This way?" Lizzie pointed the way and then followed. "Ah, there you are, my good doctor," the man said as he entered the living room.

"Takahashi," Dupré said with a huff. "Didn't I tell you I was taking the day off for personal reasons?"

"Look at you standing so well! Your treatments *are* working." Takahashi beamed at her. "Amazing."

"Of course. Don't be a fool, Takahashi, answer my question."

"Duty calls, Frau Doctor. Some of our boys dug up a sample that fits right in with your specialty. We need you to take a look."

Dupré huffed again. "Fine." Then, turning to Lizzie, she said, "Miss Namgung, we'll have to finish this conversation another day." With that, she stomped out of the room. Lizzie relaxed a little. Takahashi gave her a wink.

“Don’t mind her, she’s just evil personified,” he said, making her laugh again. “It was a pleasure meeting you. Miss Namgung, was it?”

“Lizzie. Just Lizzie.”

“Short for Elizabeth?”

“Short for Lizard, giant.”

“Ah.” Takahashi said, as if this made perfect sense. “You have a safe day then, Giant Lizard Namgung.” He followed Dupré out. Lizzie locked the door again and checked it twice.

# 4 - Old Ghosts, New Monsters

It took Mike only twenty minutes to get back to the minivan. Tracking Miller wouldn't be a problem, thanks to a GPS-linked device that he was wearing around his ankle. The anklet was made to track sex offenders, but Miller didn't need to know that. For Mike, it was just one of the many little gadgets that he had picked up when he decided to work this 'second job.' If he would be running into mythological beasts on a regular basis, he was sure as hell going to be prepared.

As the minivan rolled out of the parking garage, he got his first update on Miller's position. He was heading north, already well into the Bronx. They were moving incredibly fast for being on foot. He guessed that was why Miller had sent him back to get the van. There was no way Mike could keep pace without it. He knew that he would not be able to follow them closely, seeing as they wouldn't be traveling the major roads, but he could always find their general area. The tricky part would be locating them at sun-up. Mike fiddled with his phone at the stop lights, trying to work out exactly when that would be. He never thought he would use this fancy phone for anything other than email and texting, but was happy to have it now.

After about an hour of heading north, it was easy to guess that the beast was trying to get out of the city. Mike surprised himself by thinking of the poor woman as such. Miller must be rubbing off on him. She was still a human being, *albeit* a very dangerous one that was not in her right mind. He couldn't let himself forget that.

The time was 12:51 am. Mike headed onto the freeway and out of town. If he could get far enough ahead, maybe he could rest a bit before the 5:21 am sunrise. What would actually happen when the sun came up, he wasn't sure. In the movies, werewolves always reverted to their human form, but he knew from experience that the movies were way off. He would just have to wait and find out.

After another hour of driving, he noted with some relief that the dot on the map had not switched course. He pulled off to the side of the road to get some rest, setting the phone to wake him in two hours. He had become accustomed to functioning on very little sleep over the last few years, and particularly in the last few months. He wasn't even sure that he could sleep now, but just closing his eyes for a few minutes would help make him more useful for whatever was coming in the morning. Who knew what the sunrise might bring? Using his coat as a blanket, he made himself comfortable and closed his eyes, just for a minute.

The phone was ringing. Mike snapped it up, the bright light of day light blinding him and making him wince. He had dozed off on the job. Not good.

"Samson," he said, hitting the accept button on the phone.

"Hey baby," Melissa said on the other end. There was a feeling of relief, as if he had just had a terrible nightmare.

"Hey, pretty lady. What can I do for you?" He stretched in his seat, feeling very uncomfortable for some reason.

"Just calling about dinner. I'm thinking fish fry."

"Sounds fine to me. You know I'm not picky." Mike shuffled in his seat. Yes, something was off. Then he noticed it. His gun holster was empty. What the hell? Where the hell was his gun? He started searching on the floor of squad car. It must have fallen out of the holster while he was sleeping.

"Everything okay, honey? You sound distracted," said Melissa.

"Oh it's nothing, just seem to have misplaced something," Mike answered. He could hear Sam's excited voice in the background, but couldn't make it out.

"Hold on Mike, the boy wants to show me something." Then Sam's voice came clearly from the phone.

"Look Mom, I'm shooting the bad guys, just like Dad!"

"Jesus, Sam put that…" Melissa started to yell. There was a gun shot. Melissa was screaming. Sam was screaming.

Mike was screaming. He was suddenly wide awake in the minivan. That's not how it had happened!

"Goddamn," he panted, trying to pull himself together. An hour and twenty minutes had passed. There would be no more sleeping. Vivid nightmares had haunted him for months. They were always horrible, but also always contained that one brief moment when he remembered how it was before his wife died. Everything was okay. Even though it was so fleeting, the moment almost made the nightmares worth it. Almost.

Mike started up the minivan and found Miller on the GPS. He was out of the city now. Mike spent the next few hours tracking Miller as closely as he could. As the sun began to rise, he managed to get pretty close to his location. He knew he was in the woods to the right of the highway.

As the first rays of the sun hit the minivan's windshield, Mike noticed a distant figure running towards the van. At first he thought it was Miller, but as it got closer, he realized it was the werewolf. Mike reached for the gun in his glove compartment. This was no ordinary hand gun, but the biggest he could get his hands on: a Desert Eagle. He had read that the thing was used to take down elephants in Africa. He had no interest in hunting elephants, but was very interested in putting the biggest hole he could in a werewolf, or whatever other beastie he came across.

He checked the ammo, seven .50 caliber hollow points for maximum damage, and stepped out of the van. He hoped he wouldn't have to use the gun. That would defeat the whole point of him being out here with Miller, but if need be, he had it.

Mike could see the beast clearly now in the dim morning light. Foam streamed out of its mouth and it was limping badly, though still moving very fast. It reminded him of a dog he had seen once. Sick with rabies, the dog had simply run itself to death, dropping suddenly when its heart finally gave out. Mike had pitied the creature then, and that same pity came to him now, looking at the werewolf. Mike could just make out Miller as he came out of the woods. The man appeared to be uninjured but exhausted. His shirt was stained with sweat and dirt and he had lost the usual pep in his step, which made sense. Sprinting for six hours would take the wind out of anyone.

The beast suddenly collapsed, only several yards away from Mike, as if the sight of him was too much to bear. Mike stood still, waiting for Miller to approach and wave him over.

"Samson. Well done," he panted.

"How did it go?" Mike asked.

"Well…a few close calls, but she did not hurt anyone." The wolf convulsed in front of them.

"Is it…changing back?" Mike asked.

"Yes, it has burnt out its energy for now." Score one for popular fiction. "When she is back, help me get her to your van." They stared in silence until the creature's seizures stopped. The hair simply fell out, as did the teeth and claws. But she did not shrink or lose any of the massive muscle that she'd taken on. The evening dress had been lost over the night's activities, so Mike ran back to the van and grabbed a blanket. It was covered with his son's favorite heroes, "The Power Rangers," but he didn't think the woman would mind much. They wrapped her up and carried her to the van, laying her across the back seat. She was unconscious.

"Is she going to remember what happened when she wakes up?" Mike asked.

"Not without my help. She needs to remember, however. She is going to find herself," Miller paused, searching for the right word, "changed. I think that may be the best way to put it. She is our link to the Fallen. If she is able, I can help her lead us to the one that cursed her."

"Ah," Mike said. "That's why we've been looking for her. You could have told me that before."

Miller's timeless grin returned. "Where is the fun in that?" He climbed into the passenger seat. "I am going to need some rest. Did you sleep at all?"

"Yeah, a little," Mike answered. "Go ahead. I can take first watch."

"If she wakes, try to keep her calm. She may be frightened when she sees me. The thing inside her will not soon forget me." With that, Miller leaned back in his seat and was asleep.

Just like that, Mike was alone again with his ghosts. He fiddled with his phone, becoming addicted to a game where he had to land cartoon aircrafts. He checked for any baseball news that he might have missed, anything to keep his mind busy. His nightmare had taken away any interest in sleep. After some time passed and traffic picked up on the highway, he decided that he would drive down to the next rest stop. There, he checked on the woman sleeping quietly in the back. The swelling had gone down and she again looked quite human. Now quite skinny but muscular, she was far more attractive. He briefly wondered if the Fallen had ever considered selling curses for their fitness benefits. He could see the ads now. *I lost 100 pounds of fat in one night, and all it cost me was my soul!* He realized that he was more tired than he had originally thought. He made sure that the woman was completely covered and returned to his spot in the driver's seat.

A good hour later, he heard a moan from the back seat. He glanced behind him, seeing that the woman was coming to. Her eyes fluttered open and fixed on him.

"Well hello there, handsome," she said weakly. She tried to sit up but collapsed back onto the bench seat. "Owww!"

"Just try and relax. It was Catharine, right?" Mike asked.

The woman rubbed her head. "Catharine, yeah. Was I drinking? I'm not supposed to drink. I guess I got a little out of control there. Honestly I'm not like that. It was just a slip."

"No, no drinking, look, this is going to be hard to believe," Mike started.

"Oh, I wasn't using was I? God, don't take this personally, but I don't remember last night at all. I mean, I remember you and then it gets foggy. Wait, you didn't slip me something, did you? I mean why would you? I was ready to go." She was starting to panic a bit.

"No drugs." Mike raised his voice. "God, you talk a lot. Just wait. This is hard to explain. You had a sort of…an attack." Mike gave Miller's knee a smack. Miller responded with a snore.

"Attack?" Her voice shook at the words.

"Were you anywhere near College Hospital about two weeks ago?" Mike asked.

Catharine gasped. "Yes, yes, like a day before all that stuff went down. I delivered a package. Was it the gas? Did the gas get me? Am I sick? Am I going to die?" The words streamed out of her and she suddenly burst into tears. Mike moved back to where she was sitting and put an arm around her shoulders.

"Hey, hey, it's going to be okay. I can help you. We can help you." Well, if Miller would wake up they could.

"You can?" She put a hand on his cheek. "Oh, I knew you were special, I knew it. I mean, I never hit on men at bars like that. Never."

You mean you thought I would taste particularly good, maybe? Mike managed not to say it.

"I mean, if the ladies at church knew I was at bars picking up men and sleeping with them in the back of a van…wait, did we have sex?"

"Umm, no."

"Oh." She sounded disappointed.

"Sorry?" Mike offered. He wasn't sure what the polite thing to say was in this case.

"Then, umm, where are my clothes?"

Yeah, she was not getting this.

"Well, that is a long story," Miller interrupted. Catharine's hand dropped from Mike's face and she suddenly stared forward at the front of the van.

"Well, welcome to the party, sleeping beauty." Mike let the sarcasm drip from his voice.

"Why Samson, I didn't know you felt that way." Miller beamed as he turned to face him. Catharine became visibly tense.

"It's okay, he's here to help. You remember you met him at the bar as well?" Mike said.

"He is right lass. I am here to help."

"He, he, he…" she stuttered. "He's bad, a bad man."

"No, I am not, not to you. But the thing inside you has a reason to fear me," Miller said. His eyes caught hers in an intense stare.

Catharine tried to prop herself up. "Thing inside of me? What the hell are you talking about?"

Mike moved back. "Catharine, at the hospital you were infected with something. Do you remember anything odd at the hospital?"

"Infected?" She struggled to sit up, holding the Power Rangers blanket close.

"Cursed," Miller put in.

"Miller, you're not helping. Let me talk her through this."

"Samson, I know that you mean well, but she needs to know what has happened to her."

"I don't think this is the best way to do that," Mike said.

"Both of you, just stop. Tell me what happened. You," she pointed to Miller. "How do I know you? What did you do to me?" Miller gave Mike a questioning glance.

"Fine, do it your way. You're the expert," Mike said.

Miller focused again on Catharine. "Not so long ago, you were cursed by an ancient demon. Last night, it awoke and transformed you into one of the children of the Fallen. You became a demon spawn, commonly referred to as a werewolf."

"Hah. Right. Okay then." Catharine looked at Mike. "Is this guy all right?"

"No, not at all. But about this, he's telling you the truth," Mike responded.

"Yeah, okay guys. Look, this has been fun and all, but if you could just give me my clothes back and maybe drop me off at a train stop…" She again tried to get up, but flopped right back over. "What the hell is wrong with me? My muscles feel like Jell-O."

"I know this is hard to believe," Mike said, "and I sure as hell wouldn't have believed it if I hadn't seen it a few times. But it's true. Last night you changed. You grew fangs and fur and tried to eat me. Just look at yourself. Here," Mike pulled at the blanket, "Just look at yourself."

"Whoa, none of that." She pulled away.

"Just two minutes ago you thought we slept together in the back of a van. Now you're playing shy?" Mike dropped his end of the blanket.

"That was before I knew you people were nuts."

"Enough!" Miller shouted. He pushed his way between them and grabbed Catharine's head with two hands.

"Get off," Catharine started. Miller put his face near hers and stared directly into her eyes.

"Remember!" he shouted.

For a moment, Catharine went slack, struck by the power of his voice. Then she pulled away. This time Miller let her.

"Oh my god. Oh my god." She dropped the blanket and stared at herself. "It's true. I remember. I remember it coming, the sound, and the drums and then…and then the hunger! And it's still here! It's still inside of me!" She screamed, and then, just like that, her eyes rolled up toward the top of her head and she fainted.

"I didn't know you could do that," Mike said.

"I let you try your way, Samson, but as I think you know, this is a hard thing to believe. She had to be made to remember." Miller turned away and sat back down in the passenger seat.

"No, I mean you just spoke to her and…"

"Forget it, Mike."

"But how?

"Let's just say I have learned a few tricks over the years." He closed his eyes and immediately started snoring softly, ending the conversation.

Mike shook his head, baffled by the exchange. This was surreal. He covered Catharine and made sure she would not fall off the seat. Again he felt sorry for the woman. Her body and mind weren't completely her own anymore. How terrible that must be. He moved back to the driver's seat.

Miller was completely asleep. He looked so much younger when he was sleeping. He figured he'd give Miller another hour of rest before waking him.

He spent the next twenty minutes killing time, taking a few laps around the van just to stretch his legs. He found a tree nearby and relieved himself, and then took his place back in the driver's seat.

His phone rang.

"Samson," he said, picking it up.

"Hey Samson, it's Johnson. I didn't wake you, did I?" Johnson was the police officer he had met leaving College Hospital. Since then they had ran into each other a few times, mostly at funerals for the folks who had not made it out. The experience had bonded them and they were becoming good friends.

"Nah, just out for a ride with some friends."

"Good, figured you for an early riser. I got a case here. I know you're still on leave but thought you might be able to help me with this."

"Sure, go ahead. Doubt I know much of anything, but it can't hurt," Mike said. He was happy to talk about his real job again.

"There was a double homicide at CMDNJ the same day as the incident." No one really knew what to call the things that had gone down at College Hospital.

"Damn, really?"

"Yeah, shitty day all the way around. This one seems much more normal though," Johnson continued. "We have two dead males, Dr. Larry Conners and Wen Li, who were shot to death with an extremely high-caliber weapon at close range. The security cameras have been tampered with, so we don't have any film for that day or the week prior."

"Figures. It's never that easy," Mike put in.

"Yeah, but get this: three days before, the good doctor fired their janitor. Something about the quality of his work."

"You think it's a revenge thing?"

"It could be. I wanted to bring him in. Do you know the name 'Andres Soliz'?" Johnson asked. Mike thought about it for a moment.

"Nah, sorry, doesn't ring any bells."

"No problem. Actually I have a picture of the guy right here. Just emailed it to you. The reason I ask is 'cause I swear I saw the guy at the hospital."

"Ah, okay. Well I'll take a look. I make no promises. The stuff that went down there, well, it's just hard to talk about, you know?" Hard for people to believe was more like it.

"Yeah I'm with you. I'll never forget that day myself..."

"Yeah, thanks. I'll let you know how it goes and if I saw this Soliz."

"Alright, thanks man. Later."

Mike hung up. A moment later his phone gave a short 'bing,' signaling the arrival of a new email. Mike opened it up and waited for the image to download. It showed a young Hispanic man of small stature, maybe in his early twenties. Mike inhaled sharply. He instantly recognized the man, who was currently asleep in the passenger seat of Mike's minivan. He would know Joseph Miller anywhere.

# 5 - Meanwhile, Back at the Ranch

Travis Clayton used to be somebody, a big-shot Hollywood stuntman. Well technically, a TV stuntman. He had rubbed shoulders with big stars, like Hasselhoff, Mr. T., and the midget who played Alf. For three seasons of the A-Team, he was the go-to fall guy. If B.A. Baracus shot a guy down from a water tower, Clayton was that man. If Face punched someone off a boat, Clayton was that man. And if Hannibal blew up a group of conveniently placed barrels and tossed a guy high into the air, well, Clayton was that man. One too many falls had ended his career in stunts twenty years ago. From there it was a slow decline to what had to be the lowest place on Earth, the city morgue of Newark, New Jersey.

Clayton hated his job and loved to tell anyone who would listen. Sadly, most of these people were corpses, seeing as he worked the night shift. In this case, the night shift wasn't an all-night thing. The last thing any sane person would want to do was spend all night locked up with a bunch of dead people and a mop. It was Clayton's job to clean up after everyone left and then get the hell home. Tonight, however, a coroner was extending Clayton's stay longer than he would have liked. The man was inspecting a particularly gruesome body. It was completely white and skeletal, like it had been dead a long time.

"Excuse me, but I'm going to have to clean this area and then lock up." Clayton was trying hard to sound polite, but really just wanted to pack up and head home.

"Sorry, buddy, official police business. We'll try and keep it short for you. I'm just waiting on someone," the coroner replied.

"That someone would be me," a third man said, entering the room. He was a tall, broad Asian man. The suit told Clayton the guy was a Fed. Clayton was quick like that.

"Agent Takahashi?" asked the coroner.

"You must be Dr. Jeffers."

The men briefly shook hands. Behind the Asian man, an old woman appeared. "Let me introduce you to Dr. Dupré. She's our specialist."

"A pleasure," Jeffers said to the woman with a friendly nod. The old woman responded with a sour expression.

Clayton stepped into the hallway and started his mopping. He wasn't going to let these jackasses keep him any later than need be. He had a six pack of beer and his soaps to catch up with. He was just close enough to hear them clearly, and listened intently while pretending to mop a particularly dirty spot.

“Can you show Dr. Dupré what we were talking about on the phone?” the man named Takahashi asked.

“I have to warn you, this isn’t pleasant,” Jeffers cautioned. The old woman named Dupré snorted and Jeffers continued. “This is Sharon Deman, age 44, last seen alive last Tuesday.”

Tuesday? The body looked ancient. Clayton moved closer to the door, getting interested in spite of himself.

“So, this was after the College Hospital incident then?” Takahashi asked.

“Yes, and this isn’t the only one. I have five more bodies, all similarly emaciated and pale, all less than a week old. The press has picked it up, calling them the angel murders.”

Dupré snorted again. “Nothing farther from the truth there,” she said, her voice like sandpaper.

“Can you show her why?” Takahashi asked.

“Of course. If you’ll just look here?” A brief pause followed. “Each of the bodies has the same symbol carved into its back. Looks more like a bat than an angel to me.”

“Interesting. And what’s this on the back of the neck?” Dupré finally sounded curious now.

“It appears to be a type of mold, at least as far as I can tell. I’ve sent it out to some specialists, and we should know more in a few weeks.”

“That’s vile,” Takahashi gagged.

“There’s more.” Dupré’s voice again. “It’s growing in a straight line, down the arms and spine, almost like a nervous…” her voice trailed off. “Get this back to the Trenton lab. Takahashi, make it happen.”

There was a pause and then Dupré appeared in the hallway, almost running Clayton down. He jumped back at her sudden appearance. She gave him a wicked glare and headed up the stairs.

“I guess we’re done here,” Takahashi said. “I’ll need to get this and the other similar bodies over to the Trenton lab.”

“I thought that might be how this went. I don’t suppose you can tell me anything.”

“I would if I could. Dr. Dupré is an expert in the unusual. If anyone can figure out what’s going on, she can. Can I see any other case files that you might have on this?” Takahashi asked.

“Of course. Just keep my department in the loop if your specialist discovers something.” Both men headed out of the room, following Dupré up the stairs.

Now Clayton could finally get cleaning, but he had to admit, he would have liked to follow them upstairs and catch the rest of the conversation. He began to quickly mop the floor.

Suddenly, there was a loud metallic bang. Clayton jumped nearly out of his skin.

"What the hell?" he asked out loud. Maybe one of those folks had dropped something on their way out. Clayton peeked down the hall. Both men were long gone. He shook his head and began to scrub again.

Clang! The noise filled the room again. Clayton glanced around, seeing nothing but meat lockers. It sure sounded like it was coming from inside the room though. Clayton paid closer attention this time. Again, the loud harsh noise rattled in his ears. It was coming from one of the lockers. But that wasn't possible, was it?

"Someone in there?" he asked, slowly approaching the locker. Of course someone was in there. They were dead, that's all. He grabbed the handle but could not make himself turn it. "You chicken, what the hell are you scared of?" he chided himself. "Nothing in there but a dead guy, and he can't hurt you."

Bang*! The* noise was there again, but this time from a locker on the other side of the room. Clayton spun toward it. There was nothing there but another closed locker. Someone had to be playing with him.

"Hey, whoever the hell's doing that can knock it off!" Clayton shouted.

Another bang.

"Stop it!" he shouted. "Or so help me God…"

Someone burst out laughing and, with a flash of embarrassment, Clayton understood what was going on.

"Freddie, that you?" The laughing continued as the portly figure of Freddie Williams entered the room. Freddie was younger and heavier than Clayton. He was the security guard upstairs but he often came down to share a good bitching session.

"Stop it!" Freddie mocked. "You sounded like a little girl."

Clayton's face turned a bright shade of red. "Not nice, man. Not nice. I'm too old for that shit. You could've killed me."

"Man, just my flashlight on the other side of those lockers. Although running to the other side when you weren't looking, that took genius." Freddie was having a good laugh. "The best part was when you couldn't even open the locker!" Freddie demonstrated by walking over and opening one of the meat lockers. Inside was a dead woman, her flesh loose and white.

"Travis, she's still dead. What, you think it was a zombie?" He laughed again. Clayton took this all in. He had nothing to say. "Man, you're such a pussy."

Clayton stared, stunned, as the corpse on the tray turned its head as if to look at them. Freddie didn't notice. He was too busy laughing.

"Look!" He pointed at the corpse.

"Oh, like I'm going to fall for that shit." Freddie turned to face the dead body. It vomited in his face. Large green chunks of long-forgotten food and embalming fluid streamed from its mouth, covering Freddie.

"What the hell?" Freddie screamed. He stepped back. The dead body threw itself to the ground. It landed with a crack as a decaying bone snapped, and then proceeded to stand up. It didn't stand like a living woman, instead jerking and twitching like a puppet on strings. The eyes weren't even open. It released a horrifying shriek that seemed somehow out of sync with the movement of its jaw.

"My God!" Clayton finally managed to scream. He was rooted to the spot.

The undead thing did not charge at them. Instead, it shuffled to the other side of the room and opened another locker, freeing a new corpse, which in turn started to scream. Clayton had seen this sort of thing in the movies before, or at least in an episode of South Park. Coming to his senses, he reached for the only weapon he had, his mop. As the second dead body, this one a man, began to stand, the undead woman shuffled to a third locker.

"Freddie! Help me get them back inside their lockers!" Clayton yelled. He ran in, using his mop as a staff and smashing the undead man on the top of the head. He heard a loud crack and the dead thing fell back to the floor but didn't stop moving. It started to twitch and jerk, again pulling itself to a standing position. This time its head lolled to the side. Clayton wasn't about to give up. He smashed the dead thing's knee and it again collapsed to the floor. Clayton followed up by bringing the mop down on its head, the handle snapping in half with the impact.

"Travis! Travis! Help!" Freddie was screaming. Clayton spun to see three more of the things, which seemed to be zombies, trying to lift Freddie into the air. The three naked dead things, their eyes closed, were screeching their fool heads off and trying to get a handle on the large, vomit-covered man. But Freddie, fatass that he was, could not be lifted and the zombies collapsed under his bulk in a symphony of cracks.

Clayton dove across the room, trying to reach the security guard, but the zombies recovered quicker. They started dragging the big man along the floor by his arms. Clayton grabbed a boot and pulled back. For a second, the zombie pack slowed, but then Clayton's feet began to slip on the vomit-covered floor.

"No! Damn it Travis, help me!" Freddie yelled, kicking and screaming.

"I'm trying! I'm trying!" the older man shouted. He couldn't get enough traction. What the hell would Mr. T do in this situation? Freddie's boot slid off, sending Clayton sprawling. This wasn't working. He needed a better plan, and quickly. He ran back to get his broken mop. The zombie he'd beaten down was beginning to get to its feet again, although the knee Clayton had busted was slowing its progress. He gave it an awkward kick as he passed. Picking up the broken mop handle, he ran back to the zombie horde.

By now the group had made it to the stairs. "Hold on. Hold on!" he shouted. "I think I can stop them." Clayton drove the broken end of the mop into the back of the nearest zombie, about where he thought the heart would be. It was an old woman, her hair mostly gone. The handle entered with a popping sound and the zombie fell forward for a moment, but did not release Freddie. "Was that supposed to be a stake? That's vampires, you idiot! Vampires!" Freddie screamed.

"Shit! How the hell am I supposed to know this?" Clayton yelled. Freddie kicked out again, this time clipping the impaled zombie with his boot. The zombie went reeling back, right into Clayton, and the two fell down the stairs together in a tangle.

Clayton was covered in old dead woman as he hit the bottom of the staircase, hard. He shouted as pain erupted through his back. For a brief, horrible moment, the zombie lay motionless on top of him, like an ancient foul-smelling lover. Then, just like before, it jerked to its feet and left to join its fellows.

Clayton lay very still for a moment, panting hard. His back felt like it was on fire. He briefly wondered whether this counted as an on-the-job accident, and if he could collect worker's comp. Then he heard Freddie's screams and the zombies' screeches far above him and came to his senses. He had to try to save the man. He rolled over and started to stand, but the pain in his back was too much. He groaned, collapsing again at the foot of the stairs.

"Damn it!" He began dragging himself up the steps. He had to keep trying.

He heard more screeching, this time much closer, and rolled onto his back again, looking back into the room he had just left. The zombie he'd attacked before was slowly approaching. The dead man's neck was broken and his messed-up knee was at an odd angle. From his position on the ground, Clayton could not help staring at its family jewels swinging in the breeze. Clayton wanted to get up, he wanted to run, and he wanted to throw up. A lot.

"God, no! I don't want to die like this!" The zombie shuffled slowly forward, ignoring his pleas. Clayton rolled over again and gave the stairs another try. His back refused to cooperate and he got no farther than the first step. He couldn't move. This was it. The thing was going to eat his brains and that would be the end. Well, he regretted nothing. No wait, that was a lie. He regretted everything! Particularly the one time he went drinking with David Hasselhoff. God, what a prick.

Someone nearby was shouting. It was the Fed, Takahashi, coming down the stairs. He drew his sidearm and fired, hitting the zombie in the eye. The dead thing was knocked backed several feet.

"What is that?" Takahashi yelled, firing again at the zombie.

"Damned if I know! Shoot that sucker again!" Clayton yelled. Takahashi complied, pulling the trigger a third time. The zombie lay twitching in a puddle of its own embalming fluid. "Did you save Freddie?" Clayton asked.

"Freddie? Who's Freddie?" Takahashi asked.

"The big-ass security guard the other zombies just dragged upstairs!"

"What? There's more?"

"Jesus Christ, man! Didn't you see them?" Clayton demanded.

"No. There's no one upstairs." A sudden shriek from the zombie on the ground drew the men's attention back to the monster. It was pulling itself forward with one arm, the other dragging lamely behind it. Its head was split open and its brains could clearly be seen.

"It's not dead?" Clayton asked no one in particular.

"No, and I think that's the problem," Takahashi responded, firing again. Bullets didn't seem to faze it. It simply crawled around Clayton and started to flop up the stairs. Takahashi jumped over it, but the zombie simply ignored him.

"Where's it going?" Takahashi asked, then paused for a second, noticing a black patch of what seemed to be mold on its neck. He fired again, hitting the black stuff dead center. The corpse trembled and stopped. Its body slowly slid down the stairs, stopping inches from Clayton's face.

Clayton winced, but realized he was going to live. He sighed as he looked up and down the hallway and stairs, which were covered in green vomit and body parts.

"Damn it. Now I gotta clean all this shit up!"

# 6 - To Crash and Burn, with Love

Lizzie had a clue. It wasn't much of one, but it was a start. This Dr. Dupré was looking for Ann and Lizzie bet she knew a lot more than she was saying. She was pretty sure she couldn't just beat it out of the old woman, as that would mean leaving the house. She decided to do the next best thing, Google her.

Her first round came up with very little. Some pictures of Rene Dupré, a wrestler, a twenty-six-year-old's LinkedIn account, and a fourteen-year-old's MySpace page, filled with far too many blurry pictures taken extremely close up. Finally, Lizzie found some white papers on cell growth by a Renee Dupré, which seemed more fitting, but still nothing definite.

Lizzie also knew that she worked for the government. Which department, however, was another matter. She took the direct approach and started calling agencies, simply asking for a Dr. Dupré, but, no one claimed to know anything about her. After three hours of rejections, it occurred to her that, in fact, she had another lead. The man named Takahashi. This worked much better and on her third try a secretary at the FBI put her through to a satellite office in Trenton. There was a brief moment of panic when she heard the familiar voice on the other end of the phone.

"John Takahashi."

Lizzie decided to take a big risk and play straight. "Hello, this is Lizzie Namgung."

"Giant Lizard?" he asked, after a brief silence.

"Ah, yes, I was looking for Dr. Dupré. She left me this number as a way to get in touch with her if I remembered anything else about my friend."

"Oh she did, did she?" There was a good amount of skepticism in his voice. "And might I ask then, what she was asking you about?" He didn't know?

"A friend of mine, Ann Melakh, is missing. She was asking me questions. I guess they were related to a murder at the place she used to work."

"Oh really. That's interesting," Takahashi said.

"Isn't that what you people do?" Lizzie asked.

"Well me, sometimes. Rarely. That's generally a police matter. Her though, never."

"Oh, so should I be talking to her at all then?"

"Well the good doctor is a bit…eccentric. It could be related to one of her projects, or to something of a more personal nature. Sadly, Dr. Dupré tells me very little."

"Oh, I thought she worked for you."

"More like the other way around. She does some work for us, and in turn we do some work for her, although she does have a lab in this building," the man explained. Score! Lizzie pumped her fist in victory. Useful information!

"What kind of work does she do?"

"Oh, you know, science stuff. More than that I can't say. But there is something you should know. Dr. Dupré is not a nice person. It might be best if you forget whatever you called to tell her."

"I see," Lizzie said, honestly confused. Why should she be scared of an old woman? "Well, thank you for your time."

"Any time, Giant Lizard. A true pleasure." Lizzie hung up.

What a strange and wonderful man you are, John Takahashi. I wonder if you're single.

Lizzie quickly worked out an address for the building in Trenton. Armed with her laptop, a pocketful of anti-anxiety medication and a powerful Wi-Fi antenna extender, she headed to her car. She could use the Wi-Fi antenna to connect to distant Wi-Fi networks without even leaving her car.

She got into the car and locked the doors, confirming that they were locked three times before driving away. This little display of paranoia, reminded her just how far she had fallen. She had been getting better, but now, without Ann, she was slipping backwards. She had to find Ann for her own sanity, and soon.

Finding the building was easy enough, thanks to her mighty GPS. She even managed to get a parking spot right in front of the building. As Lizzie expected, her antenna picked up an old Wi-Fi network from a safe distance. The security was a joke, but she was used to that from government buildings. She spent several hours sniffing around the network for account IDs, passwords, and other useful information. After about five hours, she felt she had enough to get started with the real work, and so headed home. She had to pee really badly.

Returning home, after a quick bathroom break, Lizzie sat down and began to work through the megabytes of information she had picked up in her snooping. It occurred to her that to get all the information this Dupré lady had, she was going to need some help. Lizzie used only the best.

Contrary to popular belief, the best hackers in the world were not, in fact, American. Sadly, they were not even Korean. They were Chinese. They had a government happy to look the other way while its residents wreaked havoc on other countries' networks. They had a lot of practice as well. It was almost a national pastime. Lizzie knew exactly who to ask.

She found Crash on his usual IRC channel, trying to sell his usual credit card numbers with his usual level of success (not much). Even though they were in a chat room using an ancient program, running off Russian servers, on opposite sides of the planet, it still felt like she was walking into a bar filled with friends. Well, at least it would if Lizzie hung out at bars.

"Hiya Crash," she typed. The screen blinked for a moment, and then Crash's response popped up.

Cra$hU: "Well, well, well, look at what the capitalist pig dragged in."

LizardGrrl: "Long time no chat. How you been?"

Cra$hU: "Lonely, without you." Lizzie grinned at that.

LizardGrrl: "Ah you big romantic commie, you, you know just what to say to a lady."

Cra$hU: "Where have you been Lizzie?"

LizardGrrl: "Looking for a friend."

There was no instant response, so Lizzie quickly followed up.

LizardGrrl: "Not a boyfriend."

Cra$hU: "Well that's okay then."

LizardGrrl: "I need your help."

Cra$hU: "Oh no, not again. I'm not doing any more of your dirty work. "

LizardGrrl: "Ah come on. I need a big strong man to help me. Besides you'll love the target."

Cra$hU: "I believe you girls have a saying the US: no means no."

LizardGrrl: "It's the FBI."

Cra$hU: "What? You want me to help crack the FBI's network?"

LizardGrrl: "Yep."

Cra$hU: "Damn."

There was a long pause, the window displaying only a blinking cursor. Then, finally Lizzie saw:

Cra$hU: "When do I start ;)"

The next two days were a blur of computer screens. Lizzie and Crash poked at the building's network from afar, looking for a way in. It was good to have something to do and company to do it with. It didn't matter if that company was half a planet away. The whole thing came to an end, ironically enough, in one of the two hours during which Lizzie was asleep.

The computer announced in an overly excited male (not mail) voice "You've got mail," waking her from a light doze. It only did that when Lizzie received mail on a particular account, one that would be very hard to trace back to her. She shook herself awake, got herself a Cherry Coke, and brought up the message. It was from a company called "CheapPharm.net" and the subject line was "Be her Drillosaur!" The message itself said:

Get this! I found a real garbage file! Not kidding! It was actually in the recycle bin. But that totally counts. It's something from CMDNJ. Security footage I think. There are two, but the second got cut off.

"Yes!" Lizzie shouted. She followed the link provided and downloaded the file. It was in .mov format, which was easy enough to use. It wasn't very large, and she had the whole thing in thirty seconds, but it felt like a long thirty seconds. Hitting 'play,' she saw the image of a lab, Ann's lab, in black and white. There was no sound. Lizzie could see two men. One was Wen, Ann's coworker, whom Lizzie had met once. She could see his face clearly. The other man's back was to the camera, but they were talking to…yes, it was Dr. Dupré, in a wheelchair.

Dupré suddenly stood up and pulled something out her pocket. A gun. A huge gun. She fired once, hitting Wen. His head exploded. Lizzie dropped her soda. Dupré turned to the other man. They talked for a minute. Maybe the man was begging for his life. Why didn't it have sound? Dupré fired again and the mystery man was thrown out of frame. The movie ended.

For a moment, Lizzie sat, stunned.

"Shit," was all she could manage.

# 7 - Math

Newark, New Jersey, now

She remembered being a woman. She remembered warm flesh instead of cold white scales. She remembered her jaw not being filled with sharp fangs, and the feeling of her own hair falling on the back of her neck. This wasn't real. There was no way this could be real.

Ann Melakh stared at her clawed fingers, as she often had over the last few weeks. These days, she spent a good deal of the daytime sleeping or staring, just trying to come to terms with her new reality.

Suddenly, a white bag landed in her lap. She could smell that it was food, a big, greasy Whopper and fries. It may have been the best food she had ever smelled.

"Good morning, little sister."

Abraham stepped into view. The tall black man still wore the threadbare suit and top hat, a pair of old sunglasses just barely covering his ruined eyes. The black mist of the Cursed hung on him like a cloak. "Or should I say afternoon? And I thought vampires were night people." He grinned at his joke, a sickly, toothy grin that made Ann shiver. She didn't respond but tore into the bag with all of the "demon" strength she could muster. She tore off a huge hunk of the burger and swallowed it down. Food, real food!

"Thank you," Ann managed to mutter between mouthfuls. "Thank you. Thank you." Abraham's smile got a little less creepy.

"You're welcome. Some nice young lady insisted on dropping money off in my hat every day on her way to work."

"Ain't that ironic," Ann said with a smile. There were a few minutes of silence as Ann finished eating. Abraham passed her a soda to wash it down. "Thanks again. I've hardly eaten in weeks."

"Well, you're going to need your strength."

"What for?" Ann asked.

"I think it's time you stopped sulking around here. Time to see what you can do."

"What I can do? I can look like a freak, that's about it. I can't go out there!" Ann pointed to the giant hole in the wall behind her and the forbidden world beyond it. They were a good six stories up in the abandoned building that Ann had made her home. Ann had decided that the few large holes left in it by a fire were skylights, and enjoyed sunning herself, like a giant white snake. "They'll lock me up in some lab, poke at my insides. Hell, I'm half tempted to poke around in there myself."

"You do stand out in a crowd. But sometimes that can be a good thing. Worry not; the Fallen can change their shape."

"You said yourself that I'm not one of the Fallen." She looked down at the white scales. "Not anymore at least. I'm just one of the Fallen's corpses that doesn't know that it's dead."

Abraham raised his palm at that. "Stop. You have no idea what you are. No one does. That's the fun part."

"Fun? You think this is fun? Not being able to see my friends, my family? Hell, I can't even go for a walk outside!" Ann's anger boiled out of her. She was shouting now. "This isn't fun! This is shit! I'm a freak for the rest of my life, or at least until I get the balls to try and off myself…for a second time!" Ann stomped hard on the ground, shaking the building.

"Whoa, now." Abraham grabbed his cane with two hands, trying to settle himself. "Calm down. It's not as bad as all that. Many of the Fallen's discarded children can change their appearance, at least while the Fallen still live."

Ann froze at that. "What does that mean, the Fallen still being alive?"

"The Cursed, we draw power from them. When they're awake, like they are now, we can use some of their strength."

This was interesting. Ann forgot about her anger for a moment. "So, when the Fallen are alive, you get stronger?"

"Yes, stronger, healthier, younger. 'Course, doesn't affect me much anymore. I think I'm just too damn old. Used to be, when the Fallen returned, I would at least get all my hair back." He removed his top hat to show his bald head.

"How old are you, anyway?" Ann had to ask.

"Going to celebrate the big 1K next year or so, I think. Honestly, after the first few hundred you start to lose track."

"Wow."

"I know. I know. I don't look a day over 150. Probably would be better if I had a better diet. It's like they say, you are what you eat."

"What do you eat?"

"Don't you mean 'who'?" Abraham asked with a laugh. Ann stood there, shocked. "Kidding, just kidding. Little Cursed humor there. I haven't had a good meal in at least 50 years. I try to refrain. Mostly get by on dogs and cats. I'll admit to slipping from time to time, but trust me when I say they had it coming." This inspired a moment of silence. Ann was trying hard not to be disturbed by that. "But enough about little old me, looks like you can eat regular people food just fine."

"Umm yeah, seems I lack the need for the soylent green."

"What's that?"

"People. I don't eat people. I don't have one of those tongue thingies."

"Ah," Abraham nodded. "That's good. That's hard." His voice trailed off for a moment. "So see, there's one good thing. My father always taught me to be positive. Never could keep that man down."

"Yeah, yippee. Go me." Ann spun a clawed hand in the air in mock celebration, but then admitted, "Yes, that could be worse. You can't eat people food at all?"

"No, I lack the stomach for it. Literally."

"Do you really think I could change back? To the old me?"

"Well, not to the old you. There is no going back. This is what you are now." Ann felt herself deflate slightly. "But," the old vampire continued, "I'm nearly positive you could pass for human again."

"Really?" There was a small glimmer of hope growing in Ann.

"Absolutely. All of the Fallen's children can pass for human," he said.

"Well, how? Is there like a magic word or something?" Ann asked.

Abraham laughed loudly at that. "A magic word? Do you think you need to shout 'Shazam' or something?"

Ann chuckled. It felt good to laugh. "Yeah, I guess that was kind of dumb. Really though, at this point, I guess I would believe anything. So how does it work?" Ann asked.

"Here I'll show you. Look outside."

Ann obeyed. "Okay. What am I looking for?"

"Look down at the ground."

Ann obeyed again, moving closer to the edge of the gap to get a better view. The street below held a few parked cars, but no people. It was not the greatest part of town. "Okay, is this some ancient wisdom crap? What am I supposed to be seeing?"

"Just the ground," Abraham said, stepping forward and shoving Ann over the edge.

"What?" was all Ann managed before she was falling. For a few moments, panic killed any conscious thought. Then she felt something near her belly shift and her wings spread out wide, as if by instinct. She didn't hit the ground, but instead shot straight back up in the air. There was a brief moment of pure joy when she realized she was flying. Then an equal amount of fear cancelled that out and she dove for the large hole from which she had come.

She smashed hard to the ground, skidding to a stop inches from Abraham.

"What the hell were you trying to do? You evil bastard! You could have killed me!" Ann yelled from the ground. She was shaking with a mixture of fear, excitement, and rage.

"Didn't you tell me the other day you survived a seventeen story drop?"

"Well, yeah…" Ann managed to stand. "But that doesn't give you the right to throw me out of buildings. I could have died. I almost…"

Abraham was unimpressed. "Didn't you just tell me five minutes ago you wanted to die?"

"I didn't mean I wanted you to kill me!" Ann shouted. Finally, she managed to get to her feet. "I should…I should…" she stammered, "do something demon-y to you. Like tear out your liver."

"Ha! Haven't had one for years. Well, I don't think so, but if I do, you're welcome to it." The old vampire grinned. "You don't get it. You just flew. The wings aren't just for show. They work."

"Thank God!" Ann shouted. "You…you...jerk." She panted for a while, trying to make her body stop quaking. After a few minutes she said, "I did fly, didn't I?"

"You sure did. It was lovely. Never met anyone that could fly before, well besides the Fallen, but they make for lousy conversation."

"Jesus. That was surreal. I mean, besides the fear of death thing, it was kind of nice."

"That's the spirit! Wanna see what else you can do?"

Ann looked the blind vampire over slowly, unsure. Finally she said, "Okay, just no more throwing me out of windows."

"Fair enough."

For several hours, Abraham helped Ann learn the basics of being one of the Cursed. Ann was incredibly strong but was unable to change her appearance.

At last, a winded feeling came over her and she sat to catch her breath.

"This help?" Abraham asked after a while.

"Yeah, actually. I do feel better. Tired, but better."

"Good. Wait, hold on, I think I hear my lunch." Down the hall, a stray dog was yelping. "Be right back." He smiled and vanished down the hall. After a moment of silence, Ann heard the dog yelp, just once more. The silence resumed. Ann flinched at that, finally realizing what Abraham had meant. The poor creature. Abraham had been nice and helpful all day, besides throwing her out the window. She had started to forget what he was, but now the feeling of unease returned.

Minutes later, Abraham returned, grinning and looking generally healthier. Ann turned away but didn't say anything. For a few moments, they sat silently, until questions began to form in Ann's mind.

"Tell me about the Fallen. I mean, I know one is Lilith. Do the others have names?" she asked.

"Of course. The Fallen all have names. Many, in fact. Lilith herself has hundreds."

"Any I would know? I guess I'm not a huge fan of mythology, but maybe I've heard of one of them."

Abraham scratched his chin thinking about this for a few moments. "The earliest I know of Lilith is actually from a poem, very old, called Beowulf."

"Beowulf? I know that story, there was a movie. Wasn't very good."

"A movie? God, just what Miller needs, that man's ego is a thing of legend itself."

Ann suddenly stood up straight. "Wait, you mean to tell me Miller was Beowulf?"

Abraham laughed. "Actually yes, in a way. His name was Beo. He was considered a god then-that's happened a few times. A few years after Beo killed off Lilith and Asmodai, a nobleman named Beowulf showed up and took credit for it. They even made him king."

"Beo or Beowulf?"

"Beowulf. The Ancient One has been a king once before. I heard it didn't go well. Something about insisting on sleeping with virgins the night of their weddings, before their husbands."

Ann made a disgusted face. "So wait, that would make Lilith who in that story?"

"Grendel's mother. Grendel was a wolf. A particularly large one."

Ann nodded in understanding. "Wait, in the movie, Beowulf sleeps with Grendel's mother."

"I don't think that really happened, although with the Ancient One?" Abraham shrugged.

"And who is Asmodai?"

"The dragon. With mouth agape of which flames leap." Abraham almost sang the words.

"Is that from a song or something?"

"Yes, it's a chant. A sort of protective charm folks used to sing against the Seven." Abraham stood straight and cleared his voice. In a voice low and beautiful he sang:

Seven are they! Seven Are They!
In the Ocean Deep seven are they!
Battling in Heaven seven are they,
Workers of evil are they,
They lift up the head to evil, every day to evil
Destruction their work.
Of these seven the first is the South Wind …
The second is a dragon with mouth agape
From which flames leap

The third is a grim leopard
That carrieth off children
The fourth is a terrible serpent
With many heads
The fifth is a furious beast
That none can restrain
The sixth is a rampant
against god and king
The seventh is an evil windstorm
That none can with stand
Baleful are they, baleful are they.
Seven are they, seven are they, seven twice again are they.
May the spirits of heaven remember, may the spirits of earth remember.

When he was finished, he sat, stretching his long legs in front of him. After pausing a moment for dramatic effect he said. "It does lose something in the translation to English."

Ann sat very still. "The dragon. The dragon is Keith," she said.

"Asmodai is his name now. Did you know him?"

Ann swallowed hard. "I loved him."

"I'm sorry. The man you loved is gone."

"But he said he was Keith. He never used the name Asmodai," Ann said. She was fighting to stay calm. She felt the old pain of loss returning.

"The Fallen take on the memories of their hosts. When they are 'young' they are often confused. He may not have remembered or maybe, like Lilith, there is something wrong with him."

"So there is hope? Maybe I can save him?"

Abraham was silent for a long time. "No one else has ever come back from being taken by a demon, in all of the Fallen's time here." He let out a long sigh. "Don't get your hopes up."

Unfortunately, Ann couldn't help herself. There was hope. Hope she could still save Keith. Hope that she could become human again, or at least human-looking. The pain of loss was gone for the moment. For the first time in a while, she was beginning to feel almost okay.

"So that's two. Who are the rest?"

"Well there's Amon, known for its strength. And Ura, the plague bringer. Ashakku, Gallu, and Marduk."

"Wow, those are mouthfuls. I mean, I get that demons don't go by the name 'Fred,' but still. And those are all in your little song?"

"Sure. Lilith is the south wind. Amon is the furious beast. Gallu is the windstorm. Ura is the grim leopard."

"Wait, wait, back up. A grim leopard? How lame is that?"

"It's referring to disease, killing babies in their sleep," Abraham said, his voice flat but deadly.

"Oh. Well I guess that is horrible," Ann agreed weakly.

"They are not friendly folk."

A silence came over them.

"You have any family, little sister?"

"My mother. And a friend. She might as well be family." Ann wondered how poor Lizzie was doing. She was probably having another nervous breakdown. That girl pretended to be so tough, when in reality she was so damn fragile. "I should call them, go see them. Let them know I'm not dead."

Abraham didn't respond right away. Finally he said, "This is hard for anyone to accept. It might be best to wait until you learn to make yourself look more," he waved his hands in her general direction, "friendly-like, I think."

"Maybe I can just call. Let," she almost said 'Lizzie,' but something kept her from telling Abraham more than he needed to know, "my friend know I'm alive. Get her to water my plants."

Abraham laughed at that. "Alright, little sister, have it your way. What harm could a phone call do?" He tossed her three quarters. "Although I would wait for night to fall."

Ann did wait for the cover of darkness. She considered just jumping for the rooftop, trying to fly, but she wasn't ready to accept that reality quite yet. Instead she wrapped herself in her oversized coat and long scarf, as she had on the previous nights, and headed into the city.

On her way out, she couldn't help but notice the corpse of the dog Abraham had 'eaten.' It was shriveled and hairless, its skin bleached white. Her eyes moved away as quickly as possible. The image stayed with her, bringing back a flash of the body of Bill, the security guard who had briefly joined them in their attempt to escape College Hospital. A vampire had killed him as well. A vampire she had once called her friend.

Outside, she went about the difficult task of finding a working pay phone in a world that relied on cell phones. It took nearly two hours by Ann's best guess. She dialed the familiar number and a shaky voice answered.

"Lizzie?"

"Who is this?" Lizzie demanded. Ann could hear the quiver in her voice. Lizzie was scared, very scared. It must be worse than Ann had thought.

"Lizzie, it's Ann," she had forgotten that her voice had changed when the rest of her did. It was much lower, which was fitting for a six foot tall, scaly demon.

"Ann who?"

"Ann Melakh! You know, your best friend?'

"You don't sound like Ann. Who is this really? What are you playing at? Are you from the government?"

"I…wait, what? From the government? God, Lizzie you must be off your meds. I've been…sick. My voice hasn't come back to normal yet." That was reasonable. Close enough to the truth. There was a long pause as Lizzie considered this.

"Ann? Is that really you?"

"Yes it is. I swear to God. Or Brad Pitt. Whoever you prefer."

Lizzie was suddenly furious. "Where the hell have you been? Why did you wait so long to call? Do you know what I've been through trying to find you? Do you have any clue what kind of trouble you're in?"

Ann was taken aback by this. She didn't expect such a violent response. "I'm so sorry," Ann pleaded. "I've been really sick. I…"

"You know what, never mind. We need to get you off the street. Hell, they probably would be tracing your call right now if you had called anyone else but me," Lizzie interrupted.

Now Ann was really confused. "Who? What the hell are you talking about?" She was pretty sure the Fallen weren't going to tap any phone lines, even if they still had an interest in her.

"The Feds, Ann. They want you in connection with a murder. But I know who did it, Ann. I have proof."

"Murder? Lizzie, I have no idea what you're talking about. You mean at the hospital?"

"No, not at the hospital. Look, where are you? I'll come get you. We have a lot to talk about."

This was serious, unless Lizzie was on some sort of paranoid trip. Ann had no choice. "It's okay, I'll come to you. I have my own transportation now. But I have to warn you, this…disease. It causes a pretty harsh skin condition."

"Whatever, girl. Just get here and try not to be followed." Lizzie hung up.

"Oh, I don't think that will be a problem." Ann thought. She glanced around. No one was in sight. She shrugged off the large coat and scarf and spread her new wings. She took a deep breath, coming to terms with what she was about to do. Then, with a single leap into the air, she was swallowed by the night sky.

*****

Ann's heart filled with joy. Flying was beautiful. Her body seemed to hum with it. She was meant for this. For the first few moments, she forgot all her troubles and just enjoyed the freedom of it. Then she came to her senses and began working to find her way.

Navigating the way to Lizzie's place by air turned out to be a bit harder than expected. She followed the roads as best she could, dropping low from time to time to check street signs. Once she found Route 22 it became easier. She only had one minor incident on the way, when she didn't notice a billboard until she had actually flown though it. After a few moments of disentangling herself from its remains, she was off again.

Flying was amazing, landing not so much. Ann was aiming for Lizzie's front step, but instead smashed her mailbox to a pulp, bounced once and landed in a large bush. Luckily Lizzie's street was pretty empty, or she was sure someone would have called the police to report a woman with wings smashing into mailboxes.

"Ow," Ann said, picking a branch out of her mouth.

Now came the hard part. How would her oldest friend accept the new Ann? She could not imagine it going well. Ann wrapped her wings around her as best she could, giving the impression that she was draped in a white cloak. Hopefully she looked less threatening that way.

She took a deep breath and rang the bell, stepping out of view of the peephole. After a moment, Ann heard Lizzie's voice from beyond the door.

"Hello?"

"Lizzie, it's Ann."

"Why can't I see you?" Lizzie asked from behind the peephole. A fair question.

"Lizzie don't freak out. I look a little scary," Ann said. A little scary was putting it mildly.

"Oh don't be an idiot, it can't be that bad."

Ann could hear a chain scraping and multiple locks clicking free. The door was thrown open and Lizzie was there.

"Ann?"

Ann lifted one clawed hand and gave a short wave, trying to smile in the most nonthreatening way possible. "Umm, hi Lizzie."

Lizzie paused for a second to take in what she was seeing. Ann watched her eyes widen. Then, she screamed and slammed the door shut. Apparently it was that bad.

"Lizzie, wait!" She managed to get one clawed hand in and keep the door from shutting. "Ow!" Ann could still hear screaming from beyond the door. "It's Ann!" Lizzie threw her weight against the door, in an attempt to close it. She slammed it once, twice, three times against Ann's hand. "Would you please stop it, you crazy Korean bitch!" Ann gave the door a hard kick and it flew open, tossing Lizzie back. She stepped inside and closed the door behind her. Lizzie was still screaming, lying flat on her back. "Oh! Sorry about that, I don't know my own strength anymore." Ann reached down to help Lizzie up, but Lizzie started crawling backwards.

"Okay, okay, look: calm down, I won't hurt you. It's me, Ann. I know this looks bad."

Lizzie was still screaming. "Look, just stop. Relax." Suddenly Lizzie jumped back to her feet and sprinted towards the kitchen. Perhaps Ann needed to prove who she was.

"Lizzie, it's me, Ann Melakh. We met in 9th grade at Fanwood High. Umm, you sat behind me in math class. We had Mr. Matthews. You thought he was a warlock." Lizzie reappeared with a large frying pan. She charged back into the room, a snarl plastered on her face.

"Oh, hell."

The frying pan smashed across Ann's face. She fell backwards, stumbling on an umbrella stand. Lizzie followed up with another swing of the pan. It clanged off Ann's chin and she fell to the floor, her head ringing. She spoke quickly as she brought her arms over her face.

"You lost your virginity to Milton Mayfield, who was a complete loser, when you were 17."

Lizzie paused in mid-strike. "He was nice!" she roared.

"He was the head of the chess team. He actually wore a pocket protector. A real pocket protector!"

"He looked like Nick Carter from The Backstreet Boys!"

"Pssh. If Nick was 50 pounds overweight and wore glasses the size of bottle caps."

"You bitch!" Lizzie fumed and then paused. "Good God! It is you."

Tears blurred Ann's vision. "Yes, yes it is! Please don't hit me again!"

Lizzie stood back and took a hard look at her. "What the hell happened?"

"Something terrible. I need help Lizzie, help me." Tears flowing freely now, she put up her arms for a hug.

Lizzie dropped the pan but did not move towards her friend. "Um yeah, no. First I need to change my clothes. I think may have peed myself a bit."

Ann laughed.

# 8 - Going North

This isn't real. There's no way this could be real.

Catharine's mind snapped back to consciousness. It was very much like waking up to a bad dream. She remembered everything. She remembered how the horrible thing inside took her, changing her to fit its needs. Its power was incredible. She remembered its hunger, its uncontrollable urge to find...its mother? She remembered him, chasing her. The grinning man following her relentlessly through the city. He would not let her feed. He hurt her over and over again, driving her forward. There was a woman. Catharine almost got to taste her, but the grinning man stopped her. No! This isn't right. It's still in her head! It was so hungry, so desperate.

"God, save me," Catharine whispered. The man named Mike must have heard her and stepped into the back to talk to her. His voice was soft, calming.

"Catharine? How do you feel?" She liked Mike. She remembered wanting him so badly last night, but it hadn't been real. It was just the thing in her head, playing with her.

"I'm sorry," she mumbled weakly, "about last night, I mean. I'm not normally like that. I never go to bars and try to pick up men."

Mike smiled at her. "It's okay. Nothing to worry about. You weren't yourself, unless you're normally a cannibal."

She laughed weakly at that. "No. God no."

"Can I get you anything? Water maybe?" Mike offered.

"Can you get this thing out of me?" she pleaded. "It's horrible. I can feel it inside my head and it's so hungry!"

Mike placed a hand on her shoulder. "We're going to try. That's what we're here for."

Catharine was puzzled by that. "So you do this often?"

"Well, not me. No, this is my first time. But Miller has been doing this forever. Literally." Mike gestured to the sleeping man in the passenger seat. A wave of dread came over her. The grinning man. It took a second for Catharine to realize that it was not her fear but the creature inside of her's. If it was scared of him, then she couldn't be.

"What is he? What is this thing inside of me? Is it a demon?"

The man named Miller suddenly sat up. "Ah, you are back with us lass, good to see!" He sounded far too chipper. Catharine couldn't look at him. There was something about his eyes. "To answer your question, it is a demon spawn. A wee one."

"A wee one?" Catharine repeated.

"Yes, the weakest of the demon spawn."

"So are you some kind of priest then?"

Miller and Mike laughed at that together.

"No, he's not. Pretty far from it," Mike chuckled.

"No lass, although I have great respect for true men of the cloth, I am a hunter. *The* hunter, really. It's my job to keep creatures like the one inside of you in check."

"So you can get it out of me?"

"Well yes and no," Miller responded. "You are one of the Cursed now. There is no changing that. What I can do is free you from the Fallen."

Catharine was, once again, or maybe still, confused. "The Fallen?" she asked.

Mike stepped in. "This is a bit hard to believe, but just try. The Fallen are seven demons. Real life, black scaly demons that eat people or infect them with their children."

That was hard for Catharine to believe, even with the truth of it inside her. "Like fallen angels? Like Lucifer? God save me!" She made the sign of the cross in front of her. Satan had taken her and put his seed into her!

"Again, yes and no. The seven are much older than Christianity. Older than the Judaism," Miller tried to explain. "They are the origin of the demons both in religion and legend. Times and faiths change, but the seven have not. They still hunt you, I still hunt them."

"But you can free me from them? What does that mean?"

"I can take away their control over you. The demon will still be there, but it will have no power."

"But how?" Catharine asked.

"We must find the one that cursed you. We have to kill it," Miller said. His eyes lit up.

"Kill it?"

"The thing inside of you. It wants to find someone, yes?" Miller asked.

"Yes, I think…its mother? It knows where she is."

"Good. This is the plan: you lead me to it. I kill it and you do not go all furry and try to eat people again. Does that sound like a good deal?" Miller gave her a wink.

"I guess. This is a lot to take in," Catharine explained. Her head was swimming.

Mike spoke up again. "We understand it's all very hard to believe, but this is real and I think you just need to take a look at the new you to see it. If we don't kill this thing, it will take you over again."

"Tonight, most likely," Miller said.

"What?" Catharine and Mike said at the same time.

"Yes, it is resting now. But it will try to reach its master again as soon as it has the strength."

"God, no! I don't want to become that thing again!" Catharine tried to sit up, but fell back to the seat.

"Miller, there has to be something else we can do." Mike came to her defense.

"If it comes to it, we restrain her. We make sure she doesn't hurt anyone, and when it passes in the morning, we try again."

"Does it hurt when you…change?" Mike asked.

"No. At least I don't remember any pain." Catharine shook her head. "Hurts now, though. Feels like I've been stretched on a rack. But, but… I don't want it in me. It's terrifying."

"We'll do the best we can," Miller said, trying to sound reassuring. "The sooner we start moving, the sooner we arrive at our destination."

"Okay, what do I do?" Catharine asked.

"Focus on the thing inside of you. Try to get a sense of where it wants to go. I know it sounds strange, but you can do it."

She found that she could, and that it was easy. The creature was desperate to get to its mother. "North," she said, without a doubt in her mind. "It wants to go north."

"North it is then!" Miller said. "Well done, lass."

Catharine pulled the blanket tighter and again noticed her naked body. "Could I get some clothes?"

Soon Mike found her some clothes in the gift shop at the rest stop. Catharine was soon wearing a hugely oversized "I love New York" sweatshirt and a pair of "Empire State" shorts. It was an improvement, but just barely. Worse, Mike had to help her dress. She still couldn't even sit up. He was obviously uncomfortable with the whole thing, which Catharine would have found cute if she wasn't about to die of embarrassment. The whole day had a bizarre feel to it. Her body wasn't hers anymore. It felt stretched and misshapen, and Catharine felt like Mike was helping someone else get dressed and she was being forced to watch.

Mike pulled her up into a sitting position and gave her some water and a stick of string cheese. Then they headed north. It was odd, not knowing exactly where they were going. She just knew it was north. The ride was quiet. Miller tried to start a few conversations but Mike ignored him. There was an odd tension between the two, at least on Mike's side. Nothing seemed to bother Miller.

"This cheese is fantastic," Miller said, chomping down on his own string cheese. "What kind is it?"

"Fake," responded Mike.

After about two and a half hours of driving, the feeling in her changed.

"Slow down. It's…I think we're getting close," she said.

Mike obeyed. "I'll take the next exit."

They exited the thruway and came to a T-junction. Mike stopped and looked back to her.

"Left."

He complied, and continued following her directions for another 20 minutes. The way was so clear to her. It was beyond strange. At last, she shouted, "There! It's in there."

Mike pulled over. They were in front of a large office building. A small security booth and gate blocked the entrance.

"Wow. Nice digs for a demon on the run," Mike pointed out.

Miller rubbed his chin. "Yes."

"Can you see anything?" Mike asked.

"No, not at all. Catharine, sweet lady, are you positive that this is the place?"

"Yes, I'm sure. It can sense her," Catharine answered. She was certain.

"Alright then, here is the plan. We find someplace to get a good meal and rest until sundown. Mike can drop me off here then and keep an eye on you. Hopefully I can dispose of the Fallen before your time comes." Catharine shivered at the words 'your time.'

"Alright. I'm starving anyway. Let's go," Mike said, pulling the van back onto the road.

None of them noticed the security camera tracking them as they sped away.

# 9 - Lab Time

“This seems wrong somehow,” Dr. Rebecca Lawton said, as she looked through the glass over to the young woman strapped to the bench in the next room. She was naked except for several wires running into her forehead that administered an electrical shock every 15 minutes.

“Trust me, Doctor. She isn’t human and if she managed to get in here with you, you would be dead in seconds,” the man named Smith said. He was not a large man, but had an imposing presence. It may have been the wicked scar that ran up his cheek, but Lawton attributed it to something else, something much meaner.

“I’ve seen the x-rays and the sonogram, but is this constant torture necessary?”

“Absolutely, the electrical current keeps her weak. Without it, she would regain her strength and we would be unable to contain her.”

“Perhaps sedation might work?” Lawton offered.

“I can’t interrogate a sleeping captive.” Smith gave her a stern look. “Once we determine which of the Fallen she is, we can set up a more permanent holding cell. In fact, I think we should have another little chat right now.” Smith made a move toward the door to the lab. “Start the recording,” he ordered, walking into the next room.

“Yes sir.” Lawton always obeyed her boss. Although she did not care for the man, she was being paid well, and that was enough. Despite herself, she found this subject incredibly interesting. She was not sure what the “Fallen” were, exactly, but this woman could help bring the science of biology forward by years.

Smith began talking to the subject.

“Hello again, Mary,” he said, as if just running into her at church or the grocery store. Mary screamed once as a timer went off and electricity ripped through her body. For a second she thrashed violently against the bindings. Then, panting, she spoke.

“Child, I will kill you for this.”

“You might as well get in line. What makes you think you’ll get out of here?” Mary pulled against the restraints, snarling at him. She shouted at him in anger but Lawton did not understand the words. She wasn’t even sure what language they were in. Smith didn’t seem concerned.

“I told you I could make this more comfortable for you. You just need to tell me your name.”

“I have told you time and time again. My name is Mary Bodin. I live in Newark, New Jersey and I’m a nurse at College Hospital.”

“Lawton, could you please shock her again?” Smith called back to the control room. Lawton obeyed, wincing at the resulting screams. "Not that name, Mary. We know that name. We know Mary Bodin is no longer with us. We know her husband of four years, Jack Bodin, was found, a white desiccated corpse."

"I was hungry. He tasted wonderful." Mary smiled.

"You know what I am and I know what you are. You are one of the Fallen. One of the original storm demons. Tell me your name. Show me your face and I can make this so much better for you."

"Of course, I also know what you are. Who made you?"

"I was Lilith's son."

Lilith's son? What did that mean?

"Even my sister's children have betrayed us," Mary said weakly.

"So I know you are not Lilith. I know you are not Asmodai, certainly." Smith paced around the lab.

"Asmodai? Yes, of course, my brother's true name." Mary mulled over the information as if it was new to her. "Tell me the other names. Tell me now."

Smith was taken aback. "You mean to tell me you don't remember?"

"Tell me!" Mary pleaded.

"How could you not know who you are?" Smith seemed to be confused. He was backing away from Mary, moving toward the exit.

Mary roared, "Tell me! Tell me the names! I must remember my name!"

Smith walked out of the room and approached Lawton. "This is strange. Something is wrong here." Smith seemed to be talking to himself, so she didn't reply. Instead, she stared at the strange captive woman.

A few moments later, Smith's cell phone rang.

"Smith," he announced into the phone. 'Hello' was far too nice for him, apparently. "Mr. Drake. How goes your hunting party? Samson's where? Outside this building?" Smith was grinning. "I think we're going to have to ask him what he's doing here." Smith hung up the phone. "Well, well, Mr. Mike Samson, why are you up here visiting?" To Lawton he said, "I have to step out. Keep an eye on her, but for God's sake don't go in there." Lawton could still hear Mary screaming in fury.

"My name! Tell me my name!"

There was no chance Lawton was going anywhere near that.

*****

Sometime later, Lawton was busy working her way through this month's issue of Games magazine. She hadn't realized that her job would involve so much waiting. Smith had been gone for a good hour already and she wasn't sure what to do next. Mary had been muttering to herself for a long time, a sound broken only by her screams every fifteen minutes when the timer kicked off.

"The first is the South Wind…" Mary said, suddenly loud enough for Lawton to make out. Lawton wasn't sure what to do. Was Mary talking to her? She had hardly said a word since Smith left. It was better to be safe than sorry. She hit the intercom.

"Ed, can you page Smith? The subject is talking again."

"The second is a dragon with mouth agape…" Mary said, louder this time.

"Sorry Dr. Lawton, he hasn't returned."

"The third is a grim leopard!" Mary was shouting now.

"Umm, could you maybe get some security in here then?" Lawton requested.

"Can do." Lawton switched channels on the intercom so that she could talk to Mary.

"Mary?" Lawton did not know what say.

"The fourth is a terrible serpent!" Mary shouted in response.

Two large men entered the room with Lawson. "She's talking, well shouting. I think she may be trying something."

The two men stared at the captured woman. "She seems pretty secure to me."

"The fifth is a furious beast!" Mary continued. "The sixth is a rampant against god and king."

Lawton was torn. Should she shock her again? Or was this what Smith wanted? "Just be ready. She isn't human."

"The seventh is an evil windstorm, that none can withstand!"

"What the hell does that mean?" one of the men asked.

"The wind! The wind! I know my name." Mary was screaming again. "I know my name!" Her chest was suddenly expanding, the flesh tearing away to reveal something black just beneath the skin.

"What the hell?" Lawton slammed the button down for the electric shock. This time, though, Mary's scream seemed to explode from her with terrific force. The glass between the lab and Lawton's room suddenly shattered and she was tossed across the room. The lights flickered and died, and there was silence.

For a moment, Lawton couldn't hear anything. Then she made out Mary's voice, a whisper over the static.

"Gallu. My name is Gallu," Mary was in the room with them, easily picking up a security guard with one arm, "and I am hungry!"

A long, black tentacle seemed to leap from her mouth, wrapping itself around the body of the guard. He turned white and began to shrivel. He didn't scream, only letting out a horrible gurgle. In a moment, the tentacle retracted and the man's limp body dropped to the ground.

"Oh God! I need to get out of here!" Lawton thought. She tried to stand but the world swirled around her and she collapsed to the floor. Changing tactics, she crawled towards the door. Blood was getting in her eyes. She must have been sliced up pretty badly when the window exploded.

She found the still, dead body of the other man, a large shard of glass jutting from one eye. Lawton whimpered, but fear kept her moving. It was just a few feet from the door now.

Mary was coughing now. Something black and slimy poured out of her mouth and pooled on the floor. Lawton tried to ignore this, reaching the door and pulling herself up. She turned the handle and yanked, but the door only opened an inch.

"No, no! Open!" she screamed, as something hit her from behind, knocking her to the ground. Mary was above her. Her flesh was tearing off as she grew and changed into something else.

"Stay for a moment, child. I have need of you." Lawton saw something else move. The black sludge was sliding across the floor, straight at her.

Lawton managed a scream of her own as the sludge covered her face.

"Welcome to the family, little one."

# 10 - The Monster in the Mirror

Dressed in clean clothes, Lizzie carefully stepped out of her bedroom. She had not put away the pan. Okay, so it was Ann, it had to be. No one else knew what she knew, and Lizzie was very tight with her secrets. But what had happened to her? It seemed impossible.

She went back to the front door but Ann wasn't there. A trail of black blood led away from the door into the house. She was so not cleaning that up. From the kitchen she heard loud slurping noises. Holding her trusty frying pan closer, she headed in that direction.

"Ann?" she called out weakly. The refrigerator door was open and the big white monster that had been her best friend was rummaging through it. She had an orange in her mouth and was loudly sucking on it while trying to find something else to eat. The thing was completely covered in scales, at least from what Lizzie could see. She couldn't account for what was under the ripped and filthy jeans that had managed to cling to Ann's waist. Ann was tall and still skinny as a rail but on her back, a set of leathery wings twitched restlessly.

"Ann?" Lizzie repeated. The demon spun to look at her.

"Lizzie, hi! Just getting something to eat. I'm starving. Flying really takes it out of me." Her large white claws held a microwave dinner. "You don't mind, right?"

"Umm, flying?" Lizzie had to ask.

"Yeah. Look." Ann's wings stretched out and then folded neatly behind her back. "I'm like the bumblebee of the freak world. I shouldn't really be able to, but I fly just fine."

Lizzie noted that her hands were shaking, slightly, the first sign of an approaching panic attack. "What the hell happened? How is that even possible?"

"Would you believe I was bitten by a radioactive flying lizard?" Ann smiled at her own joke. It was a frightening smile, full of needle-like teeth pointing in all directions.

Lizzie stepped back. "I…please don't do that again," she pleaded.

"Sorry. Look, I know I look freaky, but it's me." Ann pointed one clawed finger at her white scaly chest. "Remember when I said I was attacked by a demon? Well, apparently it's contagious."

"What? Are you exposing me too?" Lizzie started to quake.

"No, no, not like that. Sorry, poor choice of words. Calm down, you're getting yourself worked up. Did you take your meds today?"

Tears were running down Lizzie's face. She couldn't help it. This was too much. "Calm down? Have you seen yourself? You're a monster.

A real-life horror show! You expect that not to bother me?"

"Hey, now. Words hurt, you know."

"I'll show you hurt. You left me hanging for two weeks! I thought you were dead. Dead, Ann! And then you show up at my house looking like this. God, I even talked to your mom about it." Lizzie was having problems breathing, she was so mad.

"I'm sorry. You told me I had to come. I wasn't going to until I learned how to…look normal again." The world began to spin and Lizzie fell to her knees. "Just be calm. Try and stay calm." Ann ran out of the room. Lizzie could hear her shuffling through things as she collapsed to the ground.

"Hold on Lizzie. Hold on." Ann was back now with some water and a claw full of pills. She helped Lizzie get the meds down and then wrapped her arms around her friend, hugging her until the shaking stopped. Lizzie felt the attack passing. She registered that Ann was crying. The big scaly monster was crying.

"I'm sorry," Lizzie said softly. "It was just too much. This can't be fun for you either."

Ann sniffed. "Well it hasn't been sunshine and lollipops, no. God, I'm sorry too. I shouldn't have come. I knew you couldn't handle this. I mean, who could? I can't and I'm living this." Ann's voice was soft. "You sounded so desperate on the phone and to be honest…I missed you."

Lizzie smiled at that.

"Well, girl, who wouldn't? I mean, I am awesome!" She turned in Ann's arms and gave her friend a slightly awkward hug. She made sure to stay clear of the teeth. She still wasn't sure about that mouth. Ann laughed and, when they separated, helped Lizzie get to her feet. "Thanks. So this is the new you? I love what you've done with your hair. Bald is badass," Lizzie said.

"Hah, thanks. I think."

"Why didn't you just call before? What took you so long?"

Somehow Ann's pale, white face managed to darken. "It was hard at first, after this," Ann tapped her forehead. "I hardly remember the last two weeks. It took me…some time to get used to the new me. And it hurt, a lot. But someone found me who I guess knows how to deal with this sort of thing. He reminded me that I was human and gave me hope."

"Sounds like a nice guy," Lizzie said.

"Well no, not really. He's a vampire. Creeped me out all the time, but I think he meant well. "

"A what?" Lizzie asked.

"A vamp… you know what, never mind. It's a long story."

"Tell me everything."

"Alright, but I'm telling you again, it's a tough one for me to believe and I was there," Ann said, putting some food into the microwave oven.

"I think after seeing this," Lizzie flicked at a scale on Ann's shoulder, "I'll believe a lot."

*****

Ann told Lizzie everything that happened since they had last seen each other. She explained about the Fallen, how she'd met an immortal man named Joseph Miller and a cute cop by the name of Mike Samson. She explained how her ex-boyfriend Keith and several others in the hospital had been taken over by demons. She explained how she and her new friends had escaped a pack of werewolves and how, once they had finally made it out of the hospital, had faced down a giant fire-breathing snake that had once been Keith. Ann's eyes teared up briefly while she described her rooftop chat, her transformation, and her attempt to kill herself. Finally, she explained how she had been found by Abraham and later flown to Lizzie's house.

"Wow," Lizzie said. "That's really something out of a bad horror novel, or one of those Saturday night movies on the Sci-Fi channel."

"God no! It's not that bad!" Ann laughed.

"So these Fallen demon thingies, why haven't I heard of them before? Seems like they would be hard to miss."

"Apparently they only show up every few hundred years. We were due." Ann shrugged as she answered.

Lizzie got up from the chair she had sat in while listening to Ann's tale of woe. "Well, I also have a story for you. This one is just a tad less freaky, but there was a reason why I insisted you come. I almost forgot with all this crazy demon shit."

"Oh yeah, what's the deal? You said something about the government?" Ann asked.

"I got a visit from this woman looking for you a few days back, name of Dupré. That ring any bells?"

It did sound familiar. Where had she heard it? "Vaguely. Give me a minute to place it."

"Anyway, she was looking for you in relation to a murder case."

"Who was murdered? And why me?" Ann asked.

Lizzie swallowed hard. "There was a murder, two really, at your lab. The same day you disappeared. I'm sorry. One was Wen, and I'm not sure who the other one was."

Ann was dumbstruck. Wen was such a good guy. He had a wife and a little girl. His only annoying trait was that he was too smart and too damn nice. Who would want to kill him? "God no, poor Wen."

Lizzie seemed to have more to say but paused, waiting for Ann to handle this new information. Finally, Ann asked, "Why? Do they have any leads on who did it?"

"They, being the police, do not have a clue. I checked. They are trying to find a janitor who is also on the missing persons list, by the way. But I know who did it." Lizzie started pacing.

"Okay, who?"

"Dupré."

"What? That doesn't make sense. Why would the person investigating the murder be the one who did it? That's crazy talk." Ann spun one clawed finger in a circle around her ear.

"She isn't investigating anything. That's not even her job. She's apparently some sort of scientist."

Ann slapped a hand to the side of her face. "Of course, Dr. Dupré! I was doing some research for Dr. Conners on a sample she'd sent. I remember her now. I mean, I never met her in person, but Conners really…" She paused. "Was he the other victim?"

"Maybe. The police aren't saying much. But Ann, she was looking for you. Not because she thought you had committed the murders. She knew you hadn't. You must have something she wants."

"I don't have anything. I mean, I just barely have pants!"

"Yeah, speaking of that, we have to do something. You've been walking around my house topless for too long. That's just not right." Lizzie grinned.

"Lizzie, it's not like I have boobs any more, and you might have noticed these giant wings. I can't just throw a sweatshirt on."

"Psssh, whatever. You're still a girl. We need to rebuild your wardrobe."

"Anyway," Ann said, "back on topic, I don't have anything this Dupré woman would want. She sent us a sample, just some dumb flower. Which was still in the lab, last I was there."

Lizzie was pacing again. "Okay, how about this then? What if she was looking for you to kill you?"

"Kill me? Why?"

"I don't know. Maybe you know something. Wait a tick, what if she was here to kill me?" Lizzie went pale.

"Oh come on, it's not always about you. Geez."

"No seriously. I remember it clearly. She said something about how sorry she was and what a waste it was going to be. She started to pull something out of her coat but Takahashi came in and interrupted just in time."

"Why the hell would she want to kill you?"

Lizzie shrugged. "Again, I am pretty awesome."

"Who's Takahashi?"

"FBI agent, works with Dupré. Cute guy. And tall. I would totally do him."

"You? A Fed? He must be pretty damned gorgeous," Ann mocked.

"Well, I would make him leave his job first. Anyway, I get the impression he's on our side and Dupré's working alone."

"And now you trust a Fed. You're like a whole new person."

"It's just an impression. This, coming from the girl who shows up at my door with scales and wings?"

"Okay, okay! So how do you know Dupré did it?"

"I have it on tape."

"Where the hell did you get that?" Ann asked, her voice full of suspicion.

Lizzie gave her a wicked smile. "I hacked into the FBI's network and found it."

"You what? Jesus, Lizzie, you could go to jail for that kinda shit. Like for a long, long time. And jail wouldn't be good for you. What were you thinking?"

"I could handle solitary just fine. I would just need to knife a few people with sharpened plastic spoons or something."

"Yeah, that's a good plan. What the hell, Lizzie?"

"I was looking for information on you. And I didn't get caught, so stop being my mom."

"I could never be your mom. Now *she* was a demon from hell."

"Hah, yes. Yes she was." Lizzie stopped for a moment, remembering her mother. "Look, I can show you the video."

Ann waved a dismissive hand at Lizzie. "No, I believe you. I don't think I want to see that. Can we take the video to the police?"

"Yeah, and try and explain where we got it," Lizzie huffed.

Ann seemed to be thinking. "I wonder if this is related to the Fallen."

"It's possible, I guess. There's more stuff coming. I have a friend helping me. He said he had another video."

"Well, that's a start. Obviously I'm going to have to talk to this Dupré lady," Ann said.

"And get your head blown off too? Don't tell me you're bulletproof."

"No, probably not," Ann said. "But what else can I do?"

"Can't you eat her soul or something?"

"Yes, maybe with a balsamic emulsion. No, of course I can't eat her soul, you idiot!" Ann roared.

"Well come on, you look like something out of a cheap Japanese anime. You must have some perks. I mean, besides the flying thing."

"I'm not some sorta superhero. I'm not going to put on a crazy outfit, fight crime, and call myself Demon Grrrl. This is real life."

"Okay fine, you just look like a freak, no powers, that's cool. You don't have to be bitter about it."

"Hey, once again, words hurt. Positive remarks only. Besides, I'm pretty strong."

"Oh, now we're talking. Super strength. What else?"

"God, you're like a five-year-old." She paused. "I can see things. I can tell if someone has been cursed. Or infected. However you want to put it."

"Hmm. Well, I guess that could be useful. You know what? We need to Wiki you."

"Umm, what? Shouldn't we talk about this murder thing?" Ann pointed out.

"Wiki! It's a free online encyclopedia. It's got everything. Come on." Lizzie took off to her computer.

"I know what it is, but I don't see how this is going to help." Ann said entering the office.

"Let's look up 'Fallen.' Okay. I got an Evanescence album and, oh here we go, fallen angels." Lizzie clicked on a link. "Hmmm. Less than useful."

"Try 'Lilith'," Ann suggested.

"Bingo! Wow, a lot here. Is this one of the Fallen?"

Ann nodded. "She's me."

"Wait, what?" Lizzie turned to her, baffled.

"Well, not me. The one that tried to take me over, but died somehow and I got better. Well, sort of better." Ann looked down at her scaled hands.

"So you're one of the Fallen then. Not just cursed by them."

"I was, but not anymore. I'm retired."

"Okay, that's disturbing." Lizzie shook her head. "You have quite the history." She started to read the web page. "Lilith is a female Mesopotamian storm demon associated with wind, and thought to be a bearer of disease, illness, and death." She turned to face Ann. "Wow. You go, girl."

"Stop, please. This isn't funny," Ann pleaded.

"All right, sorry, you're right. Look though, she's even listed in the Bible. The Bible! This is some serious shit."

"And the Dead Sea Scrolls… Wow, she did get around," Ann agreed.

"What are the Dead Sea Scrolls?" Lizzie asked.

"Very, very old religious documents. I think they're one of the oldest copies of the Hebrew bible ever found, but there's older stuff in them as well."

"Sounds boring," Lizzie decided.

"Look, I don't know how this is helping."

"Ah, come on. We can learn something from this. We know she exists, at least in some ancient scrolls. It's not something some crazy person made up."

"True." Ann sighed. "Try Asmodai." They briefly discussed how to spell 'Asmodai' before Lizzie worked it out.

"Okay, wow. The king of demons. Said to be one of the princes of hell and represents one of the seven deadly sins. Oh nice, he represents lust. That's the best one."

"This is creeping me out. We need to stop this." Ann got up and walked away.

"Did you meet Asmodai?" Lizzie asked.

"Yeah, although he went by the name of Keith."

"Keith? That's a lame demon name. I mean, he might as well call himself Bob," Lizzie said. "Wait…not *your* Keith?"

"Yes, my Keith."

"Damn, your ex is the mythological representation of lust? And you said he would never cheat on you."

"Lizzie! Enough!" Ann screamed. "Just stop, okay?" Tears were streaming down her face again.

"Ah, geez, girl. I was just teasing. It's what we do, we go back and forth. It's...I'm sorry," Lizzie apologized.

"Yeah, whatever. I'm going to go in the other room for a while. Maybe watch some TV. I need to work out what to do about this Dupré thing and this isn't helping." Ann left and made her way to the living room. There were more tears coming but she was fighting them. Instead of breaking down, she flipped on the TV.

*****

Lizzie watched Ann storm off. She should have known better. She really had pushed her too far. Ann had been through a lot, but it was good to know that there was some record of all this craziness, even if it was ancient myth. She decided to apologize to her friend.

Her PC suddenly buzzed. "You've got mail."

Lizzie opened Crash's latest email. This time the subject was "Wang Up," from a company called worthitwatches.org. The message was simple.

The second one at last. Remember, you owe me big for this.

Ann could wait a minute. Lizzie downloaded the video. It took less than thirty seconds.

"Now, Crash, let's see what you found this time." Lizzie started the video.

*****

Ann heard Lizzie scream and rushed back into the room.

"What? What's wrong?"

Lizzie was standing at the farthest spot in the room from the computer. "Shit! SHIT!" Lizzie was shouting and pointing at her computer. The screen showed a video that had reached its end. It showed static. "Just hit play." Ann very carefully pushed the mouse over to the play button and clicked. Her new hands made it tricky.

The video showed Ann's lab. There was Ann's back. Had her butt really been that big? She was opening a box of some sort. It was odd. She had no memory of this. Video Ann opened the box and removed a flower, the lily she had been researching. She stared at it for some time. There was something else too, something black like tar, and it was pouring out of the box. On screen, Ann didn't see it as it pooled on her desk and then made a beeline for her. It leapt from the desk to her face and she saw it. She couldn't see anything else. There was no noise, but you could tell she was screaming, trying to tear the tar from her face. The stuff was trying to force its way in her mouth and through her nose. There was even a tiny stream trying to work itself into one ear. Video Ann dropped to the floor, the screen now only showing her feet, which were kicking in desperation. A man was there, dressed in grey overalls, suddenly beside her. The janitor? He was bending over, trying to help. Then he was struck with something and fell out of frame. There was a brief shot of Ann's now-still legs, before they too slid out of view. For a moment, there was nothing. Suddenly Video Ann's face appeared close up. Her eyes were filled with the inky black of the Cursed. And now there was sound, just one sentence, full of hate.

"Dupré! I'm coming for you!"

Then nothing but static.

Ann jumped back from the computer screen, the sudden voice making the scales on the back of her neck stand up on end. That was her voice! That was her! Ann stared at Lizzie, who stared back. Finally Lizzie spoke.

"I think we found the connection."

Ann nodded. The image of her own face with those dead black eyes had chilled her to the bone, if she still had bones. She wasn't sure how demon biology worked.

"Okay, so Dupré wants to kill me because she thinks I'm one of the Fallen. Maybe that's why she killed Wen. She had no idea who opened the package," Ann said, collapsing into a beanbag chair.

"Maybe," Lizzie agreed. "But she doesn't know you got better."

"But why send the package in the first place? And how did she get whatever that black stuff was?"

"I don't know. Maybe she really is evil personified," Lizzie offered.

"What?"

"Just something someone said. At the time I thought he was kidding, but now I don't know." Lizzie reclaimed her office chair.

"Damn, Lizzie. What the hell am I going to do?"

There was silence for a while. Then, Lizzie offered, "Maybe it would be best to hide for a while. Go underground."

"Wait! Of course. I know someone who could help. He's the cop who was in the hospital with me. He knows who the Fallen are." Ann stood and started going through her ragged jean pockets. "If I still have the damn, ah!" She pulled out a destroyed business card. "Mike Samson. Toss me your phone." Lizzie passed her the phone.

Very carefully, Ann dialed. The claws for hands thing was getting annoying. The phone rang three times, and then went to voicemail.

"Hi. This is Mike Samson. You know what to do," the recorded message said. She waited for the beep.

"Hi Mike, it's Ann. Hopefully you're okay. Quick news flash: I'm not dead. Hope you can say the same. You weren't looking so hot when I last saw you. Of course, I'm not looking so hot now. Look, I have some new information on the Fallen and a little situation that maybe you could help with. Call me back." She gave Lizzie's number. Hanging up, she tossed the phone back to Lizzie. "Well, that's that. I guess for now we just wait for."

"Sounds like a plan," Lizzie agreed.

It was late enough that even Ann, who had been sleeping through the daylight for the past few weeks, was considering rest, but both of them were far too worked up to sleep. So Ann took a shower, the most wonderfully hot shower of her life. She hadn't known how dirty she was. Even with the scales and claws, the hot water and soap did wonders for her, making her feel almost human.

When she got out, Lizzie handed her a new pair of sweatpants and a shirt with no back that you would usually wear out dancing. The ties in the back didn't work, but they extended them with some old shoelaces.

"Where the hell did you get this?" Ann asked.

"You left it here like a year ago. It shows a lot more belly now, but it's better than nothing."

"I feel ridiculous."

"Just roll with it, honey. I'll see about getting you something else tomorrow."

They took a seat in the living room and watched an episode of

Seinfeld. The normality of it was refreshing. Once the show went off, the news came on. The lead news story was another body found in connection with the "Angel" murders.

"I'm sorry, the Angel murders? That may be the lamest name for a series of murders I've ever heard," Ann said.

"Yeah, I second that. Messed-up case, though. You should see the bodies popping up all over Newark. All white and skinny."

Ann sat up. "Wait. What?" Again, the image of Bill's body forced its way into Ann's head, along with the dog that Abraham had eaten for 'lunch.'

"Yeah, they aren't really releasing any pictures, but I've caught a few on the net. They're all shriveled up like…"

"Like someone sucked the life out of them?" Ann offered.

"Well I guess. I never thought about it that way. Hey, you think it's related to your demons?"

"No, I think it's related to a vampire."

"Oh come on, don't start with that. Oh wait, yeah, you said those were real too."

"Yeah, and I happen to know one that's been living in Newark for at least the last month."

"Oh shit. Really?"

"Abraham."

Could it really be him? Sure, he was creepy, but he had been helping her. There could be another vampire out there. Ann's mind flashed back to her ex-friend, now blood sucking fiend, Cynthia. What had happened to her at the College Hospital? She had to know the truth. Ann stood up.

"I have to find him, talk to him."

"What? Now?" Lizzie followed Ann to the front door.

"Yes, now. If he is killing people, maybe I can stop him. If not, maybe he can help me find out who is."

"You? Why you? Haven't you been through enough already?" Lizzie asked. There was anger in her voice.

"Because people are dying." Ann let the statement trail off. She wasn't sure where she was going with this. She opened the door and stepped outside.

"Dupré is still out there! She's going to try and kill you!" Ann turned to her friend. Lizzie's face was red with anger.

"She has to find me first." She spread her wings and bent her knees.

"How will you find him?" Lizzie shouted.

Ann stopped at that. "I don't know, but I know where to start looking."

Lizzie ran to her and grabbed her arm. "Don't go tonight. You can't just go flying around town. Someone is going to see. You'll end up in a lab someplace, being cut to pieces. Stay here. Tomorrow I'll drive you. We can look for him together."

Ann hated to admit it, but Lizzie was right. Abraham had always been the one to find her, and only during the day. It was really exactly the opposite of how you would think a vampire would work.

"You want to go outside your big safe house and hunt a vampire with me?"

"Ah well," Lizzie gave her a shy smile, "I was hoping I could just stay in the car."

*****

John Takahashi sat at his new desk, tapping the top of his autographed John Wayne photo. The office was only a week old and he was not completely moved in, but he had been sure the important things had made it in first. The photo of his wife and two girls held down one corner and the Duke held down the other. He liked the new desk, but wasn't so happy with the rest of the job.

"Sir?" a voice asked. John looked up to see one of the techs from the Newark office in his doorway.

"Yes?" he replied, replacing the photo and straightening up in his chair. The tech, whose name was Billy or Brian or something, looked nervous. John felt the same way. Billy or Brian or something had been helping set up computers for the new satellite office that had started up over at Dupré's lab two weeks ago.

"We have a problem," the man announced.

John knew the FBI had many problems, but he wasn't about to share that. Instead he simply raised an eyebrow.

"I've been going through the doctor's computer systems, trying to get them to sync with the home office. The security is terrible. I can't honestly believe anyone these days would use an unsecured Wi-Fi network."

"Yes well, Dr. Dupré is a bit behind the technology curve in some ways. Was there any evidence of an intrusion?"

"It looks like it, sir, and it looks like someone has been poking around the network. I've shut them down now, but I'm still going over what they may have accessed."

John didn't need this. He had ancient demons and reanimated corpses already on his plate. This was too…well, too real for him.

"Any leads on who might behind it?" John asked.

A broad grin appeared on the tech's face.

"Definitely. Pretty obvious really." He opened a laptop he had been carrying under one arm and showed John the screen. Security footage showed a silver Honda Civic sitting in the empty parking lot next to the building. John had walked past that same Honda Civic just days earlier.

"Very interesting. Good work. I'll take it from here," John said, dismissing the tech. He again picked up the picture of John Wayne, an idea forming in his head.

"You already know who it is?" the tech said, looking a little disappointed.

"Oh yes."

Giant lizard, you've done a very bad thing. John was barely able to suppress a smile.

## 11 - Because Timing is Everything

Joseph Miller was having quite a good day. It had started early, chasing down one of the Cursed. Though it had been a long run through the city, it had felt good to be back on the hunt. He had met a pleasant woman, who, although horribly cursed and likely turn into a terrible monster at some point soon, was quite brave and likeable. She also seemed to have taken to his good friend Mr. Samson, and while Miller admitted that he himself needed a good woman - it had been over a hundred years after all –- but Mike Samson needed to get laid more than anyone Miller had met in a very long time. Miller was fine with letting his friend take this one, once they had stopped her from transforming into a rampaging beast, of course. That sort of thing had not stopped Miller before, but Mike was a novice, and it was best to take such things slow.

Miller was also quite pleased about being on the trail of one of the Fallen. After a quick rest at the fine inn Mike had found, they would once again strike out into the evening and hopefully fell one of those beasts.

"All checked in," Mike stated, returning to the van.

"It looks lovely," Miller said, giving it a glance out the window. "A fine establishment. Do they serve spirits?"

"Yes, there's a bar, Miller," Mike said with a sigh.

"A fine establishment indeed!"

"Catharine, can you walk?" Mike asked, turning to the woman in the backseat.

"I can try."

"We will assist, my fair lady. Or at least, my brave assistant will. That is what an assistant does, after all. He assists," Miller said, popping open the van's door. The truth was, of course, that he was making Catharine very nervous. He had scared her quite a bit when he had forced her to remember the thing inside of her. That would not be an enjoyable experience for anyone. So Miller gave the woman some space and was as polite as possible, which had not stopped Mike from giving him an annoyed look. Now that he thought about it, Mike had seemed irritated with him in general that day. Perhaps he needed more sleep.

Miller grabbed the small bag that Mike had prepared and opened the door for the couple. Catharine could walk, but had to lean hard on Mike for support.

"I got some more Motrin for you. It should help," Mike said as he passed Miller.

"Thanks," Catharine replied through gritted teeth. Miller had always been told that the transformation process was not actually painful, perhaps because the demon spawn was in control at the time, but the next day was typically excruciating. Bodies did not like being reshaped.

Miller rushed past them to the elevator and hit the 'up' arrow.

"Sixth floor, Miller," Mike informed him. Miller hit all of the buttons. He truly enjoyed seeing them light up. "Miller!" Mike complained, not saying much more. Yes, Mike was clearly out of sorts.

They found their room and helped Catharine into one of the beds. It was a nice room, with two beds, a couch, a TV, and a small porch that overlooked a tiny pool. Miller slid the glass doors open to investigate the view. Almost instantly, Catharine fell asleep. Mike took off his shoes and got into the other bed, leaving Miller with the small couch. He had no intention of sleeping anymore, and so didn't complain. He instead began figuring out how the television worked, once he had returned from the porch.

"Miller, I have a question for you."

"Of course lad, fire away," Miller said. No, it wasn't this button. Perhaps the large orange one that said 'power'?

"Do you know someone by the name of Andres Soliz?" he asked. The TV snapped to life.

"Ah ha!" Miller shouted in triumph. He was getting the hang of this. There was a pretty picture of a windmill and some writing that said, 'Welcome to the Holiday Inn.'

"Miller?"

"Ah, no, it does not ding any bells…wait, was he in Spain in the 1800s?"

"It's 'ring.' You know what? Never mind. No, he was in Newark just about a month ago. Seems he disappeared about the time you showed up."

There seemed to be something about adult entertainment. Well, he was an adult looking for entertainment. Miller hit the green button. "Do you think his disappearance was related to the Fallen?" Miller asked, only half paying attention.

"No, at least I don't think so. You see, he's wanted for murder."

"Murder? Despicable act. I do try to avoid it anytime I possibly can," Miller put in. What on earth was a MILF and why would one want to see hot ones?

"Well here's the thing. You see…" Mike's cell phone cut him off. "Hold on, it's Sam."

"Ah. Say hi to the boy for me. Tell him I'll have his father home tomorrow."

Underage and wet. Perhaps this was a film about wine? Mike talked with Sam for some time, asking about school and his grandparents. Mike promised to be home tomorrow and said that he would take Sam out for a movie and ice cream. Miller pushed through the menus. This did not seem very entertaining, especially for adults.

"Miller, Sam wants to talk to you." Mike handed the phone over. Miller thought phones were perhaps the most amazingly useful thing he had ever seen. "And no Pay-Per-View." Mike snatched the remote away.

"Hello, lad!" Miller said.

"Mr. Miller, I saw a new Power Rangers today," Sam's small voice squeaked out.

"Ah, I missed it? I do always enjoy that drama."

"I recorded it for you. I think you'll like it. The white ranger has a new zoid."

"Excellent, I do enjoy a fine zoid. We shall enjoy when I return and partake in some Peps." He enjoyed the boy's company. Sam reminded him of one of his sons, many years ago. He missed his children, but pushed the memory away, not wanting to spoil his mood.

"That's Pepsi, Mr. Miller."

"Ah, of course lad, you would know. Say, since I have you here, what is a MILF?" Miller found the answer slightly shocking. "Oh, well perhaps your father is right about this 'HBO.' Goodbye for now."

"Bye, Mr. Miller." Sam hung up. Miller passed the phone back to Mike, who had apparently not been listening. The phone let out a chime.

"Well that's timing. Got another call while we were talking to Sam," Mike put in. The TV was now showing monkeys. Miller loved monkeys. "Holy shit! It's Ann."

"Ann who?" Miller asked, distracted by the monkeys.

"Ann from the hospital! You remember, the little blond girl." Of course he remembered. He had liked Ann, but had watched her die. Not even he typically lived through a fall from such a great height.

"That's impossible. She is dead."

"Well, she left a number. Hold on, I'll call her back." Mike began to dial. A knocking at the door made him stop. "You expecting any company?"

"None," Miller said. Mike got up and moved for the door. He reached for the knob just as it was thrown open, smashing him in the face. He was tossed back, hitting his head on the floor and knocked out. Miller was up in an instant, only to have a gun placed directly at his forehead.

"No moving, friend. Stay very still," a new man said. He was quite tall and very Cursed. His skin was pale and he had a sharp nose and dark hair. Miller did not know him but guessed by the age of the curse that he was a vampire. There was another man, also Cursed, behind him. As this second man walked through the door, Miller recognized him. A very, very old hatred suddenly burned in him.

"Fevre," Miller snarled. He did not truly hate many men, but had often planned for this creature to know death by his own hands, and a very slow death at that. The man was taken aback by the name, as if Miller had struck him. Miller pushed forward to Fevre but the first man kept him back by bringing the butt of the gun down hard across his face.

Miller hit the ground and spat blood.

"It's been a long time since anyone called me that," Fevre said, sitting down next to Catharine, who was still asleep. "Mr. Miller, is that you in that little Mexican body?"

"Aye, Fevre, and I owe you a great deal of pain."

"That you do. That you do. But that debt has been outstanding for many, many years now. I think it can wait a few more days."

"That gun won't stop me," Miller threatened. In truth it would, if a bullet hit him in the right place. Miller would have to be fast, but the sight of his old enemy had thrown off his timing, and timing was everything.

"Good point," Fevre said, pulling out his own weapon. "How about I just shoot this one the moment you blink a little too hard at me?" He pointed the gun toward Mike's still body. Damn him. Miller took one step back. "Good boy."

"What are you after, Fevre?" Miller demanded.

"Smith. They call me Smith here. Tie him up." This last sentence was addressed to the other man, who quickly obeyed. Miller was tied to the wooden office chair with a single, amazingly strong cord around his hands and feet.

"Now, Mr. Miller, you and I are going to have a long talk."

"If it's anything like our last one, I think I will pass. Did you know it took me nearly a month to die in that cave?"

"I did not."

"Seems that carving out my eyeballs and removing my nose was not enough. Nor was it enough when the rats came to feed off me. Would you like to know what finally killed me?"

"I…" Smith looked uncomfortable, "I'm not sure I would."

"It was water. The cave apparently floods. The first few days, I could see the water rising. On the third day it was a relief, as I could reach some to drink. On the fourth day I knew it would kill me. Finally, on the fifth day, sweet oblivion."

Smith seemed to squirm in his seat. "That does sound unpleasant."

"Oh it was, but it gave me plenty of time to think of things I could do to you. You see, time is on my side. Your day will come, 'Smith.' You will die slowly. And I intend to be there with you, enjoying every last moment of it." Miller spat out the words. He had searched for Fevre for so long. To have him here now and be unable to take his long desired vengeance was just too frustrating. The gun trained on Samson kept him in check. That, and the fact that he couldn't move his arms and legs.

"Well, it is good to have goals. Those of us who are long-lived know that better than most. But I'm afraid you'll have to wait just a little longer. Today I win again. I get to ask the questions here."

"That went well for you last time," Miller smirked.

"Nothing as vexing as last time will occur. I'll have my doctors cut you up and see what makes you tick." Smith gestured towards his partner and Samson. "Mr. Drake here has been following your friend for some time. I didn't think he was telling us everything about his little run-in with the Fallen and I suspected that you might have something to do with that. Then you show up at my front gate, completely uninvited. I have to ask, how did you find us?"

Miller showed Smith his old smile. "Why, if I told you that, it would be cheating." Drake again smashed Miller's face with his gun. The lights briefly dimmed for him. "Ow," Miller complained. "Sir. I'm going to need you to spell your name for my 'to kill' list. I would appreciate if you went slowly. Spelling has never been my strong point." The man struck Miller again.

Smith's phone rang and he raised a hand to his friend, calling for silence. "Smith here." There was a voice on the other side that Miller could not make out. "She what?" Smith was shouting into the phone. "Put her down! Use the tasers! Damn it, I'll be right there."

For Miller, everything suddenly fell into place. "You! You captured one of the Fallen, didn't you? You thought you could keep one of the Seven in a little cage. You, sir, have the rare ability to be both an egomaniac and a complete idiot at the same time." In response, Smith swore, turned his gun on Miller, and shot him. The bullet hit him in the shoulder, toppling him over, along with the chair. "Ow again. I really do dislike our encounters, Smith," he said, now looking up at the ceiling.

Catharine bolted upright in bed. "Mother!" she cried out. And the day had been going so well. Miller could hear the tearing of cloth as Catharine took on her far less attractive form.

"Shit. I worry about the company you keep these days, Miller." Smith shot the woman, twice. "On the other hand, she may offer a useful way to dispose of you. I imagine she'll kill you much faster than I did last time. Come on, we have to get back."

As Miller struggled to right his chair, the two men simply left, closing the door behind them.

Miller managed to get the seat back onto its four legs, in a maneuver halfway between a jump and a throw. The wolf that had been Catharine was now stepping off the bed, reaching towards Mike's still body.

"Hey there! None of that." He hopped backwards with the chair. A desperate plan was forming in his head. "It's me you want. Looky over here. I'm all tied up with no place to go." He sprang back two more times, making his way onto the balcony through the still-open glass door. The wolf looked up at him and recognition dawned. It howled and charged. Miller hopped back one more time and hit the railing. With his hands bound at the wrists, He just barely managed to grab the railing. Pushing with his toes, he began moving up the railing, chair and all. His shoulder was on fire but he was focused on saving Mike's life.

The wolf crashed into him, teeth biting down on his wounded shoulder. The force of the blow knocked both of them over the edge, hurtling them towards the ground.

It was a long second for Miller as he braced for what would be another death, six floors below on the concrete. He hated this part.

It turned out the wolf was kind enough to hit the ground first, landing next to the hotel's pool. The chair had flipped over and landed on top of it with a crack, but didn't break. Miller was in a perfect sitting position, the chair's legs on the wolf. It was not clear whether the crack had come from the chair or the wolf, but neither was in great shape. Amazing. If he had only done that on purpose.

"Tada!" he shouted to no one in particular. It quickly became clear that the crack had come from the chair. One of the back legs gave way, sending him sprawling backwards, directly into the pool. He was unprepared and could not get a good breath of air before he sank below the surface. The chair plummeted like a stone as Miller struggled against his bindings. If he could break the back of the chair or its front legs, he could stand up. The water did not seem very deep but the chair was quite stubborn. His lungs burning, he changed tactics and rolled the chair over, pushing up with his feet the short distance he could move them. The chair began to right itself but since it didn't have four legs, simply fell over again.

Miller's vision was going black. He fought panic and tried to roll the seat over again. Perhaps he could find a shallow area. What a disappointing way to die! He managed to flip the chair over once, then twice. On the third spin the darkness took him.

Then he was lying on dry ground, coughing and spitting water. A woman with long blond hair was holding his head.

"Ann?" he managed, weakly. It was not her. It did not even look like her. What had he been thinking?

"Sir? Sir? Are you okay? Should I call 911?"

Miller did not know this woman, but she was attractive, and had apparently saved his life. "I am just fine now, lass." He managed to smile.

"Good. Can you tell me what the hell that thing is?" The woman pointed to the wolf's still body. Black blood pooled underneath it.

"Something very dangerous. You need to get far away from here."

“It doesn’t look like it can hurt anyone now.”

“Look at the blood, lass.” The pool of blood was shrinking as the blood traveled back into the wolf’s body.

“But that’s impossible,” the woman said.

“Aye, I hear that often. Feel welcome to tell it that.”

Suddenly Mike Samson was beside him. Blood was running down his forehead. “Miller? Holy shit man, are you alright?” He was panting.

“I am now, thanks to my angel here, but we are about to have company.” Miller was grinning at his savior.

“Here, let me get you out of this chair,” Mike said, pulling a knife from his belt. He cut the strap holding Miller in place.

“Ah. Thank you.” Miller stood up gingerly. His head was spinning but that would not slow him for long. The bullet in his shoulder, on the other hand, was an issue. He put one hand on the shoulder of the woman that had saved his life. “What’s your name?”

“Ashley,” the woman said, her eyes on the wolf, who was beginning to twitch on the ground.

“Well, Miss Ashley, there are some bad things out here tonight. I suggest you run to a safe place and keep the door locked.”

“What’s going on?” At a sudden howl from the wolf, she lost interest in the answer. “Yeah, okay, good idea.” She took off at a slow run, looking behind her regularly. The wolf had gotten to its feet, and was recovering from the fall.

“Damn it!” Mike said, drawing his gun. He fired once, hitting the wolf in the gut. The bullet ripped a large hole through its midsection. The wolf let out a whimper like a dog that had been kicked by its owner, turned, and fled, holding its new wound with its hand. “I thought you said she wouldn’t change until tonight.”

“The demon summoned her. It is in trouble and is calling in the reserves.”

“Should we go after her?” Mike asked.

“We know where she is going. How is your head?” Miller asked, inspecting the wound.

Mike flinched and pulled away. “It’s not bad. I think I was only out for a few seconds. I woke up when Catharine got furry. Who were those men?”

“One goes by the name Smith now. I knew him a long, long time ago. I owe him a slow and horrible death. The other one is new but he is on my list as well.”

“Were they Fallen?”

“Oh no. Vampires.” Miller started walking towards the van.

“Shit. I hate vampires,” Mike said.

"Aye. Join the group," Miller said.

"It's 'club'."

*****

It took them only a few minutes to get back to the van. Miller quickly bandaged Mike's head. It was only then that Mike noticed the blood coming from Miller's shoulder.

"Miller, you're bleeding!"

"Aye, a bullet wound. But it's small. Once you start driving I will pull it out on my own."

"You can do that?"

"Bullets have been around for a while now. I've dealt with this before. I'd rather not, honestly, but we are in a hurry." Mike nodded and started up the van. Miller pulled a pair of tweezers from a first-aid kit kept in the van and went to work on his wounds.

"How long is that going to take to heal for you?" Mike asked.

"A few hours."

"Look, about before. I need to thank you for saving my life. Again." Miller waved a dismissive hand. "No really, thank you."

"It was nothing. I have grown fond of you." Miller gave him a grin. "Besides, it would break my heart to have to tell Sam anything happened to you." Mike nodded and pulled the van out onto the highway. There was silence between the two men for a moment as Miller tried to fish for the bullet in his arm in the moving vehicle. It was not pleasant.

"Why me, Miller?" Mike broke the silence.

"Wait, almost…got it!" Miller tore the bullet from the wound with a grunt. Fresh blood shot out onto his pants. He grabbed a bandage and held it to his shoulder. "Sorry, what were we discussing?"

"Why me, Miller? Why spend the time to find me? Why convince me to come along on this little trip?"

"You were the only one I knew here," Miller answered. "And to be completely honest, you remind me of someone I knew a very long time ago. He lost someone very special as well and it destroyed him."

"I see," Mike said. "Is this some clever way to describe yourself?"

"Not me, no. My son."

"Oh, I'm sorry. That must be hard," Mike said.

"It never gets any easier. Even with the amount of practice I have had, it still rends my heart. I know it is that way with a wife as well." Miller looked directly at Mike. Mike kept his eyes on something else. "But it's not something worth taking your own life over."

Mike shot him a quick glance, shock plainly visible on his face. "How did?" He trailed off.

"The world has changed, Mr. Samson. People have not. And I've known people for a long time now. I don't know what happened exactly, but I know a tormented soul when I see one. Let her go, forgive whoever needs to be forgiven and move on. Your life is precious. If not to you, then to your son."

There were tears coming down Mike's face, but he made no noise for some time. "I enjoy your company as well," Miller added, giving Mike a smile. "Although you still need a good lay."

Silence filled the van. This time, Mike broke it. "You know, most of the time you are a huge pain in the ass. It's like having another five-year-old, except you drink like a fish. Then you go and say something like that, and I'm actually tempted to like you again." Mike shot Miller a smile back. There was pain in his face, but maybe some hope as well.

"Well this has been an excellent chat. Now, how about you and I kill some demons?"

# 12 - The Truth Hurts

The next morning, jittery and sweating, Lizzie went to Target and bought Ann the largest hooded sweatshirt she could find. In a way it felt good to get out, aside from the constant feeling of terror.

Returning with the sweatshirt and a sour stomach, Lizzie found Ann on the computer.

"Hey now, don't be touching that. You don't have the skills," Lizzie mocked her friend.

"I'm just trying to learn as much as possible about these Angel murders," Ann replied without looking back.

"Find anything?"

"Well, they found the first body two days after the College Hospital 'incident.' They're probably calling it that because they have no idea what happened in there."

"Yeah, but the body was weeks old, according to the report I read," Lizzie added.

"Hmmm."

"Hmmm?"

"Nothing. Well, maybe nothing. I'm wondering if the body was really decayed or if that's just what a vampire does to a person."

"Umm yeah, you would be the freak expert," Lizzie said. "Here, try this on." She tossed the shirt at Ann.

"Oh God, really?" Ann asked.

"Come on, how else do you expect to play Nancy Drew?"

"Fine." Ann got dressed. It took some tinkering to get anything to fall straight. Finally, Ann said, "My wings keep cramping."

"You look fine. You ready to go?"

"Yeah, let's do this before I come to my senses."

It turned out that the Civic was just barely demon-sized. Ann's head touched the ceiling. She ended up tilting the seat back as if she was planning to take a nap.

"Comfy?" Lizzie asked sarcastically.

"Not really. You know, I always wanted to be tall, but now that I am, it's really just annoying." Lizzie laughed at that.

It took some time to find the burnt-out little hellhole that Ann had been sleeping in for the last few weeks. Lizzie pulled up in front and made sure the doors were locked once Ann was out of the car. She watched the lean figure of her friend disappear into the ruined building and wondered what the place had been in better times. Why had Ann stayed here? Her new shape was frightening, but Lizzie had accepted her. Sure, she had slept with her trusty frying pan last night (you could never be too sure), but Ann was still definitely Ann. Despite a mouth full of needle-like teeth and her claws, she really wasn't that scary. On the other hand, Ann on that video had been something else. There was something about those black eyes that Lizzie found chilling.

Thinking back, Lizzie had seen Ann right around the time period of the video. The dates were a little foggy in her mind, but she had spent a night at Ann's place drinking and watching bad movies right around that time. Hell, Ann had gotten wasted on Mudslides and had even tried to make out with her. Had that been Ann or had it been the thing inside of her? Along that line of thinking, what had that thing done while in control of Ann? Apparently Ann had slept with Keith right around then. Had he slept with Ann or the demon? Is that how Keith had become a demon as well? How would that even work? It brought a whole new level to the concept of safe sex, didn't it? Lizzie's line of thinking could only lead to bad places. If Ann had "turned" Keith, she had indirectly caused the incident at College Hospital. Why hadn't she contacted Lizzie earlier? Instead, she became a nocturnal creature, hiding here. Was Ann the one responsible for the killings? Was the thing inside her actually the murderer that she was searching for?

Lizzie was shaking again. Almost without thinking, she popped another pill. She was not good at this stuff, but for Ann, she would handle it. Ann was still in there, of that she was sure, but what about her demon hitchhiker? Sure, a vampire had told her she was clean, but he was the same one Ann suspected of murdering people. That didn't make Lizzie confident in his judgment.

A movement behind her car broke her train of thought. A little white Chevy had pulled off to the side of the road. Lizzie had seen the car somewhere before. Had it been behind them on the way here? Lizzie stared at intently. The driver did not get out. Damn it! It has to be the Feds. Of course they were watching the house. Lizzie nearly slapped herself in anger. Wait, maybe she was being paranoid. Of course, she was being paranoid. She was always paranoid. The driver still didn't get out of the car. Actually, this time paranoid might be the way to go. She was positive that the FBI was still after Ann and were watching her. Lizzie had to do something. If they caught her friend they were sure to bring her to a lab and cut her open. That's what the government did, wasn't it? Like that alien they found over in Area 51 back in the 50s. Lizzie had seen the video. Not this time.

Lizzie stepped out of the car. She had to do something.

"Lizzie?" Ann asked, exiting the building. Lizzie glanced once at her friend and dove back into the car, relocking the door. "Umm, can I get back in?" Ann knocked gently on the glass.

"Quick get in!" Lizzie unlocked the car just long enough for Ann to get the door open. "What's wrong?"

"We're being watched!" Lizzie said. She jerked one thumb behind her.

Ann craned her neck to see. "I don't see anyone."

"In the white car. It's the Feds."

"The Feds? I thought they were supposed to drive black vans and helicopters and such." There was a hint of mockery in Ann's voice.

"Do you think this is some movie? Of course the Feds don't have black vans! That would be way too obvious!"

"Oh, of course. So they drive little Chevy Aveos?"

"Well… budget cuts." Lizzie shrugged.

"Lizzie, are you okay? You can go home now. I appreciate your help, but with your…condition, maybe its best you went back to your place. Abraham isn't here. I'll keep looking and fly back to your place." As if flying like that was a normal thing.

"I'm fine!" Lizzie said too loudly. She tried again. "I'm fine, and I'll prove it." She put the car in drive. She had to keep calm. Nothing wrong here. She was just driving with a friend down a random street. Okay, so the friend was a demon and they were looking for a vampire while being followed by the federal government. Completely normal.

"Where to now?"

"Can you see that?" Ann pointed to something on the side of the road.

"The sidewalk?" Lizzie asked.

"No, not the sidewalk. There's a dark mist hanging in the air."

Lizzie shook her head. "I thought I was the crazy one."

"Trust me, just go that way. I'll let you know when to turn." Ann pointed ahead. Lizzie shrugged and continued forward. She kept looking behind her, waiting for the white car to make an appearance, while she followed Ann's directions.

"So what are we doing?" Lizzie asked, checking the rear-view mirror.

"Following a trail. Abraham said he could follow me when the demon controlled me. I think I can follow him."

"You think?"

"Well it's not like I've done this before. I didn't notice this trail before but I saw the mark on him," Ann said.

"The mark?"

"Yeah, he called it the mark of the Cursed. It's like this little cloud that hangs around people that have been infected by the Fallen."

"That's convenient," Lizzie put in.

"Here, pull over here." Ann pointed to a half-constructed office building. Lizzie brought the car to the side of the road. "It goes inside. The trail, I mean."

Lizzie still didn't see anything. "Fine, I'll come in with you. I'll prove to you that we are being followed," Lizzie said.

"Are you crazy? What part of 'vampire' don't you get?"

"All of it, honestly. I'll just step in the door with you." Realizing what she was saying, she added, "Just stay close, okay?"

Ann shook her head. "Fine." They both exited the car and Lizzie dashed around to Ann's side. Ann was still a sort of security blanket, even with scales.

"Lead on," she said.

The building in front of them was under construction, but there was a large gap in the fence, which Lizzie assumed was how the construction workers got in. The structure seemed almost complete, with some windows, but no interior walls and no doors, just a ripped piece of plastic over the main opening to the building. Once they stepped inside, it became obvious that construction had stopped some time ago. The bottom floor was dusty and covered in garbage. Perhaps the company had run out of money and the project had been delayed?

"Okay," Lizzie said. "Let's head upstairs. I'm sure we can see from there." They climbed six flights of stairs before Lizzie figured they were high enough. "Here, this should do it. Now we wait." Lizzie headed to the nearest window with a view of the street.

"I think we should keep following that trail," Ann said.

"This should only take a minute." Lizzie waved her over. "Look."

"What am I looking for?" Several minutes passed and nothing happened. "Lizzie?"

"Just a minute longer." Was she wrong? No, there it was. The white Chevy was slowing as it came down the road. "There! Same car as before!"

"Hmm, could still be a coincidence," Ann said. "But maybe for once your paranoid ass is onto something." They stood quietly, watching the white car for a long time. "So what should we do about it?"

"Hey, I'm just the sidekick here." Lizzie shrugged. "I could go and tell him off. He isn't after me."

"What? That whole hacking into a secure FBI network doesn't count as a crime anymore?" Ann offered.

"Oh well, they didn't catch me on that one." At least, she didn't think so.

"Look. Someone's getting out of the car!" Ann pointed. A man in a suit had gotten out of the car and was walking down the road to Lizzie's car.

"He better not mess with my car," Lizzie said. The man circled her Civic, peering into the windows. Then he looked at the building they were in. "Damn, he's coming in. What do we do?"

Ann shrugged. "Maybe we should just talk to him."

"Are you crazy?" Lizzie asked, giving Ann's arm a slap. "They'll either shoot you or throw you in a lab someplace."

"What else can I do?" Ann asked.

"Run," Lizzie said. There was panic in her voice.

Ann seemed undisturbed. "No, it's just one guy. He might be able to tell us something useful. I say we ambush him."

"Okay yeah. Here, take some of my meds. You've lost it."

"No really. It's a good idea. He doesn't know we're on to him. We pick a hiding spot, and when he gets close, I pop out and knock him on the head." Ann pushed back her hood. "I am pretty scary looking these days." She grinned and Lizzie was forced to turn away.

"Okay, okay, just stop doing that."

They found a particularly wide column to hide behind, which had a clear view of the stairs, and began to wait. Lizzie was terrified and coming to terms with the fact that she was just going to let Ann do this by herself. She would wait quietly behind the column, stay out of the way, and hopefully not pass out.

It seemed like an eternity passed before Ann whispered in her ear.

"Did you hear something?"

"Just the beating of my heart. That sucker is going to blow any minute," Lizzie whispered back.

"No really."

"It's the Fed loading his massive gun," Lizzie put in.

"I can hear him just fine. He's still below. No, this was a screech, like a bat. Wait, there it was again." Suddenly, there was screaming from downstairs. Ann and Lizzie both jumped. "Lizzie, come on!" Ann grabbed her arm and took off toward the sound. Now they heard gunshots.

"What the hell are you doing? Shouldn't we be running the other way?" Lizzie gasped, keeping double-time to catch up with Ann.

"That man's in trouble and it could be Abraham."

"So? You wanted to knock him out and question him just a few minutes ago."

"Yes, but he doesn't deserve to die!" Ann roared back. They reached the landing and headed down the stairs. The screaming had stopped but Lizzie could hear the screeching noise Ann had described. At the bottom of the next flight, it was louder. It was like a bat, or maybe several bats.

Ann slowed. "Wait, there's something down there," she said, looking down the next flight of stairs. "Lots of somethings." Lizzie poked her head past Ann. They were people, just standing around. In the weak light, Lizzie couldn't see clearly. "There's something wrong here, really wrong. I need to get you out of here."

"What is it?" Lizzie asked, getting scared. Well, more scared.

Ann was still staring down below them. "Something Cursed." She turned to face her friend, but then looked up. "Lizzie, look out!" Ann pulled Lizzie behind her. Lizzie saw movement behind her. A man, naked and white as milk, was reaching for her. His eyes were closed as if he was sleeping but his mouth was open in a silent scream. Ann didn't hesitate, swinging one clawed hand at him and tearing his head off in a single swipe. The body stood for a brief moment, then collapsed. There was no blood.

"Jesus, you killed him!" Lizzie screamed.

"I… holy shit. I didn't mean to do that." Ann looked at her hand. Then she bent over the body. "I don't think he was actually alive." Ann suddenly jumped back, again pushing Lizzie behind her. The headless body was getting back up! Lizzie decided that at this point the only logical thing to do would be to start screaming. She did. Ann tried again, swiping at the dead thing's mid-section. The body was launched against the wall and tumbled down the stairs. It hit the bottom with a splat.

Lizzie was still screaming. She simply couldn't stop herself. It had always annoyed her in horror movies when the victims just stood there frozen and screaming as a monster crept slowly and dramatically toward them, but here she was, doing just that. Her eyes had found the thing's head and she was transfixed by it.

"Lizzie! We have to move!" Ann's arm was suddenly around her, lifting her up. Ann ran towards a window. Over Ann's shoulder, Lizzie could see more creatures streaming up the stairs. It was getting hard to scream now. Her throat seemed to be closing up. Her body was shaking uncontrollably. Ann put her down for a moment to kick open a window. A section of the glass broke, but the hole was much too small for them.

"Hold on Lizzie!" Ann shouted. Lizzie couldn't breathe now. She couldn't move her head. The room was fading. She wasn't even going to live long enough to be killed by monsters. Death by panic attack. So fitting for her.

Ann kicked the frame out of the window. It went crashing to the pavement below and Ann turned to pick up Lizzie. Lizzie was sliding away. Something had her leg. God, no, she didn't want to die like this! She managed to convince her body to move, tossing her hand toward Ann. She was too slow. The monsters were on her, dragging her into the darkness.

# 13 - Storming the Castle

This time, Mike was prepared. Or at least better prepared. Minutes after Joseph Miller had walked into his life for the second time and Mike had agreed to his crazy request, he had begun stockpiling anything that might be useful if he ever found himself in a building full of mythical beasts again. Now that was he was about to be in exactly that situation, he wished he'd had more time. Mike missed the shotgun he'd used in his last encounter with the Fallen, but the one he'd ordered hadn't come in yet. The Desert Eagle would have to do. He also had his old Smith and Wesson 539 9mm, but he was sure that it was more likely to annoy rather than kill one of the Cursed. Mike had two bulletproof vests, which he fervently hoped were claw- and fang-proof as well. Miller had requested a sword, but Mike had instead gotten him two thin-bladed machetes that looked better suited to cleaning the back yard than to monster hunting. The problem had been a matter of discretion. It was hard to look casual when lugging around a sword and Miller grabbed enough attention as is. The machetes, on the other hand, fit well under Miller's coat.

All of the gear was carefully stashed in the back of Mike's van. Miller began to root through it as they closed in on their target.

Silence had fallen between the two men. Mike wasn't quite sure what to make of Miller, who had told him that his life was precious one moment and asked him to help storm a compound filled with unknown horrors the next.

When they reached the building, Mike didn't slow down. He kept driving, smashing right through the front gate to the compound. He had always wanted to do that.

There had been no one at the front gate and the driveway was similarly deserted. It was late afternoon. People should be getting ready to go home. That was, of course, if they hadn't been eaten, or worse. Mike put on his vest and stepped out of the car. He passed the big Desert Eagle handgun to Miller.

"Here. I think this will help you more than me. Careful, it has a lot more kick than you would expect."

Miller looked the gun over. "You are convinced this will bring down a wolf?"

"I'm not the monster hunter but if a shotgun worked, it should only take one good shot in the head with this."

"Well, let us find out." Miller smiled and walked to the front door. Mike followed closely. They found the front lobby empty. Ahead was a group of elevators and to the right were several closed doors.

"Seems quiet," Mike commented.

"It always does at first," Miller said. The lights flickered, which gave Mike a brief flashback of College Hospital. He had packed several large flashlights that he could not step and break.

Suddenly, the doors to the right burst open and five men rushed into the room, guns raised. Miller had his own gun at the ready.

"Freeze!" one of the men shouted. "Drop your weapons, put your hands on your head, and kiss the floor!"

"I don't think so lads." Miller was defiant. To Mike, he said in a lower voice, "Do as they say."

Mike slowly raised his hands. "Are they human?" Mike whispered.

"All but the one in the back," Miller answered. In a louder voice, he said, "You sir, the tall one in the back. I believe we met earlier today."

"Are you crazy, man? Drop the gun!" The man who had shouted first continued his advance. Mike thought crazy actually described Miller quite well.

Miller grinned, keeping the gun up. "What was your name again? Started with a D, I'm terrible with names…" Miller ignored the smaller man's commands.

The cursed man at the back had his gun leveled at Miller. "Mr. Miller, wasn't it? Yes, they call me Drake."

"Well, Mr. Drake, I believe I owe you this."

Miller pulled the trigger.

Mike flinched as the world seemed to slow. Miller's gun fired once as he threw himself backwards. The bullet hit Drake directly between the eyes, blowing out a large portion of the back of his skull. Black blood and brains burst from the man's head, painting the wall. An instant later, three of the men returned fire, all of them hitting Miller. Mike heard Miller's grunt of pain but his attention was focused on Drake. Somehow he was still standing. He was swaying slightly and his mouth had dropped open, releasing more black blood, but he didn't fall. One of the men grabbed Mike's arms, trying to tie them together with something. Another man near Drake was calling his name, as if he hadn't seen the man's gray matter splatter. The others were heading toward Miller to finish him off. Mike wasn't scared of them. He was waiting for something much worse. Miller had said that vampires were extremely hard to kill. So why had Miller taken the shot?

As if to answer this question, a black tentacle slid out of the back of Drake's head and grabbed the closest man by the neck. There was a scream and everyone turned to see what was happening. The man was already nearly dead, his eyes wide with terror as Drake fed on him. The vampire was not only after his blood, as was the common myth, but his muscle and fat as well. The color in the dying man's flesh was draining away through contact with the black, barbed tongue.

"What the hell is that?" one man shouted, firing his gun. The man holding Mike let go and rushed to his friend's rescue. For a long moment Mike lay still, watching the grim spectacle, before common sense reasserted itself and he jumped to his feet.

"Miller?" he asked, reaching the downed man's side.

"Samson, I thought you said these vests were bulletproof! That hurt like hell!" Miller groaned.

"I guess they are more 'bullet resistant'," Mike admitted. Miller gave him a disbelieving look. "What did you do to him?"

"I removed his disguise. Damaging the head does not kill a vampire but it frees the beast inside."

"I think you need to finish it now, before anyone else is killed." The vampire had discarded its appetizer and was moving on to the second course, a remaining eye staring dead ahead as it rocked back and forth on its heels. The three remaining men were firing their weapons at it without much success. A second tentacle slid out of Drake's mouth and reached for the next victim.

"How many of those tongue things do they have?" Mike asked.

"As many as they need. Help me get this vest off, it's crushing me." Mike opened Miller's shirt. The vest had stopped two bullets. A third had grazed his leg. Pulling open the vest, Mike could see black bruises already forming on Miller's chest. He helped him up. The vampire had a third man now, while another lay still on the floor, neck broken. The final man had had the good sense to run.

"We're next. How do we kill it?" Mike asked.

"The old-fashioned way." Miller drew both machetes and ran at the beast. A tentacle swung in a high arc at Miller's approach. He sliced it in half, spun and sliced off the second one, following with the head, an arm, and finally, a leg. As quickly as the monster had revealed itself it was dispatched. The body fell on its side.

"These will do nicely," Miller said, flicking the blood off the machetes and returning them to his long coat.

"It's still moving," Mike pointed out. One tentacle was slithering back toward the trunk.

"Hmm, good point." Miller crushed the tentacle under his boot. It popped like a balloon.

"Is it dead?"

"Mostly. The rest of it should die soon enough." He gave the head a kick. "Nasty fellow. Too bad about the others, however. I suppose I overestimated my bullet resistant vest." Miller gave Mike a critical look. Mike ignored him.

"Shall we go further in?"

"Aye, but give me a moment to catch my breath." A few seconds later, Miller added, "Trade guns with me."

"Why, something wrong?" Mike asked as he reclaimed the Desert Eagle and handed over the 9mm.

"Not at all. It is a fine weapon, but something tells me you are going to need it. I can get by with the blades. "

After a few moments, Miller headed to the door and Mike followed. They entered a room holding series of cubicles, but otherwise completely empty.

"What's the plan here?" Mike asked.

"We find and kill the demon. Kill it and this gets easier. "

"Can I make a suggestion?"

"Always," Miller said, not looking back.

"Why not try to get the regular people to help us take down the demon. Why fight two battles?"

"These people want something. It is why they captured the demon in the first place."

Mike scoffed at that. "People. You think they would learn after years of watching horror movies. The big bad monster always gets out and smashes up the town."

"Is that common in movies?" Miller asked. There was a loud crash to their right. "This way. Come on."

They entered a small break room containing a fridge and various materials for making coffee. There was a woman in a lab coat attempting to drag a much larger, unconscious man across the floor. As they entered, the woman turned to face them, her eyes the black empty color of the Cursed. Her mouth was filled with fangs and she brandished a bloody, clawed hand. She didn't, however, have the bulky build or fur of a werewolf.

"What is she?" asked Mike.

"Just a wolf, a few hours old. The demon must be desperate." Miller raised his gun and fired, hitting the creature in the chest. It dropped the unconscious man and was knocked back into the counter, destroying a perfectly good coffeepot. Miller rushed to the wolf and followed up with a boot to its head. "There you go. Now tie it up."

Their deal had been to spare the wolves as best they could. Miller had not budged on vampires, though. He would never trust a vampire, he had said, even one freed from the Fallen. In this new mad version of his world, Mike would take what he could get. He brought over several pairs of handcuffs from his overloaded coat and restrained the creature's arms and legs. It wasn't going anywhere now. Mike approached the man lying prone on the floor. There were some deep cuts in the man's chest and one arm looked as though it might be dislocated at the shoulder.

"He'll live," Mike observed.

"I suppose you don't want to just leave him here?" Miller asked.

"No. God knows what would happen to him next. I'll help him to the front door and lock him in the van. Then I'll come back and find you. The way we passed is clear anyway."

"Alright lad, the wolf was going this way," Miller pointed to another exit, "so that is the way I will go. Be careful. Do not hesitate to use the gun."

"Right, I'll see you in a few minutes." Mike drew the gun. He wasn't going to argue. If a few of the Cursed had to die, then so be it. He could only do so much.

Miller left the room and Mike tried to bring the man on the floor around. For a few minutes the man didn't respond, but he eventually let out a groan.

"Hey, can you hear me?" Mike gently shook the man.

"Ugh, what happened?" the man asked, coming to.

"That." Mike pointed to the former woman, already struggling against the cuffs.

The man stared at it. "I think that's one of the women from the lab. What's wrong with her?"

"It's a long story. Look, you need medical attention. How about I help you out of here?" Mike offered.

"Do you work here?"

"No, I'm with the police." Sort of. "My partner and I specialize in this sort of thing." He helped the man up and walked him back the way they had come in. "Can you tell me what happened?"

"There was an explosion in one of the labs…"

"That's enough, Mr. Valentino," said a new voice, from behind them. Mike turned around to see who it was. As usual, the break room was the busiest of places. There were three men behind him with guns drawn. Mike recognized one of them as the man that had come to see him in the hospital. He had gone by the name of Smith. "You know company policy. And while Mr. Samson is part of the police force, he is certainly not here on official business." The voice clicked.

"You were in the hotel room!" Mike said.

"So, you were awake for some of that. Place the officer under arrest," Smith said.

"I'm trying to help here," Mike said, not moving. "This man needs medical attention."

"That is very noble of you. However I believe your 'partner' has other plans." Smith walked over to the cuffed beast. It snarled at his approach. "And what's this? A gift-wrapped little wolf? Did you do this? I know it's not Miller's style."

"We can help her, too. We just need to kill the demon that cursed her."

"Wrong," he said, matter-of-factly. He lowered his gun and shot the beast in the head.

"Don't!" Mike cried out.

Smith fired three times into its head. "There, that should take care of that. It's too bad, she was a good employee," Smith said, poking at the corpse with a fine leather shoe.

"Why?"

"Business, my friend. She was of no further use to the company. In fact, just the reverse. For mindless beasts, these wolves can be tricky. You, on the other hand, might be very useful as a hostage, if you're good." Smith raised the gun to Mike's head. "Now tell me which way my old friend Mr. Miller went."

"Why? So you can run the other way?" Mike asked. Smith approached and pressed the gun to Mike's forehead.

"You're a funny man, but I can't let your friend destroy my specimen."

Mike didn't hesitate in answering this time. After all, Smith was exactly what Miller wanted. "He went that way," Mike said, pointing. "Not even five minutes ago. You won't be able to miss him. He'll be the little Hispanic guy kicking your ass."

The wounded man, Valentino, was leaning on Mike, looking bewildered. Mike still had his gun and his vest but didn't want to make that play unless forced.

"Jackson, check him for weapons and restrain him. Then follow me. I need to stop Miller." After giving his instructions, Smith dashed down the hall.

"Valentino, check him for weapons!" Jackson barked, training his gun on Mike.

"Sorry about this, buddy," Valentino said. Mike let him go and he slumped against the wall. "Damn it, my shoulder is killing me. You do it, Jackson."

Jackson gave Valentino a dirty look. "Alright fine, you cover him." He passed his gun to Valentino. Mike braced himself for a quick move, seeing his opportunity coming.

Jackson stepped forward. "No funny business," he said, starting to pat him down. Mike resisted the urge to laugh.

"Funny business? You mean like this?" Mike kneed Jackson between the legs and shoved him at Valentino. The wounded man managed to fire his gun once before Jackson crashed into him, causing him to let it go. Mike dropped to one knee and drew his own gun. Realizing that the two men were tangled up as it was, he stepped forward and kicked Valentino's gun clear.

"Wow, and people say the public sector is bad. You guys are jokes. Thanks for the extra gun though." Mike picked up his prize, keeping the Desert Eagle pointed at the two men. "Hostage, my ass."

Suddenly there was a low growl behind him. Mike spun, gun raised, as something large, furry, and blue crashed into him, sending him flying, his back hitting the wall on the other side of the room. It was a wolf, much larger than the last, its blue 'I love New York' sweatshirt a reminder of the woman it had been.

The wolf was looking much less friendly. Its shorts were long gone, as well as the sleeves of its sweatshirt, but it was without a doubt Catharine. It was much larger than when Mike had first seen it as a wolf in New York, and bigger even than when he had shot it outside of the hotel. Mike really hoped it had not been snacking on the way over.

Jackson rolled away and got up, while Valentino lay on the floor, whimpering. The wolf hopped forward and hit Jackson with a clawed hand, slashing the side of his body open. The wounded man was sent sprawling toward Mike, who knocked him to the right.

Then, Mike had what had to be the most ridiculous idea of his entire life. It came to him in a flash of insane inspiration that he blamed on far too much exposure to Joseph Miller. He put his gun in its holster and dropped to the floor. He lay very still, as if he was unconscious. It was either the dumbest thing he had ever done or the most brilliant.

The wolf slashed at Jackson's still-struggling body until he stopped moving. Then, satisfied with its work, looked around the room. Mike held his breath. His fear-ridden mind jumped back to a scene in a movie he had watched years ago.

"The T-rex has terrible eyesight. He can't see you if you don't move."

Of course, it had seemed idiotic. It was still idiotic now. But it led to an idea that made a certain kind of sense. The wolves he had seen so far had only killed people when they first transformed. After that, it seemed that they dragged their victims off someplace and only attacked if threatened. Mike was betting they brought them straight to their parents as potential new family members. It was a huge gamble, but Mike was also sure that if the thing got hungry, he could draw and fire the gun quickly enough. He really didn't want to hurt Catharine any more than necessary, but if he could get a free ride to the demon from her, well why not? Miller's kind of crazy was catching.

The wolf stormed around the room for a moment, seeing if any of the men kept moving again. It then picked up Valentino with one arm. Next, it came to him, gave him a quick sniff, and then picked him up as well. Mike struggled to be completely silent as it threw him over one shoulder. Then it sprinted off, moving deeper into the building.

*****

Miller had yet to find the demon's trail. He only needed to get close, to be where it had been, and he would be able to track it. He was making his way through a jungle of office furniture. How did people work here all day? Miller didn't understand.

He hated to leave Mike but the man would just slow him down. He liked and respected Samson a great deal, but his 'save everyone' mentality was taking too much time. Even if Miller agreed with it for the most part, he was a creature of habit.

"Him, in the brown coat. Get him." Smith's voice came from behind him. There was a gunshot and Miller dove under a desk. He drew the gun Mike had given him. He did not like killing normal people. Why were they on Smith's side? If they would join him instead, he would gladly buy them the first round at a tavern when this was over. Better yet, he would have Mike buy the first round. Then another bullet struck nearby, snapping his attention back to the problem at hand.

"You know, Smith, this would be so much easier if you kept it man to man. Well, man to undead creature."

Smith did not respond, but two more bullets buried themselves into the desk Miller was hiding under. Such a waste of ammunition. He hated gun fights. They were so impersonal. Well, if they wanted to play, he could certainly keep up. He crept out of cover and poked his head around the corner. He saw a man running towards him in the open. Miller frowned.

"Amateurs." He whispered to himself. He fired just once, hitting the approaching man in the knee. Mike would be pleased that he hadn't killed him. He took a deep breath and charged the fallen man, giving him a swift boot to the head and ending the man's yelling. He grabbed the gun he had dropped and dove around a desk. A bullet hit the place where he had been a second before. With the second gun stuffed in his pocket, he peeked around the next desk. A bullet missed his face by inches. This one was a better shot.

By now he had a vague idea of where the shooter was. He let off another shot and rolled away from his cover, dashing to the corner of another desk. Sneaking another look, he caught a glimpse of movement to his right. He took aim and waited. After a moment, the man popped out of cover, gun first. Miller squeezed the trigger. The man screamed as the bullet tore through the hand holding the gun. The weapon dropped to the ground and Miller rushed in, punching the man in the side of the head.

"That the best you have, Smith?" Miller yelled. He caught another flash of movement as, out of nowhere, a huge fist connected with his nose. Letting out a yelp, he was thrown across the room.

"The best distractions, yes," Smith said. "And look at you, not killing them! You've come a long way."

"And you're still the same power-hungry fool," Miller snapped back, wishing he had something wittier to say. It was hard to exchange banter with a bloody nose.

Smith charged, his arm expanding rapidly as he prepared to throw another punch. Miller wouldn't be caught twice the same way. He ducked forward, at the same time drawing the extra gun from his pocket. The punch went high above his head as he put the gun directly to Smith's crotch and pulled the trigger. Smith screamed in pain.

"I know it's been a long time since you were a man, Smith, but I would wager that still hurt," Miller quipped. Smith curled into a ball, shouting obscenities in three or four different languages. Not waiting for him to recover, Miller emptied the rest of the gun into his back. The gun empty, Miller tossed it aside and charged, drawing one of his machetes.

The vampire was not yet done. He managed to grab the charging Miller and toss him high into the air. Miller quickly recovered and landed on his feet, skidding along a desk. Sadly, the desk was about a foot too short to allow him to stop, and he slid off the end, landing on his ass.

"Ouch," Miller said, more embarrassed than hurt. Smith dove at Miller, drawing another gun as he charged. Miller managed to throw the machete, just as he was hit by a bullet that knocked him back to the ground. Mike's bullet-resistant vest took the brunt of the bullet, but Miller's chest was now riddled with bruises and the impact knocked the breath out of him. Miller's knife had struck Smith in the chest. The vampire grunted, pulled out the blade, and tossed it aside.

"You and your damn blades. Of course, now you've tossed the one thing that could do me real damage." Smith stepped over him, the long black tentacle threading its way out of his mouth and darting for Miller's throat. Miller snatched it out of the air, feeling the life draining out of him as he touched it. He would have been concerned if this wasn't exactly where he wanted Smith. He drew the second blade and sliced the tentacle off in one smooth motion. Black blood gushed from the wound and Smith fell back.

"I'm glad I brought two then," Miller said.

What remained of the tentacle retreated into Smith's mouth, blood continuing to spray like a fountain from the wound. Smith raised one arm above his face in a last ditch effort to protect himself. Miller sliced his hand off easily. "I had hoped to make this last a few days. You deserve no less, but I have a job to do." He raised the blade to slice again and paused. He had heard a familiar scream. “Damn it, you had to capture a goddamned Banshee, didn’t you?”

The wall behind them exploded, throwing debris everywhere. Miller felt himself flying, before the old familiar darkness took him.

*****

The wolf moved easily with the two men on its back. Hanging over its shoulder, Mike could hear the sound of screaming from ahead of them. It was not a sound of terror but a constant screeching drone. He remembered hearing it at the hospital where he had first met the Fallen, but still wasn’t sure what it meant. He didn’t want to move much, afraid he would tip the wolf off to his wakefulness. To his surprise, he noticed Valentino staring at him, also very much awake. Mike put a finger to his mouth to indicate that he should keep quiet. Valentino nodded lightly, his eyes wide with terror.

Mike was confident that this was the dumbest thing he had ever done, but oddly enough, it seemed to be working. Hopefully Miller had already found the demon and Mike could just jump in with a quick assist, free Catharine, and be home in time to put Sam to bed. Of course, if Miller wasn’t there, he would have a demon and at least one wolf to deal with. That would be complicated. He tried not to think of that alternative.

The scream started again, louder this time. Now it was painful to hear. The building trembled and there was the sound of an explosion. What the hell had that been?

Suddenly, the wolf dropped him and Valentino and bounded ahead through a door ahead of them. Mike quickly got his bearings and drew the Desert Eagle. He rolled over to Valentino and jammed the barrel of the gun against the man’s chin.

“I’m not going to have any more trouble from you, am I?” Mike whispered.

“No, no. God, no. I didn’t wanna mess with you last time,” Valentino said, stuttering a little. It was hard not to with a gun that big in your face.

“Fair enough.” Mike lowered the gun and dropped to a crouch. Looking ahead, he realized that he could see out of the building. The whole wall of the next room was gone, as was the one after that. The adjacent room looked like it had been another office, but the rows of furniture had been smashed to pieces. Through the wreckage he could see the thing he had come to kill. He had last seen the demon at College Hospital, where it had once been a nurse named Mary. It was still clearly feminine in outline, and had long thick dreadlocks coming from its head, which looked like snakes. Its black scales glinted in the afternoon sun. Two red, leathery wings twitched on her back. In one arm she held Smith, and was shaking him as if trying to wake him up. Mike figured it couldn't happen to a nicer guy.

"How the hell did you guys capture that thing in the first place?" Mike whispered to Valentino, who had not moved. He still seemed frozen in terror but managed to answer Mike's question.

"T-T-Tasers," he whispered back. "Electricity seems to weaken it. What are you going to do?"

"I'm going to kill it. If the demon goes down, Furry there comes back to our side," Mike answered, pointing to Catharine. The demon's voice drifted back into the room. Smith was apparently coming to.

"Wake child, you have much to answer for." Smith was trying to respond, but he could only cough blood. "Did you really think you could keep me caged like your little songbird? Would you like to hear me sing now?" She brought Smith's face up mere inches away from her own.

"No!" Smith managed. He turned his face away from the demon woman. Mike could plainly see the fear in his face. His eyes held the black emptiness of the Cursed, but the rest of his face showed clear emotion. "The Ancient One." Smith pointed. "He is here."

"What?" the demon shouted. She looked at the pile of rubble that he was indicating. An arm could be seen, sticking out. The demon tossed Smith aside, hard. "I'll deal with you in a minute, child." She stomped over to the pile and grabbed the available limb, pulling Miller free. "Yes! It is him! Our ancient enemy, helpless before me!"

It was now or never. Mike jumped to his feet and took aim at the demon. The wolf that had been Catharine noticed the movement and spun around. He had no choice. He fired once, nailing the wolf directly in the chest. The force of the bullet knocked it to the floor. Mike stepped closer to the demon and fired the gun again.

"Sorry to interrupt this reunion," Mike started, firing again, "but the Ancient One still owes me a lot of money." The first bullet struck the demon in the shoulder, the next in the lower back. He could almost hear Miller's voice in his mind, shouting, 'The head, man, go for the head,' but he didn't want to risk hitting his friend.

The demon stumbled forward, dropping Miller, then spun to face its new attacker. The demon inhaled, its chest expanding like a demonic frog, as it prepared to scream again. Mike continued to advance, lining up the all-important headshot. At the same time, the wolf got back to its feet and leapt at Mike, colliding with him just as he fired and ruining his shot. The demon's chest burst as the bullet hit it, and Mike and the wolf hit the ground.

The wolf was bleeding badly from Mike's earlier gunshot. Mike could feel the black tar-like fluid seeping into his clothes. It was weak but still struggling to save its parent. It clawed at Mike's chest but could not penetrate the vest.

They wrestled on the ground for several moments. Even weakened, the wolf was incredibly strong. Mike really hoped the demon was dead, or at least wounded enough to buy him some time. He managed to wrestle the gun up to the wolf's head. He had no choice now.

"I'm sorry," he said, and pulled the trigger. He was both relieved and terrified when it responded with a loud click. Empty. Always a bullet short, Samson.

The wolf smacked the weapon aside and dove at Mike's throat with its teeth. Suddenly, there was a small popping noise and the wolf was going into convulsions. Its teeth had just barely broken the skin of Mike's throat before jerking away. The wolf collapsed, trapping Mike underneath. It was not exactly light, but he was relieved that Catharine was alive. He pushed her head out of the way to see Valentino holding a taser to her flank.

"Now we're even," he said. He dropped the weapon and walked away.

"Hey! Wait, help me out of here," Mike called after him, getting no response. Very slowly, Mike managed to roll the heavy creature off of him. It took several minutes and left him panting. The cuts to his neck were minor. He had done worse shaving. The demon was gone, but the pools of black blood that it had left behind told Mike that he'd done some damage. Smith was gone as well. Miller, on the other hand, was just coming to.

"Ouch," he moaned.

"Miller? You okay?" Mike moved to his side and tried to help him stand.

"I hurt, greatly," Miller said. "Where is Smith?"

"Gone. He didn't look healthy though."

"Damn it," Miller swore. "I have to find him."

"What about the demon?" Mike asked. "I almost had it, but Catharine went and stopped me."

"Aye, yes, the demon first," Miller said with a sigh. "Smith has a reckoning coming though."

"How do we find her?"

"Leave that to me," Miller said, scanning the room. "She went this way." He pointed outside and then up. "She is in flight." Miller grabbed one of the machetes from the ground and stumbled outside. "Are you coming?"

Mike looked down at Catharine, then back at the taser.

"Yeah, one minute. I'm bringing a friend."

# 14 - Turning Point

Ann was getting used to operating in a state of constant terror. She'd thought she'd seen it all at College Hospital and had dealt with it okay. She wasn't always the bravest, but she did her best, and she took some pride in how she handled herself. Now though, with ten dead, naked, rotting corpses tearing at her while several others dragged away her best friend, it seemed like a good time to panic. It didn't feel like it could get any worse than this. But then again, saying something couldn't get any worse just made the universe try harder.

She had to do something. Lizzie's life was at stake. She already hated herself for letting Lizzie come here with her. Ann had known it would be dangerous, although she never expected real, live zombies. Come to think of it 'live' was probably a poor word choice.

For the first time, Ann was thankful for the white scales covering her body. The zombies' teeth could tear her clothes but couldn't do anything to the scales. She swung one of the zombies off of her, only to have another take its place a moment later.

The creatures were closing in on her, the weight of their crawling, biting bodies slowly pushing her to the ground. She didn't want to go down. She wanted to go up. She went into a squat and then jumped straight up, smashing into the ceiling above, again surprised by her own strength. Zombies flew in all directions as her arms came free. Ann landed and grabbed the nearest zombie and threw it through the window. It sailed out of view. She would like to have listened for the reassuring "splat" as it hit the ground, but the others were recovering quickly. She kicked one, sending it flying.

It was good to be strong. Yes, this time, she wasn't the one to be rescued. This time she'd be doing the ass-kicking.

A zombie jumped on her but she shook it off easily, tossing it into another. She grabbed a third and threw it out of the window. This was going to make for a messy front yard. Ann counted eight zombies left. She went to work disposing of them, swiping at the nearest and slicing off a limb. Desperately looking for Lizzie, she moved off in the direction she'd seen the creatures dragging her. Another zombie blocked her path but Ann didn't stop, instead throwing a running punch at it. It was knocked across the room by the force of the blow.

"Lizzie! I'm coming!" she shouted, dispatching another monster. The panic was dying away. She was winning. She could do this. She would find Lizzie. She could make out the faint mist of the Cursed, heading away, and dashed off after it, zombies following as best they could. Some were missing arms and one was moving along without the head that Ann had so violently removed. Obviously, zombies would not be slowed by the *inconvenience* of a few missing body parts.

The building was bigger than Ann had first thought. She ended up crossing a half-finished bridge to another equally abandoned but not quite as finished building. Here plastic, hung from rafters, separating what would someday be rooms. The faint line of mist that Ann had been tracking suddenly merged with the much larger one that she had originally seen and headed upstairs.

Reaching the top floor, she spotted Lizzie, lying still in the middle of the room. Ann took one step forward and then froze. There was something huge beyond Lizzie's still body. It took a second for her to register what it was. She had seen it before, in the psych ward of College Hospital. The demon had once been a man named Jamie. It was much larger now. There was no longer any trace of man, and yet the creature still didn't look wholly-formed. Ann recognized the gigantic arm that dragged on the floor behind it and the single wing sticking out of its back. One side of its body, which had been flesh just a few weeks ago was now black and shriveled. It's long tongue was wrapped around a man that she could only assume was the driver of the little white Chevy. Ann again briefly wondered why he'd followed them here. She guessed he wouldn't be explaining anything now. The demon dropped the corpse to the ground and stood over the dead man for a long moment, as if in mourning. Then it began to cough. The sound it made reminded Ann of a very sick cat she once had. The demon continued to cough, vomiting up a black tar-like substance that covered the dead man. It patted it gently and stood back up, turning its gaze to Lizzie.

"No! I will not allow this*!*"Ann screamed as she charged the demon. She had no idea of how she would be able to fight something so large, but it could not be allowed to touch her friend. The demon watched her approach, confusion plain on its face. She struck it in the head, her claws digging deep, its head snapping back, flinging black blood across the room. Ann didn't hesitate to dive in again, this time embedding her claws deep in the demon's chest. It responded by swinging its massive arm at her. With her hands stuck in its body, she was trapped. It hit her harder than anything she had ever experienced. It was like being swatted with a mountain. She was flying, her vision flashing red. She hit something soft and slid to the ground.

For a moment the world spun. Ann pushed herself back up into a standing position. Looking behind her, she discovered that she'd collided with a zombie, crushing it on impact. It was still not dead, however, or was undead, or was whatever you could call a zombie that was still moving. It started to twitch, one arm reaching for her. Ann grabbed the arm and launched the zombie at the demon. It was a good throw, nailing the approaching monster in the chest, but the demon batted the undead thing aside and continued its advance. Its hand reached for her again but Ann managed to step out of the way. Then, she jumped at the demon again, slicing into its back. It howled in pain as Ann followed up with a second blow, again to its back.

Suddenly there was a zombie behind her, trying to bite her ear. Ann stumbled backwards, the abrupt shift in weight making her lose her balance. The demon was on the attack again, and its big black arm swung at her like a bat, connecting. She was airborne.

She hit the wall hard and, for a moment, darkness threatened to take her. She struggled to rise, leaning against the wall and waiting for the feeling to pass. Blood was dripping from her face; her own black blood. The demon was so strong. How could she stop it?

"Well now," came a familiar voice from the down the hall, "is that you, little sister?" Abraham stepped out of the stairwell that Ann had been in just minutes ago. "Taking on one of the Fallen all by your lonesome? That doesn't seem wise." His tone was full of mirth. He looked every bit a blind old homeless man, his top hat on his head and his cane out in front of him. Both the demon and Ann stared at him.

"Abraham?" Ann asked. The real question was whether he was there to help.

"It is you! Why, I've been looking all over for you." Abraham tipped his hat to her, and then to the demon. The demon looked back at Abraham, and then at Ann. Suddenly, it roared and charged at Ann, the oversized arm flying fast. Ann dove to the side and the demon connected with the wall behind her. It had managed to punch a hole in the cinderblocks, its fist getting stuck inside. Ann saw her opening and attacked, jumping on the demon's back and digging her claws into its face. It screamed and freed its hand from the wall in a shower of cement.

"Help!" Ann shouted, as the demon grabbed her. The big hand was wrapping itself around her. Abraham grabbed his cane with two hands and seemed to snap it in half, revealing a long, thin blade. A cane sword? He couldn't just carry around a damn Uzi?

"Coming!" he said with a smile. His path was blocked by a shambling zombie, who he cut in two without pausing. Ann let out a scream as the demon began to crush her. She dug into its hand with both claws, drawing more blood, but the demon kept squeezing. Then Abraham was there, slicing deep into the big trunk of the arm. Blood spurted from the wound. The demon batted him aside and tossed Ann. It started backing up.

Ann skidded to a halt and lay very still. This kind of thing looked so easy in the movies. Abraham was pulling her to her feet. "Up and at 'em, sunshine. We're not through here yet." Ann nodded and tried to stay standing.

The demon seemed to be retreating, blood flowing from its wounds. It wasn't. It was heading right for Lizzie's still form.

"No," Ann shouted. "The girl, we've to save the girl!"

"What? Lord have mercy! Go girl, go!" They both charged the beast again as its smaller arm lifted Lizzie off the ground. The black tentacle-like tongue flopped around Lizzie's neck. The beast eyed Ann's approach, switched its footing and swung its big arm. Ann couldn't duck fast enough and it smacked her head-on. She was knocked backwards into the air, flying right through a nearby window.

She was outside, many stories above the ground but falling quickly.

"Fly! You can fly, damn it!" she screamed. Her wings were still tangled in her clothes. She ripped at the sweatshirt, spinning in the air, falling. Finally, her wings burst free, mere feet above the ground. She landed feet-first on the roof of a car, its windows exploding, sending glass in all directions as the car crumpled under her weight. Its alarm started to blare. For a moment, she crouched there, shards from the window above showering down on her.

"Lizzie, I'm coming!" she shouted and leapt back up into the air. Seconds seemed to stretch as she searched for the window she'd been tossed through. She finally spotted it and dove back in, folding her wings at the last moment to fit through the small opening.

Lizzie was on the ground now. The demon had Abraham. The smaller arm held his head, the larger one, his legs. It was pulling at him like a giant wishbone. Ann didn't want to know what it would wish for. Abraham twisted his head to look at Ann.

"Save…the girl…" he managed, screaming as he was ripped in two at the waist. Shock hit Ann like a blow to the face.

"No!" she cried. The demon flung Abraham's lower half at her. Coming to her senses, Ann ducked and dove for Lizzie's body. She wrapped her arms around her friend's body and rolled away. The demon roared at her and followed. Ann stood up, cradling Lizzie like a baby, and leapt again for the same window. The demon's oversized fist smashed the ground only inches away, but Ann was already outside. She expanded her wings and drifted to the ground far below. The demon cried after her, its mindless screams filled with hate for the thing that had hurt it and stolen its meal.

Ann touched down, much more gently this time. She placed Lizzie on the sidewalk and began to inspect her friend. She was still breathing. There was a patch of white flesh at her neck, flecked with red, where the creature had used its tongue to feed on her. Otherwise, she looked unharmed. Ann had to get Lizzie back to her car and home. She patted her friend gently on the cheek.

"Lizzie?"

Lizzie didn't move. Ann picked her back up and began to walk to her car. She was too weak to even consider trying to fly with her friend. Her disguise was in ruins and she was covered in blood, not all of it her own. She passed one or two people on the street. One turned and ran. The other gave her a long stare and just kept walking. Ann no longer cared. The horrific sight of Abraham's body being torn apart replayed in her mind. Tears streamed down her face.

At last she found Lizzie's Honda and carefully poked through Lizzie's pockets for her keys. She opened the car and put Lizzie in the passenger seat, and then rooted around in it to see what she could find. There was a water bottle in the cup holder, which Ann used to splash water in Lizzie's face.

Lizzie woke with a start, her eyes still wide with panic. She struck out, smacking Ann in the nose. It wasn't hard, but the surprise of it knocked Ann back.

"Get away!" she screamed. Lizzie kicked at Ann as she jumped for the driver's side of the car.

"Lizzie, it's Ann. It's Ann!"

"You're not Ann. You're one of those monsters!" Lizzie kicked out again. Then she noticed the keys, still in Ann's hand. Lizzie charged back to the other side of the car, punching and kicking. "Give me the goddamn keys!" Ann tossed the keys at her, completely stunned by her transformation.

"But… it's Ann…" she said.

"No! Ann's dead, you're dead!" Lizzie gunned the ignition, not bothering to close the passenger door. The wheels spun in place for a moment before the car took off.

Ann watched her go. Lizzie's reaction stung worse than any of the physical hits she had taken, twisting like a knife in her heart. What should she do next? Her only ally was dead; her only friend had left her. The demon was still out there. It had killed again today. Had she really been so foolish as to believe she could stop it? She hadn't known it was one of the Fallen. Had it just been Abraham, she could have dealt with him. But it turned out he had been as good as his word, a true hero. And she was nothing. She would have to bury him, find him a good resting place. She owed him that at least. She wiped the tears from her face and leapt once more into the air.

It only took her a few minutes to find the room that she had escaped from in the fading light. She dropped into the room, stumbling forward onto a landing. She still needed practice. The stench of the place was terrible and, even in the faint light, Ann could make out the bodies of several zombies. They appeared to finally be dead. It was good to know that they could be killed. She dragged one to the window to see it better. It was by the far the most disgusting thing she had ever seen, not to mention touched. The body was pretty decayed. One oddity that she found was a large dark spot on the back of its neck. The spot had been sliced through by Abraham's sword.

"That's interesting," she said out loud.

"Ann?" came a weak voice.

Ann stood straight up. "Abraham?" she called back, looking around in the darkness.

"Here!" It was Abraham's voice, but there was no more mirth in it. Ann could just barely make it out. It came from above. Ann walked away from the window, searching.

"Where?" was all she got out before she spotted him. Well, half of him. His torso was impaled on an iron beam that must have been knocked loose in the fight. In the spot where his legs had once been, black strings slithered like snakes.

"Help," he called out weakly.

"How are you still alive?" Ann asked, transfixed by the black tentacles. One swung out towards her, but she easily stepped away.

"Vampires are very hard to kill, but we still hurt," Abraham croaked. He pushed against the beam, trying to free himself. "Sometimes pretty damn badly," he added.

"What can I do?" Ann asked.

"Help me down."

"Of course." She stepped forward, and then hesitated. The black snake-like things snapped forward, slapping her leg.

"I can't hurt...Ann, please..." She swallowed hard and reached forward, grabbing Abraham's arms. She tried not to look as the tentacles continued moving, hitting her scales and sliding right off. She pulled once. Abraham screamed but his body didn't move.

"Again. Please," he whispered after a moment.

"Are you sure?" Abraham looked at her with his dead, empty eyes. There was such pain in his old disfigured face.

Ann braced herself and pulled again. At first he didn't move, but slowly, inch by inch, his torso began to slide towards the end of the beam. Abraham gritted his teeth, and then screamed as he came free with a wet pop. Blood gushed from the wound and Ann dropped him to the ground, surprised at the gore.

"I'm sorry! I'm sorry!" Ann yelled before her body rebelled against her control. This was just too much. For a moment, Ann was aware only of the few remaining contents of her stomach, as they forced their way back up and out of her throat.

"Thank you," Abraham said.

"Are you going to be okay?" Ann asked.

"I won't be able to take you dancing for some time." He let out a soft giggle, followed by a spasm of coughing. "But in time, yes. It's sick, you know."

"What is?"

"The demon. It's sick like Lilith was, like you were. Something killed it, but instead of freeing its host, it became a mindless beast." Abraham coughed once more, then continued. "It would have been Ura, the plague bringer. Now though, there is no intelligence in it. Its children inhabit corpses. It wanders and kills at random."

"Yeah, I noticed it wasn't like the others. I knew it before, when it was human. His name was Jamie. Only met him a few times."

"Of course you knew him, you know all the Fallen."

Ann was taken aback by this. "What do you mean?" she asked.

"Lilith was inside of you. Lilith, the mother of all monsters. It was she who made them. Brought them back into being."

"What? No, that's not possible," Ann whispered.

"You didn't know? Did you think it was a coincidence that it was your ex-boyfriend who became the king of demons?"

"I…" Ann stuttered, "I…"

The truth hit her like a blow to the head and she knew Abraham was right. Why had Keith suddenly been interested in her again? The answer was that he hadn't. She remembered her dream of waking up next to him, the black ooze spilling out of his mouth. It hadn't been a dream, but a memory. Lilith had taken him. "Why would she do that? Why would she care?"

"Demons aren't people. They're something completely different. They use their hosts as a sort of guide through man's world. People that are important to the host become important to the demon. In some ways, the demon becomes the person."

"Then this, all of this is my fault. All those poor people in the hospital..."

"No, not your fault, but your responsibility."

"What?"

"You can help stop the Fallen. Send them back," Abraham pleaded. "I can't. Not now. Not for a long time."

"I'm not Miller. I'm just a nobody," Ann said. "I'm just a shadow of them."

"The Ancient One isn't here and he is only a man. You are so much more."

"But how can I kill them? I couldn't even take out the sick one." Ann was crying.

“Because you tried to fight it on its level. You are not a demon, even if you look like one. You need to be smarter. They are weak to fire and electricity. Separate their head from their body and they die instantly.” Abraham paused for what seemed an eternity.

“This is what you were meant to do.”

For the last few days, she had been filled with hope that she would recover from this nightmare. Her time with Abraham, and then her time with Lizzie, had both made her feel almost human again. But she was not. She couldn’t forget that. She was a monster with nothing else to live for. If she could help rid the world of the Fallen then at least she would be doing something. If they killed her, well there was no loss there.

“Tell me what to do.”

# 15 - Who would win in a fight...

Mike did his best to recover what he could from the wreckage. He was happy to find his pistol. Miller had dropped it in the scuffle with Smith, and Mike would have been upset to lose it. He had also recovered one of Miller's machetes and restrained Catharine, who was still unconscious. Mike had a very hard time dragging her back to the van. He placed the taser within easy reach, just in case she came to.

Miller looked terrible. Mike insisted the man take a few minutes to rest as he went about his search. When at last he was ready to go, Mike took his seat next to Miller in the van.

"I was doing well until that wall hit me," Miller complained, as Mike looked him over.

"That does tend to slow one down," Mike joked, but for once Miller didn't respond.

"How about yourself?"

"I'm okay. A few bruises," Mike poked his finger through a hole in his shirt, "one ruined t-shirt, otherwise I'm in one piece."

Miller nodded. "You did well there. I owe you this life."

"Let's call it even for today," Mike said. "I wish I'd managed to take out the demon as well." Mike put the van in drive and pulled out of the lot, running over the gate that they had smashed through only an hour before. The building was empty now. Mike had hoped that someone had evacuated most of the day-workers from the building once the demon escaped. "Which way?" he asked Miller. Miller pointed to the right and off they went.

"So you can track it now?" Mike asked.

"Yes, as long as we move quickly. It leaves a kind of trail, but it does not last long."

"Does this one have a name?" Mike asked. "It seemed to have some sort of sonic ability. Like the old stories of banshees."

"Aye, exactly. Her original name was Gallu. She's had many names. She was also known as the windstorm. "

"Never heard of Gallu."

"Gorgon?" Miller asked. That did stir up an old memory, but he couldn't quite grasp it.

"No, sorry. It really doesn't..."

"Stop here," Miller interrupted.

Mike pulled the van over. "Is it close?"

"Close enough. Stay here," Miller said.

"Wait, what?"

"We go back to the original plan. You watch Catharine, I take care of the demon," Miller said, shutting the door.

"But I can help!" Mike yelled out of the window.

Miller stopped and turned back to face him. "I am sure that is true. You can help by keeping our furry friend here out of the fight. Gallu can kill you with a glance. It's better for everyone if I go alone." Then he was gone.

Mike couldn't help but feel a little rejected at first. Still, he had no real interest in facing that creature again and, after a few minutes of consideration, he decided being left behind wasn't so bad. He spent some time inspecting the equipment he'd recovered. Miller had taken the Desert Eagle and his two machetes, but he still had his own handgun. He gave it a good once over and checked the remaining ammo. Two bullets left. That wouldn't do at all. He unbuckled his seatbelt and headed into the back of the van.

Something moved to Mike's right. He spun in that direction but there was nothing there. He had seen only a hint of movement out of the corner of his eye. Had he imagined it? Mike glanced at Catharine. It had not been the cursed woman, but Mike reached for the taser in the center council of the van, just in case.

Suddenly, the front door of the van was torn open with a screech of shredding metal. Mike drew his gun but was unable to fire before hands grabbed him and dragged him out of the vehicle.

*****

Miller jogged forward, keeping his gun hidden under his coat. He didn't want to draw attention to himself, but Gallu was close, so close that he could almost smell the creature. Its trail hung in the air, like an after-image of lightning left on the eyes. It led to a church.

Miller marched up the front steps and pushed hard on the heavy doors. He was relieved to find that the building was empty. Having lost track of the time and even the day, he had thought that there might be a service in process.

The church itself was a drab affair, lacking the splendor of the Cathedral Basilica, which he had had the privilege of visiting (or smashing through) just a few short weeks before. Two rows of pews ran from back to front, separated by an aisle that he wandered down. The ceiling was high, with the typically upbeat large stained glass windows showing a man being nailed to a cross. He thought that the Christians were a little morbid, but he spent a great deal of his time hacking apart demons with various sharp objects, so he was not about to cast stones.

His eyes searched the ceiling, following the creature's path. It had zigzagged and crossed over itself so many times that Miller was unclear about which direction it had gone in. Had it, after so many years, at last figured out how he tracked it? That seemed unlikely.

He stumbled, rolled, and was instantly back on his feet. He snapped the gun up and then pointed it at the thing that he had tripped on. A foot stuck out from beyond a pew, by just a few inches. Miller approached it slowly, glancing around the room in expectance of an ambush. The foot belonged to a corpse, shriveled and colorless, a man of the cloth. His blank eyes stared up at the ceiling.

"Sorry, friend," Miller whispered as he closed the dead man's eyes.

"Ancient One," Gallu's voice boomed. It came from above, but Miller could see nothing. "I have been waiting."

"I am sorry to keep you waiting, but I am a busy man. If you would be kind enough to show yourself we could get this over quickly and I could get home in time for a nice pint of ale and a round of 'Power Rangers' with a young friend of mine." Miller stepped forward, spun around, and then stepped forward again, waiting for the attack, unsure of which direction it would come from.

"What have you done to us? What have you done to my sister?" the voice demanded.

Miller slowly approached a wall, trying to limit the possible directions from which the attack could come. "I assure you that I have no idea of what you are talking about. I have not had the privilege of killing any of your immediate relatives recently, although I have high hopes."

"Liar!" Gallu hissed from somewhere. "We are weak. Sick. Ura is mad. Lilith attacks her own kind. Our children have captured and tortured me. Only you could have done this."

Now this was interesting.

"Sick? I think you overestimate me. Unless you have suddenly come down with a terrible case of 'axe-in-face,' I hardly see how I could be the cause." Miller finally got his back against a brick wall. "I've had a few misbehaving children in my day, but kids of this era seem to no respect for their demonic enslavers. What is the world coming to?"

The demon screamed and the windows above Miller exploded. He dropped the gun, clapping his hands over his ears, and dove for the nearest pew. Shards of colorful glass rained down, small bits embedding themselves in his arms and back.

"You mock me? After all I have suffered, you mock me?"

Miller coughed, brushed glass out of his hair with one hand, and grabbed the gun with the other.

"Aye, mocking helps me wait. Show me your pretty face, and I will skip the general teasing and move on to the fighting."

"So be it," the voice boomed one final time. Miller peeked out from under his pew and glanced around the building. Nothing had moved.

"Perhaps I need to define showing your face. You always were slow. Now Lilith, that one was sharp…"

Gallu dropped from the ceiling, landing in the middle of the altar. Miller opened fire but the creature was already screaming. The pews in front of the demon leapt forward as if caught in a hurricane, heading right for him.

*****

Mike was slammed against the outside of the van. It had happened so fast that his head swam.

"Where is he?" Mike's vision cleared. Smith had him pinned, his eyes inky black, his flesh mangled, and his teethed gritted. His fine suit was torn and covered in both his and some poor human's blood. "Where is Miller?" Smith shook Mike hard.

"Probably kicking your demon's ass right now," Mike answered. He still had the gun and one arm was free. He used it to quickly jam the weapon up under Smith's chin. Smith relaxed his grip slightly, almost smiling.

"You know that won't kill me," he said smoothly.

"No, I gathered that. I'm betting that it hurts like hell though."

Smith laughed. "Very true. You know Samson, I like you."

"You have an interesting way of making friends," Mike said, through gritted teeth. He was being held in place by two hands. Hadn't Smith lost one? Mike glanced to the left, then to the right. The hand that had been cut off had been replaced by a five-pointed black tentacle, covered with small thorns and dripping some sort of clear fluid. Mike jerked away, making Smith smile even more.

"You like that? Another gift from your friend Miller. Lucky for me, unlike the work he did on my face, this will heal completely in…" He let Mike go, patting Mike's cheek with the dark hand to the rhythm of his words. "A few…more…hours..." Each time the hand made contact it stung, almost like a bee.

"Enough…" Mike pushed the barrel of the gun deeper into Smith's neck. He didn't pull the trigger, knowing it would be suicide.

"Oh pardon me." Smith grinned. "Am I the one who is going to die here? Oh no, wait a minute, that's you."

"Why does your hand grow back?" Mike changed the subject, hoping that by keeping this thing talking, he could buy Miller some time.

"Interesting question." Smith played along, enjoying Mike's discomfort. "I guess Miller didn't tell you all the rules. See, when the Fallen are alive, I stay young and strong, and, not to toot my own horn too much, pretty much unkillable."

"So that's why you captured the demon. As long as it's alive, so are you."

"Smart man. I can see why Miller hired you. Not smart enough, though, to know there's been a tracer on your van ever since we last met, nor to notice my good friend, Drake, tracking your movements over these past two weeks."

"Why me?"

"People don't survive an encounter with the Fallen often. I had you marked as special. Perhaps a new hire." Smith still grinned. "Of course, that's out of the question now. Your loss, though. We've got a great health plan." Smith again brought the demonic hand up to Mike's face to make his point. Mike grunted and dug his gun deeper into the creature's throat.

"I don't think it's my kind of work anyway," Mike croaked.

"Oh, I think you would have enjoyed it. My employers are all about life. Mostly their life and living forever, but can you blame them?"

In the distance, something exploded, but neither man nor monster turned to look.

"Ah, I bet that's my old playmate now. I'm afraid we're going to have to end this interview now. Don't call us, you'll be dead." Smith laughed gently, and then stopped. "Well, not my best line, but it's been a long day."

Something snapped behind Mike, but Smith ignored it, opening his mouth far too wide. The gruesome black tongue crawled out slowly from between his jaws, dripping as it advanced.

"Don't make me..." Mike screamed his final plea. He knew he couldn't kill Smith, but he could still give him one hell of a headache.

Without warning, the back door of the van flew open and Catharine's massive bulk burst out. Mike turned to look and Smith, seeing his moment, smacked the gun aside.

"Oh crap!" Mike shouted. He wasn't sure if he said it because of the big furry monster bearing down on him, the slimy tentacle approaching his neck, or the loss of his gun. In any case, this was bound to end very badly.

Catharine howled and crashed into both Mike and Smith, throwing them both to the ground with her. They bounced once and then again. Smith's tongue brushed the side of Mike's face, burning on contact. On the second bounce, Catharine's claws tore into the flesh of his left arm. Then, by some miracle, he was tossed free and thrown hard onto the street. He rolled several times, in a direction that he hoped was away from the various monsters out to kill him. He glanced around him, convinced that he was about to die.

The werewolf and the vampire were locked in mortal combat. Smith's body was fluid, seeming to double in mass to match the wolf's larger size. The cursed wolf-woman didn't seem to notice, biting down hard on the vampire's arm and digging a clawed hand into Smith's face, bursting his eyeball in a gush of black fluid. Meanwhile, Smith's seemingly endless tongue was wrapping around the wolf's chest. There was a loud snap as Catharine's jaws came together, clipping Smith's arm in half.

The severed limb dropped to the ground, but as it fell, Smith's black blood seemed to freeze solid, forming another tentacle. Mike stared in disbelief as the arm hit the ground and immediately began to crawl towards Catharine. The wolf was too busy tearing large chunks out of the vampire's chest to notice. It picked up Smith and started shaking him like a rag doll.

Mike was stunned by the ferocity of Catharine's attack. Was any aspect of the woman still in there? Before, when it had been Mike fighting the beast, had she been inside, holding some part of the creature at bay? It would certainly make things simpler if she won. Mike could just taser her once Smith was reduced to more manageable pieces and they could wait for Miller's return.

He got to his feet, grabbed the gun, and dashed to the van to retrieve the taser, beginning to hope that he might live another day. He only made it three steps, however, before he realized that Catharine was shrinking. Blood gushed from the places where Smith's long tongue had wrapped itself around the wolf. Catharine began to shrivel and lose her hair. She was still swinging though, cutting into Smith's arms and legs. She sliced again and again, bare white flesh beginning to appear underneath her thinning hair.

At last she faltered, now more human than beast. She bit down once more, this time on Smith's neck, but her once-impressive fangs snapped on contact and she let out a yell of pain that sounded far too human.

"No!" Mike rushed Smith and fired the gun from point blank into the back of the vampire's skull. The bullet did very little damage, but Smith was knocked forward, releasing Catharine's pale, shrinking form. The vampire had been literally torn to pieces by the wolf, with the bigger chunks now trying to slither their way back to Smith's trunk. The hungry tongue vanished back into Smith's still-open maw.

Mike grabbed Catharine and began to drag her away from Smith and towards the van with one hand. He glanced from her to Smith, still covering the vampire with the gun. Catharine was so light now. Was he too late?

"Damn those hairy stupid beasts. How dare it touch me?" Smith roared. He made no effort to move. Mike noticed that one leg was busy reattaching itself. "Why the hell is Miller keeping one of those damn dogs in his van? That hurt!" A leg popped back into place and Smith stood up straight. He looked at Mike slowly dragging Catharine away. "Now, where were we?"

Mike fired the gun again before he remembered it was his last shot.

The bullet hit Smith in what was left of his face. The contact knocked him off his feet again.

"Ow," the vampire said, sounding more annoyed than actually hurt. "That's going to cost you, Samson. That's going to cost you."

Mike reached the van and tossed Catharine into the passenger seat. He dove across to the driver's seat and gunned the engine faster than he'd ever thought possible. Smith was standing again, walking slowly toward them. What remained of the vampire's face did not look happy.

"Good," Mike whispered between gritted teeth. He dropped the van into gear and floored it. The grill hit the vampire with an extremely satisfying thud. Mike didn't slow down. After a moment, the body slid off the front of the van and rolled under the front tire. Mike smiled.

"Mike," Catherine's voice was weak. She was staring at him, her eyes still the dark black of the Cursed. "I tried. I tried so hard."

"It's okay. You did great." Mike attempted to comfort her while driving as fast as possible and turning Miller's tracker back on. It was obvious that Catharine needed help, and Miller might be the only man on the planet who could provide it.

"It was so…so…I think…" Her voice faded away and she began to convulse. She fell forward out of her seat, slumping to the floor.

"Oh God, what now?" Mike yelled. Was she changing back again? The tracking device made a beep and Mike slammed the brakes on the van. "Damn! Too far." He had passed Miller. Once they came to a stop, he threw the vehicle in park and dove into the back for the taser. Catharine's body thrashed for a moment while he waited in the back, unsure of what to do. Then, he slowly approached her. After one step forward, she hadn't moved, so Mike took another step. Nothing.

"Catharine?" Mike was now close enough to touch her. He tapped her gingerly on the shoulder. Still nothing. He pushed her harder and she rolled gently to the side, revealing a black pool of fresh blood. She was still bleeding. "Catharine?" he said again, confidence coming back to him. He lifted her with one arm and placed her gently on the passenger seat. A wound on her belly was bleeding freely. He reached up, grabbed the shoulder strap of the seatbelt, and snapped her in. The belt clicked into place and he looked her in the face. Empty, black eyes stared back.

"I think…" she continued, as if nothing had happened. Mike jumped back, tripping and almost falling out of the car through the gaping hole where his door had been. "I think it's dying." Mike steadied himself, taking some pride in the fact that he hadn't screamed like a little girl.

"Maybe Miller killed the demon. Maybe this is how you get your life back," he said, after a moment.

"No. I think I'm dying. We're dying." Catharine reached down and touched the wound, then brought her fingers back up to her face, staring at her own blood.

"What? No, listen, it's going to be fine. We're going to get you patched up. You and I are going to laugh about this later. I'm going to take you dancing for real and we can spend the whole evening together without you trying to eat me for once." Mike sat back down and put the van into reverse.

Catharine shook her head slowly and then leaned it against the passenger side window. "You're such a terrible dancer," she said. There was a small chuckle that turned into a cough. "Cute though."

Mike glanced at the wounded woman. She looked back and smiled warmly. Then Catharine was still.

# 16 - Path

Night fell as Ann soared. It took her only a few minutes to find a gas station. It was now the end of rush hour, and plenty of cars were still pulling in and out. At one time, Ann would have waited, but that time was past. She landed directly in the middle of the lot, much to the dismay of the patrons. Ann imagined she must look even worse than normal with her torn clothes stained with black blood. A woman fainted at the sight of her. A man took off in a run, leaving his wife and kids sleeping in the car. Another just stared, his jaw hanging slack. Ann waved a hello and headed inside the attached minimart. The clerk didn't even look up as she entered.

"Can I help you?" he asked, sounding bored and still reading a paper.

"I sincerely doubt it," Ann said. She found the aisle for car supplies. Picking up two empty red gasoline cans, she turned back the way she came, stopping only to grab a Snickers bar and a lighter from the front.

"Please come again," the clerk said in the same bored voice as she stepped out. She headed to the gas pump that the man had fled from, which was still active, and started filling the tanks with gasoline. As she went about her work, she couldn't help watching the abandoned family sleeping peacefully in the car. Perhaps they were on their way to a vacation someplace. Their life could have been hers. Instead, she was going to war.

She ripped open the Snickers bar and swallowed it whole. Then, she made sure the lighter was secure in her pocket before leaping into the air. It didn't take her long to pick up the demon's trail, now that she knew what it was. The street lamps provided enough light for that. The trail looked like the static on an old TV screen. It hung in the air, starting from the building where they had been attacked and heading north. Then it changed, growing darker and more like smoke as she closed in on the monster, ending at an old factory. Half the building had been demolished, while the other half was not much better, made up of broken glass, rusted steel, and decaying wood and brick. The smell of chemicals and rot hit her as she approached. Ann wondered if she had found all the best spots in Newark that day.

She landed on the roof and listened. At first there was nothing, but then she made out the very faint screeching she had heard when she and Lizzie been attacked. The scientist in her wondered what the noise could mean. Were zombies like bats? Sightless creatures that used sound, like sonar, to find their way?

There was a skylight on the roof, or at least the remains of one, and she crept up and looked inside. In the dim light, she couldn't make anything out. Still, she knew the demon was there. Ann let out a deep breath, fear finally starting to overcome the deep numbness that had taken her over when she had promised Abraham that she would stop Ura. For a moment, she seriously considered running, but there was no place to run to. No, she was going to do this or die trying.

Ann dropped down through the ruined skylight into the darkness. The room below was huge and cavernous. At some point, rows and rows of machines would have been busy making something, though now only garbage and debris covered the floor. Inside it was brighter than she had expected, narrow beams of city light pushing through holes in the walls and roof. Nothing moved to greet her.

Dim light or not, it took Ann some time to find the trail. She was sure it would be easier in daylight, but didn't think she would find the courage to return if she left. Finally, she found the trail by almost walking through it. The creature was close. She followed it to a smaller storage room at the end of the factory floor. It was much darker here, so Ann put the gas down and pulled out her lighter. It produced only a meager glow, but was better than nothing. Now she could see the faint outlines of bodies through the open door. This seemed like a good place to start. Ann's heart pounded and she found it hard to breathe. She stood in the doorway, stock still, struggling with fear for several moments before stepping inside.

She took the gas tank and started dousing a nearby body. She was waiting for it to spring up any moment, but it was still, well…a dead person. Ann slowly repeated the process with the next three bodies. She was afraid to breathe as she silently worked through the bodies. Obviously she could not use the lighter, nor did she want to trip over anything and fall headfirst into a pile of naked dead people. She had covered about half the room when she at last spotted the demon. It lay on a pile of bones in the center of the room and appeared to be sleeping with two fresh corpses tucked away nearby. There was something extremely fitting about the scene, like the cover of a heavy metal album that she might have listened to when she went through her retro heavy-metal/goth phase. Ann had one gallon of gasoline left. She turned to recover it, walking painstakingly slowly to the room's entrance. In the darkness, she could just make out the lone gas can. She bent to retrieve it but then noticed someone was standing next to her. She nearly screamed but managed to catch herself, only letting out a short "Eep."

The zombie stood inches from her, an old woman's corpse with a large chunk of its forehead missing. Its eyes were closed and it was naked. Some fluid was draining out of its mouth and down its chest. For a moment, it did nothing. Maybe it didn't see her? Ann took a step back and the undead thing started screeching. It might have been the loudest noise she had ever heard. Ann dropped the gas and slugged the zombie, sending it flying through the air, continuing to screech as it flew. Suddenly there was movement all around her. Ann again pulled out the lighter. The little flame illuminated the rising zombies. One pulled at her leg, catching her in mid-step, and she tumbled, sending the lighter flying forward, out of her hand.

"Aw crap." Ann swore as she watched it spin away into the darkness. Fire burst into being as the fuel caught. It ripped through the zombies, jumping from corpse to corpse and lighting up the room. For a moment, she basked in her victory, until she noticed that the zombies were not stopping. They continued to stand and shuffle. So now they were dead and on fire. "Great!" Ann muttered.

She grabbed the last container of gasoline and leapt into the air. The ceiling was high enough to give her room to maneuver, and she took refuge on top of a large beam. The zombies milled below her, reaching for her in vain. There were maybe twenty in all, bunched in a tight, flaming group. The smell of their burning flesh made Ann queasy.

From her vantage point, she noticed something odd about the walls. Symbols were everywhere, painted in what Ann could only guess was blood. She didn't recognize any of them. They seemed to be stick figures with wings, repeated over and over again.

A howl from below told Ann the demon was on the move. Dragging its oversized arm behind it, it moved past the zombies and, reaching the other side, smashed the wall. The rafter supporting Ann shifted slightly with the force of the blow.

"Wow, ugly is smarter than I thought," Ann muttered. The demon struck again, knocking out a large section of brick. Ann decided not to wait for it to bring the place down around them, and swept down from her hiding place.

"Here," Ann told it. "This will help with the smell." She splashed the remaining gas from the can onto the demon, hitting it directly in the chest. The creature was soaked and howled with displeasure. It charged at Ann but she simply took to the air again. Ura crashed into the zombie horde, tossing many of them high into the air and bursting into flames itself.

Ann took her place on the rafter again. The demon screamed, enraged, as fire ran up and down its body. It ran to the other side of the room and started demolishing the other wall. The bricks collapsed, shifting Ann's perch again.

By now, fire had spread across nearly the entire length of the wood floor. Ann noticed that one of the zombies that had been tossed was no longer moving. Perhaps the fire was working, but the air was getting hard to breathe and she needed a way out. Ann searched the room. There was the doorway she had come in through, and one oversized window, made up of small panes of glass. That looked like the easiest escape route. She leapt for it, spreading her wings and stroking them through the air once, then pulling them back. Ura had other plans for her, and managed to hit her by throwing one of the flaming zombies. Now Ann was burning. She smashed into the wall and fell to the floor.

Every inch of her body seemed to scream in pain. The flaming zombie-missile was still on her, attempting to gnaw at her arm. Trying to ignore the pain or at least control it, Ann kicked the dead thing away and used the wall to pick herself up. The room was starting to go dark again as it filled with black smoke, and flames were everywhere. Ura stepped out of the fire in front of before her. It was not burning anymore, but the black scales of its chest were charred and peeling. Before she could move, its overgrown hand was on her again, this time grabbing her by the right wing. Ann screamed as the soft skin of the wing ripped. Something like a bone snapped as the demon dangled her in the air and then slammed her down to the ground, releasing the wing. Ann tried to rise but the immense arm came down on her like a sledgehammer. She choked and spat blood.

The demon roared, bringing the arm down again. It was move or die, and somehow Ann managed to roll out of the way at the last second. She pushed off of the ground and broke into a shambling run. With fire everywhere and the demon behind her, it seemed that she was about to meet the death that she had been so ready to accept earlier. There was something about realizing she was about to die that made her want to live. Even this tortured, freaky nightmare of an existence was worth something. Ann pushed through the smoke and fire, managing by sheer luck to escape the storage room and come back out onto the factory floor.

The fire was spreading, but it became easier to see and breathe as she moved farther away. Ann jumped but could not get the damaged wing to respond, and so collapsed to the floor.

Ura stepped into the room, moving sideways. Its unbelievable bulk was still too much for the doorway. It made two attempts to get through the doorway before a loud crack came from behind it. A huge section of the wall collapsed, burying the demon in a pile of brick and steel. Ann, knowing that the debris would not hold the creature for long, struggled to her feet, despite her dizziness and the blood streaming down her face. Another section of wall collapsed to her right and fire burst out from the room behind Ura. A rafter broke free and swung from the ceiling, missing her by inches. It shattered, leaving jagged flaming shards of wood scattered across the floor. She was almost out of time. It was now or never.

A giant, black-scaled fist burst free of the wreckage and Ura's body followed as it began to pull itself free. Ann grabbed a nearby shard of the rafter and wielded it like a giant wooden stake, charging the fallen demon and driving the shard into its chest. Its protective scales, already weakened by the fire, did nothing to stop the wood. Ura screamed and then gurgled as a fountain of blood streamed out of its mouth. Ann yelled, pushing the wood in deeper, falling to her knees with the effort.

For a long moment, Ann and the demon stared at each other. Its arms twitched as it tried to figure out how to remove the spike from its chest. The smaller arm finally got a hold of it, but could not get it to budge. The other arm was far too large to be useful, and did not seem to bend correctly. The demon couldn't use it to grip the spike, and it flopped helplessly, reaching for, but never grasping the stake. The monster struggled for a few moments before toppling over.

Although every part of her hurt, the air was getting harder to breathe, and the world was in a constant spin, Ann felt relief wash over her. She had won. For a moment, she just enjoyed that fact.

Then she started hearing the voice.

"Seven are they. Seven are they." It was Ura. She didn't think it could talk. She limped to its side. "I hear them. I hear them," it continued. Ann saw that its eyes were human.

"Jamie?" Ann asked.

"I hear them. I hear them." It didn't respond to her, continuing to mutter. "The law. The law."

"Who do you hear? The Fallen?" Ann asked. She knew she should run, get clear of the building before it collapsed around her, but something held her there.

"The seven. The seven, six, five, four, three, two, one. The one who will end it all."

"End what?" Ann asked.

"Everything. The seven. I can hear them."

"One of the Fallen will end everything?"

"I hear them. I hear them say she will end it all. She has broken the law."

"Who? Who will end it all?" She knew the answer before it came.

"Lilith."

# 17 - Life and Death, but Mostly Death

"Catharine?" Mike screamed. She didn't respond. The black in her eyes was draining away, running like tears down her still smiling face. "Catharine!" He shouted and slapped her hard on the shoulder. The empty stare remained unchanged. "No! You're not dying on me. Not after all we've been through to get you out of this!" He was still shouting while keeping an eye on the road and the tracker. "You hear me? You can't die now! You're the one I'm supposed to save!" He had to get to Miller. Maybe Miller could save her. He threw the van into a hard right turn. Miller was maybe 100 yards away. It wasn't too late. He could still do this. He could still make amends. "Just hold on!"

Mike slowed the van, stuck his head out of the window, and looked furiously up and down the road for any sign of the small Hispanic man. "Miller!" he shouted. There was a small cottage and a drab-looking church to the right. Miller had to be in one of the two. A police car screeched to a halt just a few yards ahead. That might be a clue. Two officers rushed out and ran up the stairs to the church.

"Church it is," said Mike. He unbuckled Catharine. Her body slumped into a leaning position against the passenger-side door. He opened the door and checked her for a pulse. There was none. "No, no, no, no," he stammered. Maybe the officers had a first aid kit? He dragged Catharine to the street, laying her on her back and yelling for help. He would try CPR.

One of the officers heard him and turned back down the stairs, just as the large doors of the church exploded outward. Both officers were knocked to the ground and one of the doors landed inches away from Mike. Well, at least he had found Miller. As if on cue, Miller came flying out of the church headfirst. He bounced twice, hard, on the steps and then rolled to a stop.

Mike was giving Catharine CPR now, trying to find a rhythm but failing. How many compressions was it before breathing?

"Miller!" he shouted. "I need your help." He bent down to breathe into Catharine's mouth.

"Samson?" Miller asked weakly. Mike looked back up and started counting compressions, trying desperately to make Catharine start breathing again.

"Catharine's hurt. Smith found us. There was a fight. She's dying."

1,2,3,4,5,6,7,8,9,10,11,12...breathe! Mike bent over and forced air into her mouth.

"You there! Constables!" Miller was shouting up the stairs to the officers just beginning to pick themselves up off the ground.

"Officers!" Mike shouted.

1,2,3,4,5,6,7,8,9,10,11,12... breathe!

"Get away from that door! Now!" Miller sprinted to Mike's side as another police car pulled up and skidded to a stop. It was getting crowded. Two more cops were racing up the stairs to the recovering officers. One of them approached Mike.

1,2,3,4,5,6,7,8,9,10,11,12... breathe!

The officer suddenly noticed that Miller was holding a big handgun and drew his own sidearm. "Okay, let's put that weapon down!" the man shouted.

Miller ignored him and gently touched Mike on the shoulder. "She's gone."

Mike ignored him and continued to work at it. 1,2,3,4,5,6,7,8,9,10,11,12...breathe! Coming back up, Mike said, "No, if I can just keep pushing air into her lungs, keep oxygen reaching her brain, they can revive her."

"I said drop the gun!" the officer yelled. Miller pulled tighter on Mike's arm.

1,2,3,4,5,6,7,8,9,10,11,12...breathe!

"Let her have her peace, lad. I need your help with the living."

"No. Miller, we have to save her. She's the whole reason we're up here."

"What the hell is going on?" The officer still had his gun pointed at Miller.

"Const....Officer." Miller finally responded. "You need to help me get those men away from that church. Now." His tone was calm, firm, and absolute. Mike continued his CPR, but noticed the man lowering his weapon.

"Yes sir," the man said in a much more polite tone.

1,2,3,4,5,6,7,8,9,10,11,12...breathe!

The scream was too high-pitched. Mike felt it more than heard it. Sound seemed to rattle his insides and he was forced to stop the CPR as his hands instinctively slapped over his ears. A police car several yards away crumpled as if crushed by an invisible fist. The metal of the car twisted, glass shattered, and the vehicle slid several feet to the right.

Miller pointed at the demon, who had dropped from the sky to the stairs of the church. The police stared open-mouthed as Gallu appeared between them. Her black scales shimmered in the daylight, her thick tentacle-like hair stood up in all directions, and her red wings were folded up neatly behind her.

Miller grabbed both Mike and the officer and tossed them behind the van.

"Catharine! No!" Mike protested.

The demon screamed again, smashing another police car, but Miller cut it short with a shot to the chest. Gallu stiffened and took a step back, then surged forward again, diving at the nearest man. Her black tongue shot out of her mouth, but rather than wrapping around the police officer's throat, it burst through his chest like a spear, killing the man instantly.

Miller's gun clicked empty and he tossed it in Mike's direction, drawing the machetes. He charged up the stairs, only to be slammed back to the ground when the demon hit him with the remains of her latest meal. The rest of the officers were finally reacting. One opened fire, another turned and ran, while a third fumbled with his weapon, dropping it to the ground.

Mike dove back to Catharine's side and restarted the CPR. Only then did he notice that his hands were covered with her thick, black blood. For a moment, in all the madness, he looked at her face. The slight smile remained frozen there, even though the empty eyes stared towards the sky. Miller was right, she was gone.

"I'm so sorry," he whispered, as he closed her eyes for the final time.

The screams of another police officer brought Mike back to the situation at hand. Another man was dead on the staircase and Miller was going toe to toe with Gallu now. The officer nearest to Mike had run back to his squad car and was calling for help.

Mike's gun was still in the van. He had no knife, machine gun, or bazooka to help take this thing down. The only other weapon he had was the taser. If it had worked so well against the Cursed, maybe it would also do some damage to their parents. He drew the weapon and did his best to put Catharine's death out of his mind. He would mourn her later.

Miller was slashing at the demon but the creature was fast, staying just out of range. Mike assumed the large, bleeding holes that Miller had made in its chest were keeping it from screaming, but the long claws on each hand were dangerous enough. Jogging up the stairs, Mike got in range and waited for his shot.

"Miller, down!" Mike fired. Miller didn't look, ducking into a roll in reaction. The taser's cables sailed over the small man's head, but just short of the demon. Seeing its advantage, the demon kicked out at Miller's head, sending him tumbling down the stairs a second time. It then disappeared back into the church, an officer following as far as the doorway while firing his weapon.

"Get away from the…" The black tongue sprang through the opening and the officer was gone. "Door," Miller finished weakly. "Samson, how exactly did that help?"

"Ah, oops?" Mike shrugged, embarrassed. "The man at the compound said the Fallen were weak to this weapon. It's how they captured her in the first place." Mike was inspecting his pockets looking for another cartridge with which to reload the taser.

"If it can slow her down, I can finish her quickly."

"Can't. Out of charges." Mike tossed the spent weapon down. "Damn."

"What kind of weapon was it?" Miller asked, reclaiming one of the blades he had dropped. He was scanning the front door. Behind them, the remaining officer was shouting for more backup.

"It's electrical…like lightning," Mike explained.

Miller gave him a stern look. "Samson, I do know what electricity is."

"Oh, sorry, it's just most of the time you don't…"

Miller cut him off with the wave of a hand. "The question is, where can we get electricity here? Samson, what do those do?" Miller pointed to a row of power lines and smiled. It was the first time Mike had seen him grin since they had run into Smith.

"Those would work. But how are you going to…you know what, I don't even want to know. I'm going to try and get this man to safety," Mike said, pointing to the police officer. "Maybe he has a shotgun we can borrow."

"Excellent!"

Mike trotted over to the police officer, who was busy shouting into a radio. The man was sweating and his eyes were wide. "Officers down! I repeat, officers down! We need help here!"

"Officer, I need to get you out of this area," Mike said, trying to sound calmer than he felt.

"Who are you people? What is that thing?" the man shouted. Mike felt for him. He still remembered when he had first seen this kind of madness.

"I'm a police officer like you. I'm helping the…" Mike paused, thinking. How was he going to explain this? Screw it. "The FBI. That man by the church is Extra Special Agent Miller."

"Extra special?"

"Oh trust me, he's special all right. The important thing is that he needs to handle this and we need to get everyone else out to safety. This creature is extremely dangerous."

"Is it an alien?" the man asked.

"Umm sure, that's right." Mike agreed. Why the hell not? That was probably easier to swallow than an ancient demon reborn.

"I knew it! I knew that shit was true!"

Mike noticed a shotgun lying on the front seat. Perfect. He added,

"I'm going to need this," and pulled the weapon free of the car.

"Alright. Let's go kick some alien ass!" the officer shouted, waving his pistol.

"Umm no, look, enough people have…" Mike was interrupted by the now-familiar screech of the demon. He pulled the gung-ho officer down behind the car, glancing around, trying to get a view of the monster.

"Where is it?" the officer asked, joining in Mike's frantic searching.

Miller appeared first, running out of the church. Apparently he'd found a rope, tied a machete to it, and was spinning it around his head like a hybrid cowboy-ninja weapon.

"What is he doing? He doesn't actually expect to hit anything with that, does he?"

The blade leapt out into the air and found the demon that Mike could not. The rope wrapped around the creature's neck, with the blade sticking into a shoulder for good measure.

"Oh…would you look at that?" the officer said, clearly impressed.

The demon and demon hunter struggled for a moment. The rope appeared to be keeping the beast silent, but instead of the monster being pulled out of the air, Miller was lifted up off the ground. The Ancient One adjusted for this by releasing more rope, and wrapped the rest of it around his chest by spinning around. Miller kept low to the ground but was still dragged by the thing as it flew, going down the church stairs and directly into Mike's van through the hole left by the missing door.

"Oh no, not my van!" Mike yelled.

Miller braced himself inside the van, stopping his movement as he continued to struggle to bring the beast down. The demon wanted none of it and beat her wings madly, trying to escape. She flew over the van and past Mike's hiding spot but could get no further. One side of the van began to lift and the entire thing looked as though it might tip over on its side.

"Shoot it!" Mike yelled at the officer, who was standing dumbstruck and watching the struggle. The man complied and opened fire on Gallu. His first two shots were wide, but the third was dead on, striking the creature in the leg. The demon spun in the air, wrapping the rope around herself and raising the van farther off the ground.

The police officer fired one more time, and Gallu dropped out of the sky, diving through the power lines and smashing hard into a pole.

Mike gave a cry of victory, which quickly turned to into dismay as the pole leaned over and then fell toward them. He grabbed the other man and dove away as the large wooden post smashed through the middle of the police car, sending glass flying everywhere. A live electrical cable hit the ground, hissing and jumping like a snake.

Mike was getting to his feet and helping the officer up when he saw

Miller run past him. Gallu was getting up slowly, shrugging off the now slack rope, but still stunned by the collision. Miller jumped into the air and grasped the live wire as he passed, shoving it into Gallu's face in one smooth motion.

There was a loud pop and both the demon and demon hunter were flying through the air in opposite directions. Gallu hit the ground first and was still, while Miller hit the ground screaming and thrashing.

For a moment Mike did not move, taking in the scene. Miller was shrieking in a language he didn't recognize at first. He seemed to be having a seizure of some sort and the hand which had come in contact with the cable was actually smoking. Miller had known what electricity was, but seem to have no idea of how dangerous it was. Mike noticed the cable still thrashing between them.

"Miller?" Mike approached his friend's body, which was still racked by spasms. After a moment, Mike recognized the language he was screaming in as Spanish. Having worked in Newark for many years, he knew some of the language, but wasn't exactly fluent. Miller was speaking very quickly, repeating the same phrase over and over. Darkness, something, something, mother save me? "Miller! Snap out of it, man!" Miller ignored him and continued to repeat himself.

"Is he okay?" the policeman asked.

Oh yes, he does this regularly. It's his 'special' time. He suppressed the sarcastic response and replied with a simple "No." Now he would have to finish off the demon himself. Hopefully that wasn't against some sort of demon hunter union rule. He pumped the shotgun, took one step forward, and stopped.

There was music, beautiful music, which seemed deeply moving. Mike could just barely hear it and he strained his ears. It had a simple yet mesmerizing melody and was sung by the most beautiful voice he'd ever heard. Though it was faint, it seemed to consume his attention. He could no longer hear Miller's screaming. There was only the music.

For a long moment he listened, completely absorbed. The police officer behind him was mesmerized as well, but Mike had no interest in him. Gallu was next to him. Her black scaled hand brushed the cheek that the vampire had earlier ruined. The touch was almost tender. She smiled at him through fangs and somehow spoke as she sang.

"I remember you. You are special to him. I will make you special to me."

Mike's mind snapped back to reality. He tried to move, to jump back, to raise his gun, but he could do none of these things. He couldn't even turn his head as the demon walked past him, or follow her with his eyes. He couldn't breathe. He stood perfectly still.

Useful information often pops into one's head only moments too late.

Mike suddenly recalled Miller's words. Gallu was a gorgon, probably one of *the* gorgons. Mike remembered now what that was. In school, he had learned there were three gorgons, all sisters. Mike didn't remember the first two but everyone knew the third. Medusa, with her hair full of snakes, could turn men to stone with a glance. Of course, the story was a myth, but just like the tales of vampires, werewolves, and immortals, some aspects of it were based on truth. Gallu could freeze people in place, not with a look, but a song. Mike now understood that the stories of banshees killing men with their scream, sirens leading men to smash their boats on the rocks, and gorgons freezing them in stone, were probably all based on the same creature, the thing that was now behind him.

A wet sound informed Mike of what seemed to be the last policeman's death. The sound continued for what seemed like hours, while Mike tried desperately to do anything. His eyes were beginning to tear, his lungs burned, and God, his nose itched! The song continued and Mike was helpless against it.

Gallu was back then, talking to him softly through the music.

"Don't be afraid, child." She continued to grin.

She smelled vaguely of sulfur, which Mike initially thought might be a demonic 'thing,' but which he quickly realized was the smell of her burnt flesh. She leaned forward, kissing him on the mouth. Her lips were oily like a snake, and her breath was hot. The music ended with her embrace, but he found he still could not move. The creature seemed to be enjoying herself, taking her time before her tongue began gently forcing his mouth open wider. Liquid was now pouring into Mike's mouth, pushing its way inside him, blocking his throat. Mike wanted to scream, wanted to pull away, but still his body refused.

Gallu ended the embrace and continued to smile while Mike's insides revolted.

"No!" said Miller, pulling the trigger on Mike's shotgun. It was aimed directly at the demon's head. Gallu's face seemed to vanish as the shotgun blast ripped through its skull.

Mike was suddenly moving again. His stomach contracted repeatedly, expelling more and more of the foul liquid. It seemed to boil as it hit the ground, popping and hissing as it died. A moment later, Mike collapsed to the ground, his breathing coming back in great gasps. The body of the last police officer stared lifelessly at him. Mike hadn't even gotten the man's name.

"Samson. Up and at 'em, lad. You're not dead yet." Miller was suddenly next to him, trying to help him up with one hand. The other looked badly burned and was tucked in to his chest.

"Miller," Mike panted, getting up. "Am I?" He didn't finish the question.

"You're clean, lad. About the closest I've seen anyone come, but I killed her before the curse could take."

"Oh, thank God," Mike said, putting his arm around Miller, who was not all that steady himself. "Why though? Why did it kill that man, but not me?"

"Well…" Miller said slowly, thinking it over. "People like you, man. You are a stand-up kind of fellow and you have a very nice…van."

"You have no idea either."

"Not a clue." Miller grinned. "But I am not one to complain."

# 18 - Intersection

There was nothing else to be done. He couldn't help the dead and he couldn't explain once the authorities arrived. Mike said his goodbyes to Catharine and they left. This didn't sit well with him. Miller was going to leave a trail of bodies. It was in his nature. But even if his enemies were not exactly human anymore, it was still against the law. Would Mike have to cover for his friend for the greater good? Or could he convince the people in charge that this was necessary? The questions, along with everything else, made his head hurt.

Mike and Miller found another hotel in which to clean their wounds, rest a while, and try and forget. Miller had no issues sleeping but Mike lay awake, trying to deal with it all. Something was bothering him. Certainly part of it was Catharine's death, which still stung, though he'd hardly known the woman. But there was something else, something he'd overlooked, something he'd forgotten. His tired mind picked at it for hours, until it finally struck him.

"We forgot about Ann," Mike almost shouted.

"What about her?" Miller responded, drifting out of a hard sleep.

"Ann! She called, remember? Right before those two goons showed up at our door."

"Goons? Now that's a phrase I like." Miller grinned, perking up slightly. "So we did." Mike dug into his pocket and retrieved his cell.

"Hold on, I can use the call log to get her number and try to call her back."

"Excellent," Miller said, rolling back over and closing his eyes.

*****

Lizzie was not quite sure how she had gotten home. She almost fell out of the car when she arrived, dashing to her door. Her hands were shaking so hard that she managed to drop the keys twice, but she successfully unlocked the door on her third attempt. Once inside, she slapped all five locks closed, ran into her office, and closed the door, curling into a ball on the floor. She knew she was hysterical but simply couldn't stop herself. A long time passed. The phone was ringing. When had the phone started ringing? She picked it up.

"Hello?"

"Hello. This is Mike Samson. I'm looking for Ann." Mike Samson! The cop that Ann had said could help. ANN! Lizzie felt waves of shame rush over her. She had abandoned Ann at the side of the road, calling her a monster. Why had she done that? Just when Ann needed her the most, she had panicked and ran.

*****

Mike pulled the phone away from his ear.

"Is it Ann?" Miller asked.

"No, it's just some woman swearing." He tried again. "Hello?" The woman on the other side of the phone was very upset about something.

"Hi, sorry, sorry, you just reminded me. Look, my name is Lizzie, I'm a friend of Ann's and she's in huge trouble. Can you come right away?"

"I…" Mike started to respond but paused. Part of him just wanted to go home. He was sore and tired and Miller looked ill and smelled of burnt flesh. "Yeah, of course, we'll be there in a few hours."

*****

With the help of Mike's trusty GPS they found the house quickly.

"You wanna stay here or come in with me?" Mike asked Miller.

"I had best come with you. Something feels off about this." Miller opened the door and stepped out into the street.

Mike rang the bell. He was glad to have Miller with him. This Lizzie woman seemed so panicked about something and after the last few days, he could use all the help he could get. After a moment, Mike heard several deadbolts slide free.

"Mike Samson?" said a woman's voice from inside.

"Yes, that's me. Plus one." The door opened a crack.

"Who is he? He doesn't look like a cop."

"I'm a friend, lass," Miller put in. "Joseph Miller. I know Ann as well." Lizzie looked back and forth at them, and then moved back from the door. Mike heard another two chains being removed and the door swung open. Inside, he could finally see Lizzie. She was tall, Asian, and just a touch on the heavy side. Her hair was wet and her eyes were puffy.

"I'm Lizzie. Thanks for coming." She was jittery, like she was going to jump out of her skin at any moment. Mike gave Miller a quick glance.

"She's human," Miller said. "And lovely, might I add." Lizzie looked angry at that.

"Of course I'm human. What were you expecting?" she snarled.

"He didn't mean anything. We've just run into…" Mike wondered how much she knew. "A lot of unfriendly people lately."

"Wait, you mean human and not cursed right?" Lizzie said. "You're the demon hunter!" She pointed a finger at Miller's chest. "You know all about this shit."

"What is with you people and the word 'shit'?" Miller asked, a look of disgust on his face.

Lizzie ignored him. "You need to find Ann. Something has happened to her."

"So she's not here. Do you know where she went?"

"I can tell you where I last saw her."

*****

Ann did her best to run. Something inside her was broken and the thick smoke made it hard to breathe. She still couldn't fly or even walk in a straight line. She had waited too long at Jamie's side. His eyes had glazed over and he had fallen silent. The building had continued to collapse around them, and so Ann made her escape. If the demon was somehow still alive, even with Jamie dead, the fire would do the rest. His words bothered her, though. Lilith was dead, wasn't she? Otherwise, how would she be having this train of thought? How could Ann be doing anything? She didn't want to think about it. She'd had too many shocks for one day already.

The fire was spreading and she was sure the whole building would go. The old wooden floors made great kindling. The fire provided enough light for her to make out the way in front of her. It would only be a matter of time before the smoke became too thick for her vision to permeate.

Ann could make out the end of the building, and the large missing wall where the demolition crew had stopped. At least Ann had made their job easier. What would have happened if they had gotten to the end of the building and found the little nest of monsters? She stepped through the giant hole in the wall and into the night air.

A flashlight blinded her.

"Freeze!" Ann sheltered her eyes from the glare of the light. There was a cop pointing a gun at her and holding a flashlight with his other hand. Behind him were another five cops.

"Aw, crap."

*****

"I left her here." Lizzie said, pointing to a map of a particularly rundown part of Newark. Mike checked his gun and his badge. In that neighborhood, demons might be the least of their problems. "We had just been in a building over here…" She pointed to the map again. "It was full of…things." Lizzie was visibly trembling.

Mike put a hand on her shoulder. "It's okay, we can protect you.

You're safe," he said in his most soothing voice. "Can you show us exactly where it was?"

"No!" Lizzie shouted. "No, I can't. You don't understand, I just…can't!" She was almost hysterical.

"Okay, okay, just stay calm," Mike continued. "We'll find her."

Twenty minutes later, they again stepped out into the street, armed with their remaining gear and two flashlights. "Where do we start?"

"How well did you know Ann before I met you two at the hospital?" Miller asked.

"Not well. We only met an hour or so before running into you. Why?" Mike asked.

"One of the Fallen was here recently, on this very road. If Ann was here and she is alive, she isn't human. We may have to kill her."

*****

"What the hell is that?" one of the officers yelled.

"Would you believe Comic Con is in town?" Ann quipped.

"Get your hands over your head and put your face on the ground. Now!" the first cop yelled.

"Here? But it's all dirty and I'm wearing white." Ann looked around desperately for a way out. Sure, she had stolen the gas and burned down a building, but she was no criminal. Well, maybe she was now, but she wasn't about to let these men take her. She remembered Lizzie's warning about being dissected in a lab.

The first officer came closer. "Down on the ground now!"

"All right, all right! No need to be hostile!" She got down on the ground. The cop grabbed her wrists and slapped on a pair of handcuffs. She wondered…how strong was she? Ann stretched, snapping the cuffs.

"Holy…" was all the cop said, before she lifted him up and launched him at the other police officers. The three of them toppled into a pile.

"Sorry about this, but I can't stay. I'm late for a meeting of Horribly Deformed Super-Strong Monsters Anonymous," Ann said, breaking into a run. She hoped she hadn't hurt them. They were just doing their jobs. She heard the gunshots and felt a bullet tear through her damaged wing. She screamed but didn't stop running.

*****

Joseph Miller really disliked stairs at this point. It had been two days and even he had his limits. Of course, the Fallen's trail led to the very top of the building. It was old but he could see it plainly enough. So up, up, up they trudged.

As they reached the top, Miller caught the smell of death.

"What is this?" Mike smelled it as well, and then recognized it. "I would ask what died but I really don't want to know."

"Be on your guard." Miller could see something just above him. He climbed the final stairs to the top floor and flashed the light around the room. Mike drew his newly-reloaded handgun. There were a few partially-decayed bodies lying around, explaining the smell, and there was blood. Not human blood, but the blood of the Cursed. He caught movement to his right and spun to face it. His heart seemed to leap and then twist in place.

"Abraham…" The old vampire lay very still against the wall, covered in what Miller guessed was his own blood. His eyes were shut and his head lolled to one side.

"What the hell?" Mike joined him. Miller brought up an arm to stop the other man's advance.

"Stay back," he commanded.

"Another vampire?"

"Aye, another very old acquaintance." With that, Abraham's dead eyes snapped open. The wounded creature looked at Miller, shocked to recognize him. Abraham spoke one word in a language Miller had not heard spoken in hundreds of years. It meant 'father.'

*****

Ann was running faster now. Maybe she had already started to heal. The cops were giving chase but she was faster than she had realized, and she soon outdistanced them. She leapt up a fire escape on a building, jumping from floor to floor. Her own endurance and strength amazed her.

The plan was to return to Abraham and let him know that the deed had been done. Perhaps then they could find a way to get him back on his feet again. She could find him another dog or something, as long as she didn't have to watch him eat it.

*****

"Well, isn't this a prayer answered?" Abraham said weakly.

"Must be yours," Miller said, and then turned. "Mike, can you give us a few minutes?"

Mike gave him a bewildered look. "Yeah okay, sure."

Miller watched Mike head up the stairs to the roof. When he was out of sight, Miller turned back to the remains of what had, many years ago, been his son.

"I tried. I tried so hard," Abraham started. "I did not know what kind of man Fevre was. I never would have…"

Miller raised a hand to him. "It is centuries past. There is no need to…"

"Let me make my peace!" Abraham shouted. "God has seen it fit to bring you before me one final time and give me the chance to ask your forgiveness…and I am sorry."

"What happened?"

"Ura." Abraham almost spat the word. "It's sick. There is something wrong with the Fallen. I don't know what exactly, but I can sense it. And then there is the girl."

"The girl? Which girl?" Miller asked.

"Ann is her name. She was taken by Lilith."

Miller almost jumped at the name. "But I knew Ann, she was clean. I watched her die."

"She is clean still. Somehow she killed the demon from within. But it changed her."

"That is impossible. In thousands of years this has never happened."

"I thought that as well, but I saw it happen. Not before she brought the rest of the Fallen into being, sadly." Miller remembered the mindless beast in the basement. It had briefly become human again.

*****

Mike stood up on the roof, the Desert Eagle still in his hand. There was a trail of black blood that seemed to leap to the next building over. He was trying to work out how to cross when he saw a flicker of movement. He raised the gun.

*****

"She's special. I sent her after Ura," Abraham said.

"Alone? But she is just a lass."

"Not anymore. She's something new." There was the sudden sound of a gunshot from the roof.

******

"Miller!" Mike was yelling. Miller turned and ran up the stairs. He was on the roof in seconds. Mike was standing over something. "I think…I think I got it," Mike said.

On the ground was a demon, covered in white scales. No, not a demon, there wasn't a hint of the darkness on her. Her? This was Ann!

"Mike, no!" Miller ran to her side. Black blood flooded from two huge holes in her chest. Ann was staring at Mike, a shocked look on her face.

"You shot me. I can't believe you shot..." she said.

"It's Ann!" Miller yelled, trying to cover the wounds with one hand. The blood drained out of Mike's face.

"What?"

"It's Ann and she isn't a demon!" shouted Miller again as he approached.

"What? But she's all scaly and..." Mike dropped to his knees. Miller didn't know what to tell him. He was too busy staring at this new creature dying in his arms. She was beautiful, in a way. Tears were running down Mike's face while Ann's body shook.

She coughed, blood seeping out of her mouth as if she were trying to talk. One clawed hand reached up and gently brushed Mike's cheek.

"I'm so sorry," Mike whispered.

*****

Had Ann still been human, she might have guessed which organs had been ripped to shreds when the bullet entered her chest. But now, due to the minor demonic transformation, she had no idea. "All those years of school, and see how much good it did me?" She thought bitterly to herself.

She was dying, of that she was sure. The bullets had been small when they entered, but she could feel the immense holes they had left in her back. It felt like her life was draining from her and spreading out on the roof. She couldn't breathe. Air wouldn't come into her body and it felt like she had forgotten how the whole process of breathing worked. Earlier she had wanted to die, and then to live, and now the choice had been made for her. She would have laughed, if she could breathe.

Mike stared at her, his face becoming white as a sheet once he realized who she was. Miller was racing to them, looking odd in real clothes, instead of the bloody hospital gown he'd been wearing when they'd first met. She reached up and touched Mike's face gently, but didn't have the air to speak.

"No," called a voice from behind Mike. Ann hadn't noticed the woman standing behind him until now. She was dressed exactly as Ann had been when she left Lizzie's, wearing a hooded sweatshirt that covered her face, torn jeans, and nothing on her feet. Blonde tendrils of hair fell from the hood and her feet were very human.

"No," the new woman repeated, passing through Mike like a ghost. "There are things left to be done." The phantom woman pulled back the hood to reveal Ann's human face. Her eyes were the same inky black that they had been in the surveillance video. "I will show you how."

*****

Mike kept his eyes locked on Ann's as she began to shake violently. The holes in her chest started to close over, not with white scales, but pink flesh. Ann seemed to shrink as the new skin covered her. In seconds, she was there before them in torn bloody clothes that were now far too large for her small frame. Her hair was gone, and she may have been a few inches taller, but otherwise she looked human.

"Thank God," she said, as she looked at her own hands. Then her eyes rolled towards the top of her head and she was still.

Mike watched her slow and even breathing for a few moments. She was alive…and seemingly human. At least she looked human, although the definition was getting a little vague lately. He had failed Melissa, his wife, and he had failed to save Catharine. Somehow with Ann he had been given a second chance. He would not fail again. He promised her that.

Miller removed his coat and covered her.

"What the hell just happened?" Mike asked, recovering his voice.

"Something new. Something entirely impossible."

*****

Lizzie had taken more of her meds to calm her down after Mike Samson had left. She could not believe what she had done, how badly she had betrayed her friend. She wanted to go with Mike, find Ann, and beg for her forgiveness. So Ann was a horrible malformed monster. No one was perfect. The problem was that Lizzie couldn't leave the house. She had seen the monsters out there and couldn't face them again. Here in the house it was safe. For a while she slept, fitfully, until she heard the doorbell.

"I'm coming!" Lizzie shouted, getting to her feet slowly. The drugs were slowing her down. Had she taken too much? The doorbell rang again. Had Mike found Ann already? She felt a surge of hope fill her at this thought. There was a knock.

"No really, I'm coming, just give me a second." She noticed the daylight streaming in through the windows. She had been asleep longer than she had thought. The knock came again, this time hard enough to shake the whole door. Lizzie stopped.

"Mike Samson?" she called.

The last knock was so hard that the iron door leapt out of its frame, tearing the chains, the deadbolts, and a huge section of the wall with it. Lizzie screamed and ducked, just barely avoiding the door as it flew toward her. When the dust settled, a tall, vaguely familiar woman with red hair and eyes as black as tar stood in the hole that used to be the front door.

Lizzie realized that she didn't even have her frying pan.

The woman was on her in an instant, dragging her to her feet and slamming her against the wall. Lizzie grunted in pain but was too stunned to scream or even speak.

"Not so rough, Cynthia. We need her in one piece." Lizzie knew that voice.

"Yes, father." Cynthia obeyed, allowing Lizzie to drop to the ground.

"Hello Lizzie," a tall, thin man said from behind Cynthia. He was well-dressed in a tan suit, looking relaxed, with his hands in his pockets and a faint smile on his lips. His eyes were the same black as Cynthia's.

"Keith?"

# 19 - Next Time

Canada. A few days ago.

About two days earlier they had found the trail of massive footprints. Now Bill Maguire kept his eyes to the ground, searching for the next print. It had rained the night before, making the thing easier to track.

"It's a Yeti!" Johnny declared.

"Don't be an idiot," Bill answered.

"Either that or someone with size 18s is running around barefoot in these woods."

"Maybe it's just Shaq getting back to nature." Bill laughed.

"Bill, there have been stories going around about this thing forever." Johnny was taking this very seriously. "If we could find one, prove they exist, it would be huge."

"It's just someone messing with us."

"What if it's not?" The print looked real enough. If this thing was real and they hadn't stumbled upon the greatest prank ever, it would be huge. Bill might become famous.

They followed the trail. It was easy enough to track, as if the beast wanted to be found. On their second day, Bill realized something.

"Is it just me, or is this print getting smaller?" Johnny paused and looked at it hard.

"I think you're right. And there's something else. We're heading back towards camp," Johnny said.

"I'll be damned. What the hell is going on here?"

They followed the trail and, sure enough, it went back directly to their camp. As they got closer to the site, the print grew even smaller. It was now the size of a normal man. A big man, but nothing unusual. They saw him the moment they entered their campsite. He had long grey hair and a thick white beard. He was tall and broad and looked very old. Age hadn't bent him, and he still looked quite strong. He was nude, under a blanket that he had taken from one of the tents and wrapped around himself. He stared at them as they approached. Johnny raised his rifle.

"Alright buddy, what's this all about?" The strange man cleared his throat and when he talked, it came out rough, like he hadn't used his voice in a long time.

"My name is Marcel Dupré," the odd man began in a thick French accent. "Something terrible has happened. I need you to take me to the United States."

End of Book 2

# Intermission 2

September 3, 1942
Just outside Jerusalem

Samuel "Dallas" Badow slammed his notebook shut in frustration. The truck swayed back and forth, as it traveled down the dirt road, making it impossible to write. Finishing these notes had waited the past 20 years; they would wait a little longer.

Renee Dupré noted the surrender and grunted. "I don't know how you expected that to work."

Dallas looked over to his companion and fellow FBI agent. She was a large woman, just as broad across the chest as she was tall. Although not known for her great beauty or pleasant personality, her mind was unmatched. She had most of her head covered in a veil, so Dallas could not see her black hair. Even though she was several years his senior, she possessed not a single strand of silver. Dallas, his remaining hair already faded to a light grey, was jealous. Of course, Renee was not completely human, which did have a few advantages.

"Yeah, well, it needs to be done and you people have not been much in the way of conversation," Dallas grumbled back.

"There is nothing to say, although if you would like to argue again about how it should be the OSS investigating this and not the FBI, that is always entertaining."

"Leave the man be," Marcel Dupré's voice rumbled. Marcel rarely spoke, as it hurt him to speak. If Renee was large for a woman, her husband was massive for a man. Cursed years ago and trapped in the form of a wolf, Marcel was almost the width of two men, covered in thick hair, and had a mouth full of fangs that really did not work well for talking. Here he was, covered from head to toe in a large robe to try and disguise his frame, but unless lives were in danger, Marcel would stay in the truck.

"Don't tell me you are on his side?" Renee poked a finger at her husband.

Marcel raised two clawed hands in surrender, but said nothing more.

"As I said before, the OSS has its hands full with the Germans. This is much more our speed," Dallas said.

"And what exactly is this?" Renee asked.

"If I knew, I swear I would tell. Freddie asked for us himself. "

"Ah, Freddie from the old 13th. Miller's little band of merry men, still pining away for him, even after he has been dead all these years."

"He'll be back. We just don't know when," Dallas said. Renee laughed at this, as she always did when Dallas brought up Joseph Miller's status as an immortal. Dallas understood why, it wasn't an easy thing for one to believe. However, she had once grown fur and fangs and terrorized the French countryside. One would think that would make such things easier to consider. Renee, though, always had her own theory on everything.

"It is impressive how this madman made you think he was Jesus. It's been 30 years, you'd think he would get around to coming back to life."

"Renee, let our friend believes as he wishes." Marcel cut in again. Marcel was always trying to make peace between Renee and Dallas, as he was the only one Renee would ever listen to. But it never worked. Dallas had already let the comment slide; he wasn't going to get into this argument. The problem with working alongside a genius was that it was very hard to win arguments. Miller would be back at some point; Dallas had confidence in that.

A few more moments later, the truck slowed, and then stopped. The soldier driving the truck shouted back to them.

"I think this is the place."

Dallas and Renee made their way out of the truck. They were in front of large ruined building, which had been marked off with rope. It was obviously a dig site of some sort. The biggest thing to catch Dallas' eye was a large opening in the hill right next to the building, which was dug out as a sort of cave. Men scrambled about the place, but none paid them much mind.

"Private James," Dallas called out to the driver of the truck, as the young man stepped out of the trick. "Your orders are to keep Mr. Dupré in sight at all times." Private James shuddered at this. "He's waiting in the truck. If we need you, we'll yell," Dallas said, lifting the flap of the truck as an invitation to go in.

James stiffened at the sight of Marcel, but bravely re-entered. Marcel grinned, and then flashed a deck of cards.

"Marcel, if you could not take all the man's money before we get back, I would appreciate it," Dallas said.

"I'll let him keep his shirt. This time," Marcel croaked and started dealing. Private James settled in to face his defeat. "Dallas! Over here!" An older man, with long white scars covering half of his face, was waving to them near the hill. The three made their way through the camp.

"Freddie! It's great to see ya," Dallas said, as they approached.

"You too, old man," Freddie responded, as both men embraced. "Mrs. Dupré, it's good to see you as well," he added to Dallas's companion, although his voice held less warmth.

"So why are we here, Freddie? It's been, what, 10 years?" Dallas said as they left the truck.

"Twelve, actually. Since that sighting in Peru."

"Yeah, what a bust that was." Dallas shook his head at the memory.

"But why now? What's going on? Figure you would be tied up in the war."

"Believe it or not, this is about the war." Freddie stopped to wave his torch around the cave. Dallas noticed manmade stone walls. "Many years ago, this was a building of some kind. It collapsed nearly a thousand years ago, around the time of the First Crusade, and for some reason, someone buried it."

"The entire building?" Dallas asked.

"Yes, I think they were trying to hide something. We've been canvassing sites like this for any important religious items. Apparently, Hitler has some interest in collecting them, so we're out to get them first."

"What would Hitler want with religious artifacts?" Dallas asked.

"Does Hitler know of the Fallen?" Renee cut in.

Freddie took a long slow breath before replying. "It's possible. Not many living folk know of the Fallen, at least by that name, besides those of the 13th that are still with us. And, of course, you and your husband."

"We know them far too well," Renee said, anger clear in her voice.

"It is possible the Germans know something of them." Freddie said.

"I still don't see what good that would do them. The Fallen are dead; they have been for many years now," Dallas said.

"But we know the Fallen will return," Renee responded. "What if they could be convinced or controlled to work with the Axis? They would be unstoppable."

"Imagine if Hitler could bring them back," Freddie put in.

Renee stopped at this and stared at him, dumbstruck for a moment, but she quickly recovered.

After a moment, Freddie continued. "We have to assume they know something and that it's potentially dangerous to us. That's why we have people out here. They called me in because they found something."

"Something?" Dallas repeated.

"Yes, something I think you two will find very interesting." The unscarred side of Freddie's face curved up in a smile.

"Any hints?"

"It's really something to be seen. I couldn't do it justice. But if word got out, well, I think fewer folks would be skipping church on Sunday."

Dallas, Renee, and Freddie traveled deeper into the building. New construction could be seen every few feet, keeping the ancient walls from collapsing. As they traveled deeper inside the room opened to a large chamber. At one point, there was a ladder leading down several feet to a spot lit by glass lanterns.

"Here we go. Just over here," Freddie urged them forward. There was something embedded in the dirt wall in front of them. Freddie lifted a lantern toward the wall to make it easier to see. Bones. The wall was covered with white bones. The bones were small and made a slight curve.

"Is that a wing?" Renee asked. Dallas looked closer. The bones were in the shape of two massive wings. In the middle of them, a skull rested. The top of the skull was caved in, but the jawbone was clearly covered in long, jagged spikes.

"My Lord. What is it?" Dallas asked, although part of him already knew.

"Not what, who," a fourth voice called out.

All three spun to see. A tall, black man in Arab garb sat next to them. He had been so still that none of them had noticed him when they entered. His eyes were covered with a white bandage, but black stains could be seen where eyes should have been. Freddie had his gun drawn in an instant and Dallas was a second behind him.

"State your business, friend. You're not part of my crew," Freddie demanded.

The strange man only chuckled. "Peace. I mean you no harm," he said, raising his arms. "Those won't help you," he said, gesturing to the guns.

"No, but I imagine this fire might," Renee said, stepping forward and waving her torch.

"That would do a better job indeed. But there is no need for that," the man said, not moving.

"Is he..." Dallas asked.

"Yes, I believe so. A vampire, if I don't miss my guess," Renee said.

"Very good for one without the sight, Miss. They call me Abraham in your tongue and I'm only here to help."

"Help? How?" Dallas demanded.

"Well, for one, I can tell you who that is." Abraham pointed to the bones.

"And what do you get out of this? We don't make deals with the Cursed," Freddie said.

"Then explain this young lady." Abraham pointed to Renee, who stiffened. Dallas stepped forward, placing a hand on Renee's shoulder.

"Let's hear him out. But keep your distance. I was never clear on how powerful the vampires are without their parents around."

"Wise words, wise words. My father said never trust a vamp and he knew his vampires." Abraham laughed at some private joke.

"Then why don't you share, or we'll see how well you burn," Renee threatened.

Abraham smiled. "This fine specimen is obviously one of the Fallen. Not the biggest nor the strongest, but possibly the most dangerous of all."

Dallas looked back at the bones. "So, which one is it then?"

"The mother of all monsters; the oldest of them, the queen." Abraham stood up and spread his arms wide, his face stuck in a massive and vaguely familiar grin. "You never met her, but I did."

"Enough. Just spit it out, man."

"I called her queen once, but you call her..." he turned to face them, and Dallas noted for the first time the black blood running down his face like tears. "Lilith."

There was a pause as the three digested this far too overdramatic fact.

"How did you know about this dig site?" Freddie demanded.

"Now, that is a long story," he said. "But to make it short, I helped put her here many, many years ago."

Renee snorted. "Impossible. That would make you hundreds of years old," she said.

This made Abraham laugh. It sounded surprisingly warm coming from such a dour figure. "You know so little about yourself, little sister," he said, smiling, but this only seemed to make Renee ever angrier.

"I'm no sister of yours, you vile thing." She stepped forward again with the torch, but Dallas restrained her.

"We are of the same Cursed family now, little wolf," Abraham said. "How old are you now? Have you not noticed you haven't aged like a normal woman?"

"I have," Dallas put in, perhaps a tinge of jealously seeping into his voice. "You don't look a day older than when we found you thirty years ago."

"The Cursed do not age like normal folk. Oh, we grow weaker without our Fallen parents, but we age much slower," Abraham said.

"This doesn't explain why you are here. What do you want?" Freddie demanded again.

"I think a better question is, what do you want? Why disturb these old bones? Let the monster rest," Abraham said, making a sweeping gesture towards the bones embedded in the wall.

Dallas stepped forward. "There are people who might be able to use these to gain the power of the Fallen or the Cursed. We need to protect them, study them; perhaps we can use them against the Fallen the next time they arrive," he offered.

"I can't argue with that," Abraham said. "What do you know of these people?"

"We know the Germans have been gathering religious artifacts. We think this may be..." Dallas started, but Freddie cut him off.

"Dallas, stop. Why are you trusting this thing?" he asked.

Abraham ignored the insult and spoke before Dallas could respond. "It's not the Nazis you should be worried about. Other, older evils already know of this place. They may have plans of their own."

"And who might this be?" Freddie asked.

"They call themselves the Infinitus," Abraham said.

"Never heard of these people. And you think this group is more dangerous than the Nazi army?" Freddie asked doubtfully.

"Certainly not at the moment. Not to the world anyway, but to you, if you have this." Abraham again pointed at the skeleton. "The Infinitus is not large, but the group is very, very old and quite powerful. Their goal is to control the Fallen for their own reasons. My goal is to stop them and help others like your friend." Abraham gestured to Renee.

"Why should we trust you?" Freddie asked, and Renee nodded, agreeing with the sentiment.

But Abraham just laughed again. "You still don't understand. The question is, why should I trust you?" he said, standing at last. Dallas had no idea the vampire was so tall. "This place is under my protection."

"Look, I think we are getting off on the wrong foot here," said Dallas. "My friends call me Dallas, the grumpy lady is Renee Dupré, and my English friend with the winning smile is Freddie. We're all that's left from a crew that used to work under a man named Joseph Miller. Ever hear of him?"

"Aye..." Abraham said, in a perfect reproduction of Miller's odd accent. "The Ancient One and I are allies… of a sort." Abraham sat back down, perhaps comforted by this. "If you can convince me that you are in fact The Ancient One's allies, I will allow you to take the skeleton, as long as I can travel with you to ensure it arrives safely."

"All right, let me just talk it over with my comrades," Dallas said, and motioned for the others to follow him.

Freddie was the first to speak. "Dallas, what are you doing? You know Miller said to never trust a vampire."

"Yeah, yeah, I know, but to have one on our side, especially if it helps us retrieve this skeleton safely...we could learn so much," Dallas said.

"I agree with Dallas," Renee said, which surprised Dallas a little. "He has useful information and could be a strong ally."

"You would say that. He is your kind," Freddie retorted. "I don't trust him."

"You don't trust anyone Freddie. But in this case, I think you'll have to try. We'll keep an eye on him. We have more men with us as well. We've killed his kind before, if it comes to that. But maybe this time it won't. Maybe it changes now," Dallas said.

"You always were a dreamer, Dallas. You're the reason we ended up with her..." Freddie stuck a finger at Renee, who glared back at him, her face not hiding her disgust with the Englishman.

"And she and her husband have been a huge help the last 30 years. You can't possibly argue that," Dallas defended.

Freddie slowly shook his head.

"Fine, but this is on your head, Dallas."

"It always is," he said, and rubbed his balding head. "It's why I have so little hair left."

September 7, 1942

It took only four days to extract the body of the demon embedded in stone. Abraham, much to his credit, was quite helpful, which helped to calm Freddie's nerves. Dallas had a feeling the vampire would fit in well. Apart from his frightening appearance, his manners were gentle and he was quick with a joke. Surprisingly, or perhaps not, the Duprés and Abraham hit it off rather well. Dallas had never found anyone Renee Dupré liked, besides her husband, in all the years he had known her. Perhaps the common curse helped.

With the skeleton loaded onto one of the larger trucks, the party broke camp. The first truck would be escorted by one more truck and four Jeeps. Twenty English soldiers were put into the second truck and several more spread out among the Jeeps. Dallas, Renee, Marcel, Abraham, and their own American officer, Private James, took their own truck. Freddie, as commanding officer, rode in the main truck with the skeleton.

The day itself was beautiful, and Dallas again took out his pen and notebook to take notes.

Renee just shook her head. "Old fool," she snorted, but there was a note of humor to it for once. Marcel gentled slapped his wife's shoulder in mock discipline.

"What is this?" Abraham asked, whether at Renee's comment or the action of Dallas actually taking out the book, he wasn't sure.

"Dallas is updating his journal; he thinks his chicken scratches will be useful at some point," Renee said.

"Some of us are getting older," Dallas defended his work. "I've seen many things over my short time; I think it best to record them."

"Ah, passing your secrets on to the next generation." Abraham smiled.

"This really isn't the best place to write," Marcel added. To enforce his point, the Jeep hit another bump in the road, jostling everyone on the vehicle. Dallas swore as he dropped his pencil. He reached for it as it rolled behind him. To his surprise, it suddenly rolled back.

"Are we stopping?" Dallas asked.

"There is something ahead," the private said. "The whole convoy is slowing."

Abraham stuck his head out the window. "It is as I feared. The Infinitus block our path," he said.

"Get off the road and alongside the main truck. We need a better look," Dallas commanded. He drew out the small shotgun. "Marcel, Renee, are you ready?"

Marcel grunted and Renee pulled out a gun of her own. "I can handle myself just fine Dallas, as always," the large woman said.

The private guided the Jeep off the side of the dirt road and drove alongside the convoy. There was a long line of men on horses and carts blocking the road. They were moving slowly, herding some cattle with the carts.

"They look like farmers," Private James said.

"This smells of a trap to me," Marcel snorted.

"Wise beyond your years," Abraham said. "Many of those men are Cursed. We need to warn the rest of your people."

"Gun it, Private, we need to get to that head car now," Dallas commanded.

"Yes, sir." The Jeep lurched forward. Dallas leaned out the window and started shouting and waving his arms.

"Trap! Trap!" he yelled.

Two of the carts stopped and spun. Two men pulled nets off, revealing other men with guns. They opened fire on the front Jeep, killing the men in the front seats almost instantly. Another group of men started firing at Dallas's Jeep, just as it reached the front of the line.

Private James swore as bullets hit the windshield. He cut right too hard and the truck tipped, then rolled, briefly launching the vehicle into the air. Dallas braced himself against the roof as the Jeep rolled in the air and smashed into the line of armed men while upside down. For a moment, the world continued to spin, and then everything stopped.

"Everyone all right?" Dallas asked, finding himself surprisingly in one piece.

"No, of course not," Renee spat. "But I'll live."

Marcel grunted.

"James?" Dallas asked, turning to his left.

"Still with you, sir. A little nicked up, though," the young driver said. A little nicked up hardly covered the bullet hole in the man's shoulder, but Dallas was not about to argue.

"Abraham?" Dallas asked. The vampire was already out of the truck.

"Gone, Dallas," Renee said.

"Not gone far," Abraham's voice came. The door to the truck was suddenly torn off, freeing Dallas. "You need to get that convoy going. I will keep these men busy here. Besides, there is someone here to whom I owe a bit of pain."

The tall vampire was outside the Jeep, a sword already in hand. He swung his robes to the side to reveal a massive handgun. It looked more like a mini-cannon than anything Dallas had ever fired. The vampire turned and yelled, diving at the members of Infinitus. His first victim's head went flying and his second was launched into the air by that enormous gun.

"You heard the..." Dallas almost said undead creature. "...man. Let's get that truck going." Dallas pulled himself out of the wreck and assisted James to his feet. He took a moment to make sure the small sawed off shotgun was in easy reach while he followed Renee, who was already moving towards the front truck with Marcel by her side. A dark-skinned man carrying a rifle stumbled in Dallas's way. The man, perhaps hurt when the Jeep had smashed into the row of men, was slow to raise his gun. Dallas was not. At point blank range, he fired his shotgun at the man's torso, creating a gaping, black hole where his chest once was.

"Yes, definitely Cursed," he muttered to himself.

Marcel worked on making a path for his wife to follow. His blocky form ripped through a man as if he were paper. Marcel was a gentle spirit, but with his friends in danger, he was as fearsome as he looked.

Abraham was making quick work of the men around them. He fought like a demon, which, in hindsight, was about right. Another three men had fallen to his sword. Two human, one not.

The English soldiers began fighting back, coming from around the second truck and returning fire with their attackers. This made Dallas's path even more difficult, as now they were taking gunfire in both directions. The three dodged and ran as best they could, taking shots at the Infinitus as they went. The first Jeep had flipped and now was serving as cover for a group of soldiers returning fire.

"There, that's our first stop. Go! Go! Go!" Dallas yelled, as he ran. James was falling behind, his wounded arm slowing him. Renee grabbed the other arm and started dragging him forward. To Dallas's surprise, they all made it to the Jeep without being picked off by their own side.

"We need to get that truck moving. It cannot fall into enemy hands. Understand?" Dallas shouted at the group of soldiers exchanging fire. "We need to get this wreck moved so we can get the truck going again."

"Any suggestions on how you want us to do that, sir?" one of the men asked. A bullet bounced far too close to Dallas and he couldn't help ducking.

"Actually, yes. But I'm going to need cover fire," Dallas said. "Marcel! Come here."

The wolf man did as commanded, bounding to Dallas's side.

"Good lord!" one of the men shouted on seeing Marcel, but both Dallas and Marcel ignored him.

"Dallas?" the Cursed man asked.

"We're going to find out how strong you really are. Can you lift this Jeep? Just a few inches?" he asked. The Cursed man's eyes went wide with surprise.

"Whatever you're going to do, do it fast. They're flanking us!" another man yelled.

Dallas looked up to see another group of men coming from the right. "OK, look, I need cover fire for another sixty seconds, and then run like hell for the second truck. The rest of the men are there and should be able to help cover. James, you're with them."

"No can do," the wounded private said, pointing a finger at Marcel. "My orders are to stay with him. Besides, I owe him five bucks!"

Dallas shrugged; it was his funeral. He pulled out the four sticks of dynamite from his coat and began wrapping them.

"I'm just going to note that you carry dynamite in your coat," Renee said.

“Old habit. Lift here. I only need a few inches," Dallas responded.

Marcel did as he was bidden. With a mighty shove, the Jeep moved several inches.

"Remind me never to smoke around you," Renee said, watching her husband work.

Dallas finished placing the charge, but before he lit the fuse, he couldn't help but toss his own remark. "Well, look at you; it only took a gunfight for your sense of humor to come out." He lit the fuse. "Drop it and run."

Marcel didn't need to be told twice. He dropped the car and sprinted to the next truck, following the remaining soldiers and Renee. Dallas was close on their heels, dragging along James. The bullets were thick as the men of Infinitus were advancing and cover was limited. Dallas watched three more men fall in their quick dash to the next car. Renee stumbled as well, and Marcel grabbed her arm and pulled her along. The wolf man flinched several times as bullets found him, but he did not slow down.

Right on time, the first Jeep was launched to the right of the road with an explosion that shook Dallas's teeth just as they arrived at the lead truck.

"Just like old times." Dallas had to smile. "Marcel in the back. I'll take Renee!"

"She's wounded!" Marcel shouted.

"It's a scratch!" Renee shouted back, but she laid a hand on Marcel's furry cheek. "I'm fine," she said in a rare moment of tenderness. "Go."

Marcel grunted and padded off to the back of the truck.

As Dallas pulled the door of the truck open, Freddie's body dropped out into the road. He must have been one of the first hit in the fight. Dallas pushed James into the truck and motioned for Renee to enter as well.

Renee touched him gingerly on the shoulder as she passed. "I'm sorry," she said as she passed.

"Just go. See if you can get it started," Dallas responded. He bent down by the body of his friend and closed the eyes. "I'm the last one now. See you soon, old friend."

Inside the truck, Private James was shoving out the dead driver, while Renee was tearing at her own shirt.

"Renee?" Dallas asked.

Renee lifted a hand from her side. It was covered in black blood. "It may be a little more than a scratch," she said, through gritted teeth.

Dallas looked at the wound—a pulsing black hole in the woman's side, just below the breast. "Yes a little more than a scratch," Dallas agreed. He helped her finish tearing a section of her shirt to use as bandage. "Just pressure..." he said, putting the rag in place. Renee nodded a curt 'of course' and held the bandage. The truck was rolling forward.

"I can't see, sir," the private complained. The windshield was riddled with bullet holes.

"Don't worry about seeing, just worry about going. And stay low in your seat," Dallas shouted back at the man. "I'll see what I can do about the glass." Dallas leaned low in the seat, put his feet on the windshield, and began to push. "Ah, a little help?" He looked at Renee, who grimaced, then matched his position. With a scream from Renee, the windshield popped off and fell into the road, just in time for the truck to hit the first cart blocking the road.

"Go! Go! Go!" Dallas urged. The truck shook as bullets found it, but kept rolling forward. After a few long moments, the gunfire slowed as they built speed. Dallas poked his head out the window and looked behind them.

There was a man hanging on to the side of the truck. Beyond him, several other men on horseback followed.

"Doesn't look like this is over yet," Dallas said. He looked at his wounded comrades and reloaded his shotgun. "I'm going up. Private, you keep driving until you get to the airport. Run over anyone that gets in your way. It's only a few miles and there are plenty of our boys there to help."

"Marcel is still in the back. He's hurt, although he won't admit it," Renee said, pointing to the roof.

"Yeah, that may be the only common trait you two share. I'll make sure he's OK."

"Thank you. Good luck, old man." Renee actually smiled again and pulled out her pistol.

"For luck?" Dallas asked with a smile.

"More like that boomstick of yours can't hurt anything unless it's two feet in front of you," Renee said.

"Thanks," Dallas said, taking the pistol. He opened the door and pulled himself out.

The man on the side of the truck was gone. Dallas could only assume he was already inside the back. The men on horseback were gaining. He didn't have much time.

Dallas slowly made his way towards the back, hand over hand, feet constantly slipping as he worked his way across. A hand suddenly grabbed him and yanked him to the roof of the truck.

"Abraham!" Dallas shouted in surprise.

"I said I was going, no matter how much you want to leave me behind," the vampire said, a smile on his face.

"It's good to see you made it," Dallas shouted, trying to steady himself on the roof of the moving vehicle. He didn't have any luck, so he got down on his knees. "Did you get our extra tagalong?" Dallas pointed behind them.

"Yes. One down, but the next few won't be so easy," Abraham said. "Old playmates of mine." They both stared back at the riders closing in fast.

"Marcel is in the back. He can help. We only need to hold them a few minutes. Once we cross into the airport, we'll have the advantage of numbers."

"Which is why they will attack now," Abraham said.

"Can you help me get inside the truck? I don't quite have your..." He eyed the vampire balancing easily on the top of the truck, "Dexterity."

The vampire smiled. "My thoughts exactly." He swung his sword in a neat arc, slicing the canvas on top of the truck. It gave way and Dallas was suddenly falling.

"Whoa!" Dallas shouted, trying to find purchase. He stopped, inches from the floor, only because Abraham grabbed his boot and lowered him the rest of the way. "Warning would be nice next time!" Dallas shouted back up.

"What's the fun in that?" Abraham grinned, dropping to the side. "Greetings, little brother," he added, seeing Marcel.

The wolf man did not look well. His black robes were covered in blood and he lay sprawled on the ground.

"I see you have a few scratches of your own," Dallas said.

"Perhaps a few." Marcel nodded and struggled to stand. He collapsed to the ground.

"Rest." Abraham was busy cutting off the rest of the canvas, pulling it free. "There. Now we can see them."

"But they can see us," Dallas countered.

Abraham shrugged. "They won't use guns."

"Ah," Dallas responded, taking no comfort in that fact. He ran to the back of the truck and saw that the riders were almost on top of them. "Let's see if this old man can slow them down." He removed the final two sticks of dynamite from his coat, cut one fuse short, lit it, and threw it underhand as the riders grew ever closer.

The explosion killed the horse instantly in a puff of red gore. It and its rider rolled into a heap.

"Now, that was impressive," Abraham said, with approval.

"Miller thought so too. One more shot," Dallas said.

"Not that one. He and I, we have a very, very old score to settle." Abraham pointed out a rider near the front.

"Fair enough, last one anyway." Dallas cut the second fuse and again tossed it underhand. This time, the riders knew what was coming and did their best to dodge. The explosion was not quite as effective, but still knocked one more rider to the ground.

"Now we do this the hard way," Dallas said and he removed both Renee's pistol and his shotgun. He nodded at Marcel, who grinned weakly. He opened fire on the six remaining riders. He hit the closest one twice, but the man just shrugged off the bullets. So he shot the horse. The creature bucked and died, tossing the man riding it forward. The man tried to leap off the horse and onto the truck. It was an impressive attempt, but the leap fell inches short, and the man hit the ground and was nearly trampled by the next rider.

The truck swayed slightly as another man jumped onto the side, clinging onto the ruined canvas cover. Abraham was on him, slashing with the sword. The Infinitus man was faster though, and vaulted over Abraham's attack and safely onto the back of the truck. He gave Dallas a swift kick before drawing a sword. Dallas hit the floor hard and rolled, pulling up the shotgun, but Abraham blocked the shot.

"Smith, I was hoping to talk with you," Abraham said. "You've had this coming for a long time." The vampire charged, slashing again, but the new man, Smith, parried easily.

"You should be helping us, Abraham, not these apes," Smith said.

Dallas was struck by his American accent. Who were these people? He finally got a look at the new man. He was tall, with short, black hair; he was older, with a long, angry scar running up his cheek to the bottom of one ear.

"Fool me once, shame on you, fool me twice..." Abraham smiled.

"You are even more stubborn than your father," Smith spat back, diving in for another attack, which Abraham ducked.

"I'm just happy you've come out of hiding now. You'll be so much easier to kill this way." Abraham swung high, but when Smith ducked, Abraham struck out with a foot, clipping Smith in the head. Smith staggered backwards towards the front of the truck.

"The same can be said for you," Smith said, recovering his balance.

Dallas stood up himself and glanced outside the truck. Two riders remained, one almost close enough to touch. Dallas and the rider's eyes met, the dark eyes of the Cursed. The rider put his feet up on the horse's back and prepared to leap. Dallas raised the shotgun and waited. The rider leapt and Dallas fired in the same instant. The shotgun caught the rider full in the chest. He hit the tailgate of the truck and dropped to the ground below, rolling in the dust.

The last rider was suddenly on the truck as well. A woman with the same black eyes of the Cursed clung to the side of the truck. Dallas fired the shotgun again but the woman spun out of the way, landing just behind Abraham. She was tall as well, as apparently all the Cursed were; her hair was cut short, the same as Smith's. She had a pinched nose and crooked grin. She drew her own sword. Dallas felt left out, only bringing an empty gun to what was apparently a sword party. Next time, he would pay more attention to the invitation.

"Abraham!" Dallas shouted. The vampire ducked, without even turning to 'see', and the woman's blow swung harmlessly overhead. Abraham kicked backwards in response, catching the woman in the belly and knocking her back. Dallas smacked her in the head with the butt of his gun as she passed, knocking her clear off the back of the truck.

Dallas turned around to face Smith, unsure how to help Abraham without getting in the way. He did not notice the one pale hand still clinging to the side of the truck. He did not see the tall, pale woman with the crooked nose, now covered in her own black blood; pull herself up from the side of the truck. Dallas did feel the woman's sword as it entered his side, cut through his torso, and embedded itself into his spine.

Dallas shouted in pain and surprise, trying to turn back towards the woman, but the sword would not let him twist. Abraham was suddenly between them, his fist catching the woman on the chin. Her sword locked into place, she could not defend herself, and she was again knocked over the side of the truck. Dallas fell to the ground, unable to feel his feet any longer. Abraham caught him and helped him to lie down.

"Smith… behind you," Dallas managed to choke out. There was a sword sticking through Abraham's chest that Dallas was sure had not been there a moment ago. Smith leaned over, grinning. He pulled out the sword, letting Abraham drop next to Dallas.

"I do appreciate the help digging up Mother's body," the man snarled. "And someday, when I bring the Fallen back, I will remember you warmly." Smith raised the sword above his head for the finishing blow. "Say hello to your Pa for me when you see him in hell."

Smith swung, but he was stopped, much to his own surprise. One large hand held him in place. Marcel was behind him, lifting him up in the air over his head. The wolf man launched him over the side. Smith screamed once in anger and was gone.

Renee appeared by her husband’s side and helped to steady the wounded beast.

"You always did have..." Dallas coughed blood, "...great timing."

Renee looked down at to the two wounded men, one hand holding her own wound, the other wrapped protectively around Marcel's arm. There was sadness in her eyes. "Dallas..."

"Yeah, yeah, I know. I'm never going to play the piano again." Dallas laughed. It hurt when he laughed, but he had been saving that line for years.

"Which is only a good thing; you were terrible." Renee tried to smile at her own joke.

Two jokes from Renee in the same day; it must be the end of the world. Dallas reached inside his coat and pulled his notebook out. He was trying to not bleed on it, but his blood was everywhere. "I've made sure you two will be taken care of when you get home. Take this. Give this to my boss and make sure to finish what we started here."

When Renee took the notebook, Dallas couldn't help but notice the single tear was rolling down her cheek. "I..." she started.

"When he comes back, you need to make sure he sees it," Dallas continued.

"Oh, don't start that..." Renee said.

"No, no more time for arguments. He is coming back when they come back. What's in there may change everything. Promise me; promise me you'll give it to him."

Renee looked between him and the notebook. Abraham silently watched. "I'll do what I can," the woman promised.

"Good, good..." Dallas could feel his strength fading as his blood spilled out on the floor. "You two, and maybe this man..." Dallas eyed Abraham, "You are our best hope. Don't let me down."

"You were a good man, Samuel Badow," Abraham said. "It was a great honor to meet you."

"And you, Abraham," Dallas responded.

“And the best of friends,” Marcel added, tears rolling down his hairy face. The wolf man dropped to one knee, his own wounds dragging him down.

Renee picked up the thread for her husband. "Dallas, thank you for everything."

Dallas could just make the woman out, his vision fading.

He tried to talk again, but suddenly it was very hard to breathe. And cold, so cold.

"Why Renee, I believe that is the nicest thing you ever..." was all he could manage.

Then he was gone.

## Book 3

# Revelations

“Not only are there no happy endings,' she told him, 'there aren't even any endings.”

- Neil Gaiman, American Gods

# 1 - Where were we?

Blood ran down Mike Samson's nose. As much as he twitched and wiggled, he could not manage to stop it. The handcuffs kept him locked into place on the chair. He did not struggle; he belonged where he was. He had certainly earned it. His actions for the past few weeks had finally caught up with him, and so had the police. Now he waited to be questioned, like a common crook. Mike wished they would hurry up and book him. Not only so he could maybe clean the blood off his nose, but also because so many people were depending on him.

Time passed slowly in the room, making Mike's frustration grow. He was desperately trying to wipe his nose off with his shoulder when the man finally came. This man was tall and grim, with grey hair and a messy suit. A folder slid to the middle of the table and spun once so Mike could see it.

"Samson?" the man asked; his voice was oddly high-pitched for his looks.

"Yeah."

"Newark Cop?"

"Yeah." Well, this was a stimulating conversation so far.

"Detective Mathews, at your service. Seems like you've been busy."

*If only this guy knew the half of it.*

"Yeah," Mike said slowly. "Any way you can get me out of these cuffs?"

"You want to tell me what this was all about first?"

Mike rolled that question over in his mind. He was going to tell them everything. It was why he was here. Well, that and the fact that he had been arrested. But where to start?

"What do you know about the incident at College Hospital, just over two weeks ago?" Mike asked. He thought that seemed to be the best place to start.

"About the same as everyone else," Mathews said.

There was a knock at the door.

"One second." Mathews said, and went to the door.

Eric Johnson stepped through. Johnson was someone Mike knew; they had met when Mike and Ann had escaped College Hospital. Johnson had seen firsthand what had gone down there with his own eyes.

"Hey, mind if I sit in on this?" Johnson asked Mathews.

"Be my guest." Mathews shrugged.

"Samson." Johnson nodded at Mike, who returned the nod. "Let's get you out of these."

"Thanks for coming, man," Mike said. "I needed someone who might believe me."

"Yeah, that means you're going to tell me what this is all about? A car chase causing thousands in property damage? You'd better have a good story." Mathews glared at Mike.

"Yeah, it's good. But not the easiest to believe." Mike stared at Johnson, rubbing his wrists, and then at last scratching his nose. "There's some stuff I haven't told you about. I haven't told anyone about."

"I knew you were holding out on me, man, just didn't know why," Johnson said, taking a seat across from Mike.

"I didn't say anything because I didn't think anyone would believe it."

"Why don't you try us?" Mathews challenged.

Mike looked back and forth between the two men. He took a deep breath and he began to tell them the rest of the story.

# 2 - The Gathering Storm

Newark, New Jersey, a little earlier

From his vantage point in his little white Chevy, John Takahashi watched the two men carry the still form of Ann Melakh back to the minivan. His laptop on the passenger seat was still pulling up data on the men, but he recognized Ms. Melakh from the pictures, even if she was now bald.

The first man was easy. He assumed it was the owner of the minivan, Michael Gabriel Samson, Jr. The vehicle was in poor shape, with a broken grill and a missing driver's side door. This had made it easy to follow from Lizzie Namgung's place, even in the dark of the night. Mr. Samson was a Newark cop and hero of the College Hospital incident. This had made him a person of interest and was the reason why John had left his stakeout post and followed the odd pair.

The second man was harder. John only had a quick photo snapped from the window of his car to work off of. He had sent the shot to the home office, expecting the process would take some time, if it were successful at all. Surprisingly, the answer came back just as the van pulled up to a residential address. The man was, within a certain margin of error, one Andres Soliz: a man wanted for a crime John knew he hadn't committed. John puzzled this out for quite some time, wondering how this might change his plans. There was a connection here, something he wasn't clear on yet. He glanced down at the notebook; its aged pages were visible through the plastic bag it had been unceremoniously stuffed into.

*Could it be?* He decided to call Dupré.

"Good God, man, do you know what time it is?" she asked when she picked up the phone. John was pretty sure she slept during daylight hours, perhaps hanging from the ceiling, so he failed to see this as a major inconvenience for her.

"I'm sorry to disturb you..." He wasn't at all. "But I've found our missing lady."

"At last! At the Namgung woman's house?"

Yes, he had seen her two days ago there, but Dupré didn't need to know that. "From a trail that started there. Even better, she's with the man wanted for the murder of your friends at CMDNJ."

There was a long pause. "The janitor is with Melakh?" The answer came at last.

"Yes, I was surprised by this as well."

"And what was his name again?"

"Soliz," John answered, enjoying Dupré's discomfort.

After another long pause, Dupré's usual gruff voice was more polite. "Takahashi, assemble the team, we're bringing them in."

*****

Albany, New York

He had no idea how long he had been laying in the ditch before they found him, but they were both dead before he realized what he was doing. One of them—he thought it was Valentino—found him and shouted to his partner. He—or, rather, the demon spawn that had shared his body for the last thousand or so years—could not resist the smell of living flesh. He was feeding before he knew it. Jackson died next, only seconds after rushing to help. Whether he had been trying to aid his partner or his boss would never be known. He had helped Smith, though; they both had. After feeding off both of them, he felt much more like himself and his body began the task of knitting itself back together. Still, it was bad form to kill one's own employees, and the paperwork for this outing was going to be a bitch.

As he worked on the side of the road, discarding the two bleached white corpses, Smith considered his next move. By now, Gallu was long gone, if the Ancient One had not killed her. He was certain they would not get the deposit back for the office building they had rented, and he was out one very nice suit. Still, he had his health, and really, what more could a two thousand year old vampire ask for?

Someone would have to take the fall for this, and it wouldn't be him. If all these years in management had taught him anything, it was how to spread blame. This had to be Mike Samson's fault and Mike would pay. Oh sure, Smith had underestimated him and hadn't expected them to be traveling with a werewolf. Why one would make a traveling companion out of those hairy mindless things was a mystery. And there was the Ancient One, but to blame him would be like blaming the clouds for the rain. The Ancient One was a force of nature and would have to be avoided. Besides, Smith already knew of a plan to keep Miller out of the way for a very long time.

Yes, Mike Samson would pay and Smith knew right where to start.

*****

One of too many Starbucks, Newark New Jersey

The coffee shop was nearly empty, with only a single table occupied. A stunning young couple sat silently drinking their coffee, pointedly ignoring the screaming woman in the corner. The owner of the shop stood motionless behind the counter, staring at his new masters with black, empty eyes. Lizzie lay curled on the floor, wishing for death. For the woman screaming, it would come soon. She had entered the shop, ignoring the "Closed" sign, and demanded her venti skinny, half caff, no foam latte. On the plus side, she wouldn't need caffeine anymore.

Once the screaming stopped, the creature that used to be Vanessa Black licked milk foam off her lips and spoke.

"Ashakku will not come. He has no interest in family matters."

"Good, you remember more," Keith Malone said, putting down a hot chocolate. A dab of whipped cream still marked his nose.

"Yes, it comes easier now. I remember much." Vanessa nodded, then added, "More, I remember more."

"Ashakku is not my concern. For all his faults, he has always obeyed our law. If he will not help us enforce it, at least he will not stand in our way." Keith added, "Marduk is here."

At that, a massive shadow blocked the sun from the windows of the coffee shop. It was vaguely man-shaped, but far too wide. The shadow waited, unmoving.

"Cynthia, let him in, please." Keith motioned.

The tall red headed woman had been standing motionless over Lizzie. Now she snapped to attention and headed toward the door. "Yes, Father."

The door was opened, and the enormous man seemed to shrink as he entered. His clothes were ragged and just barely contained his girth. He wore a brimmed hat, which cast his face constantly in shadow.

"You summoned us …us?" the new man said, taking a place at the table. His voice seemed to echo, as if many people had spoken at once, but not quite in sync. Lizzie wondered if it was the demon version of a stutter.

"Yes, brother. We have come to pass judgment on our sister and queen. She broke our law and ended the life of our brother Ura," Keith said, before picking up the hot chocolate and taking another swig.

"There is only one punishment for the traitor. Death," Vanessa spoke, with a snarl.

"Yes death …death," said Marduk, with the same stutter.

Keith looked between the other two at the table. Finally, he put down his beverage and spoke. "There may be another way. We know the humans have weakened us somehow, perhaps..."

"No!" Vanessa slammed a fist into the table, splitting it down the middle and sending her latte flying. "We must have her death and the death of her children! She must be cast out as we were all once cast out!" Her body trembled with rage as she took heavy, ragged breaths.

Keith looked between her and Marduk.

"We agree with the beast," Marduk echoed. "Although lack her hatred for furniture …furniture."

"Table!" Keith said, raising his voice only slightly. Cynthia and the man behind the counter obeyed instantly, clearing away the wreckage and dragging over a new table.

Vanessa steadied herself and sat down. "And could I get a Pumpkin Spice Latte?" she asked politely.

The cafe worker nodded and vanished into the back to do whatever black magic was required to create lattes.

"I see I cannot change your mind; I will comply with your wishes as tradition demands," Keith said, returning to the topic at hand.

"But how will we find her when her mind is closed to us?" Vanessa asked.

"I have taken steps. Cynthia?" Too late Lizzie realized where Cynthia was going. The tall woman grabbed a handful of Lizzie's hair, dragged her to her feet, and deposited her in front of Keith.

"Ow, ow, ow!" Lizzie yelled.

"Sit, child." Keith said, nodding at the chair to his right. "This one will lead us to her."

"I will do no such thing!" Lizzie shouted, trying to sound brave, which she wasn't.

"This one?" Marduk asked. "Why… Why?"

"Lizzie has her ways. She will find our wayward sister and she will do so in 24 hours."

"What happens in 24 hours?" Lizzie had to ask.

Keith matched her look, his eyes suddenly filling with blackness.

In that moment, Lizzie realized that nothing of Keith Malone remained. The creature's look seemed to burn into her. She felt hot, and air refused to enter her lungs. A sudden powerful fear entered her mind. She tried to scream, tried to get up, tried to escape that horrible stare, but her body refused.

"Lizzie Namgung, you will bring Lilith to me in 24 hours." The demon's voice cracked like thunder in her ears, and Lizzie helplessly obeyed.

# 3 - The Calm

"There are things left to be done," the woman told Ann, as the giant wound in her chest gushed blood. Ann was dying on that rooftop; her shredded lungs were failing to find the air she so desperately needed to live. And then the woman spoke to her and something changed.

Ann sat up with a start, grabbing her chest. She sucked in air as if suddenly remembering how to breathe. She was not on the roof; where was she? She searched blindly in the dark, slowly coming to her senses. There was no pain where the wound had been, just an odd chill. Then she noticed her skin.

"Oh my God," she said, under her breath. She touched her face; it was warm, smooth, and surprisingly human. She needed to find a mirror. She kicked off a pile of blankets and stumbled off of a couch. It occurred to her that she had no idea where she was or what time it was. It was dark, that part was obvious, and it was a home, not a hospital. For that she was thankful; she didn't she think could ever visit a hospital again. Stumbling in the dark, she tried to recall what had happened. She had been on the roof of a building in Newark; she had been shot by... had Mike Samson shot her? She stopped and again investigated the bullet wound. There was no trace of damage, not even a scar. In fact, there was no evidence that she had been, until recently, a six-foot-tall white, scaly demon. Had she dreamed that? Had this all been a vivid nightmare? No, she was wearing the same clothes she had put on at Lizzie's, plus a new-to-her brown coat that was slightly singed. In fact, it was becoming obvious that she would need new clothes soon. The pants were sliding down her legs, stretched from her larger demon form, and her shirt was holding on by threads. She felt happy to have the coat; otherwise, she would not be decent for long.

To her right was a dim glow, which she was happy to discover was a bathroom. She flipped the light on and she was blinded for several long minutes. She blinked, trying to force her eyes to adjust. At last, she could see her reflection in the mirror above the sink. The sight made her cry.

"Thank God." She could not express how happy she was to see her old face staring back at her, even the too long nose she had hated since she was fifteen. No more complaints about that, ever. Her hands ran along her head, getting a feel for her latest look. She was still bald but this one negative couldn't distract her. Hair or not, she was human again, and that was something to celebrate. She wiped the tears from her eyes and started to look around. The bathroom was a complete mess, with clothes thrown everywhere. There were several toys mixed in. So there had to be children here as well.

There was a flicker of movement in the mirror and Ann spun around. Nothing there but an empty bathtub. She looked back to the mirror, again tracking motion just out of the corner of her eye. Again she turned, to find nothing. She scratched her head in confusion. Ann faced the mirror once more, this time keeping an eye on the glass and leaning in for a closer look. In the edge of the mirror, there was something.

There was a woman in the mirror, only in the mirror. She wore a hooded sweatshirt and jeans. Her face was covered, except her chin and a few locks of blond hair. And then Ann remembered everything, and screamed.

*****

Joseph Miller was dreaming. He remembered the tavern from his time in Scotland, and tonight it was filled with beautiful women who were all toasting him, telling him how great he was, how brave, and how much they really liked his pants. There was also a pink Power Ranger eating a hamburger at the next table; she seemed to be enjoying herself as well. This was not how he knew it was a dream, however. That tip-off was the large television that hung on the wall. They certainly didn't have those 300 years ago. It showed a middle-aged woman, crying. Miller tried to change the channel several times, but the others at the Tavern would not allow it, constantly calling for him to make another speech or join them in another song. In the madness that was so common in his dreams, Miller could not argue. However, something about the woman crying disturbed him. They shouldn't have a sad show on while everyone was celebrating. Besides, she reminded him of someone he couldn't quite remember. But then the crowd of beautiful women demanded another toast in honor of his pants and Miller, distracted, shrugged and cheered before taking another slug of his ale.

"All things come to an end, father," said a small boy that Miller hadn't noticed. The lad was tall, with dark skin and fine hair. His eyes were dark brown, but black tears ran down his face.

"Abraham?" Miller asked, surprised to see his son from another lifetime. The boy couldn't be older than five years here in this dream. The crowd called out for another toast, but Miller ignored them.

"All things come to an end, father," the boy repeated.

"Not everything, lad. At least not yet," Miller said and reached out to the boy.

The child stepped back out of reach. "All things come to an end, father. Even you. At the end of the world," The boy pointed to the television.

Miller looked again at the crying woman. "Who is she?" he asked.

"Maria Soliz. Your latest victim."

A woman began to scream, no, not on the television… somewhere else…

Miller was standing; awake in an instant. The dream quickly faded and he again was at Mike Samson's house. He glanced towards his usual sleeping area on the couch, which had been given to Ann yesterday. He had gladly taken the floor when they arrived at Mike's place so the woman might recover. Sure enough, the couch was now empty and Miller glanced around the dim house to catch a glimpse of where she might have gone. He guessed the time to be well past midnight. The house was dark except for the bathroom light. That would be a logical place to start. He dashed in that direction, secretly hoping the scream had been Mike's. Miller would never let him live that down. But arriving at the bathroom, he saw Ann staring at the mirror.

"Ann?" Miller asked. Nothing seemed wrong.

Ann glanced back at him and jumped again. "Miller!" Ann's pants dropped to her ankles. "Oh God." She grabbed the pants and pulled them back up. They stood staring at each other for a moment.

"It's alright, lass," Miller said. "I'm used to having that effect on women."

"I…," Ann began, but she was interrupted by a loud voice.

"Intruder! Surrender or prepare to feel the wrath of the Blue-Green Ranger!" It was young Sam, in his voice-changing helmet. He had a plastic sword pointed at Ann.

"It is safe, lad. This one is a friend," Miller offered.

"Oh, okay Mr. Miller," Sam said, pulling off the helmet.

"This is Ann; she's been on your couch for some time now."

"Oh yeah, you sleep a lot lady. Dad wouldn't let me watch any cartoons until you woke up. It's been forever!"

"Umm...sorry. Who are you again?" Ann asked.

"This is Sam, our gracious host's son." Miller introduced the youngest member of the household, although there was little need. Sam was just a smaller version of Mike. Perhaps he had his mother's eyes, but there was no mistaking where Sam came from.

Ann extended a hand while keeping the other wrapped tightly on the front of her pants. "It's a pleasure to meet you." Sam and Ann shook, which made Ann smile.

"Same to you, I guess. Does this mean I can watch TV again?" Sam asked Miller.

"In a moment. Ann, what happened? Is everything well?" Miller looked Ann over. All appeared normal.

"Yes, I'm sorry. I just... I just remembered something," Ann offered. Miller caught the fact that she was lying, but did not press. "So this is Mike

Samson's place?"

"Aye, after we found you on the roof...," Miller thought back to Ann's transformation and become more serious, "we brought you here. You've been asleep for a long time. How do you feel?"

"I… Good, I think. Cold. I could use a shower. And some food."

"I wanted to clean you up, but Samson would not let me," Miller offered.

"Ugh, remind me to thank him later. Wait, what happened with Abraham? You know him right? You didn't..."

Miller sighed. He had searched for Abraham only briefly, experience telling him to leave the vampire be if he didn't want to be found. "We found him. He's alive, lass. Our relationship is... complicated, but I hold no ill will towards him" he said. "There are very few of his kind I can say that about."

"So, wait, there are Cursed you are friendly with?" Ann seemed confused by this.

"Of course. Once they are freed from the control of the Fallen, I have no further issue with them."

"And me?" Ann asked.

"And you... what?" Miller was a bit confused by this conversation himself. What was Ann getting at? She looked extremely nervous.

"Well... I am, sort of, one of the Fallen. I guess."

"No, you're not, lass. From the moment I met you, you were clean, free of the demon's control. Lilith's control."

Ann still looked worried. "And there is no way she can… return?" she asked.

"Is that your worry? Well, that is an exciting question. No one has ever come back after being taken by the Fallen, so it's really impossible to know. But let's not dwell on such dark thoughts."

"But" Ann broke in, "you would be able to tell, right, I mean, if she did?"

"Aye, that I would," Miller said gravely. It was a depressing thought; he quite liked Ann. He had been sad to see her die the first time, and would hate to have to watch it again.

Ann seemed to breathe a little easier. "OK, good, I think. And if she does, you can't hesitate. I can't let anyone else get hurt by this, even if it costs me my life. Promise you'll kill me if it happens."

"I... what a grim thing, lass..."

"Promise!"

"Of course," Miller said, putting his hands up in defense. There was a long moment of silence.

"Can I watch TV now?" Sam asked. Both Miller and Ann looked at him, glad for the distraction.

"Shouldn't you be in bed?" Ann asked.

"Yes, he should." Mike Samson's voice came from down the hall. "What is this? Is 3 AM the new social hour in my house?" He poked his head into the bathroom.

To Miller, Mike Samson always looked on the verge of collapsing from exhaustion. Miller knew the man did not sleep much; he knew of his nightmares, and his guilt. Mike's usually grim appearance was made worse by the death of Catharine less than two days ago. Miller was glad to see Mike's eyes light up ever so slightly upon seeing Ann up and around.

"Ann. You're awake," Mike said. "Thank God. How do you feel?"

Ann visibly blushed at the question.

*Did she have a thing for Mike as well?* Miller wondered. He needed to get this man to share his secret.

"Yes, I feel great. But I would kill for some clean clothes," Ann responded, still clutching her pants.

"Yeah, I'm sure we can find something. Look." Now it was Mike's turn to blush. "About the whole 'shooting you in the chest' thing—I swear I didn't know it was you."

"Hah," Ann laughed, as if being shot was the funniest thing in the world. This succeeded only in making Mike even more uncomfortable "I guess I know how you really feel about me. It's all right; it turned out for the best."

"Well, it wasn't the best look for you, no?" Mike laughed awkwardly "I'm just glad you are okay."

"You and me both. Those teeth were a pain to floss." Ann laughed again.

"What is floss?" Miller asked.

*****

Mike Samson was glad to see Ann awake. For the last twenty-four hours, she had been nearly catatonic. He had quickly regretted not bringing her to a hospital, but then how would he explain her condition to the doctors? Not to mention what they might find when they examined her. Miller insisted that, although she was free of the Fallen, she was no longer human and never would be again. What that meant was not clear to Mike, but he would probably find out the hard way.

He moved around the house, trying to find something else for Ann to wear. Mike was still shaking the images of his latest dream out of his head. He had awoken from his regularly scheduled nightmare to hear voices in his house and he had to investigate before he had fully recovered. He shuddered a little at the memory of the dream before trying to move on. He would focus on the task at hand. Obviously, there was not much of his clothing that would work for Ann. But maybe Melissa had something... no, he couldn't do that. After a while, he settled on a pair of sweatpants with a drawstring and a shirt that was way too tight on him. They would still be large on Ann's tiny frame, but they would do until morning, when he could get to the store.

Mike took a few moments to clean the bathroom up so it was in slightly less embarrassing shape, while Miller and Ann watched.

"You don't have to do that, really. You should see my friend Lizzie's place," Ann offered, watching him work.

"Yeah, we met her. She called us and told us where you were," Mike said, while tossing clothes into the hamper. "She was worried about you."

"But she was okay?" Ann asked.

"Seemed to be. Kind of nervous, but not hurt or anything."

"She is just lovely," Miller offered.

Ann sighed. "Good. That's good. Was she, like, mad at me?"

"Mad, why should she be mad?" Mike asked.

Ann began to pace. "I brought her out with me, which was just a terrible idea. Lizzie has issues... well, I don't mean issues; I mean real medical problems. She had a breakdown when we were teenagers, and ever since then, she's been... well... fragile. And getting her involved with all of this..." Ann waved a hand between herself and Miller. "Well, it was just stupid. And when the zombies started popping up, she just freaked out." Miller and Mike both stopped moving and looked at Ann.

"Wait... zombies?" Mike asked.

"Oh, yeah. I should tell you guys about that one. Before Mike so rudely interrupted me with a bullet to the chest, I took on Ura."

"Ura?" Mike asked. "What's an Ura?"

"Aye, good lass, I wanted to talk to you about that. So you found the demon?"

"I did. And I killed it. It wasn't easy and I'm not exactly sure it was anything but dumb luck, but one demon down, five more to go."

"Well done!" Miller said, patting her on the back, but Mike was concerned.

"Why in God's name would you take on one of the Fallen alone?" Mike asked.

"Hey, I'm a big girl!" Ann said. "Well, at least I was then. I can take care of myself. Besides, this is my mess."

"How do you figure that?" Mike asked. "I mean, I get that you were the first one taken by the Fallen, but that hardly makes this your fault."

"Mike's right, lass. There was nothing you could do to prevent it, but I'm proud of you. We'll make you into a demon hunter yet," Miller said. "But you should also know: there are only four Fallen remaining. Gallu has met her end as well."

"So, zombies? Really?" Mike asked.

"Well, that's what I called them. Reanimated dead bodies. Ura was feeding off of people and then cursing them, bringing them back to life," Ann said.

"I didn't know they could do that," Mike said.

"Nor did I, to be honest. But the Fallen have yet to run out of new tricks." Miller said.

"Yes, it was all related to those Angel murders. I thought it was Abraham, actually, but it turned out to be Ura. I'm glad. Abraham helped me out of a bad place there. I don't know what I would have done without him," Ann continued.

"How about we go over this in the morning?" Mike suggested. "I need to check on Sam, and I know Miller likes his beauty rest."

"Wait, I just worked this out. Your son's name is Sam Samson?" Ann asked, and then blushed. "I'm sorry. That was rude."

Mike chuckled. It wasn't the first time the question had come up. "No, of course not. His real name is Michael Gabriel Samson the Third. Melissa, my wife, she always called him Sam," Mike explained.

"Good. Glad the poor little guy wasn't going to be stuck with that one on the playground."

Mike gave Ann the clothes and left her to wash up. Then he checked on his son, who was sitting in bed swinging a plastic sword with the lights on.

"Hey, Dad."

"Hey, Sam. Why aren't you sleeping?"

"That lady woke me up. I was getting ready to take her down, but then Mr. Miller told me to stand down."

"Sam, she's been passed out on the couch for a whole day. You had to know who she was."

Sam didn't look at his father; instead, he kept swinging the sword. "I know. I don't like her, that's all," Sam said.

Mike took a seat next to him on the bed. "Why would you say that, Sam?"

The boy shrugged. "There's something wrong with her. Before Mr. Miller was talking to her, I saw her in the bathroom. I think she was talking to someone."

That was odd. But then again, Ann was pretty odd.

"Look, she's our guest for a few days. Mr. Miller said she's OK, right?" Mike put a hand on his son's head. "And you trust Mr. Miller?"

"Yeah, of course. Mr. Miller is awesome."

"All right. Good. Just try and be nice to Ann." The boy shrugged.

"I'll try," he said, in that way kids talk when they really don't want to do something. It was as if Mike had just told him to clean his room.

"Good, now get some sleep."

"Okay."

Mike kissed the boy on his forehead and turned off the lights on his way out. He had never known Sam to dislike anyone. At almost five years old, the kid liked everyone and he was liked by everyone. Even with losing his mother such a short period of time ago, Sam was one of the happiest kids Mike knew.

Walking back through the house, Mike passed Miller, who was already asleep in his regular spot on the couch. He decided making coffee would be the next item on the to-do list.

Entering the kitchen, he found Ann standing in front of the open refrigerator.

"Ann?"

She spun quickly to face him. "Oh, hey, I'm sorry. I just noticed how hungry I am. You don't mind, do you?" Ann said, with various take-out containers in her hands. She was wearing the borrowed clothes, and the oversized pants looked ridiculous.

"No, of course not," Mike answered. "I just thought you were looking forward to a shower."

"Well yes," Ann responded, "but to be honest, I guess I don't want to be alone at the moment." She took a seat, opened a box, and began poking around with one finger in it, then thought better of it. "Fork?" she asked.

Mike handed her the requested silverware and she nodded a thanks and began attacking the food.

"I guess it has been a while since you ate," Mike observed.

He sat across from her, watching her eat. It slowly dawned on him that this was not the same Ann he had first met. Yes, she was bald now, but her features also had a sharper edge to them. Mike couldn't quite put his finger on it. And she carried herself differently. At College Hospital, Ann had been a desperate and brave woman, looking for the man she loved. Now, though, there was a confidence in her, a newfound strength. That said, she seemed to squirm as he watched her, as if something was bothering her.

"Are you sure you're OK?" he asked. "You've been through a lot."

"I'm fine, I…" Ann broke off. "It's just that… was there anyone else up there on the roof, when you…"

"When I shot you? Look, I swear that was an accident."

Ann cut him off. "No, no. Was there anyone else there? On the roof with us?"

"No. I mean, Miller came up after," Mike said.

Ann thought for a moment. "No, not Miller. Someone else."

"The vampire, maybe? Although he didn't look to be in such good shape," Mike suggested.

"Abraham? No, certainly not him. Miller said he vanished?" Ann asked.

"Yeah, we couldn't find him. Something about seeing him set Miller off," Mike said.

"Miller? You mean more off than usual?"

Mike laughed at that. "Yeah, with him it's pretty hard to tell. Then again, being a several thousand year old immortal has to make you a little crazy."

"I can only imagine," Ann said.

"So, do you think you're…?" Mike searched for the right word.

"Normal?" Ann offered.

"Well, normal is a strong word. Human was more where I was going."

Ann shook her head and look down at her hands. Her voice suddenly became solemn. "No, not human. I can still feel it; it's still here, right below the flesh. It's hard to explain, but I won't be normal ever again. I don't really know what that means yet." She looked back at him, some warmth returning to her face. "But this," she rubbed her cheek, "this I can deal with. At least I look human."

"So you might become that thing again?"

"Thing?" Ann sounded hurt, but a smile ran across her face.

"Well, I didn't mean to sound rude."

"No, it's okay. I don't know what to call it myself. It's what I am though. This here, this is just a disguise."

Mike smiled. "I don't believe that. Maybe on the outside, but this is what you are on the inside." Their eyes met for a moment before Mike looked away.

"Thanks for that," Ann added. There was a moment of silence and Ann went back to eating.

For a few moments, Mike wasn't sure what to say, but then he decided to broach a subject that had been bothering him since this whole mess had started.

"Ann, I don't think we can keep this a secret for much longer."

"What secret?" Ann asked, between mouthfuls.

"I mean, the Fallen, Miller, everything. I just don't know how to make it sound like I'm not crazy. So many people have already died."

"I don't know. I mean, I see your point, but I'm worried…," Ann started, but Mike cut her off.

He guessed what she was going to say. "No no, we don't have to tell them about you. I could see that being a tough conversation."

"They already know about me. Well, one of them does," Ann said.

"Who is 'They'?" Mike asked.

"The FBI, or some woman who works for the FBI. A lady named

Dupré. But look, here is the weird thing. Lizzie has video footage of this woman killing two of my friends. Lizzie thinks she's coming for me next."

"Whoa, murder?"

"Yeah, at CMDNJ, the same day you and I met," Ann said.

"Wait, wait. I got a call about that. The police want Miller in for questioning," Mike said.

"Miller?"

"Yes. Well, no. Miller is, or looks like, the janitor there." Mike strained to remember the name. "Soliz. Andres Soliz."

"The janitor? What? Oh my God, yes. I remember when I first saw Miller I thought I recognized him. But then he opened his eyes and he was an entirely different person. How did I miss that?" Ann looked stunned. "But what does that mean? Is Miller the janitor? Or does the janitor think he is Miller?"

"I have no idea," Mike said.

"Well, have you asked him?" Ann asked.

Mike squirmed in his chair. "No. I don't even know where to start," Mike said. "I mean, after all I've seen and all he's done. I know he is what he says he is, but I don't understand how it's possible."

Ann looked at him for a time. "Well, I guess I can see that," she said. "You like him, don't you? I mean, he is your friend."

Mike laughed out loud at that. "Yes. As much as he drives me crazy, I do like the guy. And I want to protect him and help him do his job. I'm just not sure I can do that anymore."

"Well, the FBI is out. At least until we understand more about this Dupré lady," Ann said.

"We?" Mike asked. "Does that mean you're sticking around?"

"It's not like I can walk away, Mike. I said the Fallen are my responsibility, at least to some degree. And I can help Miller like no one else can. It makes sense to work together," Ann said.

That made Mike smile again. "I'm glad to hear that," Mike said. "We could certainly use the help. I have to get back to the job in a few days. My leave is almost up, and having you to keep an eye on Miller would be a big help."

"Does he need a sitter?" Ann asked, with a laugh.

"Oh, just wait. The man is a wrecking ball!" Mike said and they both laughed.

"What about the police? You could tell them about all this," Ann asked. "I mean, you do work for them."

"Maybe. I have to understand how to tell them. I have friends in the force and so many cops saw that demon thing, Keith, leave the hospital…" Mike let the sentence trail off, seeing Ann stiffen at the name, the mirth draining from her.

"Not Keith. Its name is Asmodai," Ann said stiffly. "It killed Keith."

"Right, sorry, not Keith," Mike fumbled. This was still obviously a sore point for Ann. She sat still for a few moments and looked down at her hands. "Hey, I didn't mean anything by it," Mike added.

Ann finally looked back at him with a weak smile. "It's not your fault. Some of this is easier to handle than the rest. I'm going to go grab that shower." Ann stood up and passed him with a nod.

Instead of being bothered by this dismissal, Mike was encouraged. Ann was dealing with the events of the last few weeks. That meant she was still human. At least on the inside.

For a long time, Mike sat alone, digesting everything that had been said. It felt good to have Ann here. She was someone else to talk to about all this madness. Her 'condition' scared him a little, but if Miller was certain she was all right, then he was as well. He couldn't help worrying for her, though. She had been through so much, as had he, but had lost so much more.

He stood up and stretched, then noted the coffee machine. The call of caffeine was strong and Mike set about putting together a pot. He didn't get far. While pouring water into the coffee machine, an odd sound made him freeze. He put the coffee pot down and listened harder. Now all he could hear was the water running. Maybe it was just Ann in the shower. Had he heard something or was he getting paranoid? He decided that, with everything that had happened the last few weeks, being a little extra careful couldn't hurt.

Mike moved into the hallway, listening carefully. For a long time, there was nothing, but just as he was about to go in and work on the coffee, he heard it again. It sounded metallic. Then there were sounds of doors slamming out in the street. It was an odd time to be getting in the car. Mike walked to the front door to peek outside.

As he approached the door, it exploded inward, throwing him to the ground. He noted that too many things had blown up in the past few weeks. It had become a far too common experience for him and he would have to seriously consider some life changes if he survived whatever this was.

There was suddenly a large gun in his face.

"Freeze! FBI!"

# 4 - Thunder

Joseph Miller heard the disruption at the door and was up in an instant. Again. He wondered why the gods were suddenly against him sleeping. A man dressed in black, carrying a large gun, jumped through a perfectly good window. Perhaps the door was too tricky for him.

"Freeze!" the man yelled. Miller ignored him, lifting the barrel of the man's gun up with one hand, while jabbing the other hand into the man's neck.

"I believe the expression is 'chill'," he replied cheerily.

Another man entered in a shower glass through the window across the room. Miller spun behind the first man and kicked him towards the second. The new man pulled the trigger of the gun once before slapping the barrel up to avoid hitting his comrade. The two men collided, falling to the floor. Miller launched himself into the air and landed feet first on their backs. He grabbed one man's helmeted head and slammed it into that of his partner. Stepping off the heap, he checked both of them. Neither moved. He collected their weapons and turned towards the front door, then stopped, remembering.

"I apologize. You were right. 'Freeze' is valid too. But thank you for the gun. I have always wanted one of these," Miller said to the first man.

There was a burst of fire from the other side of the house and then a scream. Miller's first thought was of young Sam and he sprinted towards his room.

*****

Sam knew his father had told him to sleep, but he had decided instead to practice his moves. One had to be ready to fight bad guys at a moment's notice, and he knew all about bad guys. He brought his sword up over his head, and then brought it down as hard as he could on his pillow, while quietly whispering "Ayah!" because that's what you said when you hit bad guys with swords. Of course, had if it been a real bad guy he would have to shout, but then his Dad would know he wasn't sleeping.

He heard the sound of breaking glass. *At last*, he thought. It was the call to action he had been waiting for. Or maybe Mr. Miller had been drinking too much again.

Sam grabbed his helmet and dashed into the hallway. A man dressed in black, with the letters FBI in white across his chest, was in the hallway.

"Freeze! Federal agent!" the man yelled.

Sam raised the sword over his head and prepared for battle.

The bald woman, Ann, got there first and punched the man in the back of his helmet. The man flew into the wall behind him, his helmet leaving a hole in the wall where it connected.

"What's wrong with you, pointing a gun at a kid?" Ann scolded the man. Ann was wearing some very baggy clothes that Sam recognized as his dad's.

"Hey, I'm almost 5 years old!" Sam protested.

Ann ignored him and approached the man she had just punched. "Ah crap, I just knocked out an FBI agent." She touched him on his neck and was quiet for a minute. "Just seems out cold. Thank God."

Then Sam noticed Ann's hand. White scales like a snake covered her arm down to her elbow. "Oh man, what's wrong with your hand?" Sam pointed.

Ann looked too and for a moment was stunned.

"Are you some kinda monster?" Sam asked.

Looking back at Sam, Ann raised the scaly hand for him to see. She looked as surprised as he was. "I... Yes, sort of, but I'm a good monster." As she spoke, the skin on her hand grew and covered the scales again.

*A good monster?* Sam wasn't sure he had heard of such things. He thought back to his extensive Power Rangers knowledge base. He raised his sword and prepared to defend himself, just in case.

"You do know that sword is plastic, right?" Ann asked, with a worried look on her face.

Sam admitted to himself that this was a good point.

"Freeze! Face on the floor!" another man shouted. He was also dressed in black.

How had all these people gotten into Sam's house?

Ann stepped in front of Sam, arms raised. "Look, I think there's been some sort of mistake. Also, I think this man needs medical attention."

The man pointed with his gun. "Down on the ground, now!"

A white cord suddenly appeared around the man's neck. He grabbed for it, attempting to break free, but couldn't move it. He turned pink, then a little blue, and then dropped to the ground. Mr. Miller stepped over the man and waved.

"Did you just choke that guy out with a Wii remote?" Ann asked.

"Is that was this is? I figured the gun would be too loud, and honestly, Samson doesn't like it when I kill people," Miller said, tossing the game controller to the ground. Sam really hoped he hadn't broken it. "Everyone well?"

"Yeah, we're fine. But there is some sort of mistake. These are federal agents," Ann said.

"Like your police?" Miller asked.

"Yes, exactly. We shouldn't be beating them up."

"It was pretty cool though," Sam put in, and then added, "Can I have his gun?"

"No," Ann and Mr. Miller answered, at the same time.

"Let's go find your Father," Miller said. "Sam, stay behind me."

*****

Mike Samson found himself face down on the floor with his hands being tied behind his back.

"Same team, guys!" he yelled. The man tying him up did not respond. Instead, he stood up and headed into the next room. There was gunfire and suddenly Mike lost his thinly held calm. "My kid's here! What the hell are you gung ho idiots doing?" Mike tried to struggle to his feet.

Two men ran past Mike, and a third stopped by his side. "Mike Samson?" he asked, helping Mike to his feet.

"My son is sleeping in his room, I need...," Mike demanded.

The man put a calming hand on Mike's chest. He was a tall Japanese man, clean cut, in a dark suit. "We know about your son; everything will be fine," the man said in a composed tone, although the look on his face said otherwise. "I'm Special Agent John Takahashi. Please try to stay calm."

Another gunshot sounded.

"Jesus! You just had to knock on the damn door!" Mike dashed forward, but a hand snagged his wrist.

"Stay here, Mr. Samson." It was a woman's voice. "You have no idea what kind of creatures you have allowed to enter your home."

Mike turned to see a massive old woman. She must have been a professional bodybuilder. She placed a hand on his wrist, yet held him in place with ease. In the other hand, she held a enormous handgun. "Don't worry. We know how to handle their kind."

*****

Ann was one step behind Sam as they followed Miller towards the front door. The boy kept turning around and eyeing her, as if she might grow fangs and wings at any minute. She honestly couldn't blame him.

She flexed her wounded hand. She had known she wasn't human, but to see the scales just beneath the flesh still shocked her. Still, this was not the time to panic and she was doing her best to push past her condition and focus on why the FBI was breaking into Mike's house at 3 in the morning. Had they come for her?

Miller lifted a hand, which Ann supposed was the universal sign for stop.

"There, ahead, can you see?" Miller whispered.

Ann peeked her head around the corner. Mike was handcuffed and shouting at his two captors. The tall Asian man she did not know, but she recognized the woman instantly.

"Dupré!" she hissed. "And she's Cursed!"

"Aye. Very good!" Miller sounded, as if Ann was his prized student. "She isn't a demon, but her curse is old."

Ann couldn't see the difference; the black mist hung around Dupré about as much as it had around Abraham. "If you say so. But if Dupré is Cursed, what does that mean? Does the FBI know?" Ann asked, her mind reeling with possibilities.

"I have no idea. What would the fun be in that?" Miller grinned. "You say these men are federal agents? And are on the side of angels?"

"Should be. Dupré is a murderer, though. She killed two friends of mine while looking for me."

Miller rubbed his chin. "Ann, do you trust me?" he asked.

"Honestly? Not really. You are kinda crazy and your buddy over there put a pretty big hole my chest. I am fond of my chest."

"As am I," Miller put in.

"I trust you, Mr. Miller. Can I help?" Sam offered.

"Yes, Sam, I have special job for you. You stand right here and look fierce. Understand?"

"Yes, sir!" the boy said, obviously happy to be part of the plan. Sam spread his legs and raised his toy sword above his head, his face stuck in a grimace that Ann could only assume was the four-year-old's 'tough guy' face. He looked way too cute to be scary.

"Okay, what do I do?" Ann asked, still looking at Sam.

"Well, first you trust me," Miller said, grinning. "Second, you take out the man who is trying to sneak up behind us. I'm going to go make new friends." Miller dashed forward.

"Man behind us?" Ann spun and spotted the man coming from behind.

"Face on the ground!" the man was shouting, as he pointed another one of those large guns in her face.

"OK, okay." Ann put her hands up.

"I've got this one!" Sam dashed forward, waving his sword.

"Sam, no!" Ann shouted, but the man apparently had a better grasp of the situation than his coworker had earlier, and lowered the gun.

"Kid," he said, as Sam started smacking him in the kneecaps, "would you please stop that?"

Ann snatched the gun and yanked it forward. It discharged, destroying a picture on the wall. Ann followed up with a punch directly to the man's visored face, launching him across the room. She was getting better at this.

"Hey!" Sam yelled, "I called that one!"

*****

Mike Samson tried to pull away, but the woman's grip was like steel. Honestly, he was a little embarrassed. "You don't understand. My son is in this house," Mike pleaded.

"Look, I'm sure one of my men has him. We're not interested in your son, Mr. Samson," John Takahashi said. He put a radio to his mouth. "Check in."

The radio crackled a response. "Irons, checking in." There was a brief silence.

"Anyone else?" Takahashi asked. "Burns? Stone? Anyone?" There was no response.

"Missing a few friends?" Joseph Miller's voice came from across the room. He stepped into the light, that crazy smile glued to his face. Someone had given him an assault rifle, which Mike was sure had pleased Miller greatly. Takahashi and the old woman raised their guns at Miller.

"On the ground!" the woman shouted.

"Really, is that all you people can say? Honestly, I prefer to stand." Miller motioned to Mike. "Sam is safe. No worries."

"Oh, thank God," Mike said. He turned towards John Takahashi. "We're on the same team here. Let's everyone calm down and talk about this."

"That's not how this works," the old woman growled.

"Oh, trust me. You don't want to mess with Miller on this one," Mike said.

"Aye, listen to the lad," Miller encouraged.

"Miller? As in Joseph Miller?" the woman asked.

"That's him," Mike said, and Miller nodded in agreement.

"Not possible!" the woman argued.

"I assure you. That is my name."

"Joseph Miller died in 1908." The woman was waving the gun at him.

"Well, it could be a different Joseph Miller. It is a fairly common name," Takahashi offered. Mike noticed there was a small smirk on his lips.

"Quiet, you idiot! I don't care what his name is! He comes with us. He and Melakh," the old woman demanded. "You have no idea how dangerous they are."

Mike tried again. "How about everyone lowers their guns and we all head down to..." the FBI didn't have a station; where did they bring suspects? Mike had a feeling he was going to find out soon. "... wherever you want to go. We'll settle down, have a cup of tea, and not kill anyone?"

"I do like tea," Miller offered. His gun was still raised.

"How about this, instead," Mike felt the barrel of a gun pressed against his forehead as the old woman kept talking. "You drop your gun and I don't put a large hole in your tea drinking friend here."

"Hold it, Dupré. This is not how we do things." Takahashi put up a hand.

Dupré smacked the man across the face, sending him sprawling.

"This is exactly how we do things." She pulled out her own radio and barked orders into it. "Anyone still standing: get your asses to the front door. Now!" One person responded in the affirmative. "Your move, Mr. Miller." Miller's grin was unchanged.

Sam dashed out from the dark hallway and threw himself around Mike's waist. "I got you, Dad!" the kid said.

"No, Sam! Stay back!" Mike yelled, but the boy ignored him. This was not the time for his parenting skills to fail him.

"There now, father and son reunited. Quite touching," Miller said. "Do you still plan on blowing this man's brains out, now that his son is here?"

Mike was horrified. Well, more horrified.

Takahashi stood back up and wiped blood from his face. "For the record," he said to Mike, "I'm a huge fan of tea." He turned back to face Dupré. "You can't do this. This man is a hero. We can't kill this man. We don't kill innocent people, we protect them."

"John, we don't even know if he still is human. This could all be a trick. Let me do this my way."

"Then cut him." It was Ann, taking her place beside Miller. "If he bleeds red, he is human. I can tell you he is, though."

"Melakh!" Dupré snarled. She kicked Mike and opened fired on Ann. The gun went off inches from Mike's right ear and he yelled in pain. He pinned Sam as he fell forward, covering the boy with his body and shouting for him to stay down.

Miller began shooting and Takahashi dove for Dupré's gun. Mike couldn't see if he hit Dupré or not, but as he watched, the last remaining agent clubbed Miller in the back the head. Miller stumbled forward, looking stunned, and then he crumbled to the floor. He landed next to Ann, who was already lying face down in a pool of her own black blood.

*****

The FBI searched the house for several hours, but found very little. Several agents were carted away in ambulances. Miller was carried out of Mike's house in chains. Ann was strapped to a stretcher, restrained by large leather straps, with some sort of metal mask covering most of her face. Mike wasn't even sure she was alive. The bullet had merely grazed her head, but she had not moved and no doctor attended her.

Mike held Sam in the corner by the door. He had no idea what to do, how he could save his friends, if he should save his friends. This was the FBI. If anyone would know what to do with monsters, it was them. He expected to be led out to one of the cars as well, but the agents ignored him.

Sam demanded to know what they had done with Mr. Miller and why his father had let them take him. He asked over and over again. Mike had no answers. He sat in his ruined house and waited to be arrested.

Except he wasn't. The agents left and John Takahashi reappeared and apologized for the whole situation. He assured Mike that this was not how the FBI generally operated and he would help with getting the house repaired. If Mike would just call the number on this card, they could work everything out. Mike took the card and weakly thanked him. Then Mike and Sam were alone.

Mike stepped out of the house, with Sam at his side. Sam was crying, afraid for his friend. Mike didn't blame him. The business card in one hand, his other arm wrapped around his son, they sat together on the front step and watched the sun come up.

He wasn't sure how much time passed before he read the card. He was flipping it between his fingers, a nervous twitch he usually saved for writing implements. He flipped it forward; he flipped it back. He flipped it forward; he flipped it back, over and over again, simply numb. Then the card fluttered out of his hand, dropped to his feet, and landed face down. As he reached over to pick it back up and continue his mindless flipping, he noticed something on the back. A quick note was jotted down in pencil. It was three words long.

"Find Lizzie Namgung."

# 5 - Nightmare

The card shook Mike out of his daze. Why would John Takahashi give him such a note and how had he known of Ann's friend in the first place? There was more going on here than first appeared. The most direct route to action was the easiest; he would just call Lizzie on the phone. Simple.

By this time, Sam had fallen asleep so Mike carried his son back to his room, which he noted was in considerably better shape than the rest of the house. Figuring it too early to call, Mike went about the business of cleaning up. The front door was destroyed, as were four windows. The windows were easy to cover up with some heavy plastic. It wouldn't keep the place safe from thieves, but at least it would keep the rain out. The front door was harder, but it was not completely ruined. After some time, he managed to get it to at least look correct. Of course, this wouldn't stop anyone from getting in the house, but then again, it hadn't the last time either. That job complete, he spent some time cleaning all the broken glass off the floor.

While his hands were busy, his mind was whirling away at the events of the night before. John Takahashi seemed a reasonable man, but this Dupré woman was dangerous. She had recognized Ann on sight and seemed to think she was the most dangerous person in the world. That made sense—Ann wasn't human anymore. It even made sense that the FBI might be interested in Ann, since it was only on Miller's word that Mike accepted she was on the side of angels. Still, though, to break into the house like that, fully armed? It didn't add up. And if they knew who Miller was—and it sounded like they might—why arrest him? Why not ask for his help?

Mike thought back to the last few days. There was one possible reason: the FBI might want Miller for something else. The police were looking for Miller in relation to this Soliz character. Mike still wasn't sure how that all fit in. And there was the possibility they wanted Miller for his part in the violence in upstate New York, when they had taken down one of the Fallen. But if that was the case, why wouldn't they take Mike in as well? Mike was certainly in the middle of that. Catharine's blood still stained the inside of his van.

At last, ten o'clock rolled around and he felt it was safe enough to call Lizzie. Recovering his phone from a pile of debris in the kitchen, he made the call. He was disappointed when no one answered. *Of course, that would be too simple.* He was going to have to do this the old-fashioned way. He grabbed his gun and his coat, and started dialing Sam's grandparents.

"Where are we going, Dad?" Sam entered the room, his coat already on.

"You are going to your grandparents. I'm going to see what I can find out about getting Mr. Miller back."

"No way! If you're going after Mr. Miller, I'm coming too," Sam insisted.

"Yeah. No, kid. You were in plenty of danger last night. This is too dangerous."

"You need backup, Dad, someone you can trust," Sam said.

Mike knew he was just quoting some dumb movie, but he was impressed by his spirit. Mike was only going to talk with Lizzie: there was no harm in that and he had hardly spent any time with his son in the last few weeks.

"OK, Sam. You can come, but if I ask you to do something, you do it. No asking questions."

"Like drinking my milk?" Sam asked.

"Yes, exactly, but this is even more important. I say it; you do it. No questions."

"All right! We're going to go get Mr. Miller!" the boy cheered. It occurred to Mike that the minivan was missing the driver's side front door and the seats were still covered in blood.

"OK, head to the Mustang. I'll get your booster."

"And we're going to take the cool car! Yes!" Sam cheered again.

"Just get going kid." Mike smiled.

"Also, we should get some ice cream, so we're ready to handle more bad guys."

"Just go!"

*****

Mike hadn't used his Mustang much lately, certainly not since he had been on extended leave from the force. It felt good to get into his old car, like visiting an old friend. He had purchased the car right when he had started at the Police Academy, before he had gotten married. It was a memento of happier times and he couldn't help but smile every time he sat in it. Sam loved it too, and it was extremely rare that he was allowed to ride in it.

Mike fiddled awhile to get the booster seat into the rear of the Mustang. It quickly became obviously that this car was never meant to carry anyone in the back seat. Sam's knees already touched the back of the front seats and he couldn't get in or out without Mike lifting him.

Still after several tries, they were both set to go. Sam gave another cheer as they pulled out of the driveway. The ride to Lizzie's was uneventful; he mostly remembered the way from the other night when he and Miller had visited while trying to track down Ann. He had to make a guess on a few final turns and ended up having to backtrack once. Finally finding the place, he pulled into the driveway next to the same silver Civic that had been in the lot the last time. It looked like she was home. In fact, on closer inspection, the front door was hanging open. That felt odd to Mike. He remembered his short, tense conversation with Lizzie. He had never been allowed to enter the building. In fact, Lizzie had only removed all the chains and bolts so that he could see her after he had proven his identity.

"Sam, stay here," he ordered. He pulled the Desert Eagle out from the glove box.

"Aww, Dad!" came the required complaint.

"What was our deal, Sam?"

"It... yes, sir," Sam said, bitterly.

"Don't you take a step out of this car until I get back! In fact..." He fiddled with his cell phone for a moment, then tossed it into the back seat. "See the timer? If I'm not back before the timer plays music, you call 911. OK?"

"But I'm never supposed to call 911 unless it's.... Oh. Right!"

"You got it? You're my backup. You keep an eye out, OK, and call in the big guns if we need them."

This made Sam happy. "Yes, sir!" he said, grabbing the phone.

"Good."

Mike made his way to the front of the house. The door had been torn off its hinges. It was even more impressive because of the large number of deadbolts and chains attached to the door. It was apparently a bad week for front doors. *Had the FBI been here first?* It didn't make sense for them to send Mike looking for Lizzie if they already had her. No, chances were good that someone else had taken her.

"Hello?" he shouted into the house. No one answered. He would have to take a look. He dreaded going in there alone and leaving Sam in the car, but he saw no alternative. He stepped through the front doorway.

Inside the house, there were signs of a struggle, but not the massive home invasion he had suffered. Like the living room, the rest of the house looked a little messy and was decorated with questionable taste, but pretty normal. If Lizzie had been taken, it probably went down without too much of a fight.

He announced himself several times as he searched, but never got a response. He didn't want to spend too long inside the house, as he felt too nervous with Sam being outside alone. After he was sure the place was empty, he quickly made his way back to the car. He opened the door to a barrage of questions.

"Did you find him?" Sam demanded.

"No," Mike answered. "We're looking for someone that was going to help us. But I think someone took her as well. Or she went into hiding. I'm not sure."

"Dang. Do you think it was the FBI again?" Sam asked. "I thought they were the good guys."

"Me too, kiddo." There was silence for a minute as Mike scratched his chin, as he stood next to the car, trying to plan his next move. Honestly, ice cream seemed to be the way to go.

"Dad, do you know those people in the fancy suits?" Sam asked.

"What?" Mike looked up. Across the street, three people were approaching. There were two men and one woman, each dressed in a black suit and wearing shades. The 'man' in the lead was the vampire named Smith.

"Oh sh..." Mike caught himself before swearing in front of Sam, and dove into the car. He gunned the engine and put the car in reverse. A black van pulled directly behind him, blocking his path down the driveway. He put the car into first and cut the wheels hard to the right, plowing through Lizzie's front yard. At the same time, he drew his gun and fired through the open window at the blocking van. Mike had no illusions that a bullet fired left-handed out the window of a moving car had a chance in hell of hitting anything. However, it made the driver of the van hesitate long enough for Mike to get the car onto the street. He put the pedal to the floor and the rear tires of the car spun as they went from grass to pavement. Then the Mustang was off.

The van jumped forward as the driver recovered, and the vehicle managed to bump the back of Mike's car just as it began to accelerate.

"That was awesome!" Sam shouted

"Sam, keep your head down," Mike shouted back. He tossed the gun into the passenger seat, switched hands on the steering wheel, and shifted the car into second.

Mike had noticed that the three people in suits had not flinched at all at the sound of the gunfire. He could see them in the rearview mirror as they dashed into the van. It looked like he had a chase on his hands.

Mike took the first corner hard, throwing the rear end of the car out and almost hitting a stop sign.

"Who were those guys?" Sam asked.

"Bad guys," Mike answered.

"We can take them! We can make 'em give Mr. Miller back!"

Mike briefly wondered when Sam had become Scrappy Doo. "Wrong bad guys," he said. He had hoped Smith was dead. Just the thought of facing that thing down again made his stomach hurt. He needed to get away, to get Sam someplace safe.

He wondered, briefly, what Smith wanted. Maybe payback? Smith had put a tracer on the van, but Mike had gotten rid of that. Of course, Smith knew who he was; he knew where Mike lived. Had that van been following him since he'd left his house?

"Damn, damn, damn, damn," Mike chanted under his breath. If the van had not been following him before, it was now. It tore around the previous corner just as he had, almost tipping over at the turn. A second black van rounded the corner right after it. Mike shifted into third gear and made another quick left. He merged onto Route 22, a fairly busy highway, just barely missing a small blue Mazda. The first van was only seconds behind. Mike saw it clip the little blue car as it entered the highway and it was temporarily forced off the road. The second van made it through unscathed.

Mike quickly hit 60 miles per hour and wove though the traffic. Luckily, it was light at this point of the day. The second van was keeping pace, although with every quick pass, it looked as if it might tip.

"Dad, toss the gun back here. I'll shoot 'em," Sam offered.

"No!" Mike shouted.

Sam crossed his arms across his chest in a sign of annoyance. "Fine! You never let me have any fun," he grumbled.

It seemed that Mike had two choices. His first and best chance was to simply lose both vans in traffic. This seemed his best shot; his car was faster and he was in local territory. He should be able to ditch them easily enough. The second possibility would be getting the police involved. If the option appeared, he would surrender to the police. Being a cop, on leave or not, would give him an advantage. That is, of course, if Smith didn't just kill everyone involved. No, escape was certainly the preferred option.

Mike picked a street at random and turned into it, dropping down a gear and sliding around the corner with a dramatic screeching of tires. The van followed but didn't make the turn as smoothly, grinding against the guardrail with a flash of sparks.

The Mustang blew through a red light, sending traffic swerving madly out of the way. The van weaved through the chaos Mike left in his wake. He cut left, just barely avoiding a family trying to cross the street.

If he could get to the Parkway, or another highway without traffic lights, he could open the car up and make some distance. The Garden State Parkway was a good ten miles away, through some fairly congested areas. Still, he knew several interesting short cuts on the way that could help him lose his admirers.

Mike gunned the engine again as a path formed in his head. The van was still behind him, still managing to keep up. Suddenly, from a side street, the first van reappeared, and attempted to block the road. Mike swore and locked up his brakes, throwing the emergency brake in the mix for good measure. The tires screamed as he drove off the road again and onto someone's front yard. Here it was hard to keep the car straight and it actually spun a complete 360 degrees on the dirt before he managed to get it going in the right direction.

"Wheeeee!" Sam shouted from the back.

The second van barely bumped the first van as it came to a complete stop. This bought Mike more time, as he continued to tear up the front yard. He smashed through a wood fence and barreled back onto the road behind both vans. He shouted a victorious "Yes!" as his tires gained traction again and the car gathered speed.

"That was awesome!" Sam repeated his earlier praise.

Now Mike turned off the road one more time, onto a small road he knew that led through a park. It ran parallel to Route 22 and headed towards the parkway. He hoped his pursuers would assume he had taken the major route. Seeing no sign of the vans, he slowed to just slightly above the speed limit. His heart was pounding and he noticed for the first time that the windshield had a large crack in it. He wondered what else he had broken in this little adventure. At this rate, he was going to have to start taking the bus to save Miller and Ann.

"You OK back there?" he asked Sam, moving the rearview mirror down to see his son.

"Can we do it again?" The boy smiled.

*God, no,* Mike thought to himself.

At the next intersection, he cut right, again away from the major road, but still in the direction of the parkway. He followed with a quick left, avoiding traffic lights.

"Dad, look!" Sam pointed. Through the woods, to their left, a black van bounded. It bounced over rocks and smashed through a fence.

"How did...?" But Mike didn't finish his own question. He dropped down a gear and slammed the gas pedal. "Here we go again," he muttered to himself.

The van returned to the road, again several yards behind him. Mike doubled back by taking the next right and another quick right after that. The van followed, nearly tipping on the second turn but not slowing.

Mike entered the park again, determined to shake this van. About midway through the park, near a pond, he took a left up a large grassy hill. He was a little more prepared this time, so he managed to keep the car going mostly straight when it hit the grass. He kept the gear high to help the traction. Mike gained a few yards as the driver struggled to follow. The hill crested to a steep point and Mike felt the suspension on the Mustang extend as the car caught a few inches of air. He bounced hard against his seat when the car came back to the ground.

"Ow!" Sam yelled from the back seat.

"Sorry, kid. Hang on." He glanced back to see his son rubbing the top of his head.

The van appeared a moment later, catching air over the hill just as the Mustang had. It landed hard; its front wheels jammed to the right and the back end of the van snapped forward. The entire van was suddenly sideways and rolling. It landed wheels up, and slid into a group of trees.

"One down," Mike whispered to himself. He found a jogging trail and picked his way through, scaring the hell out of a young woman walking her dog.

How had the van found him? Had it just been luck? He thought he had traveled a good distance away. Maybe the vans had split up. One took the major route, the other trying the back roads. That was the most reasonable solution. Unless... Mike's stomach twisted into a massive knot. Unless they had put trackers on both cars. He punched the dashboard in frustration. What a fool he had been! But then again, the Mustang had been locked in the garage for months. The only way they would have gotten to it is if they had been in his house! He needed to find someplace safe, where he could look under the car.

He found the road again and continued in the direction opposite to what he had originally planned. If his first guess was right and he wasn't being tracked, that was the safest course of action. He merged again back on Route 22, staying just above the speed limit. *Move fast, but don't draw attention to yourself.*

The Mustang was now making a terrible grinding noise. Mike was sure he had busted something in that last jump. He was sad to learn, as an adult, that one really couldn't jump a car like The Dukes of Hazzard and expect to drive it much farther. Those Duke boys had planted completely unreasonable standards for cars in his head. Cars and women's shorts.

He didn't see the black van waiting for him at the corner until it was far too late. It barreled through an intersection, just as Mike entered. It hit the Mustang at the driver side front tire. Mike's vision was filled with the white of air bags, as the car and van wrapped together.

*****

The world came back to Mike Samson upside down. He briefly wondered if he had reached the limit of times that one could be knocked out and still have a working brain. Then fear caught up with him.

"Sam!" he shouted. There was no response and Mike fought to turn around in his seat and check on his son. Mike put a hand on the ceiling to brace himself and he reached for the seatbelt. Sticky blood rolled up his face. "Sam!" he repeated. The back seat was empty.

"Oh, he's fine," came a woman's voice. "A little cut up, but he'll be fine. Lucky for you too, driving like that."

The woman he had seen walking with Smith was kneeling by the door. She had a thin face, as if pinched, with a slight, almost mocking, smile on her lips. She had her sunglasses low on her nose so Mike could see her black eyes.

"Here, let me get you out of there." She yanked the door off the car and pulled him out onto the street. The cursed woman's pure strength terrified him. Outside, Smith was waiting. Several other men were blocking off the road, perhaps pretending to be the Feds again.

"Mr. Samson," Smith said, in a low angry tone.

"Oh, you are not going to do the Matrix thing again," the woman said.

"Is that what that is?" another man close by asked. "I hear him doing it all the time and I never got it until just now. 'Cause his name is Smith, right?"

"Yes, he's been doing it for years with whatever poor sap he is trying to terrorize at the moment. Drives me mad," the woman said.

"People, can we stay on task here?" Smith said, with more than a little annoyance entering his voice.

"Can you not make any references from movies that came out over ten years ago?" the woman sneered.

"Carter... please. Focus here." Smith pointed back to Mike. The other man laughed, but said nothing more. After a moment, Smith sighed and turned his attention back to Mike. "Mr. Samson, please don't mind my colleagues. After our last...meeting, the head office decided I needed more help. Thus, Tweedledee and Tweedledum here." Smith sighed again, then continued. "I bet you are surprised to see me?"

"To be honest," Mike said, sitting up, "I was really hoping you were dead."

"Sadly for you, I am not. But you did ruin a perfectly good suit, if that is any consolation."

"Not really, no," Mike said. He was glancing back into the ruined car to see if he could spot his gun. That wasn't likely, though. And not that it would be very useful against what he guessed were three vampires. Instead, he went another route.

"Please, where is my son?" Mike asked the woman named Carter.

It was Smith that answered. "He is safe and he will stay that way as long as we get what we want."

"And what do you want?" Mike asked, again trying to control his rising panic. He had to get Sam back; he had to make his son safe.

"Well, to be honest, I just wanted to kill you. I mean, you have it coming. I really did like that suit. But then I found this…" Smith flashed John Takahashi's business card and spun it between his fingers.

"What…?" Mike squinted at the card.

"I know, I know, it's complicated." Smith tossed the card back into

Mike's lap. "You see, the head office happens to know John Takahashi. He is a man of interest, one might say. Like yourself, except I don't have the same urge to kill him. Anyway, this Takahashi fellow happens to work for an associate of ours, who no longer finds the time to take our phone calls."

"Renee Dupré," Mike guessed.

Smith raised his eyebrows at that. "Yes, yes, very good, Mr. Samson. You continue to impress me. Yes, let's say Madame Dupré had been doing some very interesting work for the company not so long ago. Bring Renee Dupré to me alive and I will give you back your son. I may even let both of you live."

"Just give me back my son. I'll do whatever you like when he is safe."

"Hah, you should know it doesn't work that way," Smith said.

"And if I don't?" Always a stupid question, but always required.

"It's simple. I need you to bring me Dupré, or my friends and I share a lite snack of little Samson."

"No, you don't touch him! You don't touch him!" Mike shouted.

"Well then, you know what you have to do. Heck, I'll even be nice about it. I'll give you thirty-six hours to get the job done. See, I can be a nice guy." Smith turned and started to walk away.

"Please don't rush on our account," Carter said, a black tongue licking her lips.

"No! Give me back my son!" Mike screamed and charged Smith.

The third vampire caught Mike by the neck and tossed him into the air. Mike hit the ground hard and rolled until he hit the side of the Mustang.

"See you in thirty-six hours, Mr. Samson."

# 6 - Long Lost Love

Marcel Dupré had never liked New Jersey. He couldn't understand why Renee had stayed all these years. Perhaps it was for Dallas, the man that had saved them both all those years ago. But Dallas called Texas home; he only had the misfortune of working in New Jersey. Still, stepping out into the street and seeing the old office building in Trenton, Marcel could hardly complain. He wouldn't complain about anything again for a long, long time.

The sun was shining in the blue sky of a warm spring morning and he was going to see his wife as a man, not as a monster, for the first time in a hundred years. He rubbed his clean-shaven face, still enjoying the feel of it. It had been almost ten years since he had seen Renee, twenty since he had been outside the forest around his hideout. But as a seven-foot-tall, hairy monster, he could hardly get out often. He had been trapped in that hideous shape when the last of the Fallen had died—when Joseph Miller, Dallas, and his men had clashed with Asmodai in the countryside of Marcel's homeland of France, a place he now yearned to return to. Dallas had discovered him alive and once again in control of his actions, on a hilltop. Together, they found his wife in a nearby town. Renee had been lucky enough to look human at least, even if the demon had reshaped her body. With the help of Dallas and some other friends, including the recovering vampire Abraham, Marcel and his wife had managed to piece their world back together, if not in a way generally considered normal. Now, though, the Fallen had returned, and although that meant he would soon have dangerous work to do, he had finally been able to escape the form of a werewolf and rejoin society.

Not that returning to the world after living in a shack in the woods for 40 years was easy. The crowds, the smell, the noise of the modern world bothered him. He had known of it, had read anything he could, but to actually see it was still quite a surprise. Despite this, he planned on doing his best to adapt. He had been traveling for over a week now, since he had found the campers and convinced them to take him back to civilization. Stepping off the bus on the last leg of the journey, he almost wept with excitement, a reaction his wife would surely mock him for. But that was OK; he looked forward to it.

Marcel made the short walk to the park where they had arranged to meet. He checked his watch, confirming again that he was on time. He had never been to the park in the daytime, only late at night many years ago, when he desperately needed to escape. Those dangerous nights were over, though, and never again would he have to hide in shadows. He was free.

The park itself was much as he remembered it. There was now a wooden play set where several small children ran and screamed, as children were known to do. Across the way was a park bench where a single woman sat. His breath caught when he laid eyes on Renee. She was not the petite woman he had married all those years ago. The demons had changed that. But the face was still hers, with those high cheekbones. Her hair was cropped so short that she looked almost bald, and there were many new wrinkles around her eyes. Her face was set in that grim expression that he knew meant she was thinking.

"Renee!" he shouted to her.

The woman's face lit up as she turned to him. "Marcel!" she replied, and ran to him.

They embraced, and then shared a long delayed kiss. She broke away and pushed him back suddenly.

"What?" Marcel asked, a little surprised.

"Just let me look at you. Your face, I had almost forgotten." She broke off, putting a hand on his cheek. "You're crying," Renee said.

"Yes, only a little. You should be crying too," Marcel responded, with a laugh.

"I was never good at that," Renee said, but her eyes were wet. "I'm so glad you finally made it."

He hugged her again. "So am I. Even if it means the Fallen have returned, at least we are together," he said.

Renee's face darkened. "Let's not dwell on that for now. Let's enjoy this moment. I've waited so long to have you back."

"I know. And I've missed your visits," Marcel said.

Renee looked away guiltily. "I am sorry I could not see you more the last few years. I've been busy preparing for this moment."

"Well, tell me, have the Fallen been spotted? Do we still have time to find them before..."

"They are here in New Jersey," Renee interrupted, "but let's not deal with this now. Abraham has set up a place for you..."

"Here? Why would the Fallen be here?" Marcel asked, ignoring Renee's attempt to change the subject.

"Enough!" she shouted, but quickly switched back to more soothing tones, stroking his chest. "Must we do this now?"

"What's wrong, Renee?" Marcel grabbed his wife's shoulders and looked into her eyes.

She would not meet his gaze. She sighed. "I don't know why they are here, Marcel. How could I know that? I've been working with the FBI; we've already tracked one of them down just last night. I've hardly slept in weeks trying to discover their location."

"Of course. You must be exhausted. Let's go back to the lab."

"No," she shouted again. She then repeated in a softer tone, "No, I have Abraham waiting to bring you to a safe place. I'll join you there later today."

"If...if you are sure. I had hoped..." Marcel paused, not sure what to say. This was not the reunion he had pictured. "Well, I suppose I can wait a few hours more, if it makes you happy."

"Thank you," Renee said. They kissed again. "He's waiting, this way. I will have to reintroduce you two. He has never seen your real face."

"Honestly, until a few days ago, I had forgotten what it looked like myself," Marcel laughed, and Renee did as well. It was a rare sound, even to him, but it warmed his heart.

*****

Abraham was waiting by a particularly old-looking Newark Taxi. The vampire had changed little over the years; his hair was perhaps a little more grey and there was a new stiffness to his movements. With his mutilated eyes covered by dark sunglasses, he actually looked vaguely friendly, even if he desperately needed a bath and a change of clothes.

"Abraham, it's good to see you again." Marcel wrapped the vampire in a hug.

Abraham, not accustomed to such acts, responded awkwardly but honestly. "Little brother, so this is what you really look like." He smiled.

"Thank you once more, Abraham," Renee said.

"Anything for family," Abraham responded and bowed, then jerked back upright with a pained expression on his face.

"Are you well?" Marcel asked.

"Oh, don't worry about little old me; been a rough couple of days. Just need a little time and I'll be right as rain," Abraham said.

"Good, I have to get back. Can you take us?" Renee asked.

"Of course," Abraham responded.

Marcel was not sure it was wise to let the blind vampire drive.

Once inside, Renee pulled out a bag of clothes and a walker, of all things.

"Ah, yes, the disguise," Marcel said.

"I find it easier. A few know the truth, but it tends to make them uncomfortable," Renee said, placing a wig on her head. In moments, she looked more like the eighty-year-old woman she pretended to be.

When the car stopped, Renee left, walking slowly into the building.

"She is quite the actress," Abraham said from the front of the car.

"I never knew," Marcel admitted. It was a convincing act.

"What else don't you know about Renee?" Abraham asked.

"What does that mean?"

Abraham shrugged. "Maybe nothing. Let's just say I'm worried about her." Abraham pulled the taxi out into traffic.

"In what way?" Marcel asked.

The vampire paused. "Don't worry about it. I'd hate to bother you on your return."

"She was acting strangely. I had hoped we could spend more time together," Marcel said honestly.

"She's a busy lady. But if you need something to keep you busy, well I could use some help on an errand."

Marcel noted the broad smile on the vampire's face, which was reflected in the rearview mirror. He returned the smile. "Well, I'm not quite the man I used to be," he said, "but I never turn down a friend in need."

"Good," Abraham said "Some old playmates of ours are back in town and I'm not quite up to their visit. But perhaps with a little help..."

"I don't suppose you have those gifts I've been sending you?" Marcel asked.

"Already in the trunk," Abraham said.

Well, then, it would not be the reunion he hoped for, but it wouldn't be a complete waste. It was about time Marcel Dupré made himself useful again.

# 7 - A Kid's Gotta Eat

"Hey, I think the kid is coming to."

Sam moaned. He didn't feel well. Maybe he could convince Dad he needed to stay home and watch TV on the sofa today. That always helped you feel better when you were sick.

"Kid?" It was a woman's voice. Someone was shaking him.

"My head hurts," Sam complained. He opened his eyes. "Hey! Where am I?" Then Sam remembered the car chase. Had he been kidnapped? He glanced around and realized he was inside a van. It must have been one of the ones that had been following him and his dad.

"There you are, kid. Nice to see you moving." The woman sitting next to him was dressed in a suit. She was tall and thin and had a mean face. Sam had last seen her crossing the street, heading towards them. They had really freaked Dad out.

"Are you the bad guys?" Sam figured it was best to ask these things up front.

The woman snorted. "Hey, King, are we bad guys?" she asked someone in the front of the van.

A very tan man with short black hair turned and responded, "Not you Carter, you're evil-lite at best. Now Smith, he's a bad guy."

A third voice from the passenger seat all the way at the front of the van chimed in. "People, can we try and be professional about this?" This must be Smith.

"We're not really bad guys, kid. Not if we don't have to be." The woman named Carter smiled at him. The smile was friendly enough but her eyes were pitch black.

"That's exactly what a bad guy would say!" Sam accused.

"Well, he has you there, Carter," the man name King laughed from the next row.

"I suppose you're right, kid," Carter said, "but really, this is just my job. You know, like some people fight fires, some people deliver the mail..."

"If you break into 'The People in Your Neighborhood,' I swear to God I'll light you on fire myself," King laughed again.

Carter sent a dark look his way. "Don't mind him, Sam. People have been ignoring his jokes for the last 500 years. He is getting desperate." She jerked a finger towards King. "I'll tell you what: as long as you are good for us, we'll be good for you. Your dad is going to run a little errand for us and then we'll make sure you two go out for cookies and milk."

"Or maybe we'll just eat you," King offered.

"Also possible," Carter agreed, but seeing Sam's pallid face, she smiled again. "Little joke, we don't actually eat kids. Well, Smith might, but as long as you don't work for him, you should be safe."

"Carter! I thought we weren't going to talk about that anymore?" Smith yelled. "Accidents happen. I would like to see you get ripped to shreds and manage not to eat the first thing that comes along."

"You eat people?" Sam asked. He had thought maybe they were kidding, in that not funny way adults do sometimes when they're trying to be funny.

Carter shrugged at the question. "Only sometimes, Sam." That was not making Sam feel better. "What's the plan here Smith? What are we doing with young Sam here?"

"He is going to stay with Angela for the next few days," Smith answered.

"Angela? Is that safe?" Carter asked.

"Who's Angela?" Sam asked. His head still hurt and he wanted his Dad. Also, he'd never gotten that ice cream he'd wanted.

"Oh, you'll like her," Smith said. "She's your age and I'm sure she's perfectly safe. And if not, well, that is one less problem for us to worry about."

*****

Sam had bumped his head in the car accident. Carter cleaned him up and put a big bandage on his head. It was a boring white color, not at all like the cool "Cars" Band-aids he had at home.

They had arrived at a very large house, which Sam thought might be a mansion. It was pretty common for bad guys to have mansions, usually with big caves underneath. No, wait. That was Batman. Either way, the house was much bigger than anything Sam had seen before.

When Sam was cleaned up, Carter gave him a glass of water and brought him to a set of big heavy doors. She spent some time undoing the chains and locks on them.

"What's in there?" Sam asked, expecting some bad guy torture area.

"This is Angela's room."

"You keep her locked up?"

"Well, she was trying to escape, but she should be better now," Carter said.

"See, you guys are bad guys!" Sam said.

"Not at all, if she had gotten out, she would have hurt people. We're good people for keeping her safe and fed."

"So, is she some sort of monster?" Sam asked nervously.

"Some sort, yes. But don't worry: as long as she's not hungry, she probably won't hurt you."

"Probably?"

Carter smiled as she opened the door. "Yeah, probably." She grabbed Sam by the back of the neck and shoved him into the room. The door slammed behind him. Then he could make out the sound of the chains and locks being redone.

The room looked like a bigger version of his living room. It had wooden floors and a massive couch, with an even bigger TV in front of it. There was a row of windows to Sam's right, but they were boarded up so only cracks of sunlight entered the room. Something smelled terrible.

Sam took a tentative step into the room and something crunched under his sneaker. It looked like a little skeleton, maybe from a bird. There were little bones everywhere. There were more birds, and mice, and what looked like a small dog. The dog still had some skin on it, all white and tattered.

"Hello?" Sam said weakly.

A small black head popped up from the couch. It looked to be a girl a little younger than himself.

"Hello?" Sam asked again.

"Raaaaa," the girl said. It wasn't a yell, exactly; it was just a noise, a very creepy noise. The girl turned slowly to face him. Her eyes were the same black as Carter's had been and a long black tongue with little spikes hung out of her mouth, complete with drool. It slimed the couch as her head turned.

"What?" Sam asked. He took a step back and hit the door behind him. She was a monster, just had Carter had said.

"Orrrraaa," the girl said, standing. She walked around the couch, snagging old bones with her tongue as she walked.

"Um," Sam glanced around the room, but there were no other doors. No escape. He wished he had his sword.

"Orrrraaa!" The girl pointed at him. Sam dashed around the other side of the couch. The girl followed. "Ora, Ora, Ora!" she chanted. Sam assumed this was some sort of little girl death chant he had not had the luck of seeing on an episode of Power Rangers. They circled the couch slowly. She wasn't really running, and he had no real place to go. Sam just knew he wanted to be nowhere near the slimy thing.

Finally, the girl seemed to give up, and she threw something, which Sam barely avoided. It clattered to the floor. The girl pointed at the television, and then to thing she had thrown. Sam saw it was a television remote.

"Da da da ora!"

Then it made sense. "Dora?" Sam asked.

"Esss!" the girl nodded.

"So you don't want to eat me?"

"Ooo," the girl shook her head.

So he turned on the television and found an episode of 'Dora the Explorer' for the monster girl to watch.

She took a spot on the couch and stared at the show. She sang the songs and shouted what she was supposed to shout. The problem with her speaking seemed to be her tongue, which insisted on hanging out of her mouth.

Sam wanted to "fix" it but didn't want to touch the thing. He spent some time trying to push it back into her mouth with a couch pillow while she was occupied by the show. She didn't struggle at all, only bobbing her head to keep a clear view of the television.

Finally, the gross tongue slid back into her mouth and Sam gently closed her jaw. "There. Is that better?"

She didn't answer him directly, but instead shouted "Swiper!" in perfectly clear English.

Sam turned around to help warn Dora and Boots of Swiper the fox's attempted theft. He never understood why they just didn't shoot the stupid fox, but he guessed it was a baby cartoon. After Swiper had been defeated by being told "no" (*Lame!),* Sam tried to talk to the girl again. "Can you talk better now?"

The girl slowly turned to face him. Sam couldn't help but shy away from those black eyes. Those things were too creepy.

The girl worked her jaw for a few seconds, and then spoke. "Ring around the rosie, a pocket full of posies, ashes, ashes, we all fall down!" at which point she promptly fell over and popped right back up again. "Better!" she giggled.

Sam smiled back. He had made friends with his very first monster. He wondered if Dad would let him keep her as a pet. "You should try and keep that in your mouth," he said, pointing at his tongue.

"It falls out when I eat," the girl said, her attention going back to the television. Her voice was very high and shaky, but at least now he could understand her. "I ate a dog the other day. I didn't mean to, it just happened. I like dogs; I don't want to eat them."

Sam was not quite sure how to respond to that. "Umm, well, what do you usually eat?" *Don't say boys; don't say boys.*

"I used to eat good things, like spinach," she said.

Sam stuck out his tongue; he hated spinach.

"And cookies," she added, "but then my mommy made me sick. And now I have to eat things like birds and mice. Only live stuff." Her attention was still focused on the television, but she stole glances at Sam. "Except she wasn't really my mommy. I..." A puzzled look crossed her face. "I... she made me all confused."

Sam nodded sympathetically. He figured monster families must be very confusing. "My name is Sam," he said, and held out his hand to shake. The girl slapped it as if giving him five. Well, that was close enough. "What's yours?"

"Angela."

Sam had forgotten that this was whom he was supposed to be staying with. "Did the bad guys capture you too? Or do you have to stay with older monsters until your mom comes back?"

"My mom is dead. Someone named Ancient killed her," the girl said, in a very matter of fact way.

He could relate, his mom was dead too. He missed his mom. "My mom too," he said, and he patted the monster on the back gently. It seemed the right thing to do.

The girl looked at him briefly. "It's okay." She shrugged.

"How about your dad? I have a dad; do you have a dad?" Sam asked. Angela shrugged indifferently. Maybe monsters only had one parent. "Well, dads are nice when they are around. Not the same as moms, but they teach you stuff and take you out for ice cream."

"I used to like ice cream. And cookies. And spinach."

Sam made his yuck face again. "Maybe my Dad can get you some ice cream too?" Sam offered. "I'm sure he'll be here soon to rescue me."

"Chocolate ice cream?"

"Sure, whatever you like."

"Okay," Angela said. "And maybe a kitty."

"I don't think you should eat kitties," Sam said.

Angela looked at him. "Have you ever tried one?"

"Well, no," Sam admitted.

"You don't know 'til you try." She sounded just like Sam's mom.

"Okay, I guess maybe a kitty."

"Good." She turned back to the TV.

They sat in silence for a few minutes until the show ended. Sam found another Dora from the On Demand menu. He wondered if he could convince Angela that she should try watching 'Power Rangers.'

# 8 - A Bad Situation

She was dragged into the sunlight by smooth, nearly perfect hands. *Not human hands,* Lizzie reminded herself. The thing that currently tortured her looked like a woman, but Lizzie had seen the demon within. Cynthia had been with Keith since the beginning and now stayed with Lizzie to ensure her cooperation. The tall, skinny, red-haired woman dressed in a bright blue evening dress dragged Lizzie out into the street to find a car. Lizzie stumbled behind, too numb to fight. She felt terrible, sick in every way. She had suffered through two panic attacks with no meds at all. The fact that she could even move surprised her.

Cynthia was working on transportation for the both of them. She had been muttering to herself since they'd left the coffee house of doom. Keith had a car, but didn't feel the need to let his underlings use it, which was slightly ironic since apparently the bastard could fly.

As they entered an outdoor parking lot, Cynthia tossed Lizzie to the ground. "Stay," she said, as she marched towards a middle age man loading bags into a BMW. "Hello!" Cynthia waved.

The man looked up, got an eyeful (and Lord was she an eyeful, the sexy vampire lady, what a stereotype) and smiled. "Hello, do I know..," was all the man said before Cynthia bounced his head off the roof of the car. The man gave her one stunned look and began to slide to the ground.

Cynthia picked him up, opened a back door and threw him in, then pounced on top of him.

Lizzie watched this happen as if it was all a bad dream. She should shout, should run, but they would just catch her, hurt her again. Instead Lizzie watched despairingly as the vampire fed off the man.

In a moment, Cynthia slid back out of the car and grabbed Lizzie from her resting place. Cynthia tossed the smaller woman into the passenger seat and came around to the driver's side.

Lizzie could not resist looking behind her to see the white corpse.

"What do you need?" Cynthia asked, starting the car up.

Lizzie ignored the question and continued to stare at the corpse.

"Lizzie?" An angry pause, then "You with me, Lizzie?"

"Maybe?" Lizzie replied weakly. Perhaps death was better than this.

Cynthia smiled. It wasn't a mean smile at all; in fact, it was completely misplaced on the murderer's face. "You don't want to die, Lizzie. You want to help my father find our friend Ann."

"I don't want to help your... wait, our friend? Do you know Ann?" Lizzie asked.

"Of course." The vampire turned to face Lizzie. "Wait. Tell me you don't recognize me." Cynthia slid back in her seat and smiled, as if giving Lizzie a better view would help.

"Ummm," Lizzie looked hard at her, "were you in that vampire movie with Brad Pitt?"

"No," Cynthia laughed, "I wish. No Lizzie, it's me, Cynthia." The vampire ran a hand through her red hair. "We did dinner once at a bar. You nearly passed out from being in the crowd."

That didn't help Lizzie at all; that was what happened pretty much any time Lizzie went anywhere. But the name did ring a bell. Not to mention the hair. "Well," she spoke slowly, "I did know a Cynthia who worked at the hospital, but she was kinda of short and a little..." She almost said fat, but decided against it at the last moment.

"Yes, yes, that's me!" Cynthia grinned, tapping her chest. "I can't believe you forgot me."

"Good God, you look great," Lizzie admitted. Not only did she look great, she looked entirely different. She had gone from middle-aged plump to early 20s man-eater. Pun intended.

"Oh you," Cynthia flushed.

"No really, vampirism suits you," Lizzie continued.

"Well, thanks. I've been working really hard on it. Now let's go find Ann." The vampire pulled out of the parking lot, not bothering to pay the fee, just driving through the gate.

"You know, they said they were going to kill Ann," Lizzie said, still trying to take in Cynthia's transformation.

Cynthia shrugged. "Yeah, that is a shame. I really liked Ann. Well, back when I was human. Now... well if that's what Father wants, that is what we will do. We can't argue with him." Cynthia was way too chipper.

"Why not?" Lizzie asked.

"You can't argue with your parents. You have to respect your elders, Lizzie. You'll need to learn that soon enough."

"My parents are dead. Have been for years," Lizzie responded, reaching for her seatbelt as the car weaved far too quickly through traffic.

"We'll just get you new ones then. Don't you want a new family, Lizzie? You can be part of my family. No more being afraid to leave your house. No more panic attacks. You and me and Father, we'll have the best of times."

"Sounds lovely," Lizzie said, trying to stare at her shoes. "Right after we kill Ann?"

"Oh no, you and I won't do that. Your job is only to find her. We let the elders do the killing," Cynthia continued, in her happy tone. "Maybe you and I can get our nails done after, huh? Wouldn't that be nice?"

"Ah... sure," Lizzie agreed. The idea of strangers touching Lizzie's nails made her a little sick to her stomach.

"So, where do we start?" Cynthia asked.

Lizzie thought for a bit. She had no idea where Ann was or if she could handle a vampire. That would be nice: find Ann and have her get Lizzie out of this mess. But Ann must hate her. Lizzie had said such hurtful things. She hadn't meant to; it had all been too much and Lizzie had freaked out. She would give anything now to be back there, to have stayed with her friend, even if it meant dealing with those dead zombie things again. But that was impossible. Ann could be gone for good. However, Lizzie did know one other person who might know a thing about super happy vampire removal. She had a name and a cell phone number, and for Lizzie, that was more than enough. Yes, Mr. Mike Samson, Ann's good-looking cop friend who was known to hang out with that immortal demon hunter guy, Joseph something. Yes, them she could find.

*****

She directed Cynthia to Lizzie's own house. It was strange going back to the place after her abduction. Her one safe spot in the world was now violated and open to the world. Even the yard was ruined, marked with tire tracks.

"Did you have to drive across the lawn?" Lizzie asked the vampire.

"Oh, that wasn't me. I am sorry about the door though. I tend to be a little too eager to please. My therapist used to warn me about that," Cynthia said, stepping out of the stolen car and following Lizzie into the house.

Once inside, it wasn't the same either; it no longer felt safe. Lizzie quickly gathered everything she thought she might need into a bag: her laptop with high-speed internet card, a cell phone, and a change of clothes. She grabbed her meds and moved to place them in her bag, but Cynthia's steel-like grip on her hand stopped her.

"No, no drugs." Cynthia peeled them out of Lizzie's hand and then dragged her awkwardly to the bathroom to dispose of them in the toilet.

"No!' Lizzie shouted. "I need those!"

"No, you don't," Cynthia said, tossing the empty pill container into a nearby trash bin.

"You don't understand. I need those to help me keep calm. I'm not well..."

"I will keep you calm," Cynthia said, and pulled Lizzie closer. The vampire's black eyes locked with hers.

Lizzie twisted, trying to escape her gaze, but could not quite manage to break free. She could not look away. "Please, stop," Lizzie asked weakly, trying to end the vampire's version of the Care Bear Stare.

"Calm now?"

"Yes!" Lizzie almost shouted, free at last. And to her surprise, she was calmer. There was none of that building anxiety in her chest, like something was trying to claw out from inside her. She felt numb and a little uncomfortable, but composed. "Yes," she repeated in a quieter voice.

"Good," Cynthia said. "I will take care of you, Lizzie. Don't worry about anything. Father has big plans for you."

Lizzie swallowed hard at that.

Cynthia let her take a shower and get clean clothes, although the vampire did not leave her side. She was glad she had a dark shower curtain that gave her some semblance of privacy. Cynthia sat on the toilet and read a fashion magazine (which certainly wasn't from Lizzie's house).

After washing up and eating some food, she was hurried back to the car to get started.

"Okay, I need to make a call," she announced. "I think I have an idea of how to find Ann.".

"Oh goody!" Cynthia said, clapping her hands together.

Lizzie had never met anyone who said 'Oh goody' seriously before. There was a first time for everything. She dug through her cell phone's history to find Mike's number. After a few moments, she dialed.

It rang until a groggy voice answered. "Hello."

"Mike Samson? Look, I know we've only met the once, but I'm a friend of Ann's..."

"Lizzie? Is that you?" Mike Samson's voice had suddenly become alert.

"Umm... yeah..."

"Look, I need your help. It's much too complicated to explain over the phone. I know a safe place; can you meet me?"

"Umm sure... but look," Lizzie glanced at Cynthia who was watching intently, a smile across her face. How could she warn him? "Is your friend there?"

"Miller? Yeah, actually, that's why I need your help. Can you meet me at...?" Mike rattled off an address on Washington Street in Newark.

"Umm yeah, sure, but..."

"Good, see you there." Mike hung up.

Lizzie looked at the phone and then back to Cynthia. She sighed in exasperation. "Let's head to Newark," she said.

Cynthia obeyed.

*Oh, Mike,* Lizzie thought to herself, *I hope you and your little Hispanic friend are half as good as Ann said you were. Otherwise we're all screwed.*

*****

Lizzie found Mike Samson in an Irish Pub. The man looked terrible. His head was bandaged, as was his arm; his clothes were a mess, and he was slouched over a beer alone in a booth. But where was that Miller guy? It didn't look like this mess of a man could handle much of anything. What chance would he have against her super chipper vampire friend?

Lizzie approached him slowly, with Cynthia right on her heels. *Should I go someplace else and try another way? Just say I don't see him and keep looking?* Lizzie paused and looked around the room, pretending to search, while weighing her options. She only had about 24 hours left before Keith's deadline to find Ann was up and then God knew what would happen, but it was bound to be unpleasant. It was a public space and Lizzie assumed Cynthia would do nothing to the man here, out in the open. This was all a waste of time though, as Mike ended up making the choice for her.

"Hey!" Mike shouted to her. "Lizzie?"

Lizzie approached the table and smiled. "Mike," she responded, moving towards the booth.

"Oh great, him again," Cynthia muttered as they took seats in the booth.

"Mike, I want you to meet Cynthia. She's an old friend of Ann's from the hospital" *and she's a vampire forcing me to find my friend so her masters can kill her.* "We are looking for Ann and were wondering if you found her the other day." Lizzie gave Mike her best 'help me' expression, but Mike hardly glanced at the vampire, his face somehow managing to get even darker.

"Ann, Ann's been taken. Shot, too. I'm not even sure she's alive."

"Taken? By whom?" Lizzie nearly jumped out of the booth.

"The FBI."

"Oh no!" Lizzie gasped.

"They came for her in the night—her and Miller. At least he was OK, just a little beaten up. But Ann—there was a fight, and Ann was shot in the head. I don't know if she can live through that." Mike talked down into his beer, refusing to look at anyone.

"Oh, she's alive," Cynthia offered brightly, "otherwise we wouldn't have to look for her."

Mike finally gave the vampire a good once over.

Cynthia smiled back, and even her eyes looked human for a moment.

Lizzie did not understand how the black eye thing worked; they just went dark from time to time. It seemed like a poorly veiled plot device to make certain characters seem more menacing from time to time. But, of course, that was crazy.

"You know, you do look familiar. I think I missed your name," Mike said.

"Cynthia. We've met." The vampire ran a hand through her hair, almost like she was flirting with Mike.

The man rubbed his chin, deep in thought. "Wait, wait, don't tell me. I'm usually good with faces. I'll remember where we...," he said.

Cynthia leaned over the table, giving him optimal view of her cleavage. "I'll give you a hint; it was at a hospital." She playfully poked him on the nose.

To his credit, Mike's face became more suspicious. He wasn't going for the Cynthia's little show for a minute. "Hospital?" he said, backing away just a little.

"*The* hospital," Lizzie offered.

"You shot me in the chest with a shotgun, in fact. " Cynthia continued to grin, her eyes flashing back to black.

Mike paled in response. "Oh," was all he said.

"Awkward?" Lizzie offered.

"More than a little," Mike said. "Well, on the bright side, I have to say, being Cursed looks really good on you."

"I know, that's what I said," Lizzie agreed.

"Oh, you two," Cynthia blushed.

Mike took a huge slug of beer and placed it back down on the table a little too hard. "I don't suppose I can buy you a drink to make up for that whole 'shooting you in the chest' thing," he offered.

"Oh, that's sweet of you, but they don't serve what I drink here," Cynthia said, placing her head on her hands.

"Good point," Mike agreed. "So, this would mean you work for..."

"My father is Asmodai, the King of the Fallen." The vampire said it with such pride, even if it was delivered like a line out of a bad horror movie.

"And Lizzie..." Mike turned to look hard at Lizzie. "Are you... they took you from your house. That's why the door..." Mike let the thought hang in the air.

"Yeah. They want me to help them find Ann. They want to kill her," Lizzie said.

"Kill Ann?"

"She has broken the law of the Fallen; her punishment is death." Cynthia's face had become blank as she spoke.

"The law? You have laws?" Mike asked.

"Only the one. The Fallen must not kill their own. Lilith has broken that law."

"Lilith?" Mike asked.

Lizzie remembered the name from Ann's last visit. "That's Ann's demon name, apparently," she explained.

"Oh, right, sure." Mike shrugged and rubbed his eyebrows. "Man, this has been the day from hell."

"So, if you can't help us find her..." Cynthia began to stand up. Did she plan to leave Mike alone or did she have something else in mind?

"Oh, I can help," Mike said. "You see, not only did two of my friends get arrested this morning, but my house was destroyed, I got smacked around by an angry old lady, and my son, my only child, was kidnapped by vampires." Mike's voice rose as he continued.

"I'm...," Cynthia started, but Mike continued.

"I hate vampires," he said. "That whole black tongue thing creeps me out. I hit the guy with a van and he still managed to pull himself together, and then he takes my son! So, I've been sitting here for the last hour trying to figure out what I was going to do next, and thanks to you, I know."

"You do?" Lizzie asked.

Mike had been calm enough when they entered the bar, but now he seemed to seethe with hate, his face flush with anger. "Yes. And as usual it involves a lot of running," Mike said, turning to Lizzie.

"Running?" Lizzie asked.

"Running, yes," Mike repeated, glancing at the door.

"Oh," Lizzie said, finally getting the hint.

There was a sound like thunder before the table split open. Black blood gushed from Cynthia's chest. The crowd at the bar started screaming, and people ran for the exit.

"Like now!" Mike shouted. He jumped from the booth, a massive gun still smoking in one hand, and grabbed Lizzie.

The vampire stared at the new hole in her chest. "Not again!" she shouted. "You are in so much trouble, mister!" Cynthia kicked the table, sending it flying. "I really liked that dress!"

Mike spun around, shoving Lizzie behind him, and fired his gun two more times. The first shot erased the pale thin shoulder of the vampire; the second struck her in the face. Cynthia screamed, stumbling backwards.

"The bar! Get to the bar!" Mike said to Lizzie, and he then started to yell, "Fire!"

Lizzie did what she was told and headed through the stampede of bar patrons towards the bar. She turned to see Cynthia standing back up, a large black tentacle poking out of her face where the bullet had entered. Her one remaining eye was rolled back in her head, her jaw was slack, but still she stumbled forward.

Mike fired again, this time hitting Cynthia in the kneecap and knocking her back to the ground. Mike backed up to the bar, keeping his gun trained on the monster.

"Is that going to kill her?" Lizzie asked.

"No, and that was the mistake I made last time. This time, though, I have a better idea." Mike reached behind the bar and pulled out a large bottle of rum. He pulled off the top of the bottle with his teeth and spat the cork on the floor.

"Not really the best time for a drink," Lizzie noted.

"Not for me, for her," Mike answered, pointing.

Cynthia was dragging herself forward along the ground.

Mike let the bottle fly, hitting the ground in front of the vampire. He grabbed another bottle, bit down, then grunted when he realized it was a screw top. "Shit, open this one for me." Mike tossed the bottle to Lizzie, who obeyed, while he grabbed another bottle.

"Watch out!" Lizzie screamed as a black tentacle swung past Mike's face.

He barely managed to dodge, rolling to the right and creating a spiral of vodka in the air from the open bottle. Mike bounced back up and tossed it at the slithering mass of black tentacles Cynthia had become. It burst open onto the remains of her face, shards of glass sticking in what was left of her red hair. Mike vaulted the bar, and then reached and pulled Lizzie over as well.

"Hey!" Lizzie said, more out of surprise than complaint.

Cynthia approached the bar, one bloodied hand reaching the edge and pulling the rest of her up. As she stood, Mike fired again, nailing the vampire in the belly and knocking her to the floor once more.

"Matches!" Mike shouted. He started throwing around boxes behind the bar.

"Right," Lizzie understood and began her own search. She wasn't sure how many matches these places still carried, since they had outlawed smoking in public buildings, but it didn't hurt to try. She tossed aside a box of highball glasses that shattered when it hit the ground.

A black tentacle zipped around the side of the bar, snagging Lizzie's leg. It ripped through her pants instantly and pulled her to the ground. Pain ripped through her leg, like she was being stabbed. She decided now would be a good time to start screaming, but Mike was already on the case, firing two quick shots, the second bullet severing the tentacle in two. Lizzie kicked it away, still screaming.

Mike grabbed her by the arm and pulled. "Kitchen!" he said, dragging her through a door.

She had only been touched by the black thing for maybe a second, but her leg would no longer support her weight. She tried to make the limb work, but it failed to obey.

Mike dropped her several feet inside and ran ahead.

The kitchen door swung open again and Cynthia staggered through. Her face was already rebuilding itself and held a twisted smile. Her dress was torn to ribbons and covered in her own black blood. She stood, barely, leaning on the door for extra support.

"Lizzie, Father is going to be so disappointed in you," she said, eyeing Lizzie on the floor.

"No," whimpered Lizzie, dragging herself towards Mike.

There was a clicking sound coming from the corner of the room and Cynthia looked up to find the source of the noise. Mike Samson lit a rag from the newly ignited gas stove. He pushed it into the half-empty bottle of liquor tucked under his arm and turned around to face the vampire, with a snarl on his lips.

"I really hate vampires," he said. A moment later, the flaming bottle hit Cynthia directly in the face, instantly igniting her alcohol soaked body. The vampire screamed.

Mike grabbed Lizzie's arm and pulled her to her feet once more, but Lizzie still could not stand, so Mike tucked an arm under her shoulder and carried her. "I think it's time we left," he said as they reached a back door. He turned around one more time to see Cynthia lunging at them, entirely engulfed in flames. He fired again, this time at the other leg, dropping her again to the floor.

She howled in frustration and pain as the flames consumed her. Fire snaked through the room, following the trail of liquor Cynthia had made.

Mike and Lizzie limped out into the alleyway behind the bar.

"Will that kill her?" Lizzie asked.

"I hope so. I'm running out of ideas. Miller makes this stuff look easy. Do you have a car?" Mike asked.

"Well, I did. But the vampire had the keys."

"Damn," Mike said, disappointed.

"It's cool. I'm pretty sure I can hotwire it. I need my bag out of there anyway. Why can't I walk?"

They stopped and inspected Lizzie's leg. About four inches of her calf was bleached white. "Oh God, it's all numb." Lizzie poked the wound.

"I hate vampires," Mike repeated. "It looks like it will heal, but it might be a few days until you can walk normally again." He patted a spot on his cheek. "This was the same way and it's almost entirely healed. Looks like she did a better job on you though."

They made it to the stolen BMW five minutes later. There were sirens from police cars in front of the bar, so they were quickly running out of time.

Lizzie glanced at Mike. "Can you break the window?"

"Sure." He swung the gun like a club and shattered a rear window. "Shit! You know you have a corpse back there?"

"Yeah, one of joys of traveling with vampires. They bring a whole different meaning to the phrase 'fast food'." Lizzie popped the locks and jumped in, a little surprised no car alarm had gone off. She opened her bag of tricks and went to work getting the car started.

Mike got into the passenger seat, watching her. "Do you do these sorts of things often?" he asked.

"Never. But I read the internet a lot."

After a long moment, the engine came to life. Lizzie threw the car into gear and as calmly as possible pulled into the street. "There."

"Just keep it slow. We don't need to draw attention," Mike advised.

"What, you think? You mean we don't want people to notice our stolen car with the corpse in the back seat after we just burned down a local bar? Gee, I guess you're right," Lizzie retorted.

"Okay, okay," Mike said, putting his hands up in defense. "Just trying to help."

There was silence for a few minutes as Lizzie drove. A police car passed, its lights flashing, but did not stop them. Lizzie squirmed in her seat for a minute, and then spit out what was bothering her. "Thank you, by the way," Lizzie added.

"Was that your plan?" Mike asked, reloading the handgun.

"Well, I had thought you would be with the short Scottish-Hispanic guy, but yeah, there was no way I was going to let them kill Ann. I mean, even all white and scaly, she's still my best friend."

"She's not so scaly anymore, last time I saw her anyway. I'm not clear on how that works, though."

"Really?" Lizzie said excitedly. "That's great! I mean white was never her color."

Mike chuckled at that, but quickly became serious again. "How do you feel, Lizzie?" he asked, eyeing her.

Lizzie thought about it. Besides the numbness in her leg, she actually felt pretty good. Through that whole encounter, she had functioned fairly well. She had felt no signs of panic attacks at all. "Surprisingly well. A little hungry."

Mike grunted and placed the gun back in a holster.

Lizzie wasn't sure why, but that response made her very uncomfortable. "Do you have a plan?" Lizzie asked. "I mean, to save Ann?"

"Well, sort of," Mike admitted. There was silence for a heartbeat.

"Are you going to share?" Lizzie asked.

Mike shrugged. "Look, let's find a place to hide out for a few hours and I'll let you in on everything."

"Where to? I can't go back home," Lizzie said.

"Neither can I," Mike said.

"Hey, how about Ann's place?" Lizzie suggested.

"Yeah, that works."

# 9 - Head Games

The world faded in and out of existence for Ann. Her head throbbed, and in the moments she was awake—at least when she believed she was awake—she thought someone was speaking to her. A woman was in the room with her. She was wearing a hooded sweatshirt and blue jeans, but her feet were bare. Her face was almost completely covered by the hood, with the exception of blond curls that snaked out. Sometimes Ann could see the woman's teeth, which were long and pointed. Ann tried to understand this woman, tried to hold onto the words as they washed over her, but they always slipped away with the rest of Ann's world.

Over time, the pressure in her head worsened to the point of being unbearable. She screamed in pain as she finally regained complete consciousness. Following an instinct to reduce the ache, Ann attempted to move, but found she was stuck fast. She was on a slightly angled platform, with thick straps holding her into place. With her head immobilized, her eyes scanned as much of the room as she could.

The pain in her head began to fade and she could think again. She was in a dark cell, almost completely bare of furniture. There was a toilet and a sink, a chair, and of course whatever contraption Ann herself was currently attached to.

With a cold chill that ran up her spine, Ann remembered the woman. It had been Lilith

But had Lilith really been in the room with her? Ann wasn't sure if it was a ghost of the demon, or if Ann was losing her mind. She had seen Lilith on the roof when Mike shot her, but then the demon woman had spoken to her. Lilith had told her secrets, like how to change her shape, and then demanded that Ann kill Renee Dupré. Perhaps this was insanity kicking in. Ann had certainly earned it.

"Well I suppose I'll handle it like I do everything else, with sarcasm and general denial," Ann said aloud. Yes, talking to herself—definitely crazy.

The click of the lock on the door pulled her out of her musings. Ann struggled against her bonds but she couldn't even turn her head when the door to her cell opened.

"Knock, knock," came a rough voice, with a certain amount of glee in it.

Ann could guess who it was. "Who's there?" she asked, concerned this was the opening to a particularly twisted knock knock joke. There were slow footsteps as her visitor moved into Ann's limited line of sight and the ragged face of Renee Dupré came into view. *Speak of the devil,* Ann thought.

The old woman grinned as if Ann was a fine meal Dupré had just received after starving. "It's good to see you awake. I considered doing this in your sleep. It would certainly have been safer, but it lacked a bit of...," Dupré paused, "...satisfaction."

"You really dislike me, don't you? I have to be honest, before you killed my friends and shot me in the head, I didn't even know who you were. So, answer me this: what did I ever to do you?" Ann asked. Now that her head had stopped hurting, she was focusing on breaking her bonds, but she was stuck fast.

"Please, Lilith. You may have fooled the idiot running around pretending to be the Ancient One, but I know your kind far too well. Also, don't bother struggling. I designed that table myself. I had hoped you might show your demon side and tear yourself apart. Messy, but a fitting death for one of the Fallen."

*OK, so no on the dramatic busting out and kicking Dupré around,* Ann thought. "Pretending to be?" she asked. "You mean Miller? He seems pretty legit to me." Ann's mind was racing. Dupré meant to kill her, thinking Lilith was still in control, or perhaps she really hated blonds. Ann needed to escape. But she was trapped, no doubt about that. She needed help.

"Oh, don't tell me you didn't recognize him. The janitor who worked at the lab? Or was this some plan of yours? Somehow convince him he was the Ancient One? I'm sure he has some people aflutter with that concept. Joseph Miller, heroic demon hunter, back from the dead after a hundred years. What nonsense."

"Wait, the janitor?" Ann thought back. When she had first met Miller in the hospital he had looked familiar, at least until he woke up. Her head had been such a mess then, it was hard to remember—not that it was that much better now. She thought hard about any janitors she might know. There had been a few, but besides maybe a 'thank you' when they took out her trash, she never paid them much attention. What did that say about her?

"I think you are confused, lady," she addressed Dupré. "My name is not Lilith; it's Ann. Ann Melakh and yes, for a few hours, Lilith did control me. She's gone now," *Well, mostly.* "And the man who claims to be Joseph Miller is the real deal. Unless you can explain how someone gets hit by a truck and is up and running two days later."

"Impossible. On both accounts!" Dupré snarled. "The Ancient One is a myth and you are a liar." She pulled out a large gun—more of a hand cannon really—and pointed it at Ann's face.

With her head strapped in place, Ann couldn't even turn away, and had to focus on the barrel of the gun.

"This little game ends here, like it should have two weeks ago,"

Dupré said.

"Wait!" Ann screamed, desperate to buy herself time. To her surprise, Dupré did wait. Perhaps the old woman was enjoying this too much. *Is this why the villain always built those slow, easy to escape death machines for the super spies in the movies?* Ann thought fast, trying to come up with anything to keep Dupré talking. "What do you mean two weeks ago? When you killed Larry Conners?"

"No, no. I was never supposed to get my hands dirty. I'm not sure how you escaped Abraham's tracking. It was his task to kill you and keep you from returning the Seven to life." Dupré poked Ann twice in the forehead with the gun barrel. "Of course, on the plus side, now you've brought Asmodai back. I will truly enjoy killing him as well!"

*Keith, she wants to kill Keith too?* No, she had to remember: Asmodai wasn't Keith, the same way she wasn't Lilith.

"No, you can't kill him. I mean, yes, you can kill Asmodai; you're welcome to do that, but the man, the person the demon has control over, we must find a way to save him," Ann pleaded.

Dupré gave her a baffled look. "What? Why would you...," Dupré sputtered. "This is another trick."

"No, what did the man ever do to you?" Ann asked. He had done plenty to Ann, and she didn't want to see him dead.

"Not the man, the monster! It took everything from me! It cursed me! It raped me, destroyed my home, and took the man I love away from me!" Dupré screamed.

Okay, so Dupré certainly had reason to hate the demon.

"But the man didn't do any of that," Ann insisted. "There has to be away to save him—to kill the demon and not the man. I have a few ideas on how I did..."

"Enough!" Dupré cut Ann off. "There is no coming back from being taken by the Fallen. No one ever has; no one ever will. It's time I end this."

The gun fired and the lights went out.

# 10 - A Poor Prisoner

Joseph Miller had been in prison before. At one point, he had spent a very long fifty-eight years locked in a Spanish dungeon. Compared to that, this was quite the palace. He did wish it had a television, though.

He sat cross-legged on a simple bed. Across the room, there was a bench bolted to the ground, and to his right was the modern world's version of a chamber pot. The wall behind the bench was a solid black color, while the rest of the room was a dull grey. The door into the room appeared to be metal and looked quite imposing, as any good jail door should.

His hands were bound in front of him by a plastic ribbon, which he fiddled with constantly. It was very impressive, completely immune to any of his old tricks. Plastic was not entirely new to him, in this world he had recently found himself in. It was everywhere. Still, he couldn't quite get used to it. It was so alien, so unnatural. Here, it flexed with him like cloth, to a point, but held him firm like steel if he pushed too far. It was, as young Sam might say, "really, really cool".

As he struggled with his new challenge, he thought over the mistakes of the last day or so. He had assumed the best way to figure out why one of the Cursed was working with the local authorities was to get himself captured. He had not figured on Ann being shot, and he hoped the lass was all right. Seeing as they had almost killed her on sight, she was still most certainly in danger. Who knew how long it would take them to finish the job. Not long, if this Dupré woman was in charge; that much was clear. He had to rescue her, but at the moment, all he could do was pass the time and test the limits of his cell.

The wait was not as long as he had expected and soon the tall Japanese man opened the cell door. "Mr. Soliz?" he asked, "I'm Special Agent John Takahashi with the Federal Bureau of Investigations."

"Miller, actually. I think you have me confused with someone else," Miller corrected him.

The tall man held up a picture, which did—Miller had to admit—look a lot like him. "So you are not the man in this picture?"

"He is a handsome devil, but no. I believe I'm taller and have much better hair."

Takahashi laughed a little at that. "It does say here that Soliz speaks very little English, and you do seem rather fluent. Tell me then, Mr. Miller, if you are not Andres Soliz, do you know where I might find him?" Takahashi sat down on the bed, close to Miller but out of arm's reach.

"I'm afraid he is not the type I usually hunt Mr... do you mind if I call you Special Agent?"

Takahashi shrugged. "I suppose."

"Good, I like that. Special Agent. It has a nice ring to it." Miller gave Takahashi his famous grin.

"And who exactly do you hunt, then?" the agent asked.

"Oh, I think you know that. What I'm not clear on is why you're deterring me." Miller tried to meet Takahashi's eyes, but the taller man stared down at his lap.

The agent shrugged again. "Now that is a long story," he said in a low voice, as he slid in closer. He tapped something on his lap. Miller bent over to see what appeared to be a very old notebook. It tugged at his memory, but he could not place it. "You see, I think you are in fact Mr. Andres Soliz." Takahashi opened the notebook. Inside, there was a message printed in large letters, making it easy to read from a distance.

**'I know who you are and I want to help you.'**

Takahashi continued to talk, while tapping the page. Out loud, Takahashi said "... and I have to inform you, you are wanted by the local police for two counts of murder." He turned the page and the message continued.

**'but they will kill me and my family.'**

Miller looked up at the man's face, finally meeting his eyes.

"Tomorrow morning, we will arrange a transfer for you, over to the Newark Police" Takahashi continued to speak as he turned another page.

**'Your friend is down the hall and to the right.'** There was a crudely drawn map.

"I ask that you cooperate," Takahashi continued.

Another page turned.

**'They will kill her!'**

Takahashi turned another page.

**'Take this book and the key.'**

**'Just make it look good.'**

Takahashi tapped the page and stuck out his chin, his eyes clearly saying "Please, not too good," and he shut the book.

"And we will make sure your time with us is as comfortable as possible. Do we have an understanding?" Takahashi asked.

"Oh, I think we understand each other perfectly," Miller grinned. "And just so you know, I am extremely comfortable." Miller stood, bowed, and then kicked Takashi in the side of the head. The man spun off the seat, cracking the other side of his face on the wall. That had looked good.

There was no telling how long it would take before help would arrive for the agent, so he had to move fast. He frisked the man on the floor and found a gun and a small blade. He stuck the gun down the front of his pants—the absolute worst place for a firearm—but with his hands still bound, he had little choice. He then grabbed the blade and stuck it between his teeth. He scooped up the notebook and dashed through the still open cell door. He bolted around the corner as instructed. Seeing no one around, he stopped for a moment and considered. Seeing no keyhole on his bindings, he tried the knife, on a hunch. It was awkward holding the weapon with his teeth and moving his hands to cut the plastic, but to his relief, the sharp edge made fast work of his bindings. He used his freed hands to open the book. There was no key, but there was a plastic card with a large black stripe. It seemed important, so he pocketed it, before moving forward again at a quick walk. He dropped the small knife on the ground, seeing no further need for it.

The building he was in was large and very grey. He checked the hastily drawn map and slowed to make the next right, then stopped. He was passing another cell, similar to the one he had been confined in, but larger. He noted, then, that the large black wall in his cell must have been transparent on the other side, as from this position, he could easily see inside this one. Within, dead men stood and stared back at him.

"Oh my," he muttered to no one but himself. "That's different."

They had been killed by one of the Fallen, or perhaps a particularly hungry vampire, and then Cursed. These must be the creatures Ann referred to as ‘Zombies’. The faint black mist clung to each one of them. They stared with dead eyes, but did not move. In total, there were maybe twenty of them standing, with a few other bodies tied down to what looked like rolling beds. It seemed those standing had broken free, as many smashed beds were scattered across the floor. Once unrestrained, they seemed to have no plan. They stood and watched, and waited, but for what Miller did not know. It was not for him though.

"Freeze!" a man shouted.

"There's that word again!" Miller turned to face a new man aiming a gun at him. "This is getting a little dull."

The new man wore a fine suit, much like Takahashi, and a bandage on his head, much like Takahashi would soon enough.

"You again? How did you get out?" the man asked.

"Again? Have we met?"

"Earlier today, in fact." He pointed to the bandage on his head as he approached.

"Ah well, had you knocked first, I would have spared you both headaches."

"Both?"

Miller launched himself forward, grabbed the man's gun with one hand, and pulled it straight up. It fired when Miller punched the man in the throat. The man released the gun and stepped back, grabbing his neck. Miller stepped forward again and bounced the man's head off the glass. He slid to the floor and was still.

"There, you rest a bit."

That distraction dealt with, Miller focused on the task at hand. He pushed the second gun next to the first, but then remembered just how mad it was to stuff firearms down one's trousers. He took a moment to secure one of the weapons in a pocket while drawing the other gun, then made to find Ann's cell. As promised, it was not far. Again, Miller could see inside and apparently not be seen. The Dupré woman was inside the cell with Ann, and she had a very large, very odd-looking gun. Ann was strapped to a rolling bed, similar to the ones he had seen in the dead folk's cell, but this one had large heavy straps every few inches and some odd mechanics underneath. The door to the cell was open, and to his surprise, he could hear the conversation perfectly. Dupré was speaking.

"No, no, I was never supposed to get my hands dirty. I'm not sure how you escaped Abraham's tracking, it was his task to kill you and keep you from returning the seven to life," she was saying.

*Abraham?* Had she said his son's name? Miller's mind flashed back to the dream he'd had just moments before they were captured. It appeared that Abraham was more involved in this than Miller had known. But why? Miller was lost in thought for a moment, missing part of the conversation. Dupré's raised voice brought him back.

"Enough!" she was shouting. "There is no coming back from being taken by the Fallen. No one ever has, no one ever will. It's time I end this."

Miller couldn't have asked for a better entrance line. He dashed through the open door and fired one shot at Dupré's shoulder, knocking the woman to the floor. As she fell backwards, she fired her own gun, missing Ann by a large margin but destroying the sink in the corner.

Ann screamed, with her eyes shut tight.

"Ann, lass, I have you," Miller said, picking up Dupré's weapon.

Ann eyes flung open again. Her breathing was ragged, and she had a wild look about her. "Miller?! Oh, thank God. You have amazing timing."

Miller shrugged his shoulders and flashed his grin. "That I do, lass," he agreed.

Dupré groaned from the floor.

"Can you get me out?" Ann asked. Miller looked over the bed.

"Any ideas where to start?" he asked, regretting the loss of the small knife.

The lights in the hallway started flashing red, and a loud siren could be heard.

"Sounds like we're out of time," Ann said.

"I'll roll you out," Miller offered. He found the wheel lock and began to push her to the door.

"What about Dupré?" Ann asked, gesturing to the woman on the floor. She was starting to sit up, black blood gushing from her shoulder.

"You!" Dupré pointed a finger at Miller. "You idiot! Get away from her."

Miller silenced her with the same kick to the head he had given Takahashi, but added a little more torque to it. "That's for shooting a lady," Miller shouted over his shoulder.

The bed barely managed to fit through the door, and he almost tipped it as he made the first turn.

"Whoa!" Ann yelled. "Not that I'm complaining, but do you have any idea where we're going?"

"Sadly, no," Miller admitted. "My map only led me to you."

"You had a map?" Ann asked.

"Yes, we have help, just not the direct kind." Miller pushed the notebook under one of Ann's straps so it would not fall as they ran.

"What's this?"

"A clue, I think." Miller said.

They passed by the room of Cursed dead. Miller was far too busy steering the bed to notice all the dead faces turn to watch them pass. He did not notice them moving forward, as if coming to life once more.

# 11 - The Games Vampire Children Play

It turned out that having a pet monster was a lot of work. Sam just wanted to sleep. His head really hurt where he had bumped it and it seemed like he had been awake forever. But every time he was about to drop off asleep, Angela would nudge him awake. She would demand a new show, or a song, and for a little while, she demanded stories. Sam tried to tell her all about his favorite Power Rangers episodes, but the little vampire girl quickly lost interest.

It seemed like a very long time had passed and again, Angela was nudging him. "No, no sleeping. Let's play a game," she demanded.

"My head hurts," Sam said honestly. "Let me sleep."

"Ugh, you little boys do not make good pets. You never want to play," Angela said, dropping off the couch and wandering off.

*Good*, Sam thought. Now he could take a quick nap. He'd hated naps when he was younger, but now it seemed the best idea in forever. He stretched and closed his eyes.

"Here," Angela said. "Drink it." Angela held a blue can labeled Pepsi.

"That's soda. I'm not supposed to drink soda," Sam said.

Angela shrugged, then looked around the room as if about to share a big secret. "Just say that the bad guys made you drink it," Angela said, popping the top of the soda.

Sam's eyes lit up. *What an awesome idea.* Sam grabbed the can and took a big drink. It was sweet and so much better than that lame apple juice. "Do you think the bad guys could tell me to eat some cookies too?" Sam asked between gulps.

Angela smiled. "They make me eat squirrels a lot. They are really hard to catch," she said.

"I hope I don't have to eat squirrels." Sam's head was feeling a little better and he wasn't as sleepy. Soda must have magic powers, which is why the grownups didn't want him drinking it. Grownups always were trying to keep the cool stuff to themselves.

"Can we play a game now?" Angela asked.

"OK" Sam said, thinking hard. "Let's play *Escape From the Bad Guys*." He was sure his dad was coming to rescuing him. But grownups were way too slow. He wanted to go home now.

Angela scrunched up her face at the idea. "Sounds boring. I want to play monster house. You play the dada monster and I'll play the momma monster and we'll pretend to attack a village."

That did sound kinda fun, but that wasn't going to get him back home.

"OK, we can play that next," Sam agreed, but as he stood up, his head hurt again and he had to sit down. "Ow," Sam said.

"Are you sick?" Angela asked.

"My head really hurts." It was better when he didn't move, but how could he escape if he couldn't walk? Maybe Angela could carry him. She was a monster, after all.

Just then, the door began to click. Sam remembered all the locks on the outside of the door. That meant someone was coming.

"Well, well, well, you're not dead," said the woman named Carter.

"He's broken," Angela said. "You brought me a broken pet boy. I want a new one."

Carter laughed. "Well, OK. It's time for our friend Sam to take a little car trip, anyway."

"Is my dad here?" Sam asked.

"No, not yet. We're going to meet him," Carter said.

"I want to come too!" Angela demanded.

"No, sorry. You have to stay here. But I can put on a new show for you?" Carter said that last part more as a question.

"No, I want to go!" Angela stomped one foot down.

Carter ignored her and picked Sam up. The woman's touch was cold, like she had been playing in the snow.

"Can she come, please?" Sam asked. Angela was his only friend here. He didn't want to be alone again.

"Afraid not," Carter said, moving. She closed the door behind her with a loud thunk. Sam got one last look at Angela as the door closed. One small tear ran down her cheek.

"Bye," Sam said, a little too late. He felt like crying a little too.

Outside the room, there were people, a lot of people. They all leaped out of Carter's way as she came close, forming a path in the forest of bad guys in dark suits.

"Are you having a party?" Sam asked. *Did bad guys have parties?*

"It's a party for your dad. Just to be sure he behaves," Carter said.

"Hey, kid. Glad to see Angela didn't eat ya," King said, suddenly appearing from behind Carter.

"She was kinda nice," Sam said.

"Apparently, she's never kicked you in the knee," King said. "I can't believe Smith called in so many people." This he said more to Carter.

"I guess he wants to be sure. If we can get Dupré, all our issues will be solved," Carter said.

"I know, but I can't imagine the 'you know who' is going to let that happen. No matter how good this Samson guy is," King said.

They stepped outside the house. Three of the big white vans waited in the driveway. More men seemed to be getting ready to move.

"This is going to be one big party," Sam observed. "Are we going to have soda?"

"Sure kid," Carter said, putting him down in a seat in the closest van. "If you live through the rest of the day, I'll buy you a soda."

"Really?" Sam said. Maybe she wasn't so bad after all.

Sam was buckled in, and Carter went to sit in the front seat. Sam sat quietly for what felt for a very long time. He was getting the impression that this wasn't really a party. And that his Dad might really be in trouble. And with Mr. Miller and that Ann lady in jail, there was only Sam to rescue him. But what could he do? His head hurt so badly. He tried desperately to come up with an idea to save the day. It looked so easy on TV.

More men got in the car, and someone loaded several big bags into the back of the van, but they left him in the back seat to himself. Then, with a jerk, the van started to roll forward.

There was nothing he could do, nothing. He could feel the tears gathering in his eyes; he wanted to cry.

Then, there was a tug on his jeans. Sam looked down to see a small hand vanish under the car seat. Then Angela's little face appeared from under the seat. She put up one finger over her lips in the universal sign for 'Quiet, I'm trying to be sneaky'. The little vampire girl smiled at him and Sam felt much better.

# 12 - Scrum

Lizzie and Mike did not speak the rest of the ride to Ann's place. The place was exactly as Lizzie remembered: small and messy. Ann had probably last been here right before storming into College Hospital to try and rescue Keith. Since then Lizzie had visited a few times in her search for Ann, but she hadn't cleaned anything. There were clothes on the floor and a few dirty dishes in the sink. Something in the kitchen smelled of rot and the rest of the place just smelled stale and unused.

As Mike double-checked the lock on the door, he asked Lizzie to take a seat. Lizzie obeyed, not wanting to do anything more than to lie down and to try and keep her heart from exploding. She threw herself down on the couch and released a sigh of relief. She was finally safe.

Then Mike said, "Lizzie, try and stay calm."

And Lizzie tensed right back up again. Nothing good every followed those words. "What's wrong?" she squeaked, jumping back to her feet. She glanced around the apartment, but didn't find anything more dangerous than a moldy pizza on the coffee table.

"Maybe nothing," Mike said, entering the small kitchen, "but I need to know I can trust you." His eyes searched the room for a moment, before landing on a knife block. He selected the largest knife and drew it out in front of him.

"Whoa, whoa, whoa!" Lizzie shouted. "What the hell is that for? Of course you can trust me."

"Relax." Mike raised a calming hand as he approached. "I don't want to hurt you. The Fallen don't usually just let people be. They curse them; they make them into something else."

Lizzie retreated from the big knife. "I'm human! I'm human, I swear," she stammered.

"That's exactly what you would say if you were Cursed. I just need to see some of your blood."

"My blood… oh God, you've gone psycho." Lizzie glanced around the room. There was no place for her to run. They were six stories up, with only one door. She wondered if Ann had a fire escape someplace, which she had never noticed.

"Calm down. The Cursed blood is black. That way, we can make sure you're you and not about to grow fur or fangs."

"It's a little hard to be calm when big scary men have knives… OW!" she cried, as Mike snatched her hand. "Don't!"

"I'm sorry," Mike said, bringing the knife down. Lizzie screamed for a moment, then stopped. She was transfixed by the sight of her own blood running down her arm.

Mike let Lizzie's hand drop and backed away.

"Happy?" Lizzie asked, smearing her very red blood across the palm of her hand and then displaying it for Mike to see.

"Red… you're human. Thank God," Mike said. "I'm sorry. I had to be sure."

Lizzie dropped to her knees, inspecting the small wound just below under her elbow. She was gasping hard for air, but no panic attack was coming. "You can't… I can't handle this," Lizzie stammered.

Mike helped her back sit back down on the couch. "It's all right, we're done. It's safe," Mike said.

"Whose side are you on?" Lizzie snarled, now that the panic was dying down, anger was replacing it.

"Yours, apparently. Look, I'm sorry, but it's better this way. Now I know I can trust you and you know you are going to stay you," Mike said, pointing at her. He did have a point.

"And if I had been 'Cursed'? What would you have done then? Kill me, like Cynthia?"

"No, no, course not. But I probably would have had to tie you up. Keep you out of the way. I have to wonder why they spared you. They seem to want to bring everyone into their twisted little family." Mike stood back up and rubbed his chin.

Lizzie thought about this for a bit. "I have health issues," she said finally. It was not something she ever liked to admit, but it was the truth. "Cynthia tried to keep me away from my meds. Maybe there's something about them the demon guys don't like."

"Maybe. Anyway, lucky break for us. Look, I need to ask you a few questions. Then you're done."

"Done? No, not until we find Ann," Lizzie said.

Mike raised an eyebrow at that. "Really? " he asked sounding unimpressed.

"What? You think I can't help? 'Cause I'm a woman?"

"Ah no, not implying anything like that. Just not sure what a woman with 'health issues' can do against a handful of demons, an army of vampires, and the FBI," Mike said, waving a hand as if to dismiss her.

"The FBI? I can help with that. I hacked their computer systems not that long ago."

Mike looked at her hard. "You hacked into an FBI network?"

"I did. I pulled down two videos from their servers—evidence of murders they are trying to cover up."

"Murders… oh right. Ann mentioned you had videos of some friends of hers being killed. But why would the FBI keep videos on their network of a crime they are trying to cover up? Wouldn't it make more sense just to destroy the tapes?"

"How should I know?" Lizzie snorted. Also the files weren't exactly 'tapes' but Lizzie let the error pass.

"And why would one of the FBI agents who broke into my house give me this card with instructions to find you?" Mike pulled out a battered card for one John Takahashi.

Lizzie took the card and flipped it over reading the message with her own name on it. Why would John do that? He couldn't know she had those videos, could he? "I don't know," Lizzie said slowly.

"There is a lot more going on here then we know," Mike concluded.

Lizzie had to admit, he might be right.

"Did you take the videos to the police?" he asked.

"And explained that I hacked a government building to find it? How stupid do I look?"

"OK, OK. True, I could see why you might think that, but why not just drop off the tapes anonymously?" Mike said.

"Umm you can do that?"

"Of course. The tapes might have some issues getting in as evidence in court, but it would get the police looking in the right direction. Do you have the videos on you?" Mike asked.

"No, but I can get them on any computer with internet access."

"Good, let's get those. I think that might be really useful. Since you seem to be good at this stuff, there is something else I need."

"OK," Lizzie said.

"I need to find my son's kidnappers."

"Is that the plan, go after the kidnappers?" Lizzie asked.

"No, not now at least. I have a job to do."

"A job?" Lizzie just had to ask.

"They want me to kidnap Renee Dupré."

"Wow." Now Lizzie stood up. "The same woman who wants to kill Ann?" He had gone psycho.

"Yeah, that's her. The kidnappers want her in exchange for my son. For some reason, they think I can get her," Mike said.

"Why do they want Dupré in the first place?"

"It's something to do with the Fallen," Mike said,

"Umm, OK, what makes you think that?" Lizzie asked.

"These people, they're cursed. Do you know what that means?"

"A little," Lizzie said. Mike continued.

"That means, they were under the control of the Fallen, but these people escaped. If you kill the demon that cursed them, they regain control of themselves. They don't become human again, but at least they can think for themselves. Clear?"

"Sorta." Lizzie shrugged.

"It gets worse. While the Fallen are alive, these Cursed people are almost un-killable, like Cynthia. They are stronger, faster, and just way meaner. So, if they can keep just one of the Fallen alive, they can pretty much do anything else they want. They would become almost unstoppable."

"Geez, so not only do we have to worry about these demons, we have to keep an eye out for these other ex-vampires?"

"Who happen to have my son. We need to get him back fast."

"How does this tie back to Dupré?"

"I don't know. But I intend to ask her."

"But what about Ann?" Lizzie complained. "Who knows what the Feds are doing to her."

"I know, I know. But maybe if we do this right, we save everyone at once." Mike put a hand on Lizzie's shoulder and looked directly into Lizzie's eyes.

Lizzie stared back; his look was desperate. Lizzie recognized that look; it was the same one Ann had had when she had come to Lizzie to help find Keith.

"You can help if you want, but it's going to be extremely dangerous," Mike said.

"I know…" Lizzie said, trying to hide the quiver in voice. "And I'm going to help. Just no more knives."

"Deal!" Mike said. "I have a few more questions, if you're up for it."

"Yeah OK, fine," Lizzie said, sliding back down to the couch.

"Do you know where the Fallen are?" he asked, as if she was an expert on all things demon.

"I know where they were. Keith, or you know, head demon guy, seems to like this Starbucks in Newark. We went directly there after they grabbed me and he never left."

"A Starbucks?" Mike seemed unconvinced.

Lizzie just shrugged. "Don't ask me, man. I'm telling you where they brought me."

"Was he alone?"

"No, there were two other demons there. That bitch Vanessa Black, do you know her?" Lizzie had no idea how much of Ann's life Mike knew about.

"Yes, we've met. I hope to avoid meeting her again. Anyone else?"

"One other guy I didn't know. Fat. Echoed a lot."

"Echoed?"

Lizzie thought for a moment, but couldn't come up with a better way to describe the demons speech. "He just had an odd take on a stutter, but repeating full words. It was strange."

"Did you catch a name?"

Lizzie thought back to that moment the third demon walked in. *Yes, they had called him something.* "I think it was, like, Marmaduk, or something. Like that dog in the comics, but not quite." There was a brief smile on Mike's face, which made Lizzie feel better.

"OK, close enough," he said. "Thank you, Lizzie. I think that's helpful." Mike stretched, then asked "And you said they were after Ann, not Miller?"

"Right. She broke some rule or something."

"Right, right, I remember that," Mike said and was silent for a moment.

"So what's the plan here man?" Lizzie said, generally curious.

Mike smiled nervously. "It's a little complicated."

*****

Mike retired to Ann's bedroom after giving Lizzie instructions on everything they might need.

He hadn't expected to sleep. He wanted to make a few private calls and wash up a bit. How could he possibly rest with Sam in Smith's hands? But his body had other plans and sleep did not just come, it bum rushed him. One moment he was there in Ann's bedroom; the next he was someplace else.

The phone was ringing. Mike snapped it up, the bright light of daylight blinding him making him wince. He was back in the patrol car, his patrol car. Had he dozed off on the job? That wasn't good.

"Samson," he said, hitting the accept button on the phone.

"Hey, baby," Melissa said on the other end of the line. There was the feeling of relief, as if he had just had a nightmare where something terrible had happened to her. But it wasn't real. She was fine.

"Hey, pretty lady. What can I do for you?" he said, but he was distracted. There was something important, so important. He didn't have time even to talk to his wife, his wife that he missed so badly. What could be so critical? He couldn't remember.

"You have a friend here at the house. Says you know him from work. I told him you wouldn't be home for a few hours, but he insisted I call you and let you know he was here."

"A friend?" Mike asked, confused.

A new voice picked up the phone. "Mr. Samson," the voice said. "I must say, you have a most beautiful wife."

"Smith!" Mike shouted "Don't you touch her!"

"Me? I would never do such a thing." The vampire actually laughed then. "Well, maybe a just a little taste." There was a wet sound and Mike could just picture Smith's tongue leaping at his wife. Melissa was suddenly screaming. Mike was screaming.

Lizzie was screaming. Mike blinked. He was awake, back in Ann's room. The gun was in his hand.

"Whoa!" Lizzie cowered on the floor. "It's me! It's just me!"

Mike tried to slow his rampaging heart. He lowered the gun slightly. "Sorry, sorry! What are you doing in here?" he asked.

"Besides dying of a heart attack? I was just getting a pillow. Apparently, I get the couch. Some gentleman you are," Lizzie said in a huff, looking up from her place on the floor.

Mike lowered the gun the rest of the way. "I'm sorry... just a nightmare. I get these nightmares…" he began but then stopped himself. How to explain?

Lizzie popped up from the floor shaking slightly. "That is a really big gun," she said.

"How long was I out?" Mike asked, rubbing his face.

"Ah, like 2 hours I think," Lizzie responded, still keeping her distance. "And if you promise not to scream or wave a gun or cut me, I have news."

"News?"

"I got it," Lizzie said, pride clear in her voice.

Mike smiled for the first time in a long time. "I've got to make a call."

# 13 - Stereotypes

The vampire named King had been left behind. This really didn't bother him; he had minimal interest in Smith's little schemes, and being left behind meant that he could catch up on a bit of light reading. He stretched out on one the sofas and let his human underlings take care of the building's security. After some time with his nose in a book, he noticed one of the underlings was staring at him.

"Can I help you?" the vampire said, looking at the man. King couldn't remember the man's name. That was Carter's job. Instead, he gave them all nicknames. This one was 'Hireling'. The one down the hall with the bad beard was 'Henchman'. The man by the door was "Doorman' and the one pacing around the sofa was 'Expendable'. There was also Sidekick and Brunch, but Smith had taken them with him.

"Are you reading Twilight?" Hireling asked. There was a touch of disbelief in his voice.

"I am. Is that a problem?" King asked, amused by the little man's nerve.

"Well, I…" the man stammered. "I didn't think you were the target audience."

King smiled. He wasn't the target audience, true. "Oh, I think everyone enjoys a good love story from time to time. Now, don't you have something you need to do?"

"Yes sir, sorry sir." And Hireling shuffled off.

King watched him go before picking the book back up. It was always interesting to King to see where mankind would take the legend of the Vampire. King could have explained how much this transformation over the years had fascinated him and that's why he was reading up on this version of the vampire. He could have said that, but it would have been a lie. Honestly, he was just a softy for romance novels. And this one was a whopper.

His kind had made major progress over the years. Vampires had gone from undead fiends, to untouchable monsters that could change in to bats, and then to romantic creatures that sometimes moon lighted as superheroes. His favorite had to be Dracula: not quite the first, but the one most remembered. Bram Stoker had put together one badass version of a vampire. Although the whole stake through the heart wouldn't really work well, it was not as silly as some of the other ways were for disposing of King's kind. Early legends talked off inserting a coin or a lemon into a vampire's mouth: Not something that anyone wants to try. Then there was boiling a vampire's head in vinegar. And chaining a vampire to a grave with roses. Then, there was his favorite: cutting off a vampire's toes was, according to legend, lethal to a vampire. Most of these silly legends had died off over time and only the more potent versions lasted. There was that old standby—the cross. King had actually known several Catholic vampires who got a big kick out that legend. Then there was garlic. Oddly enough, there was some truth to that legend. King himself had a natural allergy to the plant. It was no more than a rash after contact, but how strange that it did something at all. Garlic, in the right amounts, might actually kill him. Maybe. He had never heard of such a thing actually happening, but there had been a few times he had considered trying it out on Smith. For the sake of science.

But if one really wanted to kill a vampire, fire was the most efficient method. Yes, decapitation worked, in that it killed what remained of the human, but it unleashed the demon within, generally a far larger problem. Fire, on the other hand, did the job quickly. The thought of open flame gave King a small chill. Fire was death and he had spent many years avoiding death.

King put this train of thought aside and went back to his book. Moments passed and then he was interrupted again by Hireling.

"Sir, there appears to be a taxi coming up the drive way."

"A taxi? Did Smith finally get tired of Carter's jokes and send her home?" King asked, without looking away from his book.

"I very much doubt they would have used this taxi," Hireling said, then added, "Sir."

"Fine," King said, standing up and tucking the book under his arm. Smith had said to keep an eye on their rented home while the rest of the group was out conducting business. King really didn't expect much, but his company did have certain enemies.

King walked over to the window and noted a large elderly man getting out the back of the taxi. King did not recognize the man, but noted the large bag he pulled out of car with him. He looked very much like a salesman. But a door-to-door salesman? Did people still do that? Perhaps the man was here to sell bibles. Oh, was he in for a surprise.

"It's probably nothing. But just in case," King made mimicked a gun with his thumb and pointer finger. There were four men total in the house with King and all four drew weapons in response to signal. It was best to be careful.

King did not wait for the salesman to reach the building. Instead, he slid his sunglasses on and stepped outside the house into the sunlight. There was no bursting into flames when a vampire walked into sunlight, nor any sparkles, but it was harder to keep the Mark of the Curse in check in direct sunlight. The black eyes all of the Fallen's children shared liked to pop up at inconvenient times, leading to many a torchlight chase away from angry mobs. A good pair of sunglasses kept that issue in check in modern times.

"Excuse me, sir," King said politely as the new man approached, "this is private property."

The old man smiled. It was a kind smile and when he spoke, it was in a thick French accent. "I do apologize. I won't take more than a minute of your time. I wonder if I might interest you in an exciting new product?"

*So, he was a salesman and a pushy one at that.* Fine, King could use a good meal. "I doubt it, but you never know," he said.

The salesman pulled a small item out of his coat pocket and pointed it him. It was a tiny gun.

King grunted. "What is this?"

"This, sir, is the finest in novelty lighters." The salesman smiled and pulled the trigger. A short blue flame burst out of the front. King took a step back into the house and the man followed, dropping his bag at the doorway as he entered. The four armed men raised their guns.

"Oh, pardon me," the man said, "there's been a misunderstanding. There's no need for those weapons. This is just a lighter. One of the finest money can buy." The man put his hands up, but his smile never faded.

"What's this all about? You're going door to door selling novelty lighters? That's an odd one," King asked. There was something strange going on here.

"Oh, I assure you, they are the best lighters money can buy. Now, I understand you may not be smokers. But think of all the other uses. You can use it to start your grill or sparklers for your children on the 4th of July…"

At this point, King grabbed the sales man and tossed him against a wall. "Enough!" King shouted. "What are you up to?"

"So, no on the lighter?" the man asked, his smile never faltering. "I do have another model in the shape of a cannon, which some people find quite entertaining."

King punched him hard on the temple and at last the smile on the man's face faded away. "Now, let's try this again. What are you doing here?" King demanded.

"Well—Mr. King, was it? To be honest, I'm only the distraction."

If King still had a heart, it would have sunk right then. He glanced back towards the bag the man had dropped by the doorway, just in time to watch it explode.

Hireling, Henchman, Doorman, and Expendable were all sent flying. Even King was knocked off his feet. The explosion was not big, but loud, and for several moments, he was disoriented. Two hands grabbed him, lifted him high in the air, and then launched him at one of his own men like a rocket. There was a collision, and a moment of tangled limbs, then King was back on his feet.

The salesman was charging, a wood stake in one hand. King almost let the stake run him through, just to prove how useless wooden stakes were against him, but this man had done too much damage already. He caught the weapon with one hand and threw out a quick jab with the other, landing his fist on the salesman's nose. It gave a satisfactory crack and the man stumbled back. King followed it with a blow to the man's kidney, then another heavy hit to the temple. The salesman crumpled to the floor, but was still conscious. He wasn't human, that's for sure, as no man could take blows like that and still be awake.

"How do you know my name? What is this about?" King didn't care which question he answered first and honestly hoped he took his time responding. He was looking forward to hurting this man.

"Both fair questions," the salesman sputtered. "But the better question would be: Who is behind you?"

A metal stake appeared in the center of King's chest. He was then lifted up and thrown to the ground. Strong hands then pounded the stake into the floor, trapping him. King twisted his head as far as he could to make out the second attacker. He noted the ruined eyes and the odd preference for bow ties.

"Abraham" he gasped.

The blind vampire knelt over him, grinning. "It's been a long time, little brother," Abraham said.

Then King finally worked out who the other man was. "Marcel Dupré," he guessed.

The salesman nodded, slowing getting back to his feet.

"I had always wondered what you looked like without all the hair," King said.

"I had forgotten myself," Marcel said, that smile back on his face.

King tried to stand, but Abraham's foot and the metal stake kept him pinned. "A novelty lighter salesman? Great bit, I gotta admit," King said. He was beaten, no doubt about that. He tried to stay calm though. Marcel was no killer. Abraham, well, that was another story. But there was a chance he could talk himself out of this.

"Where's the boy, King?" Marcel asked. "Samson's son."

"Afraid I don't know…" King started, but then Abraham kicked him in the face.

"No telling tales now, not to your own family," Abraham said.

"What the hell do you care?" King said, his temper flaring. He glanced around the room. He could see two of his men; neither of them were moving. One—he thought it might be Expendable—was nothing more than a pale corpse. "Did you feed on one of my men? Abraham, that's poor form."

Abraham reduced the pressure on King's back, just by a fraction. "My dining habits are not your concern," he said. "Please focus on the question at hand. Tell us where Smith has stashed the Samson boy and we may leave you in peace."

"Eating humans. Running me through with a stake. You are in a foul mood, Abraham." There was another kick to the head. It hurt, but pain for vampires was a distant thing. It was now more the memory of what pain once was, as what remained of most of his nervous system just barely functioned. Still, the threat of death meant something. He did not want to die.

"Answers, please," Marcel requested. "As much as I do enjoy beating you up, we are on a schedule.

"All right, all right. Smith has him and the girl. He wanted to rig up a little surprise for his dad, just in case the cop got smart."

"The girl?" Marcel asked. "Is Smith adding kidnapping children to his list of hobbies?"

"The girl. Yeah, her name's Angela. Poor thing. One of the Fallen turned a three year old girl into one of us."

Marcel let out a disgusted gasp. "The poor child," he said.

"What's Smith planning to do?" Abraham demanded. "He knows he isn't welcome around these parts."

"I don't know." Another kick to the head. "No, really, do you think that sick bastard tells me anything? Hell, he doesn't even talk to Carter anymore and they dated for like 200 years or something."

"Carter? The one that killed Dallas? She's here too?" Marcel asked.

"Yeah, yeah," King said.

"Anyone else from your side of the family we should be on the lookout for?" Abraham asked, dropping down on one knee.

"No..."

Abraham jiggled the stake.

King let out a yell. "No! I swear!" he shouted.

"Good," Marcel said. "One more question. What does your boss want with my wife?" he demanded.

"What? You don't know?" King said, surprised.

The smile vanished from Marcel and he brought the gun shaped lighter up to King's face. "What don't I know?"

King looked directly into Marcel's eyes and he knew in that instant he was dead. "I thought you knew, I mean, she's your wife..." King stammered.

Marcel flicked the lighter on.

"OK, OK, I'm talking here, I'm talking, just wait," King said.

Marcel moved the lighter forward. "Talk faster," he hissed.

"Smith hired her, years ago, funded her research to help bring back the Fallen," King explained, "but she stiffed him on the actual how to, now that Dupré's figured it out. So, he plans on getting it out of her the old fashioned..." King was about to say 'way' but at that moment, Marcel decided to jam the lighter into his eye. The vampire screamed in pain, in true agony. Something he had not felt in a long time.

"You lie!" Marcel yelled. "Renee would never do such a thing!"

King screamed again and Marcel backed away.

"I swear it," King cried. "You know, the bosses have been trying to learn the secret of bringing the Fallen back for hundreds of years... your wife, she's done it."

"For you, Marcel," Abraham interjected.

Marcel slumped back, the man looking as if King had just stabbed him. "No, it can't be true," he said.

"It is as we feared," Abraham said. He stepped off King's back and stood to the side. "King, I would like to thank you for taking the time to answer our questions so politely."

King let out a sigh. "Hey, no big, anything for Family members," he said. Maybe he would get out of this alive.

Abraham stepped in front of King. "Before we go, though, my friend does have one last novelty item to show you. It's currently sticking out of your back. Marcel, if you would?"

Marcel seemed to snap back to life. He reached over and then King heard what sounded like a click. He felt a vaguely warm feeling in his chest.

"What? What are you doing?" There was the crackle of fire and King's back caught flame.

"Fire stake. The finest in novelty lighters," Marcel explained, "and the ultimate tool for the modern vampire hunter. You see, I had to do something to keep me busy all those years in the woods."

"No, no, no, no!" King yelled. The demon in him screamed as the fire engulfed him.

"Die, monster," Marcel said and it was the last thing King would ever hear.

*****

Marcel felt miserable. They had failed to find Samson's son, but that was nothing compared to the pain of learning of Renee's betrayal. He and Abraham stood outside the burning remains of the house Smith's men had rented out as a base.

"There's nothing else we can do here," Abraham said, turning back to the taxi.

"I can't believe she has fallen this far. I was worried when she stopped her regular visits, but I never thought..." Marcel's voice trailed away.

"Your wife has a lot to answer for," Abraham said, "but right now I am more concerned with Mike Samson and the search for his son."

"In what way?" Marcel asked.

"I'm afraid Samson might do something rash. Remember Smith's demand. Your wife for his son."

"Do you think one lone human is going to storm a federal building and kidnap my wife?" Marcel said. That was madness.

"Mike Samson was chosen by the Ancient One himself to help hunt the Fallen. The same way he chose Dallas before him and countless others before that. The Ancient One does not choose people who sit and wait at bars while others rescue their children. I'm afraid if we have nothing to bring him, he will attempt exactly that. No matter what the odds," Abraham said.

"Then we need to find Smith before Samson does something we'll all regret," Marcel said.

"Perhaps you should be at your wife's side. I will continue the search for Smith." Abraham offered, but Marcel shook his head.

"Not a day before, there was nothing I wouldn't have done to be by Renee's side, but now..." Marcel paused for a moment of reflection. "...now everything is different."

"I understand, Little brother."

"But perhaps you are right. Renee and I should talk," Marcel said. He knew Abraham was right, but he also knew this would be one of the hardest conversations of his life.

# 14 - Revenge

Ann really wished she knew where Miller was pushing her. With her head still locked in place, she could only look straight up and there was nothing there to see but passing fluorescent lights and the occasional red flashing one.

"Any idea where we're going?" Ann asked.

"None in the slightest," Miller admitted, in a tone that was not the least bit comforting. As they took a hard turn to the right, Ann felt the cart tip, but Miller regained the balance quickly.

"Just stop for a minute, I'm sure we can figure out how to free me from this table. Then I can help find the way out," Ann offered.

"As soon as I find a place with some cover. We're too exposed here and I would rather not go back into one of those cells," Miller said.

This sounded reasonable. So Ann waited and watched the lights fly by. She wondered briefly if she could still get motion sickness. Oh, what a miserable thought that was.

There were voices, men shouting things like "There they are!" and "Get them!" from down the hall.

"Oh hell!" Ann shouted.

"Language, please, language," Miller said, taking another turn.

"You're not the one they're going to cut into pieces," Ann yelled. Although to be fair, Miller would make an interesting specimen as well. And a psychiatric team could have a field day.

There was gunfire. Not just that single shot stuff, but something big and machine gun like. Something Ann had only seen in the movies and at College Hospital. "Are they shooting at *us*?" she asked, before she could stop herself.

"Aye," Miller said. "I really need to acquire one of those fine weapons for myself, too." The last part he said under his breath.

One of the lights above them exploded, showering Ann with glass.

"What are you doing?" came a voice from behind them.

"Dupré said to do whatever it takes," said another voice.

Shots were fired again and Ann's cart was suddenly tumbled forward. It fell on its side, shielding Ann from the source of the bullets. The gunfire was closer now. It sounded like a handgun this time.

"Miller?" Ann called. There was no reply. "Miller?" she repeated. "Oh no."

Then the big gun opened up again, this time hitting the cart. Bullets sliced through her and she screamed in pain. One went through her calf;

another grazed a hip. Two in her back, and one more skimmed over her check. It was like being struck by lightning many times simultaneously. Her body burned with the combined pain while she continued to scream until her lungs filled with too much blood to continue. She was getting tired of being shot.

Time moved forward slowly. Ann wasn't sure if she had passed out or not.

"We have the girl. She's a little beaten up, but alive," came a voice.

Ann's cart was righted, giving her a brief glimpse of the hall. It was covered in red blood. Miller's, Ann guessed. She tried to speak, but it came out as more of a gurgle. She tried to focus, tried to force herself to heal, but her world was pain, and the power slipped from her time and time again.

"Looks like Soliz is still on the loose, though. He can't have gotten far. I'm sure I hit him."

The cart was moving again, the annoying lights moving in the other direction now. Ann struggled to breathe, the simple act of drawing air into what was left of her lungs seeming impossible. She needed to focus.

"She looks pretty messed up, man," said a man, his face appearing over her.

"She'll live. You notice her blood?" a second voice came.

"Yeah, can't miss that. It's black and thick, and I swear it's moving the wrong way."

"Holy ... I think you're right."

Ann sucked in a ragged gulp of air. *Yeessss*, she thought. *Go lungs!* Oxygen never tasted so good.

"Get her back to her cell and lock her up tight."

The cart picked up speed, while Ann reacquainted herself with the joy of breathing. "Please don't do this," she said, her voice starting weak, but gaining strength. "I'm not what you think I am."

The men ignored her and continued on.

"This is just one big misunderstanding." Still nothing. She switched tactics. "What happened to my friend? Can you at least tell me that?"

The cart stopped.

"Please... don't. She's going to kill me," Ann made the desperation clear in her voice.

The cart was shoved forward and bounced hard against a wall.

"Don't!" Ann shouted.

She heard the door swing shut and she was right back where she'd started.

*****

There was blood everywhere. His blood. Miller had to admit that the gun was extremely impressive, but he had not needed that close of a demonstration. This was not his best rescue. He had been hit several times, knocking him over and sending Ann's cart flying. His right leg was useless; a bullet had hit the calf dead center. The other hits were not as severe: two along his ribs, just scrapes really, and his left hand was now missing a chunk of its palm. Miller had dragged himself down another hallway, unable to push Ann's cart any further. He had taken several shots, hoping to at least draw them away from Ann, but the men ignored him and went right for the girl. That stung his ego a bit. After all, wasn't he the Ancient One? Didn't that deserve a little more interest? The men had not followed him, even with the trail of blood he was leaving behind him. Disappointing.

He would have to double back to try and rescue Ann again. The not walking thing would probably be an issue though. He stopped dragging himself forward and looked behind him. It was an impressive blood trail. He would have to fix that first. He pulled himself up on the nearest wall, ripping a large piece of his shirt to wrap around his leg. If he could find something sharp, he could dig the bullet out. It would heal quickly after that, but if the bullet was still in there it would take much longer and it would itch like there was no tomorrow. For now, the best he could do was to wrap the wound and slow the bleeding.

Now that he was at least somewhat more presentable, he hobbled down the hall. With his good hand against the wall and the other tucked into his chest, he made slow progress forward. Miller wasn't exactly sure how he would defend himself if someone found him, but he was sure he would think of something.

"Freeze!"

Miller was beginning to wonder if "Freeze!" was all these people could say. It did beat them just opening fire on him though. *Give thanks for the little things*. Well, now would be a good time to think of something. He managed to turn around to face his attacker. The same man he had already knocked out twice pointed a new gun at him. Miller tried not to roll his eyes.

"Sir, while I do appreciate your spirit, I've been trying really hard not to kill you. Maybe this time you could just lay down for me."

The man's gun wavered due to either fear or the head trauma Miller had visited upon him earlier. The look on his face was more confused than angry. "How did you do that?" he asked. "Before, in the hallway. You were there, and then I was on the ground. No one is that fast."

"Incredible talent and many, many years of practice," Miller grinned, happy to at last be noticed. "Should I show you again?" Not that Miller could; right now, the best thing he could do was bleed on the man.

"No, put the gun on the ground."

Miller could shoot the man as well, but that left a bad taste in his mouth. "I can't do that," Miller said, noticing a figure behind the man. "Look, I'll tell you what I'll do. I'll give you one more demonstration." Miller raised his hands a little higher. "This time, I'll knock you out from back here." He stepped back. The man watched, unsure. "Are you watching?"

John Takahashi struck the man in the back of the head with a revolver.

"Sorry about that, Burns," the tall Japanese man said.

Miller tried to clap for the agent, but remembered his wounded hand a moment too late. "Well done, sir! I was hoping you would catch on there."

Takahashi smiled weakly. There was a spot of dried blood on his face. Perhaps Miller's kick to the head earlier had been a little too convincing. "God, you are a mess," the agent said. "I thought you were supposed to be good at this sort of thing."

This comment was awarded a shrug from Miller. "Well, it's been a hundred years, I'm still rusty."

"Come on, it's not safe here."

"Can you talk now? I would love to know what is going on," Miller said.

"Security is out all over the building. We can talk while we try and get you patched up, but there is another problem."

"Oh?" Miller somehow knew this was going to be good.

"How are you with zombies?"

*****

Ann screamed in frustration and more than a little fear. The fear part she was adjusting to, but she did not like the helpless part. Being strapped to the table completely paralyzed was driving her mad. On the plus side, her body was already knitting itself back together and the pain was fading. For that, at least she was thankful. There had to be some way to escape, some way to get out of this little death trap before Dupré came back.

There was still the notebook tucked under her arm, less than an inch away from her hand. Miller had risked so much to get that to her, it had to be important. The pressure of it against her side was a comfort. Her wrists were free and she attempted to push the book further into place by tucking her palm against it and pushing. Her thinking was it would be better to have the book tucked in completely. However, when she gave it a push, it did not budge. Instead, to her surprise, one of the straps popped off.

"What?" she said in shock. She had given those straps everything she had before. Of course, that was before they had been hit with machine gun fire. Ann tested her bonds again slowly. Another strap snapped free further up her chest and a third stretched as if to tear, but she could not force it off.

Still, this was progress; she could now move her hands up to her elbows. Exploring the edge of the table slowly with her fingers, she found what appeared to be a lever holding something in place. Her fingers were not quite long enough to reach though. She tried and tried, but the lever teased her, just out of her grasp.

"Ugh, fine, you win," she again said to no one in particular. She knew what she had to do. Although she had not tried it yet, she knew she could switch back to the hideous white-scaled version of herself. Now that the secret was known to her, she could control it. .

Slowly, Ann released her hold on her humanity, letting it slip away, letting the monster—her true self—out. Her flesh stretched and ripped. It didn't hurt, exactly, but it was not enjoyable either. Her hand reached the lever and she yanked hard, allowing two more straps to release just as her midsection began to stretch. With her arms now free, she reached up and pulled on the damaged strap along her shoulders. With a grunt, she managed to snap it.

There was pressure on her head, as the strap holding it in place had not given to her suddenly expanding skull. Ann tried to reverse the change, but could not stop it. In a panic, she yanked on the strap, but it would not release. Changing tactics, she slid down the table, tearing a chunk of flesh away as payment for her freedom.

She sat up as her teeth were beginning to rearrange themselves. Her shirt suddenly rose and split down the back, making room for the red wings bursting out of her back. Ann reached forward, feeling for the levers to free her legs and feet. She rolled to the ground and let the transformation take her.

In a moment, Ann rose, the remains of her shirt dropping to the floor. She stretched her massive wings and rubbed her jaw, reacquainting herself with the rows of fangs. In the black one-way mirror, she saw her own reflection and winced.

*Well, they wanted a monster. Now, to get out of here.* She lifted the table and smashed it against glass wall. The table bounced, leaving the wall unmarked. She tried again and again, the table morphing into an unrecognizable mass of metal, until finally a crack appeared. She continued until the table was nothing more than chunks of metal, and then she tossed them aside and used her fists. The crack grew and huge sections of the wall fell away, but still she pounded. She screamed with each hit, realizing how angry she was. She was tired of being scared, tired of being a monster, and most definitely tired of being shot.

At last, her fist burst through, with a spray of plastic chunks. This caught her off balance and she began to fall through the wall. Ann steadied herself and stood back up, then enlarged the hole with a few more punches.

Her already torn and bloodied pants shredded the rest of the way as she pulled herself free.

This is going to be really awkward when she changed back. What had Miller said when they first met him at the hospital? "Step one, find pants." Wise words.

Picking herself up off the ground, she dusted herself off and scanned the hallway. She ducked back inside the room and picked up the notebook, stuffing it into her ruined pants. Back out in the hallway, the red lights still flashed and now that she was not screaming and hitting things, she could hear faint sounds of gunfire. Well, that may have something to do with why no one was around. Something else was going on. Could it be Miller was giving them hell? Ann could only hope, and she would be happy to help. As soon as she found some pants.

*****

"Please don't bleed on the suit," Takahashi asked, only half seriously, as he helped drag the wounded Miller.

"It is a very fine suit," Miller agreed, "but it makes you look like a Fed."

"I am a Fed," Takahashi replied, "and there is nothing wrong with serving your government. It just so happens that, this time, it's a little confused as to who the good guys are."

"Aye. True enough," Miller said, hopping along. He was already feeling better, the bleeding having stopped in his ribs and hand. His leg still needed some attention though. "Where are we going?"

"Dupré's lab. There's a first aid kit there. She's at our medical unit getting her gunshot wound patched up," Takahashi said.

"No offense, but I don't much care for her," Miller said. "How did one of the Cursed end up working for your government, and in charge at that?"

"Your man Badow got her in."

The name bounced around his skull for several seconds before it found a face.

"Dallas? You mean Dallas?" Miller asked, the memory of the young man he had last seen in France so long ago warmed him, then changed to pain as he realized his comrade must be long dead.

"Yes, Dallas Badow set up this FBI department many, many years ago and put Dupré in charge, knowing she would still be around when the Fallen made their return. He worked with Dupré and her husband for years, tracking down other members of the Cursed and learning what they could so next time they would be prepared. He called this whole operation Bright Steel."

"Bright Steel? Really?" Miller asked doubtfully.

"Well, if you read the journal, you'll find the man was a bit of a romantic. Do you still have it? The notebook?"

"I gave it to Miss Ann, but I'm afraid she was captured again."

"Damn. Dallas left strict instructions to give you the book the moment you arrived," Takahashi said.

"She's next on the list. Do you know where she is?"

"Probably back in her cell, I would imagine. I've lost all radio contact."

"Why, what's happening?"

"We had about twenty bodies recovered from the field, well Newark, a few days ago. They were dangerous; some version of the Cursed we didn't know anything about. We kept them contained for study. The idea was to try to trace them back to the Fallen that had created them. About two days ago, they suddenly froze in place, unmoving. Most of them had laid down on the ground, and we thought maybe they were dying. But about 45 minutes ago, they woke back up, broke out of their cell, and are now tearing the building apart."

"Ah. Samson was correct. You would think we would learn after all those years of horror movies. The monster always gets out. Always," Miller said.

"Yes, I wanted to burn the bodies, but Dupré ordered them spared until she could finish her research and we could track down the demon."

"No need. I think I know what's going on here."

They took a right and entered a stairway.

"Stairs? God I hate stairs," Miller complained.

"If you know what's going on, help me stop them. There are only a few of us here in this building and those things are tricky to kill."

Miller grunted as he hopped down the first step. "No, you first. If Dallas set this all up to help me, why are my friends and I being fired on?"

"It's Dupré. She had plans of her own that I haven't quite figured out. Not to mention power that goes all the way to the top. She's threatened or killed a lot of people to keep whatever she's working on a secret. I think the key is your friend."

"Ann?"

"Yes, she's been dead set on killing her since day one. Miss Melakh must know something," Takahashi said.

"Or be something. Ann is the first person ever to recover from being taken by the Fallen. No one has ever done that before." They reached the bottom of the stairs and walked into a large room. "What is this place?"

The room was huge, filled with long rows of tables covered with machines Miller had never seen before. Riddled throughout were hundreds of white lilies of different sizes.

"Dupré's lab. It takes up the entire bottom floor. I guess it's part greenhouse, but I don't see how the plants could possibly grow down here. Stay away from the flowers."

"Why?"

"I'm not sure; just a video I saw once," Takahashi said, eyeing a nearby bloom with suspicion.

*The man was afraid of flowers; how sad.*

"So Dupré must think Ann is still Lilith," Miller said, "which explains the desire to kill her to some degree. She lacks the sight so she cannot see for herself." He sat on a bench.

"One second, the med kit is over here." Takahashi vanished for a long moment, returning with a white box.

"Do you think you can find something to help me remove a bullet? Ah wait, never mind, this should be perfect." Miller picked up a tool off one of the tables.

"Needle nose pliers?" Takahashi looked concerned. "Do you want me to..."

Miller lifted the wounded leg onto the bench and began poking in the wound with the pliers.

"...clean them?" Takahashi finished. "I guess not."

"Ah, got it." Miller pulled and the bullet came free with a gush of blood. Takahashi flinched and turned a shade of green. "So the question is, why don't you think Ann is still Lilith?" Miller asked.

"Abraham told me," Takahashi explained. "Do you know Abraham? "

"Yes," Miller said dryly. "We've met. I found him with Ann a few nights ago, but he ran off before he could answer any real questions."

"He is a bit of a mystery man," Takahashi said. "He is in the notebook as well."

"Hmm, Abraham and Dallas, eh? Now that would be an interesting conversation," Miller said, splinting the leg and wrapping it with a bandage.

"What?"

"Long story. I would love to know Abraham's part in all of this," Miller said.

"He has been helping Dupré," the agent said. "Well and me, I guess. He set up a safe house for Dupré and her husband in Newark. Look, if you know something about the zombies upstairs, I need to know. Not only do I need to get you out of here safely, but I need to protect the rest of my men."

"Wait, who is this husband?"

"Marcel Dupré, Cursed, like her, but trapped as a werewolf. He was living in the Midwest until twenty years ago, when he had to move. Too many Bigfoot sightings in the area."

"Where did he go?"

"Where we send everything we don't know what to do with in the

U.S.: Canada." Takahashi smiled, but Miller must have missed the joke.

"Hmmm." Miller rubbed his chin and tried to stand on the injured leg. He brightened. "That is much better."

"Now, about the creatures upstairs."

"The zombies, as you call them—fitting, by the way—are not after your men," Miller said.

"No?"

"No. The demon that created them is dead. Ann killed it two days ago in Newark," Miller said, walking tentatively, testing out his leg.

"Oh, well that's good," the agent said, "but then shouldn't those Cursed die off when that happens? I mean, I thought that was how it worked."

"Apparently not in this case. No, your men have nothing to worry about. The Zombies only want one person. Ann."

*****

Ann held the notebook in one hand as she made her way through the cells. She padded silently down the hall, conscious of both her lack of decent clothing and her white scales. Her wings were wrapped around her, which she found almost comforting. In truth, she had missed the wings: they were an odd upside to this misshapen demon form. After all this insanity was done, Ann would find a way to go flying.

There was gunfire and shouting ahead, and Ann poked her head around the corner to investigate.

The same dead things she had seen in Newark filled the hallway ahead of her. Close to her, two men fired into the crowd, futilely trying to hold them back. The zombies absorbed the bullets and kept on coming.

"Zombies, why does it always have to be Zombies?" Ann whispered to herself.

One of the soldiers pitched his empty gun into the crowd in front of him. "Where the hell are Dupré and Takahashi? How the hell do we kill these things?"

The other man did not answer; he was focusing on firing his own gun into the crowd. One zombie fell but did not stop, instead pulling itself forward on the ground by its pale arms.

Ann hesitated. *I should help them, after all,* she thought. *I've become pretty good at killing those things*. But these were the men who had broken into Mike's house, shot her, and ignored her pleas. She sighed to herself. *I will not become a super villain. I will not become a super villain.* She dashed forward, putting herself between the zombies and the men.

"What the...?" one man shouted. Ann ignored him, grabbing the first zombie she could. It reached for her head, squealing in that way only an undead Cursed zombie could. She pitched it head first into the crowd. It was like bowling, but with flesh-eating corpses. Several zombies collapsed into a heap. She turned to the men. "Run, you idiots!" she screamed.

One man stared at her, his eyes wide. "What are you?"

"I'm your guardian angel. I have to save your worthless lives to earn my wings." She spread her wings for effect. "Guess we have that taken care of, now run!" she screamed.

The men did not need to be told again.

White hands grabbed her legs, and in an instant, the dead swarmed all around her. Ann stood against the tide, refusing to be pulled down. She slashed into the crowd, ripping through flesh and limbs. Kicking her legs out, she sent another two bodies flying backwards, knocking several others down in the process. Another leaped at her, its teeth clamping down on the thin flesh of her right wing.

"OW! Hey, no one touches the wings!" she screamed, pulling the offending corpse free and crushing its skull.

Ann stepped back, momentarily free of the clinging hands and gnashing teeth. The men had escaped. Now was her chance. She turned and ran. The zombies mobbed behind her.

She took the next right, gaining distance from the zombie horde. She had taken out two, maybe three. It was hard to be sure if the things were really dead. She recalled the black spot at the back of the neck that seemed to be their weak spot. Unfortunately, it was hard to be that precise with ten of the things crawling all over you. She would have to whittle them down a few at a time, all while locating Miller and somehow avoiding the guards. *It's never easy, is it?*

Around the bend were stairs heading both up and down. Having no idea which floor she was on, she picked down. Behind her, the zombies raged, refusing to give up their search.

*****

"They want Ann?" John Takahashi asked. "As some sort of revenge?"

"Exactly. The Fallen and the Cursed are a family of sorts. A twisted one, but the basic rules still apply," Miller answered.

There was a disturbance at the stairs and Takahashi grabbed Miller and pulled him down behind a table. The agent held one finger to his lips, calling for silence. Miller nodded in agreement.

Renee Dupré walked into the lab. She was mumbling under her breath as she passed.

"She cannot see us together," Takahashi hissed under his breath.

"Aye," was all he said in response, as he eyed the cursed woman.

Dupré headed farther into the lab and Miller followed, out of sight behind the tables. *What was this woman hiding?* There was only one way to find out.

"You!" a voice yelled. Dupré spun to the entrance of the lab. The white scaled form of Ann burst through the doors. Dupré's jaw dropped and she turned and ran, far faster than the old woman she was pretending to be possibly could have. Ann leaped through the air, spreading her red wings, and pounced on her. They tumbled into a heap, with Ann on top. The demon woman slugged Dupré with a right hook that made Miller feel a little proud.

"Good Lord, she's going to kill Dupré," Takahashi said, standing.

"No, wait." Miller put a restraining hand on the man.

"You've got a lot explaining to do," Ann screamed, lifting Dupré off the ground, then slamming her into the nearest table. Dupré's wig was knocked free and Ann pitched it away. "What the hell?"

Dupré reached into her pocket, but Ann saw it coming and knocked the massive hand cannon free before Dupré could let loose a round.

"No, I don't think we'll do that again. I am so tired of people trying to put holes in me." Ann decked Dupré again. "You killed my friends." Another punch—to the gut this time—and Dupré doubled over. "You made me into this monster." Ann struck out her knee, striking Dupré in the forehead and sending her rebounding off the table. "You've caused all of this!" Ann picked the woman up and lifted her over her head. "Why?" she screamed.

Dupré did not answer right away. The Cursed woman wheezed like a wounded animal for several long moments as she hung in the air. Finally, she spoke, "Why would I tell vermin like you? You can kill me now. I've done what I set out to do."

Ann screamed again in rage, slapping Dupré down onto the table. Ann slugged her again, then again.

Miller stepped out from behind a table and wobbled behind Ann. "Ann," he said.

Ann looked up, pausing in mid strike.

"Ann, that's enough."

Ann stared back at him, then looked down at Dupré's beaten form. "I... " Ann stammered. She let Dupré drop. "You don't understand what she did to me! Everything! My friends, Keith, everyone."

"I know. But killing her like this," Miller said, moving closer, "it's not going to bring them back."

Ann looked back between Dupré and Miller struggling with herself. "I am not a monster!" she shouted, bringing two fists down on the table behind Dupré. The furniture shattered, sending little devices flying. Ann stormed off to the other side of the lab, but not before Miller spotted the tears running down her face.

For a moment, Miller watched the creature walk away, destroying any furniture in her path, then he turned back to Dupré. The woman's face was unreadable, beaten as badly as it was.

As he approached, Dupré spit out a mouth full of blood and teeth. "What's your game here? I don't believe your little show for a moment. You're up to something," she said.

Miller leaned in closer. "I thought we might trade secrets."

*****

Ann struggled to regain control of herself. So much anger had been locked inside her. She had been mad—that was fair—but this had been rage, an entirely different animal. It had been with her in her prison cell and again it had boiled out from her when she had seen Dupré. Had Miller not been there, she would have killed her. She was no murderer, even if Dupré had it coming. She looked down at the dark blood on her hands—*no, claws*—and tried desperately to control the urge to go back and finish what she had started.

These weren't her urges; this was Lilith. The monster's ghost inside her head was pushing her to do its bidding. It had to be. Lilith had demanded Dupré's death from her as payment for sharing its secrets. If Lilith could still influence her, Ann was a danger to everyone around her. She had not had this issue when she was in human shape. Ann could still be influenced by Lilith when she was in her demon form.

"I need to change back. I need to be me again," she said to no one. She flexed her bloody claws, trying to remember the path in her mind to become human once more.

The transformation hit her like a kick in the chest. She fell to the floor, unable to breathe. Her body convulsed as it rearranged itself. It didn't hurt, precisely, but reshaping bones, teeth, and flesh was by no means comfortable. Ann thrashed on the floor until the pressure released and she could breathe again.

With one shaky hand, she pulled herself up off the floor and stood. The rage was gone, but it had left her weak and—*oh yeah, nude*. The ruins of her clothing lay on the floor.

She glanced around the lab and for the first time noticed the lilies everywhere. The memory of the video from the lab leaped to mind and Ann tumbled back to the floor. The tile was cold against her naked flesh, a sharp reminder she needed to find clothes fast. Then she needed to get the hell out of this place.

"Here," a voice whispered. A white lab coat dropped over her shoulders. Ann glanced up to see the tall Japanese man standing over her.

"Can you walk?"

"I… Takahashi right? You're on our side?" Ann whispered. "Did you see…" The tall man smiled; it was a genuine thing.

"While I didn't expect to see that exactly, I am a gentleman. I am on your side, and believe it or not, so are those men upstairs. They've just had some bad intel."

Lizzie was right about him, he was good looking. But there was also a large wedding ring clearly displayed on his left hand that Lizzie had failed to mention. Ann shrugged on the lab coat, trying to keep herself as decent as much as possible.

"Thank you," Ann said, struggling back up and eyeing the nearest group of flowers.

"You are a marvel," Takahashi said, looking her over. Ann blushed. Takahashi put up a hand, reddening. "Not like that. I mean, the whole shape-changing thing. God, please don't tell my wife we had this conversation. "

"Yeah, I'm still getting used to it myself." Ann leaned against the table, trying to regain her strength. "Apparently, it takes a lot out of you."

"Can you walk?" Takahashi asked again.

"I think so. Where's Miller?"

"He is talking with Dupré. I came after you. It's imperative that I get you both out of here, at least until your Mike Samson finishes his part of the plan."

"Mike… what?"

"I put him on the trail of a video that should be able to get Dupré put away, nice and legal-like."

"The videos from CMDNJ?" Ann guessed.

"Yes! Did you see them when you were with Lizzie?"

"Yes, how did you know?"

"I've had you followed for days now."

Ann recalled the agent who had been killed following her and Lizzie. Ura had grabbed him right before Lizzie. "I'm sorry about your man. I did try to save him," Ann said.

Takahashi paused at this. "We haven't heard from him. I had hoped…"

"Ura, one of the Fallen, got to him."

"God."

There was a shriek from the entrance of the lab. Ann turned to see the zombies stumbling through the door as if they had heard their cue.

"Speak of the devil," Ann muttered.

# 15 -The Best Laid Plans

"And you are absolutely sure you can pull this off?" Mike asked.

Lizzie rolled her eyes at him. "I really can't stand repeating myself," she responded with a snarl.

Mike shifted in his seat. He was more psyching himself up for what he was about to do, rather than doubting Lizzie's abilities. They were parked in front of the large commercial building that he believed housed Renee Dupré and her friends. The building was eight stories high, an old concrete thing that seemed about as welcoming as a bomb shelter. There were two other buildings on the block, one on each side, but a good ten yards away from Dupré's building. Across the street was a large but shabby looking park.

According to Lizzie, the plan was simple. Mike wasn't so sure, even though he had come up with it. He had seen the basic idea used during an attempted robbery in Newark, and the thieves had apparently gotten the notion from a television show. But Mike thought it was clever enough to work, with a little modification. Lizzie, impersonating an agent from the local gas company, would call each of the three buildings on the block to warn of a massive natural gas leak and ask everyone to leave the buildings and head across the street.

Mike's first task was to drop off one of the two bags sitting in the trunk of the car. This one contained a small canister of a chemical called methanethiol. Most people recognized it not by its name, but by its smell. Because natural gas is odorless, the chemical is added to help detect leaks. Mike would open the container and do a quick walk around the three buildings before dropping the bag off in the front of the FBI building. This would give the gas leak story a measure of plausibility, and with some luck, get the people inside the buildings to evacuate across the street into the park. It should—if all went well—put Dupré, Miller, and Ann back outside.

Mike would arrive at the headquarters, supposedly to have a meeting with John Takahashi, although this was just an excuse to be in the building when, as Miller might say, the fun began.

The other bag held a distraction. It looked a lot like a bomb, but was actually just a large amount of fireworks. It would be loud and make a lot of smoke, but not do much else. This was Lizzie's second job. She would place it behind the third building and when everyone was outside, set it off. It had a five-minute fuse, give or take, which he hoped would leave Lizzie enough time to set it, get back into the car, and prepare for the job of getaway driver. Once the fireworks went off, Mike was to use the distraction to free Miller and Ann, and then kidnap Dupré, jump in the car with Lizzie, and drive away.

The thieves from whom Mike had stolen the idea had been caught when an employee of the bank they were trying to rob had called the gas company directly. Lizzie had spent several hours working on a fix for this, blocking both cell phones and landlines.

There were a ton of problems with this plan and Mike knew it. But with the limited time and resources available, not to mention the lives on the line, it was the best he could do. He kept telling himself that it could work, but he also couldn't quite shake the quote about 'the best laid plans of mice and men'.

Lizzie looked up from her computer. "Look, I can do this. Believe it or not, I may have had some experience doing things like this in the past."

"That's lucky for us," *And scary,* Mike didn't say aloud. "But it's the timing that worries me."

"So...what...you plan on single-handedly facing who knows how many federals agents and you're worried about timing?"

Mike smiled, mostly to cover the fear that was tearing little holes in his stomach. "As Miller once said, timing is everything."

"Well yeah, he is probably right," Lizzie said, glancing back at her laptop. "We going to do this or not?"

Mike nodded his head 'yes'. This was how he would get Sam back. What choice did he have? Of course, he hadn't told Lizzie everything. He still had a few aces up his sleeve. He stepped out of the car and looked up at the building, willing himself to do this. Finally, he said, "Start the calls."

Lizzie nodded, and then looked Mike in the eyes. "Look, be careful in there," she said, trying to sound supportive.

"You too. You know, you're pretty calm, considering," Mike observed.

Lizzie shrugged at this. "Meh, this isn't my first federal crime. Although my first kidnapping, so there's that." She smiled. She had come a long way from the nervous woman who wouldn't even let him through the door of her house.

"Thanks Lizzie," he said.

"Just bring Ann back for me. And let her know I'm sorry for the way I acted," Lizzie said.

"Will do." Mike turned away and headed towards the first building, trying not to think of what he was going to do.

*****

Lizzie watched Mike leave. *There is no way this will work,* she thought to herself. *No way in hell.*

She called the first building and explained she was from the local gas company and that her 'sensors' had detected a large gas leak nearby. She asked if they smelled any gas and advised it would be best to evacuate people now, just to be safe. The woman on the other end of the line was hesitant to agree for a moment, even if her Caller ID did say Lizzie was from the gas company. In a few more minutes, Lizzie had the woman convinced.

The second call was simpler, as the man on the phone claimed to already smell gas. Lizzie doubted it, but was glad to have an easy call. She explained again that a utility truck would be there shortly and that the authorities had already been alerted and to please clear out the building, just as a precaution.

Lizzie waited until Mike was inside the FBI building before making the final call. That complete, there was nothing to do but wait, so she put the computer down on the seat next to her and watched the building. People were already starting to mill out of the farthest building.

There was suddenly an odd tightness in her chest, like beginning of a panic attack. It was a strange time for it; she had felt so calm. She reached for her bag, where she had hidden some of her meds from Cynthia not even a day ago.

Lizzie fumbled to open the bag, and instead spilled the contents out over the floor. "Shit," she muttered, as a sharp pain rumbled through her gut. It grew more intense. "What the hell?" she shouted. It felt as if something was boiling inside her, forcing its way up through her belly into her chest, and then her throat.

She vomited something black, then sat bolt upright.

For a moment she looked around the car, then picked up her cell and dialed a number. The line picked up without a greeting. "Father, I have our queen," Lizzie said.

Asmodai's smooth voice responded. "Excellent, Lizzie. I have dispatched the others; you are to serve them in any way they require."

"Yes, Father," Lizzie said.

"Oh, and Lizzie, welcome to the family."

*****

Mike entered the front door. Inside was a very small drab lobby. One man sat at a desk next to a metal detector. That was going to be an issue. He was carrying his gun and a new Taser, as well as a few other things that might be hard to explain.

"Can I help you?" the man said. He was older, grey haired, and wearing a crisp looking uniform. He screamed "retired cop" to Mike.

"Umm, yeah…" Mike started looking man over. He could be this man in 30 years. "I'm here to see Agent Takahashi. I have some information for him."

"I'll give his office a call; just give me a minute." The man began reaching for the phone, when it rang. He gave Mike an apologetic look, and then into the phone he said, "Yes?"

It must have been Lizzie on the other end.

"Gas leak, you say," the guard said. He looked worried. Mike saw an opportunity to help sell the plan. He leaned in with his most concerned face and spoke in a low voice. "I wasn't sure, but I thought I smelled something when I walked in."

The guard flashed him a scared look then continued to talk on the phone. "Yes, OK, I'll pass on the warning." The guard hung up and stood. "Well this doesn't sound good."

"It doesn't smell good either. Did they ask you to clear the building?" Mike said, looking innocent. He honestly couldn't believe this was working.

The guard walked to the front entrance and took a few deep breaths. "Damn, I smell it too," he said, and walked back to the front desk.

"Can I help? I'm a cop," Mike offered.

"Not quite sure," the guard said. "This might be a little complicated." Then he noticed something on the computer and froze in place. Mike inhaled sharply, had they been made already? Somewhere deeper in the building, he heard a siren.

"Everything okay?" he asked.

The guard did not respond for several moments. Then looked back up at Mike. The guard was pale and sweating. "Hell," he said. "Of all the…no, it looks like we have a major issue." The guard drew his gun and Mike took a step back and started to raise his hands. "I'm going to have to ask you leave the building. Do me a favor: if anyone tries to come in, please keep them outside?"

"Um, okay. What are you going to do?" Mike was confused.

The guard turned away from Mike and started down the hall. The building lights flashed once and then went out. Somewhere far away another alarm sounded. The guard looked back towards Mike as red flashing lights came to life down the hallway. "Just get clear of the building," he repeated, and disappeared into the dark corridor.

"Sure," Mike said. He noted the red lights flashing in the hallway. He flashed back to College Hospital and swallowed hard. There were no demons here though, right? Just Ann, and she hardly counted.

He waited several moments for any sign of evacuation. Nothing happened. Something had gone wrong, and Mike didn't think it had anything to do with him. The plan had already gone to pieces before it had barely started. He would have to make do. With the guard gone, he now had access to the building.

His mind made up, Mike dashed forward: his first order of business was to rescue Miller and Ann. From the plans Lizzie had dug up, there were several underground levels. If Mike were going to build a jail or maybe a lab to study the Fallen, he would start there. Or possibly in a secret cave behind a waterfall. One of those.

Unlike the mess of twists and turns that was College Hospital, this building was laid out in a pretty straightforward fashion. One main corridor branched off into offices to the right and left. The building was mostly empty, which made some sense: it certainly wasn't a main FBI headquarters. In fact, nowhere on the building was there any note the FBI was here. Or any marking for any company or government agency, for that matter. Perhaps this was intended to provide the place with some level of cover, but the lack of signage made the place stand out even more.

The staircase was easy to find and Mike quickly made his way down one flight of stairs. The next floor was less simple to navigate, as it appeared to be groups of holding cells. He appeared to be moving in the right direction. He continued on.

*****

Lizzie stood as still as possible, waiting for her masters to arrive. Some vague idea nagged at her. Shouldn't she be doing something else? Father had told her to wait, so she waited. But beyond that, there was something else, some half-formed memory. When she tried to focus on it, it slipped through her fingers. She was distracted by the sudden need to vomit again.

A large NJ Transit bus pulled into the small lot directly in front of where Lizzie waited. It stopped with a hiss of hydraulics and lowered itself to allow passengers to get out. The door opened to reveal the massive figure of Marduk, somehow contained in the driver's seat of the bus. The demon looked down at Lizzie and tipped his giant hat at her.

Asmodai was the first to step off, followed by Amon and Marduk. Lizzie bowed as they stood before her. It seemed like the right thing to do. The gesture was ruined when Lizzie again vomited black gunk at her master's feet.

"She is not well," Amon said, her voice sounding angry for a reason Lizzie did not understand.

Asmodai nodded and waved his hand behind him, signaling for others to exit the bus. The massive hairy forms of wolves lumbered out and streamed into the front of the building.

"I know," Asmodai said, turning back to Lizzie. "She suffers from the same malady our brother Ura did. The human's body was far too poisoned for the child to take hold and she will be dead very soon. But she has served her purpose." He patted Lizzie on the head and she gave him her best smile. "Perhaps she may perform one more task before she leaves this world."

"Of course, Father," Lizzie said, happy to please him.

# 16 - Getting the Band Back Together

There was blood on the floor and a man in the middle of the hallway. He was sprawled face down, his arms out in front of him, lying very still. Mike slowed at the sight and drew his gun. He wasn't sure if the man was dead or undead or something else. Mike had seen too many horror movies to ignore him. It was scary how much advice he was taking from movies of late.

Mike approached the man carefully and rolled him over with his boot. The man groaned. Mike bent over him, keeping the gun trained on the man. There was a pulse and it was red blood that trickled down his face.

He slapped the man gently on the cheek, but got no more response.

"Looks like I'm late to the action," he muttered to himself. Mike wondered if this meant Miller had already escaped or if something else was going down. He propped the man up against the wall. He considered calling for an ambulance, but decided it was probably better to wait until after he had committed kidnapping.

The blood seemed to be a trail of sorts, so he followed it. The trail was soon broken by many footprints. He was certainly onto something here. Everything led to another staircase heading down. Mike sighed loudly, checked his gun, and followed the trail.

*****

"Zombies!" Ann shouted back at Miller. She was weak, and even though her strength was quickly returning, she had no idea how she could handle these creatures as flesh and blood. There was certainly a downside to being human, but she couldn't change again, at least not for some time.

John Takahashi stepped out from behind a table and opened fire with a handgun. "So much for keeping a low profile," he muttered.

"There is a spot," Ann shouted, "on the back of their necks."

"I know, but it's hard to hit. Come on!" the agent yelled back, and pulled Ann back towards the other side of the lab. The crowd of undead shuffled forward, gnashing their teeth and screaming wildly.

Miller hobbled forward and drew a gun of his own. He fired three times and as many zombies hit the ground with a splat, tripping two more.

"The back of the neck you say?" Miller said, with a wink. He pulled the trigger again but the gun responded with only a click, announcing he was out of bullets. "Damn… Special Agent?"

"Just John, please," the FBI agent responded, as he tossed his own weapon to Miller. "You seem to be having better luck."

"Grab Dupré and get her to the other side of the lab," Miller shouted.

"She should be a bit more cooperative now. Ms. Ann, behind me please," he said, firing two more times. Ann and John obeyed. "You look lovely, by the way." Miller nodded at the lab coat.

"Well you know me and white," Ann said, flinching away from the gunfire. The wall of undead was closing in as Miller and Ann slowly gave ground. "Look, if we survive this, there is something you should know."

"Aye, lass, we have many things to talk about, but now is not the time." Three more zombies dropped to the ground, their necks cut neatly open. "It seems we're short on bullets and you picked a poor time to show us your pretty face."

"Couldn't be helped, Dupré brings out my bad side."

"That seems to be a common issue," Miller said. "This is about to get very personal, I don't suppose you have something sharp handy?"

There were only seven of the zombies left, shambling over their fallen comrades to reach them. Ann could change again, risk confronting that red rage; something inside of her almost wanted to. But fear kept the urge in check, at least until she understood Lilith's ability to influence her. No, there had to be a better way.

"Follow me." She tapped Miller on the shoulder. "We'll stop them with SCIENCE!" She tried not to giggle as she dashed through the lab. Stress did bad things to her mind.

Ann quickly spotted what she was looking for. "Gas… here we go." She grabbed a Bunsen burner and turned on the gas. A six-inch flame appeared from the end of the burner. "Hmm I was hoping for something a little more impressive. Hold this." She passed the burner to Miller, who grinned at it.

"Remarkable, but probably not the most effective," Miller said. He kicked out with his bad leg at an approaching zombie.

"I'm working on it," Ann shouted back. *Come on, there has to be something flammable here.* Ann lifted a jug of alcohol. Miller was waving the small flame at the zombies, to little effect.

Ann tore a pocket off her lab coat, sending the notebook skidding across the floor. "Damn!" She stuffed the pocket into the bottle, leaving plenty hanging outside.

"Here," she said, passing the bottle to Miller. "Light this." She dove for the notebook.

"What next?" Miller asked, holding the flaming bottle.

"Throw it," Ann yelled, "at them!"

"Ahh, I see." Miller tossed the bottle over the top of the lead zombie and into the group behind him. He then kicked the first zombie back into the rest of the group. The bottle actually exploded before it hit the ground, tossing bodies in every direction. Miller dove away, landing directly on top

Ann and pinning her to the ground.

When Ann opened her eyes, Miller was staring right at her, with a large grin on his face.

"Science is fun," he said. He rolled and helped her to her feet.

The blast had turned several zombies into flaming heaps on the ground. Two still twitched, trying to stand, although one was missing a leg and the other, both arms. The rest were still, as the fire ended them. The smell of burning flesh filled the room.

"Almost done." Miller noted the two remaining dead things. One slid across the floor hand over hand, while the other was trying to get to its feet by pushing up on a table with its chin. "I have to admire their spirit." He leaped forward and landed hard on the grounded zombie's head. It exploded like an overripe grape.

"Ew!" Ann shouted.

"Aye, perhaps not my greatest plan." He stomped hard on the black spot at the base of the neck, as the creature was still moving. It jerked, and Miller stomped again. At last, it was still.

The final zombie at last made it to a standing position. It turned towards Ann and screamed a moment before its face was cut in half by gunfire. Miller and Ann both spun to face the newcomer.

"I know that weapon," Miller laughed. "Samson!"

Mike Samson appeared through the smoke, rushing towards them. "Miller… Ann. Everyone okay?" he asked.

"Mike!" Ann yelled, happy to see another friendly face.

Miller grabbed Mike's hand and pumped it. "Glad you could join us; just didn't seem right without you at my side."

Ann threw her arms around him and kissed him on the cheek, then blushed a little. "The three of us, together again, in a building filled with monsters. Just like old times." She smiled at Mike, who smiled back.

"Yes and on that…" Miller said, "Mike, might I borrow that fine weapon of yours?"

Mike passed the gun without question and Miller fired it once, ending the remaining zombie's attempt to stand back up, face or no face.

"I'm glad to see you're both OK, but I need to find Renee Dupré," Mike said.

"Dupré? Why?" Ann asked.

As if to answer, a fire alarm sounded and all the sprinklers in the lab turned on.

"Crap," Ann said. "Follow me." She dashed to the other side of the lab to the same stairwell where she had seen John drag Dupré. She found the two at the base of the stairs. Dupré was weeping openly.

John looked at them as they approached. "What did you do to her?" he asked Miller.

"I showed her the truth." Miller shrugged in that vague mystery man way.

Mike took back his gun from Miller and pointed it at John. "She comes with me," he announced.

"I think we're going to have a problem then," came a new voice. Two men—the two Ann had saved from the zombies earlier—marched downstairs with their weapons pointed directly at Mike. "The lady stays here but you are going to have a very long stay in jail."

# 17 - Things get complicated

Mike swallowed hard as the two new men approached with their weapons drawn. It didn't matter; Dupré was the key to rescuing Sam. She was coming with him.

John Takahashi stepped between Mike and the two new men. "Everyone just calm down. I'm sure we can work this out without anyone else getting hurt," he said.

"Samson… what is going on?" Miller asked.

"They have Sam," Mike said. "Smith has Sam."

Miller's face darkened. "Why?" he asked.

"They want to get Dupré ," Mike's gun wavered over to the cursed woman, "and if that's what it takes to get my son back, that's what I'm going to do." He hoped he sounded more confident then he felt.

"Who is Smith?" Ann asked.

"The Infinitus," Dupré croaked. The entire party turned towards her.

"Who?" Ann asked.

"The man who has taken your friend's son works for a group called The Infinitus."

"Sounds like something out of Harry Potter," Ann offered.

Dupré looked at her with her ruined face. "A very powerful, very old band of Cursed," she explained. "I first met them, years ago, in Israel. Sometime later, we met again under slightly friendlier circumstances. They offered to help me in my research."

"Why don't you explain this 'research' to the whole group," Miller said.

Dupré looked at him with fear plain on her face. "All right," she said slowly. "Maybe it is time for that. Maybe it's time for the full story." Dupré swallowed hard and looked at each person in the stairwell. "I'm an old woman, much older than I look. In 1908, I was living in France with my husband when we we're attacked by the demon Asmodai. We were both tortured, then cursed, and forced to follow him. It was not long after that Asmodai was killed by Joseph Miller." Dupré paused and looked hard at Miller. "You, in some fashion."

"Aye, I remember that night. I had been tracking Asmodai for years."

"Yes, you and your crew, the 13th Unit they called themselves. Dallas was there that night and when Asmodai died, he rescued my husband Marcel on that very hilltop. Marcel had been freed from the Fallen's control, but he had been turned into a monster. Without the Fallen's power, there was no way he could turn human again. He was trapped as a beast.

"I wasn't there, I had been sent to retrieve something the demon wanted, I think the reason the demon had chosen my husband and myself. I never learned what it was though, as once freed from the Fallen's control I ran. Lucky for me, I had managed my retain my human form, such as it is.

"Dallas and Marcel found me days later. Together we spent years searching for a way to help Marcel change back. We found several other of the Cursed and helped them as well. After some time we met Abraham, and he joined us. But we never found a cure."

"So, you found a way to bring the Fallen back," Ann interjected.

"Yes, yes I did. After we found her." Dupré pointed to a skull on a table in the lab. Its jaw was missing, but where the top teeth would be, pointed needles jutted out in all directions. "Lilith, the mother of all monsters. You…" she pointed to Ann, "...in another fashion."

"No, not anymore," Ann said.

Dupré dismissed her with a hand. "It was supposed to be a controlled experiment. I had told Abraham where Lilith would reappear and he was to strike her down before she could bring about the rest of the Fallen. I had weakened her, thinking this would help. But Abraham did not strike Lilith down and all the Fallen were reborn."

"Even if Abraham had, all those people in the lab would still have been killed," Ann put in. "Their blood would still be on your hands."

"And I would do it again, if it would bring Marcel back to me." Dupré almost screamed the response.

Ann and Dupré stared hard at each other for a moment.

"What does have to do with Smith?" Mike broke in.

Dupré turned to face him. "The Infinitus help fund the research. The government, of course, would want nothing to do with it, even less with the human testing element. So a great deal of the money came from them. "

"They wanted to bring the Fallen back from the beginning. If they learned how to do that, they would be unstoppable," Miller said.

"They will never have it from me," Dupré said with a snarl. "I simply used them, a means to an end. No, the secret dies with me."

"That is tempting," Miller said in a low voice. "You've unleashed powers you don't understand. Hundreds of people are already dead from your ignorance and many, many more will die."

"I am well aware of what I've 'unleashed'," Dupré said. "It was never supposed to be like this. And you…" She pointed a finger at Miller "You shouldn't even exist."

"I get that often enough. But you know the truth of it now, don't you," Miller said.

Dupré nodded her head. "Dallas…Dallas always claimed you would be back. The fool went on and on about it, even proposed some theories how it worked. How a man could come back from the dead."

"So you never had an issue with The Fallen, but one immortal man is too much for you to believe?" Ann asked.

"The Fallen are not people. They are something else entirely. Something old, left over from another time. You cannot kill them; you can only destroy their bodies. They are as old as this planet, perhaps older. But him, he is some sort of ghost…" Dupré again glared at Miller.

"Enough." Miller raised his voice only slightly and Dupré flinched away from him.

Mike had seen Miller like this before: serious, commanding, his true age showing. It made him seem somehow less human. "Lower your weapons; we're all on the same side here," he said.

The two agents looked at each other and then back at the crowd. "It's not that simple," one of them said. "We have orders."

"Were you listening?" John said. "Dupré just admitted to murder, not to mention bringing back an Ancient Evil from the dead. If there isn't a law against that, we really need to add one."

"Takahashi, you know who her friends are. This isn't something you can make stick." The same man spoke again, although he did lower his gun slightly.

"Do as they say," Dupré said in a low tone. "For now."

The two men lowered their weapons the rest of the way.

"Good," John said. "You too." He turned toward Mike.

"Not a chance…" Mike said. "Not until I get back my son."

"Mike…" Ann stepped closer, touching him gently on the shoulder. "We'll get Sam back. All of us. And Dupré will get a nice fancy trial for her troubles."

"Yes, of course," John agreed with her.

Dupré gave John a hard glance. "It's good to know whose side you're on, Takahashi" she said.

"I'm on the side of the law," John said definitely.

From the stairwell above them, a door slammed open. There was the sound of many feet, and all heads turned to look.

"Wolves!" Miller shouted, leaping forward.

The two FBI men turned, but did not raise their weapons in time and were bowled over by the surge of werewolves.

Mike opened fired, choosing his shots carefully in the crowded stairwell. "Ann, they're after Ann!" he shouted, remembering Lizzie's story.

"Me? Why is everything after me today?" Ann complained, bringing two fists down on the head of a wolf and smashing it to the ground.

"Fall back," Miller yelled, kicking another and pushing forward.

Mike grabbed Dupré and tossed her back into the lab. The sprinklers were still on, making the tile floor slippery. He noted the big fire doors, which had not closed correctly.

"This way! We can close them in," Mike shouted.

John Takahashi jumped out of the stairwell next, his suit jacket torn, a wolf following close behind. Mike fired twice, hitting the wolf once in the neck and then in the head. It stumbled forward and dropped to the ground.

Miller leaped further up the stairs, smashing a knee into the face of the nearest wolf. It fell backwards, and Miller leaped away, to the next wolf. Mike could tell the man was enjoying this.

Ann, on the other hand, was struggling with her own wolf, holding the long clawed hands in check. The creature was perhaps three times her size, but Ann kept it at bay. Mike leaned forward and fired once, hitting the wolf in the side of the head. Ann tossed it aside. She glanced at Mike and flashed a smile of thanks, before diving forward up the stairs.

"No, Ann, this way!" Mike shouted. She and Miller were out of sight now, up the stairs. He couldn't abandon them. He started jamming more bullets into his gun.

The sound of machine gun fire rattled and Ann dashed around the corner, carrying one of the FBI agents over her shoulder. Miller appeared at the base of the stairs, firing into the crowd above them, grinning from ear to ear. He held one of the machine guns in one hand and a foot of the other FBI man in the other. He stepped backwards into the lab, firing short bursts and dragging the other man.

"Samson!" John yelled. "Help me with the door."

Mike obeyed and they pulled the fire doors shut.

Ann rushed to help as well, and the three of them did their best to keep the doors shut as the wolves threw their weight against them.

"This is just like old times," Ann quipped. She had several long bloody slashes on her face and arm. A large chunk of her side was missing, revealing the white scales underneath.

"Are you OK?" Mike had to ask.

"Yeah, Yeah I'm good." She looked down at herself. "It looks worse than it is. Just a little winded."

"Good," Miller declared, stepping in between them.

Mike noticed his limp for the first time, as he jammed the remains of a chair in between the door handles, attempting to jam them shut. "How is everyone else?"

The FBI agent that Ann had dragged in was getting to his feet. "I'm a little scraped up. Thanks to the lady there."

"That's two you owe me," Ann said.

"Two? You mean…" The color left his face…

"Yeah, I spend a lot of time with scales and wings these days. All the cool kids dress that way," Ann said, bracing the wall with her back.

"You're not human…," he muttered.

"Lucky for you," Ann fired back, and then turned back to John "Did these things escape their cells too?"

"They didn't come from here," Dupré said.

"That means…"

"The Fallen are here," Miller stated. "And they want Ann."

"Why do they want her?" John asked.

"Lizzie told me they wanted revenge on Ann for killing one of their own. They think Lilith has gone rogue and they intend on putting her down," Mike explained.

"Lizzie? You spoke with her? Is she OK?" Ann asked, concern creeping into her voice.

"She's right outside. She was supposed to be our getaway driver. She's fine though. Hopefully, she was smart enough to just stay in the car," Mike said.

"You brought her here?" Ann said, her anger barely contained.

"She wanted to help save you. She said she was sorry for something she said to you," Mike said. This silenced Ann for moment.

Miller was pacing back and forth in the room. "How many more men are in this building?" he asked.

"Most of the strike force was put in the hospital the other day, by you," John said. "There were just the four of us…"

"Three of us. Stone is gone," said the FBI agent. John rushed to his side, checking the fallen man's pulse.

"Damn," John muttered. "There is also Burns and the man at the front desk, Reck."

"That's it?" asked Mike.

"It's a small team. We can call in other agents when required, but they are all at the main FBI branch," John responded.

"All right. We need to find those two men and get everyone clear. First, we need weapons. Then we find those two men, and then you let me do what I do. This weapon is nearly spent." Miller held up his gun.

"Weapons we can do. We have a storeroom a few floors up."

"Special Agent, lead on. Son, what's your name?" Miller asked, referring to the FBI agent still standing next to the dead man of the floor.

"Irons, Jack Irons," the man said slowly.

"Nice to have you with us," Miller said. "We need to leave your friend here. It's OK, they cannot harm him anymore."

Irons was slow to respond at first, but then he shook himself and looked hard at Miller. "Yeah… yes. Let's go."

Miller clapped him on the shoulder. "Good man. Everyone together."

The party formed up and headed to the other stairwell, with John and Miller in the lead. Irons and Mike took the rear, leaving Ann and Dupré together in the middle.

Ann gave Dupré a shove forward. "You will pay for what you did to me," Ann said to her. "After all this is done, I'm going to see you in jail for this."

Dupré looked back at her as they left the lab. "We'll see."

They went up the first flight of stairs, before Mike remembered the man he had seen in the hallway. "There's one man down here a bit," Mike stated.

"Ah yes, the man with the headache. We'll retrieve him first."

"I'll get him," Irons offered.

"Mike, go with him," Miller said. "We'll keep eye out here. Be fast." Miller took up position watching the bottom of the stairs in case the wolves broke through their barricade.

Mike glanced at Dupré.

"She's not going anywhere, Mike," Ann said, noticing the look.

"All right, he's not far," Mike said and began to follow Irons.

For a moment, there was a silence between the two men as they made their way forward. It had grown darker since Mike had been here, maybe 15 minutes ago.

Mike stated this observation out loud.

"Yeah, it's like the emergency lighting is dimming. Strange," Irons agreed.

"I remember something similar at College Hospital. I wonder if it has something to do with the Fallen."

"At this point, I think I would believe anything is possible. Are you friends with the girl?"

"Ann? Yeah, we've done this kinda thing together before," Mike said.

Irons shuddered visibly. "I saw her before: the most terrifying thing I ever seen, but she saved my ass."

"She's on the side of angels."

"If that's what an angel looks like, there is no way in Hell I'm going to Heaven."

"Here he is," Mike said, dashing forward. "Still out cold."

"Burns, man, wake up." Irons slapped the unconscious man, who responded with a groan.

The building trembled and the lights flickered out.

"What the hell?" Irons shouted.

"I think this is about to get more serious. Grab him." Mike dug through his coat and pulled out a flash light. "I'll light the way."

"Nice." Irons noted the light.

"Like I've said, I've done this before. Let's move."

The building trembled again and several ceiling titles dropped to the floor. Irons began to drag Burns back the way they came, but then stopped.

"Did you hear that?" he asked.

"What?"

"Like … distant thunder."

They froze and listened. Mike heard nothing but the sound of his own ragged breath. Then there was a crack, not like thunder, but like a tree snapping. Then it happened again, louder than the first time. The ground shook.

"Move!" Mike shouted. "Whatever it is, I don't want to meet it."

They began running. Mike pocketed his gun and helped to drag Burns. The noise followed them, getting louder, faster.

"What the hell is it?" Irons asked.

"I have no idea," Mike fired back.

"Samson! Mike Samson," a voice called from the beyond the darkness. Mike stiffened at the sound. He remembered that voice. It had once belonged to a doctor. One he had met a few weeks ago at College Hospital. The woman's name had been Black.

"Check that, I know exactly what it is! Run faster!" Mike flashed the light behind them. He could make out something black and scaly down the hall, approaching quickly.

"Samson, I smell you," it shouted. The thundering noise sped up as the demon began to run.

"Oh, hell," Mike muttered. They were almost at the stair well again. "Incoming!"

"Everyone up the stairs, now!" Miller was shouting. Mike turned into the stairwell and began dragging Burns up the stairs.

The doors exploded inward, throwing chunks of concrete with them. Mike stumbled, dropping Burns. Concrete dust billowed up the stairs, making it hard to breathe.

"Ah, there you are," came Black's inhuman voice. A massive black hand reached for him. It was the size of a tree trunk. Gunfire burst out from higher up the stairs, chewing the arm up.

Ann was beside him. "Go!" she said, helping Mike to his feet. She was stuffing something into his pocket, a red note book.

"Ann! No!" Miller's voice came down from above them.

"No, Miller. I have an old score to settle with this bitch. Get what you need to get and come back this way. I'll hold her off."

"Ann…" Mike glanced up at her.

"It's OK." She smiled at him and then launched herself down the flight of stairs.

# 18 - Girl Fight

Ann knew what must be done, but wondered how safe it would be to change shape again so soon. The exhaustion from the last transformation still lingered, and there was the rage that had almost cost Dupré her life. Despite this, she followed the path in her mind that Lilith had laid out for her.

The transformation to demon came as it had before, painless except for the strange sensation of stretching. Flesh tore, and she tossed the lab coat to the ground to make room for her rapidly expanding wings. The blinding anger returned, but now Ann focused it into quickening the conversion. A cold chill sunk down into her bones as her body finished rearranging itself. She stepped out into the dark beyond the ruined hallway, white scales glimmering red in the emergency lighting.

It was larger than last Ann had seen it. Not taller, but wider, filling the hallway with its girth. Its feet were giant hooves, and large pointed horns jutted out of the sides of its head. They had grown as well, now curling around once before again sticking forward. It had been waiting for her patiently. Ann couldn't be sure why, but she thought the demon was smiling.

"Melakh!" the demon shouted. Interesting, it called her by her real name.

"Looks like you've put on weight, Black," Ann said. "Typical."

"You don't have the law to protect you this time. You have blood on your hands and you'll pay with your immortal life."

"Bring it, horn head," Ann said. It was the best she could do; smack talk with other demons was a skill she was still working on.

Black's huge arms swung down toward her, but Ann was faster. She dashed forward and dove between the demon's legs, slashing with her own claws as she passed.

The creature howled and spun to face her, but Ann just ran.

"Run, my queen, run as fast as you can. I will crush you yet," the demon shouted after her.

*****

"We can't just leave her!" Mike shouted. Miller understood his frustration.

"We won't for long. We need weapons to fight the Fallen. As much as I hate to admit it, right now she is the best equipped of us to hold them off. Amon can bring this entire flight of stairs down before we could reach the top," Miller said.

"Five more stories up, the weapons are there. Even something special for Mr. Miller here," John put in.

"Oh a surprise ... for me? You shouldn't have," Miller said.

"Faster, we can't leave her alone with that thing for long," Mike said, dragging Burns behind him.

*****

The hallway was dark, but Ann still ran flat out, one clawed finger dragging against the wall to provide some clue when to turn. The darkness had grown intense as she ran farther down the hall. It reminded her of the hallways of College Hospital. It had not occurred to her then just how strange it was for that place to be so dark. Now she wondered if the demons themselves created it.

The various cuts and scratches from the wolves were already healed and she had recovered almost entirely from her transformation. The exhaustion was gone as well; apparently, her demon form was stronger. She was really hungry though, even if it was an odd time to crave cheeseburgers.

"You have your own family's blood on your hands, Lilith."

"Lilith is dead, Black," Ann shouted back over her shoulder. "And you're next on my list, on your way to join your buddy Ura." She hoped it sounded threatening, as she had no idea how she would kill the thing that had once been Vanessa Black. Her own tiny claws could barely break the flesh of the thing. Fire might work, but that was not readily available at the moment. If she could just keep her busy long enough, maybe the others would find something that could take it down.

The demon thundered behind her, each hoof striking the ground with explosive force. The hand that had been dragging against the wall suddenly touched open air, indicating the end of the hallway. She dove right, into the opening. The demon hit the wall seconds later, plowing through it. Hooved feet were apparently not great at cornering.

Ann continued to run, knowing full well this was not over yet. She decided to try and double back through the cells to the stairwell and meet the others. She took the next right. As she moved, she noticed it was getting easier to see. Yes, it certainly seemed the demon had something to do with the darkness. She made a mental note about that.

After a moment, Ann paused to listen. In the distance, she could still make out the thundering sounds of the demon's footsteps. It was close, far too close already. Ann took off again.

As she ran, she began to wonder how the demon had found her. Could the Fallen track her, like she could track them? That thought chilled her, but it didn't feel right. Mike had mentioned Lizzie, of all people, saying the Fallen wanted revenge on Ann. But how could Lizzie know this?

Then she noticed the red lights dimming again and slowed ever so slightly, glancing around. The noise was there, but not any louder. She was close to the stairway where she had originally confronted Amon.

The cell to the left burst open. Ann covered her face and dove to the ground. A chunk of concrete struck her back.

"I have you," Amon screamed. One giant black scaled hand grabbed Ann's arm and lifted her up. The bones in her captured arm were crushed nearly instantly. While it was in some strange way comforting to learn that she still had bones in her arms, the pain was unbelievable and Ann could not keep herself from screaming.

*****

Mike was just a few steps behind Dupré, Miller, and the FBI agents as they finally exited the stairway. Burns was slowing him down. It had been a lot of stairs, and even though he was in pretty good shape, that was no small feat. There was no way he was letting Dupré out his sight.

Miller dropped back from the crowd to quickly limp by his side. The smaller man appeared hurt, but it hadn't slowed him down much. "We'll get Sam back, Mike," Miller said. "I swear."

"You're damn right we will," Mike agreed, anger helping him move forward. Miller looked at him in an almost bemused fashion. It took a moment for Mike to see the pride in Miller's face.

"You have a plan, I take it?" Miller asked. The question seemed strange coming from him. "I know that look in a man's eye."

"Well, I did," Mike admitted. "But I didn't plan on a pack of werewolves and a demon showing up."

"No one ever does," Miller replied matter-of-factly. "No plan ever survives on a battlefield."

"I'm starting to see that," Mike agreed. The building shook and the group slowed to steady themselves. "Whoa! That must be some battle down there. We have to get back into the fight."

Miller continued to slow, glancing around the hallway. They were higher up, and here the building again just looked like a standard office building, with rows of small offices interspersed among a few larger meetings areas. This hallway was brightly lit, with sun shining through large paned windows.

"No lad, that didn't come from below us," Miller said. "I'm afraid we should have planned for demons, not just the one." He raised a finger and pointed.

"What?" Mike asked. He followed Miller's finger. Something large and black flashed past the window. Mike felt his stomach drop.

"Here!" John cried. But Mike and Miller did not turn to look. The building shook again and the beast, or at least part of it, came into view. It had the head of a giant snake, with fangs larger than Mike's arm. Behind the head, a huge black trunk of a body trailed off out of view.

"Oh my..." was all Mike managed to say, before Miller shoved him and his burden to the side. The head reared back, and then dove forward towards the window.

*****

"Yes, yes, scream! That's what I want to hear!" Amon flung Ann away and for a brief moment she was flying, before striking the wall and sliding to the floor. "Oh how I've looked forward to this. For thousands of years, he always chose you. You were his special one, his queen, his beloved."

Ann fought back the blackness that threatened to overwhelm her. Her head spun and her wounded arm burned.

"But now you have betrayed us," Amon cried. "You are cast out from our family and he is mine forever."

The black hands reached for Ann again, this time grabbing her around the waist. "I can see ..." Ann said with a groan, her one good arm pressing against the giant hand, trying not to be crushed, "... how hard it must be for you to get a date."

"Funny to the end, little queen." Amon shook her in response.

Ann dug into the big hand; blood poured from the small wounds she was capable of making. No, the claws were not working. She had to do something else or this would be her end. She opened her mouth as wide as she could and bit down on the demon's arm. Her long needle teeth sliced through the scales more easily than Ann had expected, and she ended up with a mouthful of fresh demon meat in her mouth. The demon did not taste like chicken at all.

Amon screamed in pain, and attempted to throw Ann off of itself. This only caused Ann to pull away a larger chunk of the demon's flesh as she went. Ann managed to hit a wall legs first, absorbing most of the impact, and then hit the ground awkwardly while still managing to get her legs under her. She spat a large meaty chunk out of her mouth and tried very hard not to vomit. Black blood ran down her chin and into her throat. It was not pleasant, but it did beat being crushed to death.

Ann had bitten the demon's wrist, which in a human is a place with a lot of blood. This apparently held true for demons as well, as the wound was gushing blood onto the floor while the demon screamed in pain. Ann knew this would not last long, but she took a moment to steady herself. Should she run, or try to press her advantage? While her head had stopped spinning, her arm still lay useless at her side, throbbing in just barely controllable pain. No, this was not a fight she could win close up. She took off again in a shambling run.

The monster shouted after her, its voice so twisted with rage that Ann could not make out the words. It was probably more of the "I'll kill you" variety or some such anyway. It didn't matter. The stairway was right ahead. That had to be enough time for the rest of the group to get far enough away.

The stairwell was not wide enough for her to use her wings, so instead she leaped up them in great bounds. Impressing herself with her own strength, she managed to cover half a flight of stairs in a single jump. She repeated this feat several times, but then stumbled and dropped to the ground.

The stairway shook and Amon smashed through the wall at the bottom of the stairwell. It was still screaming words that were not words, but so filled with hate their meaning was clear. One massive hand grabbed the bottom of the stairwell Ann was on and pulled. With a massive crack, it gave way. Ann leaped again, this time straight up, and snagged the railing to the next series of stairs with her one good hand. The demon leaped as well, bursting through the first flight of stairs, then the third. It threw one massive arm around Ann and pulled down. There was no way Ann's one arm could support the demon and herself. They fell together into the blackness below.

*****

It was as if all the air around Mike had become shards of broken glass. He swung an arm up over his face to protect his eyes, but he still must have been cut in a hundred places. Once the sound of breaking glass faded, Mike could hear the monstrous snake head hiss. He opened his eyes almost hesitantly, slowed by shock and fear.

Miller had none of these issues. He still had the machine gun, but no bullets. It did make a serviceable club, and Miller smashed one of the giant fangs with the butt of it. The snakehead jerked back, its giant reptile eyes blinking in shock. It dove at Miller, snapping at him, but the Ancient One danced out of the way.

"Move, man!" Miller shouted.

That was the jolt Mike needed to kick him into gear. He got to his feet, another hundred tiny shards of glass digging into him as he did so. Irons was suddenly by Burns' side, and Takahashi was throwing an arm around Mike's shoulder, helping him away. The snake thing sensed easier prey and dove at them. Miller saw this coming and jammed the barrel of the gun into the monster's eye. It let out a sound like a trumpet before retreating back outside the building, with Miller's gun still protruding from its eye.

"Weapon!" Miller demanded.

"Here, just up here," John yelled back. Miller glanced one more time at the retreating demon and followed them. He quickly caught up with Irons and helped carry Burns. They could hear the demon's odd growl and the building shook again. They had to move fast.

"I'm okay, I'm okay," Mike said, waving John away. "Where's Dupré?"

John glanced around the hallway. "Shit," was all he said.

Mike's heart sank. Without Dupré all this was for nothing. "We need to find her!" Mike said.

"I know, lad, but we need to live through this first," Miller said.

They entered a large room with rows and rows of guns. Mike could see Miller's face light up in excitement. The man grabbed two of the nearest machine guns off the rack, the large grin he always wore on his face doubling in size.

"Irons, show him how to reload one of those, I need to get something from the back," John said, running past them. Irons went about showing Miller everything about the gun.

Mike hung back, panting a bit. He hurt all over. The cuts were minor, but they stung, and blood was again trickling down his nose. He picked up a gun from the rack. He still had the Desert Eagle, but it only made sense to grab another weapon. He had to find Dupré again, help save Ann, and not get dead in the process. The building shook again, bringing that last point home.

"Ancient One," John called. "Miller, I mean. Here." The FBI agent held a massive sword in both arms and what looked like a leather belt. Mike heard Miller's breath catch, like he had just seen the love of his life after many, many years. And this being Miller, perhaps he just had.

"Is that…?" Miller asked.

"It is your sword. Your friend Dallas stored it away for you all these years," John said.

Miller took the sword and unsheathed it. It was a quite large, with a broad double-edged blade and a wire wrapped hilt. The metal did not look like it had been last used a hundred years ago. Although scarred and pitted, it gleamed, and Mike caught the reflection of his own tired bloody face in the blade.

"But how?"

"Dallas was FBI for many years. After he was gone, Dupré was still around. She managed to keep a small division going since then. No one took it that seriously though. That is, until two weeks ago. After the events at College Hospital, I went and found Dallas' old notes. He knew you would be back someday, and wanted to make sure you were well armed."

"Oh, Dallas, that old fox," Miller said, not taking his eyes from the sword.

"Here, take this as well." John passed him the long leather belt that acted as a shoulder strap. On the strap were three pouches, each carrying a smaller knife. Miller threw it on without a second thought. It was a little large for him though. John noticed this. "Ah yeah, sorry about that, I honestly thought you would be taller."

"No worries, lad. You have done me a great service. A great service indeed," Miller said, adjusting the strap. Somehow, the big sword's sheath connected to the shoulder strap as well, allowing the sword to cross it in the back. Miller readied himself without even looking. The various blades in place, he swung one machine gun over each shoulder and beamed happily at Mike. He looked like a short, Hispanic, very happy, Rambo.

John then approached Mike. "Did you find Lizzie?" he asked.

"Yeah, how did you…" Mike asked.

"Did she pass the videos to the police?" John interrupted.

Mike gave him a hard look. He had to be referring to the security videos in which Dupré was shown murdering Ann's co-workers. "Something like that," Mike said vaguely. That was the reason the FBI agent had wanted Mike to find Lizzie in the first place. It made sense, but he couldn't figure out why John wouldn't bring the old woman in himself.

"Excellent, I had hoped you would work out the meaning of my message."

"But how did you even know she had them?" Mike asked.

"Believe it or not, the FBI isn't very easy to hack. The moment she had those files, we knew about it. And I intend to give her a stern talking to. She and her little Chinese friend both. But since she was doing me a favor, I didn't make too much of a fuss," John explained.

"But why did she need to get the videos? Why didn't you just turn Dupré in if you knew she was a murderer?" Mike asked.

"Gentlemen, I do hate to interrupt, but there are several demons that need slicing to ribbons, a lass in distress, and a villain to catch. The explanations can wait," Miller cut in.

The walls rattled again, as if to reinforce Miller's words. Several weapons dropped to the ground from the force of the tremor.

"Of course," John said, grabbing his own weapon. It was a rocket-propelled grenade launcher, the kind of thing Mike had only seen before in movies and video games.

Miller turned towards Irons, who was watching over a semi-conscious Burns. "You stay here and mind your fallen comrade. It makes sense to keep this room as a base of operations. Guard it and him," Miller pointed at Burns, "with your life. The Fallen don't want you, but they can use you. Do not let them take you alive. Keep the door shut and your weapons loaded, and chances are you won't have an issue. Mike, Special Agent, you are with me," Miller commanded. "We're off to save the lass first."

Somewhere nearby, glass shattered and something heavy dropped to the ground.

"Duty calls," Miller quipped, and headed towards the door. "Special Agent, you have one more man out in the field, yes?"

"Yes, the man at the front desk," John said, following. Mike remembered the old security guard at the front desk. If that was the way the Fallen had gained access to the building, there wasn't much hope for him.

"Hmm, his chances are not good, but we'll try to pass back through that way," Miller said. They entered the hallway and headed in the direction of the stairwell. Mike kept his gun pointed straight ahead, but his eyes went to window where they had seen the giant snakehead.

An odd group of shadows danced across the floor and the shards of broken glass in front of them. Miller raised an arm in a motion to stop.

"Mike, you and Special Agent Takahashi may need to retrieve Ann by yourselves," Miller said.

"What is it?" John asked.

Miller almost sang the response. "The fourth…" he began as he dashed forward and raised a machine gun. The giant snakehead pounced, smashing through another pane of glass. The huge mouth snapped shut inches from Miller. The three men opened fire on the beast. The target was so large it was impossible to miss. The head reared back through the hole it created.

"...is a terrible serpent," Miller continued. A second snake head burst through the wall behind Mike and John. Both men turned and fired as more debris was thrown across the room. A third snakehead smashed through the ceiling directly above them.

"...with many heads," Miller finished.

Mike dove to the left, but John was stuck between the two snakes. He dropped to the ground, still firing his weapon. The heads converged on the man. John rolled forward and then flattened against the wall. One of the snake's fangs sliced through the back of his jacket.

Mike continued to fire; the weapon seemed to slow the monster down. Black blood rained down from hundreds of small holes riddling the demon's sides. Miller dove into the fray, his sword raised. He sliced just under the jaw of the closest snake head. The blade cut deep and blood left the demon like a geyser, spraying the room and collecting across the floor in a pool. The injured snakehead flopped back and forth before dropping to the ground. The remaining demon heads trumpeted their strange cry, and then all three retreated out the various holes in the building.

For a moment, the men stood motionless.

"Close one," Mike offered coolly.

"Yes," John agreed, bobbing his head.

In the distance, they could hear the demon's odd trumpet sounds.

"Lads, I'll clear the way. Get to Ann; help her as best you can," Miller said, stomping to the window.

"Miller, what are you…" Mike asked.

"I'm taking this disagreement outside, like a true gentleman," Miller interrupted.

"But we're five stories up," John protested.

Miller ignored him, leaping through a hole in the wall and out of the building.

*****

Ann considered for a few moments that she might have been blinded. Her eyes were open, of that she was sure. She must have lost consciousness briefly when she hit the ground. Something was crushing her legs, and her arms were pinned. It took a few more moments for her to understand that she was trapped under the wreckage of the stairwell. She tried to move, but she was unsuccessful. Suddenly, the weight lifted, as if on its own.

"Ah, there you are," the demon Amon said. There was a happy note in its voice, as if it had just found its favorite toy. It grabbed Ann by the head and yanked her free from the ruined stairwell.

Ann had no strength left to fight. She dangled limply in the demon's clutches, one arm ruined and the other twitching uselessly at her side. Blood ran down her face and chest from many small cuts. Several of her teeth were broken and she spat them out in the demon's general direction.

Amon had not fared much better in the collapsed stairwell. One of its great horns had been snapped off, and a large metal railing stuck out its back. It appeared to be unaware of its injuries, and quite happy with its captured prey.

"Where is your quick tongue now?" the demon said, as it shook her.

It took Ann several long moments to respond. Blood from the broken teeth flowed down her throat, and she choked before she could speak. "You know I'm not her. Not Lilith," Ann croaked.

The demon's smile broadened and it pulled her closer to its face as if it were about to share a rather delicious bit of gossip. "Oh, I guessed that some time ago. You are far too small and puny to be Lilith, but that hardly matters. It's what the others think that matters. Lilith's weakness has finally given me the opportunity to take what was always rightfully mine."

There was a burst of gunfire and then a shout. "Hey, ugly!"

Both Ann and the demon looked up to see Mike and John staring down from several stories up.

"Umm, I was referring to the demon. Not you, Ann," Mike awkwardly explained.

"Thanks, Mike," Ann muttered, too weak to shout. Had she not been in so much pain, she might have thought it was funny.

The two men opened fired again in short bursts. The demon snarled and raised an arm as the bullets rained down on it. Several bullets struck the arm that held Ann and she was suddenly dropped to the ground. She lay there panting trying to gather the strength to move as the demon backed away, trying to escape back into the hallway they had come in through. The wreckage of the stair well blocked its path.

This was Ann's chance, but she knew she did not have the strength to fight the beast. Escape was the only option. She glanced up. Four flights of stairs had collapsed, opening up the area above her. Now perhaps there was room for her to fly. She did not know where she found the strength, but she managed to pull herself up and stand. Then pulling even more from that hidden reserve of strength, she leaped into the air, wings spreading out as she rose.

The men saw what Ann was doing and stopped firing, not wanting to hit their ally. The demon saw this as well and screamed in anger. It tore the metal out of its back and chucked it at Ann like a misshapen spear.

Time slowed as Ann sped up out of the demon's reach. Sheer joy filled her as she grabbed the railing to the 5$^{th}$ stairwell, then that same joy vanished as the demon's projectile slammed into her lower back and pierced her. It erupted from her belly, painting black blood and intestines on the stairwell in front of her. Pain was everywhere; it was everything, as her vision flashed red then black. She felt her grip weaken then give way, as she once again began to fall back.

Two sets of strong arms grabbed her and began to drag her up over the railing. She could do nothing to help their labors; there was nothing she could do at all. She would have screamed in pain, but her lungs were filling with blood and all that she could manage was a weak gurgle.

Mike and John lifted her broken body over the railing and dragged her across the stairwell, each bump sending more waves of pain through her body. She struggled to keep conscious, fighting back against the darkness that kept crawling from all sides. Somewhere below, she could hear the demon screaming. It just barely registered in the back of her mind through the haze.

"Is she…" John's voice asked.

"She's alive" Mike said, his face coming into focus above her then fading away back into the darkness.

Yes, she was alive, but the pain made her wish otherwise.

"It's still down there, but it's suddenly too dark to see," John said. "It's like some kind of black fog just rolled in."

Ann's vision cleared again and she started hacking up blood. Mike was trying to remove the metal spear from her belly.

"Then don't aim," Mike countered. He stopped for a moment, pointing to something on John's back. "Is that a grenade launcher?"

"Right" John agreed. "I had forgotten I had it." He unslung the weapon from his back and went about readying it.

Mike looked down at Ann with those weary eyes and put two hands on the railing that impaled her. He put one foot down on her chest. Just before he began to pull, he said, "Ann, this is going to hurt."

He was right.

*****

Miller dropped like a stone. He had been doing a lot of that lately. It was becoming a bad habit. This time, though, Miller was enjoying himself. The wind whipped through his hair as he fell, sword out, ready to strike.

He saw the demon Marduk perched on the side of the building, as if it was a giant spider. This spider only had five legs, and the legs were technically heads. The center of the would-be giant spider was vaguely man shaped, with five trunks of the giant serpents springing forth from where each limb would be, with one extra coming from where a man's head had once been. Two of the serpent head "legs" were embedded in the building, holding it in place. The one head that Miller had wounded before lay flaccid below the trunk. The two remaining heads reared back, preparing to pluck him out of the air as he fell.

The problem with Marduk was not its massive girth as impressive as it was in this incarnation. The problem was all the damn heads. With the rest of the Fallen, one clean decapitation would be enough to end the battle. But in Marduk's case, five heads had to be removed to destroy the creature. It made for a messy, time-consuming bit of demon killing and Miller was currently a man with a lot on his plate. Still, this time, he had the right tools for the job, tools that he was dying to try out.

One of the giant snakeheads dove at Miller, but he ignored it; instead, he straightened his body to increase the speed of his dive. The head passed harmlessly over him, plowing instead into the building.

Miller's aim had been true, as it usually was, and his sword first struck one of the two legs holding Marduk in place. The weapon dug deep in the demon's hide, slowing Miller's descent as it did. Miller held on and threw his weight to the side of the impaled snakehead, towards the side of the building. The blade shifted with him; it cut sideways and opened a hefty wound in the side of the demon's trunk. The blade cut down in an arc of 90 degrees before Miller's momentum slowed.

The head Miller had attacked jerked back, releasing its hold on the wall, and the demon and Miller dropped several feet, before another head latched onto the building. The head Miller was attached to suddenly lifted straight up, trying to shake the Ancient One free. Miller held fast, and with each shake, the sword did more harm.

Another head dove in on Miller, trying to bite him and pull him free, as if he were a thorn in the creature's side. Miller released one hand, grabbed one of the guns on his chest, and fired a burst of gunfire at the approaching head. His aim was off, but several bullets found their mark, forcing the head to break off its attack.

Miller swung his legs to rest on the snake head that held his sword in place and pulled. The weapon came free with a pop. With his sword free, Miller again leaped into the sky, aiming for the lower of the two legs that kept the demon attached to the wall. This time, though, the demon was prepared and detached itself from the building. Miller missed the snakehead and instead embedded the sword into the building, inches below where the target snakehead had just been.

Undaunted by missing his target, Miller swung up into the hole in the building, grabbed both guns strapped to his chest, and opened fire on Marduk.

At this point, Miller was merely one story above ground and the demon dropped all the way to the earth as bullets tore into its various appendages. The trunk of the demon bounced once on the ground, then it gathered its heads into a hissing, trumpeting mass. Two of the heads lay limp behind it, wounded, but certainly not dead. No, Miller still had his work cut out for him.

The guns clicked empty, and for a moment, the demon and the demon hunter faced each other. Two heads rose to strike, and Miller pulled two throwing blades. The heads darted forward, but did not attack him, instead they struck the ground floor window below him.

The ground trembled as the rest of the demon followed the two heads inside and soon the entire creature vanished inside the building.

*****

Mike felt the railing begin to slide free. He trained his attention on Ann's very human eyes, which kept going in and out of focus on him. The woman demon could obviously not speak; her ruined face was frozen in the most frightful look of pain and terror Mike had ever seen.

The railing came out of Ann with a pop and Mike slipped back several feet, smacking his back against the other side of the hallway. He threw the railing away and rushed back to Ann's side.

She was convulsing now, as more blood than Mike ever thought a body could hold gushed out on to the floor. Then she was still.

He wasn't sure what else he could do for her. He gently lifted her head off the ground. Her eyes spun around the hallway and then met his, just for a moment, before they rolled back into her head. He thought she was dead, her body simply overwhelmed with the damage it had already taken. But then, just as before, the blood on the ground seemed to reverse direction and began to flow back into her. Her body shrank, the pin-like teeth fell away, and the wings vanished. Pale new flesh appeared where the open wound was and crawled up her tiny frame. In just a moment, she was again the woman Mike had met at College Hospital.

For a moment, he just held her. Then her eyes opened again and she looked at him. She spoke in a voice so small, Mike could just barely make it out. "Hey" was all she said.

"Hey" he said back, smiling. "I didn't think you were going to make it that time."

"Pssh, that was nothing" she said. Then her eyes widened slightly. "I'm naked, aren't I?"

Mike looked down at her for just a moment, and then they both blushed.

"Yep" he said, not knowing what else to say.

In the distance, something exploded and the building shook again. John was still fiddling with the rocket launcher, glancing nervously at the stairwell they had just dragged Ann out of.

Mike gently put Ann's head down on the ground and went to John's side. "You got it?" he asked.

John looked nervous. "Yes, I think so," John said. He pointed to an arrow on the side of the weapon. A note said "Point this way" on the side in clear black ink. "At least I know which way to point it."

"I take it this isn't a standard part of FBI training," Mike asked.

"Not even a little. I made sure we had one after I saw that thing come out of College Hospital and fly away. "

"Wait, you were there?" Mike asked.

"I was, at the end. I was across the street with Dupré when I saw the lights. Dupré was inside the building, apparently murdering innocent people, but I didn't know that at the time. I just saw that something was going on so I took a walk over, just in time to see some sort of dragon thing burst out of the building. The most surreal moment of my life…" Then, he paused a moment. "Well, at the time. It was the next day this whole department was reactivated and I started to learn all about the Fallen and I made sure we had one of these babies." He patted the rocket launcher. Then he glanced around. "Is it just me or is it getting darker in here?"

"It's coming!" Ann yelled from her spot on the floor.

The lights were suddenly winking out. Something cracked in the distance, metal tore, and then Amon was among them, its horned head just visible in the inky blackness of the stairwell. It stared at them for a brief moment, not even 50 feet away.

John pulled the trigger without thinking.

The sound that the rocket launcher made was terrible, far worse somehow than the sound the demon made when the rocket struck it. Mike just assumed he was dead when he heard it. At this range, the explosion from the rocket would kill them all without a doubt.

Except it didn't, and Mike didn't die.

He saw the rocket hit the demon dead on. A look of fear was obvious by the rocket's red glare, even on its inhuman face. The demon reached out a hand and almost caught the rocket, as if it John had tossed a fast ball at it while yelling "Think fast!". The demon staggered backwards as it made its reach and both the demon and the rocket stumbled back down the stairwell. It was just as the demon was out of view that the rocket decided to deliver its payload.

The explosion was enough to knock both men backwards several feet and coat them with a fine white powder of building material. The floor trembled, and for a moment Mike thought the whole thing might collapse, but short of a few ceiling tiles dropping to the ground, nothing happened.

"John?" Mike asked, his ears ringing.

"Here." John coughed.

"That was incredibly stupid," Mike said.

"Yes, it was. Sorry about that," John said.

"Ann?" Mike asked.

"Still here," Ann said.

Mike slowly stood and walked again to her side.

"But I may have a small problem," she said. There was sarcasm in her voice, but Mike noted real fear in her eyes.

"What's wrong?" Mike asked. Ann had not moved an inch since he had left her side.

"I can't move," she said, panic edging into her voice now.

# 19 - An Intersection

"My lord," Marcel said, as they approached the old building, "what in heaven's name is that?"

"The Fallen have arrived," Abraham said. A creature with five snakelike heads was climbing the building like a giant spider, each head tearing a 'foot hold' in the building as it made its way higher up the face of the building.

Abraham's taxi moved through a crowd of panicking people as they approached. This demon was attacking a building in broad daylight. Some people stood and stared; others ran for their lives. It seemed as if a great mob of people was in the park across the street from Renee's building.

"I never imagined they could get so large," Marcel said.

"Marduk is the largest of them, and this is a big incarnation. And so bold, attacking like this."

"Are they after Renee? Do you think they know what she's done?" Marcel asked.

The question was never answered, although, as both Cursed men watched, the demon lurched back, apparently hurt. One of the heads dropped limp and suddenly a man was leaping out of the building at the demon. The demon and man fought, suspended in the air, with a complete disregard for personal safety, not to mention the laws of physics.

"The Ancient One," Abraham muttered.

"Here? You think? Really?" Marcel said. He briefly thought back to his old friend, Samuel 'Dallas' Badow. How he would have loved to see this.

"There is only one man in all the world who would have attempted such a tactic and I imagine he is loving every moment of it."

"My lord." Marcel repeated. "We have to help."

Abraham looked doubtful, but nodded in agreement. He pulled the taxi over and they both got out. Marcel went for Abraham's bag in the trunk, as an older man in a security uniform stumbled into him, then kept running.

Marcel ignored the assault and ran to Abraham's side. The vampire was standing motionless, staring at the battle before him. Marcel looked at the vampire, then at the monster. Marcel knew Abraham could see. Not with his eyes, but something called the sight. The sight was something rare even among the Cursed. It allowed Abraham to see the Cursed, but also other things as well. Marcel wondered what the vampire was seeing now.

"Well?" he asked.

Abraham wrinkled his nose, placed his ancient top hat on his head and began to walk very slowly towards the building. "You assist the Ancient

One. I want to check on an associate of mine," the old Vampire said, with his usual rumble of voice. "Oh, and be sure to bring an axe. This will get messy," he added.

*****

The Ancient One was quite proud of himself, perched there on a sword he had embedded into a wall while fighting a five headed demon in free fall. It had been brilliant, if only someone other than the demon had seen it.

From his vantage point, he spared a moment to take in the area around him. To his right, there was a park. People were there, staring at the building, staring at him. So, he had an audience after all. Lovely. Several of the people seem to be holding items in front of them. Miller recognized them as cell phones. Mike had one that he refused to let Miller play with, brilliant devices. But what were they doing with the phones? Calling for help? If so, why did they have the devices so far away from them? Then Miller remembered they also worked as cameras. They were photographing him. Fantastic. When all of this was done, he would have to track them down and ask to view himself in action. That would be a first.

There was the sound of something wet hitting the window behind him and Miller instinctively dropped down from his perch. With one arm, he snagged the sword and yanked it free of the wall in one smooth motion before dropping the 10 feet or so to the ground. A moment later, there was a heat so intense Miller could barely stand even at a distance. The window cracked and then began to melt with a flash of the brightest white.

Miller stepped back, reloading his guns, as the remains of the window fell away. A well-dressed man was visible through the hole. By his side was a delightfully full figured Asian woman.

"Greetings, Ancient One," Asmodai said from above him. The demon looked far better than last time Miller had seen him. For one, he was now whole again, and he stared down at Miller with two working black eyes. The creature had grown comfortable in his new incarnation, with a smart haircut and well-tailored clothes. The woman next to him was Lizzie, Ann's friend. The woman was Cursed, but there was something odd about it. The curse waxed and waned, and the woman looked as if she could barely stand. Her clothes were stained with something black. She stood, slightly slumped over, next to her master, looking a little lost.

"Demon, I had thought our paths would cross again. I was wondering if I might get my pen back," Miller said, with a grin, referring to the writing instrument he had used to blind the demon two weeks back.

The demon smiled in a bemused way, but ignored the taunt. "It makes no difference. You cannot save her. The traitor queen will die. We will tear down this building, flush her and her allies out of their holes, and destroy them. You cannot stop us." With that, the demon turned and walked back into the building.

Miller put down his guns, confused. The demon had basically just told him his plan and walked away without a fight. Why would he want to do that? Unless, of course, the demon wanted Miller to know.

Miller shook his head. That didn't matter now. He needed to get back to the fight, and fast. He looked at the hole in the building in front of him. He could track Marduk into this building with no issue, but that would be like following a snake down its hole. No, he needed a different approach.

Miller ran along the edge of the building, looking for another way in.

"Hey, hey," someone shouted.

Miller turned to see a large elderly man, neatly dressed, running towards him with an axe. By the curse, Miller could tell the man was a wolf, and Miller drew the sword.

The man slowed, though, and raised a hand in peace. "Whoa, I'm here to help," the man said. "I've come with Abraham."

"Abraham is here?" Miller asked. "Where?"

"He has run off to be his usual mysterious self and left me to help you fight Marduk," the man said. "My name is Marcel Dupré and I'm very happy to finally meet you."

"Dupré? The husband?" Miller said.

"Yes, yes, I take you've met Renee. Is she well?" Marcel asked.

Miller pushed aside several rude comments. "Last I saw, yes. But there is no time. There are three Fallen in that building. My friends and your wife are in grave danger. I need to get a message to them. Do you have a phone?" Miller asked, with a little pride that he had remembered the name correctly.

"No I'm afraid I've not gotten one yet." Marcel sighed. Then his face lit up. "But I may have another way."

*****

They had covered Ann in John's button-up shirt. The big Japanese man had stripped down to his undershirt and still managed to look exactly like a stereotypical Fed. Ann decided it was the haircut. The shirt was long on her and nearly reached her knees. It made for an excellent cover up and Ann was thankful for it.

Mike dressed her, blushing the entire time.

Ann was blushing too, but she couldn't do much else. Feeling was slowing coming back to her lower regions, giving her hope that she was not permanently paralyzed.

Mike had suggested that Ann had simply overdone it. "After all,

"Mike explained, as they walked down the hall, "the last time you were hurt that badly, you slept for an entire day." Mike had her draped across his arms. One arm was under her neck and grabbing a shoulder, the other under her knees. It was the same position he had carried her two weeks ago, when grief had over taken her in College Hospital. That now seemed almost like a lifetime ago. Then she had curled up into him, taking what comfort the stranger could give her.

Now she could not move; even breathing was difficult. She wanted to throw her arms around him again now, but her body refused. The fact that she did want to, though, did not go unnoticed. She stared up into his worried, desperate eyes. She wanted to help him, save him for once.

Ann had really only known Mike in desperate situations. They had one nice conversation in his kitchen not so long ago, but she still wondered what he was like without the monsters. What was he like out for dinner, or out for a walk in the park. How was he in bed? Did he like "The Princess Bride"?

Ann stopped that train of thought. This was not the time and not the place. Still, though, in her head, it had been all Keith, all the time for so long. This was progress. She made a mental note: If they lived through this, she was taking Mike Samson out to dinner.

"You OK?" Mike asked.

"I…yeah...I was just far away," Ann said, coming back to the present. "Do you like the Princess Bride?"

"Um, what?" Mike asked, confusion covering his face.

"Never mind. Silly question," Ann said.

The three of them stopped in front of a large metal door and John began to tap on it. "Irons? We're back," John said.

The door slid open slowly, and the other FBI agent poked his head out. "Everyone OK?" he asked.

"For the most part," John said, entering the same room. "How is Burns?"

"I think he is coming to, but he isn't ready for much action yet," Irons answered. "Where is the little guy?"

"He stepped out for a bit," Mike said dryly.

Ann gave him a puzzled look at this remark, but didn't push it.

"Rest here, I think I need more ammo." Mike put Ann down near the wounded man, who was just showing signs of waking up. "You need anything?"

"Maybe pillow and a cup of hot chocolate?" she said.

"I'll call down for room service." Mike turned and left her.

Ann lay very still for a moment, looking down at her own feet. "Move your big toe," she said to herself, under her breath. Her big toe did not move.

The man next to her, however, did. His eyes were wide open, staring at her. "You," he said, his voice full of panic. "You're one of them. One of those monsters."

Ann worked very hard to turn to face him. To her surprise, her neck was behaving much better than her big toe. "Only part time," she said, as loud as she could, trying to be funny. "Just until I land my big acting job."

"How did you get out?" the man said.

"Burns?" The man named Irons was rushing to his side.

"She's escaped!" Burns pointed again to Ann.

"Well, the situation has changed a bit. How's your head?" Irons said.

"Hurts," the wounded man said.

"We're going to need to get out of here." Mike was talking again. "We need to get everyone out."

"I agree," said John. "Backup should arrive shortly and I would like to meet them."

"Well, we can't go down the stairs we came up, and taking the other stairs puts us near the werewolves again. And I'm certainly not taking an elevator," Mike said. "Do you know another way?"

"There is a fire escape, along the west side of the building," John said.

"Good, that's my best chance of catching up with Dupré."

"You won't have to look far," a new voice said.

Renee Dupré stood in the doorway. The wounds from the beating Ann had given her only a short time ago were almost already entirely healed. In one hand, she held the giant odd shaped gun, which she leveled directly at Mike Samson.

*****

Miller ran around to the front of the building. An idea was forming, but it was dangerous, not only to him, but to everyone else around him. Miller and Marcel ran between the building and its closest neighbor in an alleyway that was at least thirty feet wide. Large enough for a rather sizable demon to get into, but not large enough to maneuver easily. A collection of metal platforms with stairs ran along the outside of the building.

"An alternate route out?" Miller asked, in passing.

"The fire escape?" The far kinder Marcel Dupré said, jogging in front of him. "Yeah, I guess you could say that." Miller still had a slight limp slowing him down.

Something exploded inside the building and both men flinched as they ran. It was nothing they could see, but the building rattled.

"It's like a war in there," Marcel said.

"Aye, a very old war," Miller said, as they reached the front of the building.

"Here, just at the desk," Marcel said, opening the door and leading Miller in. "It's been a long time but… yes, it's still here." The man held up a strange device that looked vaguely gun-shaped.

"What is it?" Miller asked.

"Just hold the button and talk." He passed Miller the item. Miller did as he was told.

"Hello?" he said experimentally. He voiced boomed in the distance, echoing his greeting through the building. "Fantastic!" Miller said with a grin. And again his words echoed through the building, followed by a loud painful screech.

"Just let up on the button when you're not talking or you'll get some feedback," Marcel said, tapping Miller's hand. "You... ah... do know what you're doing, right?"

"Of course," Miller waved the man away. He always knew what he was doing; he just didn't know if it would work.

"Attention ladies and gentlemen," Miller said into the device.

*****

"Dupré?" said Mike with a shock "What?"

"Did you think I ran? I've been planning this fight for a hundred years now," Renee Dupré sneered. She had a bag slung over her shoulders and a handgun that made even Mike's Desert Eagle look like a pop gun.

John stepped in between them. "We're moving outside. We have wounded and we need to form up with our reinforcements, who should be on their way."

"Oh, I doubt that," said Renee Dupré. "Communications went out when the power went out. And you may have not noticed—because you're an idiot—but cell phones are not working."

Mike, John, and Irons all fished out cell phones at once and confirmed her story. Mike thought back to College Hospital; cell phones had worked there, but just barely.

"That seems a little strange for…," John started.

"Ancient Demons knocked out our phones?" Irons followed.

"Not the Fallen..." Renee Dupré jabbed the point of the gun as if stabbing Mike.

"Now wait a minute…," Mike started. He didn't know what to say and he stammered a bit, trying to come up with the right words.

"Don't be an idiot," Ann said from her spot on the floor. Mike noticed she was lifting up her head. "Mike's a cop, and no offense, but he wouldn't know how to do that sort of thing anyway."

Mike gave her a nervous glance. "Well not me technically," Mike said lamely. He watched Ann's eyes go wide with understanding.

"Ah ha, so you are working with the Fallen." Renee closed in, raising her gun. "I told you he couldn't be trusted. You made up that story of your son and…"

Rage boiled up inside Mike, burning through all the weariness and pain. He raised his own gun and stepped forward, close enough and fast enough to rest the barrel on Renee's forehead. "My son is in danger," he said, the anger almost dripping from his words. "And I do not work for the Fallen."

Renee was unimpressed.

Irons suddenly became unsure as well, lifting his gun up, but was not completely sure whom to aim it at. "Explain then, how the Fallen arrive moments after you barge in here on your mission. How did they find us?"

"I'm not sure yet," Mike said, softening a bit. A terrible possibility was coming to mind. There were only two ways the Fallen could have known where and when to attack so precisely. The first one was that Mike had incredibly bad luck, and while this was true in general, Mike didn't think it was likely. The other way was that there was a spy working for the Fallen. He only had one suspect. But how was that possible? He had seen Lizzie bleed. Mike noticed Irons point the gun in his direction.

Silence filled the room for a moment. Mike's gun was pointed at Renee, Renee and Irons had their weapons pointed at Mike. He needed Renee Dupré. He needed her to save Sam's life. There was nothing more important than that.

"Samson works with the Ancient One. There is no way the Ancient One… I mean, Miller, would work with the Fallen," John said, coming to Mike's defense.

"The Ancient One was caught consulting with this one," Renee said, her gun waving in Ann's direction.

"Ann's proven whose side she is on," John said. "Right?" That last comment was directed at Irons.

"Right," Irons agreed, with a stutter, lowering his gun just slightly. "Right!" he said more confidently a second time.

"Thank you," Ann said. "Mike, how did you know the Fallen wanted me dead?"

"Lizzie. Lizzie said the Fallen wanted you dead," Mike answered. Renee's gun had not moved, so he kept his still, but now his mind was racing, thinking how to talk himself out of this.

"Right, right. But how did Lizzie know?" Ann asked, her voice cracking a bit at the question. Ann knew the answer already.

"The demons, they had her, they captured her, used her to try and find you…"

"Oh, God," Ann said. "Please not Lizzie." Ann said this more to herself then to the rest.

"But I saved her. I checked her, I checked her." He looked away from Renee, to see the tears flowing down Ann's cheeks. "Her blood ran red. She was human. I swear it was red." Mike turned to back to face to Renee, who, to his surprise, lowered her gun as well.

"She may not have gone over completely," Renee said, matter-of-factly. "For all that matters, I believe you. And you." She said that last part to Ann. "I'm sorry for your friend." The words were almost kind, coming from the cruel old lady.

"Lizzie," Ann said, to no one in particular. She let out one small sob.

Mike lowered his gun as well. Had he failed Lizzie too? This was all too much.

"Good," John said. "If everyone has convinced themselves not to do the Fallen's job for them, we need to get out of here and get some help."

Mike stepped to Ann's side and knelt next to her. "I'm so sorry. I thought I saved her," Mike said. He skipped over the part where he'd lit Ann's old friend Cynthia on fire and shot her repeatedly. This was not the time.

Ann was crying, but silently. "Not your fault," she said. Then, after a long moment, she added, "But she's not dead yet. I can get her back. It's not too late. Who cursed her? I just need to kill the one that cursed her."

"Who do you think cursed her?" Mike asked. The answer was obvious to him. Only one of the Fallen would know anything of the relation between Ann and Lizzie.

Ann shook her head, not noticing how just a few moments ago such a movement had been impossible. "Keith, of course. Who else?" she said, with a grimace.

"Hello?" a voice crackled through the speaker on the wall. "Fantastic!" The same voice added. It was Miller. On a PA system? Then, the speaker screeched with feedback and everyone clapped their hands over their ears. The sound stopped, and for a moment, nothing happened, than Miller's voice began again. "Attention, ladies and gentlemen, it would appear some of the more demonic house guests have decided that large amounts of redecorations to this building are required. I would suggest that everyone not wanting to wipe the filth that is humanity from the face of the earth, head to the fire escape on the west side of the building…"

There was a hush, then another voice… "Fire Escape… oh yes, I see if there is a fire, yes now I recall they had them in London in the 1800s. Rather clever…"

The hush returned.

"No, I'm not crazy. I did go mad some time ago, but I'm much better now." Miller seemed to remember his place. "Ah-hem. If everyone of a non-demonic nature could head to the fire escape and get out of the building as soon as possible."

"What the hell was that?" Irons said.

"Miller is a little eccentric," Mike offered.

"But he just announced exactly where the demons will find us," Irons said.

"Yes, I imagine he did that on purpose," Mike said. "He's setting a trap for the Fallen."

"With us as bait," Renee pointed out.

"I didn't say it was a good trap," Mike offered.

"To be honest, I like it just fine." Renee Dupré smiled a cruel smile and lifted her weapon.

Something exploded below them and the building began to shake.

# 20 - Bringing Down the House

"Come now," Miller said. "Let us see how good you are with that axe."

"You have a plan?" Marcel asked.

"Something of idea," Miller admitted. He didn't really believe in plans. Plans hardly ever worked out. But an idea with just enough spark of imagination—those tended to be more his style.

They ran back outside, hurrying towards where they had first met.

"A wolf fighting on our side may be more helpful," Miller suggested.

"No no, I don't do that anymore," Marcel said, turning a pale white. "You have the sight then, like Abraham."

"Of course, where do you think he got it from?" Miller said, but Marcel just gave him a confused look. Miller ignored it and pointed upwards towards a group of black cables running to the side of the building next door. "Up there. I know those cables contain electricity; it can stun the Fallen."

"And kill everyone on that fire escape. That's high voltage and if the cable comes across the metal of the fire escape, it could be quite deadly to our friends."

"Well, perhaps not then." Miller looked back and forth. "This area is narrow; there isn't enough room for beast to fight here. The people inside are armed. If we can get everyone off the fire escape safely, we should be able to take Marduk quickly."

"That's risky. I thought you said there were three demons in there."

"Yes, we may have to deal with a second. But the demon Asmodai won't attack with the others?"

"Asmodai? Why?" Marcel asked.

"The same reason your wife unleashed the Fallen in the first place. Love."

*****

"What's happening?" Irons shouted.

The sudden shaking of the building brought Ann out of her stupor. She was still reeling from the revelation about Lizzie, but that would have to wait.

"The Fallen are on the move," Dupré announced.

"It's the big one," Mike said. "The multi-headed snake thing. Damn, I can't remember what Miller called it."

*Multi-headed snake thing?* Ann thought. *Leave Miller and Mike alone for 10 minutes to fight a raging demon to a standstill and I manage to miss the giant multi-headed snake thing? Figures.*

"The fire escape! Quickly!" John shouted. He bent down to help Burns up. Mike's resilient arms scooped Ann up as well, and in the moment, everyone was running again down the hallway. There was a growing sound coming from below, like the world's largest trash compactor had just kicked into overdrive. It was the sound of solid walls and glass being crushed and torn apart.

The group took a right through a small room, and then through a large metal door marked "Emergency Exit" in bright red letters. John pushed it open, to reveal a metal fire escape that ran down the side of the building in a series of narrow metal ladders, connected with short platforms at each door. It hardly looked safe on a normal day, but now, with the whole building buckling, it looked like suicide. There was no way Mike could carry Ann down there.

Mike paused and he let the FBI agents pass. Then Renee Dupré passed as well, shooting Ann a sour look as she went.

"Leave me!" Ann said. "You have Dupré. Save Sam!"

Mike grunted, her heroic act was apparently more annoying than helpful to him. "Like that's going to happen," he said. He swung her over one shoulder on her belly, one arm tucking the back of her knees close to him. She flopped helplessly behind him, like an oversized sack, in perhaps the most embarrassing position possible. Her ass was straight up in the air and her arms dangled uselessly, almost touching the ground. She almost wished he had just left her there.

The ground shook even harder and Mike grabbed a wall to steady himself. Ann looked up to see the floor give way. A moment later, a giant snakehead pushed its way through. "

"Oh, so that's what it looks like," Ann said, then shouted "Multi-headed snake thing! Six o'clock!"

Mike didn't turn to look, but nearly leaped through the door, grabbed the first railing, and dropped down the ladder one-handed. He slid down, his feet on the outside of the ladder, almost like a fireman down a pole. He hit the 4$^{th}$ floor platform hard and stumbled a bit. Ann's breath caught as she got a brief look at the ground below her.

"I have you," Mike said.

Ann decided not to respond and just closed her eyes. They only stayed closed for a moment though, as the sound of tearing metal forced her to look. The demon was bursting through the doorway above them. Metal and stone fell away, as the monster pushed through the slightly too small doorway. Then demon head was above them, its black eyes locked on Ann.

"Mike, you're going to want to run," Ann said.

"Run? Where to?" Mike said, sliding Ann back into his arms so she could see.

Burns was moving slowly, still staggering from his wounds. John and Irons were doing the best they could to move him along. They could not move forward, and both Mike and Ann looked back at the demon. Its eyes gleamed as it reared back, preparing to strike.

There was a sound like a cannon and the snakelike creature was knocked backwards, a large hole appearing right below one eye. Ann's head rang from the sound; it had been the same weapon that had nearly taken off her head earlier.

Renee Dupré fired another shot from her strange weapon, and the demon trumpeted in pain, retreating.

"Faster, man!" John shouted at Burns. "Just a few more floors to go."

Burns stepped off the ladder, dropping the last few feet to the next platform. John almost caught the wounded man and began to shepherd him to the next ladder, freeing up room for Dupré to start her descent to the ladder.

"We can do this, people. Keep moving!" John continued. He was wrong. They couldn't do it.

The wall in front of Burns vanished in a shower of rubble, as another demon head appeared. This wall must have supported the fire escape, as the construct was torn free of the building, snapping into two pieces near where the second snakehead had appeared. The top half, which was supporting Mike and Renee, tilted slowly, with the two supports just barely holding it into place, but the bottom half broke free completely. Ann watched in horror as the remaining FBI men clung to the falling fire escape for dear life. Burns fell backwards, but was caught by one leg by the snake creature. The demon swung the wounded man back into the air and then swallowed him whole. The other two men vanished from view as Ann's view was blocked by the appearance of a third demon head.

For a brief moment, neither Mike nor Dupré moved, unsure how to continue. The fire escape only led to a very painful-looking four story drop now.

"Quick, we can still try the stairs, just use this…" Ann started to say. She wanted them to get back inside through the emergency door on this level, but it was far too late for that. One more support snapped and the shifting of the fire escape suddenly accelerated. Mike lost his footing, then he lost Ann. They both dropped to the platform, which was suddenly twisting, dumping its contents towards the earth below. As they slid to the end of the platform, Mike snagged the railing with one hand, then caught Ann's wrist with the other. To her relief, Ann was able to grab Mike's wrist back. The move had been instinctive and her grasp was weak, but she had moved.

The platform slid further to be perpendicular with the ground. Dupré's ladder swung directly below them. The old woman was desperately trying to climb up the ladder, although Ann could not fathom what she was thinking. Suddenly, the ladder gave way and Dupré jumped, grabbing one of Ann's legs. Ann screamed in pain, and Mike grunted with the extra weight.

Through all of this, the demon watched with its multiple heads, ready to attack. Perhaps it was enjoying the ample display of destruction or maybe it just wanted to finish Ann at her weakest possible point.

For a moment, they hung in a human chain as the demon looked on, licking its snake lips. The twisted remains of the fire escape were held into place by only one remaining support, and the metal screamed, trying to support weight it was never meant to carry.

If only Ann could change. Now, more than ever, she needed her other self. She again reached into her mind and followed the path that led to her transformation, but she was still too weak. It was as if the doorway had been shut in her head and she simply didn't have the strength to push it open.

There was a wild scream and a flash of metal, as Joseph Miller appeared from nowhere, flying through the air. The sword he was carrying dug deep into the first head of the demon that had appeared. Another man, much older looking, dropped just moments after Miller. The new man lacked the Ancient One's grace, but he managed to get his axe embedded deep into the lowest head of the demon, keeping him from falling any farther.

"Marcel!" Renee Dupré shouted. "No!" So the other man was Marcel, the husband for whom Renee had caused so much damage trying to save.

Ann twisted to see him clearer as he hacked at the demon head he rode like a bull. She dropped an inch, then another. She looked up: the metal support was slowly sliding out of the wall. Then, with a loud crack, it pulled free, sending the remains of the fire escape, Mike, Ann, and Renee hurtling to the ground below.

*****

Marcel had followed the Ancient One blindly up the fire escape of the neighboring building. He was still in awe after meeting this mythical man, but the conversation with the PA system had worried him. Miller didn't seem all there. But he was the Ancient One that his friend Dallas had raved about so many years before, so he was going to cut the man some slack. This particular fire escape did not lead all the way to the roof, but when they reached the top platform, Miller ran at the wall and jumped up, catching a handhold on the edge of the roof easily. This was made even more impressive by the obvious damage to Miller's leg. He pulled himself over with ease, then reached an arm down for Marcel.

"Come on, then. Time is against us," the Ancient One said and Marcel took the offered hand. In a moment, Marcel was on top of the building. On the other side of the roof, just out of sight, it sounded as if the world might be ending.

"Now, what's the plan?" Marcel asked, taking stock of the situation.

Miller ignored him and dashed across the roof, freeing his sword as he went. He vaulted over the edge of the building with a yell.

Marcel stood looking just for a moment. Yes, now he was sure the Ancient One was mad as a hatter. He ran to the edge of the building. The massive demon Marduk had smashed the fire escape to the ground, and Marcel's wife hung onto the leg of a young bald woman, suspended in the air, four stories up. He needed to act quickly if he was going to save her. Miller was slashing away at the nearest head.

"Well, when in Rome," Marcel said, pulling the axe free. He took a deep breath and leapt.

*****

As they dropped, it occurred to Ann that she didn't need to change completely. She had seen Keith only use his wings, keeping the rest of his form human. No, not Keith: Asmodai. She focused on that then, just trying for that, pushing with her mind. It did not budge.

Mike pulled her toward him, perhaps in some vain heroic attempt to take the force of the fall. They intertwined briefly, almost like an embrace, perhaps a hint of what might have been, or might be. Ann returned the hold and pulled the man close, her mind slipping back away from the path.

It was then that Ann exploded. At least, that's what it felt like. The muscles and bones in her back suddenly rearranged themselves and her wings sprung from her back, growing and stretching out in an instant. The pain was unbearable; none of her other transformations had even come close to this kind of agony. The pain was welcome though, as Ann was sure dropping four stories and then being eaten by a demon would hurt more.

Ann screamed, as every nerve, every muscle protested as she flew. She managed to flap twice, but could not do it again. Tears filled her eyes as she strained to fight through the pain and escape.

"Just glide, just glide." It was Mike's voice. "We're almost there." It was a calming voice against the storm that was in her mind and all around her. She focused on just keeping the wings outstretched. They were falling—she registered that— but slower.

Renee hit the ground first, pitching them forward. Mike and Ann hit a moment later, rolling into a ball. They stopped with Mike on top of her, looking down at her with those big dark sad eyes.

He was saying something, but she couldn't make it out. After a moment, she noticed she was still screaming and forced herself to stop.

"You did it," Mike said, had been trying to say for some time now.

Ann was panting hard, the pain in her back already fading, but the weakness was still there. "We're not dead?" she asked, just to be sure.

"Not yet," Mike said, rolling off of her.

No, he was right. It hurt way too much for them to be dead.

"Are you all right?" he asked.

"No," Ann answered honestly. Her back burned in new and interesting ways.

"You could have just let me drop. You probably would have survived," Mike said, with his voice full of concern.

"Like that's going to happen," Ann said.

*****

Joseph Miller was loving this. There was so much about this new world he didn't understand, but fighting a giant demon while suspended many feet about the ground—that he knew, and there was nothing else like it. He was made for this.

He didn't think Marcel Dupré was having as much fun. The Cursed man held his ground though, or at least his axe, and he bashed the weapon continuously on one of Marduk's heads. At one point, the axe became stuck. Marcel drew a large pistol and fired it repeatedly, while using the trapped armament to steady himself.

Miller kept the other two heads busy, leaping between the two, hacking away as best he could, as the heads continued to try and make a meal of him. He had been eaten a few times; it was not a nice death. He had no interest in repeating it.

He saw the fire escape holding his friends fall away and held his breath a long moment, until Ann went and flew away. Truly an astounding woman, making a fantastic escape. The demon didn't much care for it though. One of the heads struck out to end it, but Miller was there, unloading the guns into the side of the monster's snout. It flinched away from the gunfire and turned back to face him. It bared its teeth and dove at Miller, but Miller dove right back, leaping onto its snout and plunging his blade between the demon's eyes.

The snakehead stiffened, then dropped, but Miller was already leaping again, this time towards a nearby window. He stabbed out with his sword, destroying the glass as he entered the building. He tucked into a roll, bounced to his feet, and sprinted back to the window. The demon followed a moment later, its wounds healing already. The head passed Miller by inches, so close he could feel the odd wet heat of its scales against his face. Miller raised the sword above his head, before the demon could change direction, and chopped down, bringing the weapon in a full arc to hit the floor.

Marduk trumpeted in pain as a geyser of black blood erupted from the new wound. It yanked its head out of the building and away from Miller.

Miller paused, watching. If he could get to the trunk of the beast where the limbs combined, Miller could end this quickly. It couldn't be far from where that wounded limb had just withdrawn to.

"Try and keep him entertained!" Miller shouted, waving at Marcel. The Cursed man gave Miller a confused look, but then again, no one ever enjoyed being the distraction.

Miller made a mental note of the position of the demon's limbs. There was one at the 5th floor, and one on the 3rd. The wounded head that had just retreated had disappeared through a window on the 2nd floor. That would suggest the demon's core was near there. If this was true and since Miller was on the 4th floor that meant there had to be an undefended section of the beast nearby. Miller shook his head, demon snake logic was very complicated.

Miller dashed out to the hallway and made a left. He kicked in the next door; nothing was there. He spotted Marcel through the window in the distance. The two remaining heads now both focused on him. The one he had mounted was trying to buck him off while the second was going to snatch Marcel between his teeth. Miller didn't have much time.

He dashed back out to the hall. The next room was a bathroom but in the center was a black scaled trunk thicker than most trees. It went through the floor, tearing a hole in white tiles, straight up through the ceiling. Water was jetting out from a nearby broken sink. Miller smiled, gripped the sword with two hands, and swung with all his might.

Again, the sword dug deep, but even Miller could not cut all the way through in one swing. Miller heard the monster scream its odd trumpet scream. It first jerked forward, lifting the sword and Miller upward. Then, as the blood really began to flow, the demon jerked backwards, bringing Miller and his sword down towards the ground. The Ancient One had barely freed the weapon when the wounded section of the beast disappeared below him. He pulled back the sword and waited. In a moment, the head appeared, and Miller struck again, catching it under its jaw. Blood gushed and Marduk screamed again, but did not stop its descent. This time, Miller did not free the weapon in time and it was yanked from his hands, vanishing into the hole below.

"Damn," Miller muttered. There was no way he was going to let such a fine weapon go. He looked around the room. Following the head back directly down its hole was beyond dangerous; he needed a little extra protection. A metal door lay on the ground, smashed free of a bathroom stall from the demon's entrance through the room. That would work.

Miller quickly reloaded the guns on his chest and grabbed the door. It was just slightly smaller than the hole the creature had made. He tucked it close to his chest and then dove into the pit.

His stomach lurched as he fell straight down through the hole in the floor directly below. He braced himself for impact, just in case he was wrong. But he wasn't wrong. Demons were never one to pass on an easy meal, and just as Miller predicted, Marduk struck back up the hole and chomped down on him as he fell. Well, not so much on Miller as on the metal door. Miller kicked off the makeshift shield just as it entered the beast's cave-like mouth and jumped free. Instead of delicious demon hunter flesh (and he had been told several times he was quite tasty), the demon choked on a solid metal door. Disappointing to the demon, yes, but priceless to the demon hunter.

Miller hit the ground and rolled, coming up with guns blazing. This was the place he was looking for. The walls of the room were smashed flat and three wounded demon heads lay curled around one trunk, joining the creature's spider-like body together. Black blood was everywhere. It spread out in all directions, and spilled down the holes the monster had created.

First, Miller needed his sword back. It jutted out of the side of the head that was currently busy choking on the bathroom stall door. Miller ran towards it, still firing the guns. When he got close, he dropped the guns to his sides and leaped for the sword, snagging it out of the air.

The head thrashed back and forth, trying to dislodge the metal door in its throat. Miller hung on, digging the sword in deeper with each swing of the monster's head. He was smashed through the ceiling, then thrown to the floor, but he held on and the sword cut deeper into the creature's trunk. Miller was lifted up again, but he vaulted up and kicked off the ceiling, using the force to deepen the blade even further. The beast trumpeted and flopped to the ground, throwing Miller on his back. Air exploded from Miller's lungs and his head swam. For a moment, both demon and demon hunter lay prone, but Miller recovered faster, getting to his feet and setting himself to finish his grim work. He pulled and the sword came free with a gush of ooze. Then Miller raised it above his head. The head twitched as if trying to escape, but Miller brought the sword down and finally cut the head off completely.

The trunk thrashed wildly, spraying gore, and the other heads trumpeted in pain. Miller stepped back, panting hard. The exertion of the day was finally beginning to catch up with him. He turned to face the rest of the beast. He recognized the two heads he had wounded earlier in their first exchange; one was completely still, while the other was recovering and looked at him with one working eye. One head was slithering away, attempting to drag the rest of it with it, but it was bleeding badly and trumpeting weakly. One head was still outside; the one Marcel Dupré was apparently keeping busy, and it could prove to be the most dangerous.

"Well, well, well," Miller said, beginning to walk towards the trunk. "You were a fantastic beast, but I'm afraid there is no place for your kind here. I know you've had a long day; I've had a long day. How about we finish this quietly? I am sure this battle will live in song for centuries. Well, not song anymore. Samson says now everything is on something called 'Youtube'" Miller said with a shrug. "I'm sure it's quite brilliant."

The demon ignored him, as demons were wont to do when they were fleeing for their lives. The one moving head bit hard on a wall and dragged the rest of itself forward. The wall twisted from the weight, then was torn free. The demon spat it out and slithered on to the next one. It occurred to Miller that the building could probably only take so much of this damage before collapsing into a heap, with him in the middle. He needed to finish this quickly. He filled his lungs with a great gasp of air and pushed the pain of his body away. He screamed a battle cry, something he had learned in ancient Japan, raised the sword above his head, and charged.

He barreled across the room, not as fast as previously, but still with plenty of gusto. His scream ended when he brought the sword down on the trunk, where once a human arm was. It cleaved through completely in one stroke, as here the demon was much thinner. He lifted the sword over his head again, with a yell of triumph.

And that's exactly when the werewolves decided to make their attack.

*****

Marcel Dupré held on to his axe for dear life. For the first time, he missed his wolf form and almost shifted back to it. The extra strength and the claws could very well save his life. But he had worked too hard to be human again; he could not risk that. Instead, he did his best with his axe and his gun. The axe seemed to work, but it constantly got stuck, which turned out to be a good thing, as it was the only way Marcel managed to stay on the beast. Luckily, the demon seemed far more focused on the Ancient One than on him. Then Miller left, vanishing inside the building. There was no way Marcel could follow, so he continued to hack away at the one demon head he was stuck on. With Miller gone, another head seemed to finally take notice of him and struck out at him. Marcel repelled it with a gunshot to the nose. It stopped its attack and shook its head, then tried again. Marcel readied another shot, but never got the chance. The demon stopped in mid strike and spasmed. Suddenly, it reversed its course and retreated back into the building.

Marcel took a moment to appreciate his good fortune, but the one demon head still outside wanted none of that. It smashed itself against the side of building, trying to scrape Marcel off, as a bear might try and scrape off annoying fleas with tree bark. Marcel barely managed to roll to the opposite side of the demon, holding on for dear life. The demon head shifted and smashed the other side of its trunk into the wall, but again Marcel rolled to the opposite side, barely avoiding being crushed.

He could not keep this up much longer. A thought occurred to him, and he dug into his pocket for one of the stakes he carried. They were designed for vampires, and he had used a similar one to dispatch the vampire named King earlier. They were his and Renee's take on the classic method of dispatching vampires, with a modern twist to help make up the difference between myth and reality. These stakes were basically oversized needles, which injected a large dose of flammable liquid into the vampire, once impaled. If the plunger made it all way to the end, it lit the liquid with a small spark, causing instantly charred vampire. They had never considered trying it out on the Fallen, but it certainly couldn't hurt.

Marcel plunged the weapon into the demon's side and pushed the plunger all the way in. There was a small flash and the smell of burnt flesh wafted to him. Cooked demon was not a pleasant scent. Marcel then clicked the back of the stake off, allowing more oxygen into the wound, and a flame leaped out. The demon screamed in pain and again struck the wall. This time Marcel was not even close to being crushed, but he almost lost his grip on the axe.

Satisfied with the results of the first stake, Marcel tried again, this time aiming for the demon's eye. The demon screamed again and struck the wall once more. But this time, the wall gave away and for a moment, Marcel was inside the building. Then he was tumbling down with a mixture of brick and steel.

*****

"Must hack faster," Miller muttered, raising the sword to slice free another head of the demon. This one might have once been a human leg, but it was hard to tell now.

Behind him, the wolves raced forward. There were at least eight of them. It was the same group that had attacked them in the stairwell earlier. In the back of Miller's mind, he had known he would have to deal with the rest of the pack again at some point, but now really wasn't the best of times.

They bounded forth from the far end of the room in a line, racing to defend their demonic master from death by slicing. There were two more heads to dispose of and the demon would be gone until their next encounter, which hopefully would involve a much smaller incarnation.

Miller only needed another minute, but he only had a few seconds. The sword cut down again and another limb died. The last remaining head was still outside the building. Miller raised the sword above his head to finish the fight, when the first wolf reached him. It tackled him, knocking Miller away from the wounded demon.

The sword was knocked free of Miller's hand and skidded several feet away on the slick, blood soaked floor. Miller hit the ground a moment after, rolling with the beast, keeping the claws and deadly fangs away from any body part Miller planned on using again. The wolf was a woman, dressed in the remains of a uniform form something called Starbucks. She smelled faintly of coffee and death.

Miller had wrestled with thousands of wolves over the years and had gotten quite good at keeping them at bay. One wolf he could handle. But when the second and the third piled on, he began to get a little worried.

The wolves turned out not to be the major issue though, as a moment later, the last functional head of the demon burst through the ceiling and the outside wall. It did not strike Miller, but dropped to the floor, bringing brick and metal and plaster with it.

The building, at that moment, had apparently reached its limit of being beaten, blown up, and crushed, and it decided it would just collapse. The ceiling and the outer wall crumpled in a heap, burying demon, werewolf, and demon hunter alike.

# 21- Taking the Show on the Road

Mike pulled himself up onto shaky feet. Every inch of him hurt. Ann lay on the ground. She was moving again, but slowly. Her ability to recover was nothing short of amazing. Renee Dupré was getting to her feet as well. Mike took stock. His rifle was gone, dropped somewhere on the crazed escape from the building. He still had the Desert Eagle, the Taser, and the flashlight.

Above them, the demon battled Miller and another man while suspended in air. Mike had fought at Miller's side several times now, but he had never seen anything like this. The Ancient One leaped from one part of the demon to the next, gleefully defying gravity, striking the monster again and again with the broad sword. It was as if all the other battles Mike had seen were the warm ups and this was the main event. Mike felt useless.

"Amazing," Renee Dupré said. "Dallas was right." Her voice had a touch of awe. "But this is impossible…"

"Little sister, haven't you learned by now? Nothing is impossible."

Mike and Renee spun to face to the new voice.

"Abraham? " Ann said weakly from the ground. "You're in one piece again. Way to go."

Abraham suddenly looked down as if noticing Ann for the first time. "Oh it wasn't anything a good meal couldn't fix," the vampire said with a smile. "Looks like you could use one yourself."

"You!" Renee snarled. "You were supposed to keep Marcel safe! Now he is up there with that madman."

"Marcel is his own man, and family or not, I owe you nothing now, woman." Abraham spat the words.

"What?" Renee said, anger instantly turning to fear. Her face turned a pale white, and when she started again to speak, it was in a much kinder tone. "Abraham, please. I meant no offense…"

Abraham cut her off with a dismissive hand. "No more Little Sister. No more. You'll reap the seeds you've sown soon enough."

"Wait, you call her little sister too?" Ann chimed in, but she was generally ignored by the crowd.

"Mr. Samson. I see you did not do as I requested. Was the bar not to your liking?" Abraham said, turning towards Mike.

Mike reached for his gun, but did not draw it.

"Wait, Mike, you and Abraham?" Ann asked.

"I did what I had to do to save my son. Are we going to have a problem here?" Mike asked. The last thing Mike wanted was another fight, but if that's what it would take, he was prepared.

Abraham made no move though. In fact he seemed far more displeased with Renee than with Mike.

"Earlier today, I tried to find your son myself, but I failed." Abraham began. "Now it seems you're almost out of time." To bring this point home, Abraham reached into a pocket and pulled out an old watch. He did not look at it directly, but dragged a finger across the face and then nodded. "Yes, very close indeed. You have your hostage."

"Really?" Mike was a little surprised at this.

"I have friends in low places, as the saying goes. Or, in my case, friends in high places. Renee, you will go with him and do everything in your power to help save the boy."

"But, but I don't understand. Now is the time for our revenge against…" Renee started, but Abraham cut her off again.

He raised his low singsong voice to almost a shout. "Child, you will do as you're bid. You have much to answer for. Marcel knows, too."

"What?" Renee seemed to go even paler. "Oh no."

"You'll let us clean up your mess. Now, run along." Abraham turned back to Mike. "As I was saying, you have your hostage. I will do everything in my power to assist you once I have finished here. However, for this service, I require one boon from you."

"All right," Mike said slowly. "What do you want?"

Abraham pointed a bony finger at Ann. "You must protect this one with your life. Any harm that falls on her, will also fall to you," Abraham said. "You will get her someplace safe before the next stage of this little adventure of yours begins. Agreed?"

Mike nodded. He already had planned on that anyway. "Of course. But why are you doing this? Why are you helping me?" Mike asked.

"A son should have his father," Abraham said. "And a father should have his son."

"Well that certainly clears it up," Ann quipped from the ground. "Don't I get a say in this?" Apparently, the answer was no, as Abraham ignored Ann's request.

"Now, where is Smith planning on making the trade?" the vampire asked and Mike told him.

"Ah… of course. Typical Smith," Abraham said. "Go. Go now, but be careful. Smith is not to be trusted or taken lightly. I can't imagine he plans on letting you walk away from all this."

"I know. I have a plan," Mike said, trying to sound confident. It was hard to sound tough when you could hardly stand. Abraham just smiled and started to walk towards the fighting.

"Go. And Renee, be good. I'll be watching," Abraham said, without looking back.

Mike checked his watch, which was now scratched and covered in dust. It still worked though, and it didn't have any good news for him. Abraham was right; they had to go. Mike looked back to the battle. Large chunks of the building were flying as the demon hunter and demon battled. Mike had planned on Miller, but maybe it was better this way. There were sirens in the distance. It was time for him to go. He bent over and picked Ann up.

The little woman threw an arm around his neck. "Leave me. Lizzie is still here. I have to save her," Ann said.

"You heard the vampire. You come with me. Miller will save your friend. Besides, what are you going to do to help? You can't even stand."

Ann made an angry sound in her throat, but did not argue further.

"You coming?" Mike asked, turning back to Renee Dupré.

The old woman still looked pale. "I… I…" She had trouble starting and then in a smaller voice she added. "Yes." Then, very slowly, she followed Mike to the car.

*****

"Rise and shine, little brother. Play time is over," Abraham's voice chided Marcel. Marcel opened his eyes slowly. The old vampire stood above him, one ragged old shoe poking Marcel in the ribs.

"What happened?" Marcel asked, sitting up. He hurt, but to his surprise, not that badly. He was on the ground, covered in brick dust and a few stray chunks of debris. He glanced back up at the building. The demon was gone, as was a large chunk of the building. An entire third of the building had collapsed, leaving the remaining structure looking like an odd 'L' shape. "Is it dead?" Marcel added.

"One can only pray. Come on now. We've got to be moving on. Places to go," Abraham said. Marcel noticed he was carrying a large man who looked like he possibly worked for the federal government.

"Who's that?" Marcel asked, getting to his feet. He marveled again at how little he hurt.

"This is one John Takahashi. He has more to do in this little adventure, but he apparently needs a hospital first."

"And Renee, where is she? I lost her in all the confusion," Marcel asked.

"Alive and well, for now, but running a little errand. We'll meet up with her shortly, once we take care of my friend here."

Marcel shook his head in confusion. He then noticed the sound of sirens. "And the Ancient One?" Marcel asked.

Abraham nodded towards the collapsed building. "In there."

"We need to help him," Marcel said.

"Oh, I'm sure he'll be fine. I've arranged for him to catch up with us later. But right now, we have to go. Things are about to get very complicated around these parts and I'm not one for explanations," Abraham said, turning away and heading back to the car.

"Yes. That is true. You were never really good at those," Marcel said, and began to follow.

# 22 - How to Keep a Good Demon Hunter Down

The police arrived just in time to see the collapse. There had been something there, something outside the building, but no one could say quite what it was. Then it was gone, as several floors collapsed, spilling debris out across the street.

Reports had said there were monsters. Monsters seemed a vague term to Officer Matt Durgen. Most of the time, Matt would have laughed at that kind of report, but so many people had called it in. And then there was that incident at the hospital in Newark a few weeks back. People had called in some strange things that day and so many people had died. Suddenly, monster attacks were not so funny.

And another odd thing, people had said their cell phones had stopped working a few minutes before the monsters appeared. Several had reported that they had to get quite a distance away from the scene before their phones would work again.

And there were different monsters. Several hairy apes with claws apparently drove up to this building in a bus. Then there was the giant spider creature that was supposed to be four stories tall.

It all seemed unreal, but the reports kept coming in. Matt hadn't been far—just a few blocks away; he'd been directing traffic around a construction job. After the third call, he jumped into the squad car to check it out. He was the second officer on the scene and as he arrived, he saw the building partly collapse.

"Did you see it?" a man shouted, as Matt stepped out of the car. It was an older man; he looked like he maybe was a security guard.

"I saw the building collapse," Matt admitted. Another police car was screeching to halt behind. *Good, the more backup the better.*

"No, not the building. The thing; the giant black snake thing," the security man said. He was nearly hysterical.

Matt had seen something. Just for a moment. But he didn't think he had seen that. Officer Reynolds appeared in the car behind Matt.

"What the hell is going on here?" Reynolds demanded.

Matt didn't know what to tell him.

"Did you see it?" the security guard asked again.

Reynolds looked to Matt, who just shrugged.

"Sir, we're going to need you to calm down and tell us exactly what's happening," Reynolds said.

Matt glanced around. There was no one else close to the building. In the distance, there was a park where a large crowd hung back, just watching.

"That! That! You see that, don't you!" the security guard said, pointing. Both Matt and Reynolds followed the pointing finger.

"That I do see," Reynolds said.

"What in…" Matt started, but he couldn't quite finish. It was like a lizard, a huge black long tailed lizard with long wings. It leaped off the building into the air. In its clutches was a person. Matt couldn't quite make out the details, but he thought it might have been a woman, and he was sure the hair was black.

The monster paid them no attention; it just drifted away with its cargo.

"Is that what did all this?" Matt asked, nodding to the ruined building.

"No," the security guard said. "No, that did!"

Out of the rubble, one giant black snakehead rose. Large chunks of brick fell, and the thing freed itself. It was a monster. A real live escapee from a Godzilla movie, here in Trenton, NJ. Matt just watched, stunned, as this impossible thing freed itself.

"Shoot it!" the security man demanded.

Matt glanced down at his pistol. It didn't even seem worth trying.

The monster dropped to the ground, part of its thick trunk crushing a NJ Transit bus as it landed. At the end its body was a tangled black mass that looked like it might have been other snake creatures. It remained on the second floor as the creature recovered itself, then it dropped to the ground with a force that nearly knocked Matt off his feet. The demon seemed hurt, as it moved slowly and there were large gashes with black blood oozing out.

Reynolds opened fire, unloading his pistol in nine shots. The first few did not faze the creature, but the last few seemed to annoy it. It turned towards them and raised its head as a snake would, right before it was about to grab a mouse. Matt raised his gun as well, but backed up. He didn't mean to back up, but under the gaze of that giant thing, some natural instinct was kicking in. His hands shook and he couldn't quite pull the trigger.

Reynolds didn't have that problem. He kept pulling the trigger on his already empty gun.

The snakehead dove right at them, its mouth wide open and displaying eight crooked fangs.

"Marduk!" a man shouted in the distance. "We're not done yet!"

The monster spun around on itself, to look back at the building from which it came. There was a man amid the wreckage on the second floor, a very strange little man carrying a massive sword. Two guns were strapped onto his chest and he was covered in something black.

The snake creature went for this man with a yell that sounded oddly like it had swallowed a brass band. The new man did not flinch away, but charged right back at the creature that was several times his size. He brought the sword above his head, and just as he was about to leap into the monster's mouth, he rolled away, throwing the sword aside. He then leaped at the monster's trunk, while pulling two much smaller knives from a band that ran across his chest. The two small blades dug in, and the strange man slid down the monster, as if it was a particularly terrifying children's slide. The man hit the ground right near where the sword had landed. He dropped the two smaller blades, snatched up the larger weapon, and brought it down directly on the section the beast had been dragging behind it.

The snakehead trumpeted wildly, its body thrashing so hard that it knocked over the nearby bus. It reared up, one last time, then collapsed to the ground and moved no more.

"Now that was a fight!" the man said. He staggered suddenly, then dropped to one knee.

For a moment, Matt just watched the strange man. Several other officers had arrived, just in time. They all milled around towards the back, unsure of what they had seen. Then the man noticed them.

"Well, hello there, lads," the man said. His accent was almost Scottish and he wore a huge grin. "Don't be afraid of my friend here. It took some doing, but he won't hurt anyone again for a long time." He patted the trunk for effect. "Joseph Miller is the name."

Matt went from staring at this Miller character to the beast he had killed and then back to Miller.

"What was that?" Matt finally managed to squeak out.

"That, lad, was a demon. The largest I've seen in a thousand years. Maybe more. Really hard to keep track sometimes."

"A demon…" Matt swallowed hard.

"Aye, that's a good lad, keeping talking, I find it helps."

"And you were in the building? When it collapsed?" someone else asked from behind Matt.

"Aye, but I'm fine. I had a protective layer of werewolves to keep me safe. Their fur is surprisingly soft."

No one was sure how to respond to that, but there was apparently no need, as the man continued just fine without one.

"I don't suppose any of you have any mead? Or know where I might find some? I've been looking for a good hearty drink for an eternity. "

No one replied. Then, finally, someone managed to add something. "Did he say werewolves?"

"Oh yes… speaking of them, I doubt that was enough to keep them down for long. You all might want to keep an eye out for those." Miller stood. He still held the sword in hand, but he kept it low. "I don't suppose anyone has seen a young woman, no hair, sometimes has wings? Or a man, a little over six feet tall, always looks depressed?"

"Sir, I'm going to have to ask you to drop the weapons," Reynolds said. He was finally coming around.

"Oh, I'd rather not. Ya see, there could be more of them."

Reynolds raised his gun again. "Sir I'm going to have to insist you drop your weapons."

Miller let the sword drop and raised his hands. "All right, lad, as long as no one uses the word 'freeze,' we won't have a problem," Miller said, pulling off the guns. "I'm only here to help."

In that moment, a memory clicked into Matt's mind. He dropped the gun, and pulled out his phone and flipped to the picture. Yes, there was no mistake. It was the guy. "I know who this is," Matt said. "His name is Andres Soliz. Newark PD and the FBI have been looking for him for almost two weeks now." Matt raised the gun. "Mr. Soliz, you are under arrest for murder!"

*****

All the fight had left Ann—which worked, since she had left the fight. She sat slumped in the front seat of the car. It seemed impossible, but feeling was coming back to her limbs. Her fingers now responded to her commands, albeit sluggishly. The sensation of pins and needles was all that came from her legs and feet, yet that was a far cry better than the blank nothingness that they replaced. Her back hurt, as if her spine was laced with fire. Worse still was Lizzie, missing and cursed, doing whatever things that demon wanted of her. Then, to add insult to injury, the woman who had caused all of this sat in the back seat behind her, and there wasn't a damn thing Ann could do to make her pay. She was not in a happy place, but she hadn't given up hope.

She had Mike and Miller. And Abraham. Mike was focused on rescuing his kid, which was understandable, but once that was done, and Ann had healed up, they could track Asmodai and Lizzie down. Renee Dupré would go to jail for what she had done and her life, such as it was, would go back to normal. Well, normal-ish.

Mike Samson sat in the driver's seat. The big man looked exhausted, but focused, as he picked his way through the streets of Trenton. He was mostly covered in a large dirty coat, filled with pockets, but the skin that did show was filled with small cuts and dried blood. His short hair was matted strangely. Other men might have looked bad like this, but Ann thought it just made Mike look even tougher. He didn't have any demonic power; he hadn't lived for a few thousand years. He just kicked ass the old fashioned way and Ann had to respect that.

"I want to help," Ann said finally. "I can still help rescue Sam."

"Not this time, Ann. You're hurt. I promised Abraham I would get you someplace safe and I will." Mike was fishing in his pocket for something.

"I can help you rescue Sam, then you can help me rescue Lizzie. It's a fair trade," Ann said.

Mike found his phone and began to fiddle.

"You know talking on your cell phone and driving is illegal, right?" Ann quipped.

Mike gave her an annoyed look, which softened at the end to a smile. "Yeah, I may have heard that before. Damn it, the phone is still not working," Mike said, dropping the phone back into his pocket.

"Still?"

"Yeah, Lizzie did something to knock cell phones out in the area, to keep the police off our backs until we could get out with Madame Dupré here." Mike jerked a finger back to the old woman, who was busy staring off into space.

"Ah, kidnapping. I hear all the kids are doing it," Ann quipped, but Mike ignored it.

"I have to get this call out," he said, more to himself than to Ann.

"Who are you going to call?" Ann said, following it silently with 'Ghostbusters?', but then she thought that maybe the time for jokes with Mike had ended.

"It's complicated," Mike grumbled, trying the phone again. "Look, about Lizzie…"

"I know, you're sorry, it's not your fault." Ann cut him off.

"No, not that. Well, yes that, but also, I might not be able to help with finding her."

"What?" Ann asked.

"I want to. And when you do find her, 'cause you will, tell her I'm sorry for this," Mike added.

"Tell her yourself. What's the plan Mike?" Ann asked. She really didn't like the sound of this.

"It's compli…"

"Don't you dare tell me it's complicated again," Ann said, suddenly a little angry. "I'm not some helpless idiot. You know that. Now, you are going to tell me what the plan is and how I can help. Or, so help me, vampires will be the least of your problems."

Renee Dupré laughed at this little outburst from the back seat. Ann turned to her as best she could. "You, you don't get to laugh," Ann said. She was mad at Dupré, but the old woman was unimpressed.

"Or what, you'll kill me?" Dupré said, with a defiant snarl. "I think if you could kill, I would already be dead at this point."

"You…" Ann started, but didn't have a witty follow up. She turned away in a huff.

"It's not a bad thing, child. Not wanting to kill," Dupré said. It wasn't the normal disgusted tone of voice that Renee Dupré seemed to use on her all the time. "Believe it or not, I was like that too. A doctor, when there weren't any women doctors. I wanted to save the world."

"But instead, you kill innocent people and, oh yeah, unleash an army of monsters into the world. Nice job, sport," Ann said.

"That was the price I paid to bring back the one I loved. The same way your friend here is risking everything to save the one he loves."

"Don't compare yourself to Mike Samson. You're not worthy to lick his boots. He is not directly responsible for the deaths of hundreds of people. He didn't change me into a monster," Ann shouted. Renee didn't seem to be bothered; she didn't seem angry or scared anymore, which made Ann even angrier.

"You care about him don't you?" Renee asked.

Ann hadn't expected this line of questioning. "Yes. Yes I do," Ann said. "I mean, as a friend," she added lamely.

"You seem to care about a lot of people."

"Surprising for an unholy demon?" Ann said.

"You're not a demon."

"Oh, now she gets it," Ann said. She tried to throw her arms above her head, but it only came out as a shrug.

"And if it matters, I am sorry," Renee said.

"You're sorry?" Ann said, now indignant and confused. "You're sorry? How can you possibly be sorry? All the damage you've done. You've taken everything from me. Keith, Lizzie, my hair. I should have killed you."

"You should have. But you didn't. Because you're not a monster," Renee said.

Mike joined in on the conversation. "She's right, you're not a monster. And you're not a helpless idiot. I'm sorry. Look, maybe there is something you can do to help me. Something safe, out of the way."

"Good," Ann said.

"And I can't tell you the plan. You would just try and talk me out of it," Mike said.

Ann did not respond. She really wanted to cross her arms and pout, but the best she could do was flop her arms into her lap. So, instead, she looked out the window, avoiding both of them.

Ann sat there fuming for several minutes, until something struck her.

"The notebook!" she said, anger giving way to curiosity.

"Oh yeah, here," Mike said, reaching into a larger pocket. He tossed the red notebook into Ann's lap. "What's so special about it?"

"Dallas's notebook? Where did you get that?" Renee Dupré leaned in.

"I have my sources," Ann said, opening the notebook.

"John Takahashi," Dupré said with a snarl.

"And my sources happen to be named John Takahashi, good guess. Actually, Miller gave it to me. Said it was important. I was dying to look in it before. But I was literally dying, so I didn't have a chance."

Ann threw open the small notebook. It was old, but not a hundred years old. It was quite clear the pages had been photocopied or reprinted in some way.

"So, this Dallas guy, he knew Miller, back a hundred years ago."

"Yes, Dallas was a dear friend to my husband and me. But he worked with the Ancient One before we met. He nearly worshipped the man, and I mocked him for it."

"'Cause you didn't believe he could exist," Mike jumped back in. "All the insane things you had already seen, and that one trips you up."

Dupré just grunted.

"Oh, he is the Ancient One," Mike said.

"Yeah, once you see him in action, there really isn't much doubt," Ann added. She was flipping through the book quickly. There were notes on all seven of the fallen, but mostly just vague details. The page on Asmodai had a drawing of a small man, then a picture of what looked like a dragon beneath.

"Did Dallas draw these?" Ann asked. Renee looked over her shoulder.

"Yes," she said between gritted teeth. "That's the demon Asmodai; that was what he looked like as a man. That's the man who…". A sob, escaped her lips, and Renee sat back down.

Ann turned in shock to look at her. Renee was shaking and her eyes were wet with tears, but she did not cry. Ann suddenly felt pity for the terrible woman. Something horrible had happened. Ann flipped the page and did not ask.

The next section seemed to be a collection of notes. There was a title, then several added comments below. It took several pages before Ann realized what she was looking at. The titles were names of myths, old stories, fairy tales, and a few actual books. The notes were filled with comments on how they could be Miller. She recognized a few: there was Beowulf—Abraham had mentioned that to her. There was the story of Orion and King Gilgamesh. And many, many more. There had to be hundreds of these stories, each one with some note of how Miller might fit in.

"This is insane. All these Myths. He worked Miller into all of them," Ann said.

"He used to say that every fairy tale had a grain of truth to it. He was obsessed with Mythology for years, the old fool." Renee said in a soft voice. "I still miss him."

"You're really not nice to anyone, are you?" Ann asked.

Renee laughed. "No, no I suppose not," she said.

"I've been reading up on myths the last few days," Mike said. "When I was in upstate NY with Miller, where I met Smith for the first time, we fought one of the Fallen named Gallu. She was what they based the story of Medusa on. Or somehow tied to it. And sirens at sea, I think. You know, those monsters that use to sing songs so beautiful that sailors would smash their boats into rocks, just trying to get closer. She actually froze me in place, like a statue. And that snake thing, it could have been a hydra. Like the one Hercules fought. "

"Ah, I never liked that show. I was more of a Xena fan," Ann quipped.

"And it's not just Greek mythology, but all myths, although maybe the Greek ones are the most famous. There was a Japanese one I read about dragons that sounds a lot like Asmodai," Mike continued.

"Pandora's box?" Ann said out loud. She knew that as well, but was unclear how the story of a woman opening a box and unleashing the world's greatest evils had anything to do with Miller. There was something else about that story that had bothered her. Pandora had unleashed all the evil in the box, except 'hope'. Hope remained trapped in the box and that was apparently evil? That didn't make any sense at all.

"Hold on," Mike said, looking at the rear view mirror. He looked over his shoulder, then back at the mirror.

"What is it?" Ann asked, her belly flip-flopping.

Mike stared for a long moment, but then shrugged. "Nothing, I thought I saw something, but no, I guess it was just a bird," he said.

"Geez, man. Don't do that. I'm not sure I can still have a heart attack, but I would rather not find out," Ann said.

Renee looked behind them, searching the skies, but didn't add anything.

"Yeah, sorry," Mike said.

But Ann noticed the extra glances to the rear view mirror and a sudden gain in speed. "You sure it's nothing?" Ann asked.

"Doesn't hurt to be a little extra paranoid these days," Mike said.

"No, no I guess not. " Ann said. "By the way, where are we going?" She saw Mike grimace at the question. "Or were you not going to tell me that either?"

"Smith picked the spot," Mike explained. "Someplace where no one goes anymore, but easy to get to."

"OK, so?"

"Smith picked the place, and I know you don't know him, but he is kind of a bastard," Mike continued.

"Hah!" Renee Dupré barked from the back seat. "Smith is one of the vilest creatures to walk the planet."

"So?" Ann asked. "Does he want to meet at a trash dump or

something?" Ann shrugged.

"No, I wish," Mike said. "No, we're going back to where this all started."

"You don't mean…"

"I mean College Hospital."

# 23 - What happens at Police Headquarters stays at Police Headquarters.

Earlier that Day

Mike had told them everything up to Smith taking away Sam. They knew the rest. The police found him and the ruined Mustang not long after Smith left. They arrested Mike on the spot, what else could they do?

"So that's it?" Mathews asked. "No dramatic conclusion? No big face off?"

Mike rubbed his sore wrists and then smiled. "Not yet."

"This man with your son, the—ahem—vampire, you think he'll just give 'im back, if you do what he says and kidnap this Dupré lady?" Johnson asked. The big black man stretched and stood.

"I doubt it. I'm pretty sure he wants to kill me and Sam," Mike said. "But I plan on taking him out first."

"So, you sit here and admit you're planning on murdering someone who may or may not be a federal agent, while under arrest in a police station," Mathews said.

"I didn't say murder. I want him arrested. We could pick him up on kidnapping at the very least. Public endangerment. I'm sure there are a few extra laws we can dig up," Mike said.

"Mike, we don't know anything about this guy. Don't get me wrong; we'll do whatever we can to help find your son, but…" Johnson said, but Mike interrupted.

"But what if you caught him in the act?"

"What, while you are trading Dupré for your son?" Johnson asked. He said it jokingly, but when Mike didn't respond, he said, "What, you would really go through with this? You're going to kidnap a woman who works for the FBI?"

"Consider it a citizen's arrest if you don't want to do it," Mike said. "We got her on murder charges and I would bet money she has something to do with College Hospital."

"Based on something your buddy said, who you said wasn't even human anymore," Mathews broke in. "You're going to risk everything you have on this? This is your career. This is your life, probably your son's life."

"Does this mean you believe me?" Mike asked.

"Hell no, but I have to admit it's a good story," Mathews said.

Mike turned away from him, back to Johnson. "You know what I'm saying is the truth. You've seen these things. Now, a lot of people died in that hospital; a lot of *our* people died in that hospital. Dupré and Smith are part of why that happened. You help me with this, we get justice for those people."

Mike tried to catch Johnson's eye, but the detective wouldn't look at him.

"Samson, do you even know how many laws you've broken already?" Mathews asked. "How many people have died? The fact that you're a cop isn't going to save you. We'll do what we can for your son, but if you think we're going to let you run off and kidnap an FBI agent…"

"Who is directly responsible for two murders and maybe linked to many more," Mike shouted.

"Who maybe is responsible… where's your proof?" Mathews shouted back.

"I can get proof. I just need time," Mike said, lowering his voice. He continued to try and catch Johnson's eye, but Johnson would not look at him. They weren't buying it.

"Listen, I'm desperate. I can't do this alone," Mike said.

"You can't do this at all," Mathews said. "I don't know if you just need help. Maybe you are suffering from some sort of post-traumatic stress syndrome." Mathews stood and leaned over the table. "Look, I read your file; I know what happened to your wife."

"She has nothing to do with this!" Mike shouted.

"Yeah, OK, maybe, maybe not. But you come in here spouting one of the most outrageous, if not highly entertaining, stories I've ever heard, and you expect us all just to do everything you ask, no matter how many laws you would have to break."

"My son… my friends. This is all real. You have to believe me. Johnson, you saw…"

Both Mathews and Mike turned to look at Johnson. After a moment, Johnson looked back up at them. "I'm sorry Mike, he's right," he said finally. It was almost like being slapped in the face.

"What?" Mike was stunned.

"We can't help you. Not without real proof. All we know for sure if that you smashed up your car pretty good and admit to helping a fugitive of the law. "

Mathews smiled at this. It was a triumphant smile. He had just won. "You should get comfortable Samson. You're going to be here for a while," he said and he headed to the door. "We done here?" he asked Johnson, as he opened the door.

"Yeah, we're done," Johnson said, and followed him out of the room. The door slammed shut behind them and Mike was alone.

"Damn it!" Mike slapped both hands down on the table. What had he been thinking? The police wouldn't just help him kidnap an FBI agent. There had to be something else, some other way out of this. Sam's life depended on it. Mike racked his brain, trying to think of some other tactic, some other trick he might use. Nothing came to him.

Then the door opened and Johnson stepped back in. "Here." He slid an envelope across the table.

"What's this?" Mike asked. He opened the envelope. Inside was his gun and his cell phone. "What's going on?"

"Mike, I know you're telling the truth, but you have to know any sane man isn't going to want to have anything to do with you, officially."

"Officially?" Mike asked.

"We, officially, don't know anything about you attempting to pick up Renee Dupré for questioning about any murders. We, officially, don't know how you escaped police custody. You just walked out and no one noticed."

"I did?" Mike asked, but he was smiling. "And un-officially? You just shut off the video camera on this room, didn't you?"

"Well, the interview was over, officially." Johnson nodded back. "Mathews isn't happy about it, but he'll get over it. Look, Mike, I want to help, but the best I can do is keep the dogs off your back for a while. Maybe 24 hours, tops. And, if in that time, you happen to round up this Smith character…"

"You'll bring in the cavalry."

"Well, if there's a big enough public disturbance, we'll investigate."

"In force?"

"You bet your life," Johnson said.

Mike put his head down on the table and breathed out a sigh of relief. "Thank you," he said.

"Mike, one more thing: Even if you pull this off, you know your career is over," Johnson said.

Mike froze just for a moment. "I… yeah, I was pretty sure…" Mike was having a hard time admitting that.

"Everything Mathews just said is true. And even though I can delay this, 'cause you're a cop and I know you are telling the truth, even though I want, more than anything, to nail the people who were really behind College Hospital and the Angel murders, that won't save you. This has gone too far. Understand me?" Johnson was looking Mike right in the eye.

"I understand," Mike said. His voice was steady. Now there was no turning back.

"Good, but first there may be another way. There is someone I think you should meet," Johnson said.

*****

Mike made his way quickly and quietly out of the police station. It had been surprisingly easy and no one paid him much mind. Johnson had told him to head around the corner once he got out of the station and Mike obeyed. There, just as Johnson had said, was an old, beaten looking taxi. Leaning on said taxi was a dead man. Mike had last seen him on the top floor of a building in Newark, right before he blasted a hole in Ann. Mike drew his gun. "What the hell is this?" he shouted.

The vampire was tall and wearing a faded old tux, complete with bow tie and large top hat. His eyes were hidden behind dark glasses. "They call me Abraham." The vampire tipped his hat at Mike. "I'm here to help."

# 24 - Identity

For the second time in twenty-four hours, Miller was a prisoner. He did not resist them; he did not want to hurt these men and he was too tired to put up much of a fight anyway. The police were much more polite than the Special Agent's men had been. They had him handcuffed, this time in the metal ones, and sat him in the back of one of the police cars, which was quite a fascinating vehicle, stuffed to the brim with all sorts of gadgets he did not understand. They did not close him in the car, but kept the door open. Several men stood by him at all times and asked him polite questions. Again, they referred to him as this 'Andres Soliz,' even though Miller corrected them often. They asked to see his identification, but Miller had nothing to show them. He was Joseph Miller, the Ancient One, the great hunter, and many other names. Come to think of it, it would be handy to have that written down someplace. He tended to forget himself.

The man who had originally arrested him stood nearby. He was quite apologetic about the whole thing, explaining that it was all procedure, and he was sure once they got it all sorted out that Miller would be free to go. The man was lying, but it was a nice lie, so Miller let it go.

"So, I'm sorry, can you walk me through this again? So this thing, this is a Fallen?" another officer asked.

"Not a Fallen; one of the Fallen. They are group of demons, very old, very evil," Miller explained helpfully.

"I can't believe I'm having this conversation. But then, after seeing, that… demon, I guess I could believe anything," the officer said.

"Aye, it does help having such a fine example right here." The demon was shrinking already. Miller knew the Fallen would decay quickly once killed, but he bet this one would leave a very interesting set of bones behind.

"And you say there are more of these?"

"There are seven altogether. But several of them have already been dealt with by me and my companions," Miller answered.

"And they look like that thing?" the officer asked.

"Oh, no; they all look much different, although none look all that friendly," Miller said.

"Hey, is this my prisoner?" a new man asked. He was dressed differently, without the uniform. He was a tall, wide black man, with a concerned look on his face. He was nervous about something. He flashed a badge, just like Miller had seen Mike do a few times.

"You are from Newark? Damn, you got here fast. Yeah, this is your guy."

"I was already on my way to collect him, well before your call came in. The FBI was holding him in that building over there. I guess it didn't work out," the new man said.

"I guess not. We have more questions for him ourselves, so far nothing he has told us has made much sense. Particularly not that thing." The officer pointed to the demon's corpse.

"Yeah, that's just creepy," the Newark man said. "Although, you should see some of the stuff we've had in Newark lately. Strange days."

"No kidding," the first officer said. "We'll want to ask him some more questions of our own at some point."

"Sure, of course. No problem," the Newark man said. "Come with me, Mr. Miller, if you would." The man waved Miller to follow him.

"Soliz," added the first officer. "His name is Soliz."

"No, it's not," Miller said.

"Of course it is," the man said. "Mr. Soliz, if you wouldn't mind, please follow me."

There was a sharp cry followed by the general cries of 'what's that?' and comments about God. Miller stiffened and both the Newark man and Miller looked back towards the building. One large black shape was pulling itself free of the wreckage on the second floor. It was a wolf, one of the ones that had tried to save Marduk. The creature dropped to the ground floor with all the grace of a wounded dog. It slowly got to its feet as a second wolf joined it, then a third and a forth. It was time Miller got back to work.

"Sir, if you would be so kind. It appears duty calls." Miller appealed to the Newark man, pushing out his handcuffs. The Newark man looked at the cuffs then back at the wolves. Miller followed. The wolves were not fighting, they were fleeing. Several of the police opened fire with hand guns, but nothing large enough even to slow the creatures down. In moments, all four wolves had dashed away. One officer chased behind, but then thought better of it and let the monsters go.

"Not yet," the Newark man said and beckoned Miller to follow. Miller lowered his bound hands and did as he told. He needed to escape, get back in the fight, but something had been telling him to wait. Miller had quite a few voices in his head, and years of practice had taught him which ones to ignore and which ones to heed. This was one of the ones to listen to.

The Newark man gathered Miller's weapons and headed to his car. He did not speak again until they were both seated in the car, Miller in the back, and he in the front.

"I have him," the man suddenly said.

"Have who?" Miller asked.

"Nothing serious. Most of the blood on him isn't human," the man continued.

Miller looked around the car. Was he talking to someone else? The police car pulled into the street, waved on by another police officer in uniform. "I am sorry. Are you speaking to me?"

"No, I'll take care of him. Don't worry."

Take care of him? Well, he could use a good cleaning, perhaps a bit of shave, but he had work to do. These demons did not slay themselves. He had seen Mike and Ann escape, but what had happened to the Special Agent? And little Sam was still in trouble. No, he had work to do, and he needed to get to it now, little voice or no

"I don't mean to be a bother…" Miller began.

"Right, one second," the police officer cut him off. He pushed a button on the device, in his ear. "Sorry about that, had to check in with a friend."

"Oh, is that a phone? In your ear?" Miller asked. That explained it. He was still getting use to this technology thing.

"Yes, I guess it would seem a little odd to you. Don't worry about it."

"Friend, I have a job to do… wait, what do you mean by that?" Miller said.

"Well, a lot has changed in a hundred years," the police officer said.

"Who are you?" Miller said. "How do you know that?"

"I'm a friend of a friend, Mr. Miller. And I'm here to help. My name is Eric Johnson. I work in the same department as your friend, Mike Samson," the man said.

"So, Mike told you about me? And you believed him?" Miller asked.

"I was at College Hospital. I saw the thing that came out of there. It killed a lot of my friends."

"I see," Miller said. He didn't actually see. "Has Mike asked for your help?"

"Well, yes. But it's a little bit more complicated than that. You see, me and several other officers want nothing more than to help you and Mike. But, as it turns out, you're wanted for murder and Mike apparently just kidnapped a government official. Legally, that puts us in a bit of a sticky wicket," Johnson said.

"I see," Miller repeated, still befuddled. "You know the creature that killed your friends is still out there. I can stop it."

"Oh, trust me, I'm aware. Your demonic friends aren't even trying to stay under cover. I've already got 15 calls about a giant bird thing. People don't know what to make of it," Johnson said.

"I can track it. Let me hunt the beast," Miller said, leaning to see out the window. To his surprise, he could clearly see the demon's trail. "Although, it seems you already know where it's going."

"Well, let's just say, I have a very good guess," Johnson said, glancing into the rear view mirror at Miller. "You look just like him, you know."

"Pardon?" Miller asked.

"Andres Soliz. The guy everyone keeps mistaken you for. The eyes are a little different, but otherwise…"

Andres Soliz… Soliz, yes by now he was getting used to that name. It was who the special agent accused him of being, but even he didn't believe that to be Miller's real name. But it was more than that. He had heard the name before that as well. There was something there he had to remember. His mind reached back, trying to grasp some detail that evaded him.

"Hey, you still with me back there?" Johnson cut in.

Miller shook his head. No he couldn't remember. "Yes, my apologies. It has been a long day. I've never met this Soliz, I assure you," Miller said.

Johnson gave an "uhuh" noise of non-believing confirmation.

"So, tell me, friend, if you know where the beast is going, take me there, and I'll end it. That is what I do," Miller continued, trying to get back on topic.

"Well, no, like I said, I can't just let you do what you like. I have a job to do and until a judge says otherwise, you are wanted for questioning for a double homicide."

"Questioning? People will die. Let me do my work."

"Oh, I get that." Johnson paused and looked back again at Miller in the mirror. The man was smiling. This made Miller want to smile as well. "That's why you're going to escape," Johnson announced.

*****

Miller knew the city a moment after they re-entered it. Newark was laid out before him as the car exited the highway. There in the distance he could see the cluster of buildings where he had first awakened. To the left was the giant church he had landed in after his first fight with Asmodai. It seemed fitting that they would track the demon back here, where it had all begun. This was Mike's city, and Miller couldn't help but wonder how his friend was doing. Miller wanted to help, but fate had him at the moment, and he could do nothing but let it play out.

It was not long after they reentered the city that Johnson pulled the car over next to a small stretch of green. Here, several other police cars waited. Johnson got out of the car and opened Miller's door.

"So this is the guy," another officer said as he approached. There were five others, dressed in various uniforms, all waiting for them. Miller looked them over as he exited the vehicle. He noted the distrust and disbelief in some of their faces and the hope in others.

"It is Andres Soliz," said a particularly greasy man in a long grey coat.

"No, friends. The name is Miller, Joseph Miller," Miller corrected them. "I'm told you have a demon problem?"

"He even talks like a loon," the greasy man said. "You sure about this, Johnson?"

Johnson was busying undoing Miller's handcuffs. "I'm sure. This is the guy."

"This is your career, maybe Samson's too."

"Mike has his own problems at the moment," Johnson said. "You suddenly getting cold feet on me, Mathews?"

"Nah, I'm just an observer here," Mathews said.

"What about Samson?" Miller asked. "Do you have word of his son?"

"No, he was supposed to call me and let me know where the exchange was to be. I haven't gotten the call. He made it out of Trenton before I got there," Johnson said. Then he looked to the others. "Look if anyone wants out, this is the last chance. Anybody?" he asked the small group of men. No one moved. "I know this isn't exactly standard procedure, but our friend here, Mr. Miller is going to help us bring a little payback to that thing that killed our friends, our brothers. To make that happen, we're going to have to bend a few rules."

"Yeah," Mathews huffed. "Like let a murder suspect walk."

"He didn't do it," another man said. He held up one of the phones that showed a moving picture of Renee Dupré. "This is all over the news as of 20 minutes ago." Miller watched in amazement as the cursed woman shot two men in the head. She really wasn't a very nice person.

"Still a suspect," Mathews said.

"Well, I'm sure he'll answer all our questions when the demon is dead, won't you, Mr. Miller?" Johnson said.

"Aye, lad. That I will, although I prefer to answer my questions over a fine ale," Miller said with a grin.

"Don't we all," another man said.

Behind them, a horse suddenly trotted into view. It was the first Miller had seen since his awakening and it was a beautiful creature. Dark brown in color, with just a touch of white on its hind legs. On it rode another man in uniform, who looked at Miller with a worried expression.

"Ah, Mr. Miller may I present to you Newark's mounted police force," Johnson said, pointing to the horse. "And your ride."

The man dismounted and walked the horse over to Miller, passing him the reins over.

"This is Sally," he began. "My partner for the last two years."

Miller reached out a gentle hand and touched the beast. "She's beautiful."

The horse did not shy away from the touch, as Miller knew it wouldn't. He had developed a way with horses after a few thousand years of practice.

"Mr. Miller, you just escaped police custody, stole a horse, and have run off into downtown Newark."

"I did?" Miller asked with a grin. "Fantastic."

"The police force of Newark will have to give chase, of course."

"Of course. But lad, when the time comes, keep your men back. I know you want vengeance, but this fight is mine, and it's best for the rest of your men to stay back. Too many have died already."

"I'll do my best," Johnson said, handing over Miller's sword and two of the throwing knives. "Good luck."

"To you as well," Miller said, mounting the horse. He looked down to Sally's partner. "I'll do my best to keep your friend from harm." Then he looked to the sky, found the demon's trail, and galloped after it.

# 25 - Desperate Measures

The car slowed and suddenly turned off into a multistory parking lot.

"Mike? This isn't College Hospital," Ann said.

"You're not coming to College Hospital," Mike declared.

"What?" Ann was confused.

"I need your help. Just not on the front lines," Mike said.

"I see." Ann didn't really see.

"In case you've forgotten, you appear to be busy re-growing a section of your spine," Mike said, bringing the car to a complete stop at the top floor of the parking building. Here it was open to the elements and offered a decent view of the surrounding area. "Do you think you can stand?"

Ann opened the car door, then flopped out. "Um, no. I guess not," she said, pulling herself free of the car.

Mike opened his car door and rushed to her side. He wrapped his arms around Ann, moving her to a sitting position. "Easy. Take it slow." There she was again, in his arms. It was almost worth getting torn to pieces by a giant demon. In a moment, she was sitting on the ground next to the car. "OK, you've got a job to do," Mike continued. He handed her his phone. "Call this number, explain where I'm going to a Detective Johnson. He's the cavalry. I've tried a few times now, but whatever Lizzie did to jam the phones doesn't seem to have gone away."

Ann took the phone. This she could do, but she was still not happy about being left behind. "All right, I can do this for you. But I don't like it. And once I'm back on my feet again, I'm going to be down at that hospital busting this Smith guy's ass."

Mike smiled at that. "No, you're not. You and Miller need to stay out of this. Miller is still wanted by the police, although that should be cleared up soon. And you, you're not human…" Mike said.

"What the hell, Mike? After all this, you still doubt whose side I'm on?" Ann interrupted.

Mike smiled again and put one hand on Ann's shoulder. "Me, never. I trust you with my life. The police, though, I'm not sure what they would make of you. You need to get better; you need to find Lizzie. You need to find Miller and help him," Mike said, standing again. He opened the back door of the car, removed a large bag, and dropped it by Ann's side.

"Why does this sound like you're not coming back?" Ann asked.

"Because I'm not. The police aren't just coming for Dupré and Smith," Mike said. He looked so sad in that moment.

"But you are a cop. Why would they…?"

"I broke a lot of laws today, Ann. Not just today, but over the last few weeks. I have a lot to answer for. I'm lucky, I have some friends keeping me out of prison so I could pull this off. But when this is all done, when Sam is safe, no number of friends is going to keep me out of jail."

Ann looked at Mike, stunned. They stared at each other for a long moment, as Ann adjusted to the shock.

"Mike, there has to be a way…," Ann began.

"No, and it's not important now," Mike broke in. He kicked the bag by Ann's side. "This is Lizzie's bag. The equipment she was using is in there, plus an extra set of clothes, which you might want to take a look at." Ann looked down on the shredded man's dress shirt that was just barely keeping her decent at the moment. "From here, you should be able to see the main lot of College Hospital." Mike pointed out to the right. "If you can't get the police here in time, I'm done for."

"Right" Ann said slowly. "I don't know what to say…other than that I'll do everything I can." She put out a hand on the car door and slowly pulled herself to her feet. Her knees shook, but she held the position and looked Mike directly in the eye, then threw her arms around him. Mike flinched for a moment, then settled in as Ann hugged him. She kissed him on the cheek.

"Good luck," she said.

"Thanks," Mike said. "You too." He broke the embrace and headed around to the driver's side door.

Ann looked at Renee, who was glaring at her from the back seat.

"You and I are not through," Ann said.

"Perhaps," Renee said.

Then Ann glanced at Mike again. "Be seeing you," Ann said and Mike jumped into the car seat.

Mike gave her one last warm smile. "I hope so." Then he put the car into drive.

"Bet on it," Ann said, as she watched the car wind down the ramp back to the entrance.

*****

Mike watched Renee glare at back at Ann as they pulled away. "You don't know what to make of her do you?" Mike asked.

"She is impossible. But now I see why Abraham spared her. Perhaps I was wrong to want her dead."

"Well, well, well, an old dog can learn new tricks," Mike said. He let the disgust in his voice drip.

There was silence in the car for several moments, until Renee broke it.

"Samson, you don't know what kind of monster Smith is."

"Actually, I've got a good idea," Mike said. "But don't worry. Smith won't have you for long. I have a special reservation for you in jail."

Renee laughed. "You are an idiot," she said, giving Mike the impression she said that sort of thing a lot. "I won't be in jail for 20 minutes."

"Idiot I may be," Mike said, "but I'm not the one who was recorded murdering two people. I'm not the one who didn't destroy the videos when she had them. But I am the one who sent copies of that video to 24 different news agencies," Mike said. Actually, it had been Lizzie, but it was his idea.

"What?" Dupré said, stunned.

"I don't care what kind of connections you have; you've just become internet famous. I have a feeling all the connections in world won't save you now."

There was silence from the back seat as Mike pulled the car into the main lot of the newly abandoned College Hospital. Police tape still blocked off most of the entrance, but a section had been recently opened, probably by Smith's men.

The building had once been imposing. Now, though, it was just plan creepy. Cracked windows could be seen on the higher floors, but as you moved closer to the ground, more and more were shattered and completely open to the elements. Large stretches of scorched concrete marred the main entrance where the demon Asmodai had made its escape into the world. Mike shivered at the memory. This was the last place he ever wanted to see again and he was sure Smith knew that.

"Marcel…" Renee started up again from the back seat. "He can't see that video."

Mike exited the car and drew his gun, before opening the back seat. "Who?" Mike asked as he pulled the Cursed woman free of the back seat.

"My husband, he can't see that video," Renee said. It was as if she was suddenly a new woman. The change was so drastic, that Mike actually stopped in his tracks. Renee turned to face him, her eyes pleading. She hadn't been half as scared that he was dragging her off to meet a vampire, but for some reason this got to her.

"Isn't it a little late for pity now?" Mike said.

"No, not for me, for him. I did this all for him, to get him back," Renee continued.

"And he has no idea how many lives you've destroyed to do it," Mike said. He waved her forward with his gun and they started a slow walk towards the front entrance.

"And it would destroy him."

"Like you destroyed Ann's friends? How about all the people that died right here!"

Mike jabbed a finger at the ruined building before them. "Ann takes the blame on herself, but this is all on you."

"You're right," Renee admitted, as she followed Mike, her head bowed. "I would say, I didn't mean... Abraham was supposed to keep it contained. But I always knew some people would die, but I didn't care. Anything was worth the price of getting my husband back. Except..." She trailed off and stopped.

Mike raised the gun again, unsure what the cursed woman was planning.

"Except..." Renee continued, "when I saw him, finally after all the years, a man again, I couldn't even look at him."

"Come on," Mike pulled Renee forward, but she wasn't done.

"I hadn't seen his face in a hundred years, the man I love more than anything, and I basically ran away from him. I went right there to kill your friend, to cover my tracks, but couldn't even do that."

"For that, at least, you should be thankful. Less innocent blood on your hands," Mike said.

"Innocent... maybe." Renee seemed at last to agree. "But it would have been a mercy killing.

"What?" Mike said.

"If she is what you say she is, she has no idea the horrors she is going to face."

*****

Ann got dressed slowly. She had no choice; her body simply responded sluggishly. Pins and needles ran up and down her limbs, and her legs buckled from her own weight several times, but very gradually, she covered herself. The bag included just jeans and a t-shirt: No undies, no socks, and no shoes. But even going 'commando,' as Keith used to call it, was a major step up.

Ann kept one eye on the cell phone, brushing it with a finger from time to time to keep the screen on. There was still no cell coverage.

Once dressed, and after a moment to catch her breath, she dug through the rest of the bag. There was a laptop computer (most definitely Lizzie's, as noted by the pink and neon green lizard on the top), binoculars, a few power bars, and some sort of circuit board wired to what looked like a small car battery.

Ann attacked the food. She had no idea how hungry she was until seeing the chow. It was as if she had been programmed to kill power bars on sight. The thick chewy protein bars were hard to swallow without water, but they still tasted fantastic. Almost immediately, some strength returned to her. Now she could get to work. Something Abraham had said suddenly worked itself up out of her memory. He had just needed a good meal, and apparently, so did she.

She brushed the phone again. Still no signal. Then she had a thought and pulled out the circuit board. Carefully, she pulled a wire connecting the board to the battery. It came free with a tiny 'pop', making Ann jump and drop the battery. Something fizzled on the board, and she checked the phone again. The phone proudly displayed four out of five bars.

"A cell phone jammer," Ann said out loud. "Clever Lizzie. Remind me to bring this to the movies next time."

Ann opened the phone. The number to call was the most recent used. Mike had apparently tried it several times on the car ride over.

The phone also reported one voice mail. Well, maybe it was the person Mike had been trying to reach called him first. Ann set the message to play and then instantly regretted it. The date on the message was almost seven months ago.

There was a woman's voice on the line, not anyone Ann had ever heard before, and she sounded like she needed help.

"Mike, baby, pick up. You have to pick up! There's someone here, someone..." Then the sound of the phone dropping, a muffled scream, followed by silence.

Ann stared at the phone in terror for several long minutes.

"What the hell was that?" Ann said. That couldn't have been related to anything that was happening now; that was before any of this madness began. She hadn't been meant to hear that, it wasn't any of her business. And yet, she had and it was certainly something she could not un-hear. It took all her strength of will to put that mystery aside and finish the task Mike had given her.

The phone rang only once. "Mike!" A man's voice almost yelled into the phone.

"No, not Mike. I'm a friend. I'm supposed to tell you where he is."

"He's at College Hospital," the man said without a hint of doubt in his voice.

"He's... yes, how did you know?" Ann asked.

"I worked it out about three minutes ago while everyone else was busy chasing the madman on horseback."

It took another long moment for Ann to digest that. "I'm sorry. Did you say horseback?" she asked.

"Yes, horseback. We should be there in the next five minutes."

Five minutes? Ann stood and grabbed the binoculars. She walked quickly to the end of the parking lot. She could clearly see Mike and Renee in the parking lot. It looked like they were arguing about something. In the hospital, she could just barely make out shapes moving. Smith was already there.

"Miss, are you still there?" the voice said over the phone.

Ann turned her gaze up the road. A blur of movement caught her eye and Ann looked up. A dragon drifted by. "Oh, my stars and garters," Ann whispered.

"What?" the man said.

Ann quickly came to her senses and ducked down low. There was no need though; the creature did not see her. It simply bobbed along in the sky, with a complete disregarding physics and Ann's sanity. It had to be Keith… no Asmodai, but it was just so much larger than last time Ann had seen it. And it was carrying something.

Ann raised the binoculars again. It wasn't carrying something; it was carrying someone. Lizzie was wrapped in a claw and she appeared to be giving directions. So it was Lizzie who was doing the tracking. And she wasn't tracking Ann, she was tracking Mike's car.

"Miss?"

"Yes, sorry. I don't suppose you happened to see the dragon flying in this direction?" Ann asked.

"Dragon?"

"Yes, same thing that tore up Newark about two weeks ago. Except it's grown," Ann said.

There was short pause. "Yeah, that thing. I've seen it before."

"Well if you're heading to College Hospital, you're going to see it again." Ann peered down the road. In the distance, she could make out flashing lights.

"We're ready this time."

"How can you possibly be ready for that?" Ann asked.

"We've got the crazy man on the horse."

Just then, Miller came into view. And he was riding a horse, just as advertised. There was a small army of police cars, vans, and trucks just a few yards behind him. As bizarre as it was, Ann smiled at the scene.

"You know I've never ridden on a horse," Ann said.

"I'm sorry," the man said.

Mike had told her to stay here. Call for backup and stay far away. Mike should have known better. There was a flight of stairs to her right. If she could just make it down to the ground level in time, Miller would pass right in front of her. Ann took off at what started as a run, but ended up being a quick stumble down the stairs. While she moved, she kept talking on the phone. "Are you coming to arrest Mike?" she asked.

There was a sigh. "Yeah, most likely. Most of the other folks on the force aren't quite as loose with the rules as I am. Mike's plan was to get everyone arrested and sort the whole thing out later."

"But if there is a dragon lighting everyone on fire and a squad of vampires causing trouble, you may have your hands full." Ann stumbled on the last step and fumbled the phone so she didn't catch the next thing the man said. "I'm sorry I missed that," Ann said. Miller was almost here. "Look I'm going to have to call you back. My ride is here. Just be careful with the Fallen. Give Miller some space to work. Ciao!" Ann hung up and slipped the phone into her pants. It was a little hard to breathe, but otherwise she was starting to feel much better. She would have to invest in more power bars later.

Miller did not slow as he approached, but leaned over in the saddle and pulled Ann up into his lap. "Miss Ann! How lovely of you to join me. I like your latest ensemble," Miller said.

Ann was disoriented for a moment, but recovered quickly. "Miller, my man, you do have a way with the ladies. Not a good way, but I give you points for style," Ann said.

"I'll take that," Miller said.

"You're tracking Asmodai."

"Aye," Miller confirmed.

"You've almost got him. He has Lizzie, who is tracking Mike's car. They must think I'm still with him."

"Samson? Fantastic! And why aren't you still with our friend?" Miller asked.

"He said it was too dangerous," Ann said bitterly.

Miller grinned. "I'm sure he'll pay for that one later," he laughed.

"Do you have a plan?" Ann asked.

"Aye, but it mostly consists of chopping demons to bits with this sword." Miller jabbed a finger at the large sword at his back.

Ann shrugged. Of course that would be Miller's plan. "The vampire, Smith is there too. And Mike and his son. It may get a little more complicated than that," she told him.

Miller's grin did not falter. "Lass, it always gets more complicated than that."

*****

"Mr. Samson."

Mike spun around Renee, putting the gun to the woman's head.

"Mr. Smith," he said, rather awkwardly. The vampire was at the entrance to the building, with the woman from earlier at his side. Three men with large guns stood like suited statues behind them.

"Well, well, well, you managed to pull it off. I really didn't think you could, but you seem to enjoy proving me wrong."

"It's a popular hobby with his co-workers as well," the woman said. Smith gave her a long cold stare, before turning back to Mike and Renee.

"Dr. Dupré, so excellent of you to make it. I was worried when you stopped returning my calls that you didn't like me anymore."

Renee Dupré chuckled at that. "No one likes you, Smith," she sneered.

The woman vampire laughed out loud. "Oh, Dupré, I always liked you."

"Carter, still licking Smith's boots I see," Renee sneered. "Have you giving up licking everything else?"

Carter's face fell.

"Doctor, there is no need to be so crass," Smith said. "We're all friends here. Well, enemies who are willing to do business."

"Business, right," Mike said. He hoped no one noticed how bad he was trembling. "Where's my son?"

"He's safe. To be honest, I think Carter was hoping to have him as a snack, but you've gone and ruined that fun for now," Smith said.

"Don't be so sure." Carter said. "Let's see how this turns out first." She grinned at Mike. He ignored the look. "Samson, I have to ask, how did you get past her guardian?"

"That FBI agent?" Mike asked.

Both the vampires looked at other and laughed. "No, no, no. My old brother in arms, Abraham," Smith said.

"I sent him on an errand," Mike said. "To kill you. Now, bring me my son. Or Dupré dies."

Renee stiffened at that, but still did not struggle.

"Please, Mr. Samson. You're a reasonable, law abiding man. Do you really expect us to believe you are going to put a hole in the head of everyone's favorite mad scientist?"

"After Tesla...," Carter put in.

"Right, of course. After Tesla," Smith continued, sharing some private joke with the vampire woman. "Why don't you come inside? I've arranged a little tour of the place. I'm sure you have some great memories from here. Now, why don't you come inside before any more laws are broken?"

Mike shuddered. They didn't think he was serious. He needed to prove to them just how serious he was. "So far today, there's been kidnapping, assaulting a federal office, car theft, although technically that wasn't me, several counts of destruction of public property, and a good hundred traffic violations..." Mike lifted the gun and fired one clean shot. One of the men in the back took the slug in the right shoulder. He screamed as he was knocked to the ground. Blood gushed from the wound. "That's another assault, maybe murder. I'm not really concerned about broken laws at the moment. Now, bring me my son!" He shouted the last part. He was trembling uncontrollably now.

The other two men raised their weapons.

"No, no, you'll hit the woman," Smith snapped at them.

"Oh, enough of this nonsense," Carter shouted and charged Mike. Mike had been counting on that, and pulled a Taser out of his coat and fired. The vampire woman noticed the movement and in a display of incredible speed, snatched the small needle at the end of the Taser while in the air. She looked down at the cable in her hand for a moment before the current hit her. She convulsed and collapsed to the ground.

"Well done," Renee said under her breath. "But you would be a lot scarier if you could keep your teeth from chattering."

Mike ignored her. "My son, now! Or I kill another one of your men," Mike demanded.

Smith whistled. "That was impressive. The Ancient One chose his companion well. Tell me, what other surprises do you have in store?"

Mike was about to answer, but Renee spoke first. "The dragon with mouth agape from which flames leap…" she whispered.

"What?" Mike said. He followed her eyes up. "No, not now!" The dragon, the same demon he had chased out of this accursed place, was swooping down out of the air right at him. Mike stared at it dumbly. It had grown nearly double in size. As unbelievable as it had been the first time he had seen the creature fly, now it was even worse. It was just impossible. The long snake like body was the size of a bus and the wings now spread out a good 20 feet wide.

"Samson, down!" Renee broke free of Mike's grasp as if he was a child and shoved him to the ground. The demon spit once, hitting Renee full in the face, then turned and climbed again into the air.

Mike looked up from the ground. Smith stared from the entrance of the building. For a moment, no one moved. Renee was staring at her own hands, dripping with the demon's particularly deadly venom. Then she looked down at Mike. She spoke in soft voice. It sounded nothing like the cruel woman who had broken into his home and nearly killed his friends. "Tell him I'm sorry."

Then she burst into flames.

# 26 - Plan B

She only screamed for a moment. As unnatural white flame consumed her, she dropped to her knees, then fell face forward on the ground. Her body seemed to wither in the flame and then collapsed into itself. In a moment, the flames died away as quickly as they had appeared. Nothing remained of Renee Dupré but ash and bone.

Both Mike and Smith watched, frozen for a moment. Mike glanced away from the dead woman and clearly saw terror on Smith's face. Was it the gruesome death or the loss of his precious knowledge? Mike could not guess.

There was a noise, the sound of massive wings, and Mike looked up. The demon was coming back for a second pass. Smith and his men noticed as well.

"Inside!" Smith yelled, as he leaped towards Carter, sweeping up the vampire in one arm. Mike doubted Smith was referring to Mike, but he had to agree with the vampire. He made a mad sprint towards the entrance to the hospital.

The demon spit again, hitting the spot where Mike had been only moments before. He did not turn to look as the flame erupted from the ground behind him, but he felt the heat.

Maybe if he could get inside before Smith and his crew, he could grab Sam and then simply hide until the police arrived. There was only one vampire not accounted for and Mike was prepared for that. Besides, the police had to be near, right? Ann had to have gotten through to them by now.

The main entrance to the hospital had an airlock, a double set of doors leading to a main receiving area. The doors had been wrecked, even before Asmodai had smashed through them to escape the last time Mike had been here. Now the entrance was more a gaping hole, littered with shattered glass and mangled steel.

There were the two men carrying the guy Mike had shot. They were just inside the entryway. Mike quickly passed Smith, who was slowed ever so slightly carrying Carter. He did not see the demon, but did not stop to look either. Instead, he focused on making his body sprint as fast as possible. The array of cuts, bruises, and tender muscles were overridden by his desperate need to escape the demon and the chance to finally see his son. Mike body-checked the two goons as he entered the ruined hospital, sending them and their cargo sprawling. The move almost cost him his balance, but he stayed upright as he tore into the main entrance.

There, he ran headfirst into another of Smith's finely dressed associates. Mike had not seen him at all and all both men were thrown to the floor.

"Hey!" the man shouted.

Mike ignored him and rolled away, desperate to find Sam. He knew the area: a main front desk off to his left and a large open area that had served as a waiting room. Mike glanced around the room to find it was full of people. All were similarly dressed to the men that had been outside; all drew weapons at the sight of him. There were no less then twelve armed men staring at him as he got to his feet.

"Heads up, people," Smith yelled from behind him. Mike turned to see the demon sticking its alligator-like head into the entrance. It spit again. At this range, Mike could hear it. It was a disgusting noise, like old man coughing up far too much phlegm. Mike caught sight of Smith diving to the ground, just as he did the same. The two and a half goons, between them, were not so lucky and caught the full measure of the liquid death. The two conscious men screamed instantly, knowing death was coming. The third man did not make a sound, as he suddenly exploded into flame as he was already out cold from the gunshot wound. A small mercy.

The screams, just like Renee Dupré's before them, only lasted seconds. Mike did not stop to watch the demon's latest victims die, but barreled ahead towards the back of the room. The guns that had been pointed towards him just a moment ago were now aiming at the entrance. The demon, Mike guessed, was probably trying to kill him specifically. Asmodai and Mike's last meeting had not gone well, and he was sure the demon would hold a grudge. However, for right now, the monster was making an excellent distraction for Smith's people.

There were gunshots and Mike covered his face with his arms. He dropped low as he raced past the last of Smith's men and risked another look behind him. Smith was waving his men back further into the building, as the demon ignored the bullet wounds and pushed further into the building. Its new increased size slowed it down, as it now no longer fit back into the hole it had made just a few short weeks ago.

Mike raised his gun and fired as well, but randomly into the crowd. There was a tinge of guilt at this, but Mike ignored it. He was a desperate man and this was a desperate moment.

He made a right at the first turn of the hallway, leaving the chaos behind him. Only then did Mike recall just how large and confusing the layout of this building was. If Sam was here, it could take Mike hours to find him and Mike did not have hours. There was no power and probably no lights remaining to use it, but the hallways were brighter than at Mike's last visit. It seemed almost every door had been torn from its hinges, letting in much more light. He quickly looked into each room as he passed.

"Sam?" he shouted. He knew shouting was a risk, but he saw no better option. He checked three more rooms. All empty.

"Sam!" he shouted a little louder. He passed a stairwell and paused. This had been the place where his neighbor, Ted, as a werewolf had pinned him against the wall. He briefly flashed back to that moment, where Miller had rescued him. He could certainly use the crazy man's help now. He snapped back to the situation at hand. Should he go up a flight of stairs, or stay on the ground floor? Up seemed safer, further away from Smith, but then it could go either way for finding his son. He chose up, and entered the stairwell.

The stairs were coated in dried blood, but looked safe enough. He took them two at a time and opened the door to the 2nd floor. He chose left and started down the next hall, then stopped. In the distance, he could hear more gunfire, but now he could hear something else. It took him a moment to place it. It was a girl. A young girl. And she was giggling.

There was a brief moment where Mike was tracking the noise. He turned his head left, then right, then he turned around, and turned around again, before dashing off in what he hoped was the right direction. *Why did Smith have another child here?* Children's laughter was generally a wonderful thing, but here, in this dead place, the sound came across as creepy and ominous.

He heard the sound again. He was going in the correct direction and he doubled his speed forward, focusing on his hearing, frantic for any sound of his son. And then, as if a gift from God, he heard it.

"No, no, this way, this way. You're not dancing, you're just jumping and moving your arms." *It was Sam's voice.* He was here, he was alive, and he was critiquing dance moves? Mike's heart sung as hope filled him.

"Sam!" he shouted. He glanced into a room; no, this was not it. But he was close.

"Dad?" came Sam's voice, from just a few feet away. Mike jumped to the next room. There was his son. His legs and arms were bound, but he sat in the middle of the room looking perfectly happy. A little girl, just a little younger than Sam, was dancing around the room.

Mike dashed to his son's side, reaching into his coat for his knife. He never made it.

He was grabbed by the back of the coat and thrown backwards, inches before reaching his son. One quick bounce against the wall, and Mike slid to the ground, stunned.

"Dad!" Sam cried from the other room.

"Mr. Samson, did you really think it was going to be that easy?" Smith was above him, looking a little rough around the edges.

"Well, " Mike said weakly "a guy can hope.".

He pulled the taser from his pocket and fired in one smooth motion.

But the vampire was ready, and jumped to the left. Mike's shot missed by a good distance. Smith kicked the weapon away and followed through with a fist to Mike's chin.

Mike hated getting hit by vampires. They just hit so hard, Mike had known buses that didn't hit with half as much power. Mike spat blood and a tooth. Smith did not wait for Mike to recover and hit him again in the ribs. Then, a third blow sent him skidding across the floor.

"You know, I might have let the boy live," Smith said, walking closer again to stand above Mike, "before all that nonsense outside. I mean, I'm not a monster..." Smith's shoe came down hard on Mike's chest. He watched as Mike screamed as something inside him broke. "Well OK, maybe I am a monster. Now, though, now you're going to watch the boy die first."

Smith vanished from sight as Mike desperately tried to reach one of his weapons. The room kept shifting, not spinning exactly, but completely defeating his attempts to reach into the coat. He told himself it wasn't too late, that he could still save his son, but his body wasn't listening.

"You want your son back so badly..." Smith reappeared, dragging Sam behind him. He tossed the boy into the hallway. Sam was crying. "Here he is, just in time for lunch."

"Dad!" was all Sam could say, between fits of crying.

Mike couldn't say anything; he seemed to have forgotten how to use his mouth about the time his hands stopped working. Darkness was pressing in on him from all sides. He wanted to say it was OK, but it looked like that was going to be a lie. He managed to reach one hand towards his son, before a shoe stomped down hard on it. Smith ground his heel, and Mike managed another scream.

"This is the end of the line, Samson," Smith snarled, his black eyes burning into Mike.

"Smith!" It was Carter. "What are you doing?"

Smith looked up at the woman, confused. "What does it look like?" Smith said.

"Knock it off. We have bigger issues. Look," Carter said pointing to a nearby window. Smith glanced towards it.

"The police?" Smith asked. "Of course, the police. You think these little people can help you, Samson? You have no idea who you are dealing with..."

"Actually..." Carter said, pointing again. "The demon, the police, and that little Hispanic man on the horse."

"Little Hispanic man?" Smith stepped closer to the window. "Oh, hell! He turned back towards Mike and let out a long breath. "He is supposed to be in prison. Well, you are full of surprises. We'll make this quick, then."

Smith pulled out his gun and fired. Twice.

# 27 - Don't call it a comeback

There is an old cliché about little girls loving horses that Ann certainly fit into. She dreamed as a little girl about raising and riding horses out in some big country home someplace. She had never once had a chance to actually ride one of the animals. Now, here she was, clinging onto one for dear life as it galloped full speed, to a confrontation that would probably end her life. She reconsidered: Maybe she was just a city girl.

They were nearly there. Ann could see the ugly building of College Hospital growing closer. She shivered at the site of it. Somehow, she had known she would end up in those dark twisted hallways again.

Ann attempted to stuff down the fear and focus on the task at hand. She had to help rescue Mike's son, save poor Lizzie, and possibly kill her ex-boyfriend Keith. Each undertaking seemed more impossible than the next, particularly the last one. Still, these days, everything she did was impossible.

"There it is, lass," Miller said, pointing to the main entrance to the hospital. The demon Asmodai was sticking its head into the front door, the long snake like body curled outside up to the wings, which looked like they may not fit anymore.

"What's it doing?" Ann asked.

Miller gave the air a loud sniff. "Killing," he said, and drew the sword. "Lass, take care to avoid its spit. It's instant death for all it touches, but its range is fairly short."

Ann nodded; she had seen this when she was in this very same parking lot, when Asmodai was unleashed against the Newark police last time. Ann turned back see the flashing lights of the pursuing police slowing as they entered the parking lot. The police were stopping, setting up a perimeter around the building, as they had the last time. This time, though, they were pulling farther back, perhaps at Ann's own request for space. "I think they want to help, but I don't know what to tell them that won't get many people killed," she said, nodding her head back at the police.

"Aye, some do, some do not. Your law enforcement is of two minds about me at the moment. But after last time, they should respect that monster," Miller said. He crouched low on the horse, focusing only on the demon ahead of him. "Ready yourself."

The entrance was only a hundred yards or so head. The demon was still stuffing itself inside. Height seemed to be the creature's issue, as there was plenty of room to the right or left. It had tucked its wings in and more than half of the creature was inside, but something seemed to be slowing it down. Over the constant pounding of the horse's hooves, Ann could hear the sounds of gunfire and men yelling coming from ahead. Ann could not see

Lizzie. Perhaps she was already inside?

"Miller, I'm not sure rushing in is the way to go," Ann said, gripping the horse a little harder. Miller responded by passing the reins to Ann.

"What?" Ann stammered, as they passed through the ruined entrance. Miller gripped his weapon with two hands and stabbed into the monster's side, clamping his legs hard around the horse's sides. The sword dug in and sliced a long slash in the demon's side that continued to extend as they rode forward. Miller then pulled the weapon back and took one overhead swing at the joint where the wing attached to the scaly back. The limb was severed neatly off, spraying black blood. The demon screamed.

They burst into the main room. The head of the demon twisted back to see them. The empty black eyes still managed to display endless rage. It opened its mouth to spit, just as they were about to pass, but Miller was prepared and stabbed his weapon into the top of Asmodai's alligator-like mouth. The weapon cut through the roof of the mouth, past the demon's tongue, and embedded itself into the lower jaw, in effect pinning the monster's mouth shut. The demon bucked, as one might if one's lips were suddenly impaled, and Miller, still clutching the favored weapon, was tossed off the horse. He managed to hold the sword for a moment longer, as Asmodai tossed its wounded head back and forth, until Miller was thrown to the ground.

This all happened at terrific speed and Ann managed to process it all after she was alone on the horse for several moments. She was still barreling forward, now inside the hospital. She had no idea how to stop.

"Someone stop this crazy thing!" she shouted. Yes, she was most definitely a city girl. The horse, which had so loyally followed Miller's every command, seemed to ignore everything she did. Men in fine suits dashed out of their way. Ann barely registered them, pulling back on the reins.

"Whoa... stop... cease..." Ann begged. Then she just gave up and jumped free of the horse. She hit the ground hard, rolling several feet, before coming to a stop on her belly. "Ow" she observed from the floor. The horse carried on through the hallway until the beast was out of sight. Ann pulled herself up on shaky feet. That had not been her best entrance, but, as the saying went: any entrance you could walk away from. Well, it was something like that.

Ann took stock of the situation. She was now well inside the hospital, past the waiting room, and somewhere in the middle of the ER. Miller was towards the front and she started walking back in that direction. She had passed several men, just plain humans, on her little trek through the ex-hospital. Now, as she made her way back in their direction, she considered who they might be. Did they work for Smith? Ann knew very little about the vampire, besides the fact that Miller, Mike, and Renee Dupré wanted him very dead. She would have to be careful.

Ann could not yet run, but she continued her accelerated walking back towards the entrance. There were sounds of gunfire and more screaming coming from in front of her, so it would not be hard to find Miller again. He had to be in that mix.

There was the sound of running footsteps from behind her and Ann spun to see. A woman, very Cursed, was leading a group of four men back towards the front. The men were well armed, with large machine guns strapped to their finely dressed chests.

"Who are you?" the Cursed woman snarled.

"I, um, I'm just looking for the lady's room. Need to powder my nose. " Ann quipped.

The woman laughed just a little. "I see. You haven't seen a small Hispanic man with a preference for sharp objects around here? Or a massive black scaled demon, perhaps?"

"They went that way," Ann said, pointing in a random direction.

"Really? And I'm sorry, I didn't catch that name." Her eyes flared black, giving her a menacing look.

Ann could possibly take all five of them down, if she was running at full strength. She felt in her mind for the door that kept her demon side in check. It was still tightly shut. Ann slowly raised her arms above her head in surrender. "Hostage number one?" she said, with a nervous smile.

*****

Miller rolled to his feet, facing Asmodai. From the corner of his eye, he could make out Ann riding away, shouting at the horse to stop. Perhaps it was for the best. Miller was unsure how much help Ann could be up against her ex-love. It was hard for anyone to face a loved one taken by the Fallen. Miller knew that pain better than most.

The demon thrashed back and forth, clawing at its face, but Miller's sword stayed fast. Perhaps Miller could make this quick. He drew his last remaining weapon, one of the small ancient throwing knives, and charged the monster. It wanted nothing to do with him, though, and pulled back. The demon retreated back outside the building and Miller dashed after it, unsure how his small weapon could do much damage, but perhaps he could retrieve his sword.

Outside, the demon looked at him once, then leaped upwards, out of reach. It could no longer fly; its right wing was lying on the hospital floor. Instead, it bounded at the side of the building, hitting it some twenty feet in the air and embedded its claws in the wall. Then, it started to climb up.

Miller swore once, watching the demon escape. He would have to take the stairs and try and reach the demon, before it freed its mouth or regrew the wing. Time was of the essence. He spun towards the entrance, but then turned back slowly. Something caught his eye and it took him a moment for him understand what it was.

In the distance, he made out the line of the police. Men were gathering, preparing for what, Miller did not know. But beyond them, he saw four shapes, the outlines of the Cursed. It had to be his remaining playmates from his earlier battle, at last joining their parent. They had run on foot this entire distance. Good, they would be tired. The Wolves bounded through the police line, scrambling over cars and knocking men down, but not pausing. They would be here in a moment.

Miller looked down at the one remaining throwing knife. He was going to need a bigger blade. He spun back around and stepped back inside.

Six men with large guns greeted him.

"I don't suppose you're here to thank me for helping you with your demon problems, eh?" Miller said.

"Nope," said one large man in a black suit. A small red handkerchief peeked out of one of his pockets. He readied a large machine gun, not as shiny as the one Miller had used earlier in the day, but still very nice. Miller was going to need to borrow it.

"Employees of Smith's, then?" Miller asked. His eyes scanned the room. He needed something that could absorb bullets better than his handsome face.

"Yep," the same man answered. All six men advanced, their weapons trained on Miller.

"Pay well?" Miller asked conversationally. He stepped to the left. The front desk was not far, but he could use a distraction.

"Very."

"Really? I do see you have some fine clothes. I imagine they cost a king's ransom alone and those weapons, fantastic."

"Would you like to see how they work?" another man asked, smiling. All six men appeared to be enjoying their tactical advantage. Miller smiled his mad grin back at them. His distraction would be here any moment and he was feeling out the timing. He held the grin for a long moment, his ears straining to hear the wolves approach.

"Aye, I would. How about… now?" And like a bullfighter, Miller stepped to the left, just as the four wolves bounded into the hospital, passing Miller by inches.

*****

"You four, go see what's going on at the front desk," the vampire woman commanded. "I'll have a quick word with our good friend Hostage here." The four armed men obeyed and marched back in the direction that Ann had left Miller.

Ann watched them go, swallowing hard, concerned for Miller's sake. The vampire woman closed in on Ann, her eyes filled with the black of the Cursed. Ann thought that the vampire was going for menacing, but she had seen far worse just recently.

"Now, how about you tell me who you are?" the vampire hissed.

Ann considered several witty remarks. *'Your worst Nightmare'? Nah, too over the top. 'Just call me Buffy'? That could get her in legal trouble. 'Pizza delivery girl'? If she only had a pizza.* She was going to need to work on her snappy comeback lines.

"Ann," she finally said. "Friend of the groom."

The vampire smiled, showing all her disappointingly flat teeth. "You're a funny little woman, Ann."

"Well, thank you, I try. Everyone is always shouting and shooting in these situations. And really, I'm just getting a little tired of it. Figured I would try a little humor," Ann said.

The vampire smiled at this. She seemed to find Ann genuinely funny. Her stance relaxed a bit.

Ann took stock. She had to get away from the woman and find Miller and Mike. Yet, in her soft squishy form, she wasn't sure she could handle a vamp. She was still strong, but Ann remembered how hard vampires were to kill. Hell, Abraham was torn in two and he managed to survive. She stalled for more time, straining to think of any way out.

"Well, thank you," the vampire responded. "That is a welcome relief from all the crying and begging for one's life that I usually get. Do you mind telling me what you're doing here?"

"Well... this is where my car pool dropped me off," Ann answered. "Well, horse pool, I guess you might call it. You may have seen it running off that way."

"The horse, you were with the Ancient One?"

"Yeah, Miller, buddy of mine, a little crazy, but after the day I'm having, I'm starting to understand why," Ann joked. Sarcasm, the ultimate way to deal with life and death situations.

The mention of Miller made the Cursed woman tense again.

Ann needed to do something, quick. *What would Miller do?*

"I see. Well, Ann, how about you drop the sarcasm and give me one reason why I shouldn't kill you."

Ann smiled. "One reason, eh? How about I give you five?". She pointed her pointer finger of her right hand straight up. "One." She raised her second finger. "Two." Then followed with her ring finger and pinky "Three. Four." Then stuck her thumb out. "Five."

The vampire looked at her, dumbstruck. So, Ann made a fist and decked the creature as hard as she could. The Cursed woman flew backwards and hit the wall six feet away. Ann turned to run, but something grabbed her arm. She looked down to see one of the black tentacles the Vampires used. It was wrapped around her lower arm. Ann's flesh instantly turned a pale sickly white and the Vampire began to feed.

*****

Miller added a spin for flourish and then dove for the cover of the front desk.

The men, seeing the horrors bounding towards them, opened fire. A few bullets came quite close to Miller as he entered shelter, but most cut into the first two werewolves. Blood and fur exploded from the Cursed creatures, but they did not slow. Instead, they plowed forward into the men, even as their weapons tore the wolves apart. The Cursed clawed and bit as they died, striking down three men, before falling to the floor.

The second two wolves, who had entered the building just moments after the first, fared better and leaped over their fallen comrades and into the remaining men with little damage. One man's face caught a full claw.

The talkative man in the black suit got in a lucky shot and managed to fire off several rounds into the closest wolf's face. It fell backwards, clutching its head, and the man followed up with a kick to the creature's chest. The well-dressed man then fired on the final wolf, who was entertaining itself by disemboweling one of his co-workers. The gunfire forced the wolf back, and it dropped its prey.

Miller had to admit werewolves made an excellent distraction and he wasn't about to waste it. The gunfire stopped suddenly and Miller dashed out from behind the front desk. Two men and one wolf remained. The wolf and one of the men looked badly wounded. Only the talkative man with the black suit looked unscratched. Well, Miller could change that.

Miller let the last blade fly as he charged back into the fray. It caught the man in the black suit directly in his temple—handle first. The man turned towards Miller with a stunned look on his face, before his eyes rolled into his head and he collapsed to the ground. The wounded man was still staring at the wolf when Miller's foot connected with his nose. The man let his gun go, allowing Miller to catch, spin, and attempt to fire at the final wolf. But the gun gave a disappointing empty click.

Miller frowned, annoyed to have a rather brilliant move ruined by the simple lack of ammunition. He locked eyes with the wolf, which was bleeding from many bullet wounds. The holes were already healing as Miller watched. Bullets were being forced back out and were dropping to the ground below.

"Well, I do have to thank you for the timely rescue. The bullets look far better in your thick hide than in mine," Miller said, dropping the empty gun to the floor. The wolf lunged at him, but Miller simply vaulted over the slow monster and landed behind its back. He scooped up another of the guns off the floor and turned to face the wolf again. The wolf spun as well, slowly, as the wounds had weakened it. Confusion was clear on its face.

Down the hall came more footsteps and four more men appeared, similarly armed. Miller glanced at them, then back to the wolf.

"I know you've done so much already, but if I could just trouble you for one more favor?" Miller asked politely. The wolf took a lazy swipe, which Miller easy dodged, as he stepped in closer. He hit the creature with an uppercut, then grabbed one arm and pulled. This spun the wolf to face the approaching band of men, with Miller safely behind the beast. The men, in response, did not wait for a witty line from Miller. *Horribly rude of them.* They opened fire. It was their loss, as Miller could be very witty. Refusing to be insulted or shot to pieces, he let his friend the werewolf absorb the bullets for a moment, before dropping the beast to the ground and returning fire.

Miller cut a line through all four men, at knee level. They all screamed or swore as they hit the ground. The wolf dropped to the ground, perhaps dead, perhaps overcome with a need to nap after assisting Miller so well. Miller did not check, but ran forward and disarmed the four wounded men, gathering an impressive collection of weapons in the process.

Now that he'd had his fun, it was time to get serious. The well-dressed man in the black suit seemed to be coming to already. He would probably be a better conversationalist than the four men screaming and grabbing their ruined kneecaps. Besides, he liked to talk. Miller pulled him upright by the hair. "Now, let's have a chat," he said.

*****

Ann watched in horror as the vampire's tongue tore through the flesh of her arm. She waited for the pain to take her. Surely, this was the end. Ann looked down at the vampire, still crouched against the wall. She had a vicious grin on her demonic face.

But then the grin started to fade and the vampire's black eyes went wide. Ann realized there was no pain. She looked down at her arm. The flesh was gone and only her white scales remained. The tentacle could not do any more harm to her than a flea bite.

Now it was Ann's turn to smile. "Well isn't this convenient," she said. She grabbed the vampire's black tongue with other hand and yanked. The Cursed woman was pulled across the room, right into Ann's waiting fist.

Ann connected hard and the tongue retracted. The vampire dropped to the ground, blood running out of her nose and face.

"What are you?" she stammered.

Ann, flushed with triumph, kicked the vampire in the chest and said, "Your worst nightmare!" She regretted the phrase the instant it left her mouth. *Could anything be cheesier?*

The vampire rolled away, then pulled herself up to her feet. "My nightmare? Girl, you couldn't even begin to understand my nightmares." The vampire charged, catching Ann flat-footed. Ann had become overconfident, and as the vampire swung at her with old-fashioned fists, she realized that she should have stuck to her first thought and run.

The vampire's fist caught Ann right on the jaw and then it was Ann's turn to be launched into the air. She smashed against the wall and slid, stunned, to the ground.

"Now, as good as those five reasons were, I think I'm just going to have to kill you now, the old-fashioned way," the vampire said, wiping blood from her face. She advanced on Ann, but then froze. A thin metal blade appeared at the vampire's throat.

"Now, now, I do hate to see sisters fighting so," a rough voice said.

"Miller," Ann said "You and that timing of yours…"

But it wasn't Miller. It was Abraham.

# 28 - Reinforcements

"Little sister," the blind vampire croaked his familiar greeting. "I hope you don't mind if we cut in..."

Ann's head was swimming from the punch. She had to double check that it was in fact Abraham before her. Another much older looking man was right behind him. He was Cursed as well.

"Abraham, what... how?" she stammered.

"Abraham, let's not do anything rash," the vampire woman said. "I am rather fond of this head."

"You've had this coming for a long time, Carter." The old man stepped in.

"I don't believe we've met," the vampire, Carter, said, looking at the old man.

The old man introduced himself. "Marcel Dupré."

Ann's mouth dropped open and even Carter raised her eyebrows at the name.

"The husband," Ann said.

"Well, it looks like Renee succeeded," Carter said. "I would congratulate you, if it would help." Her eyes flashed between the old man and the sword at her throat. "You know the sword won't kill me. Not completely."

"Just the part that thinks," Marcel said. "This is for the rest." He held up a lighter. It didn't look that frightening to Ann, but she got the idea that he meant fire.

"I don't suppose anyone wants to tell me what's going on?" Ann asked, trying to reenter the conversation. "Not that I'm not glad to see you, Abraham."

"Aye, the lass has a fair question."

All spun to see Miller. He was coated in black blood from head to toe and loaded down with six different guns, one in each hand, and two hanging off each shoulder.

"Miller..." Ann stumbled to his side. "Are you all right?"

"Fine, lass," Miller said, his eyes never leaving Abraham. "The blood isn't mine. But there are several men in need of medical attention at the front door."

Carter swore. "Smith is going to kill me."

"No, I'm going to kill you," Marcel reminded her.

Then Ann remembered Abraham's reluctance about Miller and stepped between them. "Miller, this is Abraham. He is on our side. And the older looking gentleman is Marcel Dupré. The woman, well, she's working for Smith, so..."

"So, I dislike her already," Miller said. "And Abraham and I have met."

"Ancient One," Marcel said, sticking out a hand.

Miller shook it. "Good to see you again Marcel. I'm glad you survived our last encounter. You fought well," he said.

"Well, I mostly just held on for dear life, but I'm glad it was helpful holding on for dear life," Marcel said.

Ann smiled at this line. She knew exactly how he felt.

"Both Asmodai and Smith are here," Miller said. "The demon is wounded, and Smith is one floor above, with the boy and Mike. We'll sort this out later." Miller was still staring at Abraham, who had not budged nor made a sound since Miller arrived.

Ann looked back and forth between the two Ancient men. There was a tension there, but something else. Ann wanted to know more, but Miller was right. Now was not the time.

"Right. My friend Lizzie is here as well and..." Ann paused for a second, as a thought struck her. "And, actually, I think I might have a plan."

Miller finally turned to look at her. "More science?" he asked.

Ann smiled.

*****

They split up into two groups. Abraham, Miller, and the captured Carter headed straight upstairs to confront Smith and the rest of his men. The idea was to trade Carter for Mike and his son. Possibly even Renee Dupré. Ann didn't much care, as long as Mike and Sam were safe.

Ann's job was the demon and Lizzie. Ann had only told Miller she had a new weapon in mind, as she doubted Miller would even think about letting her take Asmodai, her ex-boyfriend, on alone. She intended to try anyway.

Marcel followed Ann through the remains of the ruined hospital. She did not know the man at all, but if Abraham trusted him, so did she. It was dark, but not like before. Daylight seemed to creep into the building everywhere and Marcel had a flashlight.

"Marcel, were you a doctor like your wife? I mean before the Fallen," Ann asked.

"A doctor, yes," he responded.

"Perfect!" Ann said.

"Well, it was a hundred years ago. The medical field has changed quite drastically, I'm afraid."

"True," Ann had to admit. "But that's not important. I know you and your wife studied ways to try and cure your curse. I take it that you never found anything?" She found the room she was looking for and took a step inside. "Can I borrow the light?" she asked, peeking back outside.

"Of course." He passed the light. "No, we didn't find anything to remove a curse. Although there were stories about certain ways to delay one."

"Interesting, keep going." Ann spun a finger in the air as she dug through boxes. She found a box of large syringes and pulled out five. That would have to be enough.

"Well, they were rituals really, but all of them had a potion or food—something for the patient to ingest."

"Let me guess: they contained things like garlic, Echinacea, tea leaves, and maybe olive leaves?"

Marcel smiled, clearly impressed. It was a warm thing, completely the opposite of his wife. "Yes, many contained garlic."

"Right, because it's a natural antibiotic," Ann said. "Ah, here we go." She pulled a box of many containers filled with a clear liquid.

"We came to a similar conclusion back in the 50s," Marcel said.

Ann stopped and looked at him. "And?" she asked.

Marcel seemed to be thinking.

Ann started filling the syringes, then covering the needles.

"Well, obviously it didn't work," Marcel explained, "but it did make me very sick." He smiled. "At the time, we thought it was an allergic reaction, but maybe…"

"I don't think it was an allergic reaction and, sadly, I've haven't had time to research the science behind it, but I think antibiotics are poisonous to the Fallen," Ann said.

"It's possible. The story of vampires and garlic, families using garlic to ward off evil."

"Right, and when Lilith took me…"

"Wait. What?" Marcel broke in.

"Oh, long story, I was possessed by the demon Lilith, but I got better."

"But, but… that's impossible," Marcel said, fear plain on his face.

"It was impossible, but not anymore. Yay, science!" Ann pumped one arm into the air.

"But…" Marcel seemed stuck on this. But that wasn't surprising, as it had taken his wife a very long time to wrap her mind around it too.

"The week before I was taken, I got a tick bite. Gross little thing," Ann explained. "Anyway, Lyme disease is a concern in these parts and it is transmitted by ticks. They don't even test the bugs anymore; they just put you on this huge dose of antibiotics. Doxycycline, to be precise. It was this enormous pill, no coating or anything." Ann made a face, recalling the taste. "Ugh."

"So, so, you're not..."

"Both Miller and Abraham approved. But I'm not exactly human either." Ann lifted her arm, showing the mark the vampire had made. It was already healing, but the white scales were still visible. Marcel's eyes grew wide at the view. "It didn't work instantly, sadly. Otherwise, we wouldn't be here." Ann looked Marcel directly in the eye. "Your wife...Renee, she did this. She sent the curse to me."

Marcel looked away. "I know. I can't even begin to say how sorry I am," he said. "I still can't believe she would. I should have never left her alone."

Ann suddenly felt like a jerk. Who was she to throw this at him? It was hardly his fault. She shook her head. "Sorry. I didn't mean to dump this on you. But your wife—well, let's just say I'm not happy with her." Ann put a hand on Marcel's shoulder. He gave a sniffle and Ann noticed he was crying.

"I understand. I'm not happy with her at the moment either," Marcel said. They sat in silence for a moment and the man regained his composure. "So, your plan is to use the antibiotics on the demon as a weapon?"

"Well, yes, in a way," Ann said. She gathered her ammo and passed a few to Marcel, who placed them carefully in a pocket.

"You'll have to get very close," he said.

"Yeah, I know. But I have a feeling that won't be hard," Ann said with a sigh, as they entered the hallway again.

"Why is that?"

"Because he still loves me," Ann said flatly and again Marcel was stunned.

"I'm sorry, what?"

"Well, not me. He still loves Lilith." Ann remembered the hurt in Keith's eyes the last time she had seen him. He had thought she was his lost love, Lilith. She had thought he was her ex-boyfriend Keith. If it hadn't been so sad, it would make a great romantic comedy for the WB network.

"Can demons love?" Marcel asked. That was a deep question. Did the Fallen have their own emotions or did they simply take on aspects of their hosts? Asmodai or Keith, seemed to love in his own way. Amon or Vanessa seemed to only feel jealousy and rage. Ann remembered how tenderly Ura had cared for those undead things it had created. They seemed to care for each other in their own way. Could creatures as merciless and just plain evil as the Fallen feel love? Or was it the habit of being together for thousands of years?

"I think, in their own twisted and evil way, they can," Ann said. There was a buzz and Ann dug deep into the pocket to retrieve Mike's phone. She had almost forgotten the small army of police outside. "Hey," she said. Then thinking better of it she added. "Mike's phone."

"Is this Ann?" the voice on the phone asked. It was the same man she had spoken to earlier.

"It is!" Ann said.

"OK, Ann, listen, I'm trying to buy you guys time to handle this demon thing like you asked. But I have a lot of people asking questions that I can't answer."

"Right, we're still working on it, but please keep those people back. And call a few ambulances. We have some wounded that you'll need to collect once we give the all clear."

"All right, I'm going to do my best. Damn, there it is again," the man on the phone said.

"What? You can see it? Where is it? Is it attacking you?" Ann asked. She burst ahead and entered the next room in which she could see sunlight.

"No, it's ignoring us. It's crawling down the side of the building like some centipede. Is it just me, or is that bigger than last time?"

"It's bigger," Ann agreed.

"OK, it looks like it's going back in."

"Where?" Ann asked.

"Second floor."

Ann looked at Marcel. "Oh, hell," she muttered. "I'll call you back."

Both Marcel and Ann took off at a run.

*****

Miller followed Abraham up the stairs. He had a million questions for his son, but was attempting to keep them to himself for now. When this was done, he would not let Abraham just slip into the background again. This time he needed answers.

They had hardly spoken in a thousand years, since Smith captured and tortured him in another life. Abraham had, unknowingly, betrayed the Ancient One to Smith, but Miller didn't blame him for that. That he would take out of Smith's hide.

For many years after his next resurrection, Miller sought out his Cursed child. But Abraham always managed to stay out of reach. Sometimes the vampire would help Miller on his quest in some way, but never through direct contact. After some time, he respected Abraham's wishes and let him be. But now, here they were, together.

They continued their silence as they headed up the stairs. Abraham seemed to know the building well and Miller followed. Carter slightly seethed, but followed directions with Abraham's blade at her throat. Miller had extracted information from the well-dressed man at the entrance. He knew where Mike was and about how many men Smith had left. Miller and

Abraham were still outnumbered, but they had apparently captured Mike. They had no choice.

"You're thinking far too loud, father," Abraham chided him.

"I'm wondering why you haven't run off yet. Isn't that what you do at the sight of me?" Miller said, in a whisper.

"I like to stay out of your way," Abraham said flatly.

"There's no need. As I told you last time we met, I have no ill will towards you. We could work together or perhaps just talk. This is a lonely life and family can help to lighten the blow," Miller said.

"I have yet to make penance for my sins," Abraham said, reaching the final stair.

"Old ones? Or are there any new ones I should know about?" Miller said. He hadn't meant for that to sound as cruel as it did.

"This is really touching, but if you don't mind, my boss is going to be really pissed at me and I would like to get this over with," Carter snapped. She was right.

"After," Abraham said.

"Aye, I will hold you to it," Miller said.

"Shhh," Abraham said to Carter as Miller poked his head out in the hallway. This hallway was lit by tiny plastic glowing sticks that gave off a blue light. Two men could be seen just a few doors down. Fresh blood stained the ground in front of it. Farther away, dim sunlight filtered in from around the corner.

"Is there another way in?" Miller asked.

"No time to come around the other way," Abraham said.

"All right, I'll go. They are expecting me," Miller said. "You can …"

"No. Together," Abraham said.

Miller paused for a just a moment. *What did Abraham know that he didn't?*

"All right, lad. Together."

"Joy," Carter said rolling her eyes.

Abraham took point, simply stepping out of the hallway and keeping Carter in front of him. Miller followed, a gun in each hand. He liked the guns, but against Smith and Asmodai, his sword would be so much better.

The two armed men at the end of the hall noticed their little parade immediately and shouted back into the room. In a moment, Smith appeared. He was carrying Sam. The boy's face was covered in tears, but his eyes lit at the site of Miller. Miller smiled back.

"Ancient One and Abraham. Now that's a flashback," Smith said.

"Mr. Miller, they shot my dad!" Sam shouted. "He's hurt real bad!"

"Shhh, child. Your father is still alive, for the moment," Smith said. "Hello, Carter, I see you're up to your usual standard of quality work. Did you ask to be captured or did they catch you taking a cat nap?"

"Yeah, I doubt this is going to look good on my yearly review. I think they want to trade me for the boy and his father," Carter said.

"And Renee Dupré," Abraham added.

"Well, they seem to think I care an awful lot about you. You didn't mention that Renee Dupré was dead, did you?" Smith said with a laugh.

Abraham stiffened, but said nothing.

"How?" Miller asked.

"Asmodai's first victim of the day," Smith answered. "And you have to believe I'm just as upset as you are about it, Abraham. After I went through all this trouble to support her research, arrange her kidnapping, and keep you all busy with the police. Although that begs the question, why aren't you in jail, Miller?"

"I have friends in high places, apparently. Or, it seems, Mike Samson does." Miller smiled. "The police are here for you. Mike seems to have convinced them you're behind our first little adventure in this place."

"Samson, of course," Smith said, with a sigh. "I had a feeling that is how it went down. I'm honestly not worried about the police. You see, I have friends in high places as well. However, the demon that seems to have followed your friend here—now that's a little more complicated. You see, my employers are tired of waiting for the Fallen to appear to be strong. They are tired of your constant quest to kill them. They want the Fallen's power all the time. This goal is near and dear to my heart, as well as my yearly bonus."

"I assume you have a point," Miller said. He had already guessed where Smith was going with this, but it was polite to let the vampire finish. Besides, with Sam directly in the line of fire, there was little he could do. He needed a distraction and he was out of werewolves.

"Well, since you killed my last specimen, and the woman who could make me more is dead, I need to capture Asmodai alive," Smith said. Then he held up the boy. "And if you want this little guy back safe and sound, you're going to do it for me."

"And his father?" Miller asked.

Smith made a face. "We'll see. Dear old dad and I have unfinished business."

"You and I have unfinished business," Miller reminded Smith.

"And the woman? Your sister means nothing to you?" Abraham chimed in at last.

"Sister? Carter? Abraham, please be serious. She's a co-worker," Smith said.

Abraham brought the blade in closer, drawing Carter's blood.

"Smith, you bastard. I knew you were cold, but after everything we've been through together..." Carter screamed, but the sound was cut off.

There was a crash from the end of the hall and the faint sunlight vanished. The floor trembled and all eyes turned in that direction.

Miller knew it was Asmodai, even before the long snout of the creature came into view. His distraction had arrived! Now, he just had to figure out how to survive it! The sword was missing from its maw, but blood still flowed from the wound the weapon had made. The creature barreled ahead into the crowd and opened its mouth to spit.

# 29 - A Pleasant Place in Hell

He was back in the squad car. Sunlight streamed in through the windows and outside it was a bright autumn day in Newark. He was parked near Rutgers and the small trees of the college were already beginning to turn.

Mike shook his head. For some reason it was hard to think, hard to focus. Hadn't he just been someplace else? Wasn't there something important he had to be doing?

His new phone was ringing. He fished it out his pocket and noted that it was his wife calling.

"Don't answer it." The voice came from the back seat. Mike jumped and spun around.

In the back seat was his wife, Melissa. Or what was left of her. Her flesh was pale and her eyes were cold and dead. She was wearing the dress he had buried her in.

"Melissa? What?" Mike said. Then it hit him. This was his dream—the dream that had tormented him since the day she had died. But now it was so much more real, so much more detailed. He could smell the food truck down the road, hear the students milling about outside. There was a fire truck racing somewhere in the distance. He was in his car in Newark and the city was alive around him. And the phone was still ringing.

"Don't answer the phone, Mike," the dead woman said. Mike looked at the phone, a picture of Melissa alive and smiling was displayed.

"I… why? What is this?" Mike stammered.

"You missed the call the first time. Do you remember?" Dead Melissa asked.

"Am I dead?" Mike asked. "Is this, is this my punishment?"

The phone was still ringing.

"Yes, don't answer the phone."

But he had to answer, didn't he? Melissa was calling, and she was in trouble. Mike raised a hand.

"Mike, no. Now is not the time for this," Dead Melissa said.

"But if I don't answer the phone, you'll die," Mike said, looking back to the corpse in the back seat.

"No, I'm already dead. This, all of this, is how you keep punishing yourself. You didn't answer the call when it happened. You were asleep. Asleep on the job and the one time I needed you the most, you didn't even pick up the phone."

"I… I…" Mike stammered. She was right of course. But the phone was still ringing.

"And ever since then, you can't stand to look at yourself in the mirror. You keep throwing yourself into more and more dangerous situations, finding more and more ways to hurt yourself. You say you're trying to redeem yourself, but that's a lie."

"No, not a lie," Mike said weakly.

"It is a lie. You're doing it because you can't forgive yourself. You can't stand that you failed the most important person in your life by simply missing a phone call. Miller saw it. Remember what he said."

Mike flashed back to a moment in a van. Another moment when he was risking everything, this time to rescue Catharine, a woman he hardly knew.

Miller had said "Let her go. Forgive who needs to be forgiven and move on. Your life is precious, if not to you, then to your son." And he had been right.

"Forgive who needs to be forgiven." Melissa repeated Miller's words. "You need to forgive yourself. You know, even if you answer that phone, you couldn't save me. You never could."

Mike stared at the corpse of the woman that had meant everything to him. It was like she had torn his soul apart. And she had done so by simply telling him the truth. He wanted to cry, to bare his wounded heart to the world and weep, but in this strange dreamlike world, he could not.

"But… I have to save you. You're all that matters. You are my world. My life, my love."

Melissa reached out a cold dead hand to touch his cheek, but stopped less than an inch away.

Mike yearned for that touch, even if she was dead, even if he could smell the rot on her from here.

"I'm not all that matters now. I haven't been for a long time. You can't help me anymore. There is someone else who needs your help now. He is your world now." Dead Melissa raised a bony finger and pointed out the windshield.

Sam lay curled up in the street, crying.

"Sam!" Mike shouted. He tossed the ringing phone into the back seat and began to open the car door.

"Save our son and let me go," Melissa said.

As the car door opened, water rushed into the car. The water was warm and sticky. He pushed himself up, but his legs did not work and he stumbled out, falling onto a cold tile floor.

Pain rushed back to him, his head, his ribs, his legs. His nerves screamed out all the broken parts of his body to him. And his knees—Smith had shot him once in each knee!

He was awake, lying face down on the floor of the hospital. Mike must have passed out from the pain. And, oh, what pain it was. He knew things were broken. Some ribs for sure; he could feel the pain that came with every breath. His legs, too. The deep stinging pain of a shattered bone screeched through him.

Through the haze of pain, he searched the room. There were a few men, but no one noticed him. Smith's back was turned. He was talking to someone outside in the hall. No, not talking: screaming. There was gunfire and something huge, just beyond the entrance to the room. He could hear Sam screaming as well. The boy was so close.

And there was something else. Something quiet in all the loud chaos. A child crying. Not Sam, someone else. Someone close. He rolled his head towards the sound. A little girl was crying. The little one that been dancing when he entered the room. She was kneeling over Mike and crying. Then he noticed the dead black eyes and she noticed him.

"Bad people," she whimpered. "They are bad people."

Mike didn't understand completely, but a picture was beginning to form. "Are you Sam's friend?" he asked.

The little Cursed girl nodded. Mike remembered. They had been playing a game when he had entered. But why would Smith bring this poor little creature here?

"Are you going to die?" the little girl said.

Mike wasn't sure, but didn't think telling her that would help. "No. But I'm hurt."

"The bad man hurt you. He said he was nice, but how can he be nice when he hurts Sam and shoots his dad."

"No, he is a bad man. I'm going to stop him," Mike said.

The girl was trying to stop crying. "OK," she said.

There was more screaming, and the sound of fire crackling. *The demon must be here.* Well, he would worry about that next.

He pressed down with both hands, attempting to lift himself up, but his broken body refused and his head swam. He was suddenly face down on the ground again. The little girl was on his other side. Mike guessed he must have passed out again for a moment.

"Sam's Dad. Are you OK? This is not a good place for a nap," the girl said.

"No," Mike said, panting hard. "You're right, this is bad place for a nap. What's your name?"

"Angela," she said.

"Hi, Angela, I'm Mike. I can't seem to move. Can you help roll me over?"

"OK. Like a game?"

"Sure, like a game," Mike said.

The girl lifted his left shoulder, and Mike attempted to lean over in that direction. As he guessed, the girl was very strong for her size and rolled him over with ease. What he didn't guess was the extreme pain. He screamed as he dropped on his back.

"Bad game, bad game," he yelled.

"Yeah, kinda boring," Angela agreed.

When the pain faded back to just oppressive rather than completely overwhelming, Mike began to take stock of the situation. His gun and the taser were missing.

"My gun, Angela, I need my gun. Do you see it?" Mike asked, looking around the room.

The girl looked around too, and then stopped. "Ohh... I know, hold on," she said, and then scampered off.

He didn't have much time. *Where was she going?* He needn't have worried, though. She was back in just a moment.

"There, it's a very pretty color." Angela said, pushing something into his hands. Mike lifted it to his face. It was not his gun; it was a bright orange flare gun.

"No, this won't…" then he stopped. No, this might work. Flare guns could be used to create a fire and that seemed the best way to kill vampires. "Thank you, Angela."

There were men running about the room, but no one paid attention to Mike, with all eyes focused on the horror outside the door. He was also bleeding badly and had already passed out at least three times. From this position, he had a clear shot at Smith, but he knew he only would get off one. And he couldn't fire while Smith had his son.

He aimed the flare gun slowly. Could this possible work? The flare could just bounce harmlessly off Smith's back, and what would he do then? It was also not a great covert weapon, as it was colored bright orange. Smith would notice him at any second. But then, he had to try. He looked over at Angela.

"Go hide. I'll yell when it's safe."

The girl nodded and went to the opposite corner.

Then he raised his weapon and waited for his chance.

*****

Ann ran as fast as she could manage. This day had been long and hard and whatever energy she had received from her quick meal of power bars was fading. Her back still ached and she noticed a slight tremble in her hands, but she was up and moving. And if she could move, she could help.

She spent a few precious seconds figuring out which side of the building the police must have seen the demon enter and quickly found the stairway closest to that point. She threw the door open and took the stairs as fast as she could manage, which wasn't that fast.

Marcel was right behind her. "Are you all right?" he asked.

"Just winded, been a tough day," Ann said. "Come on." In the distance, there was gunfire. "I think we're going the right way."

Ann continued forward, with Marcel staying close behind. Perhaps he thought he might catch her when she collapsed. Or maybe he just didn't want to go first. She wouldn't blame him either way.

Ann made it to the second floor and half pushed, half fell through the door. She quickly recovered her balance. To her right, the place where a window once stood was now open to the sky. Shards of thick glass were everywhere and Ann suddenly remembered her bare feet. She looked to her left. There was a woman, standing so still that Ann almost looked right past her. Beyond the woman was a scene straight out of hell, if Ann had believed in such places. Bodies burned and men ran screaming. The woman watched it all, with her back to Ann. She was dressed simply in jeans and a t-shirt and was leaning on a broadsword. It was Miller's sword. Ann's stomach flipped as she recognized the creature in front of her.

"Lizzie?" she whispered.

Her friend slowly turned towards her. Her face lit up in a smile that was by no means hers, and her eyes held no life at all. The black empty eyes of the Cursed.

"Ann!" Lizzie said, her head laying on her shoulder as if she was stuck in a shrug. The front of her shirt was covered in something black that wasn't exactly blood. "Father says I'm supposed to kill you. I hope you don't mind."

Lizzie lifted the sword and charged.

*****

Bullets flew in every direction as Asmodai entered the hallway. Miller wasn't sure if the men had panicked or had just decided to kill everyone along with the demon. He dove to the ground, one bullet skimming his ear. There was no cover to be found, so he crawled into the nearest room. He turned to see both Carter and Abraham take several shots and tumble to the ground. Bullets would rarely kill a vampire. It was one of the many disappointing things about the creatures. The sword keeping Carter in check was knocked free, but the vampire woman was too stunned to do much about it.

Asmodai let his fire spit fly, catching one of Smith's men in the arm. The man stopped firing to shake the thick goo off, before bursting into flames a moment later, flapping his arms and screaming.

Miller leaned back out into the hallway taking stock of the situation. He did not fire his weapon, but kept an eye on both Sam and Abraham. Smith had dropped back into his room and sent more men. This meant that

Sam was at least safe for the moment. Abraham was struggling to rise. Asmodai had not seen Miller; otherwise, he was sure to be higher on the priority list. And as long as he did not draw the demon's fire—the pun fully and gloriously intended—it might just thin out Smith's ranks for him. Of course, Miller couldn't let them get too thin, Mike and Sam were still in need of rescue.

The men in the hallway were now focused on the demon, who was, in turn, focused on tearing them apart. Miller waited only briefly for a break, then leaped out in the hallway, grabbed Abraham by the bowtie, and dragged him out of the line of fire.

"Still with me?" Miller asked.

"Aye," Abraham responded, mocking Miller's accent.

"Leave the pretty speech to me, lad." Miller smiled and helped lift Abraham to his feet.

Abraham wobbled briefly, then steadied himself and they both returned to the door. Another man screamed for just a moment, before the flames took him. But the demon was slowing. Hundreds of small bullet holes ran up and down its side, and one eye was missing. If only Miller had a pen for the other one.

Miller had to admit: Smith's men were brave. Fighting at this range with Asmodai was almost certain death, but the men did not hesitate. Five of their comrades lay on the floor, dead or dying or burning, and yet they did not flee.

Carter was back on her feet. She grabbed Abraham's sword and ran. Not towards the demon, but in the other direction entirely.

"Those who lived the longest are always the most fearful of death," Abraham said.

Miller wasn't sure if he was talking about Carter or the fact that they stood and watched. "Because we know better," he said. "When the moment comes, I will draw the beast away. Save the boy and his father, but try and leave a piece of Smith for me."

Abraham let out his approximation of a laugh. "Have I not always been an obedient son?"

Miller turned to face him. "To be honest, lad, you were everything but obedient," he said.

"Smith still has the child," Abraham observed.

Smith still held Sam, but the boy was motionless. With luck, Sam had fainted and he would be spared this horror.

The time was coming. Miller could feel it. He pulled out his remaining throwing knife. Well, he could let Abraham have Smith entirely to himself. Best to leave Smith with a parting gift. Miller stepped out into the hallway and let the knife fly.

The blade passed over the demon, through the hallway, and dug deep into Smith's cheek. The blade carved a black path across the vampire's face, then lobbed off the bottom of his ear, perfectly matching the scar on the other side of his face, which Miller had given him all those years ago.

Smith screamed and dropped Sam, clasping both hands to his face.

"Ah, what a priceless sound," Miller said, as he opened fire on the demon. Asmodai sprang back from the new attack, then spun around to see him.

"You!" the creature hissed.

"Gallu and Marduk send their regards!" Miller shouted. Then he turned and ran, and the chase was on.

*****

"Lizzie! Don't!" Ann shouted.

Marcel shoved her hard a moment before the sword sliced the air between them.

"Stand still. This thing is heavy," Lizzie complained, lifting the sword for another attack.

Marcel pulled a gun, but Ann grabbed his arm. "No!" she shouted. "Go help them. I'll deal with her."

Marcel nodded and ran on. The demon's back was turned to them, perhaps giving Marcel a better chance to attack. The old man ran at top speed and slammed a needle into the demon's tail, but the needle snapped. Ann saw this all over Lizzie's shoulder and realized the flaw in her plan. Well, another one. If this poison was going to work, Asmodai would have to be in human form. The needle certainly couldn't get past the hard scales.

The sword slashed sideways, but Ann was prepared and ducked under it easily. Lizzie was not fast with the oversized letter opener, and the woman stumbled about as if drunk. It was less a matter of dodging the sword and more taking down Lizzie without hurting her much.

"Stop it with the moving!" Lizzie complained.

"Lizzie, you have to stop this," Ann said. She knew this wouldn't work, but the words rushed out of her anyway.

"No can do," Lizzie said.

"No can do?" Ann repeated, dodging another lunge. "Lizzie, listen to yourself! Next you'll be saying 'jeepers creepers' and 'whoopsie daisy'"

"Hey, screw you, baldy!" Lizzie swung again. "Damn it, this looked so much easier in the instructional video." Well, that was more Lizzie-ish. "Gah, screw this!" Lizzie took a new stance and threw a kick, lightning fast. It caught Ann in the temple, and she stumbled over. Ann was suddenly on her back, rubbing her head.

"Oh my god, you really do know Taekwondo." she stammered.

"Told ya." Lizzie grinned and lifted the sword above her head for the killing blow.

Ann kicked out hard, hitting Lizzie in the shin. Lizzie's leg shot back and she fell forward on top of Ann. The sword fell as well, the edge digging deep into Ann's shoulder. Ann screamed in pain.

"Enough!" Ann yelled and she punched Lizzie in head, forgetting for a moment just how strong she was now. Lizzie was lifted off Ann by the force the blow and landed on her back several feet away.

Ann leaped to her feet, pulling the sword free with a moan and a gush of blood. Then, she was at Lizzie's side. Her friend's eyes were open, and looked human for a moment, but rolled around in their sockets.

"You punched me in the face! What kinda of friend punches you in the face?" Lizzie said, then stopped. Her eyes fluttered shut and she was still.

"Sorry, sorry, sorry," Ann chanted. She checked Lizzie's pulse, which was weak, but there. Nothing seemed to be broken. Ann had not killed her with that loss of temper. "OK, just rest now."

Ann was bleeding badly which made her even weaker. She noted the sword on the ground, and then noticed that the demon seem to be fleeing. There was no choice, there was only one way to get Lizzie back. Ann stood and picked up the sword.

"Hold on, Lizzie! I know how to fix you," she said and she stumbled after the monster, dragging the weapon behind her.

# 30 - Death and Taxes (but mostly Death)

Mike nearly cheered the moment the blade cut through the Smith's face. Mike could only assume the weapon was Miller's, because—really—who else threw knives? Had it been the 80s, he might have guessed Crocodile Dundee. So that meant, somehow, that Miller was here. *Was he with the police?*

Smith stumbled backwards, clutching his face. He dropped Sam and fired his gun without looking into the hallway. Mike assumed the words that were streaming out of the vampire were swear words, but not in a language Mike knew. Mike saw a brief flash of the demon at the door, then the creature turned and fled.

Mike fingered the flare gun. At this range, it would bounce off Smith and head right back at him. If Mike was lucky, Smith's suit might catch, but would that be enough? Somehow, Mike didn't think so. It was doubtful that vampires were that flammable. No, there had to be another way. He glanced around the room again for the taser, but did not see it. He slid the flare gun out of sight in his coat pocket.

"You! This is all your fault!" Smith suddenly noticed that Mike was awake. "You stupid little man. All my people, all my projects, just because you couldn't do what you were told. Even when I had your son." Smith walked over and grabbed Mike's shirt. The vampire pulled Mike up into the air with one hand and Mike screamed as the pain flared. "Even when I had your son."

"You were going to kill us anyway," Mike said weakly. He was sure of this. There was never any doubt in his mind of that.

"True," Smith agreed. He pulled Mike's Desert Eagle out of his suit pocket. "You know, I always wanted one of these. " He pointed the gun at Mike's face. "I could just clean this up now, but..." The gun slowly drifted over to Sam's still body. "First, I think you need to watch something."

"No!" Mike screamed and dug into his pocket for the flare gun. Smith smiled.

"Oh, yes." He pulled the trigger as Mike freed the flare gun. His head spun to follow the shot, almost too terrified to see.

The little girl, Angela, was suddenly there. Her arms were spread wide, her mouth open in a silent scream of protest. She was directly in the path of the bullet, which stuck her in the chest. The little girl folded in on herself, flopping to the ground like a discarded rag doll.

"Oh, Angela, of all the stupid..." Smith began, but Mike cut him off by shoving the flare gun into the vampire's mouth.

"Die, you god damn monster," Mike screamed and pulled the trigger.

Smith's head rocked back and he dropped both Mike and the gun. The vampire's face began to glow red and black smoke poured out of his mouth. He brought his hands to his throat as if he was choking, his black eyes wide with terror.

Mike hit the ground, but he ignored the pain. He was so filled with hate and rage, nothing would stop him from hurting Smith. The man that had tormented him, took away his son, killed Catharine. He dug his elbows into the ground and crawled the few feet to the weapon. His fingers reached the handle. He sprang up into a sitting position with a scream and opened fire.

"Die, just die!" Mike shrieked. He repeatedly pulled the trigger. The first shot went wide, but the second caught the vampire in the hip, the third dead center in the chest. Then the gun clicked empty.

Smith took the punishment without so much as a word. He continued to make choking noises as smoke teemed from him. Not just from his mouth, but his nose and ears, and then the wound in his chest. Then his eyes burst like grapes and a tongue of flame erupted from the wound in his chest. Smith toppled over at last and then burst into flame.

Mike continued to pull the trigger on the empty gun. At any moment, Smith would pop back up from the floor. "Ha! I was just kidding with the eye–bursting-burning-to-death thing," he would say. Then that long black tongue would come out and Mike would die his long overdue death.

But Smith did not get back up. Something dark and black leaped in the flames, but did not reach for him.

Then Abraham was in the room with him. And another older looking man. Mike was still pulling the trigger.

"Mr. Samson," the older man was saying, but his voice sounded far away. Like he was in another room, even though he was standing right next to him. "Your son is okay. He is breathing."

Mike kept pulling the trigger. It was starting to dawn on him that he was in shock.

"The girl?" he whispered. But Angela was already sitting back up and wailing, her chest covered in blood.

The room was starting to tilt, and for a moment, Mike thought the building might be collapsing. Then he noticed it was just his head. He couldn't seem to hold it straight anymore. The old man was still talking to him.

"Renee Dupré…" The man was saying. "Where is Renee Dupré? Where is my wife?"

Mike was suddenly cold. He tried to talk, he mouthed the word 'gone', but could not make any more noise. His head was now on the floor, and he was still pulling the trigger on the gun. The world was sideways and far too bright.

"Samson!" someone was shouting, but they were too far away now. There was some else above him. For a moment, he thought it might be Melissa and he wondered if he had done okay. But then the image was gone and he was alone in the bright whiteness of the room. Then there was nothing at all.

*****

Wherever Miller ran, the demon followed. As he ran down the hall, he turned and fired a few rounds into the Asmodai just to be sure of it. It was nice to be the demon's center of attention again. Well, perhaps nice was not the correct word.

Miller burst through the stairwell door and stormed down the first flight. He spun at the bottom and raised a gun in each hand. A moment later, the demon smashed through the doorway, sending the door flying in Miller's direction. Miller dodged the door and opened fire, emptying both guns into the Fallen's snout-like face.

The demon was too large to fit through the entrance, so it was stuck for a moment, until the doorway and a large chunk of concrete came free. Then, the demon moved down the stairs, carrying the doorframe with it like an oversized dog collar.

Miller dropped the empty guns and grabbed two more that were hanging from his neck while leaping down the stairs out of the demon's reach. He kicked the door open and ran out of the stairwell.

There was a blur of motion and one of Miller's guns was suddenly on the ground. It took a moment longer to notice that his hand was still attached to the gun and no longer on his wrist. Carter, the vampire woman, appeared from his right side, holding Abraham's sword. She was grinning like cat when she jammed the point of the blade into Miller's belly.

Miller stumbled backwards, holding the bloody stump of his arm in the air.

"Now, really, this isn't a good time for this," he gasped. He could hear the demon tearing apart the stairwell.

"You know, you are not all that great," Carter said, leaning on the wall next to him. "Smith would always shit himself every time anyone mentioned you, but really, I'm not that impressed."

"Sorry to disappoint you. However, I do have a few skills," Miller said, sliding to the ground.

"Oh, really?" Carter said.

"Well for one…" Miller opened fired with the gun in his still whole left hand. "I can shoot very well with both hands." A stream of bullets caught Carter in the chest, slamming her backwards towards the stairwell door.

"Two, I tend to be followed by rather large demons," Miller said.

The door to the stairwell flew open and Asmodai stuck his head into the hallway. It immediately clamped its teeth down on Carter. The vampire screamed as the demon swung its head up and down, like a dog trying to break a captured squirrel's neck.

Miller pulled the sword free with his left hand, then leaned on the weapon as he stood on shaky feet. He was bleeding badly. There could be no more running. He would have to make his last stand here.

Miller stood tall and readied the sword as Asmodai approached.

*****

"Samson!" Marcel shouted, but the man did not respond. Mike Samson lay in a pool of his own blood, his pulse barely there.

"Is he gone?" Abraham asked.

"Soon, without an ambulance," Marcel said.

"I wonder if the demon is immune to its own fire," Abraham asked.

"What?" Marcel said, baffled by the sudden change in subject.

"Nothing. My apologies. I was just musing on the dragon. The way the flame is delayed, I wonder if that is to protect the demon itself from its flame."

"I…" Marcel looked at his old friend. Had he gone mad?

"Marcel, old friend, I have terrible tidings and I'm afraid my old brain is trying to distract me."

"Renee?" Marcel said, his heart sinking.

Abraham lowered his gaze to the ground. "She is gone. The demon took her with his flame, just moments before we arrived," Abraham said. "I am sorry."

Marcel stood, dumbstruck. After all this, all of this misery and pain, this is how it ended? That short awkward kiss they had shared not even twenty-four hours ago was to be their last? How could this be?

"No!" Marcel stumbled backwards. "No! After we survived so much." He forgot how mad he was with her, how disappointed he was. She was still his wife and he still loved her.

The demon had taken everything from them, and then finally took her away as well. Marcel's blood seemed to boil. He would have his revenge for all the pain and suffering that monster had caused him. Renee would not die in vain.

Marcel turned from the room, his mind following a path he swore he would never travel again. The transformation did not slow him and the trail was easy to follow. Marcel would destroy the demon with the very claws that the monster had given him.

*****

Ann ran as fast as she could, dragging the giant sword. Blood was running down her chest, but she ignored it as best she could.

Down the hall, the demon burst through the doorway and disappeared down the stairs. How could she use the sword against Keith? She hoped it wouldn't come to that. She still had the needle to try. Maybe it would work; maybe she could save Keith and Lizzie in one move. She had to try.

Ann reached the stairwell. Asmodai was just below her now. She passed through the hole it had made in the wall and looked down at it. The sight of the long snakelike demon made it easy to forget its face. Ann pushed the thought aside and sprinted down the stairs, but she stumbled on the last one of the first flight. Asmodai had managed to reach its head through the door and was thrashing something about. A woman was screaming. Then the demon pushed through the door, taking a large chunk of it with it.

"Wait!" she called, but the demon did not hear, so Ann raced after it into the hallway.

Miller was there. His right hand was missing and his shirt was covered with blood. In his left hand, he held a sword. Miller and the demon were locked into place, waiting for the other to make a move. Perhaps Miller's sword gave Asmodai pause.

"My king!" she shouted, sliding to her knees.

Asmodai spun to face her. "Youuu," the creature hissed. Its face was a mess of bullet wounds and torn scales. Only one eye still functioned and many teeth appeared to be missing. The demon had paid dearly for its rampage.

"My king," Ann repeated.

The demon hung above her ready to strike, but something kept it in check.

"Ann, lass… run!" Miller shouted.

Ann put a hand up to silence him. She was thinking fast. She needed the man, not the demon. But how did one speak like a demon?

"Peace, my king," Ann said, trying to match Amon's overconfident and angry tone. "The humans have tricked you. Have tricked us. They have weakened us, turned us against each other. Surely, you know I would never kill… ummm," Ann stumbled for the right word for a moment, but then it came. "I would never kill one of the family."

The demon did not move, considering.

Ann knew the demon wanted to believe her. She almost felt guilty tricking it this way, giving it hope.

"Let me see your face, Lilith. Your true face," Asmodai demanded.

Ann briefly considered attempting to change shape again, but there was an easier way. "I cannot. The woman, Dupré, she has crippled me. I am stuck in this form," Ann lied. It did feel good to make Dupré the fall woman though. She had that coming at least.

"Dupré!" Asmodai snarled. "Is there no end to her heresy?"

"I have sworn to kill her," Ann declared.

The demon chuckled. "Then I bring you news; the woman is dead. Struck down by my flame outside this very building," the demon said.

Ann paused, overcome with a rush of mixed emotions. *Dupré was dead?* She'd gotten what she had deserved and yet...

"Does this not bring you joy?" the demon asked.

"I... I only wish to have done it myself," Ann said, covering quickly. Renee Dupré was gone, and she was conflicted about that, but Ann would deal with it later.

"I only hope she served your purpose and was worth all this pain," the demon said.

*My purpose? What did that mean?* "Of course, it served my purpose," Ann said, covering with overconfidence. But a hundred questions suddenly appeared in her mind.

Ann noticed, then, that it was shifting. Becoming human again. Its face was flattening, its spine was shrinking. The creature's legs straightened, and the long claws retracted into fingers.

Ann looked away, trying not to show how disturbed she was.

Miller lay still against the wall, watching Ann very carefully. She patted the needles in her pocket, hoping he would take that as a sign that she knew what she was doing.

"The man Samson is here as well. I will end him also," the demon hissed.

"No!" Ann shouted, a little too loudly. The demon froze and Ann remembered herself. "I have already ended his miserable existence." She almost added something about tearing out his heart and eating it, but didn't want to oversell it.

In front of her, the transformation continued. Pink flesh grew and covered black scales. Occasionally, a bullet reversed course and popped out onto the ground. Black hair popped out from its skull.

"Good, good! I had told the others. I told them that this was a human trick, that you would never betray us." The demon actually sounded happy. Not only that, but it sounded human.

Ann's heart sank and she steeled herself, then she looked him in the eye.

Keith stood before her. Or at least a version of him. All the damage he had taken as a demon remained, although it had apparently shrunken with him. Small holes covered his flesh, there was a missing chunk, black and throbbing, above his hip, and his face was just barely recognizable. A black gash rose from his chin to the bottom of his nose, splitting his lips. There was a hole under his chin and another where his left eye had been.

Ann trembled at the view. She had known it would be hard to see him like this, but it was so much worse. Some part of her still wanted to run to him, to weep into his chest until all of this went away. To be honest, that part of her made the rest of her a little sick. She was not the weak little woman Keith Malone had kicked around for all those years. She was strong now. Then she quivered slightly. *Well stronger, anyway.*

The demon approached her and placed a hand gently on her cheek. His touch was like fire.

"My queen, it is good to have you back."

"My king," was all she could choke out. Her hand went to her pocket and she slowly pulled free a needle.

"The Ancient One is wounded. Together, we will finish him, then leave this cursed place."

"Yes." She couldn't believe she was saying this, "But first, a kiss." She was impressed that her voice didn't crack.

Asmodai's eye lit up at the idea and he moved his ruined lips towards hers. Ann jammed the needle into his side and pushed the plunger as hard as she could. The demon screamed and shoved her away.

"What? What is this?" Asmodai screamed. There was hurt in that voice, real hurt.

"I'm sorry," Ann said, and to her surprise, she was. "The woman… " *creature? Demon?* "... errr… being you love is dead. I'm in charge here now. Just plain old Ann Melakh. Lilith did not betray you. Just me."

"Impossible!" the demon man screamed, as he lunged, grabbing Ann by the throat. Ann slammed another needle into Asmodai's arm. He trembled as she pushed down the plunger, but did not release her.

"That's not what your girl Black, I mean, Amon, said," Ann responded through clenched teeth. "She knew." Ann attempted to peel the fingers away from her throat, but the demon's grasp was like steel.

"Liar!" Asmodai cried. The drug didn't seem to be doing anything besides making the demon very, very mad.

"Hands off the lass," said Miller, as he entered the fray. He brought the sword down and sliced neatly through Asmodai's arm. The demon grunted in pain, then backhanded Miller with the other hand, sending the little man sprawling.

Ann dropped to the ground, but the hand still remained clasped around her throat. Ann gagged, digging her fingers into the flesh of the rogue appendage.

"You, I told you this was a family matter," the demon said to Miller.

Miller was getting up slowly. The man was pale and sweating. His shirt was soaked red with his own blood. "You couldn't stay out of it. All you ever do is destroy."

The demon punched Miller again, driving him back down to the ground.

Miller didn't stay down; he rolled away, almost as if he was in slow motion and then he started the process of getting back to his feet. He slipped on his own blood and fell again. "Funny, coming from you monster," Miller spat from the ground. "Your kind only knows destruction."

The fingers would not budge from her throat. Ann could not breathe. This was such a stupid way to die. Ann looked desperately towards Miller, but the man could hardly stand himself. And Asmodai was going to kill him. The demon stood above Miller, ready to give the final blow, but then he stopped and turned to Ann.

"Your kind always treated him like a hero." Asmodai pointed his remaining hand at Miller. "He is no hero. All of this, all of the pain brought to your people and mine. It could all be laid at his feet."

"No!" Miller shouted. The little man jumped, driving his weapon into the demon's chest. Ann could tell the blow had meant to be higher, but Miller had stumbled at the last moment and the sword caught in Asmodai's ribs. The demon shook his head and struck Miller in the face again. Ann actually saw teeth fly from Miller mouth as he tumbled back to the ground. The demon grabbed the sword and pulled it free, black blood gushing from the wound. Then he snapped the blade in half and tossed the pieces to the side.

"Yes, it all comes back to you. Did you think we didn't know?" Asmodai strode forward and kicked Miller in the ribs.

Ann fell forward, her knees buckling. She was positive her face was a shade of blue at this point. But then the hand released and dropped to the ground next to her. Ann gasped for air. Asmodai was addressing her again.

"Didn't you think it was odd that he, of all people, was chosen to hunt us? Why him? The man who couldn't die. The great hunter." Asmodai kicked Miller again.

"It was all my charm and good manners," Miller coughed.

Ann stood, still holding her throat. As she got to her feet, she saw the hand that had nearly choked her to death. The flesh was melting off the bone. Had the drug done that? Ann turned and made for Miller's sword she had dragged along with her. Her plan B. The plan she didn't think she could bring herself to complete.

"It was you, when your race had just begun. It was you that freed us from our prison. Well, one prison anyway." The demon stomped down on Miller's remaining hand. The bones crunched under Asmodai's heel. Miller yelled and kicked, knocking the demon back.

Ann reached the sword and just barely managed to lift it. She was panting hard and it felt like her lungs were burning.

"Had you not found us, how many more of your people would have lived?" the demon sneered.

Miller rolled again, this time finding a wall. Using it as brace, he stood to face Asmodai. "Had it not been me, some other poor fool would have found it," Miller said. "That was my sin and my fault." Miller lashed out with a kick, landing a blow on the wound in the demon's side. It apparently hurt, as the demon staggered slightly. "And every time I cut down one of you bastards or your children, or save another life, I make another small amends for that mistake. And someday, somehow, I will find a way to end this." Miller threw another kick, but the demon was ready this time and caught the blow mid-strike.

Ann struggled forward. She positioned the blade in front of her, like a giant spear. There was no saving Keith now. She screamed as she charged forward.

The demon held Miller's foot and for a moment the little man kept his balance. But the fight was draining out of him and staining the floor red at his feet. Asmodai simply left his arm up and Miller fell back to ground. The demon lifted his hand and the blade like claws leaped from his fingertips.

"We'll see what face you wear next time we meet," the demon said calmly. He drove the hand straight through Miller's chest. "I do enjoy killing you."

"Feeling's mutual," Miller sputtered and he threw another punch at the demon's face. The creature laughed, turned, and threw Miller at Ann who was now mere feet away. She just barely managed to drop the point of the sword, before Miller crashed into her. They dropped to the ground.

"Lass," Miller choked. "It's best not to scream before attacking from behind."

"Miller!" Ann shouted. She rolled over, resting him on his back. His blood coated her.

"See you still cry for him." The demon stood over her. "He brought you nothing but pain."

Ann turned to face him. He looked different suddenly. He flesh seemed to hang a little loosely around his face. "He is my friend," Ann said. What else could she say?

"Abominations don't need friends," Asmodai said. The demon staggered suddenly and dropped to one knee. It was weakening! The drugs were working!

"What have you done to me?" the demon sputtered.

Ann shook her head. "I… I… wanted to save him," Ann managed.

"Who?" The demon said standing again.

"The man, the man you once were. Keith Malone."

The demon smiled at this, his split lips spreading even farther apart with the act. "Then you are a fool. The man is long dead. And you will join him." The demon picked up Miller's large sword.

*****

The furious wolf that had once been Marcel Dupré burst down the hall, following the trail of destruction that the demon had left behind. It felt a bit like coming home. The truth was, Marcel had missed the power his cursed form had given him; he had been a beast far longer than a man.

Then Marcel found them. The demon was gone, replaced by a wounded young man. He stood above Ann and the Ancient One, brandishing a large sword, but there was no mistaking the creature, even in this human form. The Ancient One looked gravely wounded, lying near Ann, but all of this barely registered for Marcel. His one thought was revenge and how much easier it would be if the demon was shaped as a man. He would tear the monster limb from limb before it could change form again.

Asmodai noticed Marcel as well. Marcel registered the disgust and annoyance on the demon man's face. Asmodai spat at him. It was long thin spray of clear liquid that jetted out of the young man's mouth. The demon had done it dismissively, as if Marcel was not worth the time to destroy with his bare hands. Marcel was nothing to him, a distraction, a wayward child that would be quickly destroyed and forgotten. But Marcel had other plans. The words Abraham had planted in his mind just moments ago bubbled back up through the red haze of anger. The demon might not be immune to its own flame. Marcel leaped, knowing he could cover the last few feet to the demon in the air, even if the flame took him. And the flame did take him, it was as if he was the center of his very own sun. The pain didn't even have time to register. He reached out with what he knew would be his last effort on his earth, and grabbed Asmodai's head between his hands. The wolf man and demon collapsed to the floor. The sound of the demon's scream was the last thing Marcel Dupré would hear. But Marcel thoughts were not of revenge, or his dead wife. A questioned burned in his mind, one moment before Asmodai's flame did. *How had Abraham known?*

*****

"Down, lass," Miller cried. With a sudden burst of strength, he dove to cover Ann's face. The wolf man and the demon met in an odd embrace and then exploded into bright white flame an instant later.

"Keith!" Ann heard herself shout. She struggled to rise, but Miller held her firmly in place until the flames vanished, and there was nothing left of what was once Keith Malone but ash.

Then Ann was free and she scrambled to her feet, but her good sense came back to her and she did not move any closer. The floor was scorched black, as was the ceiling directly above it. Two burnt skeletons lay on the ground, twisted together, bones fused in places from the extreme heat of the fire.

The events of the last few seconds finally caught up to her. The wolf had been Marcel Dupré.

"Lass," came a weak voice. Ann spun back to face Miller. He was pale and shaking.

"Hold on, Miller. We'll get you help." Ann pulled out the cell phone and dialed the police who were waiting outside.

"No, Ann. Not for me. Not for this body anyway," Miller said.

"All clear, bring in the troops," Ann said into the phone. "And ambulances. We have wounded." She did not bother waiting for a response and hung up the phone. "It's OK, we can stitch you back up. The way you heal, you'll be up and running in a day or two." She knelt by his side.

"No, not this time," Miller said. He reached out for her hand.

"But, but you can't die," Ann said, her voice faltering for a moment. "I thought, I thought you were immortal."

Miller shook his head. "It doesn't…" He coughed. "It doesn't work like that. I die the same as any man. Just takes a little more effort sometimes."

"No, no you can't die. There are more Fallen out there. We need you," Ann said. Tears long held back were now beginning to flow freely down her face. Not just tears for Miller, but tears for Keith, tears for Lizzie. Tears for everything that had happened over the past month.

"I'm afraid I'm going to have to disagree with you," Miller said. He grinned at her. It was a sad thing, with the missing teeth, but it was Miller.

"Was it true?" Ann said. She suddenly had to know. "What the demon said about you and the Fallen."

Miller coughed again. "Truth be told, I had almost forgotten." His eyes wandered away from hers, and they focused straight up at the ceiling, as if he was looking for the sky somewhere above it.

"Miller?" Ann said. "Miller?"

But the man did not respond. He let out a sigh and was gone.

# 31 - Recovery

Sam didn't remember much. There was something with scales, like a giant snake, and that bad guy, Smith, yelling. His dad had come to rescue him, like he knew would happen. And then there was fire. Not like the fire when he had gone camping, this was a bad fire and Sam shuddered at the memory of it. Grandma told him he had something called a concussion, which was a hard word to say. The nurse said the worst was over and he could go home soon. No one talked much about his dad. Everyone said he was ok, but they said it in the way adults say things they know are not true. They had said that about his mom in the exact same way until she was gone and he didn't have a mother anymore.

After a long time, Ann came to visit. She looked tired and dirty, but Sam was glad she was okay. Then he saw Angela walk in behind her wearing silly pink sunglasses and carrying a stuffed animal.

"Angela!" he shouted.

"Sam!" Angela shouted back.

They giggled and jumped on the bed, until the nurse made them stop. Sam briefly wondered if the nurse was a monster too. The woman redeemed herself just a little by turning on the room's television. Angela stopped giggling and demanded Dora.

Sam noticed Ann sitting by herself and looking miserable.

"Ann. How is my dad?" he asked.

"He's going to fine," Ann lied. Sam gave her a doubtful look and she added, "I hope." Well, that was better.

"Good, and Mr. Miller?" the boy asked. Ann stiffened.

"Mr. Miller went away for a while," she said. Sam wasn't sure what that meant, but he didn't ask more.

"Okay, good. I need you to do something for me," Sam stated in his most serious grown up voice.

"Sure."

"Angela is a monster like you," Sam said. Well that was certainly one way of putting it.

"Yes. I noticed," Ann agreed.

"But she's a good monster and she's very nice, especially for a girl. She doesn't have a mommy anymore and I'm not sure monsters have dads. "

"Well, it's complicated. You see when a mommy monster and a daddy monster really love each other…" Ann started.

"No, no. I think you should be Angela's monster mommy," Sam said.

"Wait, what?"

"She's really well behaved. She doesn't eat much. Just some kitties from time to time," Sam said.

"Kitties? Wait, she eats kitties?" Ann asked in horror, just a little too loud. Angela heard and turned around to look at them.

"Does anyone have a kitty? I am so hungry," she said.

"You can't eat kittens," Ann said.

"That's what I said," Sam agreed.

"Have you ever tried kitty? They taste delicious," Angela said, then turned back to the television. Ann looked disgusted.

"You could take care of her and then you could bring her over to my place to visit," Sam continued.

"I'm not sure I'm really cut out to be a mommy for anyone … or anything," Ann said. Sam was looking at her with pleading eyes. "I don't know about being her mommy. But I'll take care of her. Promise," Ann said. Sam smiled.

"Yay! I knew you were a good monster," he said, pleased. Ann shook her head.

# 32 - Revelations and Explanations

The moon was full above her, while the city of Newark was bright below. Ann drifted silently through the night sky, searching. She had done so every night she could, since her conversation with the very much alive John Takahashi. She told herself it was to find Abraham, to find answers to the questions that plagued her, but if she was to be honest with herself, flying was simply wonderful. It helped clear her head and the fears she had for Lizzie, Mike, Angela, and even Lilith faded some.

Thirty minutes ago, she had spotted a trail. The mist that marked the Cursed trailed behind them and if she focused, she could see it and track it. Abraham had called it the sight, which was a vague term if there ever was one, but it did describe it well. She had attempted to use it once before, only to find one of the Fallen instead. This time, the trail was much smaller, much harder to see, and it led to an ancient looking theatre off Broad Street.

Ann landed on the roof, losing her balance only for a moment when she touched the ground. She stepped quickly a few times and then dropped to one knee. This was a big improvement over her usual face plant landings. She was improving.

She stayed on one knee for a moment, gathering herself to put away her wings. The transformation to completely human was painful, but she pushed through it. She did not risk her full demon form out in the night if she could avoid it, so she had taken to the skies with only the demon wings. Her power had returned to her about a day after Miller had died. Waiting at the hospital, she had continually pushed against the block in her mind. It was like a cut in her mouth that she couldn't help but find with her tongue. Then without warning, the block had faded. For some reason Ann could not completely explain, this was a relief.

Once the wings had slid away and the flesh on her back had regrown, Ann stood and shrugged on her coat. The shirt she wore had no back, to make way for the wings, so the coat helped to cover her up and make her feel more herself. The blonde wig helped as well. She brushed her fingers through the hairpiece, making sure it had not come loose in her travels.

The roof she was on had a fire escape on the right side. It went up to the floor below her, so she had to drop several feet to reach it, but that was no issue. She made her way down to the ground floor and found the trail again. It passed through a wide gilded door with a very old sign that said, "Closed for Renovations." The door was unlocked. Ann glanced up and down the street; there were a few people about, but no one too close. She pushed the door open, slid inside, and quietly closed it behind her.

The smell inside was musty, but not unpleasant. It was not the stench of dead flesh she had found in her last monster hunting expedition. That was a good sign.

With the door closed, the room she was in was dark, but beyond it, she could see candlelight flickering. Ann could still make out the trail in front of her. It doubled back on itself several times, before moving forward towards the light. Ann aimed for the light but then stopped. *Why would Abraham light candles?* Perhaps she was in wrong place; unless, of course, Abraham was expecting company? Her answer came booming into the room.

"Come on in, little sister," Abraham's voice echoed.

Ann relaxed a little and walked forward. The darkness faded and she entered the theater proper. It was like walking into another time. It had not been candles, as Ann had first thought, but gas lamps running along the halls. A beautiful polished wood floor spread out before her, covered with rows and rows of red velvet seats. The stage stood at the end, detailed in marble stone, and intricate carvings of masks and instruments. A large red curtain was in the center of it, old and faded, but still whole and clean. It did not look like an abandoned theater, but a fully functional one.

Abraham sat in the middle, leaning back in a velvet chair. His long legs were stretched out before him; his ruined top hat lay at an odd angle on his head. On the chair beside him rested a new cane.

"Beautiful," Ann said, trying to see all directions at once.

"Welcome, little sister, to my home. I had wondered how long it would take you to find it," Abraham said, spreading his arms out in front of him, laying claim to everything Ann saw.

"This? This is your home?" Ann asked.

The vampire chuckled. "Yes and no. I've spent so much time here over the years, it feels like, but I suppose I don't exactly own it. I'm a caretaker of sorts. Many, many years ago, when I first came to this county, I was much more. But that time has passed."

"You are quite the man of mystery," Ann said. She took a seat near him and looked out onto the stage.

"Thank you, I do try." Abraham tipped his hat in her general direction.

"Let me guess, you used to…" Ann paused. "You used to sing here… maybe in the 50s?"

Abraham's hat dropped to the ground and Ann smiled. It was good to be the one with the surprises this time.

The vampire gathered the hat and dusted it off before speaking again. "You have the notebook?" he guessed at last.

"Yes, there were notes there about your singing," Ann admitted. "It wasn't that hard of a leap. You must be very good. It was one of the last notes Dallas ever wrote."

"I sang as I worked with Marcel and the men. I found singing hymns tended to make folks relax when around a vampire," he said, still staring with his dead eyes at the stage in front of him. "Yes, from time to time, we all escape our lives and find happiness. I found it here once with Marcel and Renee."

"She must have been a different person back then," Ann said.

"Renee was a good woman once. She was family," Abraham said. "I'm sorry you never got to see that part of her."

"We never found her body." Ann asked.

Abraham just smiled for a moment. "We?" he asked. Classic avoidance, answering with a question with a question.

"Yeah, we. The Newark police, the FBI, and myself."

"Those are powerful friends."

"Well, she made a lot of people angry," Ann said. "She murdered my friends, unleashed the Fallen, and…" She trailed off.

"Cursed you?" the vampire offered.

"Yes, I guess that's a way of putting it," Ann said. "But she's dead now. And if it means anything, I am still sorry for your loss. I know how it is to lose family."

"How are Mr. Samson and his son?" Abraham asked.

"Sam is fine. Mike is alive, although the doctors are not sure he'll walk again. They've kicked him off the police force and there is a hearing in a few weeks to determine what they are going to do with him."

"Be a shame to see the man in prison. Sons need their fathers," Abraham said.

"John says that's not likely. The government is going to be doing its best to cover up this whole thing, although something like half the Newark Police force knows, so I'm not sure how well that will go."

"It will go fine. People don't want to believe. They'll make stories maybe even jokes about it, but it will fade in time," Abraham said.

"I hope you're right," Ann said. She wasn't so sure.

"And you? What does John say about you?" Abraham asked.

"John Takahashi is forming a new unit in the FBI. They've put him in charge this time and he's asked me to join him."

Abraham turned and looked at her directly for the first time. "You and the FBI? You want to work with the people that hunted you?"

"I do. It's the best way. There's still at least one of the Fallen still out there and Smith's little group of Cursed. There's no one better equipped to stop them than me," Ann said.

"Takahashi is a good man, but others may not be so," Abraham warned.

"John has pledged to keep my secret. Even from his bosses," Ann said.

"And you trust him?"

"I do," Ann said. "And I think I can make a difference." She let that hang out in the air before making her first request. It took her a while to work up to it. Her relationship with Abraham was friendly enough, even in the short time they had known each other, but this was taking it to a new level.

"We could use you too. On the team, I mean," Ann said.

Abraham laughed out loud.

That stung Ann a little, but she pressed on anyway. "We have the official government's power to stop the Fallen. We could help the Cursed, keep people safe."

"Would I get a new suit?" Abraham laughed.

Ann laughed back. "Maybe even a new hat," she added and then they both laughed.

For a moment, after the laughter slowly died off, neither said anything.

"No, no, little sister. I'm sorry," Abraham said, shaking his head. "Not this time."

"Oh," Ann said. It wasn't unexpected, but it still was disappointing.

"But I'll check on you, from time to time. Make sure the feds take good care of my little sister," Abraham added.

"Thanks," Ann nodded.

"I think a suit might look good on you," Abraham said. "Maybe a white one?"

"Ah, no, I don't think so. I spend enough time in white these days as it is," Ann said.

"True, true. You've come a long way though." The vampire looked Ann up and down. "You seem to have worked out how to change your appearance."

"Yeah, I'm getting better at it. I wouldn't say I'm used to it yet. Probably never will be. Yesterday, I woke up with wings and a ruined set of pajamas. So, I still have more to learn," Ann said. She was sure she would laugh at that story someday, but not yet. "You know what happened to Miller, right?" Ann said switching topics.

"Yes, the Ancient One has met his end, again," Abraham said. He didn't seem so bothered about it, but then Ann didn't really understand their relationship.

"There's something I don't understand. The police ID'd Miller's body as Andres Soliz. Soliz was the janitor at my lab. He did look like Miller, but… it wasn't really him. Was it?"

Abraham stretched then stood, grabbed the cane, and began to walk slowly towards the stage. He beckoned Ann to follow him with one hand. Ann noted he did not move like a blind man, he simply walked as if he could see everything clearly.

"The Ancient One has many secrets, even from himself," he said, slowly moving forward. "As old as I am, I cannot even fathom how it must be to be his age. He is thousands of years old. He has forgotten entire lifetimes, entire centuries. He is as mad as they come, yet never gives up. His lust for life is as eternal as he is. "

"You really aren't one for straight answers, are you?" Ann said.

Abraham reached the stage and jumped onto it, clearing the six-foot leap with ease. He then spun to face Ann, as if about to break into song. He bowed and smiled but did not respond to her comment.

"The Ancient One does not live like others. He is tied to the Fallen; their fates are intertwined forever. As long as the Fallen live, so does he." He continued, "When the Fallen are reborn, so is he. The night Lilith took you in your lab, Andres Soliz died."

Ann gasped, not at Abraham's statement, but at something clicking into place in her head. She trembled at the memory of watching the video on the computer, hunched over Lizzie's desk.

"In the video I have of that night, Lilith took me, but there was someone else there. That must have been Soliz. It makes perfect sense," Ann said, then reconsidered. "Well, as much sense as any of this does I suppose."

"Andres Soliz was the Ancient One's latest vessel. The most recent of thousands, maybe millions. The Ancient One leaps from life to life..."

"Putting things right that once went wrong, and hoping each time that his next leap will be the leap home?" Ann interrupted.

This gave Abraham pause. "Pardon?"

"Little joke, sorry," Ann said. She really would need to learn to keep her big mouth shut. "So is Miller like a ghost? Or a memory? Was the Ancient One I knew just Andres Soliz thinking he was the Ancient One?"

"No, he was the Ancient One. As much as anyone can be," Abraham said. "And so will the next man be, as long as the Fallen still exist."

"Asmodai said that Miller had caused it all. He had originally freed the Fallen and allowed them into our world. There's also a section in Dallas's book about different myths that he thought Miller might be the basis for. One of them is Pandora's Box."

Abraham grinned. "When I was a boy, my father used to tell me tales of the goddess Pandora. The all giver. It was not until many years later that I read about the story of Pandora and her jar."

"Jar?" Ann asked.

"Yes, when I heard it, it was a jar. A pithos, as the Greeks called it." Abraham sat and hung his feet over the side the stage, his long legs dangling. For a moment, he looked much younger and there was an eagerness about him that Ann had never seen before. "In the Greek version of the myth, Pandora was a curse from the Gods. The first woman given to mankind to punish them for the discovery of fire."

"Didn't..." Ann paused for a moment, trying to remember the name. "Prometheus, steal the flame?"

"Yes, and punishing him wasn't enough. Everyone had to suffer. Zeus was not the nicest of Gods," Abraham said. "So they made Pandora from clay and the Gods taught her many things. Here, her name meant 'many gifted'. She was given to men, one man in particular, who she disobeyed and opened the jar, unleashing all that is wrong with the world."

"It's like Adam and Eve," Ann added. "Men blaming women for everything."

"Yes, women's lib was a ways off," Abraham said with a wink. "But this is the Greek version of the myth. There are much older versions."

"Like the one your Father told you about. Where Pandora was a goddess," Ann offered.

"Yes, but more importantly, where a man opened the jar," Abraham said.

"And that man was Miller. Or the original Miller...err...Ancient One," Ann said.

Abraham just shrugged. "It's possible. This is long before even my time. Stories grow and change with time and these stories are beyond ancient. Stories are told and retold over generations. People are invaded and the invaders take the local stories and make them their own. In this case, they discredit the name of the old goddess Pandora, by blaming all the evils of the world on her. The sliver of truth that once ran through the original story could be long gone. "

"But it makes sense though. Why else would Miller and the Fallen be connected?"

"It does. There was even one version of the story I came across that listed the evils that escaped from the jar. "

"Let me guess. There were seven."

"Seven are they," Abraham sung back. "They were lust, gluttony, greed, sloth, wrath, envy, and pride. But then they have many names."

"Wow," Ann said, her head was reeling. It was all she could say.

"Of course, it could just be a story. Man trying to make sense of the strange world he finds himself in." Abraham stood again. He pointed to carvings that covered the edges of the stage, something a truly blind man could never do. "Mankind has always loved making up stories, acting them out in plays, now making movies and television. But there is always some measure of truth in them. Some lesson, some history for the generations."

Ann smiled. Abraham had obviously never seen reality television. But she managed to keep that comment to herself.

"So what do you think is true then?" Ann asked.

"I think the Lord God Almighty puts us all on this earth to find out our own truths, even the ones that are not—strictly speaking—true," Abraham said and he winked again.

"Well, that clears it up," Ann said, trying to squeeze as much sarcasm into her voice as possible.

"Good. Glad to be of service." Abraham hopped off the stage and bowed. "Now, if you will excuse me little sister, I do have to be moving on." He started to walk forward towards the door.

"Wait, I thought this was your home," Ann said.

"It is, in a way, but not in most," Abraham said. "But it was a fine place for a meeting."

"No, wait, there is one more thing," Ann said. She heard the fear in her own voice. "Lilith. She's still alive. I think I see her sometimes. Hear her. I'm worried, scared out of my mind really, that she'll come back, that I'll lose myself again."

Abraham stopped in his tracks, but did not turn to face Ann. "We all have our little voices in our heads," Abraham said. "Some of us less than others, but still…" Then the vampire started walking again letting the sentence trail off for a moment before continuing. "Take heart in this, little sister. The queen of demons is dead; she has no more power over you, but how much power you have over yourself is yet to be known." He reached the darkened exit, then turned and tipped his hat at her and said "With power, there is always a price. Good luck, little sister, on paying yours." Then he stepped into the darkness and was gone.

Ann could have followed; she could always follow now. But then, she didn't think Abraham would give any more answers. At least none that would calm this ever present fear in her heart. No, she was on her own. Now and perhaps forever.

*****

Abraham was watching Ann from the across the street, when the other man stepped out from the darkness. He was tall, but fat, in a suit even more out of fashion than his own. He had a messy grey beard with wild hair and his eyes were covered by a stained rag.

"She is the one, you are sure?" he asked Abraham.

"She is," Abraham nodded. Ann was making her way up the fire escape.

"Then congratulations are in order," the man said. "You've done some amazing work here. The word is that the Infinitus is in chaos. The loss of

Smith and King severely limits their field agents. The competition is out of the way for now."

"Thank you," Abraham nodded. "I did enjoy that the most."

Ann was merely a shadow now, but he could see the outline of her wings.

"And the secret of the Fallen's rebirth?"

"Gone, forever," Abraham said, as the shadow leaped into the evening air and was gone. He, at last, turned towards the man he knew as the Bishop. That was not his real name, merely a title. His real name had been lost in time and mattered little now. Now he was a Bishop in the Order of the Seven Churches and Abraham's superior.

"Ah, then, I am sorry for your friends," the Bishop said. "I warned you of such attachments many years ago."

"I did what I had to," was all that Abraham said on that subject. It had not been easy to find the Dupré's, to befriend them, and then destroy them. When he started, he hardly understood this mad quest he had undertaken. It was not until years later things began to make sense. Time had a way of explaining things. If you lived long enough.

"You did," the Bishop agreed. "Their sacrifice was for a most worthy cause. And you dealt with the Ancient One as well. I know that must be hard for you."

"The Ancient One is safely out of the way for now. I had hoped he would dispatch Carter, but it appears she got away. I'll work on correcting that shortly." Abraham tapped his new cane on the ground to bring the point home. The Ancient One, Abraham's father, would always be a sore point. It was why the Order of the Seven Churches, the Infinitus, and the Fallen had all sought him out a thousand years before.

"You won't be watching the girl?" the Bishop asked.

"No, I have a pint-sized helper keeping an eye on her. I can't have my little sister getting suspicious. Besides, my spy has a unique position and can learn far more than I ever could."

"Excellent, but the last of the Fallen? Will it play its part?" the Bishop asked.

"That is the last piece of the puzzle. It will not be easy getting Ann and Ashakku to meet, but then again, no one ever said bringing about the end of everything would be easy," Abraham said with a grin. Bishop laughed at this.

"Well, then, till next we meet. At the end of the world," the Bishop said and turned to leave.

"At the end of the world," Abraham repeated and turned back to where Ann had vanished.

# 33 - Endings

Lizzie came back to Ann several weeks later. Ann was there for her regular visit, sitting by the bed, reading a book on mythology out loud. Ann knew Lizzie would hate the book, it was far too dry to be interesting, but Ann spiced it up by reading it in bad impressions of famous people. She did Patrick Stewart for a while, then an entire chapter as Elvis, and even one chapter mimicking Miller's strange accent. It was a silly thing, but then Ann and Lizzie had always been about silly things. And sarcasm, lots of sarcasm.

Ann was reading the story of Icarus as performed by Cookie Monster, a feat of on the fly editing that Ann was quite proud of, when one pale hand slapped the book to the ground. Ann looked at her empty hands for a moment, then turned slowly towards her friend. Lizzie stared back at her.

"Lizzie!" Ann said, jumping to her feet. "Oh thank God."

Lizzie tried to speak, but nothing audible came out.

"Wait, hold on. Let me get a doctor." Ann moved to leave, but Lizzie caught her hand and pulled ever so gently. Lizzie tried to speak again, but Ann couldn't hear. She leaned in close. Lizzie tried again, and in a just barely perceptible whisper, she said "Stay."

"Of course. Of course," Ann said. Ann was crying now, as she reached for the intercom button. "She's awake. She's awake. Send a doctor."

Lizzie was waving a hand for her to come closer. Ann wiped away tears and leaned in again.

"I … am… sorry," Lizzie whispered "for everything."

Ann sobbed. "You have nothing to be sorry for," she said. She wanted to hug her friend, but instead kissed her forehead. "You just get better."

"I wanted… to save… you. Just once," Lizzie continued, her voice growing louder.

"You did, you helped Mike, so you did." Ann said back.

Lizzie paused, and seemed to focus on her face for the first time. "You looked better in white."

"I don't know, I'm rather fond of fleshy colored," Ann said, clearing more tears from her eyes.

"Oh, stop crying, you wuss." Lizzie smiled weakly. "You won't be rid of me that easily."

"Never," Ann agreed.

*****

Mike sat and looked down at his feet. The wheelchair kept him from moving his right leg at all. His left, although bandaged, was at a more common resting angle. That knee looked like it would work again in time. The right one though, the doctors had their doubts. If he was to walk again, which was not going to happen anytime soon, he would need a cane.

Somehow, they had managed to stuff him into a suit for the hearing. That had been an awkward and painful few hours, with his mother-in-law getting him ready. The hearing on the other hand, had been shorter but even more painful. Mike Samson was no longer a police officer. The hearing made it official. Had he not been fired, the best he could have hoped for with his wounds was a desk job anyway.

In the heat of the moment, he had made that sacrifice easily, to help save his son and his friends. He hadn't really been a police officer since he had met Joseph Miller. Perhaps even before that, after Melissa had died. But now the reality of the matter was sinking in and the career he had worked on his entire life was now over. His father had been a police officer as well. At least his father wouldn't have to see him broken and unemployed.

"It went about as well as could be expected," Eric Johnson said, as he pushed Mike back outside.

"Yeah," Mike agreed, still looking at his feet. "Thanks for coming, man. Really. Thanks for everything."

"Of course. Don't mention it. How many times does a man get to help round up some vampires and save a kid?"

"More often than you would think, apparently," Mike said.

"Yeah, well maybe for you. But for the rest of us, that's a pretty unique circumstance." Johnson said.

Mike didn't respond, but that didn't seem to bother his friend.

"So what now?" Johnson asked. "You got any plans?"

"Before you answer that…" John Takahashi said, limping over to meet them. His leg was still in a cast, and several marks on his face had not faded yet. Even though he leaned hard on a crutch as he limped forward, he still left the woman he had been with far behind. "Can we talk?"

Mike looked hard at the tall Japanese man. "I suppose I have you to thank for the lack of formal charges," Mike said.

"Who is left to press charges? I certainly won't and what's a little property damage between friends?" John smiled.

"If that's your idea of a little property damage…" Eric Johnson started, but Mike raised a hand.

"What do you want? " Mike asked. He didn't trust the FBI agent.

"Why you, Mr. Samson. I want you to come and work for me. I've already convinced Ms. Melakh to join us."

"You break into my house, kidnap my friends—one of whom didn't make it back—and you expect me to come work for you?" Mike demanded.

"Well, yes," John said.

"Well, no," Mike said back. "Come on Eric. Let's get out of here."

"You sure, Mike? Maybe you should listen. I don't see too many other job offers limping up to you on the street," Johnson said.

"I'm sure," Mike said, spinning the wheel chair to turn away from the agent.

"No, hold on," John said, limping to cut Mike off. "I know we got off on the wrong foot. Believe me, that's not how I wanted to meet you. But we worked well together back in Trenton."

"Fighting for your life tends to help with that," Mike said.

"But you also got Lizzie to bring her videos of Dupré's crimes to the press. Who do you think got her those videos?" John said.

Mike wrinkled his nose and stopped. He turned to face the FBI agent.

"Lizzie said she hacked those out of your network," Mike said.

"Who do you think put those files on an unsecure part of the network to begin with? It was a bit of a long shot, but I had to do something."

"Why not bring those videos to the press yourself?" Mike asked.

"Yeah, or the police," Johnson added.

"I was being monitored every moment. They threatened my family. I couldn't do anything directly," John said.

"Who is they?" Mike asked.

John shrugged. "No one you ever want to meet, trust me. Let's just say Renee Dupré had very powerful friends, who are very busy distancing themselves from her now that she's all over Youtube killing innocent people. But now with Dupré gone, we can set up this department the right way, completely under FBI control. You're bright, you think fast, you have more experience in these sensitive matters than anyone else, and you've got this instinct. I want you on the team."

"I also managed to be indirectly responsible for destroying your headquarters and killing several of your men," Mike countered.

"Chances are that would have happened anyway. I've read quite a bit about the Ancient One. This seems pretty run of the mill for him." John said.

"Find someone else. It's looking like I'm not going to be walking again and I have a kid who needs a father. I'm done with this monster hunting nonsense," Mike said and began to pull away.

"I don't need you in the field. I'm talking strictly consulting. Deskwork. And who knows, maybe we'll need to coordinate with Newark PD again."

"I'm sure you can find someone better than me to keep a seat behind a desk warm," Mike said. John grabbed Mike's shoulder and leaned in close.

"I want to hire the man the Ancient One tracked down and asked for help," John said. "Out of everyone on the planet, he came to you. Doesn't that mean anything?"

"Miller asked me because he knew I was desperate," Mike said. He was getting angry, not really at the FBI agent, but at life in general. "He knew I needed to make amends for…" he stopped for a minute and gathered himself. "I had let down the most important person in my life when she needed me most. Miller offered 'redemption,' in his own words. Part of me didn't think I deserved to live anymore and I tried to redeem myself in my own eyes." He stopped and thought about that. That was a lie. He tried to redeem himself to Melissa. But, of course, that was impossible. "But I'm past that now. I need to be a father for my son."

John Takahashi looked at him for a long time. "A matter of honor then," he said. "I can understand that." John dug into a suit pocket with the hand not holding the crutch and pulled out a business card. "If you need a way to support that son, give me call. Please."

Mike took the card and smiled. "I actually already have one. But thank you. I'll think about it," he said.

"Well, that's all a man can ask," John said. He turned to hobble away. "I think your friend Miss Ann is going to be disappointed though."

"Ann?" Mike said. He looked at the new card in his hand and thought of Ann.

*****

Lizzie was on her feet for the first time in a long time. It turned out, being in bed for a month made it very hard to do simple things. Like sit up, wash yourself, and walk. This was driving Lizzie crazy, well even more crazy than normal. It was one thing to be stuck in this hospital, but to also have other people constantly touching her when they 'helped' her. It was making her twitch in new and interesting ways.

The only reason she had not flipped out entirely was that the doctors had put her back on her regular meds. With the timing and amounts controlled by an army of insistent nurses, Lizzie was as medicated as possible. Still, she could not wait for the day she could go home, lock the door, and never come out.

Ann's regular visits helped too. Their relationship still had not recovered completely from the past few months, they spent too much time being overly 'nice' to each other, but it was coming along. Lizzie still felt guilty for abandoning Ann in Newark and saying such terrible things. She also felt guilty for getting cursed and trying to kill Ann. Ann for her part, felt guilty for getting Lizzie involved in this in the first place, which was true, Ann should have felt bad about that. But they were sisters, and sisters had each other's backs, even if one sister was a scaly demon girl.

Lizzie was making her way along the bed, forcing her legs to work. The more she practiced, the quicker she could go home. And that could not happen fast enough.

"Lizzie? What are you doing?" It was Ann poking her head through the door.

"Practicing my dance moves. What does it look like?" Lizzie said. She was panting a little from the exertion.

Ann strode to her side and placed her arm under Lizzie's. "You should be resting," Ann said.

"No, no" Lizzie shook her head. "I need to get stronger. That's the only way they'll let me go home."

"Yeah, OK, but push it too hard and you'll be in here a lot longer. Come on, lean on me," Ann said. Lizzie did so. "OK, now we're going to take a quick walk and you are going back to bed."

"Fine," Lizzie said with a grunt. Then she noticed a little girl in the doorway. She was small, very young, with dark hair and pink sunglasses. In her hands, she clutched a stuffed monkey with red boots. "Oh, Ann, I think she's lost."

"Umm, actually no. She's with me," Ann said. "This is Angela. She's been living with me the last few weeks."

"What?" Lizzie said.

"Hello," Angela said.

"Angela, this is your Aunt Lizzie. She's getting better, just like Sam's dad is."

"Aunt Lizzie?" Lizzie said. Her head was spinning. "Ann, what the hell?"

"Ahem, heck…" Ann said. "I've been trying to figure out how to tell you this."

"You secretly ran off and had a kid, like a few years ago?" Lizzie guessed.

"Hah, no, no, she is not mine. I'm watching her. She's different and... well, I guess I'm uniquely equipped to help her," Ann said. "Look, let's sit you down. There's more."

Ann and Lizzie made their way back. Ann swept Lizzie up in her arms and placed her gently in the bed.

"Show off," Lizzie muttered.

"OK, this is a little freaky. I need you to relax," Ann said.

"Uh oh. Now you've got me worried," Lizzie said.

"We think Angela was attacked when the Fallen had taken over College Hospital," Ann said.

"What do you mean, attacked?" Lizzie asked. She was looking hard at the little girl who had not budged. Then she noticed her sunglasses.

"She's a vampire."

"Oh," Lizzie said. "The poor little girl."

"She's free from the Fallen's power. But she doesn't remember much of anything before she was cursed. I think she is just too young."

"Isn't she dangerous?" Lizzie said in a whisper.

"Only to small animals."

"So, she's vampire lite?" Lizzie asked.

"Yeah, I guess you could say that. We've been looking for her parents. Her human parents, that is, but the records of who came and went from the hospital those last few days are completely gone. We've tried DNA tests, dental records, checked the missing persons lists. So far, we haven't found anything. Angela, come all the way in. Lizzie won't hurt you. I promise."

The little girl shrugged and stepped in. She glanced at the TV wistfully.

"Are you sure I won't hurt her?" Lizzie said.

"Well, your terrible hygiene might start wearing off on her," Ann said.

"It already looks like your terrible fashion sense is wearing off on her," Lizzie fired back. Ann and Lizzie shared a grin. Yeah, they were getting better.

"OK, one more thing," Ann said.

"Uh huh," Lizzie said doubtfully.

"We've sort of been living at your house," Ann said flinching.

"What?" Lizzie roared.

"Well, I've been trying to get your place fixed up, so it would be ready for you when you got better. And the extra space has been really nice for Angela… and I was kinda evicted."

"Evicted?" Lizzie said.

"I may have missed a few rent payments." Ann said.

"So, now I have a demon and a vampire girl living in my house?" Lizzie said.

"Yeah, kinda. Well, retired demon and friendly vampire girl. We would make a great sitcom."

"And you've been keeping this from me for a week now?" Lizzie accused.

"Well, I mentioned it a few times," Ann said, then quickly added "when you were asleep."

Lizzie crossed her arms across her chest trying to look stern, but then burst out laughing.

"So, you're not mad?" Ann said hopefully.

"Oh, I'm pissed. Had it been anyone but you, Ann, I would be calling the police, after I punched you in the nose."

"You do throw a pretty good kick," Ann commented.

Lizzie had forgotten about her attack on Ann's person. "Well, there's more where that came from if you sneak behind my back again."

"I'm trembling in my socks," Ann said with a smile. "I'm sorry, you weren't available for chatting."

"It's fine. We're family. Really messed up family, but still," Lizzie said

"Broken, but good," Angela said. The two adults stared at her, surprised at her sudden entrance into the conversation. The little girl shrugged. "It's from a movie. I saw it on TV."

"You like TV, I take it," Lizzie asked.

"Yes" Angela bobbed her head.

"And you promise not to eat anyone in my house."

"Just kitties," Angela said.

"You eat kittens?" Lizzie said.

"They are very fluffy and tasty," Angela said.

"Cool," Lizzie said.

"Lizzie, don't encourage her," Ann said in disgust.

"Pssh, whatever. I'm so going to be the cool aunt and I've always hated cats," Lizzie said with a grin.

"Oh, this was a terrible idea," Ann said with a grin.

"Here, kiddo, watch something on TV," Lizzie said, grabbing the remote and turning it on.

Angela hopped into a seat facing the TV.

"See, parenting is easy," Lizzie said to Ann. "Now can we move on to the important stuff and talk about me!"

"It always about you, isn't it?"

"Actually, I think it's kinda been about you a lot lately," Lizzie said.

"Yeah, I guess it has been," Ann agreed. She sat down on the corner of the hospital bed. Lizzie locked eyes with her. "I need to know some things. We've been avoiding them the last few days, but I think it's time you stop trying to protect me and tell me everything," Lizzie said. She used her serious tone of voice, but it cracked a few times due to her nerves.

"Yeah, OK," Ann agreed. "What do you want to know?"

"Am I…" Lizzie started then stopped then started again. "Am I Cursed?"

"Well, a little," Ann said.

"A little?"

"Well, when I look at you, I see a curse sometimes. It's fading though. Medically, you have a series of small tumors along your spine and a few in your head."

"Oh, that doesn't sound good." Lizzie gulped.

"Well, they are shrinking. So, we think you're going to be fine."

"You think I'm going to be fine?" Lizzie said. "That doesn't really make me feel much better."

"Well, we really don't know. It's not exactly science. I've been working with the doctors here and with Doctor Lewis to come up with a treatment plan for you."

Doctor Lewis had been Lizzie's doctor the past week. The woman was apparently a specialist in rare diseases who worked closely with the FBI.

"You're working with the doctors?" Lizzie asked, with a smirk. Ann seemed so grown up when she spoke like this. She had really matured the last few weeks. Ann seemed stronger, more confident than ever before. Lizzie was proud.

"Believe it or not, I'm a leading expert in things demony."

"An expert that says things like 'demony'?" Lizzie said. But then again, Ann was still Ann.

"Well I was going with demonish for awhile, but it didn't quite have the same ring," Ann said. Lizzie was pretty sure the term was 'demonic', but kept it to herself.

"So you are an official expert in something. Does it pay well?" Lizzie joked.

"Ah, well, actually, given time I think it might," Ann said.

"What do you mean?" Lizzie said. Her eyes narrowed.

"I've been offered a job at the FBI," Ann said.

"What?" Lizzie shouted. "Ann, no, you can't. You'll end up in some lab somewhere."

"Lizzie, its fine."

"No really, you don't know these people, now that they know what you are…"

"They don't know what I am. John Takahashi does and Dr. Lewis, but they've sworn to keep it to themselves. They both agree that if what I am got out, well, it would attract the wrong kind of attention. I'm working for the FBI as a consultant for now. Just plain old Ann Melakh, PhD student. I'm going to start training as a full agent as soon as I can."

"Ann, why would you? I mean, Takahashi is cute and all…"

"You know he is married right?" Ann cut in. "He's got kids."

"Really? Does he need a mistress then? Cause I'm flexible…" Lizzie joked. Then returned to the real subject "This is dangerous Ann."

"I think it's the only way. This fight isn't over and working with the FBI, I think we can end the Fallen."

"I get that you feel that you need to save the world, but are you sure you can trust these people? This is your life you're putting on the line here," Lizzie said.

"I do trust them. I think I'm a good judge of character…"

"This from the girl who dated Keith Malone for all those years," Lizzie interrupted, but Ann ignored her.

"And I have friends to help me out. If things do go bad. I've got you. And look how badass you were."

Lizzie shrugged. "You know, kissing up to me always gets you your way, don't you?" she said.

"I depend on your ego staying extra-large. Makes you easier to manipulate for my schemes." Ann smiled.

"Are you sure though? This is what you want?" Lizzie said, after a moment.

"I'm sure," Ann said, nodding a yes.

"All right," Lizzie said. She would support her friend, even if she didn't like it. And if they hurt her, there would be hell to pay. Then she switched gears again. "I'm serious about the mistress thing though. 'Cause I mean, wow."

"Knock it off, Lizzie," Ann laughed.

"No, really, I'm going to be living with you and apparently we have a kid. People are going to start to talk," Lizzie said.

"Well you are hot," Ann said, bending over to give Lizzie a kiss. Lizzie raised a hand and blocked her.

"Let's be honest here, I am way out of your league," Lizzie said.

"Hah, you bitch." They both laughed for a few moments. Then Ann grabbed Lizzie's hand. Ann's hands were as cold as ice. "I missed you, Lizzie."

Lizzie smiled. "I missed me, too."

*****

It was a few days later that Ann got to bring Lizzie home. Lizzie was walking better by that point, but was still very weak, so Ann borrowed a wheelchair to cart her friend outside. Angela followed quietly behind them, clutching at a doll. It was a bright spring day in Newark. It was warm outside, a preview of the intense summer heat that was coming soon. The spring flowers were already fading, making way for the deep green of summer on the small trees that lined the streets.

It felt to Ann like an end to something. Perhaps it was the change in seasons, or at last being free of hospitals. This past spring had been a time of change for her. Her world had been transformed to a nightmare and then transformed again to something new. Something she had yet to define. She had power, purpose, and good friends. But she had lost so much as well.

Lizzie twitched uneasily in her seat as they exited the building. She had been quiet for most of the walk. Ann could tell her friend was dying to get back into her house, the one place where Lizzie really felt safe. Ann didn't point out that Lizzie had not been safe there last time.

By Lizzie's silver Civic was Mike Samson. Still in the wheelchair, still scarred from last month's battles, Mike managed a smile as they approached.

"Sorry I'm late," Mike called. "It takes me a little longer to get around these days."

Lizzie looked at Mike, then gave Ann a crooked grin. It was the 'have you asked him out yet?' look. Ann hadn't. The timing was just not right yet. She would though. There was a connection between Mike and Ann now. Something she desperately wanted to explore.

"No problem. We are all moving a little slower these days," Ann said.

"Lizzie, I'm sorry for not visiting earlier. It's been a rough few weeks. But I'm glad you are on the mend," Mike said.

"I didn't know helping you with one kidnapping made us such close friends," Lizzie said.

Ann swatted her in the back of the head. "Be nice," she whispered.

"This is me being nice," Lizzie whispered back, but then she swallowed and turned back to Mike. "Thanks for coming. And…" She looked down at her hands. "I'm sorry for turning a little evil there at the end."

Ann almost smacked her again, but Mike laughed. "Not your fault," he said. "I'm just glad we got you back. And I'm sorry for getting a little intense there with you and sorry if I scared you. I'm not generally like that, honest."

"So you don't generally cut girls with knives?" Lizzie poked again. Ann smacked her again. Lizzie flashed her a look.

"No, no, I don't. Honest," Mike said.

"Well, good. You can make it up to me by taking me out to dinner. Someplace nice. With fancy clothes," Lizzie said.

"What?" Ann said with a start. She prepared to smack Lizzie again.

"But…," Lizzie added quickly. "Since I don't do fancy dinners or fancy clothes, you'll have to take my representative, Ann."

"Lizzie!" Ann said.

"Ahem. I understand," Mike said. He blushed a little. Ann could feel herself blushing quite a bit. "Well, I've made worse sacrifices." Then he winked at Ann and somehow Ann blushed more.

"And I guess I don't get a say in this?" Ann said, trying to recover a little.

"No, you owe me huge lady. Huge," Lizzie said, with a crooked grin.

*Clever, Lizzie. Very clever,* Ann thought.

Angela looked at the three adults and shook her head.

"Grownups are silly," she said, as she opened the back door and crawled in.

"We are," Ann agreed, opening the door for Lizzie. Lizzie slowly got to her feet, pushing hard on the wheel chair to stand. She then made one shaky step and collapsed into the passenger seat.

“While I have you here, Ann.” Mike started. “I did take John up on his offer. To help, as a consultant.”

“Oh good!” Ann said. She sounded a little too happy in her own ears, so she forced herself to speak in a calmer voice. “I mean, John thought you might change your mind.”

"Well if that’s settled one thing has been bothering me about all of this. Now that I have you two here, maybe it's a good time to ask," Lizzie said jumping back into the conversation.

"What's that?" Mike said, wheeling in a little closer.

"Well, OK, so Dupré brought the Fallen back through cloning or black magic or mad science or something. Right?"

"Right," Ann said. The actual method was still a mystery, one Ann planned to make sure no one ever uncovered.

"But before that, the Fallen just showed up every few hundred years on their own. Like those bugs… locusts. Right?"

"Yeah, that's how Miller put it," Mike said.

"OK, so if the Fallen were not supposed to show up now. Does this mean the Fallen are going to still show up at their regular scheduled time?"

Mike and Ann looked at each other. The thought hadn't actually occurred to Ann at all.

"I don't know," Ann admitted.

A reflection in the glass of the car door suddenly caught Ann's eye. For the first time since that day in the FBI building, she saw Lilith's reflection staring back at her. And she was laughing.

# 34 - Next Time

He was staring up at the stars as if waking from a dream. He had been dead, he was sure of that. But for him, being dead was no new experience. The act of dying itself was not what he considered a good time. But being dead, that wasn't so bad. It wasn't cold; it wasn't dark. There was no bright light, at least not for him. There was simply nothing. And nothing was not so bad.

And then just like that, with a blink, he was back. He never understood why or how, but there was no arguing it. For thousands of years, he had been mankind's protector. He'd had many names throughout time. He had been Gilgamesh, Orion, Beowulf, and Theseus. In China, he had been called Lu Tung-Pin, the great slayer of dragons. The demons called him "The Great Hunter" and "Ancient One." In recent times, he had taken the name Joseph Miller. The demons would appear; he would be reborn and hunt them down. It was the natural order of things. Perhaps it was some kind of balance between good and evil. Or maybe some God found it amusing to toss him again and again at the monsters of the world. He supposed it was a curse of sorts to never truly rest. But it rarely bothered him. After all this time, it was just what he did, what he was, as natural as breathing. Or it had long ago driven him mad and he no longer noticed. One of the two.

He took a long, deep breath and was surprised to find the air much cleaner than he expected. Perhaps he was just getting used to this new modern world he found himself in. Memories began to flood back to him. Ann, Mike, and Abraham all took turns popping in his mind. Miller shook his head to clear it as he stepped forward.

There was a screech of brakes and Miller instantly jumped backwards. A small red car with no roof missed him by inches. The owner of the car shook his fist at Miller as he passed, spouting a fairly impressive array of swear words as he did so.

"Ah yes, I don't think we'll be doing that again," Miller said, thinking back to his last rebirth.

Miller really looked around for the first time. He was in a city, a new one. Some of the lights reminded him of New York City, but the place had a different feel to it. He knew he had never been here before. Miller guessed it was early evening, as the sunlight seemed to be fading. From his vantage point, he had a clear view of high mountains in the distance. He puzzled at a string of several large letters that could be seen.

"Hollywood?" Miller mouthed the word. "What does that mean?" He grinned. Well, there was only one way to find out.

# End of Book 3

To read more go to:
**www.theancientbooks.com**

Or follow us at:
**http://twitter.com/#!/TheAncientBooks**
**http://www.facebook.com/TheAncientBooks**

# The Ancient will return!

# Afterward

The goal had been one novel. A short one, at a meager fifty thousand words in length, written for myself, by myself. Over two evenings on a wrinkled notepad, I wrote out a quick sketch of what I wanted to do. I had all these grand plans; plot twists, secrets to reveal, and jokes about pants to make. After all, fifty thousand words is a nearly endless supply. Right? Well as it would turn out, not so much. When I finished the first fifty thousand words and named it "Ancient Awakening", the story was still just getting started. How could I stop there? It would take another three years (and many, many more thousands of words) just to finish most of that first rough outline.

So with this collection, "The Ancient" series is complete. The story is done, at least as I originally envisioned it. So does that mean the story is over? Will we ever know what Abraham was really talking about with the whole "At the end of the world," bit? And isn't there one whole demon left of the original seven? We did see the other six demons die, didn't we? Didn't we? Worry not, dear reader, The Ancient will return just as promised at the end of the last chapter. In fact, he'll have a whole new trilogy to swing his axe through called "The Ancient Returns". Yep, can I name a series or what? Although it's going to be some time before we see Miller and friends again, they will return. Mike, Ann, and Miller will all be back with many new friends, new baddies, and new jokes about pants. I can hardly wait.

- Matthew Bryan Laube
  September 27th, 2013

www.ingramcontent.com/pod-product-compliance
Lightning Source LLC
Chambersburg PA
CBHW070646310726
48982CB00001B/428